TOM MIX
and
PANCHO VILLA

TOM MIX
and
PANCHO VILLA

by Clifford Irving

St. Martin's Press   New York

Copyright © 1982 by Clifford Irving
For information, write: St. Martin's Press,
175 Fifth Avenue, New York, N.Y. 10010
Manufactured in the United States of America

Library of Congress Cataloging in Publication Data

Irving, Clifford.
  Tom Mix and Pancho Villa.

  1. Mix, Tom, 1889-1940—Fiction.   2. Villa, Pancho,
1878-1923—Fiction.   I. Title.
PS3559.R79T6   813'.54   81-21543
ISBN 0-312-80887-9   AACR2

Design by Manny Paul

10 9 8 7 6 5 4 3 2 1
First Edition

for Valdi
with love
this tale of her Mexico

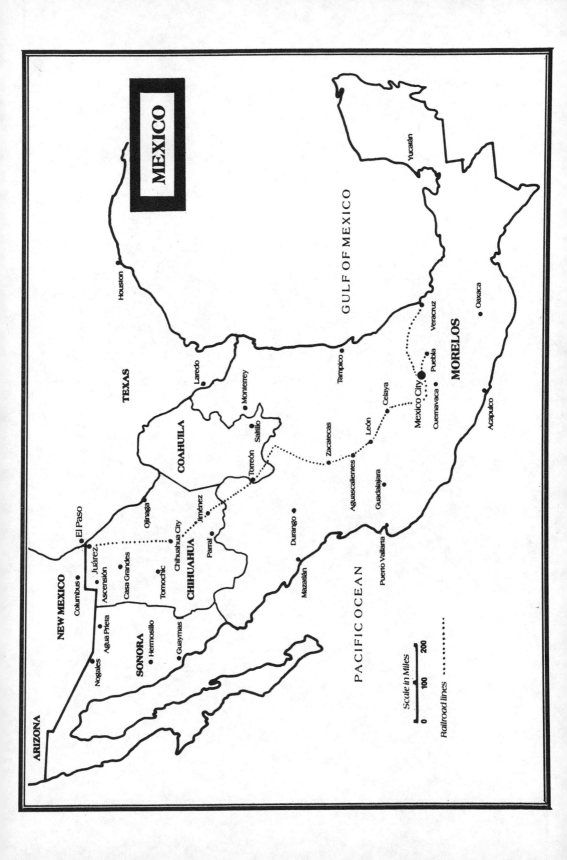

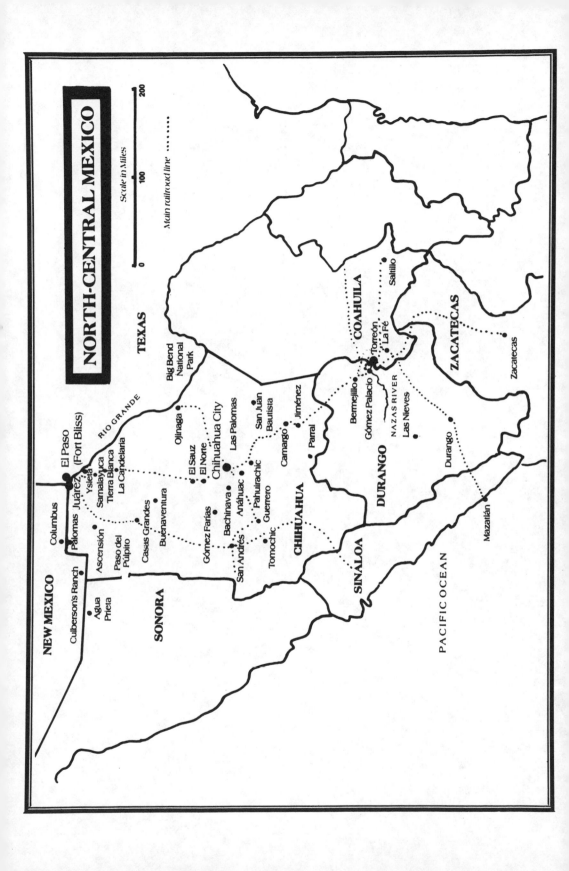

NORTH-CENTRAL MEXICO

Scale in Miles

Main railroad line ·······

0   100   200

NEW MEXICO

TEXAS

SONORA

CHIHUAHUA

COAHUILA

DURANGO

ZACATECAS

SINALOA

PACIFIC OCEAN

RIO GRANDE

NAZAS RIVER

Columbus
Culberson's Ranch
Palomas
Juárez
El Paso (Fort Bliss)
Ysleta
Agua Prieta
Ascensión
Paso del Pulpito
Casas Grandes
Buenaventura
Samalayuca
Terra Blanca
La Candelaria
Gómez Farías
Bachinava
Anáhuac
San Andrés
Tomochic
Guerrero
Pahuirachic
El Sauz
El Norte
Chihuahua City
Las Palomas
Ojinaga
San Juan Bautista
Camargo
Jiménez
Parral
Bermejillo
Gómez Palacio
Torreón
La Fé
Las Nieves
Durango
Mazatlán
Saltillo
Zacatecas
Big Bend National Park

TOM MIX
and
PANCHO
VILLA

Part One

Everybody follows them, but to where? Nobody
knows. It is the Revolution, the magical word, the
word that is going to change everything, that is
going to bring us immense delight and a quick death.

—OCTAVIO PAZ, *Labyrinth of Solitude*

prologue

I became a movie cowboy. I rode hard and performed my own stunts, did more than a hundred silents for Selig Polyscope and Fox and then ten sound films for Universal—my favorite was *Destry Rides Again*. My house in Beverly Hills had a seven-car garage. I wore a diamond-studded platinum belt buckle and diamond-studded spurs. I helped Mickey Rooney and Clara Bow get started. Jack Dempsey, Lillian Gish and Will Rogers were my friends. They were good friends; but once, long ago, in another country, I had better ones. I was on top of the world, making more money than I could spend and traveling every year to London and Paris, where I put on roping and riding shows with my horse, Tony, a white-stockinged chestnut who was so well trained he could untie my hands with his teeth. They were good years . . . but long ago, in another country, I had more thrilling ones.

The crash of '29 cost me an even million. I owed back taxes to the government. New faces like Ken Maynard and Hoot Gibson galloped across the silver screen. In 1932 I quit the movies, found a friendly banker and bought a circus for $400,000. I hit the sawdust trail around the country, until we got to Oklahoma and my new horse, Tony Jr., fell on me. My leg—and my circus—went bust. All I had left was my fifteen-minute radio program for Ralston Purina. "Made of golden western wheat . . . Tom Mix says it's swell to eat." And it was. I wouldn't have said so otherwise.

"Don't worry," Jack Dempsey said to me. "You're on the ropes, but there's always another round."

"I don't mind," I said. "The defeats are also battles."

"What do you mean by that, Tom?"

"It's a long story. Anyway, I've had a lot worse things happen to me."

"When was that?"

"Someday I'll tell you, Jack."

Around that time another of my marriages broke up. Since I had come to Hollywood I had tried three times—apparently, not hard enough.

"You're too rough on yourself," Lillian Gish remarked to me. "Do you want to know what I think? I don't believe you've ever found the right woman."

"No, Lillian. I did find her. But that was a long time ago, in another country."

"Who was she?" she said, getting interested.

"One day I'll tell you."

Maybe it's because I'm holed up here in Arizona these days, with time on my hands and a bottle of red-eye on the desk, or maybe it's because I've just turned fifty and I sense a chariot has pulled up outside in the dark. But I think the time has come to answer those good friends' questions. The fact is, I'm not the man I am because of anything that happened during my limelight days in Hollywood and on tour in Europe. All that is epilogue. The keenest days of my life—the best years, the worst time—all took place long before the name Tom Mix ever hit the bright lights and went celluloid. They took place in a part of the world that people usually associate with tiny, short-haired, funny-looking dogs. It's called Chihuahua, the northernmost state of Mexico, just across the border from El Paso, Texas, where I was brought up. In my youth I was a cowhand and rodeo rider, and then I became a revolutionist for a gentleman named Francisco Villa.

I'm going to tell that story now. There's no studio chief to tear his hair if I reveal my unseemly past. I want to spent this one last time with my old friends, some of them dead more than twenty years. I want to smell the desert, feel the heat: taste the poetry of another age, another world. A harsh world, and a bloody one, but one that has more meaning to me than Sunset Boulevard or Piccadilly Circus. And what the hell, it may not be *Destry Rides Again,* but it *is* a tale of women and gold, of revenge and revolution, and growing up . . . and a story about a love that's never quite died, at least in the dark of my mind.

It's late, I know. But life is short, as Candelario Cervantes used to say. A man can do worse than relive the part of his life that's pure Technicolor.

1

My born name was Thomas Hezekiah Mix, and my father was an un-
dertaker who had moved from Pennsylvania to El Paso, Texas—an intelligent enough move if you consider that in those years, at the turn of the
century, a great many more people were dying along the Rio Grande
than in most other parts of the country. I worked after school in his
undertaking parlor, and a Mexican fellow named Julio Cárdenas, who
glued the coffins together in the backyard, took a liking to me and taught
me to ride. I had the usual gang of boyhood chums, but Julio was a few
years older than the rest and by far the most serious; even though his
skin was darker than mine I considered him my best friend. He lived
across the river in the city of Juárez, which was bigger than El Paso but a
great deal poorer and dirtier, being Mexican, and he had the use of
some roping horses that his uncle kept by the stockyards. Even a poor
Mexican had a thin-flanked, jugheaded horse of some kind, so that Julio
was bowlegged enough for a yearling to run between his legs without
bending a hair. That was my ambition too. I went over to the stockyards
every Sunday from dawn to sundown, and I took to horses like a puppy
to warm milk.

And yet even then I wanted to be an actor. That came about because in my second year at El Paso High I played the part of Fortinbras
in *Hamlet*. It's a small part, but such a burst of applause rang out in the
auditorium after the burlap curtain fell—with me standing on the stage
waving a tin sword among the litter of dead—that I was woolyheaded
enough to think some of it was meant for me. The sound was the sweet-
est I'd ever heard. And what could I do? This was the first decade of our
century, and I had grown up on the border among riffraff and horseflesh
and corpses. To be an actor, I believed, you had first of all to be an
educated person, which I surely wasn't, and then to live in New York,
which was as distant for a boy like me as China. There was no one to
guide me, certainly no one to propel me in the direction contrary to that
advised by Mr. Greeley. I had to content myself with reading Shakespeare in the privy.

After Buffalo Bill's Wild West Show passed through El Paso I learned to twirl a ketch rope, and when I gave up my dream of becoming an actor I couldn't decide whether I'd be a Texas Ranger or a champion rodeo rider. My father hoped I'd go into the cold-body business with him, my mother thought insurance would be a nice trade, but I confounded everybody by quitting school at the age of seventeen, tucking my Shakespeare into my bedroll and hightailing it over to the Brazos, where I landed a job as wrangler in a cow camp. I was one of five healthy children, not the brightest and surely not the prettiest, so no one missed me to the point of grief . . . or else they guessed I was a quitter and would come back in my own sweet time.

A wrangler was about the most menial job you could have around a remuda, but it didn't take the range boss long to realize I had a way with four-legged beasts, and fairly soon I graduated to night hawk and then full-fledged cowhand. In a couple of years I could ride the roughstring, brand calves, throw a hooleyann and cut my way through a stampede, and I never once confessed to anyone that I was a frustrated John Barrymore. I never stayed too long at one job, for I had a restlessness big as a barfly's thirst; and I had other frustrations, the kind you can't easily talk about. Women were on my mind, but I had no contact with them other than an occasional poke in cowtown whorehouses from Tulsa to Brownsville, which depressed me far more than it satisfied any itch in my loins. I pounded away at big-breasted ladies named Honey and Sadie and Lulu, when what I really yearned for was to worship fragile creatures named Desdemona, Juliet and Ophelia. Reading William Shakespeare will poison any young man's mind if he takes it seriously.

By a dozen campfires or out on lonely ranges I dreamed of dying for love, the glory of battle, noble princes and swooning maidens . . . and what connection did that make with my gritty life? I yearned for high adventure, true love and fortune. But where did they exist? And how would a roughneck cowboy know where to find them?

So I quit ranching and spent a couple of years on the rodeo circuit. From time to time I went home for a good meal of butter beans, roasting ears and Mama's fried chicken. Then I quit the rodeo and joined up with the Miller Brothers Real Wild West Show near Bliss, Oklahoma. They paid me fifteen dollars a month plus room and board and started me out as dragman in the horse-thief act, but after a while I earned my pay in the more legitimate rodeo events such as bulldogging and bronc riding. That's where I met Geronimo, the great Apache chief, who was let out of jail to help us stage a buffalo hunt. He was supposed to shoot a bull buffalo with a bow and arrow, but he was a shaky old man and he missed, so he started shooting up the herd with his rifle and they threw him back in jail. It took the romance out of the show somehow, and I quit again and headed back to El Paso to hole up with my family. That was the winter of 1913. I arrived on a Sunday, and my father greeted me at the door in his usual way.

"Back again, eh?"

"That's right, Papa. Can I come in?"

"It's still your home . . . I guess."

Mama gave me a big hug. She thought I looked thin, and the idea of fattening me up pleased her no end. To what avail, I didn't know. She treated me like a lovable misfit, and Papa generally avoided me as though whatever disease I had might be catching. I wondered what I could do with my life to make sense of it. The next day, not having any better prospects, I felt that familiar pang of restlessness which usually signaled a change in my whereabouts.

"What ever happened to my friend Julio Cárdenas, Mama?"

"Went back to Mexico, Tom. Probably got himself killed in that revolution. He was a nice boy."

There had been a short-lived revolution the last couple of years south of the border, with an idealistic fellow named Francisco Madero taking over from the old dictator, Porfirio Díaz—but then Madero had been shot by his own generals and a new gang of thugs had seized power and imposed a kind of peace. It was supposed to be quiet now.

"I'll see you later, Mama. I'm going over to Juárez."

"Be careful," she said. "They're funny people."

"I'm still a gringo," I reminded her, meaning that even I had special privileges on the other side of the Rio Grande.

I took a streetcar downtown and then strolled in the March sunshine across the Stanton Street Bridge to Ciudad Juárez. Gambling was the city's chief occupation, and in the early afternoon you could already hear the clatter of chips and the shrieks of the keno players at Touché's Casino. Whores roamed the boardwalks of Calle Diablo, wearing shiny red dresses that they would hike up to give you a free look at their bush. Streetcars rattled by to spray garbage on anyone who chanced too close, and you couldn't smell anything else except the sour winds of tequila that wafted from the swinging doors of a hundred cantinas. The *campesinos,* the poor country folk, sprawled drunk and half-starved in the streets, mouths agape and covered with flies. Federal soldiers usually carted them away by early afternoon and the rest of the time they patrolled the city, ready to arrest anyone who mouthed off against the new government. They still invoked the *ley fuga,* a law that allowed them to shoot prisoners and then claim they had been killed while trying to escape. The women met another fate. In Old Mexico you rarely wondered why so many people were drunk; you marveled instead that in the midst of their misery any of them bothered to stay sober. They all drank *pulque* as though it were soda pop, and most of the Indian babies were weaned on it. There was no trick to making it—the juice from the heart of the maguey plant, which grew in the desert like a weed, fermented in less than a day to produce a sour milky-white liquid that would grow horns on a mule and make life bearable even to a man who knew he had little chance of living to the age of forty.

Today it struck me that there were even more white-uniformed Federals than usual, rifles at the ready, roaming in squads commanded by angry-looking officers. A few streets were barricaded, and I spotted the black barrel of a Colt machine gun poking over some sandbags. But the Mex soldiers seemed nervous, as if they were searching for something they didn't particularly want to find. I wondered idly what that could be.

Finally I stepped into a little *ostioneria*, a shellfood shop where Julio Cárdenas' mother worked, peeling Tampico shrimp and soaking them in chile sauce. I found her in the back by the smelly shrimp bucket and asked where her son was. But she didn't seem keen to answer.

"Señora Cárdenas, you know me, don't you?"

"It may be that I know you. Yes, that's possible."

"I'm Tomás Mix . . . Julio's old friend. Can you tell me where he is?"

"I don't know, señor."

"Is he here in Juárez?"

"It might be yes, it might be no. But most probably . . . who knows?"

I wasn't going to get anywhere with that Indian lady. The day was hot and I was thirsty, so I finally said to hell with it and wandered into the street. Just as I was passing Touché's Casino, a young Indian woman stepped out of an alley. She had a baby hanging from one bare brown teat, and another naked brown-eyed kid cowered behind her. The boy was crippled, the stump of one leg swathed in filthy bandages. The woman wore a torn *rebozo*.

"Señor," she whined, "just a few centavos, for the love of God. My husband is dead. My children have nothing to eat."

Just as I reached into my Levi's to fish for a dime, boots thudded in the dust. A Federal officer and two Mex soldiers rushed past me and grabbed the woman roughly.

"Hey!" I yelped. "Hold on there. She didn't do anything!" Naturally I spoke their lingo, El Paso in my formative years being more full of Garcías and Lopezes than it was of Smiths and Mixes. The officer shoved the woman and her baby into the arms of the two soldiers. Showing his white teeth, he threw up his hand to me in a sloppy salute.

"Don't worry, señor. You go into the casino . . . we'll take care of her. She's an ignorant peasant, no doubt a whore, but she knows what it means to break the law."

Gambling was illegal in El Paso, so the citizens of that orderly metropolis thronged regularly across the Rio Grande bridges to lose their money at Touché's and the other casinos. One of the soldiers' jobs was to make sure the starving women and children didn't bother the gamblers with their begging. This was the Mexico I knew. But it's one thing to know, and another to see it happen before your eyes.

"And what might the penalty be?" I asked.

The Indian woman began to struggle and wail, but no one on the dusty street paid any attention. The crippled boy limped away. I didn't know what to do. The soldiers were armed, so that even if I had been carrying a gun it would have been quixotic, perhaps even suicidal, to pull it out and threaten them. They were in their home territory. They would probably think twice before shooting me, but they wouldn't hesitate to haul me down to the local *juzgado* and throw me in the drunk tank for a night or two. Or I might find myself on a road gang for a month with the other poor souls they collected each morning. That's how I should have been thinking, and I admit it did vaguely cross my mind, but that's not how I acted. I was always impetuous, for better or for worse.

By now the boy had reached the end of the alley. The Federal soldiers let him go. They were only interested in his mother. She was young, and now that the baby had been dislodged from her breast I could see a wet swollen nipple. The baby began to wail too. "Don't worry, *madrecita*," one of the soldiers said, licking his lips. "I promise you won't go dry. . . ."

"What's going on today?" I said to the officer, when the woman paused for breath. "How come there's so many soldiers on the streets?"

"For a good reason, señor." He assumed a graver air. "You know Pancho Villa, the bandit? The enemy of President Huerta? He is in town. We're going to find him."

I knew who Pancho Villa was, or at least I knew what I had heard bandied about by a dozen campfires and a score of southwestern bars. "What's he look like?" I asked sharply, wrinkling my brow.

"An evil-looking man, señor. I've seen him once, at the battle of Juárez two years ago, and I know whereof I speak. He is fat. He has red teeth. His mouth is always hanging open, so that he looks like an idiot. In actual fact, he is feebleminded."

"Fat? Red teeth? *I've seen that man!*" I cried. "Here! About five minutes ago, in a grocery shop across from the Tivoli Casino! I remember his mouth hanging open, and I thought, Poor creature. But that was him! I'm sure of it. Yessir, that was Pancho Villa!"

The officer's eyes sparked with interest. I suppose he glimpsed the possibility of promotion. "You're certain, señor?"

"Dead certain. I've seen his picture in the newspaper too. That was him."

"What was he wearing?"

"He was dressed like a priest. That's what fooled me. I saw a pistol under his cassock. Do priests carry pistols?"

That settled it. The officer shouted to his men. They let go of the frightened Indian woman and rushed out into the street, kicking up dust as they ran for the Tivoli. Quickly I took the woman's arm and pressed two dimes into her hand. It was all the change I had, but it would buy her tortillas for the week.

"Go, señora, please. You're safe now. But you'd better scoot before they come back."

I followed her down the alley until she caught up with her crippled son. She snatched his hand. With a weak nod of thanks, she vanished. Why should she thank me? If I had saved her from the soldiers, my presence had brought them down on her in the first place. But I had no more time to reflect on it; when I reached the end of the alley the swinging doors of a cantina creaked open and the brim of a sombrero peered over the wooden slats. A hot sun flooded the alley and the street, and the face of the man beneath the sombrero was in the blackest shade. From inside the cantina, which was called La Princesa, came the tinny music of an automatic piano playing a Mexican song. I began to hurry by.

"Tomás . . ."

A hand reached out . . . it gripped my arm, yanking me abruptly through the doors.

"Hey!"

"Tomás! It's me, Julio Cárdenas. Don't you remember me?"

The gritty little cantina was hazed with cigarette smoke. At the back, near the slot machine, two bedraggled whores huddled over a bottle of tequila. I peered into a pox-pitted face that looked as if someone had mistaken its owner for a coyote and fired both barrels. The eyes were dark and intelligent, and the mouth had a sour downturn that made it look as if the man had been weaned on a pickle.

"Sure, I remember you," I said. "In fact, I came over here to hunt you down, but you're a hard man to find. Good old Julio! How the hell are you?"

"Well enough. Now, what happened in the street with the soldiers?"

Julio Cárdenas was a thin man of about twenty-five. Another man—huge, ugly, black-bearded and fierce-looking—slouched against the bar by Julio's side. I told them what had happened, and they glanced at each other. The big man chuckled hoarsely—he understood immediately—but Julio was more serious.

"Is it true, Tomás? Is it possible? Did you see Pancho Villa?"

"Are you kidding? I didn't even see a priest. I made it all up. What'll you have to drink, Julio? I quit the rodeo. Let's get drunk."

He shook his head at my offer. I noticed they were drinking orange soda pop. With the shutters closed against the heat it was dark in the cantina. I took an even closer look and realized that he and his large friend were wearing trail boots and spurs, their bandoliers were filled with cartridges and big horse pistols were stuffed into their belts. That wasn't something to remark about: everyone in Old Mexico had gone armed for as long as I could remember, but there was something about these two, some kind of wary excitement, that made me rein up for a minute. They seemed a trifle nervous too, and kept glancing over my shoulder into the street.

"Julio—enlighten me. I ask for you, and your mama treats me like a leper. You're hanging around in a bar drinking soda pop. The town's full of Federals with machine guns, and they tell me that Pancho Villa's in Juárez. What's going on? Is the goddam revolution starting all over again?"

"You don't know what's happened?" he asked, narrowing his dark eyes.

"*Hombre,* if I knew I wouldn't ask. And I don't even want to ask," I added, "if it's going to rub your fur the wrong way." I knew enough to be closemouthed around Mexicans when they were drunk, which was often, and I had an idea it might be wise to shut up completely when they were dead sober, which was practically unheard of.

"I thought you knew," Julio said, "because you tricked the soldiers. It's true. Pancho Villa is here in Juárez. He was hiding in Texas, but he crossed the border after he heard President Madero was assassinated by Huerta. That pig, Huerta, sent Villa into exile before it happened."

"So what's Pancho Villa going to do about it?" I asked. "Will he fight Huerta now?"

"Fight? Of course he'll fight. Who else is there to do it? Do you think Carranza can fight? Villa will fight, and Villa will win."

Pancho Villa was a name to stir men's hearts, but at the time he was more of a myth to me than a reality. His real name was Francisco—Pancho was just a nickname—and his name before *that* had been Doroteo Arango, back in Durango before the hacienda owner's son raped his sister (or so they said by the campfires) and young Doroteo killed him and bowlegged off into the sierra at the age of fifteen to take his new name and become a bandit.

But anything I tell you won't make much sense unless you know what had been going on in Mexico since I had been born, and for a long time before that.

It was March of 1913, as I've said, when I walked—or was yanked—into that cantina, and for years Mexico had been ruled by one man, Porfirio Díaz, whom they had called "The Iron Hand." He kept the peace with the aid of the Federal army and the red-jacketed *rurales,* his licensed thieves who pretended to be police. Díaz made a few people very rich and a lot of people very poor and miserable, which is a system you would think the majority would refuse to tolerate for very long, but from what I had read in my history books it had been successful in a great many countries for centuries. Three years ago, in 1910, Díaz had just celebrated his eightieth birthday when that scholarly little fellow,

Francisco Madero, rallied the people and started a revolution. Men either loved Madero or considered him a jackass. The fighting lasted about a year, and it could have gone either way except that Díaz developed a toothache, lost part of his jaw to a quack dentist and finally, in terrible pain, left the country on a German steamship. He took up residence in Paris, where the good dentists are. Madero was elected president.

Now Madero was an honest man, but apparently a man had to be more than honest in order to govern Mexico. The revolutionary generals became restless. One of them, a former mule driver named Pascual Orozco, sold out to the northern cattle barons, defecting with six thousand former *rurales.* Madero's chief general, Victoriano Huerta, a bullet-headed, brandy-drinking Indian who boasted that his closest friends were named Martell and Courvoisier, ordered the little president confined in the national palace for his own safety. A few nights later Madero was taken out and shot. Huerta assumed the presidency. Orozco became his commanding general.

As for Pancho Villa, when the revolution had first begun back in 1910, he decided to fight for it rather than against it—banditry, I suppose, already being a kind of natural opposition to property and the status quo. Villa was different from most of the mountain gunmen in that he came to be a true believer in the cause and a devoted follower of the one they loved to call, with weepy affection, "the little Señor Madero." Pancho collected his share of scalps and medals, rose to the rank of colonel and won a big battle right here in Juárez, which made him famous. After Madero was elected president he retired, but then he got into trouble with General Huerta for stealing a horse from some rich hacienda owner. At the last minute a telegram from President Madero called off his execution, and Pancho was thrown into prison in Mexico City. Disguised as his own lawyer, he escaped and made his way through the mountains to exile in El Paso. He had been there ever since, until Madero was assassinated two months ago.

If there was any revolution still drawing breath, I had heard it was led by a new star named Venustiano Carranza, an older gentleman with a distinguished white beard parted in the middle and blue-tinted spectacles that hid his eyes. He was east of here in the state of Coahuila, and there was another independent revolutionist general to the west named Alvaro Obregón. Confusing? No American could follow the ins and outs of Mexican politics. The chiles killed each other off so fast you didn't know from one day to the next who was on top and who was six feet under.

"Does Villa have an army?" I asked Julio, in that smoky Juárez bar. "Is he going to join up with Carranza?"

"Venustiano Carranza!" Julio snorted with disdain. "We call him 'Don Venus.' He smells of scent and he drinks chocolate with his pinky in the air. He makes proclamations, but he does nothing. And he has no *cojones.*"

That was about the worst thing you could say of a man in Mexico, that he had no balls.

"Well," I said, "they tell me that Pancho Villa has plenty of *cojones.* Can't he lend one or two to Don Venus, so they can lick Huerta and Orozco together?"

Julio's vexed expression softened a bit, and the huge man behind him smiled at me with broken white teeth out of a bearded face the color of burnt toast. He murmured something that I didn't catch. A random shaft of sunlight touched his face . . . something glittered. I realized he had only one good eye and the other one was glass. He had the kind of brutal mien that you would describe to little kids if you wanted to scare them into eating their porridge. Finally he laid a thick hand on Julio's shoulder and rumbled, "We have to go. That other one's not going to show up."

Julio said, "Tomás, it was pleasant to see you again. What you did in the street for that woman was a good thing. Consider that the revolution owes you a favor."

"Hang on a minute." A thought finally wandered into my skull that accounted for their standing in that bar drinking soda pop and the way they kept glancing over my shoulder into the street. "Are you a Villista?" I asked Julio bluntly. "Are you going to meet Pancho Villa?"

Julio started to grin—then murmured, with obvious prudence, "Possibly."

Looking back now, I can see more than a few times in those years when I made decisions that determined the course of my life. I almost said ". . . changed my life," but from this distance I no longer believe that. No doubt I hungered for adventure, sensed big doings, glimpsed glory on the horizon—but there was surely more to it than that. I knew it, and it was never my nature to shy away from new occupations. Saving that Indian woman from the Federal soldiers in front of La Princesa may have begun the chain of events, but I don't believe now in a fate that falls on men however they act. I believe in a fate that falls on a man *unless* he acts.

"Take me along," I said boldly. "If you owe me a favor, I'll collect it right now. I'd like to meet Pancho Villa."

The bearded, one-eyed giant butted his jaw out and said, "Who is this boy?" Actually he called me *pendejo,* which is Mex for a piece of pubic hair. I bristled, but I was in no position to take offense. I introduced myself and so did he, with some reluctance, and we shook hands limply—I taking care not to squeeze too hard, because greasers don't like that sort of Yankee pressure, having lived with it through most of their history, and simply offer their hand to show you they haven't got a broken bottle in it. The giant's name was Candelario Cervantes. He had already raked me over from topknot to boots and seen I wasn't armed, and I guess I didn't have the look of a troublemaker. It's no easy trick to see yourself as others do, but I'll try: I was lean and on the tall side, with straight hair, brown eyes and a habit of sticking out my jaw to make it look firmer than it was. A callow youth, you might say, looking to be a man. I didn't know it then, but Candelario Cervantes would become just about the best friend I'd ever had. I still think about him, and some of the advice he gave me over the next three years still governs my life. But then he had a decision to make too, and everything would have been different if he had decided otherwise. He didn't. Perhaps, like me, he couldn't.

Even with his glass eye, he was the boss of this pair. The one good eye gazed at me as if waiting for a message. Then, abruptly, clapping a hairy-knuckled hand on Julio's shoulder, he grunted his approval. So we left the cantina to take a short walk, and I began the longest journey of my life.

2

"The eagle suffers little birds to sing."

Indian women pounded tortillas in the doorways of scattered huts. Their eyes gazed at us without expression as we tramped through the narrow back streets of Juárez. Naked children played in the dust and the rotting carcass of a dog provided a feast for the buzzards. Candelario Cervantes' boots rang out merrily with the music of danglers that he had added to the rowel axle of his spurs. Now and then we ducked into alleyways, where he and Julio peered out, pistols drawn, to survey the street—but apparently the Federal soldiers didn't venture this far from the heart of the city.

After a while we came to a ruined adobe house isolated from view by some stands of cactus and sword plants. Two horses were tethered outside in the unpitying sun . . . and I knew we had reached Pancho Villa's lair.

A stooping man bulked out of the door; he straightened up, blinking into the glare. He was a fat, olive-skinned fellow who carried a rifle loosely in one hand, and his chest was crisscrossed with two cartridge belts, the brass tips of the bullets glinting in the hot light. What made it unlikely, and odd, was that under the bandoliers he wore a shiny blue business suit, white shirt and black string tie. The man had a large curved nose, bushy brows and mustache, and there was a shrewd look in his brown eyes. He nodded in a friendly manner to Candelario, then jerked his head inquiringly toward me.

"A friend," Julio said.

That sufficed, and the unlikely fat guard in the business suit stepped aside. We ducked our heads and entered.

The one shadowed room of the hut smelled powerfully of tobacco, gun oil and old sweat. Rifles stood stacked against a wall. There were no chairs, only wooden boxes, a little stone fireplace, some chile peppers hanging from a frayed string . . . and a cot with a man lying on it. He was in an apparent state of exhaustion, one gorillalike arm dangling to the dirt floor. His eyes were open a crack, and I could swear they gleamed greenly in the darkness, like the eyes of a bobcat surprised in its cave. But he was totally still. He had a bushy reddish-brown mustache over a mouth that drooped open, just as the Federal officer had described, almost as though he were an idiot. His fleshy cheeks were stubbled with beard and his curly brown hair was matted with sweat.

I knew him from the pictures I had seen in the illustrated Sunday supplements in the *Herald,* except that in the pictures he was always heroically astride a black stallion, flourishing a long-barreled pistol. This was Pancho Villa.

The one dangling hand made a little gesture of welcome. Julio and Candelario hunkered down slowly on their haunches by the side of the cot. That was a Mex trick I'd never learned and didn't care to learn, priding myself on knowing how to sit like a good American, so I dropped my butt down on one of the wooden boxes, instructing myself to keep my mouth shut and let things lazy along at their own pace. Pancho Villa hadn't even acknowledged my presence with a nod, much less asked who I was. He looked like a punchdrunk boxer taking a long count, and I wondered if he was going to drift back to sleep or whatever state of coma he had been in when we jingled and jangled through the door. He didn't give any sign that he intended to get up from the cot.

"Forgive me," he murmured to the others. "I'm still in mourning . . . and therefore I'm not myself. I keep thinking of what happened in Mexico City to the little Señor Madero." The others made little grunts and mews of sympathy. Villa broke in, his voice rising. "To him," he said emotionally, "I owe everything." Remarkably, the catlike green glow in his eyes suddenly blurred with tears. "I was a bandit, and by explaining the revolution to me, he helped to make me a man with some purpose. Such a little fellow . . . but he had the great heart of a saint! He was a father to me, and he was a scholar. And by God, he had *cojones!"*

Raising his sleeve from the dirt, he wiped his eyes. Then, like a mountain cat about to pounce, he switched those cold green lanterns on me. He spoke in a hard high-pitched voice.

"You have rifles for me, meester—yes? And bullets?"

Rifles? Bullets? I didn't know what he was talking about. I just gaped.

"This is not the man, *jefe,"* Julio piped up uneasily. "That other one didn't show up. The other one's name is Wentworth. Rodolfo's crossed the river to find out what's happened. This is a friend," and he nodded at me.

"A friend of whose?" Villa demanded, I think annoyed at his mistake.

I decided I had better answer for myself, for there's no way of telling what Mexicans will do to cover up an embarrassment. I may have been Julio's youthful friend, but Villa was his *jefe*, his chief. "A friend of Julio's, Mr. Villa," I said. "And a friend of the revolution."

Villa allowed himself a narrow, fleeting smile. "But there are many revolutions," he said calmly. "There was the revolution of Señor Madero, who is dead for his troubles. There is Emiliano Zapata's revolution—the Plan of Ayala. There is Venustiano Carranza's revolution—the Plan of Guadalupe. You understand that every revolutionist has a written plan of what he promises to do—all except me. My plan is only in my head, because I don't know how to write. I'm an illiterate, a buffoon and a killer—according to my enemies." He chuckled softly; so did I. "Now, my young gringo, tell me . . . of which revolution do you call yourself a friend?"

I was in over my head, but the thrill of sitting there with Pancho Villa, in the flesh, pushed a speech out of me.

"I didn't know Señor Madero. And I haven't heard much about Zapata except that he wears a big hat and comes from the south. Huerta sounds like a first-class sonofabitch, and Julio says that Carranza has no balls. So I'm a friend of your revolution . . . chief. I don't like the Federals, and I'm not doing anything important right now. If you can use an extra hand in your army, I'd like to join up."

It was something beyond youth and having nothing better to do with my time that was moving me. There was an air about these men— Pancho Villa particularly—that made me want to be part of what they might do. They had a purpose in life, and I knew already that it had to be a more worthwhile one than mine. They were hardy and dedicated men. I wasn't—not yet. But I wanted to be.

Villa sat up so smoothly that you couldn't see where the leverage came from. He wore a pair of crisscrossed cartridge belts over his khaki shirt even while he had been dozing, and a Springfield rifle lay on the far side of the cot. One paw of his, the one hidden from my sight, grasped a black pistol that had probably been pointed at my belly the whole time. Villa was a big man, and when his face moved into the patchy light I saw that his eyes weren't green at all, but more the color of mustard.

"How are you called?" he asked me.

"Tomás Mix, Señor Villa."

"And how old are you?"

"Twenty-two, señor."

"Tomás rides as well as Rodolfo," Julio muttered from behind me.

16 /

"And of course he speaks English. That's useful, chief." He had to be on my side whether he liked it or not, because he had brought me here, the wisdom of which he might now be wondering about.

"Are you prepared to die?" Villa asked me.

"I don't see that I have any choice," I said. "Better later than sooner, that's all. And let it be quick."

"You must have some Mexican blood," Villa said, grinning. "Have you ever killed a man?"

I shook my head.

"Could you?"

That stumped me for a moment. Here I was, setting a torch to my flimsy bridges and fixing to become a revolutionist with the bandit Pancho Villa, and I knew as much about bloodletting as a hog does about Sunday. "I could learn," I said. "I guess I could learn pretty damned fast if the man I had to kill intended to kill *me.*"

"You know how to shoot?" His eyes were still locked steadily on me, but I knew he wasn't angry anymore and he didn't dislike me. Later I would learn that Pancho Villa usually made his decisions about men in a few seconds and rarely changed his mind. He trusted his instincts as few others had the courage to do.

"I've fooled around with a gun," I told him. "I know you don't pull the trigger with your big toe. But I don't claim to be a Joe Lane."

Villa frowned. "What is a Joe Lane?"

"Fellow with the rodeo up in Dallas. Puts on a shooting exhibition. He can slip a pistol bullet into an empty cartridge at twenty yards. Dead center, so that it's all joined up again."

"That's impossible," Villa said flatly.

"Impossible? No, sir. He's the best shot in Texas."

"At twenty yards? With a pistol?"

I didn't want to be thought a liar. "Hell, chief," I said, "I've seen him do it a dozen times."

I bit my tongue, and now there was nothing in the world I wanted more than a change of subject, because what I had told Pancho Villa wasn't precisely true. I had lied, then got carried away trying to prove I wasn't a liar, and I had told a worse lie to do it, which I guess is the way of the world. The truth was I'd only heard that Joe Lane could do that stunt back in his prime, before he took to a diet of Tennessee sour mash.

Villa jumped furiously to his feet, and that made me jump up too, bewildered by his intensity. "We'll go outside," he said, with heat. "I tell you, it's impossible!"

He had made a decision, and we trooped out the door into the blistering sun. I heard black-browed Candelario address the unlikely fat fellow who had been standing guard in his blue suit, calling him Hipólito; I realized then that he was Pancho's older brother. Pancho himself, in the light, looked to be a man of about thirty-five, barrel-chested but with a good spring to his rolling gait. I had always assumed he was older, but I should have realized that revolution was a young man's game. He snappily told Julio to stay with the horses and marched the rest of us around to the back where there was nothing but barrel cactus and a busted-up stone wall. The desert of Chihuahua shimmered in a yellow light. It was hot enough to slip hair on a bear, and you would have had to prime yourself to spit. I felt uneasy. I had figured out what Villa was going to do. It would either make a fool out of him or a liar out of me.

He led us through the dust to the stone wall, where he pulled a brass cartridge from his belt, put the flat end into his mouth and began to work it loose. Under his bushy mustache I could see that his teeth were stained the color of rich topsoil. He finally separated the cap from the powder, letting it spill to the ground in a thin gray stream. Candelario farted gently. A single black buzzard sailed aloft, silent as sin, in the bone-white sky . . . nothing else moved. Not even Villa, who just stood, arms akimbo, studying the shadows of the wall. After a minute he bent, worked the empty cartridge between two stones, and with the butt of his pistol gave it a single tap. He walked back to the hut and we trooped after him—twenty long paces.

But hitting that target would still be like hunting for a whisper in a big wind. Señor Villa, I prayed . . . shoot straight.

He raised the pistol quickly to chest level, didn't bother to use the sights, steadied a split second, then fired. The gun made a light, dry snap; chips of stone sparked off the wall. There was a little echo and the bitter whine of the ricochet. Hipólito Villa and Candelario ran to the wall, spurs jingling, while Pancho Villa hooked his left arm through mine and said softly, "Come on, Tomás!"

Candelario squatted, then bellowed, "You did it, chief!"

Villa's face was nearly blank, but I caught the flicker of a red-toothed smile. We reached the wall and peered down. I couldn't believe it: the right edge of the cartridge had been shattered to pulp by the bullet.

"I didn't hit it exact center," Villa said glumly. "Almost, but not quite. You see? I told you, it can't be done."

Candelario beamed. "Try it again, chief."

"Why break your balls trying the impossible?" Villa still held my arm in his warm grasp. "Now tell me the truth, meester"—and again I saw the green flicker in his eyes—"this man in Dallas . . . did you really see him do this thing? This thing which I've just failed to do?"

I could have kept lying, I think, and got away with it. He wasn't angry. But it seemed I was being given a second chance. He hadn't really failed, and suddenly I didn't want to fail, either. I swallowed hard. "No, sir. I heard about it, but I never did see it. I lied. He's an old man. They say he could do it when he was young."

"You won't ever lie to me again, will you?"

"No, señor."

"I believe you." For a minute, Villa contemplated. "You know," he said, quite seriously, "I think if I practiced I could do it. But since this other gringo sonofabitch didn't show up, we're short of bullets. I might have done it with one shot when I was younger. It's not that I'm old, but I've been with a woman. Last night, and the night before . . . I can't count the nights. Days too. You see, I lay my life bare to you, as with all my friends. When you spill your juices, it unsteadies your hand. I like women too much—that's one of my principal faults. I respect women and therefore I often marry them, but most of all I like to fuck them. Sometimes I can't help myself . . . do you know what I mean?"

"Yes, chief," I murmured.

"Try to stay away from women, Tomás. Sometimes, of course, it's impossible, but if you try and succeed you'll be a better man. Bullfighters have told me the same thing. They ought to know. Now, what's bothering you?"

I had been thinking about the shooting and finally voiced my puzzlement. "You didn't aim," I said.

"Aim? No . . . ah, wait. I understand! You're a good American cowboy . . . you ride, but you don't shoot. That's something we'll have to fix. Come along! This won't be a waste of bullets."

Together we walked through the dazzling light to the thin strip of shade behind the hut. The others tagged along, interested. Villa handed me the cartridge belt and pistol, still warm from his grasp. The butt fit snugly in my hand, and I strapped on the belt.

"Go ahead," he said. "Take a shot. Give us your best."

I sighted carefully down the barrel at the cartridge case, took a deep breath and pulled the trigger. There was more kick than I had expected, and the pistol jerked up into the air. Candelario trotted down to the wall and inspected the target.

"About a hundred yards into Chihuahua, chief . . ."

"Awful." Villa rested a fleshy hand on my shoulder. "I like you. I don't want to see you get killed. Actually, it's a wonder you're still alive, telling lies and shooting as badly as you do. Now pay attention . . . I'm going to share a secret with you that's worth more than a million dollars. It could mean the difference between life and death to you. Don't you think your life is worth more than a million dollars?"

"You bet your ass I do," I said.

He guffawed, showing red teeth. "What a fool this is! Listen, my friend . . . I'll tell you another secret which might save your hide equally well. This is Mexico! Your life isn't worth more than ten pesos here. That's the price I would have to pay some down-and-out *pelado,* some nobody, if I wanted to hire him to kill you—which of course I'd never do, because if I wanted you dead I'd simply shoot you myself. And there would be no one in this world to object. You understand?"

I nodded unhappily. I understood all too well.

"Cheer up," Villa said. "We're going to be friends. I'm going to teach you many things. Now pay attention again. Listen closely. First calm yourself. Look at the target. . . . Shut everything else from your mind. Love it a little. Not the way you would love a woman, but the way you would love part of yourself . . . like a hand, or your cock. Between you and the target there must be no distance . . . distance is an illusion. I spit on distance. Is it nonsense to you, or do you understand?"

His voice droned, yet soothed, and I had the feeling as I stared at the target that it had moved closer to me. I saw the cartridge clearly. Villa's voice came from very far off.

"Wrap your middle finger around the trigger. It will feel strange, but do it. Remember, there is no distance. You don't have to aim. The bullet will find its way. Raise the pistol and fire."

I did as he told me and squeezed off a second shot.

"Son of a whore!" Candelario sounded amazed. "Only four inches to the right!"

Villa beamed at me. "Well done, cowboy! You've learned in five minutes what it took me five years! If you go out there every day with five rounds and a clear head—and if you haven't fucked a woman the night before—you'll become a marksman." He clapped me on the back, and I don't think he could have been more pleased if his own shot had lodged dead center instead of clipping the cartridge's edge. I was feeling pretty frisky myself. "If you're loyal to me," he said, "you'll never have anything to fear. I like you, and my friends like you. Candelario! What do you think of this boy? The truth!"

"He's lucky," Candelario replied.

Villa considered that for a moment, then nodded vigorously. "We need men who are lucky," he said. "In fact, we need every man we can get. So!" He turned back to me. "Do you still want to join us? Do you have any idea what we're fighting for?"

"Land and liberty," I said. I had read that in the *Herald.*

"Good! *Very* good! Listen—" He grasped my shoulders. "For nearly four hundred years the people of this miserable country have been slaves. First to the Spaniards, who stole our gold and gave us religion. Then to the rich Mexicans, who stole our land and gave us pulque. If the revolution triumphs, the poor will get everything back that they lost. Then—so that they can keep it!—their children will learn to read and write. The little Señor Madero explained all that to me before those bastards, Huerta and Orozco, killed him. So now we follow Señor Carranza, the First Chief, and we're blessed with a common enemy. Huerta controls the Federal Army—it's the same army that Díaz used to keep the people in line. They're professional soldiers, which means that the people are their natural enemy. Orozco, on the other hand, has a volunteer army, the Redflaggers, that he pays in silver. Their task is to kill revolutionists. Their flag is red, and so are their hands, with the blood of the people. They're mercenaries, by their own choice. To them we'll show no mercy."

"How many of them are there?"

"A lot," he said grimly. "The pay is good."

"And how many men do you have in your own army, chief?"

"Five here. That's counting you and me. Four waiting for me across the river in El Paso. That's . . . let's see . . ." He counted rapidly on his fingers. "That's nine."

"That's *all?* I thought you already *had* an army!"

"I'll get one."

"Nine men?"

"With nine men, loyal and brave, I can recruit nine thousand more. Then I'll need horses for them to ride, trains for them to travel on, food for them to eat, rifles for them to shoot and bullets to put into the rifles." A pop-eyed smile lit up his face. "None of this will be very difficult. The people know me. They'll follow me. Look how easily I convinced you to do it, and you're a gringo." His eyes grew a shade more solemn. "I need men like you, Tomás. You're young, but you're clever and you want to learn. Moreover, as Candelario said, you're lucky. Once we have a real army, you'll have the rank of captain. If I forget, remind me."

A captain! I hadn't counted on that at all, but it made me feel wonderful.

3

"He may at pleasure whip, or hang, or torture."

A Yaqui Indian woman cooked our meal inside the hut. Like most Yaquis she was a nutty-brown color, flat-nosed and silent; I judged her more young than old. As she passed close to Villa, on the way to the little fire she had built on the broken dog irons, he gave her a friendly pat on the rump. It occurred to me then that she might be the woman into whom he had spilled his juices the night before, so that his aim at the cartridge was just that hairbreadth off. She was cooking frijoles, with some bits of brown meat simmering in a pan, waiting to be rolled into the tortillas. The smell of meat in that tiny space set my mouth to watering. From the pocket of his dirty shirt Candelario produced a crumpled pack of Sweet Caporal cigarettes which he offered round. Hipólito dug a bottle of mezcal from a dark corner, and it passed from one man to another. Although that frontier scamper juice could draw a blood blister on a rawhide boot, I took a healthy swallow. I had always heard that Villa didn't drink alcohol, and it proved to be true: he let the bottle pass by him. They were talking idly about a man named Urbina who was waiting somewhere to the south in Durango to join up with them . . . when we heard the hoofbeats of trotting horses outside. Everyone fell silent.

"Just two," Villa said, even before Julio went out the door. Then the hoofbeats slowed, and I heard a Mex voice say something indistinctly. Hipólito peered out, black and bulky against the white light that would have fried us if we had let it beat its way inside.

"It's Rodolfo, with some gringo."

Looking over his shoulder, Candelario cried, "That's Wentworth! The bastard who didn't show up at the cantina!"

"Be easy," Villa ordered. He had the natural instinct to keep men calm, and then they looked to him to point in the right direction.

A moment later a short, middle-aged American wearing rimless eyeglasses and a dusty tan business suit fumbled slowly through the door, followed by a big Mexican in a heavy brown-and-gold sombrero that could have shaded two smaller men. It brushed against both sides of the doorway. The American was busy rubbing his ass, which I guessed was saddlesore—he didn't strike me as a horseman—and he tried to restore his lost dignity by busily slapping the dust from his jacket.

The Mexican, Rodolfo Fierro, looked about thirty years of age. He was over six feet tall and sturdily built, with a neat mustache, gentle brown eyes and a handsome face. He wore the outfit of the *charro,* the gentleman rider—tight black pants, glistening hip-high black boots and a loose-fitting blue-striped cotton shirt. It occurred to me that if you took any of the men surrounding Pancho Villa, including his brother, down Commerce Street in Dallas, the citizens there would give you a wide berth to avoid infection by this plague marching their way—for they were the most ferocious lot I'd ever seen. Except this man. I could have brought Rodolfo Fierro into my mama's sitting room for coffee and biscuits and not been ashamed. He looked like the Mexicans I had seen in the movies, plucking languidly at a guitar and crooning "La Paloma" to shy señoritas on grilled balconies. This man, I decided, was *civilized.* In the light of later events I would think back often on that meeting, breathtaken at my perceptiveness.

"Chief," he said liltingly, and even his voice had a musical quality, "I found Señor Wentworth in El Paso, and I was lucky enough to persuade him to come visit you. He wants very much to explain why he isn't able to provide the rifles and bullets he promised you. He's tried to explain it to me, but since I'm only an ignorant railway worker turned revolutionist, I don't truly understand. I know he'll do better with you."

He offered this with such soothing politeness that I thought, Good grief, how did this big sweet fellow fall into such rough company? Candelario was right. I was a *pendejo.*

As an El Paso merchant, Wentworth knew the lingo, and he

launched right away into his defense. He had the rifles, new Mausers; and he had ammunition for them. But they were in bond at a warehouse, and his partner—well, not exactly his partner, but a man with whom he was doing business, a man named Felix Sommerfeld—had gone off with the papers and the keys. Sommerfeld was seventy miles away in Columbus, New Mexico, and wouldn't be back for at least a week. It was all Sommerfeld's fault.

"I know this Sommerfeld," Villa said. "He's a Jew. I've dealt with him before."

"Then you know how difficult he is." Wentworth spoke with a new righteousness. "Not to be trusted."

Villa nodded. "I trusted him two years ago. Would you believe it, Señor Wentworth? I asked him then for three hundred Springfield rifles."

"Ah, you see?"

"But he delivered them to me! Not only on time, but on credit. He charged me three percent interest, that's true, but I didn't think that was unfair. He has to live too. The Jews are called 'The People of the Book,' did you know that?"

"He's in Columbus," Wentworth said stubbornly. "And he has the papers."

Villa turned to Wentworth's calm escort. "Rodolfo, do you know any more about this matter?"

"Yes, chief," Rodolfo Fierro replied smoothly, as if this were a play they had rehearsed many times. "After Señor Wentworth didn't meet Candelario and Julio, I asked around. By great fortune I stumbled on Señor Sommerfeld, who had just returned from Columbus, earlier than expected. He's a very straightforward fellow, even if he looks like a frog, and he told me that he had sold the rifles to Señor Wentworth. But since that time, he said, Señor Wentworth had met at the Gateway Hotel with two Mexicans recently arrived from Coahuila—where, if my memory doesn't play tricks on me, I believe that Venustiano Carranza, the First Chief of the revolution, has his headquarters."

Villa turned to the American, offering a friendly smile. "Why didn't you say that you'd been approached by Carranza? He and I fight for the same cause. How can there be a conflict?"

"But Carranza—" Wentworth stopped, as if he had thought better of it.

"Do you know the wisdom of King Solomon?" Villa inquired. "The two mothers claimed the same baby, so the king said, 'We'll cut it in half.' He could then tell by their reaction who truly owned the baby. I learned the tale last year when I was in prison in Mexico City, from a book. The solution isn't exactly the same, but it's still very simple. We can divide the supply of rifles and ammunition. Half for Carranza, whom I serve, and half for me. Never mind that you promised them all to me . . . I understand the ways of business. A man must stay friendly to all factions."

Wentworth's eyes narrowed. "Half the guns would be enough for you?"

"Do we look like we've got a fucking army here?" Villa, barking his high laugh, peered into the corners of the hut. "How many rifles do we talk about? Five hundred? Two hundred would be more than we could carry! You can sell the rest to Carranza, even Obregón, as you've arranged. Where is your warehouse?"

"Missouri Street, a block west from the railroad yards."

"And the papers?"

"You don't need them. It's illegal to take guns across the border."

"And the keys?"

For some crazy reason Wentworth's face took on a smug smile. "I just remembered—I have an extra set in my saddlebags."

"Excellent." Villa turned to me. "Now I'll teach you something, Tomás. If Rodolfo hadn't gone to find this man, we wouldn't have any guns. He would have sold them to Carranza—in fact, he would have sold them to Huerta if the bastard had bothered to make him an offer. But the guns had been promised to me. Now tell me. Do you think Señor Wentworth behaved honorably?"

"No," I said. That was the obvious answer, and clearly required of me.

"Can we ever trust him again?"

Not so obvious. "Maybe he's learned a lesson," I said, thinking of my lie about Joe Lane.

"No," said Villa. "But he'll learn one now. He tried to cheat us, and what a man does to you once, he'll do again . . . if you let him. Rodolfo—?"

"Yes, chief?"

"Execute this man as an enemy of the revolution."

"Here?" Fierro asked. "Or outside?"

"Outside would be better. It's a small room, and I have sensitive ears."

Wentworth turned a sickly blue color. His eyes seemed to pop from behind his glasses as if he were being strangled. "Señor Villa! . . . ." His voice cracked. "Half the guns is fine! All, if you need them! I don't want to be difficult! I have to tell you more about Felix Sommerfeld—" Abruptly then, he turned to me, as if seeing me for the first time. He whispered pitifully in English, "Please, whoever you are—for God's sake, help me out of this. . . ."

Villa asked me what he had said.

"He wants me to help him," I explained, and now my voice shook too. My previous answer had helped to condemn him. I felt dazed by the events, but there was nothing I could do to halt them.

"Yes, do that," Villa said. "Help him out the door, Tomás. Rodolfo, this is Tomás. He's just joined us, and he's a clever young man. Tomás, this is Rodolfo Fierro, who is like a brother to me. Some men call him my butcher. He doesn't mind."

Wentworth wobbled down on his knees; his trembling legs wouldn't support him any longer. I saw the dark stain spreading down his trousers.

"General Villa, this isn't fair . . . this is a mistake!"

"I'm not a general yet." Glancing down, Villa saw what I had seen. "Jesus! He's pissing! . . . and he's going to shit in a second and stink up the room. Do it here, Rodolfo—and quickly! I'll cover my ears."

Before Villa had time to stuff his thumbs into his ears, Fierro slid a long-barreled black pistol from his belt and jammed it snug against the back of Wentworth's neck. Villa was right—the boom of the shot was like a small thunderclap echoing against the close adobe walls. My ears rang and Wentworth's forehead splattered redly open. He plunged forward as though someone had reached up and yanked him powerfully to the dirt. The body twitched a few times, then accepted its death and lay still. A moment ago, a man . . . now, a corpse. Garbage. Julio Cárdenas crossed himself. I nearly vomited but managed to hold it back.

"Take him into the desert." Villa gave the order to Candelario, who bent immediately to seize Wentworth's limp legs. "Wait . . . did he shit?"

"I don't think so. Rodolfo was too quick." Candelario wrinkled his nose, then looked carefully. "No, he didn't. Should I bury him?"

"What for? We won't be here tonight. Get the keys from his saddlebags. Give the horse to Tomás. We're going to this damned warehouse in El Paso to get the rifles."

Candelario got a good grip on Wentworth's patent-leather shoes and began hauling him out the door, leaving a streak of dark blood speckled with white pulp in the dirt. I'd never seen a man's brains before, and I noticed, as my stomach kept heaving, that they looked like oatmeal.

Rodolfo Fierro stepped to one side to let the body slide past. Putting away his pistol, he sniffed the air. "Is the food ready? I'm starving."

Villa called out, "Manuela!"

The Yaqui woman by the fire nodded and began to stuff the meat into the tortillas. There was a cardboard box full of bent tin spoons. She handed the first chipped plate to Villa, who grunted and took it. They were all squatting in a semicircle on their haunches, and I did so too. It wasn't as uncomfortable as I had imagined.

Villa handed me the plate of food that the woman had meant for him. "Here, Tomás. Tell me if Manuela cooks as well as your mother."

I thought that his offering me his own plate was a kingly gesture of hospitality; I tried to forget that I had just nearly puked watching a fellow American murdered in cold blood. "Good," I grunted, spooning up some warm frijoles, although the sight of Wentworth's splattered brains from the corner of my eye nearly ruined my appetite.

"Eat a taco, boy. That's real beef, not dog."

Villa reached over and snatched the plate that Manuela was just in the act of handing to Candelario.

It wasn't until a long time afterwards that I realized Pancho Villa never took any food that was given him. He always made someone else eat it or else nibbled a bit from the plates of common soldiers, fearing that somewhere in this world there might possibly—just possibly!—be someone who would have reason to poison him.

There was no poison in the food that day. We six men hunkered down to our plates, nodding to one another and exchanging small talk, just like a hundred relaxed mealtimes I had passed with cowhands around campfires back in the Brazos. I kept thinking about Wentworth's body heating up outside in the afternoon sun, and how I had just witnessed an execution, and I wondered did he have a wife?—kids?—a mother who would miss him? And then I looked around and suddenly realized I was alone in this agitation. For my new friends, Wentworth was as forgotten as the fly killed at breakfast. They had other things on their minds. What was a single life? They were planning to conquer Mexico. To do that they would have to destroy a Federal army fifty thousand strong.

And that's how I met the band of men I would ride with for the next three years. One of them had already made my imagination a captive to his visions. Pancho Villa! *Muy matador,* as the Mexicans say— a killer. But he was going to make me a captain, and a man.

That night I sauntered up to the watchman at Wentworth's warehouse on Missouri Street, and while I engaged him in conversation Candelario stepped up behind the poor fellow and buffaloed him with the thin end of a Colt pistol. We loaded the Mausers on the backs of mules and set off through the darkness, until at dawn we were downriver opposite the little Mex town of Ysleta.

A hot sun was cooking up above the Franklin Mountains, rising fast. A dry wind gusted out of the desert from Texas, clearing the mist on the far bank of the Rio Grande, which my *compañeros* called the Rio Bravo. Even now I remember that the river smelled of dead fish. In my saddlebags I carried twenty spare cartridges for a Mannlicher rifle, a supply of Bull Durham tobacco, a barbed-wire cutter and my leather-bound copy of Shakespeare. With Pancho Villa and Rodolfo Fierro leading us, our horses pranced through shallow water. Upriver on the mud flats, Candelario Cervantes cursed the mules, swaybacked under the rifle crates. To get those rifles a man had been killed—I could still see his brains flying past my nose.

Candelario waved his big straw sombrero and bellowed, *"Viva el revolución! Viva Mexico!"*

The early-morning sparkle of the river glinted off Pancho Villa's answering grin. He wore an old cotton jacket and a dirty brown hat, and he had a paunch from drinking too much strawberry soda pop and eating too much peanut brittle. He sat his horse the way most men sink into their favorite easy chair, not a crack of daylight between his rump and the bowed saddle. I would come to know that man well. I was twenty-two years old, I didn't have a dime in my pockets, and like most young cowhands I liked to tell folks I could gobble up centipedes for breakfast and barbed wire for supper and it wouldn't harm my digestion a hair; but I knew that in crossing this river in such company I had never done anything in my life so reckless, so ridiculous . . . and so splendid. This is one thing, I swore, I won't quit until it's finished.

What I'm trying to say is that in those days I may have been a little crazy.

4 "Assume a virtue, if you have it not."

Alkali dust boiled up from the horses' hoofs. The desert of Chihuahua lay bone-white and dry, while to the west the craggy shoulders of bronze-colored mountains heaved up from the plain. Nothing grew but saguaro cactus and maguey. Nothing lived but the turkey buzzards aloft and the lizards below. Our sombreros cast black shadows on the baked earth. A killing sun beat down, and saddle leather creaked wearily. . . .

The mules carried the five hundred rifles and the fifty thousand cartridges. The next phase of Villa's plan had begun: his great trek in the spring of 1913 through northern Chihuahua to recruit his revolutionary army. From nine men, he had said, we had to become nine thousand, armed and ready to fight. How could he do that? I rode Wentworth's horse, a mutton-headed gray with knock-knees and one rheumy eye. It had been given to me with hardly an apology. I was still an outsider.

"Where are we going?" I asked my boyhood pal, Julio Cárdenas, who rode with me through that bleak landscape.

"Ascensión," he replied.

"Where's that, Julio?"

"To the south. Not far, but it will take awhile."

"What's in Ascensión?"

"Maybe a few goats. It will be our base. We'll train our men there."

I remembered that he wasn't usually a talkative fellow, this pox-faced man. He had the face of a monk, with thin lips and piercing eyes under tufted black brows. To make conversation and lead up to the big questions, I asked him how he had met up with Pancho Villa.

/ 27

"I fought with him at Juárez two years ago, Tomás, when we took the city for the little Señor Madero. So did my wife."

"You're married now? Wonderful! Gosh, I didn't know that. Congratulations!"

His wife, he told me, had been a *soldadera*. She hadn't fired a rifle but had cooked food just behind the front lines for the men. The position had been overrun by the Federals. She had been captured and shot.

"Shot? What do you mean, Julio? *Killed?*"

He nodded, and I mumbled something about being sorry. Then I remembered the words he had used. "But you said she was captured. She was a prisoner."

"That's what they do," he explained. "So do we."

"You shoot the prisoners?"

"Tomás, they're bad men. In Juárez with that woman, you saw something of it. But there's worse. If you're patient, you'll find out."

I did my best. Toward early afternoon we reached a little pueblo called Samalayuca, baked by the breathless sun to the color of the desert. It meant nothing to me then: I had no idea that one day I myself would be taken here to be executed. How could I know? That was far in the future, and I knew nothing. An ancient church greeted us, and then a dusty white street with adobe huts, a cantina, a few squawking chickens and a wrinkled old woman in black with a water jar on her head. Candelario pounded on doors and found some eggs, a pile of brittle tortillas and a clay jar filled with tepid water. The peasants hid from us. I had never been to Old Mexico south of Juárez. If a man died here and went to hell, I figured he would wire back for blankets. The land was dry as a tobacco box, and the people in it looked withered, with shriveled skin and bent backs. Did they know the revolution was starting again? Did they know that Pancho Villa and the rest of us were going to give them land, liberty and literacy?

I had voiced the thought aloud, and Julio answered, "They know, but they're too weak to care. They don't fight, so we leave them alone."

We ate in the cantina. Two thin, knotty, brown Indian boys limped in, wearing homemade sandals and filthy breechclouts. One seemed no more than thirteen. They stared at us—our appearance, armed, unshaven, barbaric, would have frightened most grown men, and they were only boys. But Villa measured them with a friendly look, so the boys drew near.

"Señor Villa . . . is it really you?"

"I'm no ghost."

"Is it true what the men say? Do you go to fight again?"

"Naturally."

"Can we go with you, señor?"

"If you loved the little Señor Madero, and if you're prepared to e . . . yes, you can come with us."

The younger of the boys laughed shrilly. "Will you give us rifles?"

"In time, *muchachos,* when we have enough of them."

I had been standing next to him during this conversation, but something puzzled me. I looked down at the boys' feet, "Why do you both limp?" I asked.

The boys glanced at Villa, as if for permission, and he nodded his round head.

One of them spoke, explaining that they were Yaquis. They and their fathers had worked on the cattle ranch of a rich landowner, Luis Terrazas, who now paid Orozco's salary. They were whipped like oxen, paid in metal disks that could only be exchanged for goods at the hacienda store. When the revolution began the Yaqui men fought for Madero. After he assassinated Madero and took power, Huerta decided that the Yaquis would be an unstable element in the north. He sent Orozco's Redflaggers into the desert villages. The Yaqui men were shipped to henequen plantations in the south, while the boys and others like them were tied to stakes. The Redflaggers skinned the soles of their feet with bayonets, so that they could never run away and fight.

"Show me your feet," I said, and they lifted them to reveal the wounds.

"You'll get horses too," Villa said. He patted the boys' heads, dismissing them, and they limped out.

"You see?" Julio turned to me. "That's what we fight against—men who would do that to children."

Then an older man came in, carrying a rusted sword and an ancient carbine. Empty cartridge belts crisscrossed his bare chest and the scars of old bullet holes puckered his shoulder. He had fought for Madero back in 1911, he said. He wanted to fight again, and he was accepted into our company. But he brought bad news. Abraham González, the pro-Madero governor of the state of Chihuahua and an honorary godfather to Villa—the man who had supplied him with money when he was exiled in El Paso—had been arrested by one of Huerta's generals. On his way to prison in Mexico City, the Federal officers hung González from the rocketing train. He was torn to pieces under the steel wheels.

"Filth!" Villa growled. His eyes sprouted tears.

He wiped them and strode to the little adobe hut, where he knew there would be a telegraph key. A pockmarked old man cowered behind a battered desk. Villa ordered him to tap out a message to the Federal general in Chihuahua City.

MURDERER: KNOWING THAT THE CRIMINAL GOVERNMENT YOU REPRESENT WAS PREPARING TO EXTRADITE ME FROM TEXAS I HAVE SAVED THEM THE TROUBLE. I AM HERE IN MEXICO READY TO MAKE WAR UPON YOU. FRANCISCO VILLA.

To everyone's surprise, less than twenty minutes later a message

/ 29

ticked back. General Rábago, the Federal commander, was prepared to let bygones be bygones. "You have no army," he said, "but I'll give you a whole division and make you a general to boot." And in the name of President Huerta, he offered Villa a bonus of $50,000, to be deposited in an El Paso bank if he would accept the appointment.

"This man has no shame!" Villa cried. He wired back promptly. TELL THE PIG HUERTA THAT I DO NOT NEED THE RANK OF GENERAL AS I AM ALREADY COMMANDER OF TWELVE FREE MEN. FRANCISCO VILLA.

We were twelve now. He counted the Yaqui boys and the man with the rusted sword. I thought that showed some style. He was an actor too. He wasn't Hamlet, not by a far cry, but he could certainly do Henry Five.

Pancho Villa detached Candelario and the Yaqui boys westward, mounted, with the mules and rifles, to Ascensión. The rest of us headed south, deeper into the desert of Chihuahua. We wandered past gutted pueblos, populated only by old crones, gaunt men, children naked in the dust. The dust was everywhere—in your hair, up your nostrils and between your teeth. As soon as the sun set like a blast furnace behind the hulking mountains, the chill struck at our bones. We wrapped ourselves in serapes up to the ears, like mummies, while the horses shivered on the picket line. Dawn came. We set out again, hunting for some stray scrawny hen or even a prairie dog. On the roads, little more than wide tracks, we passed heaps of stones topped by crude wooden crosses to commemorate some violent death. It might have taken place yesterday or a century ago. There was no telling.

A few ragged men rode up out of the shimmering heat haze to join us. Toward late afternoon we would see small patrols of Federals, dark figures cutting a trail of white dust through the desert, but we avoided each other. I wondered what Villa was accomplishing, until it got through to me that his purpose at this stage was simply to recruit and spread word of his presence throughout Chihuahua, before we settled down to training, or whatever we would do, in Ascensión. Sure enough, when we reached a place called El Progreso, fifty *campesinos* from the nearby haciendas, men and beardless boys alike, were gathered at the edge of town to join us. Most of them were armed with only machetes. "Don't be killed!" their women wailed. The boys cheered—they might have been marching off to a Sunday baseball game. Then in San Lorenzo a gang of nearly two hundred mine workers joined us. Their leader said to Villa, "Señor, we are at your disposal. When can we ‘ght?"

"Are you prepared to die?" It seemed to be Villa's favorite question ‘olunteers.

"Look at these poor souls," the man said. Indeed, they were a ragged lot, with swollen bellies and protruding cheekbones. "The mine owners have starved them for a hundred years. Why should they not be prepared to die? They have nothing better to do in life."

But they had no rifles. How could they fight? Villa sent them off through the desert toward Ascensión.

We came upon a thin steer grazing alone among the cactus, pitifully trying to nibble at the dry green spikes. A reata circled above Villa's head and flew lazily through the dark violet air, looping neatly over the cow's neck. The animal bellowed weakly, but it could hardly move. Rodolfo Fierro bent from his saddle, with one slash of his machete dropping the beast to the earth in a spray of bright blood. Death seemed to be Fierro's reason for living. Julio told me that it was said he had once shot a stranger in Chihuahua City to settle a bet on whether a dying man falls forward or backward.

"And which was it?" I asked.

A macabre argument raged; no one could remember.

As darkness fell an unseen horseman passed by, iron spurs ringing. Villa sniffed the dry air. "We can't light a fire. I smell the Federals. . . ."

Fierro skinned the steer expertly, and the men ripped the meat from the carcass. They ate it raw. I had never believed I could do that, but hunger and a new life change a man's tastes. "You like it?" Julio asked me, blood staining his narrow jaw. He chewed steadily.

I grunted something that wasn't either yes or no.

"But it's good for you, especially if you're going to fight. When the battles start, sometimes we have no time to cook. That's all we eat. It makes us brave. Are you brave in battle, Tomás?"

"I'll find out," I said, and then began to wonder.

At yet another dusty pueblo whose name I no longer remember, the black shadow of Candelario Cervantes appeared out of the alkali haze, leading a herd of twenty cattle. The mules and rifles were safe in Ascensión. He and the Yaqui boys had rustled the cattle from a hacienda to the north. "Did we do the right thing?" he asked Villa, scratching at the lice in his beard. "They wandered into our path . . . I couldn't resist."

"You did right, *compadre*. The function of the rich in this miserable country is to feed the poor."

But this gave Villa an idea. He had some of the cows butchered for steaks, and then after the rest of the meat had been salted and hung out to dry in the sun, he detailed a force of men under Candelario to ride a few miles east to the estates of Luis Terrazas, the hacienda owner who was Orozco's patron. Two days later Candelario's gang of rustlers returned, driving a herd of nearly two hundred fat beef cattle, whooping like banshees and firing their guns into the air. For a minute Villa looked annoyed—we didn't have that many bullets to spare. But then he grinned and gave Candelario an *embrazo,* the obligatory Mexican hug. I think, because he was a peasant himself, he understood the nature of his men better than any regular army general could have done. Aside from eating raw meat, nothing made them feel braver than hearing a little boisterous yelling coupled with the din of their own gunfire, even if their precious bullets were only watering the desert with lead.

Then Villa explained his notion: Candelario and Hipólito were to take the herd north to Columbus, in New Mexico. "You remember Wentworth, the one who tried to cheat us? He spoke of a man named Felix Sommerfeld. I know this man. He has a partner, another Jew trader named Ravel, who lives in Columbus. They're in the business of selling rifles and ammunition. We have no money yet, but we have the cattle. Trade for them, Hipólito. Beef for guns. Make a good bargain."

Sitting hunched on a cane chair in an adobe hut in a godforsaken pueblo called Espindoleño, Villa wrote out a list of the supplies he needed. Writing didn't come easy to him, and he gripped the pencil until his knuckles showed yellow. Twice he tore through the paper with the point—not in anger, but because he was pressing so hard, trying to translate his thoughts into these impossibly difficult squiggles. Julio and I were standing nearby, smoking some cigarettes I had rolled from my sack of Bull Durham. With the smoke wafting past his nose, Villa's concentration broke. He looked up and saw me. Then his eyes widened.

"Madre de Dios! It must have been providence that sent you to me, Tomás. . . ." Smiling wonderfully, showing all his red-stained teeth, he thrust the note at me. "Translate this into English, and write it out neatly." He wrapped an arm around my shoulder and moved me outside into the sunlight. "Can I trust you?"

I wondered exactly what he meant by that, remembering with considerable unease how he had punished Wentworth for a breach of trust. So I thought it prudent to show some enthusiasm.

"You can trust me," I said. "I'll never lie to you again. I'm on your side."

"I believe that. I want to tell you how I'm going to win the revolution, so you won't think I'm some kind of Moses wandering in the desert, waiting for God to give him a new set of commandments. Look at this map." We bent down and he dropped it in the dust between us, smoothing out the wrinkled edges. There was Mexico spread before me, from its long northern border with the United States, through the high central plateau and Mexico City, then narrowing and swinging east to the Yucatán peninsula. Pancho Villa couldn't read, but he had studied the map so often that he knew the shapes of the names as well as the veins on his brown hand.

"Here we are," he said, pointing, "in the desert of Chihuahua. Carranza is to the east in Coahuila, with General Pablo González. Obregón, who is also on our side, is in Sonora, to the west. Zapata's near Cuernavaca, south of Mexico City, in the state of Morelos. Those are the leaders of the revolution. The Federals and the Redflaggers, unfortunately, are everywhere—we're like little islands in an unfriendly ocean. So the first thing to do is consolidate our forces, which is what I intend to do when we reach the pueblo of Ascensión."

His own objective, he explained, would be to gain control of the state of Chihuahua. To do that he would have to achieve three things: control of the main north-south railroad line that meandered all the way from Juárez on the border to Mexico City on the high plateau; the capture of the major industrial cities of Torreón, Chihuahua City and Zacatecas; and finally the capture of Juárez itself.

"The railroad is the key," he went on, "because not only will we cut the link between Mexico City and Huerta's garrisons in the north, but we'll be able to move freely on it. And Juárez is the prize, because then we'll have a port of entry for arms and supplies from the United States." Once he controlled Chihuahua, he said, Mexico City would collapse like a piece of soft fruit between a hammer and an anvil, with Zapata in his small southern base of Morelos playing the part of the anvil.

"And then," he grinned at me, "the revolution will be won. Don Venus Carranza will be interim chief of state, we'll elect a new president and maybe we can live happily ever after. What do you think of my plan?"

"I think you need a big army, and rifles, and bullets, and maybe even some machine guns and artillery. And a lot of luck."

"Good, Tomás!" He looked pleased, as if I had said something brilliant. "That's what I think too. And that's why I've given you this list. I want you to go to Columbus with Candelario and my brother. After you've translated it, give the list to the Jews. Tell them, if they ask, that I wrote it out myself—it's best they don't think I'm a barbarian." He considered for a moment, squinting into the sun. "There are two gringo generals at Fort Bliss. Their names are Scott and Pershing. This Jew, Felix Sommerfeld, knows them both. Find out from him what they think of me, and if that pig Orozco is in touch with them. Go to El Paso if it's necessary. . . . Hipólito will give you the money. Is all that clear to you?"

I nodded gravely, delighted with his trust.

"And get rid of that fucking blind nag I wished on you. Tell Candelario to give you a decent horse."

Candelario found a big chestnut that belonged to one of the mine workers. He was twelve or thirteen years old and stood over fifteen hands high, with a good topline and heavily muscled hindquarters. I took the ring bit out of his mouth, slipping in a hackamore to keep him from getting cold-jawed, and I could see he appreciated it. Within an hour we had provisioned ourselves with water and jerked beef, and we set out with the herd for New Mexico—a trip that would introduce the next piece in the new jigsaw of my life. But if the first huge angular piece was Villa, this next shape—rounder by far; you might say, an hourglass figure—connected at only one narrow bridge. And it would bring me an entirely different sort of trouble for the next two years.

The chaparral slashed my cheeks, and the cholla cactus pricked my legs and gashed the chestnut's flanks, but he stepped along with a natural fox trot and I hardly ever had to tickle him with my spurs. Candelario quickly found out I knew more about trail driving than he did, and so he and I were the point riders while the Yaqui boys rode swing and Hipólito drew the disagreeable job of riding drag, getting the dust of the whole herd kicked into his teeth. His good blue suit was a mess. The rippling line of mountains seemed to march beside us—gray, forbidding, desolate beyond a man's understanding. The heat turned the land into a cauldron. At night, under diamond-hard stars, coyotes howled like wounded children. I shivered under my serape, rubbing my icy feet together until sleep canceled the pain.

Just before dusk on the second day out, the chestnut picked up a stone in his shoe and I dismounted to cut it out with a hoof hook. Riding herd here for a single year would kill a good trail horse and burn ten years of weather into a man's face. Candelario swung down out of the saddle and tromped over to me, boots kicking up pebbles.

"You look unhappy, Tomás. Are you all right?"

"Candelario, this is the most godawful place I've ever been."

"Isn't it? But let me tell you a story I heard when I was young. When God was busy making the world, He said, 'I'll try an experiment. I've given some countries rivers—to some I've given forests—to others, beautiful women. With this land I'm making now, I'll give it . . . nothing!' You see, God had a sense of humor then. But He repented. Nothing, after all, seemed too harsh a gift. He had to give it something. So He said, 'I know. I'll give it *rocks.*' And He did, and He called it Chihuahua."

We trotted through the wilderness toward Columbus. . . .

Candelario told me how he had lost his eye. He was from Camargo, a town south of Chihuahua City, and although he had been brought up on a ranch he began working in a potash mine when he was eleven. A twelve-hour day, six days a week. His father was a foreman there, and his mother, when she wasn't in the final day of a pregnancy, sold tacos on the street. She had sixteen children, ten of whom had lived.

"The unlucky ones, as she would say. My father, naturally, was deeply in debt, and the debt fell on his sons as well. One day when I was fifteen I came home and my father told me I was betrothed. My bride was to be my cousin Annabella, who was pregnant. 'Not by me,' I protested. He knew that, and she had been a maid at the hacienda, so it was all fairly clear. I married Annabella and we had our first child, a daughter. There was a fee due to the church at the time of the marriage, then another one at the christening. I couldn't pay it, so it was paid for me by the hacienda owner, and my debt kept growing."

"Why didn't you just quit?" I didn't tell him that in the past it had been my specialty.

"Under the dictator, Tomás, if you ran away from a job or debt, you could be shot on sight. There was even a bounty to whoever brought you in. I was a slave until my twenty-seventh year. My mind as well as my body. Asleep! The revolution awakened me."

As soon as word spread of Madero's uprising, Candelario joined a local brigade. He knew how to ride, but he learned to shoot only after he slit a Federal officer's throat with a machete and stole his rifle. When his own captain was killed near Tecolete, the brigade was given to Pancho Villa. Camped outside Juárez, the little revolutionist army was eager to fight, and Villa sent a patrol upriver to draw fire from the defenders.

"I was in that patrol," Candelario recalled. "I was shot, and the bastards left me there. I dragged myself to the riverbank and then passed out. I assumed I was dead . . . it's a strange feeling, hard to describe. Not truly unpleasant. But Villa had seen all this through his field glasses, and he knew I still lived. He sent Julio out to get me. So I owe my life to them both. I lost an eye—the bullet cracked it like an egg—but I was very lucky. And a one-eyed man, they say, brings good luck wherever he goes."

It was in that same battle that Julio's young wife had been captured near the railroad station and then shot.

"Poor Julio! He had married for love, which is often a mistake but in this case seemed to work. He is a serious man, and religious, although I don't know how a revolutionist can believe in sin and Jesus and the rest of that shit the Church forces down your throat. Anyway, since she died he won't touch another woman." Candelario sighed, and then his good eye sparkled powerfully, making the glass one look even deader than usual. "I, Tomás, am just the opposite. Sometimes I feel cursed. I can't do without women, and I think of them all the time. When I ride, when I eat, when I try to sleep—why, even when I'm fucking one, I'm already thinking of the next one I'm going to fuck! Isn't that a curse? I love them too much. Perhaps that's my fate." He cast a quick look at me to see if I was scandalized. "I hope you won't be offended by this, but I like the gringo women above all. Their skin excites me. And among the gringos, especially the yellow-haired ones. The chief won't touch a woman who doesn't look like Moctezuma was her grandfather, but those blond pussies drive me wild, even if I know the bitches have dyed them." His tongue flicked across his lips. "Hipólito says there's a whorehouse near Columbus that has two blond sisters. They're famous . . .

they come from New Orleans and have French blood. We'll see. Do you crave women, Tomás?"

If he knew how little experience I'd had with them, he would have laughed at me, and I didn't want that. But I was saved by the bawling of a cow that had become tangled in the chaparral. I trotted off to help her, and so Candelario was forced to wait for his answer . . . but not too long.

The United States Cavalry had set up shop on the western edge of Columbus, in the state of New Mexico. When we crossed the border we gave their pup tents and pine barracks a wide berth and brought the herd in well to the east, where we bedded it down behind some small buttes that humped up from the desert. The morning was hot, and there wasn't enough grass there to chink between the ribs of a sandfly. Carrion crows wheeled lazily in a faultless blue sky. Hipólito Villa, in charge now that we had reached our destination, decided to ride into town right away and start negotiations with the Jews.

"You have my brother's list, Tomás?"

I tapped the breast pocket of my denim shirt where I kept my dwindling sack of Bull Durham. We rode off on the yellow plain, Hipólito in his dusty suit, with Candelario waving goodbye and chewing his lips thinking of the French whores.

Columbus was a recently built New Mexican cowtown of little importance and perhaps three hundred souls. Trying to make something of it, the good citizens had built a few hotels and a movie theater, and Hipólito told me there was a gambling emporium next to the whorehouse on the road that led north to Deming. It was a sorry place, and I had seen a dozen like it stretching from El Paso to Brownsville. Old Glory drooped over the depot of the El Paso & Southwestern Railroad, and riding up the main street, which these optimistic settlers had called Broadway, I spotted a Woolworth's and a Popular Dry Goods and the Crystal Theater, which was charging twenty cents admission to see Mabel Normand in *Race for Life.* The desert stretched like a flat brown carpet in all directions. Hipólito disappeared into the Commercial Hotel to find his man.

Ten minutes later we were sitting in Peache's Lunch Room at a big table with a red-and-white-checked cloth, spooning up split-pea soup and making small talk with Felix Sommerfeld and Samuel Ravel. I liked both of them, which surprised me, because I'd never had anything to do with Hebrews before and had been brought up believing they all wore little black caps and had beaks that touched their chins. Sommerfeld looked much as Fierro had described him—a white-faced frog—but to be more exact, and kind, he was a man of about fifty with a hairless face, a relaxed smile and two keen pale blue eyes that gleamed from behind gold-rimmed glasses. When he laughed, his belly rippled under his white linen suit and his watch chain jingled. He was never without a Murad cigarette in his hand, and the fat pink fingers were stained brown right up to the knuckles. Sam Ravel, by comparison, was a tall man in his early thirties who wore Cheyenne chaps, calfskin boots and a black Stetson; he had a hawk nose, dark observant eyes and an air about him that made you glad he was on your side rather than against you. But Felix Sommerfeld, I found out, beneath his plumpness, had plenty of leather as well. They bought the whole herd from us outright, taking our word for it on the count but reserving a look-see to make sure the cattle were healthy and offering a fair price of twenty dollars a head in greenbacks. Over the pea soup I explained to them that we didn't need cash; it was arms that we wanted. I handed them Villa's list.

Felix Sommerfeld studied it. "That seems reasonable, and if there's a difference either way we'll sort it out later. When do you need delivery?"

"Right away."

"Next week's more likely," Ravel drawled. He was from San Antonio, and he had put in a few years with the Texas Rangers, which of course didn't stop him from riding the other side of the fence now that he was a civilian. It gave him advantages too, since he knew whose palm couldn't be greased and who would take the *mordita*—the little bite—as the Mexicans lovingly called it.

"What about transport?" I asked.

"We'll lend you wagons," Sommerfeld said.

I thought that was friendly of him, and it gave me an idea. I knew how badly Villa needed bullets. "Look, Mr. Sommerfeld," I said, "we can provide you with a lot more cattle, probably as much as you can handle. It's wandering loose over half the state of Chihuahua." I guess they knew that was a lie but didn't much care. "Why don't you give us an extra hundred thousand cartridges, and one more machine gun with a hundred belts of ammunition? We'll deliver the cattle for them in two weeks."

Sam Ravel turned to Hipólito, who was busy tearing into his fried chicken with one hand and guzzling a cold bottle of Carta Blanca beer with the other. "I need to know," Ravel asked in Spanish, "if this man speaks for your brother."

Hipólito wiped grease from his mustache. "Yes, Tomás has my brother's trust."

That made me feel well, and Ravel nodded. "All right," he said, "I can live with the idea of another hundred thousand cartridges and a machine gun on credit." They were certainly fine men to do business with.

Toward the end of lunch I hazed the conversation round to matters Villa had wanted me to find out about. "I'll tell you what you want to know," Sommerfeld said. "President Wilson doesn't like Victoriano

Huerta—an attitude that Sam and I also share, in case it's escaped your attention. Wilson was appalled by Madero's murder. That means he won't allow any American arms to reach Huerta, and he's given orders to Pershing to seal off the border. That embargo applies to Villa and Carranza too, but it's a long border. The problem is, Huerta's being supplied by the Japanese . . . and I suspect the Germans as well. Did you know that?"

"No, sir."

"Keep it in mind. Beyond that, Wilson's most in sympathy with Carranza, because he likes Carranza's calling himself a Constitutionalist. Isn't that his title—First Chief of the Constitutionalist Army?"

"That's what they call him," I said, "when they're being polite."

"What Mr. Wilson knows about Mexico," Ravel said sourly, "you could stuff into a small taco."

Understanding the measure of their sympathy, I spoke more freely. "Villa wants to know what the Americans think of him."

Sommerfeld puffed at his cigarette, puckering his features so that he looked more like a frog than ever. "They think he's an illiterate bandit, a ruffian, and a hell of a man. And now, young fellow, there's something *I'd* like to know. What in the devil are *you* doing riding with him?"

"He's going to make me a captain," I said, chuckling.

"With pay?"

"We haven't discussed that yet."

"Haven't you any other reason?"

I was young. I couldn't tell him the nature of a young man's dreams. I said, "It's a long story."

Sommerfeld said pleasantly, "You should tell it to my daughter. She likes long stories, and she's a great admirer of Villa's revolution."

"I'd be glad to, sir"—which was a downright lie, if his daughter looked anything like Felix Sommerfeld.

"She may have a few doubts about Villa," he explained, "but none about what he stands for. She used to distribute that newspaper for Ricardo Flores Magón. *Regeneración,* it was called. In fact, she got into a little trouble over in Juárez because of it, but that's a story she'd have to tell you, and she's a bit shy about it." He may have seen a dulled look in my eye then, because he said, "You know who Flores Magón is, don't you?"

I nodded my head affirmatively. I didn't want to seem too much of a country bumpkin.

"I see. How about Bakunin and Marx? Do they interest you?"

There was a different tone to Sommerfeld's voice now, a kind of probing that made me decide not to press my luck.

"No, sir, I never met those two."

Sommerfeld and Ravel thought that was a witty remark, or at least they laughed good-humoredly, but then they changed the subject. Ravel was taking the evening train, the Drummer's Special, back to El Paso to arrange the supplies and wagons. He told me that he owned the Commercial Hotel here in Columbus and he would be honored if I'd spend the next few nights as his guest. He said he hoped I wouldn't take offense, but I smelled as though I'd been reared in a wolf's den and could use a hot bath, and any man who'd been riding a cattle trail could appreciate a night's sleep in a feather bed. Clean straw was tempting, but I explained that I didn't think Candelario and my friend in the blue suit would understand, and I'd bunk down with them on the edge of town where we had sheltered the herd. We all shook hands. I promised Mr. Sommerfeld I'd meet him in the lobby of the hotel at noon the next day, to wind up our paperwork.

When Hipólito and I were riding back to the herd, he loosened his black string tie and began to chuckle.

"What's so funny?"

"You are, Tomás. Why didn't you take the hot bath and the bed? The ground is hard. A bed is soft. Maybe he would have found a woman for you. Then you could have told Candelario and driven him mad."

"You understood?" I asked, more than a little surprised. "You speak English?"

"Naturally. When the revolution's over, I'm going to be a businessman. Did you think I was a peasant like Candelario and the others? The best part of business is to shut up and let someone else do the talking." He leaned across his saddle and patted my shoulder, and his fat face creased with a smile. "But you did well, asking for more bullets. I didn't think of that. You could be a businessman too. Maybe we'll be partners. Would you like that?"

"I wouldn't mind at all," I said, feeling less like a fool than before.

"In that case," Hipólito said, "make sure you don't get killed, and then you'll have a future."

5

**"It is the purpose
that makes strong the vow."**

That night, after we had made sure the cattle were snugged down under the watchful eyes of the vaqueros, we trotted out of Columbus on the north road to Deming. Candelario was looking forward to the evening's entertainment, and he let out a yell that might have made a wolf hunt for cover. But when Hipólito jingled the coins in his leather purse and announced that our first stop was going to be the gambling hall, Candelario's howl ceased and his head snapped round. His one good eye glared in the moonlight.

"What did I hear you say? You want to gamble before you fuck?"

"I'm feeling lucky," Hipólito explained.

"You'll lose all the money! Nothing will be left for the women!"

"If we fuck first," Hipólito said, "we'll be too tired to gamble. I'm worn out already. Fucking makes me sleepier."

I could hear Candelario's teeth, like galloping hoofs, grinding and gnashing in his jaw. "Listen, my fat friend," he sputtered. "Let me enlighten you as to your nature, which you should know already, but apparently you've forgotten. You'll gamble all night until there's nothing left. If you're lucky you'll lose it quickly. And what then? Where should I put my pecker, in my horse's ear?"

"Whose money is it?" Hipólito demanded.

"It belongs to the revolution."

"Is the revolution meant to pay for you wallowing in the cunt of some French whore?"

"Is it meant to pay for you at the roulette wheel?"

"Candelario, you're a peasant. In harder times I may have been a bandit, but in my soul, as I've told Tomás, I'm a businessman. I think ahead. I can read the eyes of the men sitting across the poker table from me, and I can see which numbers turn up more frequently on the wheel. Don't worry so much . . . I'll win the price of both those whores for the whole night."

"Then divide the money."

"There may not be enough," Hipólito admitted.

"Coño!"

"Imbecile!"

Mad enough to gnaw a gap out of an axe, Candelario leaned across his saddle horn and gripped my arm with fingers that were like iron bars. "Tomás, you decide. But bear this in mind—he plays poker like a Mexican, which means he can't believe the next card isn't going to give him a magnificent hand. So he raises every bet. Now, choose! The gambling first, or the women first." He snarled at Hipólito, "Does that suit you?"

Hipólito leaned close to me too, and the evening breeze brought me a full whiff of him, all stale sweat and cattle and sour river mud. "You're sensible," he said. "Never mind that I called you crazy. And you like money. One day you'll be my partner. You don't let your cock lead you around by the nose, do you?"

At the time I thought not, so I shook my head. I said, "You'll both abide by me?"

"You have *my* word," Hipólito said.

"Candelario?"

"Hijo de puta! Should I swear on my mother's life? For the love of Christ, tell us your decision!"

That whiff of Hipólito had made up my mind. I knew that Candelario and I had to be giving off the same aroma; it would have backed a skunk into a corner.

"Every whorehouse I've ever been in has a big tub downstairs," I said. "That gets my vote. A hot bath first. Then . . . we'll see."

That decision was about as popular as an ulcerated tooth, but they were both men of honor, and after they groused and complained for a while, they finally agreed. Candelario was a shade more warm to it than Hipólito, because he figured it would at least get us inside the whorehouse first, and it did. It was a quiet night, and the only other customers were a couple of beer-sodden troopers up from Camp Furlong. The iron tub was there, just as I had predicted, and not only was it vacant and full of steaming hot water, but it was big enough for three grown men or other combinations. We stripped down and jumped in. The madam—a Mexican woman named Doña Margarita, who was said to be sympathetic to the revolution—took a quarter from each of us and then extracted a silver dollar for what she claimed was a bottle of genuine scotch whiskey. We passed it back and forth while we soaked in the big tub and discussed the state of our souls. The hot water flowed round my aching hide, smooth as molasses and soothing as a mother's touch. The whiskey heated up my insides, and the bath wrinkled my outsides a ruddy pink. The bottle of whiskey somehow got to be empty. Another one somehow took its place. Hipólito told us a tale of his youth when he and his brother were bandits in the Sierra Madres.

". . . Pancho knew that the cry of the gray dove was a warning that men were near. Usually *rurales.* . . . "

His voice began to falter, and soon he started to snore. Candelario had begun a song of the desert, but it faded too. His good eye rolled in his head, and it had no more expression than the one made of glass. He reached for the whiskey bottle outside the tub, but his hand never made it. His snores grew louder than those of Hipólito.

I was headed in that direction, or at least not far behind, when a door opened at one end of the cellar and the body of a handsome blond woman swished by, her yellow head atop a pile of wondrous curves nodding pleasantly at us in the tub. She took some towels out of a chiffonier at the other end of the room and then flounced back. She wore a skintight blue silk dress, and from the rear, just below her belted waist, it looked like two boar shoats fighting under a wagon sheet. I awoke in a hurry.

"Excuse me, ma'am . . . señorita . . ." I cleared my throat of the sour taste of whiskey. "You do work here, don't you?"

"Yes, *chéri*. My name is Yvette."

"Are you from New Orleans, Yvette?"

" 'Ow you know that?"

"And you've got a sister?"

"Ah . . . my sister. *Oui—si*. She is Marie-Thérèse."

/ 41

"Would you mind waiting a minute while I wake my friend here? There's some business I know he'd like to discuss with you."

The blond and curvaceous Yvette was willing, and I shook Candelario until I thought I might rattle the glass eye out of its socket. But all he did was add some grumbles to his snores and finally slide a little farther down into the warm water. Hipólito was equally uncooperative.

"They are not very interested," Yvette said, smiling. I could see the carved line of her lips beneath the red color. "But what about you, *chéri?* I am ready, and so is my sister."

I thought, Get thee behind me, Satan. But if he obliged, all he managed was a hard shove forward. I asked her what we could do about my friends, as I didn't want them to drown while I was taking my pleasure, and in that lovely French accent she told me not to worry, she would send someone down to keep an eye on them. Anyway, once the water cooled they would wake up. "They always do, *mon jeune ami,"* she said sweetly.

You could have hung all her towels on my pecker, and then some, as I followed Yvette upstairs to a second-floor bedroom. Marie-Thérèse, almost a twin of her sister, bounced in a little while later to see what all the shouting and thumping was about, but it was only me expressing my feelings, and by then I was so carried away by French ways that I asked her to stay too.

I had scooped up Hipólito's purse for safekeeping, and around two o'clock in the morning, after I had paid my debt, I limped downstairs to see how my *compañeros* were faring. Some kind soul had hauled them out of the tub and dumped them into a single feather bed where they slept in each other's arms like two bedraggled, soapy-smelling, large brown angels. But when I shook them back to the world of the living, they had headaches built for elephants. Whatever Doña Margarita poured into those bottles of scotch whiskey surely had never crossed the Atlantic Ocean. Hipólito began to sneeze. Candelario, as he pulled on his boots and dusty clothes, groaned. "Aaargh . . . what now?"

"Let's go home," Hipólito said, "before I get pneumonia."

Soon we were mounted and back on the road to Columbus. The sky was solid with stars, and the night had that fine, quivering and thrilling silence that you know only in the desert. It was bitter cold, but I didn't care. Candelario finally spoke. His voice was hoarse and sad.

"Tomás, I wish to ask you a question."

"Go ahead." But I was on my guard.

"Have you no shame?"

I explained that I had tried my best to wake him up . . . and I had a witness in Yvette. But he had passed out cold.

"You weren't drunk, Tomás?"

"Certainly I was drunk."

"Ah," he said sadly, "you're younger than we are. In that way, life is cruel." The horses' hoofs clopped along the road, raising puffs of unseen dust. "And so now tell me what happened."

"What do you want to know?"

"Everything, hombre! First of all, who did you fuck? Did you find either of the Frenchwomen?"

I admitted I'd found Yvette first.

"First? Son of a whore, don't torture me like that! Am I not your friend? Don't we ride together for Pancho Villa? I want to know everything!"

As best I could, I told him how I had pranged Yvette, and then Marie-Thérèse. I could hear his teeth gnashing again, so I kept the detail to a minimum, but that wasn't good enough for him.

"How many times, *hombre? Válgame Dios,* be honest!"

"Yvette twice. And then Marie-Thérèse . . . let's see, once, I guess."

"Ya te chingaste!—now you've fucked yourself! You're lying! Did you hear that, Hipólito? Three times, he says! By the Virgin, that's not possible, not in your condition, in that short a time!" He growled, twisting his head toward me—but then he gave a mighty groan and gripped the pommel of his saddle to keep from falling off. I told him I wasn't lying, but I decided I had better leave out the last part where both women had bent on their knees, coaxing my pecker out of its doldrums and putting it between their two sets of lips to torture the last drop of jizzum out of me. He would never have believed it.

"And did they moan and groan a lot? Did they tell you they were dying? Which one was better? Describe their breasts and their private parts, Tomás. I need to know."

"Let him be," muttered Hipólito.

"What for? Should I be sorry for him? I'm the one who got nothing! Except you, you hairy oaf! Farting beside me in the bed, while he was upstairs fucking his brains out!" He addressed himself to me again. "So? Will you tell me?"

When I finished with a more detailed description he gave a small, pained grunt, and he was silent for a while. Then he spoke quietly. "Tomorrow I'll find out for myself if you were telling the truth . . . there's only one way to do that. Meanwhile, I believe you. And I'm proud of you. You didn't disgrace the army of Pancho Villa."

Satisfied, he slumped back into his saddle and closed his eyes. Soon he began to snore. Hipólito sighed into the darkness, too weary to talk.

I gazed up at the stars, glittering with such cold majesty, thinking that at least for now, this moment, the chestnut jogging comfortably under my drained loins, life was sweet. Not noble, but surely sweet. It was one more crooked and fleshly detour on the road to true love . . . but where in this dark world, under what far star, was the one to show me the straight and holy path? Where indeed? I would find her sooner than I ever dreamed, but it would take me years to know her. And then it would be too late. If we had the power to see our future in advance, as in a witch's crystal ball, we might be wiser men for it—but no happier, no better. It often occurred to me that we might even choose not to go on living.

A few minutes before noon of the next day I showed up at the Commercial Hotel to give Felix Sommerfeld a final count of the herd. The little lobby was pleasantly cool, and a pretty girl was sitting in one of the red plush chairs near the mahogany staircase. My first impression was one of lustrous brown hair, a high pale forehead, lively blue eyes, a beguiling smile. Then she got gracefully to her feet, gathered her rustling pink skirt and planted herself in my path. No, she wasn't pretty. Up close she was the loveliest creature I had ever seen.

That was wonderful enough, but when she spoke my name I thought my heart would break right through its rib cage. It gave a heave that happens only once or twice in a lifetime.

"Is it Mr. Mix?"

"Miss?"

"Mr. Thomas Mix?"

"Yes, miss." With one hand I grabbed my sombrero off my head, and with the other I began scratching my chest. I didn't itch, but I didn't know what else to do with my hand. I tried to remember everything I knew about etiquette. Did you bow? Shake hands? Before she had opened her mouth to speak, I realized that in all my life I'd never met anyone who measured up to this girl.

"You're here to meet my father," she said. "I'm Hannah Sommerfeld."

This was hard to believe, after my assumption about the unfortunate evils of heredity, but there was no way to debate it with the young lady, and I was only grateful for the fact that I knew her father at all. The only parts of Felix Sommerfeld I could see reflected in her face were her ivory skin and her blue eyes; the rest came from a provident creator. Her brown hair, with a few strands curling above her tiny ears, was neatly coiled above a forehead that didn't own a blemish. Her nose was gently curved—you might even say beaked if you were in the mood to criticize, which I wasn't—and under it, her mouth was small and friendly. Her chin would have been almost too firm if it hadn't suggested to me the proud princess of a fairy tale. Her eyes shimmered like water in sunlight. She wasn't tall, wasn't short, she was just right. She looked to be about nineteen or twenty. And her breath smelled of mint and rose water.

"My father will be late, Mr. Mix, and offers his apology. Can you bear the thought of entertaining me on the hotel veranda, until he gets here?"

I could bear the thought, and with a strangled grunt I said so. We walked toward the veranda, her pink dress swirling like tall grass in a high wind. I had to catch my breath.

"How do you find Columbus, Mr. Mix?"

"Oh, it's fine . . . just fine."

"You've been here before?"

"No, no, I haven't. I haven't been here, not ever. But it . . . it seems like a nice little town."

"It's ugly, Mr. Mix. That's the price of progress."

"Yes. That's so, Miss Sommerfeld. I guess . . . it certainly is."

I felt like a child—an idiot child. I had nothing to say that was any better. The color rose to my cheeks; I wasn't embarrassed, just overwhelmed. By then we had walked out the side door of the hotel to the veranda, where we had some privacy and could still observe the street. A few horses and buggies moved through the dust, and a big red Locomobile sputtered by in the opposite direction. Hannah Sommerfeld chose a wicker chair with some shade, and I stood uncertainly in a slanting bar of sunlight, shifting my weight, then leaned back against the white painted railing.

"My father told me we had a friend in common. And of course," she said, "I know with whom you're associated. I find it fascinating."

"A friend?" I had developed this awful habit of repeating her words. "We have a friend in common?"

She beamed a sunny smile at me. "Ricardo Flores Magón. Didn't you mention that you knew him?"

I had done it again. Opened my mouth—or in this case, as I recalled, nodded agreement, which came to the same thing—and stuffed my boot in it. I had told a lie. A small lie, and mostly from an urge toward politeness; but a lie's a lie, and now I had been caught out.

"I'm sorry, Miss Sommerfeld . . . I believe I must have misunderstood. You know how it is with Mexican names. Ricardo Flores Magón? Who might he be?"

She wasn't annoyed. If anything, she seemed pleased, because it gave her the chance to explain it all to me. And it pleased me too, because she had a warm, cultured voice that I could have listened to all afternoon. Ricardo Flores Magón, she said, was one of the early revolutionists who had opposed Díaz, but he had done it generally from a distance, making fiery speeches and publishing a newspaper in Texas, then in California. Hannah Sommerfeld, at first, had helped his organization smuggle copies of the paper to Mexico in Sears Roebuck catalogs, where the forces of Madero grabbed them up and read them to the *campesinos.*

"How—I mean, why did you do that, Miss Sommerfeld? Wasn't it dangerous?"

"Dangerous?" She flashed her dimples at me. "I'm not a man, so it was all I could do. What *you're* doing is dangerous, Mr. Mix, and I can't tell you how much I admire you for it."

Trading cattle for guns? I cleared my throat. . . . "Tell me about this fellow Magón," I said.

A spot of color, the heart of a rose on a bed of snow, flushed her cheeks as she quoted one of her champion's speeches. She spoke in flawless Spanish, cadences rising and falling as if she were an actress on the stage. I hardly heard a word; I just watched her eyes and her pretty cupid's-bow mouth.

" 'Workers, listen! Revolution is the logical consequence of the thousand crimes of a despotism! It has to come, unfailingly, with the punctuality of the sun banishing sorrowful night! By blood and fire it will come to the den where the jackals who have been devouring you for forty years are holding their last feast. Go to it, not like cattle to the slaughterhouse, but as men conscious of all their rights. Break your chains on the heads of your executioners!' Isn't that splendid?" she asked me.

"Wonderful, Miss Sommerfeld!"

"A little flowery," she said, "but he's appealing to a simple people. I can forgive him his excesses. At least his heart is in the right place." And she smiled at me gently, as if we were conspirators.

Magón, she told me, had set forth the basic principles of the uprising to which all the leading revolutionists agreed. "He was the first one to cry, 'Land and liberty!' He is for the protection of the Indians, the end of peonage and forced military service, freedom of the press, and the granting of rights to illegitimate children." She then related how she and her parents had visited Mexico City three years ago, on the occasion of the centennial of the war for independence against Spain. "We saw things that almost made me ashamed to be an American. While we and other foreign guests ate off solid gold plates at the receptions, the poor in the streets couldn't find corn for their children. William Randolph Hearst, as you probably know, owns a part of Mexico that is actually larger than some countries in Europe. That's capitalism with a vengeance. Don't you agree, Mr. Mix?"

I said fervently that I did.

"I really didn't have to ask. If you didn't believe it, you wouldn't have volunteered yourself in the cause of liberty." Her eyes glowed forcefully into mine. "Are you a student of Karl Marx, Mr. Mix?"

I decided that if I was going to get anywhere I wanted to go with this girl, I would have to stop telling tall tales. "No, Miss Sommerfeld . . . your father asked me about that too. The plain truth is that I'm just a cowhand and rodeo rider, and it's a long story how I got myself hooked up with Pancho Villa."

"I would be delighted to hear it."

"I think it would bore you to the point of tears." I remembered Fierro blowing out Wentworth's brains. "Kind of gruesome. Besides—"

"I'm not a fool, Mr. Mix. I was educated in Philadelphia, but I've been born and brought up on the border. If I may use a cliché, I know you can't make an omelet without breaking eggs."

It was no cliché to me. Then I remembered something that had been mentioned yesterday in Peache's Lunch Room. "Your father said you got into trouble over in Juárez, Miss Sommerfeld, doing something for Flores Magón. He wouldn't say what it was, and he thought you might be shy about telling it, but I'd really like to know."

"Why would you like to know?" she asked.

"Because," I said, trying to match her bluntness, "everything about you interests me."

That was a clear statement and she fielded it cleanly, without comment or blush. I liked that. Then she told me that a little over a year ago the forces of Flores Magón ran into trouble distributing *Regeneración* in northern Mexico. Díaz had decided that its message was a bit more than pesky and had begun to check the bulk mails flowing across the border. So Hannah Sommerfeld had come up with an idea. More than that, she had put the idea into practice, a second step which is always significantly more difficult than the first. She and a group of Magonistas had donned Salvation Army uniforms, then crossed from El Paso to Juárez with the usual drums, trumpets and bags of literature. But in this instance, folded inside every copy of the pamphlets exhorting the sinful souls to Jesus, there was a page or two of *Regeneración*. It worked perfectly the first Sunday it was tried, so Hannah and her group made the mistake of trying it the following week, but by then the *rurales* had been tipped to the deception, and they arrested the little group of gringo counterfeit soul savers and threw them into the Juárez jail for a night. The next morning, after listening to Hannah's threats and yells from dusk to dawn, the *rurales* let them go. Bedraggled and lice-ridden, the gringos, led by Hannah, walked back acoss the border to El Paso.

"Daddy was furious. Still, I think he respected me for what I had done. But he forbade me to do it again, and since I respect his rights as a father, I've not been back to Juárez since."

I had never met anyone before who could be described as a pure idealist, but I think the term fit Hannah Sommerfeld. It didn't fit me; I was an adventurer. I had to know more about this girl and thought it wise not to tell her too much about myself. I saw a light in her eyes, as she looked up into mine on that hotel veranda, that I knew would fade if I unmasked my own motives. So instead I asked her questions about life in Phildadephia, and didn't she find it dull on the border, in the main, after she'd had a taste of civilization? "I mean, except for your trips to Juárez . . ."

Yes, she admitted, it was a quiet life, unruly at times, but she had an aunt back East who sent her books to read, and she was herself a subscriber to *McClure's Magazine,* which serialized Booth Tarkington. She had read all the bestselling books by Mary Johnston, George Barr

McCutcheon and Robert W. Chambers, and I had to admit, a little shamefacedly, that I hadn't had the time lately to keep up with their works.

"Well, who knows how much you've really missed," she said, correcting her own enthusiasm. "The judgment of the future is always in doubt. In literature as well as politics. Or, as it's been better said— 'What's past, and what's to come, is strewed with husks and formless ruins of oblivion.' " She blushed. *"Troilus and Cressida . . ."*

I looked at her for a moment in silence. It had occurred to me, even in the height of my intoxication, that I was being swept off my feet by a pretty face, by the shining vitality of her youth and by the fact that she was *there*. But now I knew better.

"Yes," I replied. " 'And the whirligig of time brings in his revenges.' . . . I believe that's from *Twelfth Night."*

Now it was Hannah's turn to be surprised, and she made no attempt to hide it. I was delighted. Progress was being made. Then Mr. Sommerfeld appeared on the veranda, gave me a firm handshake and Hannah a fatherly peck on the cheek, struck a match to another Murad and suggested we head over to Peache's for lunch. "I think our talk might tax you a bit, Hannah, but you're welcome to join us." He had an extremely self-satisfied expression, and when I took a moment to look him over, having feasted on his daughter's face for the last half hour, he wasn't as ugly as I'd thought the day before.

"Mr. Mix is anything but taxing," Hannah said softly. Despite the noonday heat, I shivered.

Her father took me by the arm as we marched along the boardwalk toward the restaurant. "Be warned, my young friend. She's already broken the hearts of half the junior officers at Bliss." Deep in his throat, as though he were gargling, he chuckled.

But at lunch we kept the talk pretty much on track, sticking to the subject of arms and cattle and the future of the budding revolution. Still he could see I'd taken to his daughter like honeysuckle to a front porch, and for reasons I couldn't fathom, he didn't appear to object. This afternoon, he said, he was going to ride out with his foreman in a buggy to inspect the herd. "But you stay here if you like. I'm sure Hannah would be pleased to show you around our metropolis of Columbus, what little there is of it."

"Oh!" I cried. "That's very kind of you. Columbus must be a fascinating place! I'd *love* to see Columbus!"

Those nonsensical exclamations told both him and Hannah everything there was to tell about how I felt.

We had crossed the border to the U. S. meaning to get in and out fast. Mexico was where the action was, where Pancho Villa was supposedly creating an army and would soon create a revolution. I wanted to be part of it all. But that wasn't to be, at least not yet. Ravel and Sommerfeld took three days to pull the gun consignment together. Hannah Sommerfeld could have gone back to her home in El Paso anytime she wanted to, but she hung around in Columbus with her father. I saw a great deal of her, and not much of Candelario, who passed most of his evenings up on the Deming road. He and Hipólito had divided the remaining spending money, and Candelario had sworn off scotch whiskey and taken to drinking the heady wine of France. Hipólito went straight to the gambling casino, where he lost his share in three hours of stud poker, and I began to wonder if I wanted him as my business partner. From then on he stayed at the camp with the vaqueros, except for one evening when he and Candelario went to the movies in town. The admission was twenty cents, but Candelario, because he had only one eye, insisted he would pay only a dime. He wasn't the kind of man you argued with too long, and so he got to gawk at Mabel Normand for half-price.

Meanwhile I was falling in love. That's not quite correct; the truth is I had fallen in love at first sight, and the time that I spent now with Hannah Sommerfeld, walking up and down the hotel veranda, riding in the desert or listening to her explain the keener points of Karl Marx, was just plunging me deeper into that state Shakespeare had likened to lunacy. *Love is merely a madness,* he said, *and deserves a dark house and a whip as madmen do: and the reason why they are not so punished and cured is that the lunacy is so ordinary that the whippers are in love too.* I had never understood that passage. I do now.

And yet the Bard was our common meeting ground. To the soft accompaniment of squeaking saddle leather and the tinkle of bridle chains, we quoted back and forth to each other from the passages we knew and loved best. I told her I had once played the part of Fortinbras, and she said that back in Philadelphia, at school, she had been Portia in *The Merchant of Venice.* For a brief moment her eyes seemed about to film with tears.

"It was humiliating, Tom. I didn't want to do it, but I was afraid to say no for fear I'd make it worse. They already thought I was oversensitive on that score."

"Because of Shylock?"

"I hated him, and myself for feeling that way. You know it's Portia who has to stop him from taking his pound of flesh. I still remember the line—'Thou shalt have nothing but the forfeiture, to be so taken at thy peril, Jew.' I nearly choked on it."

"Is it hard for you, Hannah? Still?"

"You should ask my father. But he would say no. He would praise America, because he comes from a poor German immigrant family that had nothing. And now, here on the border, I would say no as well. I've been made fun of in the past, when I was a child, and even at school. But no more."

I could understand that. Her beauty overrode all distinctions. Added to that were her intelligence, a kindness and sympathy that revealed itself to me more and more each hour, and her dedication to the downtrodden on the other side of the Rio Grande. She was a suffragist too—she didn't wear trouserettes, but she went regularly to emancipation teas—and I respected her for it. She was no flamboyant Ziegfeld girl—she was a princess. No, not a princess, but *the* princess, the one I had conjured up as a boy by the campfire. She poured out her heart to me and I emptied mine to her, told her of my past and how I had seemed to fail or give up in everything I tried, and she said: "But now, Tom, that's all over. You're on the right track. And I have total faith in you."

I loved her for that and found it impossible to confess the flimsy grounds on which I had first joined Pancho Villa's revolution. If she cared for me it wasn't just because of my looks and my passion for Shakespeare. Her father was right: she could pick and choose from all the best men of El Paso and the young officers at Fort Bliss. Maybe some of them would shy from her because she was a Hebrew, but those were the myopic and demented ones. No . . . what dazzled Hannah, what made her look up at me with that radiant light in her blue eyes, was her picture of me as a captain-to-be and a lover of liberty in the Constitutionalist Army, riding at the side of the great general-to-be Pancho Villa. I wasn't worthy of that vision, not yet, and I knew it. Whenever I thought of where I had been rutting like a goat the night before I met her, up on the Deming road with Yvette and Marie-Thérèse, I wanted to get down on my knees, kiss the hem of her skirt and beg forgiveness for my sins.

A telegram arrived for Hipólito at the Commercial Hotel—it was from Villa, and he had a new list of supplies we had to order in El Paso. That meant taking the train there and spending at least two nights. We wandered around the city, stopping in at Sam Ravel's office in the Toltec Building and picking up other items at Heid Brothers and the West Texas Fuel Company. Villa wanted saddles and some uniforms and hats, and prairie hay that Heid's said would be shipped from Kansas. There were some small amounts of other items that puzzled me, like a case of canned asparagus, Washington State salmon at ten cents a can, Maine sardines and Bayer's Strawberry Soda Pop.

"That's for my brother," Hipólito explained. "We'll buy him a few bags of peanut brittle too. He likes that above everything, but he didn't dare ask for it." We picked up the peanut brittle at the Elite Confectionery on Cleveland Square, which Hipólito told me had been Pancho's favorite hangout during his year of exile. "He loves their pistachio ice cream almost as much as peanut brittle, but we can't take that across the desert."

The two days and three nights in El Paso away from Hannah seemed like a week. I had never been in love before. I didn't know how painful even a separation of two short days can be. So I urged the thundering train on, toward Columbus. The truth was that the thought of Villa and his mission was beginning to fade. I wanted *that,* but I wanted *this* too.

The craziness of my dilemma soon got through to me. Hipólito and Candelario announced that they were ready to pull stakes the next day at dawn. The wagons full of rifles and cartridges had arrived, and the clothing as well. All the socks were red and the shirts every color of the rainbow—not exactly what we'd ordered, but we had to have something to take the place of the men's rags. Ravel was a wizard and had produced everything on credit. The hay, the saddles and the coal would come later.

Hannah and I had a pink lemonade on the hotel veranda. "I'm sorry you're going," she said. "It may be wrong of me to tell you this, but it makes me sad. . . ."

"It does me, too. I thought about staying, but—"

"Yet it's so exciting. I'll think of you often. Maybe it's childish of me, but you're like a knight riding off into battle in a far country, to slay a dragon. Not really, but you must know what I mean." She blushed deeply. "You're like . . . *my* knight."

I took her in my arms and kissed her—it lasted only a few seconds. Carried away by the evening breeze, the softness of her lips and the mint on her breath, I whispered: "And you're like my princess, Hannah."

"Oh, Tom . . . truly?"

Her lips parted; I was sucked into them like a leaf into a twister on the prairie. Kissing her the second time made my heart nearly break out of my chest. My head spun and my pecker began to rise. I had to back off. Words bubbled in my brain like popcorn on a hot stove. I couldn't stop them; they just flew from my throat.

"I love you, Hannah. I'll come back to you."

It was madness: to find true love at last, and in order to keep it I had to give it up. Not forever, but for as long as it took Pancho Villa to win his revolution. I had to leave Hannah, or I would never be worthy of her.

I kissed her a third time, more passionately, and now she trembled too. I told her I would come back to her as soon as I could, but I didn't know when that would be.

"I'll wait," she said . . . and that was all I needed to know.

Mr. Sommerfeld stepped out of the hotel, harumphing and scraping his boots to give us some warning, and when he came up to me there was a mellow, paternal smile on his round face. I told him I had to go. "Good luck, Tom," he boomed. "Come back in one piece."

I didn't want to kiss Hannah good-bye in front of him, so I just looked for a moment into her eyes and thought I saw the beginning of a tear. The sunlight struck her hair, making it shine like honey. "Good-bye," I said softly. Then I ran into the street, like Bronco Billy in a two-reeler, jumped on my horse and quirted him out of town. I never looked back. I rode in a daze to our camp at the butte east of Columbus, full of joy because Hannah was mine and equally full of sorrow because I'd had to leave her.

Candelario was waiting for me, sitting astride his bay. The grin on his bronzed face almost split his cheeks wide open. "Tomás!" he whooped from afar. And when I got closer, he said gleefully, "A wonderful thing has happened!"

"What might that be, Candelario?"

He tugged at his black beard. "First tell me why you look so glum."

"I'll get over it," I promised, but without much conviction.

"Good. I have news that will not merely make you happy. It will make you feel blessed! What would you like more than anything else in this world?"

"Huerta's resigned? Orozco had a heart attack? The revolution's over?"

"No, *pendejo*. We still have to kill Huerta and all those other bastards, but that's no problem. We'll roast them over a slow fire." He was trotting his horse next to mine, and we had reached the wagons.

"Candelario, what in hell are you—" Then I saw it . . . saw *them*.

They were together in back of one of the supply wagons. Yvette's slender, black-stockinged legs dangled over the edge, waving slowly back and forth as she gazed out at the horizon, where the first streaks of a rosy sunset marked the sky. She wore high heels and a blue silk dress and long gold earrings. Her breasts, popping up from her bodice, resembled white melons. I remembered how my head had been buried between them so that I almost lost consciousness. Marie-Thérèse, standing next to her, was putting pins in her dyed-blond hair and preparing to wrap it in one of Candelario's bandannas. When she saw us, she waved merrily, bracelets jingling. I reined up.

"Candelario, you're crazy!"

"Never in my life have I done anything more intelligent."

"You can't take two women down to Chihuahua, to the desert—to wherever the hell we're going! How will you . . . what will they . . ." I began to sputter.

Farther out on the plain Hipólito and the vaqueros were boiling corn in an iron pot over the campfire. Candelario smiled wolfishly and stroked his horse's neck. "You don't understand how we fight battles in Mexico, Tomás. The women always come along. They make the tortillas. They tend the goats. They follow us everywhere. They are very useful." He spread his arms as if he would embrace the world from horizon to horizon.

"How wonderful the revolution is!" he cried.

"Yes, but these aren't Mexican women. They won't tend goats. Do you see Yvette on her knees, pounding tortillas? They're—mother of God, you know exactly what they are!"

"They were very unhappy at Doña Margarita's," he said gravely. "They told me so. There is no business. When they came out from New Orleans they thought they would get rich here, but the town is too small. With us there will be plenty of work. By the Virgin, they'll never get off their backs! And when their work is finished, they will be there for us."

I looked at him sharply. "For *us?*"

"Ah . . ." Candelario sighed. "I can't handle them both, my friend. To my sorrow, but not to my shame. A man isn't a man if he doesn't face reality. The tall one with the gorgeous teats, Yvette, is very fond of you. She wondered why you never came back."

There was no way around it. I laid a hand on his reins, checked his horse, and told him that I had fallen in love with Hannah Sommerfeld.

Color rushed to his cheeks, and he leaned across to embrace me. "Tomás, that's wonderful! I congratulate you both." Then he drew back. "But what difference does it make? Your Jewish sweetheart will be here, and you will be in Chihuahua. The desert nights are cold."

"Candelario, I *can't.* I'm in love. Don't you see what that means?"

He didn't, and with a heavy frown he told me that Yvette wouldn't see it, either. "Anyway, they're coming. It's all settled. Think about it . . . that's all I ask for now." And then his mood changed, and he laughed boisterously, clapping me on the shoulder with one hard hand. "Wait until the night before the first battle. When you realize you may never come back, that you may lie dead in a ditch within hours . . . you'll change your mind. There's only one big lesson to learn in life. It's *short.* If you know that, you know all there is to know."

That didn't make me feel too happy. Dead in a ditch? It had never occurred to me. I was going off to fight for Hannah's vision of land and liberty, not to die for it. That would make no sense at all. I had to be worthy of Hannah, and I would do that by helping Pancho Villa destroy the tyrants and raise the *campesinos* out of bondage. But die? Oh, no.

That wasn't part of my plan. And neither was the idea of becoming a faithless libertine. I had found something more precious than gold, and Candelario and his French whores would have to do without me. I was a man with a heroic purpose.

6

"If to do were as easy
as to know what were good to do . . ."

The first morning on the way south toward Ascensión we passed a gutted, burned-out pueblo. We saw the fires smoldering from a distance and approached it cautiously, rifles drawn, but we needn't have worried. Only the broken shrieks of old women greeted us. There were a dozen survivors at most. Corpses lay everywhere, on the dusty main street and among clumps of cactus where they had tried to flee. Some of the corpses were women and children, even babies. They had been shot and then bayoneted. The women's breasts were sliced off and lay at their sides, chunks of bleeding meat. The pueblo was called La Perla.

"Who did this?" Candelario demanded grimly.

An old man—he had survived by hiding in a well—told us that it had been a detachment of the Federal Army, not the Redflaggers. They had come at dawn.

"But why?" I asked, nearly sick to my stomach.

The old man explained that six youths from the town had quit their jobs on a nearby hacienda and gone south, he didn't know where, to join up with Pancho Villa.

So the plan was beginning to work, but at a terrible cost. This was the revenge taken by Huerta's government forces.

We helped the villagers bury their dead. It took the better part of a day—there were more than sixty victims of the slaughter. Nearly three decades later I still remember the stench, the sight of mangled flesh, my bloodstained hands. . . . Water wasn't enough to scrub them; I had to use sand and stones. Like nothing that had happened before, it made me see the nature of the enemy we would fight, and why we were going to fight him. No one ever had to lecture me again, or talk about land and liberty and literacy. I didn't even need Hannah's inspiration. I *saw*. I never forgot La Perla . . . which, as it turned out, was just as well.

Ascensión was formed by a cluster of cracked adobe huts that looked like children's blocks thrown carelessly in a heap. A small lake cooked in the sun on its northern edge, but nothing grew except maguey and stunted corn. A lazy hum of noise floated through the breathless air—cocks crowed, burros heaved racking sobs, babies wailed for the tit. A line of black-garbed Indian women trudged back and forth to the lake, bearing water jars on their heads. You never looked out across the desert without seeing a twister, spinning its way to nowhere.

We arrived at night with the supply wagons. I couldn't see anything of the town in the darkness and didn't want to, for I was bone-weary from our trek from the border. I didn't talk much during that ride, not after La Perla—I just daydreamed of Hannah Sommerfeld in a better and cleaner world. We foraged hay for the mules and let the horses loose to graze in the chill night. All I wanted was to bed down, so I built a little fire of cornhusks on the edge of town near the wagons, chewed some beef jerky, slipped my boots under the serape with me so they wouldn't freeze stiff during the night, and got ready to pass out. The French whores were giggling in the back of their wagon.

Candelario came galloping back from town and I heard him talking excitedly to Hipólito. A battle was taking place to the south, in a city called Casas Grandes. Villa was there with two hundred men who had joined up while we were in Columbus. Our soldiers by nearby campfires began to stir. Red holes pierced the darkness as they lit cigarettes, and soon came the sound of black coffee on the boil. Stiff and cold, with blurred eyes, I crawled out from under my serape and saddle blanket.

"What's happening?" I asked Candelario.

"The chief attacked Casas Grandes. A Yaqui runner just brought the news. He doesn't know how it's going, so we'll ride down there and see. You don't have to come, Tomás."

"Why not?"

"Hipólito's staying to guard the wagons. Stay with him."

I had stuck with Pancho Villa in order to fight for a just cause, to become a captain and hero and keep the love of a good woman . . . not to trade cattle and guard supply wagons. "If you can ride without sleep," I told Candelario, "so can I. Let's get down there and kill Redflaggers. They cut the soles off the feet of Yaqui children. And if they're Federals we'll kill them too." I was thinking of La Perla.

He grinned at me in the hot light of the campfire. "Get some coffee. Stay close to me."

The men poured out into the night. The desert was freezing and we rode swiftly, bundled in serapes, sombreros jammed tight over our ears so that we looked like a herd of traveling mushrooms. My big chestnut clipped along at a choppy fast trot, a natural gait for a cow horse that he could keep up all night if he wasn't crowded, and so steadily that I nearly fell asleep again to the drumming of hoofs, the ringing of a hundred spurs and the creak of saddles. We passed the ruins of a monastery and then another gutted village, but now we had no time to stop and bury their dead. A half-moon cast a cold light on the mountain that girdled the horizon. A battle—a real battle! I was in love for the first time in my life, and now, within a matter of hours, I might be killed. That was an idle thought; I didn't believe it for a moment. I listened for the sound of gunfire but heard nothing. Dawn broke as we neared Casas Grandes, pale light streaking across the desert. A few sleepy Indians watched us, crouched in the shelter of some mesquite trees. Their serapes were rags, and they were barefoot. How could they sleep? How did they survive the Chihuahua winter? God only knew.

But when we trotted into Casas Grandes, the battle was over. A haze of thin dust and bitter smoke covered the town. We had taken it. We had won—but I had missed it all!

This is how to survive the revolution, I thought, and come back whole to Hannah Sommerfeld. But it would never make me a captain and a parfit gentil knight.

* * *

At seven o'clock we were sitting on some broken cane chairs in the plaza, drinking the last of the tepid coffee we had brought in canteens from Ascensión, letting the rising sun thaw our bones. Julio told us about the battle—bloody but brief. Pancho Villa stood nearby, the back of his rough shirt salty with sweat, listening. His hair was a matted tangle; he was eating an apple and cooking pork skins in a skillet of bubbling brown oil over a drum full of burning corncobs. Men wandered by, limbs bound in bloodstained bandages, their hollow-eyed horses following. Even as Julio talked you could hear the men recounting their exploits.

"I shot the fool right through the heart!" . . . "The Holy Virgin protected me, Carlos" . . . "*Hombre,* the barrel was so hot I couldn't touch it". . . .

Villa, Julio and I rode out to a corral to see the prisoners. There were about sixty of them sprawled in the dirt, while Rodolfo Fierro pounded round the enclosure on his big sorrel stud. He punished the horse, but I could see he was a fine rider, erect and at ease, the silver spurs on his heels jingling and flashing in the sunlight. He had fought well in the battle, Julio said; he had led a charge. A group of ten revolutionists lay about cleaning their rifles and drinking tepid beer that had been looted from some shop. A thin young man named Juan Dozal, with a great flowing mustache over a weak chin, was in command. The sun slanted more strongly now across the desert, casting a misty golden light and deep indigo shadows. This was the loveliest hour of the day, always fresh and reviving with its warmth. Dozal raised a cheer.

"*Viva Francisco Villa! Viva el revolución! Viva el muerte!*—hurray for death!"

Dark half-moons of fatigue were graven beneath Villa's eyes as he faced Dozal. "Have you searched these prisoners?"

"Yes, chief. Nothing on them but lice."

So this was the enemy. They didn't seem very formidable, but then no soldier did without a rifle. I wondered if any of them had been at La Perla—it hardly seemed possible. Some were boys, not yet twenty. Most wore cowhide sandals, and a few smoked hand-rolled cornhusk cigarettes. I saw one beg a real cigarette from a scrawny Villista, a youth his own age, who gave it gladly. "Take it, poor little one," our fellow said. "Ah, you're wounded? You can bear it? That's good. Where are you from? Juárez? No, I've never been there. I'm from San Juan Bautista . . . it's beautiful there. Cold in winter, yes, but . . . ah, you'll never see it . . . poor little one!"

I turned to Julio. "Why would these men fight for Huerta? How can they try to destroy the revolution?"

"Because they're stupid, Tomás. Drunk in a cantina, they hear some flannelmouth proclaiming that the government isn't responsible for their suffering. Díaz was a lover of the people. Huerta is compassionate.

Madero was a homosexual. Villa is paid by the gringos. The Church will give them life everlasting." He snorted. "Give them a jug of *pulque* and they'll believe anything."

The sun rose higher, the desert beginning to throb with heat. Julio looked unhappy at his own explanation. "Tomás," he said, "I was lucky. I went to school for a few years. I got books from the library in El Paso. These people can't read or write their own names. How can they think clearly? How can they know the revolution is their only hope?"

"They're your brothers," I said. "Teach them."

"Did you learn that in Sunday School?" Julio spat violently. "There are good brothers and bad brothers. Didn't Cain kill Abel? The man I call my brother is the one who guards my back."

Some paces away, Pancho Villa had been thinking, and he turned to Rodolfo Fierro, dismounted now, laying a heavy arm across his butcher's shoulder. I heard Villa clearly. He wasn't trying to hide his words.

"Rodolfo, my friend, I've realized that we have a problem. It's obvious that we can't release these men and let them go south to Chihuahua City, where they'll be rearmed by Orozco and free to fight again. It's equally obvious that we can't make slaves of them, which would mean we were no better than the hacienda owners. And I'm not going into the business of constructing prisons—we're going to capture so many men before the revolution's won that I would need a whole brigade to guard them. So . . . what do you suggest?"

"With respect, chief," Fierro answered, "it seems necessary to shoot them."

"Somehow that's what I thought you'd suggest. Do it, then. Ask Dozal and his men to help. Is there a well nearby?"

"About a hundred yards toward town."

"Move them near the well before you begin. After they're shot, dump them in."

I had listened to all this. So it wasn't only *they* who shot the prisoners. We did it too. Julio had said so, I now remembered. I turned to grab Julio's arm, but he had walked away toward his horse, and a moment later he swung into the saddle. He believed it was necessary, but he didn't want to see it.

Before I even knew I would do it, I stood before Pancho Villa. Rodolfo Fierro saw me first. He turned to look at me, almond eyes narrowed with curiosity. The sun had risen farther into a stainless sky, pouring its savage heat across the desert. Sweat slid down my forehead. My heart beat more rapidly.

"Chief . . . don't do this."

Villa stared at me a moment, puzzled. Then he sighed, and his shoulders seemed to sag a little. The heat beat down.

"What do you mean, Tomás?" His voice was level, not unkind.

/ 57

"It's inhuman. They may do it, but why should we?"

He considered a moment more. He still wasn't angry. He was patient and very serious. Finally he said, "No, it's a quick death. That's not inhuman. That's always preferable."

His patience made me bold.

"Chief, before you do this, why don't you ask if any of these men want to join us? Some of them are professional soldiers. They've had some training. Others may have fought against their will."

"That's true," he replied. "And I considered it. But they fought so poorly that I decided they're worse than useless. More important, they bayoneted some of their own officers. That's disgusting, and it doesn't give me the feeling that I want such men at my back. Without loyalty, a soldier is an armed animal." He turned to Fierro, who waited stolidly. "Shoot them, Rodolfo. I give you the order."

He mounted his horse, a fine black with a white flag on his forehead, and as soon as he was in the saddle he looked less weary, no longer bowlegged and pigeon-toed; even in his dirty clothes he looked like a chief. His brow puckered and he squinted into the sun, then down at me.

"You spoke your mind, Tomás. I like that . . . sometimes. Not many men have the courage to do it. They know I have a nervous trigger finger."

Courage? I had challenged him, accused him of being inhuman. I hadn't thought about courage. But then he was gone, trotting off toward the town. Behind me Fierro beckoned to Juan Dozal.

"Juanito," I heard him say—cold-blooded as a rattler with a chill— "we're short of ammunition and this lot isn't worth sixty bullets. Line them up in ranks of three. I think a bullet fired from five yards will go through three men without much difficulty, if you shoot straight through the heart and don't hit bone." Dozal nodded appreciatively. Then yet another thought occurred to Fierro. "Juanito, ask them to line themselves up according to height, so that you don't have a tall man standing in back of a short man, or vice versa. You understand?"

"Yes, señor. So that their hearts are all in a line."

"Correct. Otherwise you'll shoot a tall man through the heart, and it will just part the hair of a little fellow in back of him. And the other way round, you'll hit the tall fellow's belt buckle."

That's how it was done. The shadows of the morning shortened on the edge of Casas Grandes. The heat increased. The prisoners went off to the well like docile sheep, obligingly lined up as Dozal requested, and then he and Fierro and the squad of revolutionists went down the line and shot them through the hearts. Fierro was right: the bullets penetrated three men. The boy who had begged the cigarette died silently. The boy who had given him the cigarette pulled the trigger without emotion. At least it was quick. The bodies were tossed into the well, limp sacks of meat. I wondered about death. A flash of pain, then . . . nothing. No more regret, hunger or longing. No joy, but no lack of it. Put that way, it was almost acceptable. An indignity in the going, but a necessary one. In that, none of us had a choice.

The buzzards coasted aloft in the brilliant blue sky, wondering how to get at the offering. The sun rose higher, a burning yellow disk.

"You know," Fierro said to Dozal, "next time we could try to see if it works with four."

I mounted and turned my horse toward town, toward my friends. That's when I might have gone back to Texas and Hannah, separating myself from all this butchery. But a man acts, or doesn't, for reasons that only get through to his brain a long time after. Scorpions sting. Buzzards eat dead flesh. Men ask, "Why?" I asked, but I had no clear answer.

We used to say of a man up on the Brazos that "he'd do to ride the river with," which meant he wasn't the sort to turn tail and scoot for safety when the water was high and frothy and the herd might sweep down on him any moment. That's the kind of man I wanted to be. I would kill no prisoners, but I was riding the river with Pancho Villa.

The women in Ascensión beat the laundry with mesquite branches. Children howled, fighting in the dust. The gear we brought back from Columbus had been distributed right away, and it was common to see a Yaqui sprawled in the shade of a tree wearing his breechclout, red socks and an orchid-colored shirt with French cuffs, a Mauser rifle cradled lovingly to his chest. His sombrero was usually decorated with pictures of Francisco Madero and the Virgin of Guadalupe. He may never have picked any grapes in the Lord's vineyard, but he wasn't taking any chances.

Villa had set up his headquarters in a small house on the main square. The day after we returned from Casas Grandes he sent for me, and I found him with Rodolfo Fierro and Juan Medina, a bony, freckle-faced ex-Federal colonel. They were poring over some new military maps that Medina had brought from Torreón, where he had deserted. Villa looked dirty but cheerful, and as usual he was reclining on an unmade bed. They were talking about Casas Grandes, and I asked him who he had left in command there. He smiled faintly.

"The buzzards, Tomás." He took a sip of coffee from a tin mug. "I'll continue your education. At this stage of the revolution, territory means nothing. What matters is to break the spirit of the enemy, and access to supplies. I will take cities—if I have to, by the dozen!—but then I don't give a damn about them unless they're on the main railroad lines. The railroad is like the arteries, pumping blood to the body." He congratulated me then on what I had accomplished in Columbus. "Hipólito told me you were clever, and you upheld their honor at Doña Margarita's." He was especially pleased about the extra cartridges and the second machine gun—"I didn't say for you to do it, but you thought as if I were standing in your shoes, and that can't possibly be bad. The red socks and purple shirts are a joke that I don't entirely appreciate, but I suppose in war one must learn to laugh as well as cry. I'll deliver the cattle you promised. These Jewish merchants are important to us. It's a sad truth, but the more we Mexicans kill each other, the richer the gringos will get."

Then he asked me what they had said about the situation in El Paso. I gave it to him word for word.

"Tell Sommerfeld not to worry. I won't cross the American border." He punched a stubby finger at the map on the floor next to his cot. "I'm going to take Torreón, on the railroad. I've told you, that's the first key to the north."

A woman came out of the back room—young, dark, big-breasted and fairly pretty. She carried a tray full of hot tacos, which she set down on a small table.

"This is my new wife," Villa informed me, waving a fat hand at her. "I married her yesterday, to celebrate our victory. Her name is Esperanza Rodriguez. Well, now it's Esperanza Villa Rodriguez. That makes her very happy, to be married . . . doesn't it, my dove? Esperanza, this is Tomás. He is my gringo."

With hardly a flicker of expression on her walnut face, the woman nodded. But I frowned. Rodolfo Fierro said, "Chief, don't forget about the silver."

Villa told me that while I was gone Fierro had ambushed a mining train and carried off two hundred bars of silver. He wanted me to ride again with Hipólito and twenty men to El Paso, where I would trade the silver for more arms and clothing.

"And no red socks this time! I want army uniforms from the stores at Fort Bliss—thonged hats, cavalry boots and saddle blankets. Sommerfeld can arrange it. And I want more sardines and peanut brittle. Tell them all that I'm going to take Torreón. Spread the word. Let them think I have a big mouth."

He didn't have to ask a second time. I was furious that I'd missed out on Casas Grandes, and I wanted to fight, but even more than that I wanted to see Hannah again. The gladness showed on my face, and of course Villa took it for an eagerness to serve. I was about to go when he motioned me back with a crook of his finger. He was silent a minute, his face puckered and his eyes nearly closed. The woman still stood by the table, while the tacos grew cold. Again I saw the mind that never abandoned anything, as he said: "Esperanza, it was thoughtless of me to say that Tomás was my gringo. He didn't like that . . . I could see by his face that he was hurt. He can hide nothing, this boy!" Villa smiled gloriously, widening his eyes. "It's not the easiest thing in the world for me to apologize to someone. But I know when I'm in the wrong, and I'm man enough to admit it. He is my gringo, that's true. But I also feel toward him like a father toward an illegitimate son." He smacked his thigh. "When he comes back from Texas, get one of your younger sisters for him. He won't marry her, as I did you, because one day he's going to marry Sommerfeld's fat daughter and become a rich businessman, but he'll keep her warm when the winter comes."

He lay back on the bed languidly, nodded at me, then at Fierro and Colonel Medina. "You can go now. I want to fuck my new wife."

So once again, sooner than I had dreamed, I rode up through that unfriendly desert with Hipólito Villa, shepherding a wagonload of silver, but this time to Texas, and this time with two extra titles stitched to my belt. I wasn't just Pancho Villa's scribe and cattle trader—I was his gringo and honorary bastard. I didn't much care. It wasn't just for Hannah's sake that I wanted one day to wear the uniform of a captain. I would do a sight better as a businessman in El Paso or Columbus with a title to my name, and already I could see the invitations that read: *Mr. and Mrs. Felix Sommerfeld invite you to the wedding of their beloved daughter, Hannah, to Captain Thomas H. Mix, Retired. . . ."*

That was my dream. But Hannah was my reality. Before we reached El Paso I had the shakes, and when I went round to the Sommerfeld house on East Yarnell Street, I was as nervous as a longtailed cat in a roomful of rocking chairs. What had I done to deserve her? Surely in the ten days I'd been gone she had thought it over and decided I was a mongrel and a long cut below her station. All those young officers at Fort Bliss would be sending her roses, knocking resolutely on her door day and night. They were real officers in a real army. I had seen such men when I was a boy, stared in awe as they trotted by on their fine horses, sabers at the side of their dress khakis and scout hats cocked at just the right angle. How could I compete?

But first I did my business with Felix Sommerfeld in his office downtown, ordering the hats, boots, cartridges, tins of sardines and tuna, and then Sam Ravel came by and we talked about Mexican politics and the war. They were impressed with my tale of Villa's quick victory at Casas Grandes. I left out the epilogue about the prisoners.

"He's expecting a lot more men. Some fellow named Urbina is bringing a brigade from Durango. You know who he is?"

Ravel frowned as he lit a cigar. "A bandit and a drunkard."

Sommerfeld said, "Why don't you stay here with us, Tom? Work for us as an agent. We could use a man like you in Columbus—a man Villa trusts."

"I couldn't do that, sir."

"And why not?"

"Because Villa trusts me. You said so yourself. He expects me to come back."

"Perhaps when it's all over. You could certainly think about it. What are your plans for the future?"

"I don't have any. That might work out fine, in Columbus . . . then. I could certainly think about it." I was pleased, and when Sommerfeld invited me to supper at his house that evening, I was delighted.

"I won't tell Hannah," he said, with an impish twist of his mouth. "We'll make it a surprise."

But when I arrived at East Yarnell a few minutes before six, the hour for which I had been invited, my worst fears were realized. Hannah was standing on the veranda with a short, stocky young man in dress khakis and shining dark leather boots, with a lieutenant's bar on his shoulder. He wasn't the acme of military perfection that I had conjured up in my vision, but he didn't have to be; he only had to be *there*. Hannah's chestnut hair caught the smoky red light of the setting sun. She wore a lemon-colored dress, and her bosom swelled toward her throat like two perfect globes covered with white silk, straining upward to break free. The lieutenant couldn't seem to take his eyes off them. Calmly, Hannah introduced us. His name was Martin Shallenberger. He was pleasant to me and completely correct, and I hated him.

After five minutes of inane polite conversation, he left. I glowered after him, then turned to Hannah, trying to smile.

"I'm sorry if I interrupted you."

"I didn't know you were coming, Tom. When Martin dropped by, Daddy called me upstairs and told me. I didn't know . . ."

She flung herself into my arms and kissed me. I felt the fire of her cheek.

"Oh, Tom! I've missed you . . ."

So I knew where I stood and asked no more questions. For the next two weeks I was two persons—the daytime man, impatiently doing the revolution's business until the evening came; and the evening man, head reeling and heart surging in the company of that most adorable creature. Mr. Sommerfeld seemed pleased, and not once during that time of courtship did he ever bring up their being Jewish and my being a non-believer. I gathered from Hannah that they didn't take their religion in too strict a manner and in fact only went to their church once a year on some special holiday called Yom Kippur. Hannah herself quoted Karl Marx, who apparently had called religion the opiate of the people. In any case she was an only child, beloved and used to getting her own way. Mrs. Sommerfeld, a quiet and pretty woman from whom Hannah inherited most of her looks, just smiled and chatted amiably at the dinner table and, when the right moment came, said: "Put out your cigarette, Felix. Let's retire and let the young people talk."

I thought she was wonderful.

But it wasn't easy. All the women I had known until then had been border whores and washed-out cowtown beanery waitresses. I'd had no experience with a girl of education and breeding. I brought her flowers and courted her in what I thought was a proper manner. Not too fast, not too wild—except I wasn't taking one thing into account. Hannah was a hot-blooded girl. Night after night on the davenport in the family parlor, we sparked and whispered sweet endearments in each other's ear, and her fur grew awfully damp. One night we were huddled there as usual, holding hands and gazing steadfastly into each other's eyes. I told Hannah then that I would be leaving for Ascensión in a few days. She had known that, but still the realization struck hard and turned her eyes dewy.

A minute later she was all over me, her mouth sliding around my lips and her hands gripping the back of my neck until it ached. Her breasts crushed my chest. The blood drained from my head, making me dizzy.

I don't know how it happened, but the next minute my hand was inside her dress, fondling those silky globes, and her nipples were stiff as strawberries on a winter morning. That wasn't the only thing that was stiff, but she didn't seem to mind this intruding presence, just kept pressing herself against me and letting out moans that loosened my hinges a lot faster than I liked. . . . And then, tangled as we were on the davenport, with Hannah crouching over me, my leg snuck between her thighs, and she was rubbing against it like a dog with fleas against a gatepost. I felt the damp heat of her private area go right through my leg to the bone. Her groans became so loud and reckless that I tried to clamp a hand over her mouth, for fear Mr. Sommerfeld would come pounding down the stairs with a shotgun to keep his daughter from getting killed . . . or from something worse.

"Hannah . . . we can't!"

"Can't what?" she gasped.

"That . . ."

"We're not doing *that*. . . ."

"Stop it, Hannah!"

Her mouth closed over mine like a hot oven. Her hand grabbed my pecker right through my pants. She bucked and twisted, her body jerking like some poor soul in the midst of an epileptic fit.

And then she cried out: "Oh, God . . . *Tom!*" Her teeth hooked into my lower lip, drawing blood. In the grip of her hand I went off like a Mexican cannon, all spurt and no target in sight.

"Hannah. . . ."

She was purring over me like a cat that's just lapped up a stolen saucer of sweet milk, and the stain that spread halfway down to my knee didn't seem to bother her at all. I was ready to apologize once I got my breath back and could unfasten my lip from her teeth, but I never got

/ 63

the chance. She nibbled at me for a while, and her own breathing eased halfway back to normal, and then she was telling me that she loved me. It was the first time she had ever said it.

"I love you too, Hannah."

"Sweet Tom . . . say it again."

We smooched for a while, then I excused myself and went to the bathroom and wiped my slippery pants as best I could with a bandanna. I was in a daze, and so worn out that I would have had to lean against a building to spit. When I wandered back to the living room Hannah had rearranged herself and brushed her hair. In the lamplight she looked beautiful, aglow like a sunflower. She threw herself into my arms as if she wanted to squeeze the tallow out of me, and I gave as much—though not as good—as I got.

A few minutes later she whispered, "You're not just leading me on, are you, Tom?" Her voice was shyer, huskier, than before. "We will get married, won't we?"

"Yes," I said stoutly. "I want that more than anything."

And so when I left El Paso the Monday following, I was engaged, although we agreed not to tell anyone until the revolution was over and I had gone into business with her father or Hipólito. But how long would that take? We still hadn't fought anything like a real battle; Casas Grandes was too small to count. Good God, we didn't even have an army! I suddenly wondered if Pancho Villa was only a dreamer—I knew there were men like that, who can plan marvelously but never *do*. And even if he could do, that other big question remained. Could he *win*?

"How soon?" I badgered Hipólito on the ride back. "When will we fight?"

"Be patient," he said. "Aren't you having a good time? Pancho knows what he's doing. We need more men, and then we need to train them. And we can't blood a new army in the rain. When the rains are over, in September, we'll attack."

"September!" I yelped. "That's three months from now! Listen, Hipólito, I didn't join up with the revolution to sit on my ass in Ascensión and run up to Texas to trade cattle and silver. It's *dull*. I want *action*. I want to fight!"

"You'll see plenty of fighting," he said quietly. "More than you like. And the day will come when you'll wish you were sitting on your ass in Ascensión in the rain, and think that trading cattle and silver is heaven on earth."

But I doubted it.

Worn out from crossing the desert, Hipólito and I reached the camp to find that two emissaries from Carranza had also arrived. One was called Manuel Chao, a heavy-lidded, bucktoothed man; the other was a dapper little fellow named Jesús Acuña, a lawyer. When we went round to Villa's house to give our report, they were there, dressed in natty suits and bow ties, sweating in the afternoon heat. Villa's appearance momentarily startled me, because he had put on a badly frayed and shiny brown suit which looked as if it had been hauled out of a ten-year-old trunk—wrinkled, dusty and coffee-stained. He smelled as usual from meat and tobacco. Hipólito had told me his brother had never owned a toothbrush in his life, just scrubbed his teeth occasionally with a finger dipped in salt. But that reddish color came from the iron oxide in the soil of northern Durango, where he had been born. The conversation was already well under way when I poked my nose in, and from what Acuña was saying I gathered that it was the desire of the First Chief that all revolutionist forces in the state of Chihuahua be placed under the command of General Obregón over in Sonora. Carranza had great faith in Obregón, and he was sure that Villa shared it.

Villa chewed that over, in his sleepy way, and finally nodded. "Yes, I know of this General Obregón. Of course, it's only lately that he's become a general, thanks to the First Chief's appointment. I'm trying to remember . . . did General Obregón offer his services to Señor Madero back in 1910, when the revolution began?"

"Obregón controls the state of Sonora," Chao explained. "Things are peaceful there. In Chihuahua there's nothing but ferment and Federal troops."

"And me, señor. There is also me."

Acuña coughed discreetly. "Señor Villa, the First Chief wishes to formally confer upon you the rank of brigadier general."

"In time," the chief said, wonderfully casual. "Meanwhile, Obregón. Ah . . . yes, *now* I remember! During the revolution of the little Señor Madero, he was a farmer! In Huatabampo, as I recall, raising chickpeas. Chickpeas sold pretty well. Has he won any battles lately?"

"Sonora is quiet," Acuña said.

"Has Señor Carranza won any battles lately in Coahuila?"

"The First Chief is not a general. He is a lawmaker. He has no army. He has only his ideals, his unchallenged rectitude, and the loyalty of those who acknowledge him as First Chief."

"And no one is more loyal that I," Villa replied fervently. "But in case it's escaped your attention, I have won battles in the past for Señor Madero. I have a little army now here in Ascensión, and I command it, and I shall win battles in the future. So until the day that there's someone who does more than sit on his ass in Sonora, I'll keep command here. I accept the First Chief's excellent Plan of Guadalupe—which doesn't say much that's new but certainly offends no one—and with all due respect I ask the First Chief to keep his snout out of my trough if he ever wants to become President of Mexico, which he says he doesn't, but you know how these things happen. Please excuse my rough language, because I'm only a peasant turned soldier. And try to understand that there isn't anything on earth I wouldn't do for the First Chief, except let him tell me how to go about my business."

Acuña coughed again; he adjusted his necktie. "It will be discussed further, I assure you, Señor Villa, and we'll report your recommendations word for word. There's another matter that the First Chief asked us to bring up. He's very upset by stories he's heard about your men taking women from their homes and forcing them to stay in Ascensión. And he's equally upset about the theft of so much cattle in the state of Chihuahua. It gives the revolution a bad name. Complaints reach the United States, and we need badly to keep the friendship of their President Wilson."

"One thing at a time, señores." Villa raised his fat brown hand with its broken fingernails. "First, the women. I've never met the illustrious First Chief, as you know, but I understand he's been married for many years to the same woman and is a man of temperance in all respects. On the other hand, it's well known that I've had more than one wife. Let me add, without meaning to boast, as it's strictly a matter of taste, that I've had some experience with women in general—perhaps more than the First Chief—and it's my observation that you rarely can take a woman under your serape with you unless she's willing. The women of Chihuahua, they say, are born with their legs already spread. What can my poor soldiers do when these hungry creatures thrust themselves so eagerly upon their cocks? It's too much to ask, Señor Acuña, that they should say no. Could you? No, don't answer—that was my little joke." Here his voice hardened a bit. "And now I want to talk to you about the cattle. The cattle, señor, belonged to the enemies of the revolution—the landowners. So it is not theft, but warfare. Besides, they are traded for guns with which to fight Huerta. This need not be discussed further." He took a shallow breath. "As for President Wilson, I'm given to understand by my young American friend here, Señor Mix, that although Mr. Wilson thinks of me as an illiterate bandit and a ruffian, he also thinks I'm a fine fellow, and he's considering inviting me soon to his house in Washington for tea and tacos—which of course I won't be able to do because I'm going to be too busy taking Torreón and Juárez. Isn't that so, Tomás?" And he turned on me, without so much as the hint of a smile.

I didn't hesitate. "Yes, chief. That's what I just heard in El Paso."

Returning his attention to Chao and Acuña, Villa said, "You may tell Señor Carranza that I respect his struggle to keep order. The First Chief knows where his strength lies. In return I ask him to respect my struggle, which is the winning of the revolution. He should be informed that with our victory at Casas Grandes the revolution has truly started. I invite him to be its most illustrious spectator. For that he doesn't even have to leave Coahuila. We'll let him know when we've taken Mexico City, and he may enter in triumph."

When the emissaries finally left, after promising to provide some badly needed artillery pieces, Villa shucked off his brown jacket, slung it on the dirt floor and collapsed on the bed, head drooping and held between his hands.

"When they arrived," he said gloomily, "they sniffed as if they were in a pigpen, and they looked me up and down as if I were the head pig. Nothing good came of this meeting. But maybe they'll leave me alone now and let us win the war." He looked up eagerly. "Tomás, did you bring my peanut brittle?"

7

"The web of our life is of a mingled yarn."

From one day to the next, or so it seemed, the ragtag mob of volunteers became an army. At first they drifted into Ascensión in pairs, then by the dozens—then whole mounted bands under their own commanders, all of whom knew Villa, had heard of his return from Texas and were prepared to swear their allegiance to his cause.

Four hundred men arrived from Coahuila, another five hundred from Chihuahua City, another three hundred from San Luis Potosí. A gang of hungry, sullen brigands appeared from the wilds of Sonora under the command of a bandit chieftain named Calixto Contreras; they looked as if they would cut your throat for the fun of it and to hell with the going rate of ten pesos. The leaders, I learned—somewhat to my surprise—had all fought for Madero in 1910. The first among these equals was Tomás Urbina, a former bandit and Villa's oldest pal, who rode in from Durango with six hundred of his men, well armed and well mounted on those hard mustangs that breed wild in the sierra. Urbina was a stocky man of forty, with a big mustache and small animal eyes that never quite focused on you. From so many years of outlawry, spending his winters in the damp caves of the western Sierra Madres, he had developed a rheumatism that kept him in constant pain. He was illiterate, as were quite a few of the revolution's commanders. He made his mark by drawing a heart with a small bullet hole in its center. It seemed appropriate. He traveled with a branding iron, and wherever he went he would cut out a few choice calves, brand them and send them back to his mother in Durango. He carried three magnificent general's uniforms that his mother had sewed for him and that he planned to wear when we rode into Mexico City, and a twelve-gallon jug of aguardiente that was never empty. Candelario told me that Urbina had wanted to bring his mother along with him on the campaign, but she had refused. "Whenever he gets drunk," he explained, "he tries to shoot her." But

Candelario never told me why. Matricide being impossible at a distance, Urbina dictated telegrams to her which always read, in one version or another: "Sainted Mother, I am well despite my damned rheumatism. I pray for your safety and continued good health whenever I am sober. Your loving son, Tomás Urbina."

Villa at this time was closest to Urbina and Rodolfo Fierro. They smoked fat black cigars together, and when he toured the camp he would drape a long arm around Rodolfo's shoulder and say, "Well, my animal, how does it look? Does it smell right?"

But Pancho Villa trusted no one totally. When it grew dark he would wrap himself in a serape and walk out of town to bed down in the desert, making a pillow of stones. At dawn he always returned from an entirely different direction. He had the instincts of a hunted cat.

It was a difficult time, that summer of 1913, because we all hungered for action. Villa had already announced that his first real target was the city of Torreón, five hundred miles down the railroad track from Juárez and almost halfway to Mexico City. He then planned to fight his way north to Juárez, which he had called "the real prize." He studied Medina's military maps until they were almost in rags. Deep into the night he talked with men who had come from all over stricken Mexico and could give him eyewitness reports of the enemy's strengths and weaknesses. We all wanted to begin, but before we could do that the army had to be sorted out, armed and trained, which meant first teaching the men to load and fire the new rifles and impressing upon them the need to follow orders given by officers. It was a tedious and often staggering task, but Pancho Villa organized it and then accomplished it. From the look of the several thousand mustachioed cutthroats—men and boys alike—who spread in all directions on the desert and out by the lake, I don't think any other man could have done as well, or even dared to try.

Starting in early June, summer rain struck the plateau like bullets. Clouds humped over the mountains, darkening as the day wore on and then rolling toward us at almost exactly the same hour every afternoon, as if God had looked at His watch and said, "Go." The rain swept through the streets of Ascensión, turning them to mud. After a few hours the torrents ceased, the clouds raced away and the air was fresh and blue until nightfall, which came upon us like a swiftly thrown black sheet. The rain turned the desert green, so that the horses grazed and grew sleek. But we could not fight well in it; we could certainly not travel easily through it. So we waited and filed our spurs, and got drunk and dreamed of glory.

I shared an abandoned house on the main plaza with Julio, Hipólito, Candelario and the two French whores. That was an uneasy situation, but I explained to them that I was all but engaged to Hannah Sommerfeld and that my fidelity was a matter of honor. Yvette and

Marie-Thérèse, jolly girls, seemed to understand, although now and then I caught Yvette staring at me from under her long lashes in a way that made my mouth grow dry. I couldn't help remembering what she and her sister had done to me out on the Deming road. Some nights, when I heard Candelario and one of the others carousing with them, and their groans and piercing laughter filled the darkness, I had trouble sleeping. Candelario thought I was crazier than Urbina.

"*Hombre,* I don't know what you've got in your pants, but it must be something special. Don't you see the way they look at you?"

"I have an obligation, you fool."

"Your obligation is in El Paso. Yvette and Marie-Thérèse are here in Ascensión. It's a matter of geography."

"Not geography. Honor! Jesus, you're a Mexican, you know what *that* means."

He sighed and went away, but the next day he started pestering me again. I could bear that easily; what I minded was the way Yvette and Marie-Thérèse brushed against me when we were in the kitchen together, or when I passed them on the way to the privy. It always seemed that a silk-clad hip would slide against mine or a strand of blond hair would float against my cheek . . . and it worked on me. I was as horny as the next fellow, and Hannah had waked something in me that cried for attention and wouldn't go back to sleep.

I held firm to my virtue until a moment came when it seemed I had little choice. Or I was too weak, pitted against the adversary of my goatish nature, to make the right choice. My downfall wasn't Yvette's fault, or even Candelario's, although in their separate ways they tried their best to fracture my resolve. It was Pancho Villa's. That man dominated my life.

One cool evening after the rain had freshened the air and darkened the dust, Esperanza Villa knocked lightly on our door. She was in company with a blushing, plump girl whose name, she told me, was Carmelita. Candelario and the others had gone out drinking in a local cantina with our own girls, trying to drum up some business for them in an effort to make them rich as well as happy. After I opened the door and was introduced to Carmelita, I made some noises like a jackass, trying to figure out what the visit was all about. I peered into the darkness. The chief was nowhere in sight.

"Señor," Esperanza said, smiling, "Carmelita is my sister."

Oh, Lord. I remembered Villa's promise, after he had called me his gringo and then felt bad about it, to gift me with one of his new wife's younger sisters. If I wasn't sure, Esperanza quickly rid me of any doubt.

"My husband Don Francisco Villa says"—*she* didn't blush, or even blink—"to have a good time, but please try not to make her pregnant.

There are already too many babies in the camp. They keep him awake during his siesta."

"Hang on there, Esperanza—"

But she left without a further word, sliding off into the darkness in her bare feet, vanishing like a shade. I was left with my mouth hanging open.

I turned to Carmelita. She was short, about twenty, and not at all bad-looking if you liked smooth young skin and an ample handful of flesh. Mexican women tend to pork up before they're anywhere near old, but she was on the cusp. I noticed, too, that she had been freshly scrubbed and her black hair smelled of lemons. She smiled at me pleasantly, showing a missing tooth and several made of silver, and walked straight into the first open doorway, which happened to be the room where I slept. Her sense of direction was perfect.

I didn't know how to handle this. It was one thing to say no to Candelario, another to insult the chief. He was making an offering, and it was family. How would a Mexican react if you gave his wife's sister— offered wholeheartedly—a dry pat on the rump and said, "Scoot . . ."? And not just any Mexican. This was a gift from Pancho Villa, who was going to take Torreón.

A candle burned on the oak table in the main room. I carried it before me to the bedroom and shut the door softly. Then I turned to face Carmelita. I was about to discuss the matter sensibly, to see if we could come to some arrangement that would save me from the chief's wrath and Carmelita from a loss of pride. I intended to behave like a gentleman; I had read enough books to know how gentlemen behaved. But Carmelita hadn't been told there would be a problem. She was already out of her rebozo and sandals, and just as I set down the candle she shucked her dress to the floor. When the cotton snaked loose and all that smooth, coffee-colored flesh shone in the moonlight, my pecker shot up into the air like a mean mustang jackknifing from the chute. I had no control over the beast. I suppose it didn't know that it was meant only for the girl I loved. It was a matter of bad communication between brain and lower parts.

The fact that I was a coward didn't shock me. I just hadn't known that I was a lowlife and a man without principle, incapable of keeping to his deepest resolve. But I knew it now. It was a lesson I would learn more than once. I wondered if, like Candelario, I was cursed. In any case, my condition was beyond repair. I looked down, gave a mighty groan, and then stripped off my clothes and climbed into bed.

For all the pleasure I got out of it, I might better have jacked off and prayed that no hair would grow on my palms. Carmelita lay flat on the ripped old sheet, just about as responsive as a large lump of dough. I kneaded it, I fondled it, but it just never baked. Twice during the night I worked myself up into a hot lather and pumped my seed onto the sheet, heeding the chief's admonition not to make any more babies, and twice Carmelita showed her silver smile and said, "It was good, señor?"

"Awful, if you must know," I said the second time. But I said it in English.

The third time, in the cool dawn, waking from a restless sleep, I tried to get her to mount me, thinking it might give her an unexpected pleasure. She explained that she had never done it that way.

"How is it accomplished, señor?"

"I lie down on my back, like I'm doing. You sit on top of me, Carmelita." I grasped her fleshy hips. "See?"

"Like riding a horse?"

"That's exactly it."

"I would feel funny doing that. But if you insist, señor, I'll do as you wish."

"I won't insist, and would you mind not calling me señor? My name is Tomás. Here, we'll try another way. Get up on your hands and knees . . . hunch over . . . like that." This other way was one of the subtleties I had learned from Yvette and Marie-Thérèse on that memorable night in Columbus. "Now, just lower your shoulders a bit—"

She twisted her head around just when I cupped her breasts in my hands for some leverage. The sight of her dark wet bush protruding between her cheeks had engorged me again. Yes, I was cursed. But there was confusion in her eyes.

"Señor, how are you going to do it?"

"Just like this . . ."

"Like the *dogs?*"

She flopped right down on the bed, flat, squeezing her cheeks tight together, leaving my quivering pecker in the air—homeless. From the mattress, to which she pressed her forehead, she said stolidly, "I am not a dog, señor. I am a woman. Human beings don't do it like dogs."

A few minutes later, my flesh seeming to have a stubborn will of its own, I climbed aboard her docile body for the third time, in the missionary position, and within a couple of minutes that was that. Afterwards, as she dressed, she giggled good-naturedly.

"Are all gringos so perverted, señor?"

I couldn't find an answer, and when a respectable time had passed I said, as gently as I could, "You can go now, Carmelita. Thank you very much."

"*De nada,* señor." For nothing—and I believed her and began to think even more highly of the French whores. So I was punished. Of course, Candelario and the others knew I had been partying—they had trooped in during the night and immediately sniffed the aroma floating from my room—and when I ushered Carmelita out the door and appeared in the kitchen wearing my skivvies, bedraggled and scowling, they howled with laughter and wouldn't stop sticking their knives into me. Candelario kept pounding the table and winking at me with his one good eye. I suppose he assumed that the barriers had now fallen to my reunion with the French whores. But Yvette didn't say a word. Sitting on a rickety chair and eating a hardboiled egg, she glanced at me for a moment with a wounded expression, then tossed her hair proudly and turned away. . . . What could I say? *It wasn't me, Yvette. You know I'd never be unfaithful to Hannah. It was that mean critter who hangs out down there in my pants. . . .*

I didn't say that to her, but I couldn't stay completely silent. I drew her outside into the shade and told her that Carmelita had been a gift from Pancho Villa, an obligation I couldn't easily refuse. But the words sounded hollow even as I spoke them.

"You must do what you have to do, *mon chéri,*" Yvette said coolly.

"Look . . ." I took a straighter tack. "I didn't have to. I could have made up some excuse. I was wrong, and I feel rotten about it."

She sensed the truth of my distress, and her hand touched me gently on the cheek. *"Tu es jeune,"* she murmured, and I didn't understand, except that I knew in some way I was forgiven.

After that we were always friends, and it stood me well, for one day, with a casual word, she and her sister would save my life. But that was far in the future, not to be foreseen. . . .

I bolted down some cold frijoles and lukewarm black coffee, muttered some unfriendly words to Candelario and the others, then stomped out of there and headed for the lake. I needed to cool down. All fucking and no fighting made for one hell of a revolution.

A hot morning sun baked the surface of the lake. Horses had been watered and now they boiled up the dust as they trotted out to be grazed. Goats cried out to be milked. Thousands of people camped by the lake, spreading like a squirming human stain along the shore. New men drifted constantly into the camp, and most found it unthinkable to travel without their families. How would this army move? Villa had better know. I was worried about other things, such as the fragile state of my apparently corrupt soul. It wasn't much past eight o'clock and the sun was already frying my brains, so I wandered a bit past the jungle of makeshift tents and twig fires, peeled off my clothes and dove into the blue-green water. It was a little soapy, but nicely cool. I splashed about, tired, out of sorts, annoyed with myself, and at the same time, like a rutting hog, dumbly content. I left the lake about fifty yards down from where I had jumped in, swimming the Australian crawl as fast as I could, so that when I grabbed the overhanging limb of a dead jacaranda tree near the shore and hauled myself out of the slime that collected on the bottom, I was winded and puffing. I heard a hiss.

"Who . . . ?" I croaked.

I wasn't alone. A girl crouched there under the jacaranda tree, wearing a drab brown dress so that she blended in with the earth, which is why I had failed to see her in the first place. As I heaved myself up, buck naked, she clapped a thin hand to her mouth. I just shrugged—none of the women around the camp paid the slightest attention to a naked man swimming. As the Mexicans said, a man has two peckers, one for fucking and one for pissing, and women could look at your pissing pecker without even blinking. Your fucking pecker, of course, either turned their eyes dewy or gave them the right to whack it with a broomstick. What I had brought up with me from the lake was certainly my pissing pecker. But when this young girl saw it she collapsed in the dirt.

"Please, señor! For the love of Jesus, don't!"

I didn't think she could have been more than sixteen. I could have waved gallantly and gone back to my clothes farther down the shoreline, but somehow I wanted to assure this frightened child that she wasn't in any danger, that I wasn't a mad gringo rapist risen from the depths of Lake Ascensión. And, I thought, if I take just one more step in any direction, she might decide to scream after all, and a brother or father might come on the dead run whirling his machete, which I don't need. So I stayed put, up to my knees in the cool shallow water.

"Señorita, I'm not going to do anything bad to you. The fact is, I've just got out of bed with someone else. It was a long night. We did it three times, whether you believe that or not, and I couldn't do it again now even if I wanted to. Which I don't."

She was a cocoa-colored girl, far more Indian than white, and when she raised her face I saw that she had long black hair, dark-chocolate eyes, high cheekbones and a mouth that was too wide for her face. She was pretty enough, but not beautiful, although such judgments, I've learned, are subjective and always open to change. I also noted that her eyes were red from crying, her cheeks streaked with tears. Her hair was powdered with dust and tangled as if she had been rolling in the mud like an animal. Her brown sack of a dress was ripped down one shoulder. I felt sorry for her. She had a problem, but I didn't know its nature.

"Listen, *muchacha*, I'm going down the shore and get my clothes, and then I'll be right back. If you run away, I'll come after you. I'm no damned Sonora bandit. I'm the gringo captain on Villa's personal staff. So you stay put. And don't worry." I finished more kindly. "I just want to help you."

The girl barely breathed. *"Sí, mi capitán. . . ."*

"And you can get up off your knees. This ain't church, and I'm not God. I'll be right back, you hear?"

When I reached my clothes I couldn't see her through the mess of scrub, so I jumped into my Levi's and stuffed myself into my shirt on the way back, arms waving like a windmill in a tornado. She was obediently waiting for me, sitting with her back against the dead jacaranda tree, legs splayed out in the dirt. Her head was bowed forlornly.

I settled down beside her on my haunches. "Come on, now. Whatever it is, it'll turn out all right. And I won't do anything to you, on the honor of my mother." This was the most serious vow you could make among Mexicans, and for the moment it seemed to win her over.

"*Aieee!* Help me, señor. . . ." She keened the words, raising her dusty head. "There is a man," she whimpered.

Well, there almost always is. "A boyfriend? A lover? You had a fight and he beat you up, is that it? Did he leave you for someone else?"

"No, *mi capitán*. A man here in the camp. I hardly know him."

I was already regretting I had come up with that windy about being a captain on Villa's personal staff, but I was stuck with it and I'd worry about that part later. I just didn't want Villa to find out about it, particularly after his having faced me down for my tale of Joe Lane and the bullet dead center in the cartridge.

"What's your name, girl?"

"Rosa Navarro de Guaycavo," she said formally. "At your orders, *mi capitán*."

I told her my name was Tomás and she could call me that.

"Yes, Captain Tomás."

"No. Just Tomás."

"Yes, *mi capitán*."

"All right," I sighed, "if you insist. Now, what's the problem?"

Tears leaked out again. Hadn't anyone ever been kind to her before?

"Señor, I am from a pueblo called Tomochic, which you may never have heard of, but it is to the south. In the high sierra. We are Tarahumara . . . that is a tribe of Indians, very old. My father was a Mexican, an officer in the *rurales*. He left us many years ago. You know the Tarahumara?"

I admitted that I didn't.

"It's of no consequence. For the last year I have lived in the city of Casas Grandes with my husband—"

"Your husband?" I couldn't hide my astonishment. "Good God, how old are you?"

"Fourteen, *mi capitán*."

Fourteen, and married already. That was the Mexican way. I shook my head sadly. "You have kids?"

"No, señor. I must be barren, for we tried."

"Well . . . go on."

"My husband was from the city of Camargo, and older than I by two years. He was not Tarahumara. About a month ago he was transferred to Corralitos, to guard the railway switches there. So that we counted ourselves fortunate when we heard what happened to the men in Casas Grandes." Word about the prisoners had spread quickly, and I saw her point.

"Yesterday afternoon," she said, "the Villistas came to Corralitos—it's a distance of perhaps twenty miles from here. They attacked the Federal soldiers, who ran away, all but my husband. I told him to go, but he swore he wouldn't leave me. I tried to convince him that was foolish, they would shoot him, but he said he would offer to join them—he didn't care for which side he fought as long as he could be with me. So he threw down his rifle and went out with his hands in the air. They shot him before he could speak. *Aieee!* I saw it. I watched him die."

Now a glaze came over the girl's eyes, even though the tears had dried.

"I came running out of the barracks and fell on his body. The soldiers picked me up. They told me not to cry, that my husband was a coward to surrender, and a bad man to have fought for Huerta against the revolution. They said I must come with them to Ascensión. Before I left I begged them to let me bury my husband, and they said they would do it." There must have been a well handy, I thought. She stopped for a moment to catch her breath. "On the way I began to bleed. My curse had come early. I cried and I was bleeding, so they left me alone. They were not unkind to me. But when we got here, a man came out—an officer, I think, because they reported to him, although he wore no insignia and fine clothes as real officers do. The officer looked me over, from head to ankle, very slowly, so that I became embarrassed and turned away. Then he said, 'I will take care of the girl.' And he took me to a house. He told me to make food for him. I cooked enchiladas and some corn. But later he said, 'Come to bed. I'll cure you of this sadness.' I told him, 'No, my husband is only dead a few hours.' He said, 'This will help you to forget him,' and he tried to take me by force. I screamed and kicked, but he was a big man . . . and then I told him I couldn't because I was bleeding and unclean. He didn't believe me. He tore off my dress and saw that I told the truth. Then he said, 'Stay here, I can wait until you're better.' And he left. I ran away in the darkness to the lake. As you see me. I slept here." She indicated a patch of damp ground between the jacaranda tree and the shore. "But now I must go back to him or leave Ascensión . . . and I don't know which to do."

Although it was a common enough story these days, I certainly felt sorry for her and believed that she and her young husband must have been a nice pair of lovebirds. But I didn't understand the end of it one bit.

"What do you mean, you have to go back to him or leave Ascensión?"

"He claimed me. He is an officer. What can I do?"

That was uncommonly simple thinking, but she was just a simple Indian girl, and I could see that she believed what she had said. Still, to my way of thinking it didn't seem right.

"Do you want to stay with this man?"

"Señor, what else can I do? I'm alone here . . . Tomochic is very far away. They took the horse from me. Who will feed me? Most of these people don't like the Tarahumara. We never surrendered to the Spaniards when they came to our mountains looking for gold. We hunt wild horses. I can ride like a man, and without a saddle. We are poor, but we never go to the cities to work. The real Mexicans of whiter blood think we are lowborn mountain dogs."

"How do they know you're Tarahumara?"

"Señor, they know. It's in my face, and my speech. I didn't speak good Spanish until my husband taught me."

I couldn't tell one Indian from another, and to me she was just a kid; a little foolish, but reasonably pretty and in trouble, which overpowered what sensible thinking I might have done otherwise.

"Listen, Rosa. I do know Pancho Villa personally, and I've got some influence there. Not much, but I guess it's enough to handle this kind of situation. I'll find you a place to bed down tonight, and I'll feed you. And then you can figure out what to do. You don't have to go back to this other man if you don't want to. You're not a slave."

"Do you want me as your woman, señor?"

"Now, wait . . . hold on there." I felt my cheeks go hot and undoubtedly red. "I didn't say that. Let's do one thing at a time. You asked me to help you, and that's what I'm trying to do. I'll be your friend, okay? For a while, anyway. Until you . . . until you get over your curse . . . yes?"

I finished up lamely. A girl on her own in Chihuahua, where there were nothing but soldiers and people on the move, couldn't fling out the door and get a job as a waitress or take in laundry as she would have done in Texas. She couldn't even be a whore, because everyone else was giving it away . . . except for Yvette and Marie-Thérèse, and they were special. If she wanted to survive she had to have a man or live with her family. There was nothing in between.

"I tell you what you should do first." It was a dandy idea, I thought, because it postponed a resolution of her dilemma. "You can go for a swim and clean yourself up."

She hesitated, then tossed the dark hair off her face. "I don't know how to swim."

"Then just kind of squat. Get the mud out of your hair. With all due respect, you're a mess. I won't come in after you," I promised, "and I won't grab you when you come out. On the honor of my mother."

A sly smile appeared. "Do you truly have a mother, *mi capitán?*"

I grinned back at her. "I've got a mother in El Paso, Texas. And three sisters, and a fiancée."

"But how can I bathe? I am unclean. I have my curse."

"You won't die. My sisters do it all the time. It's a hot day; you'll dry off quick. And your hair's a hell of a lot more unclean than the other place. Go on in, girl."

She considered all that, then finally nodded. "You don't have to turn away. I am not ashamed."

Rosa slipped off her dress. Under that shapeless brown sack I hadn't seen much more than the outlines of a young girl's slim body, although it was clear enough that she had a generous portion of what constitutes a female. And she was right—she certainly didn't need to be ashamed of the way nature had fitted it together. She was a little taller than the average Mexican girl, with well-curved brown legs and muscular thighs, a flowering black bush between them, hips on the slim side, strong shoulders and a narrow equator. She wasn't stooped yet like most of the women were from their years of grinding corn. It was her breasts that stood out: not just in a manner of speaking, but rising out of her ribs in a swollen and perfect curve as in pictures of Greek statues in museums. They might have been a little too big for the rest of her body, but that wasn't anything that a man with some tallow in his bones would grouse about, and they were tipped with the neatest pair of brown buttons I had ever seen, although I hadn't seen so many as to make me an expert.

But I had to catch my breath and half turn away, lest she see my pecker come to attention in my pants as if Old Glory were passing by on parade. How many times was that to happen to me, and with how many women? Was that my fate in Mexico?

She didn't hurry. She walked off into the water as if she didn't have a care in the world and this was the Fourth of July at Galveston Island. Her rump swished from side to side, beyond her control, in a way that made me almost bust the rivets off my Levi's. I watched the smooth arch of her back slide into the cool water and I had a sudden vision of her husband rotting in some well out by Corralitos, and how he had been graced by life's lottery to enjoy all that, but now it was gone to him forever and was some other man's booty. I had a pang of sorrow for that boy that swelled inside my heart with almost as much intensity as I felt in the lower region.

After she had dried her hair in the sun and put on her dress, I walked with Rosa back to the house in town, keeping an eye skinned for this so-called officer who, in her view, had claimed her. I didn't really want to lock horns in debate with him until I'd had a word with Villa, and when I got home—it was that, for the moment at least—Julio, Hipólito and Candelario were swilling coffee and playing dominoes under a framed print of Mary and Joseph in the manger. Their shirts were open to the waist, letting out a powerful aroma. They wore cartridge belts and pistols, and sweat dripped from their faces to the rickety wooden table. Taking one look at them, my Indian waif turned pale. I may have done the same. Was the officer one of *them?*

But Rosa was only frightened at the malevolence of their appearance. I had grown used to it, but I realized that if you came on that trio fresh, you might appeal to all the saints in heaven for protection.

"What's *this?*" Candelario jumped to his feet; his head almost banged the ceiling. Grinning cruelly, he stroked his black beard. "You spend the night with one, and in the morning you turn up with another! You gringo bastard! Have you no shame? No respect for Mexican womanhood?"

"It's the same one," Julio said dryly. "He's just given it to her so many times that she's lost thirty pounds."

Candelario took the privilege of a closer look. "She's Tarahumara. Are you not, señorita?"

"True," Rosa said.

"The worst women in all of Mexico, Tomás. They have vinegar in their blood. They steal horses."

"No, señor," Rosa said. "We catch them wild, then eat them for dinner."

Candelario became suddenly friendly; he liked her spirit, and so did I. "Listen, girl, this is our gringo *compañero.* He crossed the Rio Bravo with Pancho Villa. We too were there. He has no ambition to die young, so be careful with him. Don't break his back. Don't bite off his *cojones.*"

My cheeks were scarlet by then, and they howled brutishly, pounding the little wooden table and upsetting all the dominoes. When they quieted down I told them Rosa's story, about her husband and the skirmish at Corralitos, and the man who had claimed her the night before. For her husband it was clear they felt nothing. He was a Federal soldier, an enemy, and they probably would have shot him too. To the other part of it, however, they paid some attention.

"It sounds like Urbina or Contreras," Julio said thoughtfully. "Except that a little blood wouldn't stop either of those roosters."

Hipólito laid a chubby hand on my shoulder. "If it was Urbina, it's been pleasant knowing you, Tomás."

Candelario said, "He's right. This is serious. Remember what the chief told you. Don't aim. Just shoot and pray."

I couldn't really tell to what extent they were joshing, but I knew that Mexicans didn't settle arguments with their fists. They believed that if God had intended human beings to fight like dogs, He would have provided them with teeth and claws.

"Can't the girl do as she pleases?" I asked, frowning.

Candelario tugged at his mustache. "Do you think this is the first dance at the cotillion in El Paso? The girl is pretty, but she is of no significance. What is of significance in this matter is the honor of men."

Rosa hadn't said a word. I had read *The Three Musketeers,* and I wondered, if there were going to be any kind of a serious scrap with this unknown officer, whether they would be willing to play the parts of Porthos, Aramis and the other fellow, the melancholy one whose name I had forgotten. I also wondered if I really wanted to be D'Artagnan. I surely wasn't in the market for a fourteen-year-old girl I might have to drag along with me wherever we were going to fight this long-awaited war.

I said, "I'm going to talk to Villa about her."

"That's a good idea," Julio decided, "but make sure he's not looking for a newer wife."

They howled again. Rosa stood by with no expression on her brown Indian face. I guess in her own way, at the time, she subscribed wholeheartedly to Candelario's theory that women were of no significance in such matters, and as far as she was concerned her fate was now in the hands of superior forces—namely, men—and whatever it was, she would accept it. So I left with her, and my *compañeros* picked the spilled dominoes from the dirt floor and resumed their game, jostling and shouting. I wasn't D'Artagnan.

In the street some boys were playing leapfrog on the back of a tired old sow, and a pack of mongrel dogs snapped at each other in the dust. One of them, I noticed, was stuck inside a bitch and whining pitifully. Rosa smiled, but not I. It's a warning, I thought glumly. Then in the blaze of the morning I spotted Pancho Villa, Rodolfo Fierro and Tomás Urbina emerging from the shadows of the chief's house across the street. They looked businesslike, and I assumed they were off to inspect matériél or new troops. I decided it would be better to postpone this problem to another time. But with a word Fierro detached himself from the other two and strode toward us, out of the shade into the brazen sunlight. Since we had brought the new supplies from El Paso, he had outfitted himself with U. S. Army puttees, hip-high cavalry boots and a white Stetson. He cut an imposing figure: tall, robust, with smooth skin and wide sloping shoulders, his silver spurs inlaid with turquoise—Pancho Villa's butcher.

I was about to tell Rosa who he was when she touched my arm gently. "That is the man," she murmured. "That is the officer who claimed me."

Rodolfo Fierro? I had to hold back a groan. God, I thought, I would rather it had been Villa himself!

He came straight up to her, ignoring me completely. He was his usual polite and chilly self, which I knew by now wasn't a mask but simply the only way he knew how to speak.

"Señorita, you didn't return last night. That was wrong of you."

Rosa showed no fear. Why should she? She didn't know that Fierro was a killer of men, that he pulled the trigger of his pistol with as much emotion as a man usually saves for slapping mosquitoes. And she had me at her side to protect her. I had promised, hadn't I?

She answered him with equal politeness. "Señor, I didn't want to stay. I told you that my husband's body was not yet cold. I slept alone by the lake. Now I have found another man. I will stay with him."

"Hold on a minute—" I got that much out, then stopped, not knowing what more to say. But my flesh began to leak sweat.

"This man?"

"Yes, señor."

Fierro's brown eyes shifted to me. They weren't cold or angry . . . just curious. He measured me while I waited, my heart beneath my sweaty shirt starting to beat like a telegraph key. We both carried pistols. I hadn't any idea what I was going to do when Fierro challenged me, which it seemed he must if his honor and machismo were at stake. The best thing, I realized, was to tell him the spotless truth. The girl was wrong. She had found a man with whom *she* wanted to stay, yes—but that man, namely me, hadn't been consulted. Still, I held my tongue. I had made a promise. Even more, I didn't fancy sending a homeless widow kid off into Fierro's clutches. From what I had seen at Casas Grandes, his tastes might have been pretty unpleasant.

But I had to face something else, and quickly. Could I kill for a woman? I truly doubted it, even if she were mine. More to the point, could I die for one? No doubt about that answer. Life was sweet, and I had Hannah waiting for me, and I wanted to grow old in her arms and rich in her father's business. This Tarahumara girl had put me in a boghole of her own devising; she assumed that if I took her in tow it had to be because I wanted her to pound my tortillas and share my saddle blanket. No, señorita! I'm engaged. I won't die for you. You'll have to wriggle out of this on your own.

Fierro shifted his eyes from me back to Rosa. His business was with her. He didn't deign to argue right and wrong with the likes of me.

"This man is one of us, but he's a gringo. He's not clear about certain things. Have you slept with him?"

"No, señor. I told you, I slept alone by the lake."

"Then he has no reason to be offended when you return to my house. Do so now. I have business. Then I'll come to eat."

Rosa didn't budge. I wondered if she was enjoying this—it wouldn't have been unnatural for a young girl to conjure up a fantasy that two men were arguing over her. But I don't think so. Looking back on it now, after all these years, I think the Tarahumara, once they decide to ride through fire, spur forward and will their blood to ice. And Rosa was Tarahumara to the bone.

"Señor, I don't wish to go. I will stay with the captain."

The captain! Then, truly, I was almost willing to die. Fierro jerked his head toward me, and finally there was an expression in his eyes of amusement mixed with scorn. I was only saved, if that's the right word, by the fact that Villa and Urbina had ambled across the dusty square and finally appeared at Fierro's side. Villa walked in his awkward pigeon-toed gait, arms thrust out at the side by the bigness of his chest. He was pulling at the curly ends of his mustache, and he shot a gob of spittle into the dust.

"For Christ's sake, what's going on?"

My fear that Fierro would ask what Rosa meant when she called me a captain prodded me to speak first.

"Chief, it's the matter of this girl. I was coming to your house just now—I wanted to ask your permission for her to stay with me awhile. She's fourteen. Her husband was one of the Federals shot yesterday at Corralitos. I'll care for her until she can get back to her family in To-mochic. She's Tarahumara, as you can see."

Villa eyed me keenly. "What about my wife's sister?"

"With respect, she didn't please me."

"Oho!" He laughed with great mirth. "So, Tomás! You too are an expert with women . . ." Then he looked suddenly puzzled. "But why, for such a simple thing, do you need my permission?"

Fierro had opened his mouth to speak, but again I darted in. "Last night," I said, "when our soldiers brought her to camp, Rodolfo took her with him. She ran away. He claims her now. The girl doesn't want to go with him."

"So . . ." Villa sighed. "I must be Solomon once more, as I was with the rifles. Unfortunately, if you divide a woman in half to please two men, one gets the half that fucks and the other the half that whispers pleasant things in the darkness, and neither is much good without the other, not even considering that they'll both soon rot if they're sepa-rated. But still . . . I think the problem has a solution. Which of you has fucked her?"

"Neither of us, chief," I said.

"But you took her to your house, Rodolfo!" He frowned, for his solution had gone up in smoke. "For God's sake, what the men say—is it true?"

This was news to me; I hadn't any idea what he meant. Fierro darkened for a moment, then got hold of himself and eased back into his calm attitude.

"She came to my house," he said quietly. "But she was bleeding, and so I let her be. Then she ran away. She is Tarahumara, as has been stated. They are not so quickly tamed."

For the first time Villa examined Rosa, his pop-eyed glance roving appreciatively up and down her body.

"Do you ride, girl?"

"Yes, señor. I traded my mother's tit for the saddle."

Villa clucked his tongue a few times, like a chicken, and then made up his mind. "I'm a busy man. I have much to do today. Moreover, I don't want any bitterness between my friends, and to encourage it over a stray woman would be so stupid that I wouldn't respect myself for having made a choice. So there is a simple solution. Neither of you will have her. I'd consider taking her myself to end the quarrel, because I like what I see, but that would only lose the love of both of you." He turned to Fierro. "She ran away from you. What women do once, they'll do again. That will make you crazier than you already are. Count yourself lucky to be rid of her." His paunch rippled silently with a chuckle. Then he turned to me. "You'll thank me one day for this, Tomás. This kind has a sharp tongue. They lack the dignity of a true Mexican woman, and they use unseemly language, as you just heard. Let her find another man. You'll see, it won't take more than a few hours."

My luck had been running kind of brown ever since I had come out of the lake, and I thought his solution wasn't bad at all. But the girl had other ideas.

"I want *this* man, señor." She inclined her head toward me.

Villa's back arched. He wasn't used to a female stating her preferences so clearly, particularly when she was a child, alone in the world and obviously at the mercy of the men around her, to most of whom she was considerably less valuable than a horse or even a good saddle. And of course she was implying a willingness on my part that wasn't there. But I was in too deep, like the dog in the street—which had been an omen even more than a warning—to back out. With bite in his voice the chief said, "There are plenty of good men in the camp. Are you so choosy?"

"It's a matter of honor," Rosa said flatly. "I have promised myself to this man."

He didn't know how to reply. You couldn't easily spit in the face of honor. But whose honor was she talking about? Villa ground his teeth. If he let her have her way he was either going to have to contradict himself or eat crow, neither of which pleased him. He was the leader now of five thousand men, and he couldn't let a girl bully him into a decision. He looked at Fierro, who for the first time had an expression of annoyance on his smooth and handsome face. He's willing to give up the girl, I thought, as long as I don't get her . . . but he can't accept her choosing me over him. I could see that clearly. Villa opened his mouth to decide.

"Chief, let our Tomás have her." The gruff voice, startling me by its closeness, came from Candelario. "We're planning a little fiesta tonight. Life is dull when we're not fighting. This would please us."

Spinning around, I almost bumped into him, standing behind me with Julio and Hipólito. Absorbed in the dealings with Fierro, I hadn't even heard them troop up through the dust. Dirty, warlike and mustachioed, legs widespread, thumbs hooked into their gun belts, they looked like an armed Praetorian guard. Guessing I might find trouble, they had ambled along to make sure I could handle it. So after all, I was their D'Artagnan.

Hipólito said, "She can cook for us. Our Frenchwomen do the other thing well, but then they lie about. Even if we kick them, they don't move. This one is young and strong."

Fierro's eyes were cold now, and he looked at the three friends as if he were measuring each of them for a pine box. They returned the look with equal hostility, and I had the first inkling then of how much they despised him. He was the outlaw wolf—Villa's animal. I had over-simplified, thinking that they were all Mexicans, all revolutionists, and therefore held each other in equal esteem.

But Villa couldn't say no to his brother and two who served him so faithfully that they would die if he crooked his finger. Moreover, they had solved his problem. He looped an arm about the butcher's shoulder. "Rodolfo, it's settled. Unless you choose to object, which I hope you won't."

"It's of no consequence," Fierro said calmly, with eyes like cold ice. "Besides, she has a foul mouth."

"You have more sense than Tomás." Villa wheeled on Candelario. "Are you inviting all of us to this fiesta?"

"We'd be honored, chief. If you don't mind seeing us drunk and disorderly."

"I'll suffer it. You have all day tomorrow to rest, which you'd better do"—he paused dramatically—"because on the next day we're going to ride south and fight. At Torreón."

A hoarse murmur of approval and excitement rose from every man's throat. We had all been waiting for this day. It was to be the beginning of the battle to conquer Mexico. I felt twin stabs of fear and expectation—and I thought it was time, in the midst of everyone's jubilance, to assert myself.

I turned to Rosa. "Go home. We have some chickens in the back. There's a goat you can milk." I didn't have to fake the sharpness. This girl had nearly got me killed.

"Yes, señor," she said obediently, and off she went. And we couldn't help it; we all turned to watch her as she walked through the dust, the firm cheeks twitching and rolling from side to side even beneath that shapeless brown sack. She couldn't help it, either. Only Rodolfo Fierro didn't watch her. He lit a cigar and stood contemplatively, gazing out at the heat shimmering above the prairie and the hazed mountains. I had an enemy now, I realized, and the wrong one.

The fiesta before the battle lasted all night. Calixto Contreras from Durango carried his own orchestra with him—eight villains in huge sombreros who played cornets and drums and trombones, so that they sounded like a Bavarian oom-pah-pah band at a barn dance in Abilene. Before the party began Esperanza came by with a pink cotton dress that she carefully explained was a gift from her husband, Señor Don Francisco Villa. When Rosa appeared in it, black hair washed and shining, a few of the men who had casually handed her over to me that morning must have had second thoughts. If she was in mourning for her husband stuffed into a well out in Corralitos, she hid it well. Barefoot, dark eyes glinting, healthy young breasts bouncing to the beat of the drum, she danced half the night. She was a pretty child, and I couldn't keep up with her. Pancho Villa danced with her, and she told me later that his hand slid down to her bottom and gave her little affectionate pinches every chance he got.

"Not so little, to tell the truth. This chief, he took a handful of almost everything I have. He must have been a good bandit."

I had a minute alone with Villa during the party, while the musicians took time out to douse their heads in buckets of water and there was something resembling quiet. Unlike everyone else, Villa was sober. If we were leaving in two days to fight, I asked, what should I do with Rosa? He threw an arm about my shoulder.

"Tomás . . . if you have anything of value, take it with you. You may never see Ascensión again. We're an army now, and armies fight or die. From now on we'll move and strike, like a fox in the chicken yard, until the north is ours. After Torreón, we'll take Chihuahua City and Juárez. After that, Zacatecas on the high plateau. And then," he said, narrowing his eyes, "we'll visit Mexico City, and I'll give an *embrazo* to Señor Emiliano Zapata, who will come up from the south with his calf eyes and his ridiculously big hat. I admire that man. I want to meet him."

The music started again and we couldn't talk more. At six o'clock in the morning, as the sun began to rise, Rosa leaned against my shoulder and said wearily, *"Mi capitán,* can we go to bed?"

I eased off with her to my room and she shut the door. There was just the one narrow bed with sagging springs, the sheets stiff from my night with Carmelita. My big Texas saddle and Mauser rifle and other gear lay in the corner next to a clay jug of drinking water. The music still blared from afar, and from the same distance we could hear the voices of men and women laughing and Urbina shouting drunkenly. Rosa put her hot head on my chest, sighing. I cleared my throat.

"Rosa, I have to tell you something. . . ."

"Yes, *mi capitán?"*

Retreating, I dropped down on a little cane chair that had only three legs.

"Rosa, you're only fourteen, but try to understand. There's this girl in Texas. I'm engaged to her. I'm in love with her."

"You told me that by the lake." Her dark brown eyes didn't blink. "I heard you well."

"It means a lot to me."

"Did you not sleep with the other one? Carmelita, you called her. You said you did it three times."

She wasn't accusing me; she was just stating a fact of life.

"I did. That's true. But . . . damnation! Yes, I did, but that was a mistake. I mean I had to, Pancho Villa sent her to me—" My voice trailed off. The sun slanted through the wooden shutters into the room, and motes of dust danced in the warm morning air. My head felt suddenly heavy.

"Rosa, I can't. That's all there is to it. I promised to take care of you, and I'll do that. I swear I will. But not the other. I don't want to shame you, so we won't tell anybody." My hand fluttered in front of me, waving at the room. "There's just the one bed, you can see that. We'll have to share it. But . . . try to understand."

She lowered her head. There was only one thing she thought she could offer me, and I wanted no part of it. It wasn't merely a reward for my kindness in giving her a home and saving her from Fierro's unpleasant clutches. From her point of view, even though she was just a girl, there was one natural act that took place between a man and woman, and that was in bed. If the rest of life was drudgery, bed was the vital center, the moment of truth. She turned around, unknotted her sash and pulled the pink cotton dress over her head, folding it neatly on the brass footboard. She was naked, and her brown back glistened with tiny pearls of sweat from the dancing. Without a word she climbed into the bed and pulled the tattered sheet over her nakedness. She turned her head to the wall. She never spoke.

I had to get some fresh air. I knew I couldn't sleep yet, not in the narrow bed with her while she was still awake and probably getting ready to cry. I slipped from the room and out the front door into the oven of the street, blinking at the glare. Behind me I could hear Hipólito snoring, and the blatting of trombones wandered to my ear through the still air. I walked in the direction of the lake, thinking that a swim would cool me down and clear out the ache between my ears. My boots kicked up white dust and I jabbed my toe hard at a rock, sending it skidding into a broken wall. Damn! I thought. Why did I ever get into this? What do I need it for?

The town stank of sour pulque. As I passed beyond the chief's house, Rodolfo Fierro stepped from the black shadow of a doorway. He was dressed exactly as I had seen him yesterday, and there was something in the neatness of his pants and dark blue shirt—as well as the thin lines graven into his olive cheeks—that made me think he hadn't slept since then. His beard was stubbled, and I knew he was a man who shaved carefully every dawn. When his eyes checked me, I halted in the dust. Again I thought I had better get in the first words.

"It was a good fiesta," I said. "Plenty of booze and spare women. You would have been welcome." My voice was just a hair on the high-pitched side.

But his, when he finally spoke, was calm, steady as a boulder, smooth as blackstrap. He knew exactly what he was going to say.

/ 85

"What happened here yesterday, señor, was unseemly. The girl means nothing to me—that, of course, you understand. And I would not argue in front of Francisco Villa, as you also understand—"

This was ridiculous. "Listen, Rodolfo," I said, "we're talking about a *kid*. And her husband had just been *shot!* Didn't you understand that too?"

He went right on as if he hadn't heard. "You shamed me, señor. But to have killed you in front of Francisco Villa and your friends would have been wrong. Nevertheless, what you did was unforgivable, and it is necessary for me to kill you. Or I have no honor among men."

I couldn't believe this. But then I realized the words came from the arctic depths of his soulless being. I glanced quickly down, but I knew what I would find. I wasn't armed. I had unbuckled my holster when I walked into the house with Rosa. The sun throbbed on my bare head. I had forgotten my hat too. And then Rodolfo Fierro spun on his heel, turned his back and walked toward the house. I stood there, thunderstruck. Hadn't he just said he was going to kill me?

"Hey, there!" I yelled angrily. "Hang on!"

I jumped after him and almost grabbed his arm to twist him round again, but he turned under his own volition and stared down at me. For the first time there was an expression on his face; he was startled.

"You can't tell me you're going to kill me and then just walk away! What the hell kind of a trick is that?" I demanded. "What's the matter with you?"

His mouth gaped open and his eyes blinked rapidly. He almost smiled—there was a certain foolish twist to his lips. But then he became himself again, glacial and malevolent.

"Señor, you have some big *cojones*. I see that now, although I didn't before. That's good." He nodded solemnly, as if to settle the idea into his head and give him breathing room. Then, quite matter-of-factly, he said, "Have no doubt that I will kill you. And it will be quick. You needn't fear. At the proper time, in the proper place."

I barked at him, "And when is that supposed to be?"

"We will both know."

With that engimatic conclusion to our conversation, he turned once more and stamped into the house. I didn't follow him this time. I didn't have big *cojones,* I realized; I had undersized brains. If I had touched him the first time when I chased him, he would have killed me. That's what he had been waiting for . . . that's what he needed, then or now, to satisfy his honor. That, or an order. I wouldn't need to fight in a battle—I could get myself killed anytime I wanted by Rodolfo Fierro.

Under a sizzling sun I shuffled back down the street to our house, bumped through the front door and into the shadowed room where Rosa slept. I flung off my clothes. The brass headboard rattled when I crawled into bed behind her. She stirred, but she didn't wake. Her black hair, with the scent of a gardenia that had wilted there during the night, flowed over my chest. Somewhere, far away, in some other cool room, Hannah also slept—but alone.

I'm a dead man, I thought, and I've only just begun to live.

8   "Courage mounteth with occasion."

Bugles screeched at dawn. A thundering, clicking ringing filled the cool air. Men struggled in a rising haze of dust, catching mules, cinching harnesses, leading horses to water, adjusting girths and snaffles, strapping spurs to boots, stuffing salt pork into their mouths and snatching hot mugs of coffee from greasewood fires. The lean Durango mustangs pawed the earth nervously, backs humped up until the vaqueros could cosy the ring bits into the tender roofs of their mouths.

Serapes flapped like flags in the wind, and the sunlight tilting over the eastern desert glinted off five thousand rifles. Pancho Villa's army was ready to move.

The horsemen trotted southward. Behind each troop plodded a few dozen women, babies sucking at their brown breasts as they led mules that swayed perilously from side to side under sacks of corn. Our column stretched for five miles across the desert, a tawny line of men and beasts obscured by the brown cloud of dust that hung in the choking air. In every village groups of neutrals stood silently in the streets to watch us pass by, but next to them they had their few precious belongings wrapped in bundles, ready to flee. The army seemed to swallow everything in sight, chickens and pigs and even stray women, as I imagined a whale would do as it moved ponderously across the ocean, mouth agape for all the little fish. I rode my big chestnut gelding, and Rosa walked next to me, refusing to mount behind—it would shame me, she said, to share my horse with a woman, and later, when the men laughed at me, I would be angry with her.

But in Bachinava, where we camped one night, Candelario commandeered some horses from the local police stables. He brought round a gray and a skewbald mare with an old broad-horned saddle.

"The gray will be a good spare horse for you, Tomás. The mare is for your woman."

I slanted an accusing look at him. He knew how I felt about Hannah and my fall from grace with Carmelita. But then I realized he meant well, and so I thanked him properly. He didn't know that Rosa was only in my care until she could go home to Tomochic, and I had promised not to shame her by letting the men know that we lived like brother and sister. For a while I thought of trying to give her as a gift to Hipólito . . . until I realized how shameful it was to treat a human being like a horse or a sack of corn. Saint Peter would never have recognized me as a candidate for wings, but I figured I might make some amends for my hoggish ways if I offered that young girl some genuine kindness. Rosa mounted the skewbald as smoothly as any bronc buster I'd ever seen, riding it stiff-legged in the Mexican fashion and crooning to it all the while in order to get better acquainted. This was no Sunday horse lady out for a canter in the park.

And I kept a weather eye peeled for Rodolfo Fierro. I had told the others about our dawn meeting on the street, and this time they didn't crack jokes. Fierro, on his part, ignored me, but whenever his big silver spurs jingled around my horse I felt my guts turning to fiddlestrings. I considered that it might possibly please Hannah in some kind of giddy romantic way that the man she loved had died fighting for land and liberty in Mexico; but it wouldn't please me.

"Don't worry about it," Julio said. "The solution is simple. In the first battle, we'll kill him."

"You can't do that," I said, shocked. "He's on *our* side."

"He is on no one's side," Candelario replied. "He is not a revolutionist. Do you think he cares for anything but himself? He loves no one, except perhaps the chief, but only because the chief allows him to open the door to his destiny. He loves the killing. There are men like that, who had nothing before the revolution and will have nothing after it. The revolution gives them life, a purpose, however grisly it may be. He is *matador,* no more."

But I made them promise it wouldn't happen that way, that they wouldn't shoot Fierro in the back during a battle. I might kill, but I would never murder, and to instruct others to commit it for me was no better. I would handle it myself, when the time came. And when would that be? *We will both know.* Those were Fierro's words.

We plodded through a range of gaunt mountains to the banks of the Nazas River, close to Torreón, in a fertile area called La Luguna, filled with cornfields and big irrigation ditches flowing with cool water. Bales of sparkling white cotton lay rotting in the sun near a deserted mill; Villa had advertised that he was coming and the people didn't doubt his word. Before that, in the pretty pink town of Bermejillo, he picked up an automobile, an open seven-passenger Dodge, and decided that he would travel in style until the gasoline tank became empty. He didn't know how to drive, but Colonel Medina did. The Nazas was in flood, so that our artillery and heavy supplies had to be carried across on rafts. Just as the old Dodge reached midriver on the raft, a cable broke and the car was swept away by the powerful current. Villa ruefully watched it go, then turned to Medina with a red-toothed smile.

"You just lost your job, my friend. But don't worry. I'm going to make you my chief of staff instead of my chauffeur."

We camped on the Nazas, from where we would launch our attack on Torreón. Our trek to the south had taken two weeks. A nearby hacienda had been abandoned, so Villa made it his headquarters, and the army spread out for a mile along the winding river. I found a spot in the shelter of some cottonwood trees, drawing a bit away from Candelario and the others, who tended to argue and drink far into the night and then keep me awake with all their grunting and humping of Yvette and Marie-Thérèse.

Rosa and I hadn't talked much on the way south—we were too busy herding the livestock and keeping an eye out for Federal patrols. When she kindled a fire and spread our blankets by the river, I sat with her in a peaceful, brooding silence, listening to the crickets and the purl of water against the bank. I rolled a cigarette and smoked it, then leaned back, hands under my head, looking up at the stars. It was a warm night, and a thin moon shed a pearly glow. Rosa lay down beside me, keeping the distance that I had ordained as necessary. But after a minute she shifted just a bit, laid her head on my chest and began quietly to cry.

I stroked her hair. Her crying kept up for a few minutes and then gradually stopped, and I felt her breast heave as if she were shaking something loose from inside herself. She wiped her nose with the sleeve of her blouse.

"What was the matter, Rosa?"

"I think of my husband," she said softly.

That was better than I had hoped for. I dreaded being the cause of her misery.

"What was his name?"

She took a shaky breath. "May I not tell you that? It will be easier for me if you know nothing about him, because then his shadow cannot fall in front of you. You know that there was much love between us. But he is dead, and you are alive. And I am young, and I am with you."

With her head on my chest I started to speak, but then thought better of it. She had moved me with her words, and I didn't have anything in kind I could respond with. And there was the problem of what she assumed and I didn't. Only the night before I had dreamed of Hannah wearing a white wedding gown.

Rosa sat up and looked down at me, dark eyes still blurred. But I saw a lurking uncertainty. I nodded.

She said, "That morning by the lake, in Ascensión. Do you remember? You had been with another woman, which you said meant I was not to worry . . . you couldn't take me because you were too tired. But I think that was not the reason. Will you tell me the real reason?"

"In the first place," I said, a little impatiently, "I wouldn't do that. I couldn't force myself on anyone."

/ 89

"And in the second place?"

"I told you, Rosa. I'm engaged to a girl. I want to be faithful. When this is over, if I don't get killed, I'll marry her."

"It was not that you found me unattractive?"

"You're very pretty."

"Truly? You believe that?"

"Well, sure. Of course I do."

She tossed her hair back, trying to smile. But the sadness hadn't left her eyes. The crickets began to sing a little more quickly, as the night cooled down. From afar I heard Marie-Thérèse giggling, and the sounds of a guitar striking up.

Women have that special silent way of letting you know that something's bothering them. If you don't coax them into spitting it out, they sulk forever and a day. Even if she wasn't my bedmate, she was traveling with me and under my care, and I couldn't have that.

"Come on, Rosa. What is it?"

"Also that morning . . ." She looked down at her bare feet. "You told your chief, Francisco Villa, that you would care for me until I could go home to my family in Tomochic. Did you not say that?"

"I guess I did. I don't exactly remember."

"You did. And I wish to ask you one thing." She struggled a moment or two, then crawled against me again and got the words out, muffled into my chest. "Unless I displease you, which of course is possible, I ask you not to send me back to Tomochic. There is nothing for me there. And if I displease you, tell me in what way. I am not a foolish girl."

That didn't seem to commit me to much, and I nodded.

"I will try to please you . . . even if you won't let me in the other way. I am Tarahumara, but all that they say about me is not true. My tongue is quick, but it's not spiteful. I will try to please you," she whispered again.

"Go to sleep, Rosa."

The guitar had begun to be plucked more vigorously, and we heard men singing a ballad about some forgotten battle and a lost love. Rosa curled in my arms, smelling of smoky firewood and a fresh scent that came from her flesh . . . it had to be the pure scent of youth. She was a child who needed to be cradled to sleep. I felt that, and I guess my pecker did too; it didn't twitch at all. I wasn't troubled; my love was far from here, and I was faithful. Rosa's forehead was warm in the hollow of my neck. We were almost asleep in the heat of the night, soothed by the guitar, when she giggled, a kittenish sound that I probably wasn't meant to hear. And then in a tiny voice, the kind children use when they deign to tell you their most precious secrets, she whispered in my neck: "I know you are not a captain. But it doesn't matter."

"I'm glad."

"I'll only call you *mi capitán* when we're alone . . . *mi capitán.*"

I thought about that for a minute and then whispered, "Go to sleep, Rosa. You're displeasing me."

The night before we were to storm Torreón, Pancho Villa called a meeting of his commanders at the Hacienda de las Lomas. He had spent a month planning the attack. He never, as long as I knew him, left anything to chance. He studied the terrain and even sent spies into the cities, disguised as peasants, to plot the enemy defenses and manpower. He organized the medical units and the placement of artillery, the food and the ammunition, the disposition of reserves. He did it without fuss, quietly, making no written notes, operating from instinct as much as knowledge—it was all balanced in his mind at once. And then, when the battles began, he himself led the men into the field.

Now, before Torreón, he had decided to organize his force in a more military manner.

"Come along, Tomás. This will be instructive."

The big room of the hacienda, thick with cigar smoke and the rank odors of horse and sweat, was lit by candles that sent black plumes swirling through the breathless air. Pegs were driven into the walls to hang saddles and bridles, and outside the hacienda a great fire blazed. A harpist, an old albino who had been the hacienda's caretaker, played balled after ballad, while the men gathered round the fire to sing and smoke their cornhusk cigarettes.

Sitting at the head of a big scarred mahogany table, his unshaved cheeks glowing in the fierce light thrown by the candles so that he looked like a barbaric medieval tribal chieftain, Villa held forth to the leaders.

"Señores, this will be an army now, not a rabble. We'll start as a division, which means we must have a commanding general . . . brigades, with other generals . . . regiments and battalions. That's how it will be done."

"A moment, Señor Villa!"

The interruption came from Manuel Chao, the bucktoothed fellow who had first visited us in Ascensión and was once again present as an emissary from Carranza. This time he wore a uniform and carried an ivory-handled pistol in a yellow calfskin holster. "I have a letter here from the First Chief," he said. "It bears his signature and seal. If I may be permitted to read it aloud?"

A murmur went round the table. Chao unfolded the letter, typed on crisp blue notepaper, and began to read. It authorized him to take command of all the revolutionary forces in the state of Chihuahua. That meant us—there were no others. Villa scraped back his big armchair, started to rise, then thumped down again, his eyes popping.

"Jesus Christ! First he wants Obregón, a chickpea farmer . . . now you! What did you do, Señor Chao, before you became a paper general?"

"I taught geography in Monterrey, señor. I also have studied military history."

Villa turned to me at the far end of the table, where I sat behind Urbina, who clutched his demijohn of aguardiente on his lap. "Make a note of that, Tomás. He taught geography and studied military history. We may need something to inscribe on his tombstone. Give me that letter," he growled.

Chao handed the blue notepaper to him. Villa held it over one of the sputtering candles—it caught fire immediately. He didn't let go until it nearly scorched his fingers and then let it drop to the table, where it curled into black ash with a glowing edge. Chao's jaw jutted forward. One hand dropped to the ivory butt of his pistol.

"Go ahead," Villa said coldly. "But be sure you can bite a bullet in midair. Before you have that pantywaist pistol out of its ridiculous holster, I'm going to shoot you right between your big buckteeth."

Chao hesitated, then raised both hands from his lap. He tented them together on the surface of the table. "There's no need for discord, Señor Villa . . . just as there's no need for insult." He coughed nervously. "How do you propose to organize this division?"

"First we'll vote on a commanding general. I'll accept nominations."

"I nominate Francisco Villa!" cried Urbina.

"Any others?" Villa asked.

Everyone shrugged. "In that case," said Villa, "I myself will nominate Manuel Chao, the geography teacher who's been recommended by the First Chief. That way we'll have some kind of vote. And we'll know who believes in what."

Hands were raised in the smoky air. Villa was unanimously elected chief general. He didn't vote, and neither did Chao. Villa thanked his commanders graciously; then he appointed them generals. Rodolfo Fierro, Hipólito and Candelario were named colonels. Medina became chief of staff and artillery commander. Julio made major. "We'll call this the Northern Division," Villa said, "since we're all men of the north and this is the heartland of the revolution. Is that agreed?" His generals and colonels thumped their fists on the table in unison and then drank a toast from bottles of French cognac that had come up from the hacienda's wine cellar—first to the revolution, then to the sacred memory of Señor Madero and finally to Don Venus ". . . whose firm principles," Villa intoned, "guide our minds at all times, even if they can't do so well with our bullets."

From the nine ragged men who had splashed across the Rio Bravo in March, we were now a force of nearly eight thousand: the famed

Northern Division. Its memory, in Mexican legend, would never die. Shortly before midnight when the meeting broke up—for the next day we were going to storm Torreón—Villa's hand settled on my shoulder.

"Tomás, in Juárez I made you a promise. I didn't forget. You're a captain, attached to my personal staff."

I thanked him . . . I felt thrilled.

"I know that you told your woman that you were already a captain. That was impetuous of you. But I forgive you because you're young. And loyal, too. Now you can go to her and not feel like such a damned fool."

That man knew everything.

At dawn the outlying Federal cannon began to bombard us on the banks of the Nazas. The earth shook . . . gouts of smoke swirled among the cottonwood trees. I mounted my horse and whipped him along a burro path toward the hacienda. All around me boots dragged jangling spurs, cavalrymen checked reins and stirrups, hoofs pounded. A pillar of brown dust, like smoke from a burning city, rose into the air. Mist packed under the trees, rolling across green fields, and a weak orange sun peeked above the mountains. The birds, who didn't know that a great battle was about to take place, began to sing . . .

Villa had already assembled most of his staff. "Let's not waste time," he said sternly, "or we'll all be food for the buzzards."

He would take one brigade and advance down the right bank of the Nazas, with Calixto Contreras attacking on the left bank toward Gómez Palacio, Torreón's twin city. The population of the two cities numbered almost three hundred thousand. This was no knitting bee, for the Federal general, Murguía, commanded a full division with a regiment of artillery.

Villa turned to me and said, "Tomás, do you want to fight?"

A little surprised, I replied, "That's why I'm here, chief."

"My staff officers don't sit around at the rear with binoculars. The others know that . . . I wasn't sure you did. Go with Candelario's battalion," he ordered. "And remember, with your pistol you don't aim. But with your rifle, line up the sights low and dead center." He slapped the cotton shirt that covered his belly, crisscrossed with full cartridge belts.

A shell splashed in the river, and my stomach heaved. I'd never been in a battle before and I had no training as a soldier . . . not that many of our troops were much better off. I didn't want to die, and even more I feared being gutshot or having a chunk of shrapnel tear my balls apart. Checking reins and stirrups, thinking about all the awful things that could happen to a man's body, I mounted my horse and almost slipped right out of the saddle when he wrinkled his spine to get the kinks out. Mule-drawn caissons and gun carriages rumbled past us. The gunners unlimbered, and Medina ran round screwing on the sights and cranking the levers. Far to the east we could see the smokestacks of factories and the stony peak of La Pila guarding the city from the north. Whips cracked. The mules strained forward and troops of horse kicked mighty clouds of dust in our faces. Like any sensible cowhand I wore a big blue bandanna round my throat. Now I raised it up over my nose— Jesse James in Old Mexico—and started to sweat.

We moved slowly toward Torreón, through a narrow valley flanked by low hills. We were bunched together in a mass, thousands of horsemen with wagons following. I was glad we weren't fighting Apaches or the advance would have been suicidal, but the Federal Army fought by the book and waited for us. Our horses trampled the burnt yellow corn into rubble. I heard the crackling rip of rifle fire ahead, and then a shell burst with a dull *bar-ooom* in front of Villa, who rode ahead of the troops.

"Deploy! . . . spread out!"

The brigade fanned out as the valley widened. It was a warm, muggy morning with elephant-gray clouds clustered on the horizon, threatening rain. I spotted some adobe houses and then an automobile wrecking yard in our path. In the distance the buildings of the city formed themselves vaguely out of the haze. Suddenly I realized Torreón wasn't just a word, an image—it was a *place*. We rode at a choppy trot, which made it difficult to fire, while pods of cotton floated by like snow. A few bullets whistling by made a tired sound. I pulled my rifle from its scabbard and took a snug check on the rein. Off to my left then, a horse was hit. Braying like a donkey, it spilled its rider into a prickly-pear cactus. He jumped up from the dust, cursing and pulling thorns out of his arm.

"Don't kill them all, boys! Wait for me!"

Julio yelled at us. "There are Federals in the wrecking yard!"

Behind some rusting automobiles I saw white shapes with peaked caps. The muzzles of their rifles puffed with smoke. We were about three hundred yards away, easy range for a sharpshooter, but they were snapping off their shots too quickly and too high to do any damage. Julio gave the order to fire. At least fifty of us cut loose at once, and even at that distance I could hear the spang and whine of bullets hitting metal, so that if you were sheltered behind the wrecks it must have been a terrifying clamor. The white shapes disappeared. There was no more return fire.

This is easy, I thought. This suits me fine. If this is war, then I'd a damn sight rather take part in it than face Rodolfo Fierro's pistol. A shell exploded off to our right, but it wasn't aimed at me. I slammed the bolt, aimed, fired and heard the shattering of glass—a car window. Then from far away Candelario shouted an order to gallop. I put my knees into the big chestnut. Off he went like a quarter horse, hind legs churning, supple in the withers and lightning between my legs, Hipólito at my side on his roan. We must have been two hundred men in that charge . . . and suddenly the wrecking yard was in front of us and I could make out twisted license plates, crumpled fenders, and a big jack lying in front of a rusted Stutz-Bearcat whose insides had been stripped down to the chassis.

We were almost at the yard when the Federals popped up like ghosts from behind stacks of black tires and let off a volley at us. None of us was hit. The Federals turned and ran toward the adobe houses across the dirt road. Almost immediately they began to fall—Candelario and another troop of cavalary had outflanked them. Remembering La Perla, I fired until my rifle was empty, not having any idea whether or not I hit anyone. The dust billowed up like a yellow fountain.

I reined up in the wrecking yard behind the shelter of a clapboard shack, dug a fresh box of five rounds from my cartridge belt and rammed it home into the Mauser. My breath came in shallow gulps. The chestnut nickered—he wanted to keep moving. A score of Villistas, including Julio and Hipólito, had stopped to reload, and I grinned foolishly at them through the smoke. A man next to me stared at the mess of his bloody hand. A few red-soaked, white-uniformed bodies lay on the ground, either dead or twitching. I had seen corpses laid out neatly in my father's undertaking parlor, but here they flung themselves about in the most awkward way possible, legs twisted and necks bent back at ridiculous angles. I was trying to figure out what useful thing I could do next, when a nearby man, busily trying to adjust a loose cinch, jumped suddenly off his horse and lay down full length in the dirt, making a pillow of his hands. What in hell, I wondered, is *he* up to? This was no time to take a siesta. Then I saw bright red blood flowing from his neck. The man was dead. I said aloud, "Oh, lord!" Rifles began cracking murderously at close range.

I yanked at the rein and my horse spun, crawfishing, as the Mauser flew out of my hand and bounced with a clang against the hood of a car. There were Federals hidden in the wrecking-yard office not twenty yards away, firing at us as fast as they could.

Men tumbled from their saddles. Blood jetting from its throat, Julio's horse slid out from under him. He jumped down, crouched behind the flailing body, laid his rifle across the withers and began to pump bullets through the windows of the clapboard shack. The other men scattered through the dust like boys playing hide-and-go-seek. I pulled my pistol, spurred between a battered black hearse and a Winton touring car and almost trampled Hipólito, on his knees behind a fender of the hearse.

He yelled up at me, "Idiot! Get down! Shelter yourself!"

I vaulted from the saddle and hit the dirt with a shock that nearly drove my spine through my neck. For a minute bells rang; the world turned fuzzy. Working the bandanna loose from my face, I smelled grease and the dizzying odor of spilled gasoline. I was safe behind the hearse. The firing slacked off, the smoke swirling downwind. In a battle the enemy always had to reload—there was always plenty of time to think and worry. I gulped some hot air into my lungs and wiped the sweat from my eyes. The sweat rolled down my forehead as if someone had dumped a pail of warm oil over me. Why had I ever looked forward to this?

I peered round the fender. A bullet spanged off metal . . . now they *were* shooting at me. But that quick glance told me that the Federals in the office were surrounded—they had no chance, unless we just lay back and traded shots with them all day until we got tired of it and went away. Not a bad idea, I thought, when suddenly there was a deafening explosion—and the tire in front of me whooshed out its air, flattening before my eyes.

"What was that?" I yelled.

At my elbow, as if we were at a tea party, Hipólito said, "Don't shout. I can hear you quite well. It was a grenade."

"A grenade?" I felt my bowels loosen. No, it wasn't a tea party. Despite the birds chirping and the sun shining, this was a battle, in a war. Grenades could kill or blow your balls to shreds. I didn't want to die, or be maimed, not now, not ever. Somehow I could deal with bullets, but not with grenades. I muttered to myself for a few seconds, then leaped to my feet, enraged. "Come on!" I shouted. "We have to rush these sons of bitches!"

Maybe I had read it in a magazine somewhere: some tale of Teddy's Rough Riders at San Juan Hill. I yelled, *"Adelante! Forward!"* and sprinted toward the shack, blood pumping in my ears, tugging at the trigger of my pistol. Fifty men followed me, weapons rattling like a chorus of hammers on iron buckets.

The shack splintered apart. Federals began tumbling out the door. They fell on their knees, shrieking to surrender. My pistol was empty before I reached the wall of the shack. I slid to the ground there to reload. By the time I had finished, scorching my fingers on the barrel, the gunfire had stopped. A gang of our men had broken into the shack and were herding the rest of the enemy out at rifle point.

Julio trotted up to me, thin face streaked with blood. A bullet had taken away part of an earlobe. His eyes looked like targets, huge white circles centered with black bulls. He bent to my side.

"Where are you hit, Tomás?"

"I'm not hit. I'm fine."

"But, *hombre,* you're bleeding. . . ."

I glanced down. There was blood in the dirt where I sat. It was soaking redly through the Levi's on my left thigh, staining them a rich grapelike purple that glistened in the sunlight. I could see the rip clearly. I hadn't felt a thing. Scrambling to my feet, I still didn't feel anything.

"Take off your pants, Tomás."

"What? Here?"

"Are you shy?"

I pulled down my Levi's, and a knife of pain flew from leg to brain and back to my leg again. Just below my underpants, damp with sweat from crotch to crack, was an ugly dark red gash and a sliver of thin black metal about an inch long sticking out of my thigh. I stared, then babbled, "Well, look at that . . . just look at that. How about that? I'll be a cross-eyed baboon if I know where *that* came from."

"It's a grenade fragment."

"Is that what it is?"

"You'd better go back, Tomás."

"You don't look so hot yourself with that red ear. Are you going back? If you go, I'll go."

Julio grinned like a coyote out of his bloody poxed face. Without warning, he threw his arms around me, giving me a hug that nearly cracked a rib.

"Tomás! My friend! You were brave! You were like a lion! *You led the charge!*"

I grinned foolishly, a little embarrassed. Then suddenly I felt dizzy, and stumbled, and sat down in the dirt. The world grew fuzzy and gray. Hands lifted and carried me. I shut my eyes.

When I woke, most of the fighting for Torreón was over. Machine guns putt-putted nastily from far away, and the sun baked down through the sultry late-afternoon air. My wound was being dressed in a makeshift aid station outside the city, swabbed with iodine and bandaged by an old crone who was certainly no nurse.

"*Aieee,* poor little one," she crooned. "You're lucky to be alive!"

"I think so too, señora," I said, opening my eyes.

"I have a son your age. No, wait . . . that one's dead. But it's all right, I have five more. Two with the Federals and two with your General Villa! One is a Redflagger . . . he's the naughty one. Do you have a cigarette? Give me a cigarette for good luck. . . ."

Wreaths of black smoke spiraled up from Torreón. As dusk settled I sipped a bottle of warm beer and watched the men limping back along the road. I recognized an unshaven filthy soldier from our battalion. His name was Ignacio García. He had been shot in the shoulder, and his arm was in a sling ripped from some Federal's shirt. I waved him over and said, "How did it go, Ignacio?"

"Wonderful, my captain. I was brave as a bull. I killed many bad men."

/ 97

He told me that the battalion had penetrated deep into the city, and Villa had ordered them to rest while he brought up his reserves. Only a few had been killed.

"What about Colonel Cervantes?" I asked.

"A one-eyed man can ride through hell and come out carrying sunflowers. But I haven't seen him, that's true. . . ."

Nor had he seen Hipólito or Julio. Despite the pain in my leg, I saddled my horse and set out in the direction of the city. Dark groups of shawl-wrapped figures sat by the roadside, women and half-naked children who had huddled in the ditches during the day. A river of wounded men flowed by, and a baby wailed from the darkness. The dead had been cleared from the road, but horses lay with stiff legs splayed in the air.

The battalion had established itself in the ruins of a brick school-house. I found Candelario, Hipólito and Julio in one of the classrooms, each sitting behind a small wooden desk. Heads pillowed on the wood, they snored in unison as if the music teacher were waving her baton. When I clumped in with my boots on the concrete floor, Candelario opened one malevolent eye, looked me up and down, then groaned.

"Mother of God, it's come back from the dead."

"It went back to the Nazas. . . ." Julio grimaced as he tasted his own mouth. "It crept under a blanket with that girl and got eaten alive."

"Certainly," Hipólito croaked, "one can see that something bad has happened to it."

Julio shook his head disapprovingly. "You know what the chief says. If you fuck before fighting, your hands will shake."

I was glad to see them all alive and didn't care what fun they made of me. I was one with them now, blooded in battle, and I had liked it—that was a truth I couldn't deny. No raw meat and still I had been brave, had led a charge. I had taken a giant leap toward becoming the man worthy of Hannah's faith. What more glory could there be? Later—but sooner than I wished—I remembered that Shakespeare, who had been my mentor before Pancho Villa, had said that we were to the gods as flies to wanton boys. And before they killed us for their sport, no doubt they let us buzz and draw a drop of blood . . . let our flies' hearts swell with pride and a sense of heroic purpose.

The next morning I moved slowly through the gardens of the city, where the smiling women of Torreón served coffee and sandwiches to hollow-eyed soldiers. Blue butterflies drank deeply from the bougain-villea. A streetcar, drawn by galloping mules, rattled past, bulging with drunken men. I watched while our dead were carried in trucks to the hill of La Pila and burned, the pyres scorching the blue sky. The women of

Torreón threw bunches of marigolds and pink dahlias, silk scarves and embroidered hats, as if a torero were circling the ring for tribute. The soldiers tossed the hats back. The silk scarves they knotted round their sweaty throats, or draped them over the staring faces of the dead.

We had taken the first city on Pancho Villa's unwritten list, and in the evening he received a report of what the Federals had left behind as our reward. It included six machine guns, thirteen artillery pieces, forty locomotives and the attached rolling stock. So there was something to celebrate. Villa ordered all available food distributed among the poor; surgical supplies from the new military hospital were handed out to the civilian doctors. Five hundred tattered prisoners were then penned into the hospital until they could be sorted out and a final decision reached as to their fate.

Late that night a fiesta was given for the officers of the Northern Division at the Casino de la Laguna. The French whores danced the can-can on the banquet table. To watch Urbina, you might have thought walking was a lost art—he fell down three times, sent off a telegram to his mother, then went to sleep on the banquet table with Calixto Contreras snoring under it. The señoritas of Torreón garlanded us with flowers, but I was weary and cleaved to Rosa, who wore her frilly pink dress from Ascensión and literally danced her shoes off. Villa arrived with two women. One of them was Esperanza, his new wife. The other, Juana Torres, was the daughter of a Torreón cotton manufacturer. She had black eyes and breasts that looked hard as pears. Villa left with both of them. He also had a wife from Chihuahua City named Luz Corral, but that was before my time and I didn't know where she was these days.

Rosa and I left the party while it was still dark and walked the few blocks back to the Hotel Salvador, which had been taken over by Villa's staff, and that now included me. A group of drunken soldiers sang on a street corner. A guitarist crooned through a barred window at a señora whose husband was off fighting in some other battle. Rosa linked her arm with mine. "Thank you, *mi capitán,*" she murmured, "for taking me with you."

Thinking back now, it must have been inevitable, although I had warred against it as best I could. My best just wasn't good enough—not now, in Torreón, after one battle, with another one surely looming ahead and the chance that life would be snuffed out as easily as a burning match in the wind. I only understood that after the grenades had exploded in the wrecking yard and the blood had flowed from my leg. It could as easily have been my heart. Hannah would never have forgiven me for what I did, but Hannah would never understand how a man felt when he realized finally that Candelario was right: life was short. Short, brutal, always hanging by the most slender of threads. If you didn't take the goodness it offered you, what was left? And didn't the brave deserve the fair?

We reached my room in the Hotel Salvador, undressed, and I turned out the light. I had seen Rosa's body often enough, first at the lake and then on our journey south, paraded before me in innocence. It wasn't the body of a child. I knew her breasts and the buttery curve of her hip. But stroking them, kissing them, they came alive in a way I had not imagined possible. It would never have been this way if it had happened in Ascensión, when her young husband's death was fresh and I was sunk in the trough of my guilt over Carmelita.

I touched her satin skin, listening to her sighs of pleasure. The scent of her youth gradually gave way to a muskier scent, a womanly blossoming. Strong trembling hands gripped my hips and demanded that I mount her.

She cried out not as a girl, but as a woman. "I want you, Tomás. . . ."

I slid smoothly and deep into a snug, yet marvelously oiled velvet channel, tightly gripped as I had never been gripped before, astride and yet saddled as the solid muscles of her legs clutched at me. I was drowning in her thick black hair, gasping in the sweat of her neck. Rosa was strong, vital, young. Toward the end she groaned and dug her nails into my back. Her head thrashed on the pillow. So she had been pleasured too—it was not in her nature to pretend. That was new for me too. I couldn't hold back then, and I poured into her, while she gripped me in the vice of her limbs and crooned my name.

We drifted to sleep under the blanket in each other's arms. Before we slept, she whispered, "Was it pleasant for you, *mi capitán?*"

She wasn't being sly. I said, "Yes, Rosa. You please me."

We woke to a cool and lovely autumn morning. I hadn't thought once of Hannah, and then only when I was shaving, wondering if she would like the mustache I had started to grow. Rosa and I went for a walk, listened to the mariachis in the sunshine of the park, then had lunch in an oyster shop.

"I've never eaten them, Tomás. They're so gray. How do they taste?"

"Try one."

With her spoon she lifted a small oyster, swimming in red sauce with chopped avocado. She placed it carefully on her tongue.

"Ah!" She smiled happily, relieved. "They taste of chile!"

We ambled back to the hotel for a siesta. Just after we had made love, someone knocked stoutly on the door. It was a soldier to tell me that General Villa wished to see me, at my convenience . . . which meant right away. I dressed quickly, tried to wish away the weakness in knees and loins, then walked upstairs. He was in the bridal suite, its blue velvet walls decorated with oil portraits of Spanish grandees. He lay collapsed on a settee with silk cushions, drinking coffee from a silver decanter that stood on a teak table. He wore only baggy pants and his boots, which hadn't been cleaned from the battle and still smelled of horseshit. His chest was hairy and he looked flabby in the gut, but that had to be deceiving; you couldn't ride a horse the way Villa did and be internally soft. Juana Torres was with him, smiling demurely, dressed in a silk bathrobe from which her breasts jutted like twin cannons. Hipólito and Rodolfo Fierro sprawled in easy chairs, each with a bottle of Canadian whiskey and a crystal glass.

Villa was talking with three well-dressed men, two of whom had distinguished silver-gray hair, while the other was portly and bald. They were bankers. The chief was explaining that he would require a loan of 600,000 pesos to re-equip his army and distribute food to the hungry of Torreón.

"We could plunder what we need," he said gravely, "but that would give a bad name to the revolution, besides displeasing Señor Carranza. I wish things to be done in an orderly and legal manner. Will you cooperate, señores?"

The bankers asked hesitantly what security would be provided for the loan, and if interest would be paid.

"Why quibble over interest? Charge what you think is fair. As for security, it's all around you." Villa waved diffidently out the window, where his soldiers roamed the streets and slept in the plaza. A marimba band played on the shaded platform in the center of the park. The sun was shining, and birds sang vigorously. Now and then some shots were fired . . . just exuberance.

"Let's assume that all will be arranged by tomorrow afternoon. From now on, señores . . . you serve the people! Be proud."

He dismissed the bankers, who murmured various compliments on his victory and then scuttled out.

"Scum. I had half a mind to shoot them, but I needed the money. The fat one is a Spaniard. I may shoot him anyway."

He turned to Juana Torres, who was looking at the photographs in an American movie magazine. "Get dressed, my dove," Villa crooned. "Order us something to eat. Chicken, plenty of it, and more hot coffee, and sweet melon. French wine for Captain Mix."

When she left he patted his belly. "Tomorrow," he announced, "I'm getting married." He eyed me speculatively. "Tomás, you're an educated man, certainly more than this oaf I call a brother, and this other animal. I want your opinion on the matter. Is it right or wrong?"

"To marry Juana Torres?"

"That's what I have in mind. Didn't I just say so?"

I cleared my throat so that I could give an enthusiastic blessing, but he raised his hand.

/ 101

"Before you answer, consider. The Torres girl comes from a good family. It would have made her unhappy to be seduced by me and then abandoned, and of course I'd never consider violence. *But I had to have her.* So I promised marriage. Isn't that the answer? When I lead her to the altar, she'll weep with joy. If there's a sin in the eyes of God because I've got more than one wife, the sin belongs to me, not her. So . . . is this right or wrong of me?"

He didn't care what any of us thought. He was just thinking aloud with a convenient audience. But something was required of me.

"How will Esperanza feel about it?" I asked.

"She's my wife already. For Christ's sake, I'm not planning to divorce her! That would be cruel."

"And the other one? Isn't there a wife in Chihuahua City? Luz Corral?"

"Ah, that's different! Luz Corral is my *real* wife. She understands everything about me."

I thought that made her an extraordinary woman.

"And can you find a priest in Torreón who'll help you commit bigamy?"

Villa chuckled. "If I've got a pistol in my hand, I can find a dozen. Even a bishop."

"Chief," I said, laughing, "maybe you've discovered the solution to the problem that's been troubling men for the last two thousand years."

"That's interesting, Tomás." His face grew sober. "I never thought of it that way. I just do it to save time, and to make the women happy."

Satisfied with our approval of his new domestic arrangements, he turned to military business: there was the question of the five hundred prisoners in the military hospital. He had a new plan. "This time we'll give the Federal enlisted men a choice," he said. "They can join us or be shot. We'll shoot the Redflaggers, of course, as well as all the Federal officers. The officers are educated men. They should know better than to fight against the revolution and the people."

Hipólito was to collect the men for the firing squads and take charge of sorting the prisoners into the correct groups. I was to keep an accurate count on paper. Fierro would be responsible for the final arrangements—his specialty.

Villa dismissed us, saying that Juana Torres had tired him and he would sleep.

I doubt if he realized what he had set in motion. For a while I wondered if it were a test, or some sort of punishment for the way I had bearded him in Casas Grandes over the killing of those prisoners. But probably he didn't think at all; the mind behind the sleepy eyes was already gazing northward toward Chihuahua City and Juárez. We were his aides, he trusted us and there was a job to be done. He couldn't know how it would change all our lives.

9

"The gates of mercy
shall be all shut up."

The military hospital was a massive new white building abutting the stockyards on the fringe of the city. Fierro had found a car, a Studebaker, with a chauffeur who wore a braided sombrero and propped his rifle against the gearshift. Fierro wore the white Stetson that he had now fashioned to a sharp point, a striped blue shirt with red suspenders and his natty cavalry puttees. He never spoke to me unless it was absolutely necessary. Whenever I remembered that he had promised to kill me, a chill washed through my insides . . . I never let my guard down. One thing was in my favor: he was too correct in his fierce loyalty to Villa, who was as much his master as any man could have one and not be a slave, to ever do anything of which he suspected the chief would disapprove. He was the faithful wolf whose eyes never revealed his passion . . . if he had any beyond killing. It was whispered among the men who disliked him that he really didn't care for women—after Rosa, I had never seen him with one—and that in his youth he had lain with men. But I couldn't believe that. I knew that all homos were simpering men with fleshy lips and that they hung around places like the YMCA in Dallas. Not Rodolfo Fierro, the wolf, the death dealer.

When we left the hotel, Hipólito started out to find men for the firing squads, but Fierro called him back. "Don't bother," he said languidly. "The men are tired. I'll arrange all that when the time comes."

Hipólito was an easygoing sort who couldn't have cared less about details, and he agreed.

We stared about us. Fierro seemed shocked, and he turned to Hipólito. "Is this a hospital? No, it's a madhouse. . . ."

Most of the prisoners had cots to sleep on, but they had been given no food for nearly three days. If there hadn't been a trickle of water from the hospital faucets, they would have died of thirst. Through an oversight, no officer had been in command until just a few hours ago. The wards stank foully of shit, piss and vomit. The Redflaggers had guessed their fate. Some of them gibbered, even frothed at the mouth, huddling against the walls when any of us approached. Some fell on their hands and knees and tried to lick our boots. I had to kick one away . . . I clenched my teeth and did it.

The new Villista lieutenant in charge of the hospital guard presented himself, and I recognized him. He was Juan Dozal, who had helped Fierro execute the men at Casas Grandes. Somewhere along the route to Torreón he had received a promotion.

Dozal, weak-chinned and mustachioed, eager to please, told us that a dozen of the prisoners were already dead and had been dumped out-side in the hospital gardens. It was a hot afternoon, and we could smell them. During the night some of the Redflaggers had attacked the Federal enlisted men, trying to strip them of their uniforms. Men had been battered to bloody unconsciousness, even death, for the sake of their soiled white shirts and peaked caps. Many of the Redflaggers had torn their uniforms to shreds and thrown them away, so that they were naked. The Federal officers, understanding their special peril, had ripped off their insignia; but if you looked closely you could see the tiny pinholes on their shoulders. A man's life literally depended on the way he was dressed.

"My colonel," Dozal said to Fierro, "if you've got to pick out the right men to die, you're going to have a difficult time."

"I don't think so," Rodolfo said good-naturedly, surveying the writhing mass of men. "Let's not tax our brains too much. Those who are dressed as Federals will be spared—unless, of course, they refuse to join us. But it looks as if most of them have fought hard for the privilege."

"And if they're naked, my colonel?"

"If a man's naked, we'll shoot him. We'll assume he's a Redflagger or an officer. We may make a few mistakes that way, but they won't be the sort of mistakes we can live to regret."

They screamed with terror—kicked, shoved and spat—when Fierro approached. They knew who he was. He took over the operation, did the picking and sorting, while Hipólito smoked a cigar and I kept count in a schoolboy's black notebook. I still have the notebook, stained with blood and weather. This is what it tells me.

Dead already:	12
Federal soldiers who chose to join us:	253
Federal soldiers who said no:	3
Federal officers:	17
Redflaggers:	64
Men of unknown description:	155
Total:	504

The three Federal soldiers who chose not to join us had lost their wits during the night's scuffle and were incapable of understanding Fierro's polite question: "Will you fight for General Francisco Villa and swear allegiance to the sacred memory of President Madero?" Two hun-dred fifty-three men swore on the lives of their mothers and children and the blood of Christ, and they would have signed a contract with their own blood if they had been asked. A squad of men led them off toward town. Their cheers of *"Viva Villa!"* faded slowly away.

The last four categories on my list, a total of two hundred thirty-nine men, were herded outside by Juan Dozal's soldiers into the stockyards. By then it was late afternoon, growing chilly. The penetrating wind of the high plateau had begun to blow. The sun skimmed the tops of the gaunt mountains to the west. We walked slowly through the hospital gardens to the edge of the corrals, where Fierro surveyed the terrain for five minutes without saying a word. Occasionally he grunted deep in his throat as his plan for the execution took shape. He had thrown a dark serape over his shoulders to ward off the wind. The wind of La Laguna was fabled in song; the people liked to say that it couldn't blow out a candle, but it could kill a man. Today the wind would not have to work alone.

Dozal and his squad of soldiers had only their thin jackets, and they were cold. They moved about restlessly, rifles pointed at the prisoners, while Fierro stood like a tall statue, vigorous legs planted wide on the earth.

"My colonel," Dozal asked, "what are your orders for us?"

Fierro seemed to waken from a dream, and he turned to measure Dozal. "Do you have a good supply of bullets?"

"We have plenty."

"For rifle or pistol?"

"Both."

He draped an arm over Dozal's shoulder and walked with him to the wooden fence, topped with barbed wire, that shut in the condemned men. The two were beyond earshot. Hipólito and I and the other men stood shivering, while Fierro and Dozal began a long discussion. I could see Rodolfo pointing in various directions, and Dozal kept wagging his head. The stockyards were empty of cattle. The prisoners, some wearing ragged uniforms, most naked or nearly so, sat on their haunches in the pen nearest us. They were the most pitiful lot of human beings I had ever seen. But most seemed to have accepted their fate. Their screams and mewling had given way to stunned silence. And they were very cold. The pen led through a narrow cattle chute to a second similar enclosure, and then the same sort of chute led to yet a third pen, somewhat larger. Beyond that lay open plain dotted with cactus and a few adobe huts, and then the looming brown bulk of the mountains. There were some adobe walls too, and a well with an iron bucket that clanked monotonously against a forked post, and adjoining the third and final pen was a small house that must have served as the office for the stockyards. The sweet smell of cattle dung came to my nostrils with the gathering wind.

Suddenly one of the prisoners stepped boldly across the dirt yard to where Hipólito and I leaned against the fence. He was a haggard but well-set-up man of about thirty, with pale skin and dark, intelligent eyes. He wore the torn uniform of a Redflagger, so he surprised me by speaking in an oddly accented but fluent English.

"Colonel," he said, "I can see that you're an American. Is that not so? Yes, surely it is. You're a volunteer in the revolutionary cause. I request the privilege of a word with you. My name is Miguel Bosques, if you please. I am a schoolteacher."

A little startled, I said, "I'm not a colonel, Señor Bosques. Just a captain. There's nothing I can do for you."

"That's not so, Captain. You can do me the honor of listening to what I have to say. Surely, under these ghastly circumstances, that's not too much to ask from one human being to another."

"All right," I muttered uneasily. Beside me, Hipólito cocked an ear.

The man spoke with dignity, but I sensed that he was about to plead for his life. I kept shifting my weight from one foot to another.

"My name is Miguel Bosques, as I have said, and I am a schoolteacher. I taught the English language in Gómez Palacio in a small private school for the children of the wealthy. I spent much of my youth in Tampico, which you may know is eastward in the state of Tamaulipas, and there my father labored for Lord Cowdray's Eagle Oil Company of London, England. This accounts for my small command of your language. I apologize for any insufficiency."

"You speak it fine," I murmured.

"Thank you. You are kind. I wish to say this, sir. You see I wear the uniform of a volunteer in the Redflag army of General Orozco, who is the enemy of General Villa. I wish to say that I do not wear this uniform by choice, but rather by force and lack of alternative. I am not a political man, although I am most assuredly an attentive student of Mexican politics. Perhaps that explains why I am not a political man." He smiled a little—a remarkable feat, I thought, under the circumstances. "I am, actually, a poet, although I have not yet been honored by publishing of the little I have written."

Oblivious to my discomfort, he told me his story.

It seems that Huerta and Orozco were running short of men to fight the growing threat of Villa's Northern Division. There weren't enough volunteers, so they had organized press-gangs in all the major cities. In Mexico City, Bosques related, they had seized seven hundred men who were at a bullfight and marched them off under guard to the Chapultepec Barracks. Others had been taken from their homes and jobs, if the jobs were menial enough. Bosques and his two younger brothers, one a bank clerk, the other a printer, had been standing in the streets of Torreón one night about three weeks ago, watching a fire that was destroying a movie theater. Naturally, a big crowd gathered. The army moved in and asked the women and children to withdraw first, for there was danger of the building collapsing. The several hundred men left were then cordoned off with ropes and told by an officer that if they had nothing better to do than stand around and watch their city burn to the ground, they might as well be of some use and fight for its survival. Two men tried to run. They were shot on the spot. A few doctors and lawyers lodged furious protests. They were excused. But when Bosques told the officers he was a schoolteacher, one of them said, "Good. You can teach your new comrades that to disobey orders is punishable by death." And they were driven off in trucks to the barracks in La Cruz, where they were issued torn uniforms and rifles without bullets.

"We were not given bullets until four days ago," Bosques said, "when it was known that General Villa was intending his march on Torreón. I did not fire a shot until the attack in actuality began. . . . Then I fired into the air. It was my wish to cause harm to no man. I could not do that, sir. My brother Roberto was killed in Gómez Palacio, not a hundred yards from where he had lived with his family. My other brother, Isidoro, is a prisoner here tonight as well. He is married, and his wife is expecting to give birth. I, fortunately, one might say in these circumstances, am a widower. As soon as opportunity presented itself—I speak now of the battle for Gómez Palacio—I laid down my arms and surrendered. And now I ask you, Captain, not meaning to impose too much on your time, if it is justice that I and my brother should die here in a cattle pen, when I am a schoolteacher and poet, and he is a printer of words, and we are the enemy of no man."

Quickly I glanced at Hipólito. His face gave nothing away—this Miguel Bosques hadn't appealed to *him*. I shivered, for it had struck right into my innards when he said he had fired into the air and hadn't wanted to kill any man.

"Hang on a minute." I spoke a little more roughly to Bosques than I felt. Then I took Hipólito aside.

"Did you understand?"

"Most of it. He uses large words, that fellow."

"What do you think?"

"I think this is a shitty war, Tomás."

"What can we do?"

"When Pancho and I were bandits, we killed a man only if he wouldn't part with his silver or his supplies, or if he fought back. We killed the *rurales,* but they were pigs. Now I'm a revolutionist. We kill peasants and schoolteachers." Hipólito hawked and spat into the dirt, in the same way that his brother spat on the carpet of the Hotel Salvador.

"Could you shoot this schoolteacher?"

"Rodolfo will take care of that. He's in charge. I'll just smoke a cigar." He fumbled in the pocket of his suit. "Do you want one, Tomás? They're good for your nerves."

"I'm going to talk to Rodolfo."

"What for?"

"Because I have to."

He was still with Dozal, issuing orders. A case of cartridges lay on the ground at his feet, with two extra pistols, the wind swirling the dust around his leather puttees. I excused myself for interrupting. In Fierro's presence, politeness seemed to come naturally, and I had an even better reason.

"Rodolfo, one of the prisoners spoke to me."

"Ah? About what? Does he have information?"

"He has a tale to tell."

I repeated Bosques' story. Fierro listened with great attentiveness, never coughing or scratching his jaw, as if I were telling him the most fascinating thing he had ever heard. I finished by saying, "I don't think this man deserves to die." And then, more lamely, "If we allow him to live, he could be useful to us."

Fierro grunted, put a hand on my shoulder and smiled at me. The weight of his hand felt like a ton, but he wasn't pressing.

"Tomás, I'm going to tell you exactly what our chief would tell you if he were standing here." His voice was as smooth and as icy as his smile, the resonant tone of a man whose destiny is unquestioned. "If you talked to all these prisoners, every single one would tell you he was conscripted against his will. Every one of them would tell you he was a schoolteacher, or a poet, and you'd probably find enough medical students to cure an epidemic of cholera. Every one of them would tell you he only fired his rifle into the air. Every one of them would talk eloquently of justice. Aren't they human? Wouldn't you do the same?" He didn't pause for an answer; his brown eyes were clear and certain. "And remember this too, Tomás. This man, this so-called schoolteacher, has begged for his life. But you can never save a man's life. You can only postpone his death. Isn't that so?"

This time he waited for my reply.

"Maybe," I said, "but that's not the point. He wants that postponement."

"He's a fool." And then for the first time, although there was to be one more, Fierro revealed his mind—his heart, if he had one—to me. Even his eyes changed, growing cloudy. He seemed to be talking to himself more than to any listener. "After all," he said quietly, "death isn't the worst thing that can happen to a man. It's a reasonable answer to a generally unsatisfactory life. We Mexicans know that, and so we don't fear it. Naturally, from instinct, as this schoolteacher illustrates, we try to avoid it . . . but when the moment comes, we know how to face it. When my time comes, I ask only one thing—that it be quick. Then must come a long sleep, without care or memory. I pray for that. That can't be bad, can it?" He waited again.

"No," I said, through clenched teeth.

The cloud vanished from his eyes.

"In any case," he said calmly, "the man is lying. You're young. He guessed correctly that you would be impressionable. Go to him. Tell him that he was absolutely correct in asking for justice, and he shall receive it. He shall have revolutionary justice. And then report back to me. I'm going to need your help."

There seemed no way to argue. Fierro was in command, not I, and his decision was clearly unbending. My leg ached and I still felt weak; I was glad to get away from him. I passed by Hipólito, who was smoking his cigar and leaning against the knotted fence, apparently unconcerned. He had known the outcome in advance. Bosques, however, awaited me with a look that made me cringe inwardly. The man had dared to hope. It showed in the gleam of his eyes and the way his knuckles whitened as he gripped the fence rail. Compassion might have made him buckle, and I couldn't bear to face more pleas.

I spoke flatly. "You'll be shot with the others."

He let out his breath, one of the last he would take in this world. "I see . . ."

His voice was almost without expression—it held the lightest touch of scorn. He wanted to know one thing more. "May I ask the name of the officer with whom you spoke?"

"Why? All right . . . his name is Colonel Fierro."

"And your name?"

"Mix. What difference does it make?"

He didn't answer. He turned his back and sauntered toward the mass of silent men, huddled together for warmth, vanishing among them. At a distance you couldn't tell one from another.

The sun still hadn't dropped below the mountain peak. The earth was dappled with shadows. I confronted Fierro again. I couldn't keep the hatred from my voice.

"You need my help for something?"

"Lieutenant Dozal's men are cold," he said, "and he's confessed that he doesn't think too much of their marksmanship. So—here." He tossed me a serape he had taken from one of the soldiers. "Put this on, Tomás, or the wind will chew your bones. Pay attention. Here's how we'll do this."

Fierro had decided to have some target practice that would test his skill and relieve the boredom of a simple mass execution. A squad of soldiers guarded the two hundred thirty-nine prisoners in the first pen. Ten at a time, as Fierro had decreed, they would bring the prisoners through the narrow cattle chute into the second pen. In single file they would enter the chute leading to the third pen, where a few of Dozal's shivering soldiers would await them with fixed bayonets. The bayonets were a cure for any reluctance. At a wave of Fierro's hand, the ten men would be shoved into the third and largest pen and told to run for the far fence, a distance of some fifty paces.

Fierro would shoot them as they ran. If any man could reach the last fence and clamber over it without being killed, he was free. . . . No one would chase him, and Fierro wouldn't fire at any man who had gained the safety of the plain. Once there, a man could make his escape into the foothills of the mountains. Each group of ten would be followed by another, until all had passed through the final pen and were either dead or escaped.

/ 109

My job was to sit next to Fierro and reload his three pistols as they fell empty. The wooden box of ammunition had been splintered open so that the bullets were easily accessible. Dozal would stand by with a spare pistol in case any one of the three jammed. As for Hipólito, he could wait in the car. There was a bottle of Canadian whiskey in the glove compartment—Fierro had seen the chauffeur squirrel it there when we left the Hotel Salvador.

"What do you think, Tomás?" he asked, almost pleasantly. "Do you think I can get them all before they climb over the last fence? Or do you think some of them will manage to escape? What's your guess?"

"Rodolfo, I ask to be excused from this detail."

"You do? Why?"

I was in no mood to offer clever explanations. "It disgusts me."

"But I'm not requiring you to shoot them, Tomás. I'm only requiring you to reload my pistols."

He looked at me with great intensity. I felt an evil force flowing from the man. This was the moment he had been waiting for since I took Rosa from him in Ascensión.

"I ask to be excused," I said again, and my voice began to tremble.

He considered that for a few moments, then shook his head firmly. "You're an officer by appointment of Francisco Villa," he said. "This is part of your duty. Consider my request to be an order."

Perhaps his eyes glinted once. If I refused, he could shoot me. He had Dozal as a witness to explain to Pancho Villa. If he pulled his pistol I would do the same, because Rodolfo Fierro was less than a whole human being, and I would take the consequences. One of us would die— or both. For if I killed him, Villa would surely have me shot. But the glint faded immediately and was replaced by his maddeningly bland look.

"Refusal would be foolish, Tomás. You think this a repugnant task, but I assure you that it's necessary. These men will die. It doesn't matter how." His lips curled in the shadow of a smile. "But," and his tone hardened, "if you fail to carry out my order—if you don't load the pistols as I've instructed—Lieutenant Dozal will shoot you. Lieutenant? You've understood?" He didn't even bother to glance over his shoulder.

In the gloomy light, Dozal nodded. I remembered what he had done at Casas Grandes, helping Fierro to prove his theory that a single bullet would kill three men. If there was any man who wouldn't hesitate, this was the one.

Whatever pride I had felt before, after being blooded in the battle for Torreón, ebbed away from me in a single rush. To be brave in battle with your friends was one thing; to calmly and knowingly sacrifice your life for strangers was another. In that I was a coward. What Fierro demanded of me was loathsome, but if I didn't do it I would surely die. He knew how I would choose. He didn't even wait for me to nod my acceptance.

"Let's begin," he said to Dozal. "I don't want it to grow dark before I finish. Tell the prisoners how it will work."

"It's being done, my colonel."

A low moan reached us from the first pen, where Dozal's sergeant was explaining the details of the game to the huge lump of Redflaggers. One naked prisoner broke from the pack, trying to leap over an adobe wall in the direction of the hospital. A volley from three revolutionists sitting on the fence hurled him to the ground.

The sergeant wasted no more time. He began to extract ten men from the formless mass, shoving them at pistol point through the chute into the second pen. I could hear him clearly now . . . the wind blew but made no sound. "Don't resist," he cajoled. "Come on, boys . . . this way you have a chance."

Fierro took up a position directly in front of the stockyard office, his back braced against the adobe wall. I knelt on one knee to his right, with the box of cartridges in front of me and the two extra pistols lying on a torn blanket that had been spread between us. To my right, Dozal slouched with the fourth pistol in his hand, ready to kill me if I abandoned my task. We were at a central point in the third pen. If the men ran in a straight line from left to right, trying to cover the distance in the shortest possible time, which would be natural, the range would vary between twenty and thirty yards.

Just then a small bird, a crow, flew overhead and alighted on the far fence, the one that would lead to freedom if Rodolfo Fierro kept his word. It sat motionless, tucking in its black wings. Fierro raised the long barrel of his pistol and fired. The report was a dry, light snap. The bullet passed harmlessly through the air, and the alarmed crow quickly fluttered up and away toward the mountains.

"Come on, boys!" Fierro smiled. His deep voice easily carried across the stockyard to the prisoners, who writhed like a mass of snakes in the gray light. "You see that I missed! . . . I'm not such a good shot! A running target is even more difficult. So! Who's first?"

The first group of ten bolted from the chute into the third pen. They ran like crazed goats. Fierro extended his right arm straight out and with his left hand gripped the right wrist. He fired five shots, then dropped the pistol on the blanket, where I picked it up with my left hand. With my right hand, holding the second pistol by the barrel, I slapped the butt into his waiting fingers, as a nurse delivers a scalpel to a surgeon. "Good, Tomás," he murmured. He fired six more times in rapid succession, and I delivered the third pistol.

He had only to fire four bullets from that one before the group of ten men sprawled all over the pen in the dust, dead and dying. One man had reached the final fence, but he was hit before he could even grip the wooden rail. Fierro smiled again. The shot at the crow had been to calculate the wind.

"Let's have another ten," he called brightly. I had already reloaded the first pistol and was at work on the second one, removing the exploded caps and stuffing the steel cartridges into the chambers. Dozal bent to Fierro's ear.

"What about the wounded, my colonel?"

"Don't let them suffer, Juanito. Tell your men to finish them off."

Dozal shouted the order. The soldiers who crowded to the fence of the second pen, that they might have a better view of the slaughter, raised their rifles and poured a volley of bullets into the three or four prisoners who still writhed in the dirt.

The second group of ten catapulted from the chute. This time one of them, a Federal officer whose pants flapped in rags like a rodeo clown's, launched himself directly at us, hands raised to strangle Fierro if he could reach him in time. His face was hatred at its most pure. Fierro neither flinched nor fired at him. He remained entirely concentrated on the other nine who bounded wildly across the pen. He simply said, "Lieutenant . . ." and Dozal raised the fourth pistol and shot the officer in the chest when he was no more than four strides from us. The man hit the ground with a noise like that of a falling log, muttered something to himself . . . then lay still.

The other nine men died in the midst of their mad race. Again one reached the fence, planting a boot on the lower rail before Fierro's bullet drilled a red hole between his naked shoulder blades and he sagged across the bar, bent double and coughing blood.

Now the prisoners realized that there was no hope of escape, that Fierro's aim was good enough and the illusion of freedom beyond the far fence was as unattainable as their youthful dreams of riches and love and glory. They began to sob, to wail dementedly. "Little Jesus . . . blessed saints . . . Mama!" Apparently they didn't agree with Fierro's thesis on death. A few refused to go, and Dozal's soldiers quickly shot them down. And so the rest kept coming—a third ten, a fourth ten—then more. Fierro fired in a rhythm as regular as that of a ticking clock. He saw no men in front of him, only darting, crawling targets. The prisoners stumbled over the corpses of the men who had run before them. They slipped in pools of blood, sometimes colliding with another, battering him out of the way in their frenzy to reach the gate not merely to freedom but to life itself. If it hadn't been a carnival of death, their antics might have seemed comic. They dodged and jostled, kicked, beat on human obstacles with clenched fists. One man, incensed that another blocked his path, stopped to smash him in the face; the other man struck back, and they began to trade blows in the midst of the massacre . . . until Fierro's bullets dropped them both to the earth, still feebly swinging. The Villistas on the fences shouted encouragement at the fighters and the runners, made bets, howled with mirth when a man turned a particularly absurd cartwheel after Fierro's bullet broke his spine.

Mounds of bodies began to grow in the yard as though some strange human plant, with a hundred heads and double the amount of out-thrust arms and legs, were pushing its way up with unbelievable speed from an earth fertilized with its own blood.

The wind still blew coldly. A flaming ball of red sun touched the bare crest of a peak that was shaped like the breast of Juana Torres. The sun's fading light matched the color of the stockyard earth.

The yard had become a slaughterhouse. Dozal's soldiers increased their fire into the heaps of dead and wounded, taking no chances that a man might feign death and so escape. Now and then an arm jerked loose from the pile, touching off a salvo of gunfire until it stiffened into death. The gunfire and the screams of the prisoners grew strangely distant. I felt the coldness of the bullets that I fed into the revolving chambers and the damp grip of the pistols fresh from Fierro's hand. The barrels had grown so hot that my fingers were blistered. Each steel-jacketed bullet with its tapered, beautiful shape would soon embed its point into a man's stomach, or his brain, or his madly beating heart, stilling it forever. I tapped them into the chambers and felt them lock into place with a dry click. Even in the cold wind I was sweating, and when I glanced at Fierro I saw that his forehead as well was beaded with the passion of his effort. But his eyes never wavered. His rhythm didn't vary. He was a machine. He had made one of me too. More than an hour had passed when the last group of men was finally booted through the chute. The number was uneven, and so the soldiers who dispatched them at bayonet point toward that grisly obstacle course sent a group of thirteen—an unlucky number, but for one man it would mean life. Perhaps the soldiers thought it would be the final test of Fierro's marksmanship. The sun had dipped below the mountain, leaving a wake of garish orange streaks against the royal blue sky. All was in shadow. If Fierro had been less proud, less vain, he would have ordered Dozal's men to shoot the last thirteen, for the dusk would make it difficult for him. He had to be tired. But his vanity and dedication to his task made it impossible for him to give that order.

The thirteen men ran, stumbled, crawled, zigzagging forward through the heaps of dead. Fierro fired as rapidly as he could.

Three fell, then three more, then two. . . .

He leaned forward intently, sweating, left hand locked to his right wrist. The hammer clicked on an empty chamber. I handed him the pistol, and he fired. Three more men twisted to the ground, none dead but all nearly so, tears bursting from their eyes, as through their pain they realized that all hope of life was lost.

My hands were blocks of stone, and I was late in reloading. Some stubborn feeling, some final hatred of what I had helped to do, gripped me . . . I let my hands go slack. The pistol slipped to the earth. Fierro glared at me.

"Lieutenant . . . may I?" He turned to Juan Dozal.

He was not to be denied his chance. He leaned quickly across to snatch Dozal's pistol. The only two remaining survivors had reached the fence, where a pile of corpses led up to it like an irregular flight of soft, yielding steps. The bodies steamed in the cold air. With a bound, both men danced to the top of the heap at the same time, gripping the fence rail in a last desperate effort to climb over. Fierro's pistol snapped twice. Once of the men cried out, a terrible sob that pierced the twilight. He fell back slightly, reeling like a drunkard, blocking Fierro's view of the second man. Fierro fired again, and the figure atop the pile jerked but didn't fall. It had been pinned to the wooden post by the blow of the bullet.

Behind him, the second shadowy figure hesitated, then vaulted over the fence into the plain. A howl went up from the troops in the second pen—half a cheer, half a shout of rage at being so cheated. They fired their rifles into the darkness where the man sprinted toward the first hills. But the mounds of dead took the impact of most of the bullets, and the others whistled off into the evening. The fleeing man became only a faint shape, running low to the scrub, then indistinguishable from the cactus. He vanished.

So one had escaped. One had survived. One among more than two hundred.

Fierro's arms dropped heavily to his sides. He let the pistol slide from his grasp. It bounced once before it settled on the blanket. He raised his right hand, the trigger finger purple and swollen, then rubbed it tenderly, wincing as he felt pain.

He frowned down at me. "If you hadn't been so slow at the end, Tomás, even that one wouldn't have got away. Still, it wasn't bad shooting . . . I could have done worse. Don't you think so?"

"Yes," I said hoarsely, "you could have done worse."

"And so could you."

He meant that I would have been shot if I had failed to help him. Dozal would have seen to that. But the one gesture I had made at the end—the hesitation with the last pistol—had given one man back his life. Poor comfort, but all I had.

Fierro ordered the bodies burned, and we walked back to the car. Hipólito and the chauffeur were asleep, the empty whiskey bottle between them on the front seat. The soldiers, gathering firewood and trotting to keep warm, began to sing softly in the gathering darkness.

10

**"And if words will not,
then our weapons shall."**

In order for me to tell my story properly, another man must tell his own. He wrote in a journal which I have translated from the Spanish. The journal is a ledger, a long, thin, hardbound green volume normally used for keeping accounts of debits and credits in a business—perhaps a small grocery shop. I came upon the ledger three years after the killing at Torreón, in the saddlebags of a dead man's horse. That was no accident. But that part of my tale comes later . . . in the ghost town of Las Palomas, where Miguel Bosques, Rodolfo Fierro, Lieutenant Patton and I faced our final reckoning and paid all our debts.

from THE SCHOOLTEACHER'S JOURNAL

Fort Bliss
El Paso, Texas
December 20, 1913

One of my great regrets is that I could not begin this journal at an earlier date, but for the past two months my right hand, with which I normally write, has been bandaged and partially paralyzed. On that awful October evening, just as my brother Isidoro and I reached the fence in the Torreón stockyards, a bullet from Colonel Fierro's pistol struck me in the wrist, shattering the bone. Thanks to Lieutenant Patton, I am receiving treatment from the post surgeon, and there is excellent hope of full recovery. Today the bandages came off.

In the event that these pages should ever fall into other hands:

I, Miguel Bosques Barragán, thirty years of age, was born in the city of Goméz Palacio on January 27, 1883, the oldest son of Antonio Bosques Triano, a carpenter, and Encarnación Barragán, a saint. My parents are dead. My wife, Carmen Bosques Copeda, died in childbirth in 1910. The baby did not survive. I did not remarry.

Both my younger brothers, Roberto and Isidoro, were killed in October 1913 by the revolutionary forces of General Francisco Villa, in Torreón. I dedicate this journal and my life to their memory, for they were pure young men with not a drop of malice in their souls, and I write this account of my recent life because it has lost nearly all meaning for me. Educated as an idealist, I now find myself opposed to every form of idealism. I believe only in facts, and even there I am wary, for what one man swears to another will surely contradict; and I view history as a compilation of the self-serving statements of men who have much to justify and even more to hide, hardening over the years into a literature of lies. I live for only one thing, that most soul-destroying of all human motives: vengeance. This shames me but does not deter me from my purpose.

My escape from Torreón was surely miraculous, as if the hand of God had singled me out not merely for salvation, but to carry out His will, however dreadful it might be. My brothers and I had been unwilling conscripts in the volunteer army of General Pascual Orozco, the former revolutionist who had offered the services of his army to Victoriano Huerta, now President of Mexico. My brother Roberto was killed by an exploding shell in the battle for Gómez Palacio. In that same battle, neither I nor my brother Isidoro fired our rifles. "It's wrong to kill," I told Isidoro. "These men of Villa's think they are fighting to free the people of Mexico from slavery. They mean us no harm beyond their duty as soldiers." With many others, we surrendered to a squad of Villistas, who made us lie on the floor of a grocery shop for half a day. Another prisoner told me of Roberto's death. Isidoro and I wept. We were struck several times in the kidneys and head with rifle butts. We were hungry, but we were given no food, although it was all around us in the shop.

Then we were taken in a truck to what had been the military hospital of Torreón. During the night there was fighting among the prisoners; many men were beaten to death. Isidoro and I hid in a toilet.

The following afternoon we were taken into the stockyards to be shot.

I could not believe at first that this would happen, but the other men told me that the army of Francisco Villa showed no mercy, that they killed merely for the love of killing and became crazed by the sight of blood. I began to realize that we would die. I could not accept this, because I valued the gift of life and believed that evil could not possibly triumph over innocence. Even in that awful hour, I was still an idealist.

Then I noticed two men standing nearby. One was a well-dressed fat fellow with the face of a wild boar. The other was slim, tall, fresh-faced and young. I realized from his features and his gait that he was an American, a volunteer with Villa's revolutionary army, perhaps therefore an idealist like myself. When I addressed myself to him in English, he could not hide his surprise. I told him my story and asked if he considered it just that Isidoro and I should die. My only shame is that I did not plead for the lives of all the prisoners, but I knew that was far too much to ask.

The American, Captain Mix, listened politely but refused to answer my question. He went off to confer with another officer, Colonel Fierro. When he returned, his jaw was set, his eyes were cold. He spoke with no feeling.

He said, "You will be shot with the others."

The killing began. It was done personally by Colonel Fierro and Captain Mix. One fired, while the other quickly reloaded the pistols. They were like a well-trained team that had rehearsed many times. We were pushed in groups of ten through a cattle chute and made to run across a yard toward a fence. We were told that if we could cross that fence we would be free. But it was soon clear that this was impossible. Colonel Fierro was too accurate a shot. Captain Mix was too swift at reloading his pistols. The men died like hogs being butchered for All Saint's Day.

I took my brother to one side. "Let the others go first," I said. "Perhaps they will spare the last of us."

But these were only the words of a man postponing the dreaded inevitable. Isidoro began to cry. I thought for one insane moment that when my turn came I would rush toward the two officers and try to kill them with my bare hands. Then one of the prisoners did precisely that and was shot down by a third officer long before he reached the murderers. Clearly, there was no way.

But it was growing darker, and by the time our turn had come, the sun had

116 /

set. The killing ground lay in shadow. Many bodies had piled up near the fence of the corral that led to life. I said to Isidoro, "Run low to the ground behind the other men. He always shoots the swiftest first. Leap upon the bodies in front of the fence, if you get that far. As you run, pray." We were a group of thirteen, three more than had ever gone before, which made me think we had a slim chance.

I ran cautiously, trying to crouch low behind the piles of dead, Isidoro at my side. Just before we reached the fence, a bullet struck my wrist. I cried aloud in pain. Isidoro and I clambered up the hill of bodies, which slipped beneath my feet like jelly. He was between me and Colonel Fierro. As he clasped the rail, he shouted terribly, *"Miguel!"*—and I knew he had been hit. For a second I stopped; I wanted to take my beloved brother in my arms and hold him while he died, and comfort him, and die with him. But there is an urge for life that is stronger even than love. With my one good hand I found purchase on the wooden post and shoved myself over, even as more bullets found Isidoro's body that stood between me and the colonel's pistol.

I struck the earth on the other side of the fence and ran low into the field. Of course, Colonel Fierro had lied to us. His men fired at me as I ran, but the darkness saved me. I ran until I could not run anymore and fell face forward in the dirt, my heart pounding, my lungs seared by an almost unbearable heat, my hand soaked with blood. I lay there, unable to move, waiting for them to come. I heard nothing except the bark of a dog, the braying of a distant burro. No horses' hoofs drummed on the plain in pursuit.

After a time I rose slowly and began to walk through the darkness toward the mountains. I was cold and hungry. I was bleeding. I saw no shelter.

I thought of Isidoro, a nameless wreck of flesh and bone in a heap of mangled dead. I did not think I would live through the night.

January 9, 1914

This morning I gave Lieutenant Patton another Spanish lesson. Although he often makes jokes, he progresses rapidly. At our first lesson he asked me to teach him to curse in my language. I told him a few words and translated them, and he said, "Christ, Bosques—I've got to talk to *soldiers!* Don't you know anything more salty than that?"

He repeated my next phrases so seriously and accurately that I blushed. To say such things to a Mexican would result in a quick death.

But I owe much to this man.

January 12, 1914

After my escape from Torreón, I spent the first night and all next day in a small abandoned farmhouse in the foothills of the mountains near the pueblo of La Fé, a railroad junction. There was water in the well, some old clothing in a bureau and some feed for cattle and chickens in the barn. I ate crushed eggshells and grain that I scooped from the dirt, forcing it down my throat with a tin cup full of water. I also found half a bottle of tequila, hidden under a pile of straw, and used it to clean the bullet hole in my wrist. Some strips of torn underwear served as a bandage. I had lost blood and felt too weak to travel yet, so I slept. Waking at dawn, among the rags of clothing I rescued a torn shirt, a pair of filthy trousers and a serape that had been a feast for moths and smelled as well of horses. I tore my Redflagger uniform into strips, stuffing them under the straw in the barn. I tried to think carefully. To return to Torreón was out of the question, for it would be too dangerous to be a man of military age out of uniform. I thought of going south, but if Villa's army marched in that direction I could easily be swept into its net or conscripted again by the Redflaggers. But I could go north—I could cross the Rio Bravo to the United States. What was Mexico but a land of death and cruelty in equal proportion? All that was good would perish. Evil would triumph. I knew the revolution to be a tragedy, the government to be a macabre comedy. One way or the other, the soul of the Mexican people was doomed to a certain strangulation.

So at dusk I set out, moving south through the foothills to the small railroad junction of La Fé. But for my wound I looked like any ragged *campesino* in flight from the war. I lacked a pistol. I had only the nearly empty bottle of tequila and another of cold water from the well.

Few lights showed in La Fé, but near the junction there was a cantina for the railway workers. I heard the sounds of male laughter, the strains of a guitar floating through the gloom. Half a dozen horses were tethered outside, snorting in the cold. A bar of light shot into the street from the cantina's swinging doors. I found shelter in the darkness behind an empty house, and there I waited, my arm throbbing. But no train came. How could it? Torreón was now in the hands of the revolution! I had tried to think carefully, but my mind was blurred by grief, fever and pain.

The horses snorted again, blowing gusts of steam into the night air. I knew how to ride; I would have to steal one. I approached them slowly, not wanting to frighten them, but the old serape smelled of the beast it had once covered and that put them at ease. One of the horses was a big young sorrel with full saddlebags and a rifle stock protruding from a worn scabbard. I realized then that the men inside the cantina were not railway workers, but soldiers. On which side?

I pondered for a minute, then dismissed the question. What did it matter? All men under arms were my enemies.

Just as I unlooped the sorrel's reins from the post, the cantina doors flung rudely open and a drunken man lurched out. He had already unbuttoned his pants and was peeling back his foreskin, readying himself to piss, when he saw me standing by the horses.

"Hey . . . who are you?" he called. "What are you doing there?"

He was a Villista, a lean young man with a bushy mustache and tilted-back sombrero. With one hand he fumbled at his penis, trying to stuff it back into his pants. With the other he tugged at his pistol. My mouth grew dry.

"Señor," I said, "don't be angry, I beg you. I was just—"

"You were just going to look through my saddlebags, you piece of garbage!"

"No, señor. On the Virgin, I would not do that."

"Scum! Wouldn't you?"

I tried to smile crookedly. With my left hand I raised the empty tequila bottle. Spare this besotted peasant! But the soldier, unsmiling, kept tugging at his pistol. His drunken fingers were clumsy, and with the other hand he still shoved at his penis. Grumbling another curse, seeing I was unarmed, he decided to button himself properly before he shot me. He looked down.

With all my strength I swung the bottle at his head. It caught him on the nose, making a dull crack. Gasping, the man sank to his knees, raising both hands to check the outrageous spurt of blood from his nostrils. For a moment I held back . . . but if I tried to mount the horse and escape, he could easily shoot me or cry for help to his companions in the cantina, where the guitar still sounded its melancholy chords.

With my wounded right hand I plucked the sombrero from the man's head, then smashed the bottle on the top of his skull. I felt his head split. He slumped to one side, stretched out in the dirt, drawing up his knees. Then he lay quietly. His blood looked black in the darkness.

No noise had penetrated to the cantina. I jammed the fallen pistol into my waistband, then swung up on the horse. I rode off at a quick trot, following the dim North Star through the windy night, along the line of the railroad tracks that gleamed a dull silver under a rising three-quarter moon. A coyote howled from the mountains.

I had killed a man for the first time in my life. It had not been difficult. I felt nothing. It made me realize what I was capable of doing, given the need and the chance. I had the need now; I would find the chance. That was my fate, as it had been the soldier's fate to die at La Fé. In every man, as in nations, a revolution can occur, and afterwards there is no looking back other than with bitterness and hate. There is purpose without conscience.

I rode through the night to Bermejillo. Passing myself off as a Villista wounded in the battle for Torreón, I found a doctor who treated my wrist. He was afraid of gangrene and asked me to come back the next morning. But again I rode north by night to the railroad junction of El Norte, where I let my horse go and in the evening clambered aboard a freight train bound for Juárez. I huddled in a car full of beef carcasses and slabs of melting ice, so that I shook all night with the cold. South of Juárez, as the sun broke loose from the misty Sierra del Hueso, the train slowed. I jumped off and then walked all day in the heat of the desert toward the town of Ysleta. There I forded the muddy Rio Bravo, into the state of Texas.

As soon as I reached the far shore, five soldiers rode toward me at a trot. They were mounted on fine horses and wore the olive drab shirts, puttees and peaked scout hats of the United States Cavalry. Four were Negros, with thick lips and wide flat noses. They halted in the dust, and the one white man, an officer with two silver bars on his shoulder, said haltingly, with an awful accent: *"Quién está usted? Porque* do you . . . damn it, man, do you speak any English?"

"Yes. Perfectly. I am a schoolteacher. A refugee from the massacre at Torreón. My name is Miguel Bosques, at your service, sir."

"Very well. Hey . . . you've been wounded!"

"By the Villistas in Torreón."

"Captain Boyd, U. S. Tenth Cavalry." He saluted me, and I imitated the salute, which made him smile. He turned to one of his mounted soldiers, a man black as coal.

"Take this Mexican to the clinic at Bliss. Have the sawbones look him over. Then bring him to Lieutenant Patton and let him tell his story."

"May I retrieve my weapons, sir?"

Boyd smiled. "I'll take care of them for you. You're in the United States of America now, Mr. Bosques. You won't be doing any shooting here. And no one will shoot at you, either—not if we can help it."

I mounted behind the sweating black soldier and rode with him at a trot to Fort Bliss in El Paso, Texas, where I was to begin life almost as if I had been born a second time.

Fort Bliss was no longer an actual walled fort meant to fend off Indian attacks, but a compact post set on a mesa behind the town, without a single tree in sight. The wooden buildings seemed fairly new: there were barracks and stables and a parade ground where a tired-looking officer with an upraised sword was trying to teach a troop of mixed Negro and white soldiers to wheel their horses in formation. He kept shouting, "Colummm . . . right!" and then "Col-ummm wheel . . . left!"—with the result that the horses jammed into each other's flanks and the troop became scattered over half the parade ground. I wondered what it had to do with war, but then I was not a soldier.

The post surgeon cleaned and bandaged my wrist with hardly a comment, except to say I was lucky the bullet had exited, and then my escort took me to an office in regimental headquarters, knocked on the door and shoved me through ahead of him. A man smoking a pipe looked up from his desk.

"Lieutenant Patton? Cap'n Boyd sends this greaser to you, with his compliments."

The lieutenant was a tall, slender and healthy-looking fellow with hard blue eyes and close-cropped sandy hair. The big meerschaum pipe was clamped between his teeth even when he wasn't smoking it. He was about my age, I judged—somewhat old to be just a second lieutenant—but when he stood up to shake my hand he looked, as they say, every inch a soldier. I noticed that he had several diplomas on the walls of his office, handsomely presented in gilt frames: one from the Virginia Military Institute, another from the United States Military Academy at West Point, his Expert Rifleman and Expert Pistol Shot certificates, and of course his commission signed by President Taft. There was also a letter from the War Department commending him for having taken fifth place in the pentathlon at the Stockholm Olympics, and a framed scroll stating that George S. Patton, Jr. was Master of the Sword in the United States Army. The scroll hung between photographs of the lieutenant, mounted on various polo ponies and with a mallet cocked over one shoulder, and on the glass surface of his desk stood two other photographs: one of a very pretty dark-haired woman in her wedding gown, and one of him as a youth standing rigidly next to what I later learned was his father, a stern-looking man in a tweed suit, with a flaring mustache.

Lieutenant Patton dismissed my escort, then offered me hot coffee and buttered toast, which I accepted gratefully. Then he asked for my story. I began with my conscription outside the movie theater in Torreón and ended with my greeting from Captain Boyd.

When I finished he said, "Shithouse mouse! Is that what you people call a war? It's just plain butchery!"

"It's a revolution, Lieutenant. There's a difference. In order to kill one's own countrymen, one must work up not so much hatred as a certain amount of cold-bloodedness. After that, all else follows naturally."

"Well, we had our own Civil War here. They didn't play that one according to the rules of the Hague Conference, although I don't recall them using prisoners for target practice." He thought for a while and then said, "Look, Bosques, I'll tell you straight out—I don't give a hoot about Mexico. It's just another big thorn in the ass of Uncle Sam, and right now it's tying me and five thousand other men down in this hellhole, when I'd a damn sight rather be in Washington with my wife, or getting set to go over to Europe and *cherchez les femmes*. But if you're willing to talk, I'm willing to learn about what's going on down there. Because I'll tell you the simple truth—we don't know beans from pineapples about your country and all these goddam generals you people let loose all over the place. Maybe you can enlighten me."

One thing that surprised me about the lieutenant was his high-pitched voice. It was almost like that of a woman. He was conscious of it too, for he made certain efforts to drop it lower. But when he became excited, which was often, he forgot. I was tired, but the lieutenant's energy was infectious, and since he was my host—in fact, my potential savior—I felt I owed him an effort at the enlightenment he had asked for.

"Where are you from, Lieutenant?"

"I'm from God's country. The state of California, in case you were wondering. You know where that is?"

"What Mexican can ever forget? It used to be ours. Is it pretty?"

"Hell, no. It's not pretty. It's beautiful."

"Green and fertile?"

The lieutenant's expression grew wistful. "Why, you can grow pears and sweet corn and two crops of wheat, and the cows are so full of milk they knock on your door in the morning and say, 'Hurry up.' I mean yes, hell . . . it's fertile. It's so green in summer that it hurts your eyeballs."

"Do you have rivers and lakes and rainfall?"

"We've only got the Sacramento and the Merced and the Russian, and Lake Tahoe and the Klamath, and a slice of the Pacific, so I'd have to say yes. And we have our share of California dew. Not enough to drown you but enough to wet your socks, as the folks like to say in Pasadena. What's all this got to do with the price of eggs, Bosques?"

"If you come from such a place, Lieutenant Patton, you will find it difficult to understand Mexico. Look out your window. Be kind enough to tell me what you see."

He didn't have to look—he had done that often enough. He shifted his pipe, and for the first time his blue eyes twinkled.

"Nothing," he growled. "A whole lot of piss-ass nothing."

"That's what you will find in Mexico. As you say—a whole lot of piss-ass nothing, for nearly a thousand miles south of the border."

"But you grow bananas. I know that for a fact. I love 'em. Sweet as sugar."

"Yes, bananas grow in the coastal jungle," I said. "But a nation doesn't live on bananas, Lieutenant. Or on poor corn that's only fit for animals, although we pound it down to make tortillas. On the central plateau, the only part of Mexico habitable the year round, we have no rivers larger than the smallest ones in your country. We have no lakes of any size. We have no rainfall except during the summer months, so for nine or ten months of the year the land is parched. When Cortés returned to Europe after conquering Mexico four hundred years ago, the king of Spain asked him what the land looked like. He crumpled a piece of parchment and dropped it on the table. 'Like that,' he said. A few oases like Mexico City, Morelia and Cuernavaca, and thirty million people live there in that expanse of piss-ass nothing. Live there, starve there . . . die there. Death, not bananas, is our greatest crop."

Lieutenant Patton drummed his thin fingers impatiently on his desk top. "But you've got oil. Plenty of oil."

"No, sir, forgive me . . . *you* have our oil. You and the English and the Dutch. We supply more than a quarter of the world's fuel, but Lord Cowdray's Mexican Eagle Oil, Standard Oil, Royal Dutch Shell and Royal British Petroleum—the profits are theirs. It is the same with the mines, the iron and steel factories. The largest landowner is William Randolph Hearst. The rest of the country is owned by our own rich, such as Luis Terrazas. They live in Texas and New York and Paris, where they *cherchez les femmes.*"

Patton eyed me keenly. "You sound like you may have fought on the wrong side, Mr. Bosques."

"No," I said, smiling. "I am not a revolutionist. We had our first revolution a hundred years ago against the Spaniards. Wisely, they fought only briefly, to save their honor. They impaled our leaders' heads from spikes and then left the country to us. They had taken all of the only thing they ever valued—our gold. What was left after that, you can see from your window. Why squabble over it?"

"So what's this goddam revolution all about?" Patton demanded.

I had wondered exactly what he might want from me in the way of information, and how I could best help him. Now it became clear that I could supply him with a point of view that wasn't available to him from his fellow officers.

"The land," I said quietly. "The poorest and most miserable Mexican loves it, even though he knows it's useless. Given the means, he'll fight to the death for it. That's why the revolution will succeed, Lieutenant. In love, under arms, we are a passionate people."

The lieutenant considered all this and seemed satisfied. "What about your leaders? There's Huerta—Carranza and Obregón—Villa and Zapata. Who's the right man to take over if the revolution succeeds?"

"The one who survives, Lieutenant."

"Christ, you *are* a cynic. Well, it's refreshing after all the claptrap I hear around this post. All right—here's what I really want to know. Can any of them fight?"

"Huerta is a drunkard," I said, "who leaves the fighting to General Orozco, who leaves it to men such as General Murguía, who left Torreón in the middle of the night when things looked bad. On the other side, Carranza thinks of himself as a biblical prophet. He leaves the fighting to others. Zapata can fight, but he doesn't like to move out of the south where the people protect him. I don't believe he's capable of ruling. If you don't mind my using a classroom phrase, his political base is too narrow. Obregón controls the state of Sonora and professes loyalty to Carranza. He is said to be clever."

He eyed me shrewdly. "You haven't mentioned Villa."

"The best for the last. Pancho Villa can fight. It's everybody's mistake to underestimate him because he looks like a fat bandit in dirty clothes. He worshiped Madero, and they say he has no ambition to become president. He is a peasant, like Zapata, and equally ruthless. The people either love him or hate him. Carranza, on the other hand, is neither loved nor hated—just respectfully tolerated."

"Sounds like the men to watch are Carranza and Obregón."

"If I were you, Lieutenant, I would watch Villa."

Lieutenant Patton smiled. "But you're not exactly objective on that score, are you?"

"I have no feeling for or against Pancho Villa. It was not he who put my brother and me into that corral. I speak only of his chance to rule."

He leaned back in his wooden swivel chair and contemplated me for a while with his pale eyes, constantly tapping his fingers on the desk. "What are your plans, Bosques?"

"Not to return to Mexico."

He made his decision, the final one that would shape my destiny. He stood up and said, "Stick around, if you like. I want to talk to you some more. And I want to learn Spanish. Things may pop down there soon—that's what Pershing says, and Black Jack's always right. In fact, until you make up your mind where you're headed, I can find quarters for you. Even employ you. And we'll try to do something for your hand. How about it?"

For me it was hardly a decision. It was inevitable.

"I have nothing else to do. Thank you, Lieutenant."

"Don't thank me yet," he said, chuckling. "This isn't California. This is the asshole of the Yoo-nited States." And he waved his slender hand out the window at all that lot of piss-ass nothing, which was to be my new home.

11

"And if I have a conscience, let it sink me."

I heard the steady crack of Rodolfo Fierro's pistol. I saw the mass of prisoners slipping in their own blood. I listened every night to their screams. What could I have done? . . . I asked the question a hundred times and received no answer. In his brutish way, Fierro had carried out revolutionary justice. He had said so, and it was true. I could have shot him and Dozal both. The price of interference would have been my life; I would have gone to an inglorious death as a man who refused an order. A martyr . . . and not even that, for martyrs need witnesses to their martyrdom. The witnesses would have died too, for Pancho Villa himself had pronounced the sentence.

I told no one but Rosa. On those bad nights when I couldn't sleep she rubbed my back with coconut oil, and in the day she bathed the shrapnel wound on my leg with some desert herbs and then coated it with powdered alum. Her hands were gentle.

"There was nothing you could have done, *mi capitán.*"

"I keep saying that too, Rosa. But I was there. I saw it, just as I saw what they did at La Perla. But this time—*we* did it."

"Fierro did it."

"And I helped."

"Kill him, Tomás. You'll feel better about it."

"No, I won't. It won't change what happened."

"He is evil." She echoed my thoughts.

I hadn't been born to comprehend Rodolfo Fierro. I didn't then, and I don't now. How could a man exist who was purely evil? If there was a God, how could He create such a man? And if there wasn't a God who could be held responsible, how could men tolerate that bestial existence among them?

But Fierro's death wouldn't purge me of my sin. Perhaps one day I would face a moment—an ordeal, a choice—that would allow that. I was young. I had to believe that life offered such chances. It does, of course. But they have to be seen, and seized; and you dare not fail.

The revolution didn't grind to a halt because one of its lesser captains was sunk in a bog of remorse. Villa was gathering momentum, and in November the Northern Division attacked again. He organized an elite force of cavalry called the Dorados—the Golden Ones—equipping each man with two good horses, two Colt pistols and a 7-mm carbine, and giving the overall command of the unit to Candelario. Torreón had been stripped of everything useful. Villa decided he couldn't afford to defend it when the Federals still held Chihuahua City and the gateway of Juárez; we needed every man. So we abandoned La Laguna and headed north on the forty captured railway trains, our horses in the open stockcars, with Villa riding in a caboose that he had painted fire-engine red and converted into his traveling divisional headquarters. Esperanza and Juana Torres sewed red curtains for the windows and matching counterpanes for the foldaway bunks—the best of friends now that both had the status of wife. The rest of our men rode in the passenger cars and on top of them as well, firing rifles into the air or taking potshots at unlucky coyotes. Women camped on the rocking platforms, building fires of twigs and cow chips to bake their tortillas. A few young soldiers slung hammocks between the wheels of the train as it chugged north from Torreón, smoking marijuana and sleeping just a few feet from the steel rails. A spirit of casual madness had already begun to infect the army. Death was always a companion on the revolutionary journey, and what did it matter how it took you by the hand?

Our trains halted ten miles from Chihuahua City. Rosa waited with the rest of the women in the nearby pueblo called El Charco. "Don't worry, *mi capitán,*" she said, when we parted on the eve of battle. "I will be all right, and so will you."

I smiled at her. "You're sure?"

"Yes," she said solemnly, gazing at me with her clear child's eyes. "I would feel it if you were in danger. On the morning that my husband was due to die, I woke with a fever. It only lasted an hour. I had dreamed of blood pouring from the earth. So I knew, but I was afraid to tell him. But I would not be afraid to tell you, and if I ever dream again, or have that fever, I will not let you go to fight."

Her belief was so strong, even if it was only a child's faith, that it gave me a kind of faith too. At first I didn't think too much about it, but I know now, in some arcane way that I could never fully explain and certainly never justify, that her faith protected me. I threw myself into the battle without thought of losing life or limb. I was brave again—although, after what had happened in Torreón, it gave me no solace.

Our assault on Chihuahua City was bloody and fruitless; the Federal artillery outnumbered and outgunned us. Villa himself was nearly blown to bits by an exploding shell that killed two of his doctors. Could we lose? I had thought after Torreón that we were an unstoppable juggernaut, that Villa's careful organization and rallying genius would prevail over any kind of defense. After three days of useless fighting and heavy losses, he assembled his generals in the red-painted railway caboose. "This can't go on," he said grimly. "Our left has been shattered. Our right is about to cave in, and our center is pinned down. But I have a plan."

The bulk of the Division, he explained, would entrain for Jiménez, a hundred fifty miles to the southeast, with all the women and children. The Dorados and one mounted brigade, under his personal command, would ride that night to the nearby railway junction of El Norte.

"We'll steal a train there and take it straight up to Juárez," he said to the generals. "When I was in prison I read something like this in a book. It was about a revolution in ancient Greece, which was in Europe. They built a big wooden horse and hid a batallion inside it, which they somehow got into the city held by the government troops. Then they jumped out and took the city by storm. The revolution triumphed. That's how it will be in Juárez, except we haven't got time to build such a horse. So we'll use a train."

Calixto Contreras muttered that it broke all the rules of warfare that he understood. Juan Medina said, "My opinion is that we won't get farther than Samalayuca before the Federals bombard the shit out of us. How can we possibly get the train into Juárez?"

"You'll see," Villa replied cordially. "Any more questions?"

I said goodbye to Rosa before she boarded the southbound train with Yvette and Marie-Thérèse and all the other women. I asked her if she'd had any dreams lately, the past few nights, and she blushed and bit her thumb, like a little girl.

"Yes," she said finally, raising her head. "But not the bad one again. I dreamed of a child. I don't know if it was *hembra* or *macho*. You held it in your arms."

My heart seemed to slow a bit. "You're not—"

"No, *mi capitán*. I am not. Go to Juárez and don't worry. It will go well for you there."

"You mean we'll take the city?"

"I think so. But more, it will be good for you. Don't ask me what I mean. If I knew, I would say. I will wait for you in Jiménez. Go well, Tomás," she said gravely.

"And stay well, Rosa."

I didn't think anymore about the idea of a child, not for a long time. It was a complication I didn't need in my already complicated life, and the easiest way to deal with the possibility was to banish it. That same cold and windy night, the Dorados and one mounted brigade took a wide sweep around Chihuahua City. Bundled in serapes up to the eyeballs, the men looked again like a herd of traveling toadstools.

Candelario rode next to me. "Do you understand all this, Tomás?"

"Not much," I said, shivering.

"Do you know of these Greeks?"

"I remember they got licked pretty good by the Romans."

A coal train chugged into the yard from Juárez at one o'clock that afternoon. Villa ordered Candelario to take it, with instructions to shoot any soldiers that might be aboard but to spare the engine crew. At the same time Villa and twenty men stormed the El Norte railway office.

"Don't shoot the telegraph operator," he ordered. "But don't let him get any messages out."

Six Redflaggers were surprised in the office and shot before they could get to their rifles. Villa quickly ordered them dragged to a back room. The telegraph operator, an old man who had been drinking pulque and eating a plate of enchiladas, crossed himself and prepared to die. But Villa clapped the hot barrel of his pistol against the man's gray temple. "You can finish your meal later, señor. Right now, wire Juárez in your regular code. Our telegrapher here will watch"—and he nodded at me. "He understands English too, so if you add anything or don't follow my instructions to the comma, I'll splash your brains from here to the wall. . . . Now, what is the name of the conductor on the coal train?"

"Velasquez," the telegrapher whispered.

"You're positive?"

The old man nodded vigorously, sliding his tongue over dry lips.

"Good. Wire this. 'DERAILED. NO LINE OPEN TO CHIHUA-HUA CITY. EVERYTHING BURNED BY FRANCISCO VILLA. SEND SECOND ENGINE AND ORDERS. VELASQUEZ.' Have you got that?"

"Yes, Señor Villa."

"You know I've got a nervous trigger finger. Make sure you send the message exactly as I dictated."

A few minutes later the key began to click rapidly as the Juárez railroad yard answered. "NO ENGINES AVAILABLE. FIND TOOLS. ADVISE AND WAIT FOR ORDERS WHEN BACK ON RAILS."

"Tomás, stay here with two men," the chief said. "Let this old fellow finish his lunch. If he tries anything funny, shoot him." And he winked at me with one bloodshot eye.

He went outside into the hot sun, ordered all the coal dumped from the train and loaded his brigade of nearly two thousand men and all their horses aboard. He worked like a coal heaver, kicking mules in the belly, shoving horses up the rickety inclined boards. Dust boiled up in the railroad yard, the air so gritty you could hardly see. It took more than an hour, but Villa came back dripping sweat, black with coal dust, jubilant. This time he brought Calixto Contreras and Juan Medina with him, also begrimed from head to boots.

"Now, my friends! If luck is with us, you'll see how it works." He turned to the telegrapher. "Send this. 'ON TRACKS. NO ROADBED OR WIRE SOUTH. BIG CLOUD OF DUST ON HORIZON. LOOKS LIKE VILLISTAS. VELASQUEZ.' "

/ 127

No sooner had the man finished tapping the key than a message came clicking right back.

"BACK INTO JUAREZ IF POSSIBLE. WIRE AT EACH MAJOR STATION."

"Backwards?" Villa groaned. "I don't remember the Greeks doing it that way. Well, if we must, we must."

Fierro, a railroad engineer during part of his prerevolutionary life, took charge of the train, although he admitted he wasn't too sure of himself traveling backwards. That separated him from me by at least half a dozen railway cars, and I didn't complain. We chugged that way through the barren desert toward the north, and everybody went to sleep stretched out in the coal dust, exhausted from the night's ride and the day's vigil, until we reached the first station of El Sauz, festering under the afternoon sun. Candelario and a squad of Dorados took care of the few Federals who lounged around in the railway office, and then we telegraphed: "IN EL SAUZ. SEND ORDERS. VELASQUEZ."

Juárez answered: "PROCEED NORTH. TRACK CLEAR FOR YOU ALL THE WAY."

We did the same in Ojo de Laguna, El Mocho and La Candelaria, all through the afternoon and evening. Each time the reply came back: "PROCEED NORTH. TRACK CLEAR."

The chief kept grinning. "These people couldn't be nicer to us. Do you suppose they'll have a brass band at the station, to welcome their men who escaped the clutches of Pancho Villa?"

At Samalayuca, only twenty miles south of Juárez, Villa sent his last wire and issued his final orders, deploying the brigade for a three-pronged assault on the garrison.

A few minutes past midnight of November 15 the train bumped its way backwards into Juárez railroad station. The Federal garrison was asleep, and the Redflaggers were whooping it up in the town. Wasn't Villa getting his mustache tweaked in Chihuahua City? Before they knew it, two thousand gray-faced cavalry were in their midst, and they were prisoners of the revolution. I was with our boys when we raided the gambling casino of the famous El Touché, scooping up $150,000 worth of dollars and pesos from the stunned croupiers. Touché himself cried, "Who are you people?" He couldn't recognize anyone, because we were covered with coal dust from the boxcars.

"Get me a basin of water," one of the raiders, a stoutish fellow, commanded, and a croupier did so as the pistol waved in his direction. The man scrubbed himself, then showed his red teeth in a fine smile.

"Francisco Villa, at your service, you buzzards."

At three o'clock in the morning the battle for Juárez was wrapped up in a neat ribbon, ready for the history books. We had a port of entry and supply base. We hadn't lost a single man. Rosa's prediction had proved right, and I decided that Pancho Villa could have licked Hannibal and Napoleon and still have had something left over to take care of William Tecumseh Sherman. I slept for a few hours on the green felt of a craps table in Touché's and woke at dawn, stiff-limbed, and hungry. I had some fried eggs and chicory coffee in the street, but the sight of the Indian women behind their charcoal fires brought an image of Rosa to mind, and suddenly I wasn't quite so eager to cross the Stanton Street Bridge and pound on Hannah Sommerfeld's door. One look into my eyes, I thought, and all would be clear. Wouldn't she instantly see my faithlessness?

O heaven, were man but constant, he were perfect! Oh, faithless dog! Oh, wretch!

Oh, damn!

I knocked instead, that evening, on the front door of the Mix house on Noble Street, and it opened almost immediately. My mother peered out at me in the dusk with a frightened little smile. She looked well—gray-haired, with bright eyes, a few fresh lines etched into her forehead. She wore her familiar red-checked kitchen apron, and from inside the house I could smell hot tomato paste wafting toward the street.

"What do you want? If you're a salesman, please come back tomorrow morning."

I suppose I had changed. For one thing I had grown a mustache, and I wore a sombrero, and those months in the desert of Chihuahua with Pancho Villa had turned me leaner and harder-looking than when she had last seen me.

"It's me, Mama. Your son Tom."

She folded her arms around me. I was in time for dinner—the family always ate when the parlor clock chimed six—and we had fried chicken in tomato sauce and roasting ears in butter, clabber cheese and pecan patty, everything she guessed I had missed. I told my folks and sisters some tales of the campaign which made it sound like a frolic in the barn, complete with mariachis and dancing señoritas, with an occasional battle going on somewhere else which I would only hear about when it was won and the bodies had been carried away. I didn't want them to fret about me.

Papa finally got down to business. "How much they paying you, Tom? What's a captain get in the chile army?"

"All the tacos he can eat."

"Be straight, son."

"Papa, it's not a lie. We don't get paid, not yet. But we don't lack for anything."

"You've got to think about the future, boy. And security!"

The future? That was tonight, maybe including tomorrow. Security meant about as much to me as a kind word to a steer during a stampede.

I was lucky to be alive, I thought, after what I'd been through in Chihuahua. The funny thing is that Mama and Papa didn't ask me anything at all about Pancho Villa, and pretty soon I realized they didn't believe a word I said about what I did with him. To them he was a storied name in the newspapers and I was a footloose black sheep, and they somehow couldn't fit the two together. Come to think of it, the juxtaposition did seem improbable.

After supper, unable to bear my cowardice any longer, I went to see Hannah. Luck was with me, or else love was blind. No matter how much I dodged and shifted my gaze, she never once asked me what was the matter, or whether I'd met some other girl in Mexico to account for my uneasiness. I suppose it never occurred to her that I could stray, and when I was with her then it seemed as farfetched to me as my fighting at Villa's side. Rosa fell out of my mind like a stone into a well, just as Hannah had done in Torreón.

"It's extraordinary, Tom." Hannah sat with me on the parlor davenport, clasping both my hands. "No one ever dreamed it would happen so quickly! First Torréon, and now Juárez. How many men can say precisely what they're going to do and then go out and do it?"

"Villa's one of them," I said. "So far."

"And what will he do now? Will he take Chihuahua City, or will he head straight for the capital?"

She made it sound so simple, as if the chief had only to turn his horse and his brigades in a certain direction and the Federal Army would melt away like butter in the sun. Perhaps it was so. At the time, it seemed that way.

"I don't know," I said. "He's got to catch his breath. But he'll move quickly, whatever he does."

Indeed, within a few days the rest of the army under Urbina had moved north and reinforced us in Juárez. The women didn't come, and I was glad of it; I didn't think I could have handled Hannah on one side of the border and Rosa on the other. Villa established his headquarters in the old Customs House, and the American reporters swarmed round. He was a famous man now. "General Villa," one eager young man asked him, "do you speak English?"

"*Sí,*" Villa replied. "American Smelting and Refining *y* sonofabitch."

After that session he sent for his commanders. "Boys," he announced, "I've just heard from the press that the Federals don't believe we know how to fight. They think all we can do is sneak into cities at night when the defenders are asleep. So let's show them."

His reasons were more profound than that, but he liked his little jokes. The Federal garrison from Chihuahua City was advancing north along the railway in eleven trains. Villa had promised the American authorities in El Paso that there would be no fighting within cannon shot of the border, and in any case he was never a man to defend a city. He chose to attack in the desert at a place called Tierra Blanca. He ordered a review of his troops on a cool November morning, and at the same time he sent Rodolfo Fierro south with orders to destroy the railway line. Within sight of the approaching Federals and under a constant artillery bombardment, Fierro and a squad of volunteers coolly blew up the tracks. After the parade in Juárez, our brigades didn't return to their quarters. We trotted toward the railroad depot and entrained for Tierra Blanca. Villa led the first cavalry charge, and the battle lasted four days. When it was over I was exhausted, dazed, filthy with dust and covered with lice—so were we all—but the Federal Army was in flight. Three days later they decided to abandon Chihuahua City and flee for the safety of the border. Villa cut them off at a town called Ojinaga, just across from Big Bend National Park. He killed more than a thousand Federals, and not just Juárez but the state of Chihuahua was ours. All the supply lines to Texas were open, and we no longer had to worry about our rear or flanks. Controlling the vital railroad line, Villa had only to re-equip the Division and drive south, city by city, pueblo by pueblo, until he reached the final goal of Mexico City. Victory seemed inevitable, and close. The more I thought about it, the more remarkable it became. Just nine short months ago, nine men had crossed the Rio Bravo at Ysleta. Now we were nearly ten thousand.

I didn't fight at Ojinaga. Before he left, Villa said to me, "I don't need you under arms right now, Tomás. Stay in El Paso and help my brother. I've told him to drive a harder bargain than before, and the Jews will need someone to complain to. They like you, so be sympathetic and suggest some sort of compromise between what Hipólito asks and they offer. They'll agree, and we'll be better off. That's the way to do business, according to Mr. Carnegie and Rockefeller. They should know. I'm always willing to take advice from men as smart as I am."

I didn't say no. I always worried that my luck might run out one fine day on some battlefield. Hipólito had also been ordered to take over all the gambling in Juárez and get it going again—the revolution could use the money. He told me to come into Touché's and try the wheel anytime I needed extra cash. "I guarantee," he said, "that you won't lose." He rented a little furnished house on Montana Street in El Paso and then went out and bought three new suits: a gray worsted, a blue serge and a black velvet. He had always wanted to be a real businessman and an entrepreneur—it was certainly more elevating than helping to arrange for the slaughter of prisoners. I had always suspected he was a revolutionist more out of loyalty to his brother than from deep conviction, but I didn't love him any the less for it . . . we all find our fate, if we're patient enough. He also found a young woman named Mabel Silva, a cashier at the Hidalgo Cinema, and within a few weeks they were engaged. I was glad for him.

So for the next months, well into the new year of 1914, I lived in a back bedroom in Hipólito's house in El Paso, while Pancho Villa and the rest of the Northern Division took Ojinaga and then skirmished southward, clearing up the last few pockets of resistance that lay north of Chihuahua City. A big article appeared in *Collier's* magazine; it called the revolution "Villa's uprising." That didn't please Carranza. And then General Pershing invited Villa to a meeting in El Paso to take place in January of the new year. The chief accepted immediately and got word to me that he wanted me to be there as his interpreter.

I spent every minute of my spare time with Hannah, and kept working for Hipólito as a go-between to Sam Ravel and Felix Sommerfeld. Our orders now were by the trainload, and we signed for everything from five carloads of canned Maine sardines to wide-brimmed Texas scout hats with which Villa wanted to equip the whole Northern Division. We couldn't hope to get the men to wear matching uniforms, but if everyone wore the same kind of hat instead of an assortment of straw sombreros it would help to keep our boys from picking each other off under the belief that they were Redflaggers. Both sides already carried the red, green and white Mexican flag, so there was confusion enough.

In the day, when I wasn't inspecting our consignments, Hannah and I went riding in the desert and ate ice cream out of silver cups in the Elite Confectionery, and at night we spooned on the parlor davenport until I thought my Levi's would pop. She became inflamed so quickly that I couldn't do anything about it, but I didn't dare to think of going all the way with her before we were married. I knew she wasn't that kind of girl. Still, there were nights when she seized my pecker with such dedication that I thought, I may be crazy, but I swear she wants it. She would twist under me on the davenport until I felt every tuft and bone of her vulva pressing into the muscle of my thigh, and then she'd see stars and go off like a rocket in her own way. I was always looking out for her mother on the staircase. It wasn't satisfactory—after Rosa, I certainly knew better—but it was all we had.

One night I was so excited, and her virginal body was so reckless under me, that I couldn't help myself. I blurted: "I want you, Hannah. God, I want you . . ."

"No, Tom! Please!"

I apologized right away, but it put her in a bad mood and I went home that night with a dry bandanna.

Most of the time she liked to talk about the future, just like my father, and she prattled on happily about the wedding and what part of El Paso we'd live in, and which of her girl friends would be bridesmaids, and whether we'd go to New Orleans or Niagara Falls on our honeymoon, while I just nodded and slipped in a word of approval every now and then. I didn't truly mind, because I loved to listen to her voice and see the flush rise to her cheeks when she talked about things that moved her.

"You do love me, don't you, Tom?"

"You know I do."

"When do you think it will all be over? When do you think we can get married?"

"Well, now that we've occupied Chihuahua City, Villa says that Mexico City's the key, the seat of power. But before that we've got to take Zacatecas, which is on the way. And then we have to deal with Don Venus, and Zapata down in Morelos. . . ." And I would go on, mapping the upcoming campaign and lecturing about strategy and the peculiarities of the different generals, and not really answering her question. But who could tell?

"By the summer, do you think?"

A little impatience crept into her tone, and something else too. I began to realize that during the winter her revolutionary zeal had started to wane. Her hero, Ricardo Flores Magón, had been bypassed by Villa and the other generals, and after the last few battles she had heard some disturbing reports about how the revolutionists were stripping the pueblos of food, carting off the women . . . even killing prisoners.

"Do you know anything about that, Tom?"

"Well, the people know that an army's got to eat. Most of the time they're glad to share with us. Sometimes we loot . . . sure. I mean not me, but the fellows who don't know any better. They're dirt poor, you know—well, of course, you know. Sometimes, yes, hell, they grab whatever's in sight."

"And the rest? The women? Killing the prisoners? Some people are starting to say that Villa may be a great general, but he's also a brute. An animal! He has three wives, they say!"

"The poor fellow," I murmured.

"Oh, Tom! It's no joke. He sets an example for his men, and they set it for all of Mexico. If he simply takes what he wants and shows no mercy to those he's vanquished . . . it's uncivilized! The revolution will end in tragedy."

I asked her again, for she needed cheering up, why she thought our honeymoon would be more memorable if we went to Niagara Falls instead of New Orleans.

The day after that conversation, on a fine January morning, I took the train south with a load of coal to talk to the chief about his arrangements to meet the American generals. The winter sky was a crisp blue, and the soldiers in the rattling railway car sang cheerfully. Candelario was waiting for me at the depot in Chihuahua City.

"I'm glad to see you," I said. "I was going to look for you. What's happened to the women? Why is it taking so long?"

"That's your fault," he yelled. "All the trains are going north to the border to bring back supplies! There are none left to go to Jiménez.

Tomás, what am I to do? I miss Yvette and Marie-Thérèse. I'm a simple man—when I get used to something, I crave it. Don't be so damned conscientious. Delay some shipments! We won't fight anyway until this damned meeting in El Paso is over."

"I'll see what I can do," I said cautiously. But it suited me fine for Rosa to stay in Jiménez for the time being; I didn't want to complicate my life any further. So when I met with the chief in his headquarters suite at the Fermont, a five-story pink-colored luxury hotel in the center of town, I said nothing. After we had discussed the timetable for meeting General Scott and General Pershing, Villa decided to show me the city. I had never been there, he pointed out, and Chihuahua City was practically home to him. He didn't seem in a hurry to head south and retake Torreón. I wondered why, and he told me.

"Because, Tomás, winning battles may be the only purpose of a war, but not of a revolution. We have to take time out to show the people *why* we fight, and whom we fight *for*."

Outside the hotel, at the curb, stood a shiny green Packard touring car that he had requisitioned somewhere along the line, complete with a villainous-looking chauffeur named Martín Lopez. But Villa called for two horses.

"I need to get into the saddle. I've been here two weeks and my ass is getting soft like a woman's. Riding in a car always makes me think I'm sitting in a movie theater. You see only what the car lets you see."

It was a warm day, with fleecy clouds hanging over the mountains. Chihuahua was a pleasant city with wide streets and pretty parks, and it had been left more or less intact as a result of Orozco's hasty withdrawal. Thousands of its citizens, including the police force, had fled with the Federal Army, fearing Villa's wrath for sins real or imagined, so Villa had put the Northern Division to work. Whole battalions were delegated to run the streetcars and telephone exchange, the electric plant and the slaughterhouses. He told me he had lowered the prices of bread, meat and milk, so that not only his soldiers but the poor of the city could eat well, at least for a while. We passed the Plaza Hidalgo, and there on the grass, before a crowd of shirt-sleeved citizens, a military band in brilliant purple uniforms was playing a pretty one-step named "Tierra Blanca," in honor of the battle.

"You see how the people smile, Tomás? This isn't music to make them forget their troubles. It's to remind them that the soldiers are their servants."

As we left the park a small boy, dressed in rags and chewing a piece of sugar cane, followed us. He stayed in the shadow of the horses and just looked up, his large brown eyes fastened on Pancho Villa. Finally, when the chief noticed him, he reined up and peered down. The boy must have been eight or nine years old.

Villa leaned from the saddle and snatched the sugar cane. He bit off a piece and began to chew it with his stumpy red-brown teeth. The boy said nothing.

The chief laughed. "Aren't you angry, boy?"

"No, señor."

"And aren't you afraid?"

"No, señor." In fact, the boy was utterly calm and unblinking.

Villa frowned ferociously. "The bandit Pancho Villa is going to steal all your sugar cane! Watch out! Don't you know that Pancho Villa came into the world to rob and kill?"

"I didn't know that. Are you really Pancho Villa?"

"Yes," Villa said solemnly. "And now I want you to tell me why you followed us through the street."

"Señor Villa, I like to look at you."

"And why do you like to look at me?"

"I don't know," the boy murmured.

"Will you sell me this piece of cane? How much did it cost you?"

"Two centavos, señor. You can keep it if you like it."

Villa reached into his pocket and took out a peso coin, which he flipped so that it spun brightly in the sunlight. The boy caught it in the air.

"What will you do with the money? Buy more cane?"

"Give it to my father."

"Ah, you have a father. A mother too?"

"Not anymore, señor."

"And why are you out on the street? Doesn't your father send you to school?"

"No, señor, he can't do that."

"Can't? What do you mean, *can't?*"

"Because I help him in his store. He sells bananas and mangos. He is all alone except for me. This is the siesta hour—I don't have to work."

"So you don't go to school *at all?*"

"No, señor."

Villa turned to me across our horses, his voice high and quivering. "Listen to me, Tomás. This child, without knowing who I am, follows me down the streets of Chihuahua and even wants to give me what he eats—this bit of cane that cost him two miserable centavos, which is certainly all he had. Can you tell me why? I'm not handsome. I'm not dressed in the fine uniform of a general. Why does he do such a thing unless he senses in me the soul of a man who struggles for the salvation of just such children as himself? There is no other explanation." Villa's eyes shone like emeralds. "I dedicate my life to this boy, and that's why I fight. He will be a better man than I. But to do that," he suddenly shouted, so that the boy flinched, "he must go to school! He must read and write! To make him work is a crime, a crime worse than murder! If you kill a man, you put him out of his misery. If you make a boy such as this work, if you keep him from school, you doom him to that misery." Villa turned back to the boy. "Go tell your father," he said, "that Pancho Villa orders him to send you to school tomorrow. If he doesn't follow that order, he will be shot. Do you understand? Will you swear to tell him?"

The boy didn't reply and didn't so swear, which I could well understand.

"All right," Villa said, sighing. "Where is your father's store?"

"Not far, señor."

With one powerful arm Villa hauled the boy up into the saddle. He sat snugly behind the horn, in front of General Pancho Villa. Despite the boy's worry, I could see the sparkle in his eyes. The world must have seemed to lie at his feet, and be glorious.

We rode down some narrow dirt alleys to a part of the city that shouted its poverty and degradation. The shutters were closed, so Villa dismounted with the boy and pounded with his fist on the closed door. After a few minutes it opened to disclose a weary-looking Mexican in a frayed shirt and torn trousers. His shop with its mangos and other fruit was about as big as a large closet. Two hammocks were slung in the back from hooks on the walls, but if they hadn't been slung at angles they wouldn't have fit.

Without wasting any time on pleasantries, Villa said, "Señor, I am General Francisco Villa. What is your name?"

Looking confused, sleepy—wary, too—the man gave his name. ". . . at your orders, my general."

"My orders are that you will send your son to school, beginning tomorrow, or you will be shot."

"School?"

"You know what that is, don't you?"

"*Shot,* señor?"

"You know what that is, too."

The wretched man pleaded his case. "Señor General, if I sent him to school, who would help me in the store? I have no wife," he pleaded. "My daughters work in a sausage factory. They give me nothing. Without the boy's help, I can't run my store. How will he eat?"

"I know nothing about your store," Villa shouted. "I care that your son goes to school! And I tell you that if you don't send him tomorrow, you'll be shot. If the greed of the rich deprived you of your schooling, as it did me, and you are so poor that you have only this ridiculous hole in the wall you call a store, then . . . *go out and steal!* Steal whatever it is you need to send your son to school! If you steal for that reason, you have my solemn word I won't shoot you. But if by not stealing you force your son to remain a filthy street urchin who will be as miserable all his life as you are, and perhaps even turn to crime and drunkenness—for I smell pulque on your breath, señor, if you wish to know the truth—you have Francisco Villa's solemn word that you'll be shot."

The man turned pale and wrung his hands, and that's when I butted in. By now I knew Villa's temperament fairly well. He always meant what he said, and although he was capable of changing his mind on a whim, it was never something you could count on. The boy's father was close to death, if not from a bullet, then from fear. The boy, however, remained remarkably serene, and more than anything that was what moved me. He had faith. I had to make sure it was not misplaced.

"Chief," I said quietly, "if you send this man out to steal so that this kid can go to school, he's liable to be shot before anyone finds out you gave him permission. You've strung him on the horns of a dilemma that he can't solve. You've given him a choice as to who will shoot him."

"I'll give him a paper," Villa proclaimed, "with my signature."

I wanted to laugh, but I knew that wouldn't convince him. "How many of our men can read?" I asked. "And if they can, they'll be reading it after he's dead." I decided to press him a little harder. "Listen, chief. You can't cure an evil by curing the symptoms. If there's a drought and the cattle are starving, you can fatten 'em up with a load of grain—but they'll go right back to starving unless you move 'em to decent pasture. This man and his son aren't your problem. The problem is they're *poor*. If he steals, he might be better off for a while, but it's going to make the man he steals from even poorer. Is that a solution? And what's more, I'll bet you a peso there's no free school in this quarter. So what can the man do except die?"

Villa had listened to me carefully, brow furrowed in a mixture of concentration and annoyance. But he didn't blow up or reach for his pistol. He thought awhile, then turned to the wretched father.

"Is that so? Is there no school in this quarter?"

"None, Señor General. And the few schools in the other quarters are so full they turn their own children away. This is a fact. You can ask. You owe your officer a peso."

Villa didn't remark on this boldness or bother to point out that he hadn't taken the bet. "What is the name of this street?" he demanded.

"Calle Aldama, señor."

"Tomorrow we'll tear down a house here and build a school. Until then, we'll use that shoe shop next door as a school. I'll send a teacher. Tell the other fathers to have their children here at ten o'clock tomorrow morning. Tomás?"

"Yes, chief?"

"Do you have any money with you? I gave this kid my last peso for his sugar cane."

I fished around in my pockets and came up with a five-peso note and a two-dollar bill. Villa took them and handed them to the man.

"This is for your trouble, señor."

I left him then, but the next morning the chief sent for me again, and we rode once more through the streets of Chihuahua City to Calle Aldama. We halted in front of what had been a shoe shop. About fifteen children were crowded in there on wooden stools, including the boy with the sugar cane, and a young woman stood before a wobbly blackboard with a bit of chalk, scratching out the alphabet. Across the street twenty men from one of our brigades pounded with sledgehammers to destroy two old adobe houses. All over the city, Villa said, beginning today, gangs of soldiers under civilian engineers were tearing down such buildings, making way for forty new schools. Each of the children who attended were to be given ten pesos a week to bring home to their fathers.

"Well, Tomás? Does Alvaro Obregón do this? Does the illustrious Señor Carranza, the First Chief? He declares new national holidays. Does he build schools? Does he pay the fathers of the children so that they accept the sacrifice? Can I hold my head high when I meet your General Pershing?"

"Yes, chief," I said. "You can do that."

He was an actor, no doubt of it, but it seemed he was more than Henry Five. Come to think of it, Shakespeare would have had to write a whole new play to do him justice. I had a fresh rush of faith, almost equal to that of the boy with the cane. The only thing I wondered about was where all the money would come from to pay for this construction, but when I got back to the hotel Candelario enlightened me. Villa had already asked Carranza for five million pesos to finance the planned spring offensive toward Mexico City, but the First Chief protested that he didn't have it. He was supporting two other divisions as well— Obregón's in the northwest, General Pablo González's in Coahuila. Villa confiscated the state printing presses in the basement of the old Governor's Palace, put two local artists to work and began to print his own currency—three million pesos' worth on the first run. There were eagles and swords and the usual olive branches, and one side carried twin portraits of President Madero and Abraham Gonzalez, the pro-revolutionary governor who had also been murdered by Huerta, so that the bills quickly got to be called *dos caras*, or "two-faces." All the former government money was declared illegal and had to be traded for the two-faces. Then Villa promptly shipped the incoming supply of cash up to El Paso to pay for more coal and guns. A move, I reckoned, worthy of J. P. Morgan.

The next day, again, the chief asked me to meet him in front of the Fermont, but this time he waved a hand at the Packard. "Get in, Tomás," he said, and I stepped inside. Washed and waxed, gleaming like a jewel in the sun, it had matching green leather cushions and a glass partition. I put my boots up on the jump seat. So this is what it was like to be rich. I could learn to like it.

"We'll go to my house," he said. "This is a special day. The schools are open all over the city, and your inspiration helped it to come about. I invite you for lunch."

"What house?"

"To meet my wife."

"I've met her. I mean I've met them."

"No, no. My *real* wife, Luz Corral. I've told you about her, haven't I? She's been hiding in the mountains, but now she's here in Chihuahua, although I'm going to send her to Texas. This is still no place for her and the child, not until the revolution's won."

"You have a child? And a house?"

"I have plenty of children, without doubt, but this one bears my name. Tomás, you ask a lot of dumb questions. Luz cooks well. We'll have a fine lunch."

I was too flabbergasted by the revelation of this domestic existence to go on bleating any longer. The house wasn't far away, just outside the center of the city, and Villa told me that it was called Quinta Luz in honor of its owner. "I met her here in 1910," he said, "just before the revolution began. It was love at first sight, which is the way I still am, as you know. But it took awhile to persuade her to marry me. She was much too level-headed. Finally I promised to buy her this house, and that did the trick. Here we are."

From the outside the brown stone building didn't appear very sumptuous, but inside it was enormous, with sagging armchairs, pictures of Villa and his wife on the walls, a Mexican flag, glass cases with cheap bric-a-brac, an old oak desk and several main rooms that led to a large courtyard of worn cobbles flanked on all sides with other rooms—forty in all, Villa claimed.

"Who lives here?" I asked.

"Luz and her family. Parents, cousins, aunts and uncles, cousins of cousins, orphans . . . I can't keep track. She'll take in anybody who has a hard-luck story. I pay for it. I want to keep her happy. If I don't, she nags at me."

Luz Corral greeted us in the patio. She was a handsome woman in her early twenties, on the bosomy side, with light brown hair, calm gray eyes and a queenly bearing. She was so different from Pancho Villa's other two wives that it was hard for me to believe that he had chosen her.

"This is my *güera,*" he said tenderly. "My *chulita.*" Both were affectionate words for fair-haired one. He had told her all about me, he explained. His belly heaved with a low chuckle. "I didn't say that you were my gringo, Tomás."

She had a kindly manner, and she said, "You take good care of my Pancho, don't you? He claims all his officers do. He never has the time to take care of himself. And he always speaks well of you, Captain."

My Pancho? The general, who had led the charge into Torreón, just smiled. We ate lunch in the patio in the welcome shade of some lemon trees, surrounded by potted plants, clinging purple bougainvillea and little patches of sunflowers. A pair of bright green lovebirds screeched in a cage that hung from a branch of a lemon tree. Half a dozen small children galloped in and out of various doorways, playing games and calling shrilly to each other.

"Teo, do you want me to bring out the child for Captain Mix?"

Teo! I realized that had to be a private nickname for Doroteo, the name he had been born with in Durango, where as a youth he had sold wood from the back of a burro. I think if a man ever called him that, Villa wouldn't bother to yell for Rodolfo Fierro, He would just shoot him on the spot.

"Where's my *angelita?*" Villa called, grinning.

Out came his little angel, dressed neatly in a navy blue cotton skirt and white blouse. She must have been about three, a pretty child who looked like her mother, which was lucky. She didn't have much to say, and after she buried her curly head in her father's chest and he bussed her all over her cheeks and ears, so that she giggled and whispered, "It tickles, Papa," she went dutifully to her mother, who patted everything back into place and then sent her off to play.

Pancho Villa—the Lion of the North, the conqueror of Juárez— smiled his half-idiotic, pop-eyed smile. He might have been an accountant come home for lunch after a busy morning at the office. I was privy to a domesticity that I wouldn't have thought possible, and if anyone else had described this scene I would have guffawed. When lunch was over, Luz Corral clapped her hands and said serenely, "I have a present for you, Teo."

A cunning smile spread over Villa's features, and he winked at me. He said, "The last present she tried to give me, Tomás, was a knife in my belly."

"Ah, well!" Luz tapped her spoon on the tablecloth. "You know why!"

"Because of Esperanza . . ."

"Is that the one from Ascensión or the one from Torreón?"

"Ascensión. The one from Torreón is called Juana."

"I did make a mistake. I should have put the knife in *their* bellies."

"They're not to blame, *chulita.* They only do what they think is right for them. I lie to them, and they believe it." He coughed. "Why don't you have them live here with you? The older one, Esperanza, sews very well."

"I have a seamstress already. You haven't met her, because she's too pretty. What does the other one do besides look at you adoringly, and the other thing?"

"Not much," Villa admitted, and looked uncomfortable. "Where is my present?"

Luz swept out of the patio, trailing her long skirts like a young queen. Villa bent quickly toward me.

"That went well. Naturally I brought it up on purpose, because she would have done so sooner or later, and this way it was easier. I'm glad you were here, Tomás. She doesn't like to make scenes in front of my officers. What do you think of my *güera?*"

"She's a remarkable woman, chief."

"I think so too. She won't like it when I send her away to Texas. But I'm going to rent a fine house for her and buy her a Dodge car. She wants to learn to drive. Can you imagine? A woman! But why shouldn't she?"

Luz Corral returned with something wrapped in tissue paper, and when she deftly peeled the paper aside it uncovered a tan pith helmet, the kind you see on African explorers going up the Nile after crocodiles.

"What the hell is *that?*" Villa demanded.

"If you can't see what it is, I'll give you spectacles as a present." Luz frowned.

"I have a hat," he said grumpily.

"A dirty sombrero. This is something special—I had Hipólito send it from El Paso, and before that it came all the way from Abercrombie & Fitch in New York. This is the kind of helmet that Colonel Roosevelt wore before he became President. He wore it at the battle of San Juan Hill. It will keep your head cool in the desert."

"Roosevelt wore one? Did he really?"

"I've seen photographs."

Villa set it slowly on top of his head, and it fit well. With his curly mustache he looked like pictures I had seen of Englishmen in India, except that his cheeks were too brown.

"Will you wear it?" Luz asked him. "Do you promise?"

"Well . . . yes. I'll wear it."

"Captain, you heard him promise. Tell me if he doesn't wear it."

We pushed our chairs deeper into the shade of the lemon tree. Luz Corral went away, and Villa turned the pith helmet over and over in his hands, as if it might bite. Luz returned with three small glasses and a bottle of Spanish anisette. "Do you like anisette, Captain, or would you rather have whiskey?"

"Señora, I've never had anisette."

"It tastes of licorice. It's strong, but excellent for the digestion."

Villa was going to drink too. When I realized that, I was startled. He caught my eye and winked again. Then he drained his glass in one swallow, coughed, turned slightly red, but quickly recovered himself. I drank the anisette and it was nicely warming in the belly, and then Luz Corral disappeared again, skirts trailing on the cobbles.

"Say nothing to anyone about this," Villa commanded, indicating the empty glass. "It helps me to fuck her, which I intend to do now that lunch is over. It's been very helpful having you here, Tomás. When she gets back, make some excuse and leave. Tell Lopez to come back at seven o'clock sharp and say that I'm urgently wanted by one of my generals. Have you got that?"

"Yes, chief."

/ 141

"She's a remarkable woman. That's the word. I love her as much as I did on the day I first set eyes on her. Who else would give me a hat like this to wear in battle?"

"I can't imagine."

"If I had my life to live over again, I wouldn't change a thing. Not many men can make that statement. This anisette goes straight to my balls. It makes my head swim." He patted his stomach. "You know, I was crazy when I was younger. Luz helped calm me down. For that alone, I love her. A wife is essential in a man's life, like an anchor for a boat. You can keep it coiled on the deck and throw it out whenever you find yourself drifting. Do you know that I've never seen the ocean? Not even the Gulf of Mexico. But someday I will." He belched. His voice was lazy, his eyelids drooping, although the eyes themselves showed a certain impish sparkle. "Go now, Tomás . . . she may be awhile. She's probably primping and getting ready for what she hopes will happen. And it will! I'll make some excuse for you. Seven o'clock sharp—have you got that?"

"I've got it."

Lopez drove me back to the Fermont, and I gave him his instructions.

A few minutes before seven I looked out of my window to spot the Packard pulling away from the curb, on its way to rescue the commanding general of the Northern Division from the arms of his adoring wife.

12
"Shall I be frightened when a madman stares?"

On a softly warm January day of 1914, I met the train that brought Pancho Villa north for his historic meeting with Generals Scott and Pershing.

We rode on horseback to the center of the new International Bridge between Juárez and El Paso. Villa dismounted, and General Hugh Scott, the commander at Fort Bliss, shook his hand firmly. Scott wore yellow gloves because two fingers of his right hand were missing; he was a thick-bodied Indian fighter with a white mustache and a face that resembled a walrus, and he massacred the Spanish language with the same vigor that he had applied to the Apache nation. Black Jack Pershing, the general who commanded the whole border area, hung back a little and was less hearty in his welcome, although he was always correct—a tall, graying, rawboned man in his fifties with squared-off shoulders and a steel ruler sewn into his shirt where his spine should have been. Both Americans and their gang of officers looked slick as paint, and the chief had spruced up for the occasion too, wearing a dark bow tie and a new butterscotch-colored tweed suit that almost fit.

Obregón was also there—come over from Sonora as a military representative of Carranza—a short, barrel-chested man with penetrating green eyes, whose family had emigrated from Ireland a few generations ago and changed the surname from O'Brien. He wore a rumpled white-duck uniform, and he needed a shave. He had been doing well lately, winning several battles against superior Federal forces, so that he and Villa outdid each other to be friendly.

"I bring you the compliments of the First Chief, *compañero,* and we both congratulate you on your great victories in Chihuahua."

"Ah, *compañerito*"—Villa used the diminutive, for Obregón was a head shorter—"I accept your compliments and congratulate you on *your* victories in Sonora."

Once this eloquent and momentous speechmaking on the bridge was over, the Americans took everybody to Fort Bliss in a caravan of automobiles, Old Glory and the Mexican flag whipping together in the breeze. In the open Dodge staff car the generals discussed horses and saddles, including the new McClellan saddle the American army had just adapted from the Hungarian cavalry, and with Obregón keeping fairly silent—he was an infantry general, a believer in trench warfare rather than cavalry charges—the others were like three big kids talking about their favorite toys. Pershing spun a couple of yarns about fighting with Teddy Roosevelt in Puerto Rico and then campaigning against the Moros in the Philippines, and Villa's eyes grew wide and respectful, because the man was modest and yet knew what he was talking about. Scott translated and I kept quiet; I was just thrilled to be in such august company. They talked of the impending war in Europe, and Pershing spoke forcefully. "We'll be in it with the French. The English too. No doubt at all, no matter what Mr. Wilson says."

At Fort Bliss, Scott had organized a military parade of his troops. We all sat in a wooden grandstand to watch. The American cavalry did look smart on their Oklahoma-bred saddle horses, and they performed some crisp maneuvers. Scott wheeled out his light artillery and had them pop away at targets on the desert. They hit them all.

"Señores," Villa said sincerely, "I'm glad we will never have to fight you."

We all laughed politely at these words, and we would all have reason to remember them.

Afterwards we watched a few innings of a baseball game between two of the cavalry battalions. Pershing tried to explain what was going on, but Villa quickly became bored. Scott seized the opportunity. "General Villa," he asked, "have you read the pamphlet I sent you? The Rules of War of the Hague Conference?"

Villa said, "I'm going to have it translated and distributed to my soldiers."

"You'll abide by it?" Scott asked, pleased.

"I don't want to lie to you, General Scott. I've studied it, and my officers will be ordered to read it . . . if they can read. But you must admit it's a pretty funny book. We both know that war isn't a game. It's savage and disgusting, even though it sometimes brings out the best in a man. If I'm in a cantina and a fellow pulls a knife on me, as happened in my youth, I'm going to shoot him. I'm not going to dig around in my pocket for a little book that tells me the correct way to do it. Would you, señor?"

Scott didn't smile. "To what do you object, General?"

"For one thing, the rules say you can't use soft-nosed lead bullets, because they spread. That makes no sense to me. They do the job."

The American general tried to argue, but Villa suddenly turned to Pershing and began asking why the men on the bases didn't simply run to home plate if that was the object of the game, and Pershing, who loved baseball, replied at length and asked Scott to translate. The rules of war were not discussed again.

Then we were all taken to Scott's house in the foothills behind the post for tea and cakes. Rodolfo Fierro, the best-dressed among us except for the Americans in their neat khakis, wandered through the sitting room, inspecting the spinnet and the Currier & Ives prints. As usual, we avoided each other carefully. But Fierro forgot to take off his white Stetson. Villa shouted at him across the room, "Take off your hat, you brute!" He turned to General Scott. "Forgive me, señor . . . that man is an animal." Scott seemed a little embarrassed, but Fierro just grinned like a naughty boy who had been scolded for his table manners.

I ate the best pineapple upside-down cake I'd ever tasted, and I gave Mrs. Scott my praise in English. General Pershing turned to me with a cool look. The great man had finally recognized my presence. "I thought you were American, but I wasn't sure. I didn't catch the name."

"Mix, sir. Captain Thomas Mix."

"You're a Texan?"

"From right here. El Paso."

"Will you be offended if I give vent to my curiosity and ask why you're an officer in General Villa's army, and how it came about?"

"I won't be offended at all," I said. "It came about by accident, you might say, a year or so ago. But I serve General Villa now because I believe in his cause."

That was the first time since Torreón that I had been able to come out with that and mean it, wholeheartedly, and it made me feel good. I was thinking of the boy with the sugar cane and the forty new schools in Chihuahua.

The general nodded, satisfied. "Were you formerly in the American army, Captain?"

"No, sir. I was a cowhand and a rodeo rider."

"That's interesting," Pershing said, and I could almost see his mind filing it away in a neat compartment.

Villa asked me to translate this conversation, and when I finished he threw a bearlike arm around me. Then he turned to the Americans.

"This man was with me when I crossed the Rio Bravo. Sometimes he acts like a *pendejo,* which I won't explain since there are ladies present, but he fights like a tiger, rides like a devil, and buys guns like a Jew. I trust him as if he were my illegitimate son and commend him to you with all my heart. When the revolution is over, if he can't find a job—as sometimes happens with soldiers—make him a captain in your army. He'll serve you better than most." Villa squeezed my shoulder. "In fact, right this minute, in honor of the occasion, and also because he deserves it, I'm going to promote him to major. Congratulations, Tomás."

He shook my hand limply, and there was a light tattoo of applause in the room, mostly from the ladies, who knew very well what a *pendejo* was if they had been around El Paso for any length of time. I felt wonderful, and at the same time I felt like a fool. General Pershing coughed politely and shook my hand with a hard grip. I could see a glint of amusement in his slate-blue eyes.

"My compliments, Mix. You certainly must have an interesting officer corps. May I ask how old you are?"

"Almost twenty-three," I said.

His leathery smile grew broader. "Well, at this rate you may outrank me before you're thirty. Try to let me know before we meet again . . . Major."

"That would be my pleasure, sir." And then Pershing turned back to resume his conversation with Obregón, no doubt forgetting all about me . . . for neither of us could look into a crystal ball and foresee the future that would bring us together in the burned-out town of Columbus, and then the mountains of Chihuahua.

A few days later President Wilson lifted the arms embargo to our side. Pancho Villa, still in Juárez, grinned like an old dog having its belly scratched. He was positive he had made such a good impression on the American generals that they had immediately telegraphed their feelings to Washington. In a barber shop on my way to see Hannah I picked up a copy of the El Paso *Times* and read that the government of Germany was up in arms over Wilson's move; their ambassador to Mexico screamed that the Americans wanted to take over all of Central America. He publicly offered to support the fading fortunes of General Huerta if that old drunk would sign a pact to confiscate the British oil refineries in Tampico. To show good faith, three shiploads of German arms sailed from Hamburg to Veracruz, which the Huerta government still held. Villa just chuckled. "If the Germans back Huerta," he said, "the Americans will back us even more."

Then came my twenty-third birthday, falling on a warm Sunday in February of 1914, and Felix Sommerfeld invited me and Hipólito to a little celebration lunch in his rose garden. We both bathed, I put on a suit and tie, and we left our pistols behind at the house. Sam Ravel brought his wife, who was dark-eyed and might have had a touch of Mex, and Hannah looked lovely in a white cotton dress with her light brown hair curling in ringlets to bare shoulders.

In the rose garden Mrs. Sommerfeld's maids served us cold rare roast beef and red wine, and a chocolate cake with twenty-three candles. I was treated as much like a son-in-law as a newly commissioned major. But I sensed trouble; I noticed the way Hannah tapped her long red fingernails on the tablecloth all throughout lunch. And then, after I had blown out the candles and received a polite hand of applause, as well as a blow on the back from Hipólito that nearly made me cough up my last glass of wine, she spoke up.

"I'm not to be put off anymore, Tom, like a mere woman who doesn't deserve an honest answer . . . not by you or by Papa. This time I want to know about General Villa. People are beginning to call him a beast and a murderer. Is it true?"

I cleared my throat uncomfortably. "You might better ask that question to his brother, Hannah. He understood every word you said."

"Does he speak English? One would never know. But if you're afraid to answer, so I shall."

She turned boldly on Hipólito, and I had to admire her for it. "Is your brother really such a beast, Colonel Villa?"

Hipólito worked that around for a while in his mind, while he refilled his wine glass. Then he shrugged and said, "Yes, miss, he is."

That made Hannah rein up a bit. "Oh . . . I see. He is. Of course. How candid! Then what we've heard from the refugees, what we read about him in the newspapers, is all . . . true?"

"I don't read the newspapers, miss," Hipólito explained.

"Does he kill all the prisoners he captures?"

Hipólito didn't seem at all angry. Only the tip of his big nose was red.

"No, miss. Most, but not all."

A hard look of outrage appeared in Hannah's eyes, although she kept her voice within the same tight octave. Her lips thinned. "Don't you consider that brutal, Colonel Villa? Brutal and uncivilized?"

"My brother can't afford to feed them, miss. We give the food to the people, who are hungry. And if we let these men free, they go back to General Orozco and get another rifle. Let a man shoot at you once, it makes you feel unfriendly to him. Let him shoot at you twice, it makes you feel a fool."

Felix Sommerfeld suggested that we go into the house for cigars and brandy.

"No, Papa!" Hannah cried. "There's more that I want to know! May I not ask questions? Is it forbidden? Am I not allowed to satisfy my interest?"

"Your interest—" But he bit off his words, and Hannah's blue eyes glittered. A flock of birds chirped in the coral trees, and the smell of roses was sweet. Hipólito sat in his white iron garden chair, wearing his new suit, puffing clouds of smoke from a Havana cigar, drinking French wine and looking as if had been doing it all his life. It was hard to remember him from the battle at Torreón.

"And is it true," she pursued, "that your brother steals money from the banks in Chihuahua City and Juárez?"

"He always gives a paper, miss. He says it is a loan." Hipólito shrugged his shoulders. "But you are right. He will never give it back to the bankers. It is stealing."

"Then I'm right, and he's nothing but a common bandit! And it's said that at Torreón he ordered one hundred men shot down in a corral! Is that true too?"

Felix and Sam Ravel stirred uneasily; but Hipólito kept the same smile in place on his round cheeks.

"Miss Sommerfeld," he said, as pleasantly as before, "for many years in Durango my brother and I and General Urbina were bandits together. This is known. We steal, we gamble, we get drunk. We spent the money—poof! Now my brother is general of ten thousand men, and he has not a peso in the bank and not a pair of shoes. For himself, he wishes no more than to finish the revolution and learn to read better, and to have four wives who will be nice to him when he is old. In this, yes, he has much greed. Will he grow old? I don't think so. He has one great dream . . . to take all the money from the bankers and give schools to the people, and to take all the land from the haciendas and give to the *campesinos,* as the little Señor Madero before him wished to do. Tell me truly . . . do you think this is wrong?"

Hannah regarded him sternly, for of course he hadn't answered her question. Then her father said in a firm voice, "The gentlemen will have brandy and cigars in my study. Ladies?"

The ladies stayed in the garden. In the study, which had oak paneling and more leatherbound books than in the local public library, Mr. Sommerfeld poured out big snifters of French cognac and offered a box of Monte Cristo Havanas.

"I apologize, Hipólito—and to you too, Tom—for my daughter's rudeness. Youth is guilty of certain misplaced . . . well, excess enthusiasm."

"Miss Sommerfeld is too pretty to be angry with," Hipólito murmured gallantly.

That subject was closed, and the talk quickly veered to politics, where I was bound to be a listener. Sommerfeld and Sam Ravel told me a lot I didn't know. Like Hipólito, the main contact I had with newspapers was in a privy.

Apparently, according to Sam, Victoriano Huerta's fortunes were sinking fast. After the fall of Juárez some senator had stood up in the Mexican Chamber of Deputies to denounce Huerta's poor conduct of the war, and the next night they found the senator's body in a ditch. The congress flew into a rage, so Huerta dissolved the whole body and carted off more than a hundred of its members in tram cars to the prison. President Wilson didn't like that, especially when Huerta celebrated by getting publicly drunk and then appointed an entire company of army officers to take the places of the imprisoned congressmen. Ravel chuckled. "Now, instead of rapping a gavel to come to order, they blow a bugle."

Sommerfeld puffed out his cheeks and looked more like a frog than ever. "Tom, Huerta's ripe to fall. The United States will move soon to recognize the revolutionary government. That will be decisive. Villa and Carranza will win, and Mr. Wilson will give them each a hug on the White House lawn."

"That would be fine. Then Villa can have his four wives and I can be a retired major of the Mexican army. The only problem," I reflected, after another sip of that warming brandy, "is what Villa and Carranza will do on that White House lawn. I'd hate to see blood spilled over President Wilson's shoes."

Ravel spoke emphatically. "If Villa plays his cards right, Carranza will cool his heels in the waiting room. Tell him that, Tom. Don't let him do anything foolish, like what we heard happened in Torreón."

So they knew. What they didn't seem to know was my role in it, and I would never tell.

After coffee Hipólito announced that he had to go over to Juárez and look in on his casinos, and he asked me to go with him. Mr. Sommerfeld decided he would drive us to the Stanton Street Bridge in his new Buick roadster, so we all piled in and headed downtown. The wives stayed home, but Hannah surprised me by saying that she wanted to come along. I would have thought she'd had her fill of Hipólito and me for the day, but sometimes girls are as hard to read as Mexicans, and she was all smiles and perky chatter. It was such a pleasant springlike afternoon that Mr. Sommerfeld parked the car on Paisano Street and we strolled at a leisurely pace down Stanton toward the bridge, looking into shop windows. I walked with Hannah, who took my arm and murmured a soft apology for her outbursts over lunch. She quoted Shakespeare, which always touched me.

"Do you remember, Tom, from *Richard II?* ' 'Tis not the trial of a woman's war, the bitter clamor of two eager tongues . . .' "

I whispered in her ear: "I love you, Hannah."

Her father and Sam Ravel walked behind us with Hipólito, still talking politics. We had just stopped at an intersection to let an automobile pass. I wasn't even aware of what was going on . . . I don't think anyone was. Two men stood across the street from us in front of a notions store, and it looked as if they were having a hot argument. Hannah and I started walking toward them—it just happened to be the direction we were heading. At first I thought they were both American officers from the post. One of them was a tall, suntanned man with smartly creased cavalry twill trousers and a silver bar on his epaulet—a handsome devil. The other looked to be a Mexican, although he was dressed in U. S. Army summer khakis without any insignia. Then the Mexican broke off the argument and reached into the officer's holster. Before the officer could do a thing, the Mexican skinned out faster than an ant from a burning log and was moving rapidly toward us. The barrel of his pistol came up level in the direction of me and Hannah.

I thought, This is crazy. There's a madman loose in town. Or maybe he was drunk. I grabbed Hannah and tried to push her out of the way. At the same time she grabbed me, just trying to hang on for protection; so we collided and danced a little foxtrot on the sidewalk. And while that was going on, the officer, a lieutenant, came galloping with blood in his eye after this demented fellow who had snatched his pistol. A few other people on the sidewalk ducked into storefronts or behind parked cars. In El Paso, over the years, they'd had plenty of practice.

Several things happened at once. Hannah disentangled herself but didn't scream or run away. Later she claimed that she knew the madman wasn't looking to shoot *her*. And although he had the pistol steady now, he hesitated. She was too close to me, and she was quite right—she wasn't his target. Then we were both shoved roughly to one side as Hipólito and Sam Ravel stepped in front of us. Ravel had a black .22 revolver in his hand that he must have carried in a shoulder holster under his white linen jacket.

"I'll shoot you if you don't drop that," he said in a piercing voice, and you'd be a fool not to realize he meant it. Before the Mexican could digest that and react, the lieutenant reached him on the run and snapped a hand down on his wrist.

"You dumb sonofabitch!" he yelled. He wrenched the pistol from him. The man's face seemed to twist with as much anguish as pain.

Then I recognized him . . . he was the schoolteacher who had approached me in the stockyard at Torreón, begging for his and his brother's lives. How could he be alive? But he was there on Stanton Street in El Paso, and of course it soon got through to my numbed brain that one man in that last batch of thirteen had made it over the fence. This was the man.

Bosques, I remembered. Miguel Bosques . . . the name had stuck in my memory like a poisoned thorn. His words had haunted me, but now there were more than words to do that. He stood before me as a living accusation. If he spoke now, how in God's name could I reply?

The lieutenant, his face drained of color, had his pistol pressed tightly into Bosques' ribs. Bosques fixed me with a look of pure hatred. Ravel stepped forward, brandishing his .22.

"What the hell is this all about, Lieutenant?"

"I apologize," the lieutenant said, still white beneath the rosy tan. "Lieutenant George Patton, Thirteenth Cavalry, Fort Bliss. I know you. You're Samuel Ravel."

Then he turned, more ice than fire, although he spoke in a high-pitched voice. "Is your name Captain Mix? Do you recognize this man?" He nudged Bosques with his pistol.

If I had said I didn't, I think the lieutenant would have taken Bosques off and staked him to an anthill.

"Yes, I know him," I said. "From Torreón."

Lieutenant Patton's expression didn't match the one on Bosques' face, but it made me feel less like a major than ever before.

"You're a brave young lady," he said to Hannah. "You put yourself in risk a moment ago. I'll tell you one thing—the man isn't worth it." He holstered his pistol and faced Bosques. "Consider yourself under arrest. Keep your mouth shut and come with me." Then he clamped Bosques' arm and marched him out of there, across the street and in the other direction from the bridge.

Hannah looked pale now, and her father had taken her by the waist and was supporting her. Ravel gazed after Bosques and Lieutenant Patton as they disappeared around a corner. Slipping the .22 back under his jacket, he turned on me.

"For God's sake, what was *that* about?"

Sweat had broken from all my pores. Bosques had kept his mouth shut, but I didn't know what to say. I surely wasn't going to tell them the story of Rodolfo Fierro's massacre of the prisoners and the part I had played in it.

"Come on, Tom! They knew your name!"

I stiffened even more, deciding there was only one good way to handle this. "Mr. Ravel, it's a long story, and not a very pretty one. I don't want to talk about it."

Then Hipólito stepped forth to have his say, quietly enough, but everyone heard him.

"I will tell you one thing, señores. Forgive me, Tomás—I think it is necessary to speak. That man was a prisoner in Torreón. And, in a manner of speaking, we let him go. You see, miss? That is probably why my brother shoots them. We let that one go, and now he wishes to kill Tomás. Since he is Mexican," he added, "he will never stop trying."

13

**"Fortune brings in some boats
that are not steered."**

So Torreón still haunted me. It began to seem that I would never be
free. . . .

A few days later word got through that the women had at last
arrived in Chihuahua City, coming up on a special train from Jiménez.
That night, guitars must have twanged and bedsprings creaked all over
the city. I needed to get down there. Rosa would be looking for me, and
I didn't want her to come north to Juárez or El Paso. I couldn't handle
that. Thinking back, I don't see how I handled the situation *at all,* considering my youth and inexperience in such matters. It wasn't finesse, it
certainly wasn't foresight, and I have to spring to my own defense and
make it clear that I wasn't in any sense keeping my options open. No, I
was acting out of simple need. It was wartime—even if there was a long
lull now in the fighting, while Villa solidified his hold in northern Chihuahua—and wartime is a poor stage for high moral decisions. The normal rules of life just don't seem to have much sticking power.

The incident on Stanton Street had turned me nervous as a teased
snake. Besides Rodolfo Fierro there was now a second man in this
world, close at hand, who had reason to kill me—and for this man I
couldn't dredge up any blame or vows of bold defense. Miguel Bosques
had no way of knowing that my hesitation with Fierro's last pistol had
helped to save his life. When I was honest with myself too, I knew how
flimsy an argument that would have been against his rage. In his eyes I
had helped to kill two hundred men, one of whom had been his brother.
The shame of that act marked me, and I couldn't help wondering if
Bosques had been spared to bring about some awful form of retribution.
Divine or not, I had to fight against it. Sam Ravel did some sleuthing
among his friends and told me that Bosques had been put in the guardhouse at Bliss for two months' detention, which gave me about as much
comfort as a barbed-wire fence gives shade. One day soon, when this
was over, I would be living in El Paso—good God, it was *home!*—and he
would be there. If Ravel knew any more details about why Bosques
hated me enough to shoot me down, he didn't say. Neither did I.
Hannah sulked when I refused to talk about it. I told her I'd be back in a
week or two. Let sleeping dogs lie, I thought. But make sure they don't
jump up and bite.

When I reached Chihuahua City I went straight to the Hotel Fermont, which was now official headquarters of the Northern Division's
general staff. Candelario was there with Yvette and Marie-Thérèse, and
he took time out from his reunion to peer out the door of his room,
bleary-eyed and sweaty-haired, and tell me that Rosa was in the soldiers' camp in the suburbs of the city called Las Granjas. He had wanted

her to come to the Fermont, but she had refused. When I asked him why, he gave me a sharpish look with his good eye and said, a little sternly, "She's only a child, Tomás. Children don't like to go places alone."

"But she—she could have—"

"Go find her, you fool." He shut the door in my face.

I took the rebuke. Poor girl, without me she had no status, no rights. And she *was* a child. I felt awful. It was nearly three months since I'd seen her and I had just assumed she was all right, that she could get by on her own. She was among her own people, so why shouldn't she? Because, I realized, she believed that she belonged to me, and the fact that I hadn't accepted it as a reality didn't make it any less true for her. I hurried out to Las Granjas, taking a mule-drawn streetcar and then striding the last mile on a dusty road under a hot sun, so that I arrived at the encampment sweating. I found her without any trouble. She was sitting cross-legged in the shade of an adobe hut, scratching something in the dust in front of her. I stopped for a minute, before she looked up and saw me, and gazed at her. I tried to look at her for that minute as a man might who didn't know her. She had something of the same forlorn look that I had seen when I first met her by the lake in Ascensión: head bowed, thick black hair spilling down past her shoulders. But when she raised her head I didn't see a terrified Indian waif. I saw a nubile adolescent girl, eyes suddenly alight with pleasure bordering on joy, as if she had just come downstairs at Christmas and found her heart's desire under the tree. A great ripe calmness seemed to flow from her, surround and infuse her.

She rose gracefully as I held out my arms. And then the sweet child jumped into them and held me tightly, body hot against mine. A little moan broke from her lips.

"Rosa . . ."

"*Oui, c'est moi,*" she said. "*Comment allez-vous, mi capitán? Tu m'a manqué . . . Quand est-ce que tu est arrivé?*"

Then she looked up at me shyly.

My mouth hung open. "What did you say?"

"I said I missed you. I was glad to see you. I am happy to see you." She began to laugh. "When did you get to Chihuahua City, Tomás?"

"But you spoke in French! Wasn't it French?"

"Marie-Thérèse taught me. It was such a long time waiting for you in Jiménez . . . there was nothing else to do. I don't know much. A few words. I practiced what I would say. I memorized it. I won't speak it again if it displeases you," she said, as she saw my face growing cloudier all the time. "But if you would teach me some English, *mi capitán,* that would please me most of all. What good will French do me? Who can I speak to? Wouldn't you like it if I spoke English to you?" Her smile had vanished. "Don't be angry with me, please. I know I am a foolish girl. . . ."

I wasn't angry, and she certainly wasn't foolish. She was wonderful. The cloud was one of astonishment. I had always seen her as a simple Indian girl who shared my bed and took care of my needs and comforted me, and who would wait for me in the docile manner of her race, even if she claimed to drink horses' blood for breakfast. I had known that in time she would grow into a woman, although I hadn't believed I would be around to witness it. Grow, yes. But I hadn't known she would *change*.

"Let's go back to the hotel, Rosa. I have a room there."

Two hours later she was in my arms again, and two minutes after that, with the shades drawn against the afternoon sun, we were peeled down to the buff and between the sheets, her fur all wet and brown belly bucking. Should that have shamed me? For one thing, I was horny. For another, after my nightly sessions on the Sommerfeld davenport and the encounter with Bosques, Rosa was an island of wholesomeness in an ocean of personal lunacy. We stayed in that room for the better part of two days, consoling each other in the way God seemed to have had in mind all along when He tore the rib out of Adam. She never asked about Hannah and whether I had seen her in El Paso, and I never said a word. I had told Hannah I would be back in two weeks. I knew I had some thinking to do until then.

Rosa had asked me something, and I didn't forget. One evening we were sitting in our favorite *ostioneria,* eating a bucket of fresh shrimp and oysters, when I suddenly leaned forward across the little wooden table and said: *"Este es* a plate. *Y este es* a spoon. *Aqui,* a fork. What you're eating is an oyster. *Te gusta?* You like it?"

She nodded solemnly and repeated the words. She mixed up fork and spoon, but on the second try she got it right.

Back in the hotel I produced a notebook, a fountain pen, a bottle of ink and two sharpened pencils I had bought that morning in a nearby *libreria.* I handed them to her.

"You want to learn to read and write. If I can, I'll teach you."

She seemed a little stunned. In Mexico you only learned to read and write if you were in school, and no one from the Tarahumara villages of the high sierra had ever seen the inside of a school, much less been enrolled in one. Moreover, if you learned, you learned from a teacher, a real teacher. If a man was fortunate enough to know how to read and write, it was considered beneath his dignity, and a waste of time as well, to teach the art to a woman. He was supposed to teach her to obey and to please him in bed; the rest would only spoil her. I knew that was why she hesitated.

"I haven't got a book for you yet," I said, "but next time I'm in El Paso I'll find one. You'll have to do most of the work on your own. The alphabet, the beginning stuff, isn't hard for me to teach. I know you can learn it."

Still she didn't say anything. I think she knew it would change her life. It would make her a person she hadn't been born to become, and that's a frightening prospect for anyone—man or boy, girl or woman. I knew, because it was happening to me there in Mexico: I was moving further and further off the path of my life as I'd thought it ordained when I was a youth and left home to be a cowhand and rodeo rider. We all want to change and grow, but we prefer it to happen gradually, when we're not looking. To will it, and know we will it, is like stepping off a familiar road to climb a high mountain. There may be a paradise waiting on the far slope, but you know it's a hard journey beckoning, and you may be lost before you can ever reach that slope . . . if it truly exists.

"It would please me, Rosa," I said. "If you want to, you can do it. And then you'll have pleased yourself. That's the best thing you can do in life."

She picked up the notebook and with her fingers began to leaf the pages. They fell open, and she ran her fingertips on the smooth white page, empty but for the ruled lines. That was like her life. If she wanted to, she could fill it with whatever composition she liked. Her fingertips stroked the page. She stroked it the way she stroked my body, gently and with wonder. Then she looked up. Her dark brown eyes were a little filmy, not wet but blurred ever so slightly with some soft shine.

I still remember her eyes that way . . . even now . . . full of the deepest pleasure, aglow with love, with gratitude and grave promise.

"I will try, Tomás," she said. "Yes, I will please myself."

The next morning, after Rosa's lesson, the chief called me to his suite. Candelario and Urbina were there, and then Rodolfo Fierro entered, silver spurs jingling. His presence never worried me as long as Villa was in the vicinity, and today he hardly glanced at me.

"Chief, I have good news," Fierro said. His usually mild brown eyes gleamed with excitement. "Don Luisito still claims that he has no money. But now he also says that he knows where there is some."

"And where might that be?" Villa inquired.

"In one of the steel columns in the Banco Minero de Chihuahua. One of the columns is full of gold. The Spanish bankers hid it there when they left—it was too heavy to carry. But—and this is the problem— Don Luisito doesn't know which column."

"Are you sure?"

Fierro shrugged his sloping shoulders. "I had a long talk with him, while Lieutenant Dozal put a rope around his neck. Under the circumstances, I don't think he lied."

I knew a little bit about this matter. Don Luis Terrazas had been one of the richest men in all Mexico, and in the early days of the revolution, more than a year ago, we had rustled his beef and sold it to Felix Sommerfeld. Knowing that Villa hated him because of his wealth, he fled Chihuahua City as soon as Juárez surrendered. He was now in El Paso, where he rented the estate of Senator Albert Fall of New Mexico, whose later claim to fame would be the scandal of Teapot Dome. One of Terrazas' sons, Luis Jr., whom they mockingly called "Don Luisito" even though he was in his early fifties, had stayed behind. He was supposed to be slightly dimwitted and had tried to convince Villa that he was really sympathetic to the revolution and not responsible for the way his father had tortured the peasants and accumulated his millions. "In that case," Villa said, "contribute all your money to our cause." But Don Luisito wept and claimed he had nothing, only the silk shirt on his back and his good name.

Villa at first tried to ransom Don Luisito to the old man for $150,000, but Don Luis replied: "Not a peso." Don Luisito wept again when he heard that. Then Villa sent Fierro and Dozal to have that little talk with him.

"Anything's possible," Villa said now. "Let's go to the Banco Minero and find out for ourselves. Get some engineers and an electric drill. If the sonofabitch is lying, we'll shoot him." He picked up his pith helmet and set it at a jaunty angle on his head.

So it came about that Candelario, Urbina, Fierro and Juan Dozal, whom I knew from the Torreón stockyards and who was now Fierro's aide, piled with me and Villa into the Packard and were driven by the chauffeur, Martín Lopez, to the Banco Minero de Chihuahua on the Paseo Bolivar. Villa ordered the bank closed for the day. After some soldiers had herded the confused clerks and customers out the door, Dozal locked it from the inside. The soldiers were told to stay by the car. While we waited for the engineers to arrive, we examined the huge steel columns. There were three rows of three columns supporting the high ceiling, on which was painted a fading mural showing the Spanish conquistadores, led by a fair-bearded, blue-eyed, armored Hernán Cortés driving a near-naked Moctezuma and his Aztec warriors into the lake of Tenochtitlán, which in those days was the name for Mexico City.

Villa grunted with annoyance. "Now you know who built this fucking bank. I wish I could spit that high. But since I can't . . ."

He pulled out his pistol and fired a single shot that struck the painted image of Cortés in the left eye. The echo reverberated through the empty bank.

"Now he looks like you, Candelario."

Urbina went round, tapping each column with the butt of his pistol. It was early enough in the morning for him to be still sober. "They all sound solid."

Finally the two engineers arrived with a big electric drill, and Villa told them to plug it in.

"Where do you want us to drill, my general?"

"Will this thing go through steel?" Villa asked.

"Slowly, my general, but yes, it will."

"Show me how it works."

The engineer snapped on the drill. It whined and buzzed, biting easily into some marble in front of a teller's window. Then he flicked the switch and it whined to a stop.

"You can go now," Villa said. "Leave the drill."

The engineers looked puzzled, but they saluted and left the bank. Dozal again locked the door.

He and Candelario did the drilling under Villa's watchful eye, while Fierro, Urbina and I hovered behind him. It just didn't seem possible that any one of those massive steel columns could be hollow and contain something so elusive as gold, and it occurred to me that Don Luisito might be more dimwitted than anyone realized. They went right down the first row of columns, drilling holes both low and high to make sure. On the first column the drill bit snapped off before it was an inch into the steel. Fortunately the engineers had left their toolbox with spare bits, and Dozal unscrewed the broken one and inserted a thinner, sharper bit.

It took nearly an hour to inspect the first three columns. A second bit snapped off, and Dozal screwed yet another one in its place.

"That sonofabitch!" Urbina cried. He turned to Fierro. "For Christ's sake, how badly did you torture him?"

"He swore on the cross," Fierro said stolidly.

"That cost him nothing. This is his way of getting a quick death."

"Wait." Villa's command brought them immediately to silence. "Shut up, all of you."

He studied the remaining six columns, his eyes narrowing to half-blind slits. I remembered how he had studied the wall and the shadows in Juárez before he fired at the empty cartridge. Both Dozal and Candelario were dripping sweat, for Villa had ordered the windows closed. The bank was like a hot, airless mausoleum.

"Try that one . . ." Villa pointed to the last column in the middle row.

I don't know how he knew, and I don't think he could have told anyone. He smelled it, or he had the kind of calculating mind that no other man in the room could understand. Candelario did the drilling. After the new bit had whined its noisy way through less than half an inch of steel about two feet off the floor, it suddenly made a different sound.

"That's it!" Villa yelled, and Candelario flipped the switch. "Bore some more holes in a half-circle around the column. . . . Not too deep! Be careful! Rodolfo, go outside and get a shovel—anything that's heavy. Something that we can swing."

Fierro ran outside the bank and was back with a pickaxe just as Candelario finished a neat half-circle of holes. Fierro stepped forward eagerly, but Villa halted him with one stiff hand and grasped the pickaxe with the other. He was like a torero who couldn't think of giving up the kill, the moment of truth, to any others of his troop. He swung the pickaxe sideways, powerfully but not wildly, as a batter tries to hit a clean line drive to center field. The flat of the curved blade struck the column exactly where the holes had been drilled. The column split and crumbled. Under the thin steel layer there was only plaster.

Gold pieces popped out as if someone had thrown them . . . striking the marble floor, rolling and jingling.

Urbina scooped one up. "Pancho! For the love of God," he cried, "Hit it again!"

Villa swung a second time. The column split wide open, and gold streamed out in a smoky cloud of plaster dust, piling itself at our feet in heaps. Some of the glittering coins rolled merrily along the marble, but no one chased them. There was a hole in the column as big as a man's head. Villa dug his fist in. He opened his fingers and began to scoop out gold. There were ten-peso pieces about the size of an American dime, and Spanish gold peseta pieces of varying sizes, gleaming richly on the floor and in our palms as nothing else does in this world but gold. Urbina's eyes nearly exploded from their sockets. He sifted the coins back and forth in his calloused hands, listening to the heavy clink as they slid against each other. Villa kept scooping, reaching down into the hollow column as the gold kept tumbling from above, then shoveling it out onto the floor in larger and larger shining bursts. Finally it seemed that he had it all. But he stopped, concentrated for a minute as he had done before, then reached up into the column with one hand. We heard his knuckles rap some hard surface. He turned back to us, eyes alive with the passion of the hunter.

"Rodolfo, go out and get heavy sacks—as many as you can find. Tell no one what's happened. Candelario, I think there's another partition in the top half of the column. Drill another half-circle. About here." He tapped the steel column at the level of his head.

After fifteen minutes of Candelario's sweaty work, Villa struck again with the pickaxe. With three blows he opened a second hole . . . and yet more gold poured out, far more than had been in the bottom half. Falling from a greater height, it jingled and chimed on the marble floor, some of it rolling halfway across the bank. A couple of pieces dropped into my boot. I pulled them out. The second hoard was all Yankee twenty-dollar gold pieces, stamped with the screaming bald eagle. Urbina said, "Mother of God!" His face twisted with emotion.

Fierro and Dozal returned with the sacks. Most of them were stenciled FLOUR, PROP OF U S GOVT. Working together for half an hour, down on our knees on the cool marble, we filled thirty-two sacks.

Out of breath, Urbina massaged his aching rheumatic shoulders. "Pancho, how much do you think it is?"

"We'll find out later. What we'll do now is bring it back to the

Fermont. No one will speak about this. Only the seven of us will know. If any one of you tells another man—I don't care which one of you—I'll have him shot. This will be the Division's treasury. The time will come when we'll need it." He turned specifically to Urbina. "When you drink too much and feel like boasting, remember what I've just said. If anyone speaks, he signs his own execution orders." He looked at the rest of us—Fierro, Dozal, Candelario, Lopez and me—to see that we got the message too.

Fierro commandeered a truck, and it was late afternoon before we loaded the flour sacks aboard and drove back to the hotel. Lopez parked at the back entrance, and Villa ordered a laundry room on the ground floor cleared of sheets and towels. We all staggered back and forth from the truck to the room until the sacks were safely away. All of us stank with sweat, but we were elated. Villa produced a big iron padlock, snapped it on the laundry-room door, then dropped both keys into the bottom of his holster. "That's the safest place," he said. "I may be naked, but I sleep with my pistol under my pillow."

"Aren't you going to count it?" Urbina asked, amazed.

Villa eyed him idly. "What's the rush?"

The group dispersed reluctantly, and Candelario and I went to a nearby restaurant on Avenida Cuahtemoc. Candelario, who had worked the hardest, wolfed down a bowl of fish soup and then ordered a leg of mutton with potatoes.

"What do you make of this, Tomás?"

"I trust the chief," I said, spooning up my soup.

"But the others? Not Rodolfo. And Urbina, less."

"Rodolfo will do whatever Villa tells him to do. If Villa told him to put a pistol in his mouth and pull the trigger, he'd blow his brains from here to the border. Urbina . . . well, Villa has the key."

"And Lopez? We hardly know him."

"Villa will make him an officer and keep an eye on him. You'll see."

"I don't like this Lieutenant Dozal. I have only one eye, but I've trained it to see for two. He kisses Fierro's ass too much."

"He almost shot me once." For the first time I told Candelario the story of my part in the massacre of the prisoners at Torreón four months ago. He listened, fascinated. Then he shrugged.

"They would have died," he said, "one way or another."

"But it wasn't quick. It was awful."

Before I could unburden with everything else that was on my mind, Pancho Villa rolled into the restaurant and thumped down at our table, straddling the chair backwards. "Give me what's left of your mutton leg," he said. I passed my plate and he scooped up the rest of my frijoles too. Candelario's plate was as clean as if a dog had licked it. After he had eaten, Villa wriggled one of the keys to the laundry-room padlock out of his holster and slapped it down in front of me. "Go count the gold. It will take awhile. Let me know tomorrow how much there is."

"Alone?" I asked.

He glanced at Candelario. "Do you want to help him?"

"Why not?"

"All right. Both of you then. It will be quicker that way."

We left the restaurant, with Villa still gnawing on our mutton bones. Candelario, who always spoke his mind, said, "Don't be offended, Tomás, but the chief's trust in you now and then surprises me."

I was thinking the same thing. Why *did* he trust me that much? A bastard son can stray, and even princes of the blood have been known to betray their kingly fathers for the lure of gold. Perhaps it was because he had already tested me when he sent me to the border with the wagon of silver, and in our business with Ravel and Sommerfeld I had handled hundreds of thousands of dollars and never skimmed a dime. He was the kind of man to keep track of that. On the other hand, he may have looked at the alternative choices and decided he could be worse off than by picking me. Or else he thought I feared him too much to steal. If that was so, he was wrong. I didn't fear him anymore—a mistake for which I would soon pay—and although I considered myself an accomplice to murder and a faithless philanderer, I wasn't a thief. I winced at the labels I had just so casually attached to myself. What had happened to me in Mexico? It was important to understand, but I didn't know how to go about any kind of fruitful introspection. More important, what would happen to me when I left? That was easier to think about. The future always is, when you're young.

Counting the gold was a more tedious task than I had imagined. After a while the glowing pieces lost most of their meaning and all of their attraction for us, but we had time to talk, and so I asked Candelario the question that was probably troubling me more than him.

"What are you going to do when this is all over?"

"Counting the gold?"

"No, you fool. The revolution."

"I'll tell you if you promise not to laugh."

"Would you care?"

"I suppose not. All right, I'll tell you. You know I come from Camargo. I have my wife there, and four children. Two of them are sons. Frankly, I don't miss my wife, but I have great love for my children. I'm thirty-one years of age now. So—when the revolution's over I want to go back home and open a restaurant. A good restaurant, with tablecloths and real napkins, with waiters who wear white jackets." He glanced up from the gold to see if I was laughing, but I wasn't.

The rest of it spilled out of him, and I had the feeling he had never spoken of this to anyone else. "I'll run the restaurant myself. I've always wanted to eat as much as I liked and get fat . . . even fatter than Hipólito. Have you ever noticed how jolly the fat people are? That's because they don't deny themselves what they truly crave. I crave food all the time, almost as much as I crave women. Tomás, you have no idea how hungry I get . . . I think I may have a tapeworm. But I control myself, because you can't be fat and fight well. Villa can . . . but not I. And then," he said, nodding his head and scratching his beard, "and then! With the money from my restaurant I would send all my children to school and order my sons to become lawyers. There's no future in being a revolutionist—the lawyers will carve up everything. To eat well, to have educated sons who can take care of you when you're old . . . that's the only way to live." He frowned, for the constant chink of the gold coins was irritating, like a faucet that drips all night. "So now you know, and I'm pleased you didn't laugh. And what about you, Tomás?"

"I'd like to be an actor." I don't know where that came from—I had thought that ambition was dead. "But I guess I'll get married and go into business with Felix Sommerfeld."

"What kind of an actor?" he asked.

"A real actor, on the stage. Or in the movies."

"I'll pay my peso to see you. Everything is possible."

"You don't find it funny?"

"If that's what you want to do, do it. Believe me, otherwise, after the revolution you'll be bored stiff. This is a better life than you realize."

Candelario and I worked well into the evening with a few sheets of paper torn from a notebook and two stubby pencils. Around ten o'clock we were both yawning, and the work wasn't half done.

"Let's finish tomorrow," he said. "This gold bores me."

"Who would have believed that?"

"But it's so, isn't it?"

I slept with the key and my pistol under the pillow. Rosa asked what the key was for.

"The laundry room. I'm counting sheets and towels."

In the morning Rosa told me I had slept badly. "You jerked around and pulled at the covers. You talked in your sleep."

"What did I say?"

"It was in English. Once I thought you said you were cold. Is *cold* not the word for *'frio'*? You said it several times."

"I wasn't cold. Counting the sheets and towels is a great responsibility."

"Aieee . . . mi capitán!"

We made love then, and after some rolls and coffee in the restaurant, Candelario and I went back to the laundry room and began counting again. Around noon someone rattled the padlock outside, and we both drew our pistols.

"It's only me," said Pancho Villa, chuckling through the thick door. "Don't shoot."

Candelario let him in, and he sat down on a sack of gold, wriggling around until the hard edges no longer disturbed his ass.

"We have only two sacks left, chief." I wiped the sweat from my

160 /

forehead with my sleeve. The windowless laundry room was even hotter than the Banco Minero.

"How much is it so far?" Villa asked.

I studied my pieces of paper and added the last figures to the total. The pencil was pretty well chewed.

"There are four hundred fifteen thousand six hundred and sixty pesos. We've counted eighty-one thousand two hundred and twenty-five Spanish pesetas, which is about one hundred sixty thousand pesos at the bank exchange rate in El Paso. In dollars, so far, eighty-eight thousand six hundred and thirty dollars. At two pesos to the buck that's—well, it makes a grand total of about seven hundred fifty thousand pesos."

"These fucking Spaniards bled Mexico dry, didn't they?"

"And then there's the last two sacks. They're full of double eagles."

"Keep them," Villa said carelessly. He nodded at Candelario. "You take one." And then, to me, he said, "The other's yours."

"What did you say?"

"I said keep them. Are you deaf?"

I didn't know how to reply. Candelario's face held the blank expression of the desert at noon.

"Don't you want it?" Villa asked me.

"I don't know, chief. No . . . no, I really don't want it."

"You're crazy, as Hipólito always says. You could have stolen anything you wanted, but you didn't. Take it. You both worked hard." He wagged a finger at me. "If you intend to marry Sommerfeld's ugly daughter, which my brother tells me is sure to happen, you'll have to show her father something more than your nice teeth and your good posture. Just don't tell any of the others." He addressed Candelario then. "Do you accept this gift as well?"

"Why not? It's the same as stray cattle. It's bad luck to say no to good luck."

Candelario was undoubtedly thinking of getting fat in his restaurant and his sons becoming lawyers.

"Tonight you can both come here," Villa said. "Wrap the two sacks in sheets and take them away. One of you keep the spare key. I might lose mine under someone's pillow and forget whose." He grinned, showing his red teeth.

He had said it was settled, and so it was. I hadn't counted the last two sacks, but I knew there had to be at least $15,000 in each one, for they were both filled with American twenty-dollar pieces.

I was rich. There was a time in my life, not so long ago, when I thought that all I wanted was true love, high adventure and fortune. True love had come my way in the person of Hannah Sommerfeld. I suppose that the life I had been living as a Mexican revolutionist had its share of adventure—although high or low, I didn't care to say. And now I had a fortune in a flour sack. I had all a man could want. I wondered why it didn't make me feel any better. It might have been the shadow of

Torreón that took the warmth out of other things, but I suspect it was a realization—the years have only clarified it—that you're not a different man even if your bank account swells. The glow of gold merely illuminates your other worries. Sometimes I think that Mammon might have sworn an oath that nobody who didn't love money should ever have it.

That gold became a problem quicker than a man can get grassed on a mustang. Furtive as thieves, Candelario and I each carted our sacks out of the laundry room just after midnight chimed on the cathedral tower. By the time I got it up to my room in the Fermont my heart was dancing a polka and sweat dripped down my cheeks. What do you do with a sack of gold double eagles? I couldn't very well walk into the Banco Minero when the sun rose and deposit it, and it wouldn't fit under the bed. I left it sitting in the clothes closet, gave Rosa my pistol and told her to guard that closet with her life. I ran out into the hotel corridor to find Candelario, who was staying up on the fourth floor. We nearly collided with each other on the staircase, he running down and I running up.

"Jesus, Tomás! Where did you hide it?"

"That's just what I was coming to ask you."

"But this is a very weighty question. I left Yvette and Marie-Thérèse with my pistol to guard it. Let's sit down and think."

He had a full bottle of tequila with him, so we drank while we thought and came up with some pretty wild ideas, but none of them made much sense, even to a pair of drunken men on a dark hotel staircase in the short shank of the night. We thought of burying it outside of Chihuahua City, but I vetoed that with the glum idea that the tide of war might change and we would never see this part of Mexico again; we discussed carrying it south with us in our saddlebags when the army finally moved, but Candelario pointed out that if a bullet ever struck one of the saddlebags the whole battle would grind to a halt while the soldiers threw down their rifles and scrambled for the gold that would pour out like a waterfall.

"Then where, Tomás? I can't think straight."

"The gold is a curse. I read a story once in Aesop—"

"Please don't tell me stories," Candelario said. "Tell me where to keep the gold. This is a curse I can live with."

"Listen! I've got it. I know what *I'll* do. Rosa can ride like a man. It's only a hundred miles west to Tomochic, and her family's there. No one goes to Tomochic—it's up in the high sierra. She can bury my sack there."

Candelario's good eye narrowed. "You trust her this much? Are you crazy?"

After just a brief hesitation, I said, "Yes."

"Which question are you answering?"

"Was there more than one?" I asked.

"You'll have to tell her what it is. You can't say it's rocks."

162 /

"I'll tell her it belongs to the Division's treasury. So if it goes bad between us, she won't do anything foolish. She'll think Villa will know about it."

"That's not such a bad idea," Candelario decided. "You'll have to send a couple of soldiers with her to protect her."

"But then they'll know."

"We'll have them shot afterwards."

"You see what gold does to a man? If you want to kill our own soldiers, why don't you desert and fight for Huerta?"

"You really think she can make it on her own, Tomás?"

"That's Tarahumara country all the way."

Candelario studied the empty tequila bottle with great solemnity. "Why not? We'll give it to her."

"We?"

"If it's good enough for you, it's good enough for me. When can she go?"

"Tomorrow night. Bring your sack to my room."

"This is madness," he muttered. "If I wasn't drunk, I'd never agree to it."

But in the morning, sober, we agreed that it was the best solution to the problem. Candelario went out to requisition a pack mule for the gold, while I explained it all to Rosa.

"Can you do it?"

"Yes, *mi capitán,*" she said proudly. "I know a back trail through the mountain from here to Anáhuac, and from there I will cross the sierra by way of Baquiachic. I will bury the gold behind our corral and tell you exactly where."

That evening we rode with her to the outskirts of the city. We watched until her skewbald mare and the laden mule had vanished in the gathering chill of dusk, through the pass of San Martín that led to the desert.

Candelario groaned. "There goes our gold! She'll ride all the way to Guaymas and open a whorehouse. No disrespect intended, Tomás. It's not easy being rich."

"Well, if she goes to Guaymas," I pointed out, "we'll be poor again. We'll have no worries. So we can't lose."

Five days passed, and I did little but think of Rosa. It had been a mistake to send her alone into the mountains. Anything could happen. She was only a child—fifteen years old now—but I found that hard to bear in mind because she usually acted toward me as a grown woman acts toward a grown man. It was a fretful but interesting time, those five days, and I began to see that the simplicity with which I had ordered my life wasn't so simple after all. There was Hannah in El Paso; there was Rosa in Mexico. There was I, shuttling back and forth without conscience or fear of consequences. It couldn't last, and one day I would have to leave. Rosa knew that—I never lied. But that vision of my easy honesty gave me no comfort. When the time came, it would give less to Rosa. The fairest thing, I thought, would be to tell her now, to send her back to Tomochic.

But I don't want her to go. I want . . .

I don't want . . .

One day, I prayed, I'll be old and calm and wise and not want *anything,* and that will mean freedom, and I'll never be able to hurt a human being again.

In a week we would attack Torreón, which we had been forced to abandon in order to concentrate all our forces on the border. To keep them busy, Villa ordered his Dorados to drill as he had seen the American cavalry do it on the parade ground at Fort Bliss. He sent for me. "I'm going to Juárez," he said. "We need more supplies, and I've got to make sure Luz is happy in El Paso. Julio's coming, and Rodolfo and Dozal. You'll come too. You'll have a chance to say goodbye to your Jewish sweetheart."

It was a trip he should never have taken, but we had no way of knowing. "Give me another day, chief," I said nervously. Rosa was still not back from Tomochic.

"Why?"

"Just one more day. I have things to do."

"You can meet me there," he said, a little annoyed.

That evening there was a knock on my door, and when I opened it Rosa darted in, covered with dust and looking weary but pleased with herself. I hugged her for a full minute before I let her speak. I wanted her to know that she was more important to me than gold.

"The trip was nothing," she said—which wasn't true, because she'd had to cross in the darkness through the sierra at more than ten thousand feet. "It was pleasant to see my mother and sisters. The first night I went out, when all slept, and buried the sacks behind the corral." She described the location of the adobe hut and the exact hiding place. "I worked many hours to bury it, *mi capitán.*"

"Good girl. In case you forgot, I'm a major now."

"May I not still call you *mi capitán?*"

I loved her then and knew it beyond doubt.

14   **"And every tale condemns me for a villain."**

When I reached Juárez, Villa's caboose was parked as usual in the railroad yards. I found him at Hipólito's house, and we went together to see

Sam Ravel to discuss the movement of supplies. Felix Sommerfeld was away in Columbus. "That doesn't matter," Villa said afterwards. "When one Jew agrees to something, you can count on the other as well. They're brothers," he added instructively. "If not by blood, then by wallet."

The following day, after Villa had been to see Luz Corral in her new house on North Oregon Street, Juan Dozal appeared at the railway caboose, bringing word from an Englishman named William Benton who wanted the favor of an audience. "It has something to do with his land," Dozal explained. "He found me in a whorehouse last night, so naturally we couldn't discuss it at length. He wants to come this evening."

Villa scratched his jaw thoughtfully. "I know of this Englishman. He owns a ranch south of Juárez. He always had the protection of Luis Terrazas, but now he's out of luck. He has a bad temper, and he's a stubborn man. Why should I meet with him? Can't you handle it? Nothing good can come of it."

"He was very pleasant in the whorehouse."

"Most men are, Juanito."

Villa frowned and started to shake his head. At that point he was one breath away from saying no. That would have been the right decision. But how was he to know it? How were any of us to counsel him? He should never have come to Juárez in the first place; but who can know the future? It seemed to be of minor significance, whether or not he granted an audience to an aggrieved English landowner in Chihuahua. History often turns on such casual shakes or nods of the head, and I've sometimes thought that the earth may only be what it is because of a series of unconnected and casual nods. But perhaps that's not so; perhaps our natures are condemned to find a way of expressing themselves . . . and if we say no to our fate on Monday, we'll find ourselves saying yes on Tuesday.

"All right," Villa said, sighing, as though surrendering to something. "Tell him he can come. But he'll have to leave his pistol at home."

Dozal nodded and then left.

In the late evening Juana Torres broiled tenderloin steaks in the kitchen of the caboose. Villa picked a few bits of well-done meat off every man's platter and made that his dinner. At eleven o'clock Dozal arrived with the man he had described as an Englishman—Mr. William Benton. He was about fifty-five, a wizened, sunburned man with small snapping eyes. The first thing I noticed was that, contrary to Villa's request, he wore a gun belt and pistol. Benton, too, was in the grip of his nature—and his doom. But Villa said nothing about it, so I relaxed.

Benton spoke perfect Spanish, though with an odd accent. He had lived in Chihuahua for thirty years, he told us, and he had paid hard cash to Don Luis Terrazas for his ranch and some tin mines. He had built the place up from nothing until it was worth twenty times what he'd paid for it.

/ 165

"I know your ranch," Villa said impatiently. "Hacienda de Santa Gertrudis."

"No, no. Ye dinna know it. It's called Los Remedios, near Santa Ysabel."

"What's the difference? One ranch is just like another if it's owned by an Englishman."

"In the first place," Benton bridled, "my ranch is nae like any other. And in the second place, damn it, I'm a Scotsman. From Aberdeen."

Villa laughed harshly. "All Englishmen drink whiskey until they're red in the face. All Englishmen in Mexico look down their long noses and live off Mexican oil."

Benton had a short pug nose. His dark eyes seemed to grow almost black.

"General Villa, pay attention to me," he yelled. "I don't live off bloody oil! I made that blasted desert bloom like the Scottish highlands! And then this so-called general of yours, this Urbina, came around last week and told me he was taking over! And he'd do me a bloody great favor and let me manage the place!"

Villa asked, "Did he offer you a price for your land? He was ordered to do so."

"You think I want any of this two-faces junk you people hand out? What am I supposed to do if you bloody well lose your damned revolution? It won't even be good for toilet paper, man."

Villa's eyes sparked. "You Englishmen don't—"

"I'm a Scotsman!" Benton cried. "Are ye deaf?"

"What are your political sympathies, señor?"

"If you win," the Scotsman growled, trying to calm down, "that's fine with me. If Huerta wins, I can live with that too. I speak my mind, and I'm afraid of no one. I sell my cattle to the highest bidder. No man alive can ever say I cheated him."

"Be assured I won't say it, either, señor. I'm going to pay you a fair price for your ranch and your cattle," Villa said, "and whatever the hell else you've got lying around in Santa Gertrudis. Then you can go home to London and get drunk in your club like the rest of them. And weren't you told by Juanito to leave your pistol behind tonight?"

"You're a bandit and a fool!" Flushed, Benton jumped to his feet, shouting. "And I was a bigger fool to come here! Do you think you can rob a Scotsman and get away with it, Pancho bloody Villa?"

I don't think he meant to pull out his pistol. But in his rage his hand dropped to the butt. He gripped it tightly, probably more to control his itch than anything else. Villa thought otherwise. The gun belt around his own thick waist was stuffed with gleaming steel cartridges that looked like miniature torpedoes. The handle of his pistol protruding from the scuffed holster gleamed with the polish of use, as if the warmth of his palm had given it a permanent sheen of sweat. He laid the long blue-black barrel on the table, pointed at Benton's stomach. His eyes were narrowed, and when I saw the green light in them I knew he was out of control.

"Disarm him," he said coldly to Julio.

Benton's eyes flickered and blazed . . . but he was no killer. He let Julio pry his fingers from the handle and take the pistol.

"You Englishmen!" Villa raved. "You think you can do what you please in Mexico! You count Luis Terrazas as your benefactor—that Spanish pig! I'm sure you never cheated *him,* but I'd like to hear the tales told by your *campesinos.* You came here to threaten me! No, señor! You can't do that! The man is not born who can do that to Francisco Villa!" He wheeled on Julio and Fierro. "I won't waste a good bullet. Take him out and execute him."

Benton cried, "You wouldn't dare!"

I thought it time to get my two cents in. "He wasn't going to shoot," I said sharply. "And his friends will know he came here."

Julio agreed with me. His long face twitched. "It's a bad thing, chief."

Fierro and Dozal said nothing. Villa kept his angry gaze fastened on Benton, who returned it in kind—but he spoke to me and Julio. "You don't understand these things, either of you. The harm is done. Do you think I can let a man live to boast that he called me a fool and then drew his pistol, and I did nothing?" He spun around on Fierro. "You heard me! Take him out of my sight!"

"Here in Juárez, my general?" Fierro asked carefully.

"Handcuff him," Villa said. "Go down to Samalayuca. Julio, take some soldiers to dig a grave. Tomás is right. We don't need an uproar."

"Wait, chief." I broke in again. "You can't do this."

He glared at me. "What do you mean? *What* can't I do?"

"Shoot this man in cold blood. He's not an enemy. He's not a prisoner. He didn't try to cheat you the way Wentworth did. He hasn't fought against us. You can't do it."

The glare turned his face the color of cream. I had learned that when a man's face turns red with rage, there's usually little danger of his taking violent action. But when his face turns pale, he is out of control. And this wasn't any man—this was Pancho Villa.

"You go too far, Tomás," he said softly.

I hated this. I hated my fear, but I hated even more what Villa had declared he would do.

"I can't let you kill him," I said.

Villa smirked, but not a drop of color flowed back into his cheeks. "Because he's an Englishman, Tomás? Because he's white like you?" His cold voice cut like the blade of a knife. "Is that it? You don't mind killing Mexicans, even unarmed Mexicans, but you object to killing one of your own kind. Is that what you tell me?"

Perhaps it was partly true. But only partly.

"The man is innocent," I said. "I won't let you do it."

"You're a fool. That means," Villa said, "that you'll have to die with him."

"You'd regret that, chief. I'll regret it even more, but afterwards you'll know you were wrong. You'll know I was right, and you'll hate yourself for the rest of your life."

That speech took all the courage I had. I didn't think there was anything more I could say after that. I caught Julio's eye. He was staring at me in undisguised horror. He believed I was already a dead man. Behind him, in the shadows of the hissing lamplight, Fierro regarded me with cool, impersonal eyes, but there was a flicker of anticipation in their depths. I suppose he thought he would receive the assignment, and nothing would please him more. He would keep his vow and the love of his master at one stroke. At his side, Juan Dozal looked at me scornfully.

"Give me your pistol, Tomás." Villa had still spoken coldly, with just a touch of regret. "Carefully."

I took a deep breath. "What about Benton, chief?"

"I've given my orders about Benton. I can't change them."

"Then I can't give you my pistol," I said.

I thought he would shoot me then. I had driven him too far, and for a moment he no longer knew who I was, no longer knew I was a man who had fought at his side at Torreón and Chihuahua, a man to whom he had entrusted the Division's gold and had called his illegitimate son and promoted to major in front of General Pershing. He would remember eventually, but then it would be too late.

"Disarm him too," he said, giving the order to Dozal. Now his voice quivered too. "Take him with you to Samalayuca. Get rid of him. Julio, stay with me."

Dozal moved swiftly. I was in too much of a daze to resist. And resistance would have been impossible. I hadn't known what I would do, but I knew what I couldn't do, and that was shoot Pancho Villa. I had been bluffing, and the bluff had failed—I had asked to die, and my wish was about to be granted. Dozal slipped the pistol from my holster as easily as a child is robbed of a toy.

The world seemed to grow dark; perhaps my eyes were dimmed with tears. I moved in a trance, out the door of the caboose, with Dozal, Fierro and Benton following me. A few strangled sounds came from Julio's throat, but he knew that if he objected he would become a victim of Villa's wrath as well. There were no goodbyes. Benton never said a word. He was a braver man than I. He had accepted his fate. It was crazy—all of it was crazy. But it was happening.

Still in that trance, I let myself be led to the other end of the railroad yard. In the darkness Fierro talked to some men, and five minutes later Benton and I were shoved into another caboose attached to an engine. The door slammed shut and was locked from the outside. The pitch-black caboose stank of rotting meat and old piss. I sank down in some damp straw, and almost immediately the engine shivered into life and began hauling us out of the Juárez yards, south toward Samalayuca. I couldn't see Benton's face. He was crouched only a few feet away from me, but he might as well have been on the other side of a wall.

"Be brave, laddie," he said. "Ye did the right thing. Ye have to die now, but so do we all. Yer bloody general will pay."

The right thing? I stared into the inky darkness. I felt neither courage nor fear, and I experienced no sense of satisfaction. I felt only a drowsy sadness, as if I were dead already. I didn't want to talk to Benton. He meant nothing to me, I realized. I had thrown away my life in the cause of conscience; I had failed the simple commandment of survival. Was that the right thing? I began to wonder. But it was too late.

An hour later we reached Samalayuca. The caboose jerked to a halt . . . the engine sputtered and then shuddered to silence. A bolt rasped from outside, and the door of the caboose slid open. A moon gave a bit of light now, and the charcoal gray outline of a sombrero and a man's head appeared at the door.

Dozal's voice said cheerfully, "Get out, señores."

Standing by the track, I realized that we were not in the railroad yards, but at a lonely part of the desert near the sleeping town. Stars blinked down. The stars were beautiful . . . I would never see them again. Fierro and half a dozen soldiers stood to one side, while Dozal shepherded us at pistol point to the shelter of some tall saguaro cactus. The cactus was a lovely, ghostly silvery green in the moonlight. Goodbye, Hannah. *Adios,* Rosa. Yes, life was short.

Fierro handed some shovels to the soldiers and ordered them to dig. In the dark, some twenty yards away from the cactus, the soldiers began to dig a crude trench that would serve as a grave. Benton, totally calm, peered down and said to Fierro, "Listen, amigo, make a deeper hole. The coyotes will drag me out of that one."

Perhaps he believed that his bravery would be impressive enough to save his life. He didn't know Rodolfo Fierro. For Rodolfo it was just another job of work. He nodded; the soldiers dug deeper.

"This one is mine," Dozal said happily to Fierro, digging his elbow into my ribs and waving his pistol in the moonlight. A cigarette hung from his lips, glowing cherry-red and dropping sparks. "That's what the chief ordered."

Fierro considered a minute. He had heard Villa's words too. It made no difference which one of them pulled the trigger and dispatched the bullet that would end my short life. Fierro had his reason for desiring the chore, but he must have decided that an order was an order . . . he always listened carefully to what the chief said.

"All right," Fierro said, walking off into the darkness toward the open grave where the soldiers and William Benton waited. The darkness seemed to absorb him. The moon had edged behind a lone cloud.

"Can I smoke a cigarette?" I asked Dozal. I didn't have much of an urge for one, but it seemed a proper thing to say, and it would prolong my existence for just that extra few sweet minutes.

"Well . . ."

"It's not much to ask," I said, my mind racing. Perhaps every man's mind races when he's about to die.

"All right."

"I don't have one."

"Jesus. Here. Be quick."

Dozal was a stupid man. I was a desperate one. I hadn't fully realized the extent of my desperation, or my will to live, until he gave me the opportunity. He was more than stupid. He was willing and eager to kill me; he had reminded Fierro that it was his privilege. I bore that in mind. He reached into his pocket for a crumpled pack of cigarettes, shook one halfway loose and let me take it.

"Give me a light, Juanito."

But he wasn't stupid enough. He had no matches, and in order to give me a light he would have to shove the pack into his pocket and then puff at his own weed before handing it to me. He must have realized that his hands would be occupied, and if I were rash enough to try any tricks, that would be the time for me to do it. His pistol came up level with my stomach, and with the other hand he flipped the cigarette at my feet. Even in that eerie darkness, I could see him grinning.

"Take it," he said. "Smoke fast."

My heartbeat grew violent. Oh God, I thought, I'm going to die. He'll probably shoot me when I bend down. The bones of my knees cracked and my fingers shook as I scrabbled in the dust for the end of the cigarette that wouldn't burn my fingers. I almost laughed aloud. What did it matter if they got burned? That would be the last pain I would feel before the big one. As I bent, something slipped from my shirt and dangled on the ground, glittering slightly in the faint starlight. It was the spare key that Villa had given me for safekeeping, tied round my neck by a piece of pigging string. The moon darted out for a moment, then was swallowed by its cloud.

"What's that?" Dozal asked, when he saw the glitter.

"The key to the laundry-room padlock," I said. "Where the gold is. You better take it before blood gets all over it. Blood makes keys rust."

The thought of the gold must have excited him . . . maybe deranged him. He lowered the pistol, stepped forward and made a grab. Maybe he thought I was going to throw the key away in a fit of spite. He had nothing to fear from me—Fierro and the others were twenty yards away. But if he couldn't see them in the suddenly moonless night, I realized, they couldn't see us. With both hands, as he clutched at the key, I seized his right wrist, the one with the pistol. He grunted with surprise and annoyance. I twisted the gun into his neck and then squeezed his hand as hard as I could.

The shot shattered the darkness . . . the bullet nearly tore his head off.

Off by the grave, the soldiers threw down their shovels with a dull ringing thud. Fierro called calmly from a black distance, "Good, Juanito. Bring the body over here."

"In a minute," I called back, pitching my voice higher—not difficult, under the circumstances.

I let Dozal slide to the ground, wiped my bloody hands on his shirt, then turned and bolted across the desert. Alive! It seemed a miracle. I didn't stop until I had covered half a mile. But I heard no pursuit. I didn't even hear the shot that was meant to kill William Benton. That puzzled me, until I found out later there was no shot.

I spent the next day in a small fleabag of a hotel in the area called "Little Chihuahua," on the El Paso side of the border. I didn't know what to do. I was glad to be alive, but it seemed that I had no reasonable life worth living. I contacted no one I knew, not even Hannah or my family. I didn't dare go back to Hipólito's house—his loyalties might have been divided if he knew what had happened, but not divided evenly. For a time I thought of heading east to the Brazos and starting a new life in the cattle country under another name. I didn't do that. There was Hannah to think about, and there was Rosa back in Chihuahua City. Finally I decided it was time to talk to someone, and I chose Sam Ravel. He was a man of savvy and experience. After a decent night's sleep I went to a barber shop, paid a nickel and soaked under a hot shower so that I looked halfway presentable, took a streetcar to Cleveland Square and walked into Sam's office in the Toltec Building around ten o'clock in the morning. It was pleasantly furnished with some plaques and souvenirs of his days as a Texas Ranger. Some beautiful red Navajo carpets had been stitched together to form a bigger carpet. Sam looked grim.

"Where the hell have you been?"

"That's what I came to talk about, Sam."

"What happened with William Benton?"

"That's a long story," I said.

"You'd better damn well tell it to me." His hawk's eyes glittered. "Benton left a note with some friends. He told them where he was going. Now it's rumored that he was shot in Samalayuca. The American consul in Juárez wants to see Pancho Villa. He also happens to be Mr. Wilson's personal representative here on the border."

"What does the American consul have to do with it?" I asked. "Benton was a Scotsman."

"*Was?* So you *do* know!" Ravel leaned across the desk, clasping my wrist. "Listen, Tom—I'll tell you something about the English. You can murder a man in the streets of London, and whether you're a Mexican or a Turk, all they'll do is hang you for it. But if you murder an Englishman abroad, they send gunboats and the Royal Marines, and they've been known to declare war if it suits the course of empire. Now they've dumped it in Mr. Wilson's lap. He's hopping up and down."

I trusted Sam Ravel and had come here to tell him all that had happened. And so, finally, I did.

"Good God," he said softly, when I had finished. "I guessed most of it, but not the part about you. No one's spoken about you. I've seen Hipólito. He didn't say a word."

"Maybe he didn't know."

"Tell me this, Tom. In the caboose, with Villa, was Benton going to pull the pistol?"

"I didn't think so. But Villa did."

Just then Ravel's office boy came in with the afternoon paper, the *Herald.* It had black banner headlines that read: PANCHO VILLA REPORTED TO HAVE MURDERED LOCAL ENGLISHMAN. It also said that Mr. Marion Letcher, President Wilson's man on the border, had been ordered to investigate the incident. The story quoted from the French and British newspapers in Paris and London, whose editorials were screaming for Pancho Villa's head on a plate.

"This does it," Ravel said, slamming the paper down on his desk. "If he denies it and they catch him out, he's finished. But if he does confess, he'd better have a damned good story. And witnesses." He looked at me keenly. "What are you going to do?"

I hadn't known until then. But now it seemed fairly clear.

"I'm going back to see Villa."

Ravel's look became even more searching. "Tom, you can't do that. He'll kill you. He said he would, and now you've shot one of his officers to boot."

"I think he'll have cooled down about that by now. I think he'll need me."

"You're insane."

"No. It's the only thing I can do. It's the only thing that makes sense."

"Not to me, my boy."

"Well, I know him better than you, Sam."

Did I? I would soon find out. Maybe I *was* insane. I was certainly betting my life on it.

"One favor, Sam. Don't tell Hannah what happened—to me. I don't think she'd understand."

"Do *you?*"

* * *

A few soldiers stood guard about the red caboose in the Juárez railway yards. The last time I'd been here, I remembered, I had thought my short life was at an end. Whatever happened now, I had picked up a few days of existence that I wasn't supposed to have. Maybe my luck would hold. Still, after crossing the International Bridge, even though it was a cool day, I began to sweat.

The soldiers knew me and didn't know I was supposed to be dead or on the run. They saluted sloppily and I returned it, mounted the two iron steps and opened the door. The first person I saw was a man who I guessed to be Mr. Marion Letcher, the President's representative. He was ruddy-faced, plump and short, wore a gray business suit and apparently had brought Pancho Villa a telegram that had come directly from Secretary of State Bryan in Washington. When I came in, Villa had just finished telling his side of the story. He wore his butterscotch-colored jacket, and the pith helmet sat on his little desk—probably to invoke the image of Teddy Roosevelt. His stubby brown hands were tented calmly in front of him. He looked up at me.

At first he blinked a few times. His face colored a little, and he smiled sheepishly.

"Hello, chief," I said.

He cleared his throat . . . then he frowned. Perhaps it had occurred to him that I might be here as a witness for the opposition. He couldn't be sure. But what he couldn't do was shoot me to insure my silence—not in front of Letcher, who had turned to me, raising a ginger-colored eyebrow. The only other one of our officers in the caboose was Julio. He was grinning at me wildly.

"This is Major Mix," Villa announced, taking the gamble. "He was here that night. He'll swear to the truth of everything I've told you."

Letcher nodded, obviously unconvinced. "Who pronounced the sentence, General Villa?"

"I did, on behalf of the Northern Division of the Constitutionalist Army."

"And where is the body?"

"It is buried, señor."

"Can the grave be located?"

"All my graves can be located, señor."

That didn't go over too well, and Letcher frowned. He then repeated what Ravel had said, that if you killed a British citizen abroad, for whatever reason, the entire population of England, Scotland and Wales rose up in arms. "Some members of Parliament have called for the British Navy to sail," he said stiffly.

Villa chuckled. "Señor, if a British battleship sails through the desert to Chihuahua, I'll surrender immediately."

Letcher responded to this wit with a weak smile and then a demand to see the formal order of execution.

/ 173

"I've already told you what happened," Villa said. "Why do you need papers?"

"President Wilson is confident the order was in writing and in correct form."

"I want to make your President happy," Villa said enthusiastically, picking up what he thought was a broad hint. "I'll have them for you this evening. Major Mix will deliver them."

Letcher, somewhat confused, finally left. Villa turned to me, laughing.

"Tomás, write up some good papers that I can sign. Make them very legal, with 'aforesaids' and 'therefores.' Lots of seals. Use the typewriter." Then he stopped, got to his feet, waddled swiftly round the desk and threw his arms around me. "Jesus Christ, I'm glad to see you. You're like Lazarus! I can't tell you how glad I am!" When he stepped back, I saw his eyes were dewy with tears.

"It's all right, chief," I said.

"You forgive me?" he said hoarsely.

"I wouldn't be here if I hadn't forgiven you. But it wasn't easy. If the moon hadn't gone behind a cloud, and if Dozal hadn't been so stupid, and if Rodolfo had decided to do the job himself . . ."

"I know, I know. You were right," he groaned. "I would have hated myself for the rest of my life! I knew it an hour after you had left, when I came back to my senses. But it was too late then. I sent Julio to the yards to stop them. You had gone. Tell him that it's so, Julio."

"He sent me," Julio confirmed. "I wanted to ride after you, but I knew I couldn't catch the train."

"I'm sorry about Dozal," I said. "I wouldn't have killed him if it wasn't necessary. And if the sonofabitch hadn't been so glad to get the job."

"Fuck Dozal," the chief said. "The only one who cares about him is Rodolfo."

As if on cue, Rodolfo Fierro stepped through the door, ducking his head so that his Stetson wouldn't scrape the door frame. When he looked up and saw me, he stiffened.

"Tomás is back," Villa said flatly. "And I rescind my order to kill him. Do you hear me?"

Fierro said nothing. He stared at me with apparent calm, but I knew what emotions he must have been fighting to control.

"If you shoot him," Villa added, shoving a finger in his chest—"and I mean for any reason whatever, including things that may or may not have happened in the past—I'll hang you by your *cojones* from the tallest tree in Mexico. I'll hang you until your tongue turns black and you beg for a quick death. And then I'll have you shot. Do you understand?"

Fierro still said nothing.

"Do you understand?" Villa shouted.

"Yes, chief," Fierro whispered.

So I had been reprieved, not just from the death that had been ordained three nights ago in the caboose, but from the death that had been sworn in Ascensión. Life was certainly full of twists and odd turns. I had been saved from two deaths, and I had my honor intact. I was almost ready to cry from gladness.

Villa winked at me and then turned back to Fierro. He had remembered why we were there. He still had to resolve the problem of William Benton.

"Listen, Rodolfo—pay attention. I've made some promises to this American consul, or whoever he is. Can you find the Englishman's body? Because if you can't, you can start digging a hole for yourself."

Fierro, for the first time that I had ever noticed, looked shamefaced. He actually blushed. He took off his Stetson again and smoothed his black hair. He shuffled his feet.

"Oh, Jesus." Villa grew pale. "What is it?"

"Chief, I can find the grave. That's no problem," Fierro said. "But I didn't shoot the man. I remembered your saying that he wasn't worth a bullet. So after the soldiers dug the grave deeper, as the old *inglés* requested, and after the unfortunate death of Juanito, I picked up a shovel and hit Señor Benton over the head." He cleared his throat uncomfortably. "And, obligingly, he fell into the grave."

Villa gasped, digging his nails into the wood of the table. *"Alive?"*

"I doubt it," Fierro said cautiously. "I hit him hard."

"You doubt it? You didn't look?"

"It was very dark, my general."

Villa's big curly head sank like a rock into his hands, so that he was staring into blackness. He was making one of his rare efforts to control himself, and if it had been any man but Rodolfo Fierro, I think he would have shot him immediately for such craziness. Finally he looked up. His fury had ebbed, but he spoke coldly.

"Go to Samalayuca—tonight. Dig up the body. Pray to God, in whom I doubt you believe, that you didn't bury him alive. But either way, alive or dead, shoot him wth a rifle through the heart. Shoot him three or four times, from about ten paces. Then take the body down to Chihuahua City." He turned to me. "Tomás, get started on the papers. Say that there was a trial with four staff officers present. Say that one of them was appointed to defend the accused man. Say anything you please . . . but for the love of God, make it sound good! Then add an account of the execution, which took place in Chihuahua City, and say that after he was shot he was given a blow on the head—an act of mercy—in case the poor man was still by chance alive. God in heaven! Do it now, Tomás, please. And you, Rodolfo . . . get out of my sight, and for Christ's sake do exactly as I told you. Don't use your famous initiative."

/ 175

Fierro, almost trembling, left the caboose.

The chief tried to smile at me, to make light of it, but his smile slowly drained away. Julio came over and squeezed my shoulder. "You're back from the dead, Tomás."

"Let's get drunk tonight," I said, "and celebrate my revival."

I worked most of the afternoon on the papers, drafting them by hand and then typing them slowly on Villa's banged-up portable Remington. He signed them, and so did the rest of the Division's staff officers there in Juárez, excepting Fierro, who was away on his ghoulish mission. Then I delivered the papers to Mr. Letcher.

I was still troubled by a reason just a hairbreadth away from my grasp, and I decided to talk to Sam Ravel about it. His sympathies for Pancho Villa weren't going to be dampened by a single murder—they would only fade if the murder were discovered in all its gruesome detail. I went round to his house on Fort Boulevard and caught him just as he was about to go to bed.

"You're alive," he said.

"Seems that way."

"You're awfully lucky, Tom."

"So far," I said. "You never know what's round the bend."

He sat with me on the porch, wearing his striped flannel pajamas and a silk bathrobe, while we drank a brandy in the cool night air and I told him the rest of the story. As I got near the end, he gasped. He jumped to his feet.

"Oh, my God! Do you know what will happen when that body's delivered here?"

"That's what I came to ask you, Sam."

"They'll have an autopsy! They'll see that the bullet wounds didn't bleed. And if Benton suffocated in that grave, they'll learn that too! Tom, go back right now. Do anything that's necessary . . . but stop Villa before it's too late."

I found the chief in the caboose, munching on a chocolate bar. When I told him what I had done, he groaned.

"You were right. I shouldn't have had him shot in the first place. And you were right to talk to Ravel. But now . . ." His swollen hands fluttered in the air, the fingers stained with chocolate. "I don't know what to do. . . ."

"Can't you find a Mexican law that says, after proper burial, it's not permitted to disturb the dead?"

"There must be such a law somewhere."

"And then get some doctor in Chihuahua to say he performed an autopsy *before* the burial. With the correct results."

"I'll get four doctors. That's good, Tomás."

"And something else. The English recognize the Huerta government, don't they?"

"Yes. The bastards."

"If they don't recognize your authority, what right do they have to meddle in your affairs? Deal only with the Americans. They'll make plenty of fuss, but it'll die down after a while. At least we'll hope so."

He gave me a chocolate-smelling hug, but when we disengaged he looked despairing again. "Why should this happen to me? I'm just a simple soldier. I want to do the right thing, but there are so many choices to make. Look, I almost had you shot! My head buzzes sometimes like a hornet's nest." Tears filmed his eyes. "Protect me from myself, Tomás. . . ."

I doubted I had the wisdom and strength to do that. And I didn't know how to comfort him.

Later that night a distraught Carranza telegraphed him from Nogales, and Villa mournfully telegraphed back with most of the details. For once they were linked in something: the revolutionary cause shouldn't suffer because of one hacienda owner's death, even if he happened to be a Scotsman. The First Chief instructed Villa not to permit any investigating commission to enter Mexico; that would violate its sovereignty as an independent nation. He would take the heat off, as best he could. He begged Villa not to speak with reporters, and Villa promised gladly. That was the last thing he wanted to do.

"Maybe old Don Venus isn't so bad after all," he murmured.

Rodolfo Fierro came back in the morning like a dog who had rolled in the mud all night. He gave a full report; he had done everything exactly as instructed. It looked to him as if Benton had been killed by the blow with the shovel—but of course he had to say that. The only problem was that rigor mortis had set in. After they managed to remove the handcuffs, they couldn't bend the arms back to Benton's sides without breaking them.

"Get out of here," Villa said wearily.

But the Benton scandal wouldn't die. Letcher wasn't at all pleased when I visited his office and told him that an obscure law signed by Benito Juárez back in 1859 wouldn't allow the body to leave the country. I moved back in with Hipólito. Hannah, whom I finally visited to explain my long absence, but to whom I didn't tell the tale of my near execution, was enraged. Bright pink spots appeared on her cheeks.

"I think," she said, "if you're still determined to see this through to the end, you should offer your services to Obregón."

"Hannah! How could I do that?"

"Isn't he a revolutionist too? And a more honest one than Pancho Villa!"

"I'm loyal to Villa." More loyal, I thought, than you'll ever know.

"But *why*, Tom?"

Why indeed. There was a question that needed pondering, but the answer was so simple that it brooked any sensible debate. I was loyal because I had offered my loyalty and it had been accepted. The bargain had been struck a long time ago, in Juárez, and then sealed when I had taken his captain's commission and gone into battle at his side in Torreón. I still believed he was the only one who could lead the revolution to victory. He had almost had me shot, but I had driven him to it with my stubbornness. I had truly forgiven him. I believed in the revolution—and with all his baffling rages, I still believed in the man.

"How can you?" Hannah's lip curled. "Everything I said about him at your birthday party is true! I know I once thought differently, but if you don't change your beliefs when you're faced with facts, you're a child and a fool. I don't care what you and Daddy say. The man *is* a beast! And a barbarian . . . and a murderer! When he had Mr. Benton killed, there were people in this town who wanted to cross the river and hang him from a cottonwood tree!"

"Yes," I said with a sigh, "killing Benton was certainly a mistake."

"A mistake?" For a moment her mouth hung open. Her lip trembled. "To kill a man in cold blood? Tom! You talk like a Mexican bandit! What have you become?"

I wondered . . . then and later.

We had some fine autopsies performed in Chihuahua City, and they were printed in newspapers throughout the United States and Europe, but always with big question marks in the accompanying commentary. The furor in England began to simmer down. The Royal Navy didn't sail, although the messages from President Wilson, relayed through Letcher, grew increasingly cooler and disapproving. All our gains with the generals at Bliss seemed to have melted away, and it appeared that we had lost an ally, one we couldn't afford to lose. Sam Ravel didn't like that. Neither did Pancho Villa.

He had finally arranged for the needed coal and artillery that had brought us to Juárez in the first place, promising a delivery of two million new pesos, and he had made sure that Luz Corral was comfortably installed in her new house.

"Let's get out of here," he cried that day, slamming his fist on the kitchen table in the caboose so that the plates rattled. But then his voice turned gloomy. "I want to win the revolution, Tomás, not play games with consuls and newspapers and doctors. Let's go back to Chihuahua City. Then let's go south and make war on Victoriano Huerta." He spoke with what I thought remarkable honesty. "That's the thing I do best. Maybe it's the only thing I know how to do."

And I? What did I know how to do? Stay stubborn, and play my double game with Hannah and Rosa. I suppose, if anyone had been able to dissect the pattern of my life, the way I had dissected a frog back at El

Paso High, they would have quickly concluded that I was doing little more than aping the master, Señor Don Francisco Villa. I was treating Hannah the way he treated Luz Corral, and Rosa occupied the same place in my scheme of things as Esperanza and Juana Torres did in Villa's. True or false? If you talk like a Mexican bandit, maybe you think like one too. But it wasn't entirely true, or entirely false, and that was the rub. I wasn't a Mexican bandit. I wasn't Pancho Villa. I was a youth learning to be a man. That's rarely easy, and there are lessons that can only be learned in the doing. One of the hardest was taught to me on the night that I went to say my goodbye to Hannah.

I was invited to the Sommerfelds for dinner, and at the table the conversation centered mostly on the new opera house planned for Houston and the state of the performing arts in Texas. It was lively talk, but I took no part in it. I was watching the rise and fall of Hannah's bosom and occasionally meeting the unsettling glances she threw at me from beneath her dark eyelashes. Sam Ravel went home early. Felix said his liver was acting up again and dragged himself off to bed. Mrs. Sommerfeld followed. It took me about five seconds before I crossed the room and kissed Hannah. When I disentangled from the kiss I was helpless as a cow in quicksand, and I knew if we sat there long enough we would have a repeat of an old scene, with Hannah playing soprano and me hitting the high notes in the tenor part. I didn't want that tonight.

"Would you like to go for a walk, Hannah dear? I need some fresh air."

In the street the chill night wind of early April blew off Shadow Mountain. Hannah took my arm, pressing her hip against mine. "Tom, I'm going to miss you so much!"

"And I'll miss you, too."

We walked for a while in silence.

"Do you remember," Hannah said, "what Daddy once told you? That he and Sam wanted you to work for them? Have you been thinking about it?"

"Yes, I have. 'Who seeks, and will not take, when once 'tis offered, shall never find it more.' Does that answer you?"

"Tom, I'm so happy. Couldn't you . . ." Her voice trailed off uncertainly.

"Couldn't I what?"

"Couldn't you stay? Do you have to go back this time? Couldn't we get married *now?*"

Just then we came to Hipólito's house. I saw that no lights burned, which meant he was out somewhere with Mabel Silva. A wind blew, rustling among the new leaves of maple trees. Hannah shivered against me. "Can we go inside for a few minutes? I'm so cold."

She had been there once before, in the parlor. It didn't take long before we were in each other's arms, and it was a short step from the parlor to my bedroom. But we had never been alone like this. A flask of brandy stood on the rickety table, and we sipped from a bathroom cup that I scrubbed free of toothpowder stains with my bandanna. The wind buffeted against the windows until glass creaked. The room had a frayed carpet and a musty smell coming from damp walls, and I saw a poorly sewn patch on the pillowcase. I hadn't made the bed this morning.

"It's not exactly honeymoon cottage," I said.

She smiled nervously. "Just so long as there are no bedbugs. Give me a minute, dear. . . ." And she faded off to the bathroom, locking the door behind her. I didn't know what would happen; I was truly innocent. And therefore guilty. I shucked off my boots and lay down on the bed, still dressed. I stared up at the peeling paint on the ceiling.

A few minutes later the bathroom door opened. Hannah appeared—first a tentative arm; then, slowly, all of her. In the slanting yellow light of a lamp glowing on the table, she was naked.

I caught my breath—this wasn't what I had expected. The soldier would leave for war with more than blessings and a silk scarf as token. She had come here to offer herself to me. I understood the gravity of the gift and how it would bind us; I didn't doubt for a moment that she understood it too. Something in me wanted to protest, but I couldn't find the words or the motive. Arching my head, I gazed across the room . . . at the girl I loved. Her face turned bright red, and she flung her arms violently across her breasts.

"They hang too low," she whispered. "Please don't look. . . ."

It was true. Bound by her woman's secret undergarments, I had never noticed it before. She had never been naked in front of me.

But I cried out, "No, Hannah! They're beautiful!"

With a sob she jumped quickly into bed, burying her head on my chest. She began to unbutton my shirt. "Turn out the light, Tom. . . ."

"Must I?"

"Oh, yes!"

I thought of Rosa in the shadowy room of the Hotel Fermont in Chihuahua, where a candle always flickered beside the bed that I might better see the look in her eyes and the slow flushing of her lips . . . but the image unsettled me deeply and I banished it. My clothes fell to the floor. I snapped off the light. How could I, how could any man, say no?

The bedsprings creaked. Hannah was uncertain, almost clumsy, and my heart went out to her in a rush of love.

"I'm so dry, Tom. . . ."

"You're scared. . . ."

"But I want you. I want you *now.*"

"Maybe we shouldn't. I can wait, Hannah, if you can."

"No, I want you!"

All that dry humping on the davenport had made the next step a difficult one. That had been wild, dangerous, a child's adventure into a topsy-turvy world, and this was grown-up, real. I still found it hard to believe that it was happening, and perhaps she did too—I couldn't believe that she had planned it. I understood the enormity of the thing she was doing, from her point of view, but I had lived in revolutionary Mexico for a long time, where sex was as simple as a meal. Finally the heat of our bodies came together, she pressed my neck down hard with one forearm, shifted her thighs apart, and with the other hand gripped my pecker to guide it toward the right place.

"I'm ready, Tom. . . ."

I had first to reach up, gasping, and unlock her arm. I was being strangled. Then I began to press.

"Ouch!"

"Are you still dry?"

"Do it, do it. Darn it! Go ahead . . . oh, God!"

"What's the matter?"

"It's killing me. . . !"

"Hannah, we don't have to. Let's wait."

"Go slower. Oh, why am I so tight!"

I licked her ear a bit with my tongue, calmed myself down, braced on my elbows and let things stay the way they were for a while. She was breathing quickly.

"What are you doing now, Tom?"

"I'm just resting, Hannah."

"No, do it. We haven't got all night. Just go slowly . . . yes, like that. That's better . . . *oh!*" Seizing my hand, she bit into the soft part of the flesh above the wrist, the way a man having his leg amputated might bite a bullet.

"Ouch! Don't do that!" I cried.

"Tom—it hurts so much! It's not *fair!*"

I eased away, not that I had got anyplace, and flopped next to her side, rolling her over and drawing her into my arms. She cried for a while. I stroked her and wondered when Hipólito would be coming home, and if the rains would come early or late this year, and whether the new artillery would do the job this time at Torreón. . . .

"Let's get dressed. Don't cry, darling. It wasn't the right time. Not the right place, either. It will be better, I promise you."

"It will, won't it? When we're married . . ."

"That's right. When we're married."

"When, Tom?" Her body stopped shaking, and she sniffled. "I want that so much. Do you have a handkerchief?"

"No, but use the sheet. Soon, Hannah."

"Why do you have to go back? Can't you stay? We could be married right away."

"All right. Let's get married. I mean as soon as I come back. As soon as we've taken Mexico City. That won't take long, and that will be the end."

"Definitely?"

"I've made up my mind."

/ 181

She shivered, but she laughed quietly as she huddled against me. "You mean the native hue of resolution is no longer sicklied o'er with the pale cast of thought?"

"Exactly." This was the Hannah I loved. "And this enterprise of great pitch and moment—you and I—will not have its currents turned awry. Will not, by God, lose the name of action."

"Tom, that's marvelous!" She laughed again, but I heard the quiver in it. "And as soon as you get back, we'll get married?"

"Right away. Why should we wait? Hell, we've waited long enough." Be all my sins remembered, I thought.

"Can I tell everybody? Can we announce it?"

"Sure, you can."

"I'll be good for you . . . you'll see. I was frightened tonight. I want you to make love to me so much."

"I know that, Hannah. I adore you for it."

She wept against my cheek, the warm, salty tears sliding into my mouth. I felt confused by the rapidity of the decision. And yet, hadn't it been inevitable, written in the stars from the day that we had met in the lobby of the Commercial Hotel in Columbus? I kept telling myself I was the luckiest man on God's dusty earth. This is what I had always wanted, what I had dreamed of since I was old enough to dream a man's dream. I hadn't been trapped into it. How could you be trapped into marrying the girl you loved?

In a little while, amid giggles and whispers and reassuring touches, Hannah and I got dressed. I took her home. From the darkened doorway, under a trellis of honeysuckle and roses that had also closed their petals for the night, she blew kisses. I whispered good-bye. I wondered then how I would tell Rosa when I reached Chihuahua City. But there was no solution yet, and I let it pass.

Walking back through the black and windy streets to Hipólito's house, I had some more disquieting thoughts. Even if you ride the river with a man, the time's got to come when you reach the far bank. But I had never done anything to make up for Torreón. In that, no matter how much I had chipped in to help Pancho Villa win his revolution and send urchins to school, I had somehow failed. And now I was leaving Mexico. The wind gusted even harder. Time healeth . . . so they said.

15

"Whose church-like humors fit not for a crown."

In his suite at the Hotel Fermont in Chihuahua City, his voice sounding like a rusty gate hinge, the murder of William Benton behind him if not forgotten, Villa poured out his heart to me.

"Tomás, I've been thinking, and it doesn't always come easy. Tell me if I'm wrong. Don't be afraid. I trust you wholeheartedly. Your life is as dear to me now as my own. When I think of how I wronged you, I could weep." He was unshaven, and his eyes looked like red holes peering out of an icecap. "But this is what I want to say. No one man is more important than the revolution . . . isn't that a fact?"

I agreed with that and told him so. He put a hand to his breast.

"I may be impulsive, but I'm not a complete idiot. I see the awful things that I'm capable of doing, but still I see that it's morally impossible in this squalid country for any man not to be a revolutionist. But to justify all that we do, someday we'll have to change the very face of the earth—yet we dare not give up. And I! I must lead, but I mustn't stand in the way of something decent that could come after. Advise me."

It sounded like fuzzy thinking to me, although I knew he was still upset over the Benton affair, and I didn't take him too seriously. As it turned out, I was right.

"How, chief? What is it that you want to know?"

One of his problems, he believed—one that he could control—was that he didn't appear respectable. If he had, Mr. Letcher might have given him the benefit of the doubt. So . . . should he buy a general's unform?

"Well, nothing fancy. You don't want to look like Napoleon, or Kaiser Wilhelm waving his sword at the Yellow Peril. No sashes or medals. But on the whole, it's not a bad idea."

. He banged on the door to my room three days later, just as Rosa and I were contemplating a siesta. He wore a new tan tunic that buttoned tightly over his paunch and right up to his jowls, a visored military cap and a brand-new pair of shiny cowhide boots.

"How do I look?"

"Good. How do you feel?"

"Hot. And my feet hurt." He ripped open the top button of the tunic, and it popped. "That's better." He hesitated a minute, then turned to Rosa. "What do you think, my Indian dove? Am I not irresistible?"

"To most women, yes," she said.

"Oh?" Villa frowned. "And to whom would I not be so?"

"To those who have not had the joy to meet you," she replied prudently.

He raised an eyebrow at me. "Your dove has grown sharp claws," he murmured. "She suits you, Tomás."

He had also brought with him a jovial, middle-aged man in rumpled civilian clothes whom he introduced to us as Dr. Ludwig Rauschbaum. He looked Mexican, but he was a German-born physician who had emigrated to Chihuahua ten years ago. He was one of the doctors who had provided the autopsy on Benton. His Spanish was awful, but he had excited Villa's imagination by telling him that if he ate no meat it would cure his terrible temper.

/ 183

Rauschbaum explained it again for my benefit.

"Man is an animal, *ja?* This is so, *ja?* But he is so little! So *schwach!* Weak, *ja?* He must kill other animals or he die. Not enough bananas. I speak of millions of years ago, *ja?* So he kill, and he eat the meat. Zebra, antelope, monkey—I speak of Africa, *ja?* Long ago. Now he is different! He is civilized! But he still eat meat, *ja?* And he remember. Deep inside him, even if with his brain he don't know, he remember. He eat the meat, and he think—kill! *Töten! Angreifen!* The meat get him excited, *ja?* Meat is bad. Make you crazy."

"Are you going to do it?" I asked Villa.

"Yes. I'll try anything."

"Ja, gut," Rauschbaum said happily. "Fruit and vegetables. *Auch keinen alcol."*

"Do you speak any German, Tomás?"

"I think he means no hard liquor."

"Then I understood. I don't drink liquor anyway," Villa explained to Dr. Rauschbaum. "If I did, I would be impossible."

I hadn't yet told Rosa about the clarity of my new plans with Hannah. That was a subject we never discussed, although I thought the time was fast approaching when it would become necessary. But when I got back to Chihuahua City, one night in a cantina, thinking that he would be pleased, I told Candelario. He didn't smile and clap me on the back as I thought he would.

"Let me give you a piece of advice," he replied, "if it doesn't offend you."

"You think I'm making a mistake," I blurted. "You think I should stay with Rosa! But you've never even *met* Hannah!"

"What I think about that," he said, "is beside the point. In these matters no man can counsel another. Just do what your cock tells you to do, then you can't go wrong." He lit one of those crumbly Mexican cigarettes and with his stubby fingers held it between his teeth, puffing hard until the ash glowed a bright cherry-red. His eye glinted sharply, but his voice was calm and purposeful. "What I have to say is this. Before you tell your woman that you're going off to marry someone else—get the gold out of Tomochic."

"You don't think . . . ?"

"Who knows? Just remember, half the gold is mine. I would be unhappy to lose it. Not that I worked very hard to get it, but when you have something for a while, even if it came to you as a gift from heaven, you get used to the idea that it's yours."

"Rosa wouldn't do that!"

"Rosa is a wonderful girl. She has the best tits I've ever seen, and a brain, and I love her like a sister. But in this life, my friend, anything is possible. Don't tell her about your marriage until we have the gold. That's all I have to say."

It was still April of 1914, and I didn't think we would get to Mexico City until early fall, when the rains ended, which meant that I would be at least half a year more in Mexico. Candelario's reasoning didn't impress me; I would have trusted Rosa with my life. She had known about Hannah from the beginning, and I had told no lies to her since then; but it struck me that it would be an unnecessary cruelty, this far in advance, to announce my impending marriage. When the day came, when it was time to leave, I would tell her, and I would go quickly.

And, of course, it was easier this way. . . .

By the end of April the Northern Division was ready to strike southward. The new Belgian artillery and Pennsylvania coal had arrived from Sommerfeld's warehouses. The Packard broke down because Martín Lopez had never checked the oil, cracking the block, but Pancho Villa quickly ordered Hipólito to send a new engine and six spare tires from El Paso. He fired Lopez, commissioned him a lieutenant and made his brother Pablo the chauffeur. He added a new company of Dorados, promoted Julio to colonel and gave him its command under Candelario.

As the day of our great move approached, Villa decided that he lacked a qualified artillery commander for the attack he planned. Some time ago a Federal general named Felipe Angeles, long suspected of being a Madero sympathizer, had been sent by Porfirio Díaz to Europe to study with the French army; he probably would have been shot if he had not been the oldest son of a rich Mexico City family. Returning from France, he had joined Obregón's forces in Sonora, and it was rumored that he was responsible for the big victory against the Federals at Hermosillo. After the capture of Juárez, Felipe Angeles had telegraphed his personal compliments to Villa, casually adding that his greatest wish as an officer would be to serve under him.

"I need this man," Villa said to me. "He's everything I'm not. Do you know that he speaks four languages? How can one man do that? You'd think his mind would burst with so many words. Angeles knows more about artillery than Medina will ever learn—these Belgian guns are complicated. I'd even give him command of the Division if he wanted it. What can I do?"

"Ask for him. If Angeles likes you so much, Obregón may be glad to see him go. But keep the Division for yourself," I counseled.

Villa fired off a telegraph message that day, and in the evening he received a reply. He could have Felipe Angeles. He was delighted, and even more so when Angeles arrived in Chihuahua City with one hundred first-rate loyal artillery officers and gunners, most of them former Federals.

"Now we'll win," Villa said. "I never had any doubts, but if I did, they're gone."

/ 185

The next day we received word that Obregón had been named chief general of the Army Corps of the Northwest, which by Carranza's fiat included the state of Chihuahua. Villa himself was still only a brigadier general. Carranza also announced that he would move Constitutionalist headquarters to Chihuahua City, timing the move so that he arrived after the Northern Division had chugged off for battle in the south.

"Piss on it," Villa said. "I'll fight the revolution—let them fight over the titles. Obregón knows enough to stay out of my business."

But later he grew dejected. "Why do they try to humiliate me, Tomás? Is it the Benton affair? I've pledged my loyalty a dozen times. What more can I do?"

"I'll tell you one thing. If Carranza's coming to Chihuahua City, you can move that gold somewhere else."

Instead, he had a steel door built for the laundry room in the Fermont. He told the commander whose brigade would stay behind in the city that it contained the divisional pay records and other important documents. Two keys were made. Villa wore one around his neck on a cheap brass chain, and the other he gave to me. I had never told him how the padlock key had helped save my life.

"You won't steal the gold, Tomás. You have enough already in Tomochic."

Candelario hadn't told him . . . surely not Rosa. He would never tell me how he knew, and I would never ask. I had come to enjoy these mysteries. This key I didn't hang around my neck—I didn't anticipate needing such distractions a second time—but instead asked Rosa to sew it into the back pocket of my Levi's, which were worn so thin that no one would consider stealing them. The poorest *campesino* had better pants.

And then, suddenly (it seemed to happen almost capriciously, but I knew better), Villa announced that we were ready and would attack. He always did this, let his army savor its triumphs for a while, celebrate, rearm and solidify its position, and then when he smelled the restlessness of the men and their readiness to do battle again, he would seize on the moment and whip them into a frenzy of war.

This was to be our final campaign. Our objectives were Torreón, which Villa had abandoned to seize Juárez, and then the fortress city of Zacatecas nine thousand feet above sea level. From Zacatecas to Mexico City was only two hundred miles with a good railbed and a straight paved road. There were no Federal garrisons of any size between it and the capital. Villa said, "When Zacatecas falls, they'll feel our breath on their necks. Then Huerta can decide. A last battle, which he can't win, or surrender. You'll see, Tomás—after we take Zacatecas, the war will be over."

I barely had time to kiss Rosa goodbye before the Northern Division struck to the south with ten full brigades and two regiments of artillery under Felipe Angeles. The women would follow in a caravan of trains, and Rosa would go as usual with the French whores, who treated her almost like a daughter to be cared for and protected from the rabble. A torrent of dust rose from the corrals. Horses milled and stumbled, while vaqueros coiled their reatas and cut out their mounts. Men strapped on their cartridge belts, buttoned their thin cotton jackets; women shrilled advice and goodbyes. For miles near the Chihuahua railroad yards the desert seemed to writhe with troopers urging their horses toward the boxcars. In a great caravan the trains grunted forward, mile by mile, through the foothills of the Sierra Madre Mountains.

Night struck, with a rising chill wind. The engines clicked southward, streaming fire from the coal boxes, thin lines of brilliant red sparks vanishing into the darkness. A few hardy women soldiers cooked on the swaying platforms; inside, guitars twanged a dozen different songs. The engines labored up grades. It began to rain . . . the women wailed, then groaned miserably. The men sitting next to me shouted with glee, "To Torreón!"

"*Válgame Dios!* How drunk we'll get!"

Two roosters wandered up and down the aisles, eating crumbs and cigarette butts. Someone thrust his rifle out the window and fired a clip of bullets at the desert. The train jerked forward with a screech, a clank, then gathered speed . . . toward Torreón, again.

Bermejillo fell, and Villa found a working telephone there at the tiny post office. Miraculously, after cranking it and plugging in here and there in the switchboard at random, he got through directly to General Velasco, the Federal commander in Torreón.

"Who is speaking?"

"Francisco Villa. Your servant, my general, who begs you to end your useless resistance and save the lives of many Mexicans."

"That can't be done, General Villa."

"Too bad, because we're coming for you in just a moment."

"You will be welcomed properly."

"Good. Fix supper."

"We'll have something warm for you. Are there many of you? I'd like to tell my chefs."

"Not so many, Señor Velasco. Just a couple of regiments of artillery and fourteen thousand men."

But the Northern Division, with its pent-up energy and awesome power, was not to be denied. Gómez Palacio fell, and we stormed Torreón. We were approaching a hill outside the city with Candelario's Dorados when Villa noticed six or seven long-haired Otomi Indians standing near some cottonwood trees. The men were half-naked, and one of the women clasped a baby at her breast. As the baby sucked, they watched us silently.

/ 187

"For Christ's sake . . ." Villa yelled to me. "Ride over there! Tell them they could be in our line of fire!"

I reined up in a spill of dust and finally found one of the Otomis who spoke some Spanish. I explained the situation.

"But, señor," the man said humbly, "this is where we always stand to watch the battle for Torreón."

The battle took ten days, and it was hard. This time there was no marimba band on the grass outside the Hotel Salvador, no fiesta at the casino. Blood ran darkly down the worn cobblestones as if bulls had been skinned after a *corrida*. I walked my sweating horse carefully down from La Pila to the Plaza de Armas, following the relentless course of that muddy crimson stream.

When I saw Villa in the familiar bridal suite at the Hotel Salvador, he was still covered with dust and dried sweat. Felipe Angeles was with him, bathed and shaved, but there were black shadows under his melancholy eyes. The map of Mexico was spread before him on the coffee table. Angeles wore a brown cashmere sweater with leather elbow patches, and his handsome profile, flared mustache and dark sunglasses made him look like a gentleman pirate. But his voice vibrated with passion. "My general," he said to Villa, "in every campaign there is a single decisive battle in which the body and spirit of the losing side is broken. If the victor presses on, resistance crumbles. Now you must push to the south with all speed."

"And Velasco?" Villa spoke coldly and angrily.

Seven thousand Federal soldiers under General Velasco had escaped Torreón and were heading east along the railroad line. Villa didn't argue with Angeles' military theory, but it troubled him deeply to have a large intact enemy force in his rear. During the battle he had taken time out to telegraph our supposed ally, Carranza's favorite general, Pablo González, asking that González cut the eastbound railroad line—the only one Villa had been unable to reach. But González for some reason had neglected to do it. Now, from the hotel, with Angeles, Villa telegraphed once again, begging González to attack.

He received his reply in a wire direct from Carranza. "I do not recall ever having ordered you to take Torreón in the first place. I congratulate you, but you are under the command of General Obregón and must clear all orders through him."

"These bastards! Are they serious?" Villa brooded awhile, biting his fingernails and tugging at his mustache. "How can I speed south with such people protecting my flanks? My men can barely stand up."

So the momentum created by the decisive battle was lost. Angeles' advice went unheeded. Villa called a halt to the advance on Mexico City.

"I must go north," he said, when he had finished brooding. "I must meet this man, Venustiano Carranza, whom I serve but who doesn't serve me."

Like many events, such as the Benton killing, the meeting with Carranza was to change the course of history in Mexico—for it subtly began the change in Pancho Villa's purpose as a revolutionist. And anything that changed the course of the revolution, I realize now, changed the shape and direction of my life as well.

Give me the place to stand, and I will move the earth, Archimedes said, two thousand years ago. What he neglected to say is that the earth moves too. The tides sweep both ways. Men have the ability to change history and seldom can resist the beckoning of that chance. History reciprocates. The dance of life goes on—more a tug-of-war than a dance. Sometimes we are movers, sometimes we are moved. Buddha, I once read, called the process "the wheel of life." To liberate himself from that relentless process, a man has to disengage—has to get off the wheel, stop dancing, thumb his nose at the tides. How can he do that? Long before I left Mexico, with the aid of two women, I would begin to find out. And that knowledge, that action, would color the rest of my life. It would make me the man I became, the man who could accept success and failure, wealth and poverty, misery and its cloudy opposite, with equal calm. It would make me untouchable. It would darken my soul, because I had seen and done too much.

But that spring of 1914, in Chihuahua, I was still on the wheel, still a victim of history and of myself. And of Pancho Villa.

We drove up to Chihuahua City through the rich cotton fields of La Laguna and then the flat northern desert: just Villa, Felipe Angeles and I, with one bouncing truckful of soldiers as escort. Villa slumped thoughtfully in the front seat of the Packard, munching chocolate and sucking on some lemons that the chauffeur had bought for himself. "I haven't eaten meat for ten days," he announced. "Except once or twice, when I forgot. I'm going to be gentle as a rabbit. You'll see."

The reception for us was at the governor's palace, where Venustiano Carranza sat on a throne whose arms were carved in the shape of lion's paws. I looked forward to meeting him almost as much as Villa did; after all, he was our leader, and in some ways—even more than I realized then—the future of the revolution lay in his hands. The First Chief was a tall, imposing man in his late fifties and, so seated on the throne, he might have been an emperor except that he lacked a uniform, and his air of serene rectitude, his flowing white mustache and thick white beard, made him look more like God. He had a habit, when he was listening idly to anyone, of combing his beard with the pointed fingernails of his left hand, so that the beard became parted in the middle. He wore a well-cut dark blue pinstriped suit which disguised his portliness, and dark-blue-tinted spectacles which made it difficult to read his expression. I knew that he had trouble with his eyes, that they rarely stopped watering and were sensitive to bright light. He seldom went outdoors. When they were introduced, Villa stepped forward and gave Carranza a hearty hug. But the old man seemed to shy away from it, as if he hated to be touched.

Afterwards we all drove to Carranza's new house, a splendid, thick-walled, porticoed mansion on the edge of town, with a lovely flower garden and bubbling Moorish fountain. It had recently been proclaimed as Constitutionalist headquarters. But then we entered an uncomfortable sitting room dimmed into chilly darkness by the closed shutters. Carranza didn't take off his glasses except to wipe his dripping eyes with a cream-colored silk handkerchief. The room smelled dank and sour. About six of Carranza's advisers and secretaries sat behind him on carved French chairs. Villa sprawled in an easy chair in front of him, flanked by myself and Felipe Angeles on hard wooden benches. I had been introduced as the chief's secretary, but that apparently didn't rate a shake of the First Chief's hand.

"And now, General Villa," Carranza said benignly, when we had settled ourselves and exchanged some small talk, "tell me why you've come to Chihuahua. I'm at your service, as always, to answer questions and enlighten you in any way possible."

Villa took him at his word. Why, he wanted to know, hadn't this crazy General González cut the railroad line and advanced on Velasco from the rear?

"Ah, General Villa . . . you ask me a military question. I am a statesman, a lawyer, a former senator and governor of the state of Coahuila under President Madero. You, who correctly concern yourself with matters that you know best, such as fighting, should know the answer to your question far better than I."

"But I don't, señor," Villa said. "If I did, for Christ's sake, I wouldn't ask."

The First Chief dabbed at his eyes with the silk handkerchief. "There must have been some circumstances that did not permit it. I have the utmost faith and trust in General González. He is a man utterly loyal to the Constitutionalist aims, an educated man who understands the need for obedience." Carranza sighed softly, as a teacher might with a backward pupil.

Villa scratched his head; the dust flew. "And now," he inquired, "why is this obedient General González marching in a lateral direction toward the port of Tampico, when our objective is supposed to be Mexico City?"

Carranza in turn inquired of Villa if it wasn't true that in the area of

La Laguna the Northern Division had captured more than a hundred thousand bales of cotton.

The chief looked puzzled. "Yes, that's so, but I asked you why—"

"And I answered you, although perhaps more subtly than you're used to. We must have a port from which to ship that cotton abroad. Tampico, toward which González marches—at *my* orders—is that port."

"Señor!" Villa laughed. "We can send the cotton by train to the United States!"

"I am not pleased with the attitude of the United States," Don Venus proclaimed. "Are you not aware of what is happening at Veracruz?"

We all knew something of it—rumors, anyway—and Carranza explained the rest. The first of the German ships dispatched from Hamburg, *Ypiranga,* was due to dock at Veracruz with a cargo of fifteen million cartridges and two hundred machine guns for Huerta's army. A German cruiser hovered off the port, as did various American gunboats and three Yankee battleships. An incident had already occurred; one of the American gunboats had run out of fuel, and a German supplier on the Tampico canal had unaccountably offered to sell them what they needed. A party had been sent ashore. The Federals, nervously awaiting an attack from González to the north, promptly arrested the Yankee sailors, held them a few hours, then received orders to release them. But the American Admiral Mayo had demanded a formal apology in the way of a twenty-one-gun salute, which he promised to return. Huerta stamped his foot in Mexico City, saying that his men had even helped the sailors load their damned fuel—and in any case why should he salute the ship of a gringo government that didn't recognize his authority and was openly supplying his enemies?

"But this is the best thing that could happen," Villa said warmly to Don Venus. "If Huerta doesn't apologize, the gringos may take some action. That'll put a firecracker up the ass of that bullet-headed drunk!"

Carranza smiled. "Such a salute would violate our national sovereignty, General Villa, just as much as if I had allowed the Americans to inspect the grave of Mr. Benton, whose death caused us so much embarrassment. If you'll bother to study the history of our country, you'll realize that for four hundred years Mexico has been the victim of foreign imperialism—the Spaniards, who took our whole country; the Americans, who stole half of it; and the French, who gave us the puppet emperor Maximilian. And now the Americans wish to interfere once again! History cannot be allowed to repeat itself. If they arrive and are made welcome, who knows that they'll ever go? In this matter, I place the soul of Mexico before the revolution."

Villa squirmed in his seat. "Señor, nothing comes before the revolution. How do you explain the soul of Mexico to a peasant who hasn't enough corn to feed his children?"

"In time," Carranza replied affably, "peasants will be taught such things. That is the purpose of our proposed Constitutionalist government." He fended off any further comment by turning toward a bottle of chilled French rosé wine that stood in a silver bucket on the table. The blue-tinted spectacles still hid his eyes. He poured a small glass of wine for himself, then offered one to Pancho Villa.

"Will you drink with me to the noble aims of my Plan of Guadalupe, General Villa?"

"I don't drink, señor. But if you have some hot coffee, I wouldn't mind a cup. It's cold as a witch's tit in here."

Don Venus said, "I admire your abstinence, General. I deplore the effect of strong drink on the Mexican nation. In fact, it is my aim, during the short period that I will be interim chief of our country, to forbid the distillation of pulque, which I consider a curse on our national family life and productivity. I will encourage the people to replace the swilling of pulque with the moderate imbibing of chilled light wine."

Villa chuckled. "While you're at it, you could also ask God to replace corn with caviar. And pray for snow in summer, so there's ice to chill the wine."

The First Chief didn't comment, just rubbed his hands together nervously. Then he picked at the skin of one thumb. Shortly after that, the interview ended with a limp handshake.

Once we were in the Packard and on the road south, Villa threw his hands in the air. "Son of a whore!" He shook those hands as if he were throttling an invisible demon. "I didn't understand half of what that man said! The words, yes . . . but the meaning? *Válgame Dios!* Before I met him, despite everything, I swear to you—I respected him. But when I hugged him at the palace, the feel of his body made my blood run cold. What is he? Shall I tell you? A sluggish old man who lives in a dark, damp room and detests the light. Is this a statesman? No . . . it's a half-blind court clerk! Wine instead of pulque! Did you hear him? I'll have to tell that one to Urbina. He may go over to fight for Huerta. . . ."

On the hot winding road to Torreón he sank into a lethargy. But then, after a while, he spoke again.

"Felipe, I'm a peasant. But you're an educated man, at least as much as he. You understand all his words. Tell me truthfully—do I do him an injustice?"

"I know Carranza well," Angeles said. "He believes in intrigues. He surrounds himself with toadies and parasites, with jackals. They have only to agree with all his pronouncements. That's why he tolerates this oaf, General González, who failed to cut the railroad line. He despises you. That's surely obvious. Have you never wondered why?"

Villa nodded, apparently undisturbed; the question had already been answered. But his brows knitted. "Did you smell something in that room? Didn't you sniff it?"

"Just the dampness," Angeles said. "The perfume on his handkerchief. The wine."

"There was more. Listen to me. I trust my nose . . . it's saved my skin more than once. I smelled an odor in that beautiful house, in that fancy room. Even more, I smelled it in his manner, and he can't hide it even behind his dark glasses—at least not from a peasant and a former bandit. What I smelled was the odor of ambition. A secret greed! Despite his repeating endlessly that he's only interim chief until we're victorious, this man dreams to become President of Mexico . . . and more." He grunted deep in his throat, like a hog. "He doesn't see me as the general of an army that will help him win the revolution. Don Venus hopes to be another Porfirio Díaz, to rule alone and forever. And he sees me as the chief obstacle to that demonic dream."

Villa considered a moment and then said firmly: "In that, of course—by all that's holy—he is not mistaken."

16   "Do you not know I am a woman?"

Huerta refused to salute the American admiral at Tampico. President Wilson heard the news while he was preparing to tee off at the fourteenth hole of his golf course and immediately left to convene first his cabinet, and then Congress, in order to debate the gravity of the insult. As a result, if you can call it that, on April 21, 1914, the U.S. Marines landed in Veracruz and got a toehold on Mexican soil.

Pancho Villa chuckled. "It's Huerta's bull that's being gored, not mine."

But Huerta wasn't unhappy. He must have thought it would distract the revolutionists and unite all of Mexico behind him in the hour of national humiliation. For a short time it looked that way: the American Club in Mexico City was burned to the ground, the new statue of George Washington in some plaza knocked off its pedestal and shattered. The German freighter, *Ypiranga,* off-loaded its bullets and barbed wire anyway, at a more southerly port. Carranza sent grave notes of protest in all directions, to Secretary of State Bryan and to the visiting German military attaché in Mexico City, Franz von Papen.

Villa met with a group of American reporters. "Mr. Wilson is my friend," he said, "and one of my most trusted aides is a gringo. Your navy may have been foolish in attacking Veracruz, but listen to me, boys—it can stay there as long as it likes. It can bottle up the port so tightly that not even a drop of whiskey gets through to Huerta. And now that I think of it, that's a sure way to make him surrender."

Carranza dithered and protested. We attacked Zacatecas, the last obstacle before Mexico City.

Under a brooding sky and in a warm June rain, the fortress city fell to the assault of the Northern Division. Zacatecas was the decisive battle that Angeles preached, but it lasted a week and there was none bloodier. I watched as the bodies of the dead were thrown into mine shafts or stacked on flatcars to be hauled into the desert. Others were soaked in gasoline and burned, and the stench stayed in the city for a week. The bodies, as the flames began to eat at them, flung themselves about as though some part of their souls still felt pain. Again, though I struggled against it, I remembered the men in the corral at Torreón. . . .

Villa, keeping to his vegetarian diet, recruited almost all of the living to our side. Then, the day after Zacatecas finally surrendered, we ate lunch under some mesquite trees at an outdoor restaurant. With us was Carranza's newly arrived personal representative, the lawyer, Jesús Acuña, who had first visited us in Ascensión with Chao. He bore papers appointing him the new provincial governor. I could tell that Villa didn't like the man, but he was polite to him throughout most of the meal. Acuña ate delicately, declining to pick up his chicken leg in his hand. He drank chilled white wine, which stirred memories.

"There's still good meat on those bones," Villa pointed out. "Don't be offended, but if you don't want it, I do. There's no disease I fear except clap, and you can't get that from a chicken leg." He was hungry after the long battle, and he attacked Acuña's plate like a famished wolf. Dr. Rauschbaum had been banished; the meatless phase of Pancho Villa's life was suddenly over.

An avocado salad arrived, and so did a squad of our soldiers, escorting two dusty Federal officers who had somehow lost their boots. They had been hiding in a house nearby on the outskirts of town. A woman had betrayed them. The Villista soldiers, themselves former Federals, were unsure what to do with the captured officers.

His teeth still grinding into the new governor's chicken leg, Villa solved their problem without benefit of debate.

"Shoot them."

Acuña sputtered and shifted uncomfortably in his chair. "General Villa! Is that really necessary?"

"Señor Acuña! I've spared all enlisted men. But your patron, Don Venus, has himself invoked the decree of Benito Juárez in 1857, that all captured enemy officers are to be executed, since they're educated men who deliberately fight against the revolution. Would you have me refuse his orders? If I did that, we wouldn't even be here in Zacatecas."

One of the Federal officers, a captain, a small fellow with a waxed mustache, stepped forward and looked Villa straight in the eye.

"I have no objection," he said calmly. "You may be sure that if we had won the battle and you were my prisoners, I would shoot you in the same way. And with special pleasure to you, Señor Villa, since I am a soldier doing my duty, and you, señor, are no more than a bandit living on what you steal from the Mexican people."

That fellow had nerve. Perhaps he thought it would win a pardon for him. Benton had thought so, too.

Villa, unruffled, kept on eating. He turned to Acuña. "You see? Here's a brave man, although misguided. He's going to die, but he speaks his mind. Why deprive him of believing that he dies for a good cause at the hands of a bandit?"

Acuña paled. Then the second officer, a lieutenant, much bigger and fiercer-looking than his companion, fell to his knees in the dirt. "General Villa! It's not right!" he cried. "They told us we were coming north to fight the gringos! If I had known it was your army attacking, I would never have fought! I swear it on the life of my mother!" He began to sob, and he pissed his pants.

Villa's nose wrinkled with disgust. I knew how he felt about such incontinence. "You're a hell of an officer," he said, and he turned again to the escort. "Carry out my orders."

The young soldiers exchanged uneasy glances. Acuña spoke up. "General Villa, must it be done here? We're eating. We're happy over our triumphs. For God's sake, I beg you, spare us the sight of death at such a moment."

Then Villa's eyes really blazed. Throwing his chicken leg in the dust, he jumped to his feet.

"Death bothers you, señor? So it does me! I've just come from Zacatecas!—from Torreón!—battlefields that stink of death, that are soaked with the blood of our own men! You chocolate-drinking politicians," he shouted, "want to triumph without knowing how that triumph is achieved! But you *must* know, señor! And you must always remember!" He leveled a blunt finger at the soldiers. "Carry out the order!"

The captain, the little brave one, said, "General Villa, it's obvious to me that your men are reluctant. They won't shoot straight. To that, I seriously object."

"You have reason," Villa replied. He pulled his own pistol. The squad of soldiers quickly scattered. The officer on the ground staggered to his feet, and the smaller man closed his eyes. Villa fired twice at each, once while they stood, and then once while the fallen bodies twitched on the ground. Blood trickled down the slight incline of the earth toward the luncheon table.

"Don't touch the bodies," he ordered, holstering the pistol. He thumped back into his iron chair. "Eat, señor," he instructed Acuña, as he himself began to spear his avocado salad.

The bodies lay there throughout the rest of the lunch. Acuña ate bravely, taking big mouthfuls to show his spirit, until at last the trickle of blood reached his feet. He moved the shiny toe of his black shoe slightly to the left, to avoid it. But the blood gently changed course, as if to search him out, as if it flowed at Villa's orders, that Acuña might always remember. His toe retreated, and the blood of the two officers, mingled in one muddy river, stubbornly followed it. Acuña, in the midst of his caramel custard, turned gray in the face and excused himself. Behind a nearby tree, he was sick. Without another word, he left. That evening in the telegraph office—where we had our man, of course—he sent a wire to Carranza giving full details of the incident.

The rains would never have stopped us from taking Mexico City. This time Villa was determined to fight in rain and mud or sleet and snow, for the Federals in the capital dared not retreat farther south into the waiting guns of Emiliano Zapata. But we needed coal, and we had captured none in Zacatecas. Ravel and Sommerfeld agreed to send us five hundred more carloads. It didn't arrive, and no amount of angry telegrams to Hipólito could elicit more than the usual Mexican promise that it would be sent *"ahorita,"* which meant, literally, right away. If he had said "tomorrow" or "next Tuesday" we would have had hope, but the bold "right away" had the unmistakable meaning of "Who knows when?" Everything was in short supply. The Northern Division had swelled to 22,000 men, with more than 15,000 horses, hundreds of cannon and machine guns—and the women and children had to be fed too. No longer a guerrilla army, it was a huge organization gobbling bullets and tortillas at a rate that alarmed any of us who stopped to consider it. Now that it was summer, the remuda could graze for miles throughout the blooming desert, but by October the land would be bare and the bushes would be following the dogs around. We had to store provisions as squirrels do nuts for winter.

Carranza promised us coal. It would come from the docks in Tampico . . . *ahorita.*

"It doesn't matter," Villa said to me. "Huerta knows we're here. He knows what to expect. He won't get a night's sleep until he hears our cannon, and then it will be too late for him. Let him sweat. By September, if he can last that long, he'll be a broken man. The waiting is always worse than the battle, especially for the army that knows it will lose."

The revolution made you as homeless as a poker chip. Rosa arrived at last from Torreón. Tired of hotel life, I quartered myself with her in a small abandoned house on the hill of La Sierpe, a thousand feet above the city. There the air was brisk and blue, the trees grew green under the deluge of afternoon rains and the summer winds blew gently. The house had crawling purple bougainvillea, leafy tomato bushes, eucalyptus and even a laden banana tree. Candelario and Julio came up often with the

French whores, although Julio still behaved toward them like a monk, and Rosa and I were like a young married couple having friends to lunch and dinner. Candelario was always able to liberate a wandering chicken or suckling pig, and Rosa would kill it in the backyard and barbecue it. I had bought a schoolbook for her the last time I was in El Paso. Every afternoon I gave her a reading or writing lesson, and sometimes in the evening, when we were alone, we listened to the rain drip from the leaves in the garden, and we spoke in English.

"The weather is nice today, Thomas, was it not?"

"Yes, Rosa, it was fine. How about tomorrow? Do you think it will rain tomorrow?"

"Yes, it is rain tomorrow. It is rain tomorrow and past tomorrow."

"It *will* rain tomorrow. And the day *after* tomorrow."

"I think so too," she said, kissing me.

She was quick. I was proud of her and proud of myself, and the waiting for what would happen or not happen in Mexico City wasn't bad at all because we had each other on the hill of La Sierpe. I began to see the magic that can spring to life between a pupil and teacher, and how each becomes dependent on the other if the teaching is from the heart and the learning penetrates. I wondered if Pancho Villa, in his way, had become linked with me through that process, as I was being linked now with Rosa. I remembered my Greek history: she was Galatea to my Pygmalion. She was sixteen now. Once she had been a waif, a burden; then a child concubine, a sewer of buttons. That seemed so long ago.

Hannah was far away, and not just in uncrossable miles. There was no way I could write to her, for the mails to the border were restricted to military dispatches. And even if I could have used my position to slip a letter into the daily pouch, what would I have said that wasn't a lie? I didn't miss her at all; that was a terrible thing to realize. Did I need her the way a man needs the woman he's going to marry? Hannah fed my imagination and my wispy dreams of the future. But living the life of a revolutionist in Mexico, nothing was left to imagination. And I had no future now, not there on La Sierpe. I was a soldier with his woman, a soldier between battles, living only in the present.

Rosa and I went out every Sunday to the bullfight, and sometimes in the morning, before it grew too hot, we would walk through the parks of the city and sip a lemonade in the shade of an oak tree. At night there was a cantina we liked, where guitarists came from all over the city to play until dawn, and one night a violinist, who had played with the national orchestra but now was a revolutionist like the rest of us, wandered in and began fiddling Beethoven sonatas, so that the bar fell silent and tears sprang to every listener's eyes. Not far from town we discovered an abandoned mineral spring, and when we tired of the guitarists we would ride out there and bathe naked in the starlight, letting the hot,

/ 197

sulphurous water soothe our bones. Those nights I slept like a baby and awoke like a satyr.

The one sin that didn't come naturally to me was gluttony. I needed no more than what I had. And so we waited in Zacatecas for the coal, while the rains beat down.

Early one morning in July, I woke to the rapid pounding of hoofs on dirt. In the quiet, soft air, I heard my name shouted. Candelario and Julio pounded on the timbered door—the beams of the roof shook with the urgency of their fists. I struggled out of bed, where Rosa and I had just greeted sunrise in the proper amatory fashion. I threw on some clothes and opened the door. Despite the cool morning, Candelario and Julio were sweating. Their horses were ground-tied, flanks heaving. Candelario flung his great arms around me, and the strength of his embrace made me gasp.

"Tomás! It's over!"

"Hombre . . ." I managed to shove him away. "Calm down. What are you talking about?"

"The revolution is over! *We've won!* Do you understand? Huerta's quit! He got drunk with Orozco . . . sailed from Veracruz on some German battleship. . . ."

He was out of breath; his face streamed with sweat. Julio shook his fists into the air with glee.

Villa had been right after all. Zacatecas had fallen. . . . Huerta, staring into a glass of cognac, had glimpsed his destiny. And I could go home now, home to Hannah and my real life. Major Thomas H. Mix, Retired . . .

Yes, it is rain tomorrow, mi capitán.

I stirred from my reverie. They were waiting for me to whoop with joy, to break out the tequila and share their exultation.

"Amigo, that's the best news I've ever heard." I tried to sound convincing. "Tell me more! Who's taken over in the capital?"

"Some little politician," said Julio, not quite so joyously. "I can't even remember his name. But he's Carranza's man—naturally, a real pantywaist. No *cojones.* The Federal Army is disbanding. Orozco's quit too. Obregón's moving south from Guadalajara. So is González, west from Tampico."

"And we?"

"Ah, we!" Candelario's laugh boomed in the morning stillness. "Angeles just found out that the railroad tracks are torn up for a hundred miles to the south. And even if that weren't so, you can be sure that fucking Don Venus won't let the coal get through to us. He's going to bottle us up here so that he, the deliverer, can ride into Mexico City on a big white horse, all alone. A Spanish conquistador! Fuck his mother!

His grandmother too! He's publicly called the chief a murderer . . . the Benton thing again, and something to do with some officers who were shot for lunchtime sport after we took Zacatecas." Candelario's good eye gleamed. "But the chief didn't care. Listen, Tomás! Listen to this! There's going to be a big revolutionary convention in Aguascalientes. A fiesta to end all fiestas, beginning next month, after Carranza's had his day. Everyone will be there! All the generals and politicians—Zapata, Obregón, González, Carranza. Everybody! What a time we'll have! The girls will make a fortune! That's where they'll decide everything—the land, the vote, the new president."

"And who will that be?" I asked.

"Not the chief," said Julio. "But not Carranza, either."

I should have been more elated. I think, in that moment, I had been briefly granted the vision of a clairvoyant, not that much clairvoyance was necessary. You had only to understand the natures of the men involved to glimpse the outcome. I went inside the house and told Rosa. I told her quickly, gave her a big hug and then went outside again, because I didn't want her to ask me the one question I couldn't yet answer.

That night we all went to town and got drunk. Gangs of our cheering soldiers passed by us on the gas-lit streets. Arms linked together, weaving down the wet cobblestones, they sang a raucous verse to the tune of "La Cucaracha." It went like this:

> With the whiskers of Carranza—
> I'll make a new *toquilla!*
> For the sombrero—
> Of my general, Pancho Villa!

Their exuberance was to be expected. Everything that Villa promised had come true. He had rallied the people, armed them and led them to victory. He had taken Torreón, then the railroad line, then Juárez, Chihuahua City and Zacatecas. Even more quickly than he had predicted, Mexico City had fallen. Along the way he had made more than his share of mistakes, but in the end it didn't seem to matter. He had won. Now, I knew, he wanted to carve up the big haciendas, distribute land to the poor, build schools for the kids—and then he would retire, surround himself with his wives and learn to read. And I? I had survived nearly two years of fighting and hardly been scratched. Rodolfo Fierro had once promised to kill me, but now he would never have the chance. There was that fellow Bosques in El Paso, but I had a hunch he would stay there only as long as his friend Lieutenant Patton remained at Fort Bliss, and I knew that young officers moved from post to post almost as often as cowhands from pasture to range. Bosques would have to learn to live with the pain of his memories . . . and so would I. It was over. I had become a man. Not quite the man I had dreamed of being, but something more substantial, at least, than the youth who had banged into the Juárez cantina on that March day of 1913 to find Julio Cárdenas.

That's what I thought, in idle bursts, as we drank our way through the cantinas of Zacatecas during the next weeks and prepared to go with Pancho Villa to the historic Revolutionary Convention at Aguascalientes. I wouldn't quit before that. I had told Hannah I would leave when Mexico City fell, but I had thought it would fall to the Northern Division, and I had to be in at the end to see how it all worked out. That was the actor in me. I couldn't exit before the final curtain. I had to hear the bravos and witness the bows.

We also heard, during that time, that down in Morelos the little brown-skinned Zapatista soldiers were singing a verse of their own to the music of "La Cucaracha." It went this way:

> With the whiskers of Carranza—
> I'll braid a great reata!
> To lasso a horse—
> For my general, Zapata!

I wondered what the soldiers of Obregón were singing, and the soldiers of González, and if Carranza himself were humming anything into his long white beard. But I didn't really care. When we weren't out celebrating, I sat up on the hill of La Sierpe with Rosa, in the shade of some grapevines with a breeze whispering through the eucalyptus tree, quietly making my plans. There was a certain bittersweet felicity to that season. Day by day, Rosa's English improved, and it gave pleasure to us both. I put off telling her that I was leaving; I had decided that could wait until after we finished up at Aguascalientes. Who really knew how long the convention might take, or that there might not be an unforeseen aftermath? I must have sensed then what I know now: that nothing works out as planned, and there are no happy endings in life. There are no endings at all, except death. There are only pauses, the ends of acts and scenes . . . and then the wheel begins to turn again.

I didn't reckon with Rosa. I may have thought of her as a child, but she knew she was a woman. A woman with a right to a life, and a right to know where that life was going. One evening, after yet another wild celebration in town, we came back to La Sierpe, and the night air was so cool and vibrant, so fresh after the rains, that I suggested we sit outside on the stone terrace and drink one last tequila. I may have been a little drunk. Rosa poured a glass for me but none for herself. She rarely drank. In the bars, while Candelario and the others popped the cork on one bottle after another, she sipped sweet soda pop. She was only sixteen.

Scudding clouds moved across the face of the moon, then left it whitely bare, then masked it again, and I was reminded of the night I had nearly been shot by Juan Dozal.

And suddenly Rosa spoke. "Tomás . . . what will you do now? Will you go back to Texas to marry? Or will you stay with me? I need to know."

She had spoken quietly, but in the silence of the night I heard every word. She hadn't equivocated. She hadn't spoken shyly, either. She had spoken deliberately, as a woman who needed to know.

I let the breath slide from my lungs. I hadn't meant to groan, but it was indeed a groan that escaped my lips into the night air. She had always needed to know, and I hadn't seen it. I had played the fool, and fools are cruel when they don't understand the depth of their foolishness. Did I once believe that I was innocent of the sin of gluttony? There on La Sierpe, scathed by her quiet words, I knew better. And now honesty was somehow no longer easy or simple.

"Yes, Rosa. When the convention's finished in Aguascalientes, when there's peace, I'll go back to Texas. I'll marry Hannah. That's her name." I remembered her refusal to tell me her dead husband's name, because his shadow might fall between us. For the same reason, I had never told her Hannah's name. But now she knew. The shadow had fallen. "I'll stay with you until then," I said, "if that's what you want."

"What I want," she answered, "is for you to stay with me. Not until then. Forever."

The moon popped out again and cast a cool light on her face. I hadn't lied to her; I hadn't tried to be clever or apologetic or patronizing. I had tried to match her simplicity and to be honest. I hadn't known how she would respond, but I had assumed she would either accept my declaration in some kind of stoical Indian way, or else cry. What I hadn't bargained for was a forthright declaration of her own desires. And I hadn't glimpsed the full truth of those desires. I had been blind.

"Rosa, I told you in Ascensión . . ."

"I know what you told me in Ascensión," she said, "and since then. I remember well. I hear well. But I had thought, Tomás, that you might have changed in your feelings. I thought—"

Her voice broke in mid-sentence. She didn't go on. Her head tilted away so that I might not see, but her effort failed; the moonlight struck fully now on one cheek, and I saw the single glistening tear sliding down from the corner of her eye toward the bare brown shoulder above her blouse. She didn't bother to wipe it away. That would have been a theatrical gesture of which Rosa was not capable. She kept her hands tightly together in her lap. She was sitting on a small webbed cane stool, legs tucked neatly beneath her long skirt.

I knew what she thought. She thought it had been good between us, that it couldn't possibly be any better between me and anyone else. We were lovers and friends, we were as intimate as brother and sister, we were as linked as teacher and pupil. And in her eyes we were man and woman, mated. I wondered how it was possible to look at it any differently, except for the fact of Hannah and my allegiance that had existed before I had met a child by a lake, and that was cemented now by what had happened in Hipólito's house and the subsequent promises. My promises had all been to Hannah. I had made none to Rosa. She had never asked for any . . . except that I not banish her to Tomochic unless she displeased me. Had she ever displeased me? I couldn't remember a single instance. I was starting to detest myself.

"I love you, Rosa," I said, and wasn't surprised to hear my own voice break too. "You know that. You're a bountiful woman. There is no one else in the world like you. You've made me happy. I tried to do the same for you, but . . . I didn't succeed." I saw her mouth start to open, to protest, so I plunged on. "No, don't say it. I know I succeeded. . . . I know you were happy with me. I don't mean that. I mean I can't make you happy now, and I always knew this day, this night, would come when I would have to tell you . . . have to say good-bye. So in that sense I didn't succeed. I may have cheated you. I don't really know. I tried not to. But now, with Hannah—"

"I don't want to hear of her," Rosa said, speaking firmly, breaking into my hopeless speech. "I hear from your voice that you mean what you say. I cannot argue with you. I cannot beg. It would only make me cry, and it would achieve nothing. I never thought I could want a man who did not want me, but that seems now to be the case. Still—"

"Rosa, that's not so."

"Yes, I am sorry. I didn't truly mean that. I know you want me, but I also know that you want someone else, and want her more than me. You never lied to me about that. I am not angry with you." She lowered her head. "I am just sad."

Then, with swift grace, she stood up.

"I am going to bed, Tomás. I am very tired. In the morning I will leave."

My heart ached; it felt as if there were a bruise deep in my chest, spreading from behind the ribs to all parts of my body. I didn't want to hurt her anymore. I didn't rise to stop her, or embrace her, or do anything that would make it worse for her—or for me.

"Where will you go, Rosa?"

"To Tomochic. I will take the mare and the saddle, unless you need them."

"They're yours. Now listen to me." I spoke from a sudden darkness, into a darkness, for the moon had vanished again behind a long, lumbering gray cloud, and the starlight was dim. "The gold in Tomochic is yours. The gold you buried for Candelario and me. Half of it is yours. It's a gift, Rosa, from me to you. Please take it."

"But the gold belongs to the revolution," she said, puzzled. "You told me that before I buried it."

"I lied. I didn't know you that well then, and besides, half of it was Candelario's. He knew you even less. It was a gift from Villa to me. I want you to have it. It was taken from Mexicans; it belongs to Mexico. I want to give it back to Mexico. For me, Rosa, you're Mexico. Take it."

"No. You fought for it."

"I fought for Villa, damn it—not for gold. I didn't want it then and I don't want it now. Listen to me! You can buy land with it, or horses, or both. You can do whatever you want with it. You can go to school. You can become someone. You can become independent. You can be whatever you want to be in life."

I caught the flicker of a smile. "No, Tomás," she said softly. "I can't be what I want to be. I want to be your wife."

I winced but didn't reply to that. "Take the gold, Rosa. I'm not paying you off. I'm giving you something . . . with all my heart."

"I will never touch it," she answered sharply. "It will stay buried in the corral. It will rot there, if gold can rot. If you want it, you will have to come for it. You know where it is buried."

"For God's sake—!"

"I don't want to talk about it anymore. I'm grateful, Tomás. You mean well. You are a kind man. You gave me many gifts. I know you're not paying me. But I don't want it. I mean what I say. I vow before the Virgin that I will never touch it." She crossed herself. "And now I am going to bed."

I couldn't have stopped her and didn't try. I sat in the moonlight for an hour, alone, until the bottle of tequila was empty . . . as empty as my heart. I slung the bottle into the darkness and heard it shatter on the mountainside. An owl hooted, annoyed. Then I went inside and crawled into the bed behind her but didn't touch her, just as the morning after the fiesta in Ascensión, after Fierro had told me that one day he would kill me, and after I had made my first speech to Rosa about fidelity to Hannah. So much for fidelity. So much for Rosa. So much for becoming a better man. I listened for Rosa's quiet breathing. She was asleep, I realized. She wasn't at peace, but she was a child, and she could sleep. I lay awake until nearly dawn.

In the morning, because I had drunk tequila and she had drunk soda pop, she was up before me. When I woke from a short sleep, dazed, her saddlebags were already packed and she was tightening the cinches on the old skewbald mare. She wore her traveling clothes, a black skirt and a rough rebozo, and a flowered kerchief tying down her hair. Her fine breasts were hidden beneath the shapeless garments. She didn't even kiss me goodbye. She mounted the mare while I stood on the porch, an undoubtedly comic figure if there had been other eyes to see, wearing long johns, bleary-eyed and with tangled hair . . . as her hair had been by the lake on the day I met her. She was dry-eyed and seemingly confident. I loved her terribly.

"Goodbye, *mi capitán.*"

"Goodbye, Rosa."

Perhaps I didn't believe she would really go. But she did. She rode off on the dirt road and never looked back, and after a few minutes she vanished from sight, and then the dust slowly settled.

"Take the gold!" I shouted after her into the morning silence. It was a fine Mexican morning, crisp and dewy, with a clear bright blue sky, a morning that should have been one of glorious promise. "Take the gold! It's yours!"

I bent to one knee and laid a palm on the dusty Mexican earth. I shut my eyes against the hurting glare.

True love. High adventure. Fortune. I had found them all . . . then lost them all. Rosa had never displeased me. It was I, in the end, who had displeased her.

Part Two

Villa? Obregón? Carranza? What's the difference? I
love the revolution like a volcano in eruption. I love
the volcano because it's a volcano, the revolution
because it's a revolution.

—MARIANO AZUELA, *The Underdogs*

17

"The cankers of a calm world and a long peace."

from THE SCHOOLTEACHER'S JOURNAL

Fort Bliss
September 20, 1914

Lieutenant Patton receives a steady flow of intelligence reports from Mexico which he discusses with me, and my comments are then passed along in written form to his superiors. He told me that General Pershing no longer greatly esteems Francisco Villa—despite his recent remark to the newspapers that "Villa is the man of the hour"—but thinks Venustiano Carranza is a more noble sort of leader, armed with dignity rather than a pistol. General Scott, on the other hand, still admires Villa not merely as a resourceful field commander but as a man of powerful purpose and seems to turn a deaf ear to any tales of Pancho's villainy. Thus, a steady stream of conflicting reports reaches President Wilson from his generals on the border, and it is no wonder that to us here at Fort Bliss the White House seems almost paralyzed by indecisiveness.

"Wilson will have to make a choice one of these days," Lieutenant Patton confided to me this morning, in the midst of his Spanish lesson. "Villa or Carranza. But from what he hears, it's kind of like choosing between syphilis and the clap."

September 27, 1914

. . . my life is not unpleasant, although I have the feeling now and then that I am merely marking time. I am paid well and regularly, have a comfortable room at the post barracks, eat with the enlisted men and am learning to shoot a rifle—one of the dividends of my relationship with the lieutenant, who treats me more like a trusted friend than a menial servant.

I have met a young woman in town. She works as a chambermaid in the Gateway Hotel, and she is twenty years old, widowed with a child. She lives across the river in Juárez with her uncle but sometimes spends the night with me. The experience makes me feel that I am coming alive again. I think less about Colonel Fierro and Captain—now Major—Mix. But that is not what I want. I want to remember. The incident in El Paso last February, when I tried to kill Captain Mix, revealed the depth of my intentions to Lieutenant Patton. He was shocked. Like most Americans, he has the proper humanitarian emotions, but like most Americans he lacks the background of suffering with which to understand the thirst for vengeance, the dark need to destroy at all costs. Taking its place, as in the lieutenant, is an induced thirst for law and order tempered by a wavering sentimentality. He even apologized for placing me under arrest.

"I know how you feel. But Jesus, if you had shot the man," he cried, "we would've had to *hang* you! Can't you see that it leads nowhere? Forget revenge, Bosques . . . live your life!"

"I could forget revenge," I confessed, "if I could forget the horror. But that seems to be impossible."

"You know what I believe?" he said, in an uncharacteristic manner. "If each day all color is reinvented by the sun, then the chance to be present is worth all risk. Life is very full. Life is good. You just have to believe that and make the best of whatever comes your way. Stay awake and ready."

"I'll try, Lieutenant. I'll follow your example."

In two months' detention in the guardhouse I ate better than I ever had during thirty years in Mexico. During that time Lieutenant Patton came to visit me three or four times a week, ostensibly for his Spanish lesson. He has begun to reveal himself to me. A strange man, gifted but fundamentally unsure of himself—a horseman, hunter, steeplechaser, football player, swordsman, ardent student of military history—above all, a soldier. And yet, at the age of thirty, still a lowly lieutenant, he feels that glory and opportunity have eluded him. I suspect he knows that his superiors consider him a dilettante and dislike him because he owns the finest string of polo ponies between Fort Riley and California and is married to a beautiful woman with eight million dollars. He is convinced that hostilities are not over in Mexico, that the United States will somehow become involved and that the revolutionists—in particular, Villa—are our natural enemies. But one afternoon during his Spanish lesson he made a revealing statement.

"I don't care who we fight," he said, "as long as it's a long war and a good big one, and I get my share of it."

He sees a war against Mexico as the only chance to make his mark before it is too late, since Mr. Wilson seems more determined than ever to keep his country out of the European conflict. He cried, "Look at me, Bosques! I lie around shooting ducks and drilling men on a parade ground . . . playing polo . . . reading the *Iliad* and the *Odyssey* for the third time. Christ, I'm a soldier! I've had a good time in life, sure, but I've worked hard. And yet . . . have I done one solitary thing worth doing? Shithouse mouse! *Hijo de puta!* Don't you see? I want to write my name on something bigger than a section-room bench or a stock certificate!"

After the Benton killing last April he sent a plan to General Pershing that called for a fast cavalry strike across the border to retrieve the body. "Let Villa get in our way," he told me, grinding his teeth on his pipe. "We'll go through him like crap through a goose."

Meanwhile, in Mexico, the revolution has triumphed. Does that mean the end of war and suffering? The people of Mexico City might supply an interesting answer. The capital was occupied in August by the army of Alvaro Obregón, who immediately declared martial law. Then he began to take revenge on the civilian population, most of whom, since they had lived under Victoriano Huerta's yoke for two years, had been supporters of the government. When Obregón entered from the northwest he found a dry city—silent, sullen and hungry, and, above all, thirsty, for the pumping machinery of the city's water supply had been dynamited by the evacuating Huertistas. Obregón seized all available water and food for his troops. The poor, naturally, suffered the most. They began by eating the stray cats and dogs; they wound up trapping rats in the sewers. Children loitered near the military barracks and tried to sneak between the soldiers' legs for a few sips of water being given to the horses. It was an informal rule among the Obregonistas that anyone over twelve caught stealing water from the horses was shot.

Obregón levied a tax of twenty million pesos on the merchants of the city, ostensibly to relieve the suffering of the multitude. The merchants and bankers refused to pay it, and the city quickly became a scene from a painting by Hieronymus Bosch. Corpses were collected in milk wagons every morning by volunteers and burned in Chapultepec Park, the stench borne as far south as Xochimilco by the swirling winds. The sewer system, untended, overflowed and made the city stink like a slaughterhouse.

Carranza, during this macabre period of "peace," sits quietly in a luxury hotel, refusing to enter the National Palace, for by his own words in the Plan of Guadalupe he has disqualified himself for the presidency—"unless, of course, the people insist." His photograph has been taken a hundred times, always looking distinguished, always signing some decree. Emiliano Zapata, who has never met Carranza but nevertheless despises him, has refused to leave Morelos. Francisco Villa, a lion with sheathed claws, camps with his powerful army outside Zacatecas. All hope seems now to be centered on the Revolutionary Convention which begins any day in Aguascalientes. Every faction will be represented. At best, what can come of it other than a more refined definition of chaos? At worst, it will be a fatal struggle between irreconcilable forces: Villa and Carranza. If they can make peace, establish law and order, agree on who shall rule the country, there is hope. If not, there will be war. Men will march off to die with bugles and banners, to the cheers of children. Isn't it the easiest way to resolve human differences? How prosaic this sunny world would be if the knife and the bullet had not been invented. . . .

Law and order! Such fine words, which one hears often here, and now even

/ 209

in Mexico since the Revolutionary Convention is about to start. But they neglect the raw root of human passion. At best, like cages for vicious animals, they keep men at bay from each other. For a time.

18

"The bow is bent and drawn, make from the shaft."

One October night at the Morelos Theater in Aguascalientes, where they had been flag-waving and going for each other's throats for nearly a month, they showed movies. The theater was so jammed you could easily button up the wrong fly. The revolution's leaders were packed holster to holster in the aisles—Carranzistas, Obregónistas and Villistas—even the little cocoa-skinned Zapatistas, with their sleepy eyes and gigantic sombreros, who had finally agreed to show up and sulk in public. Cigarette smoke hung from the balcony like a solid gray cloud, as if a bomb had just exploded. The air was barely breathable, and you had to wonder when some of these fellows had last seen a bathtub.

A large white cotton curtain hung on the stage, flanked by two limp Mexican flags. That was the screen. The movie promised to be a panorama of the revolution, a collection of newsreel bits that some enterprising journalist in Mexico City had pieced together. I arrived late with Candelario and Julio, but as soon as they realized how crowded and hot it would be in the theater, Candelario objected.

"We can use our time better. Do you like Frenchwomen, Tomás? By pure chance, I know two. You're on your own now, my friend. What a blessing! Let's get drunk and find them."

But I hadn't been to the movies in a year, and the film might be important. Since Rosa had left Zacatecas and we had journeyed to Aguascalientes for the Convention, I had spent most of my nights in cantinas, or gazing up at the stars that glittered so coldly and implacably in the autumn skies. It seemed to me that on the high Mexican plateau the stars were closer to the earth than anywhere else I knew. It was an illusion . . . but what wasn't? I had heard it said that their light, streaming down on us with such mocking certainty and wondrous beauty, had existed billions of years ago and had only just reached us, and for all we knew those same stars might not now exist. Which meant if there was anyone up there and they could see our planet, they viewed a barren earth, antique and uninhabited except for crawling things. A desolation. I wished I knew. Rosa, in Tomochic, if she arched her head to gaze at the night, would see the same stars, glimpse the same mystery. That was all we shared now.

Outside the Morelos Theater, Candelario kept arguing that we were wasting our time. *"Hombre,* there are no seats! Is this movie going to show us something we haven't already seen?"

"I want to see it," I said doggedly. "And I have an idea. That screen is just a cloth curtain. I'll bet if we go backstage and sit behind it, we'll see perfectly."

"Yes," Candelario said, "but backwards."

"Does that mean," Julio asked, brandishing a nearly empty tequila bottle, "that we'll be retreating when we were really advancing?"

Full of tequila and stubborn energy, I had my way. We trooped round to the back entrance of the theater. For a few pesos the stage-hands were glad to rummage in the prop room and find chairs for us directly behind the screen, so that we sat with our boots resting comfortably on some greasy coils of rope. No one in the audience could see us; we couldn't see them, either, but we could hear them. These were the ranking officers of the various revolutionary divisions, the leaders of Mexico, struggling to find a solution to the conflict between Villa and Carranza. They hooted at each other like banshees.

At midnight the movie started. A bellow of approval surged like a thunderclap as the titles flashed on the screen. We had some trouble reading them backwards, but I had guessed right and we could see the images perfectly. As the action began, the theater grew hushed.

First came a file of long-haired Yaqui soldiers, marching to the beat of a drum which you could see but couldn't hear. They marched for two minutes, while the audience stirred restlessly. Then Obregón appeared, standing like Napoleon by an artillery piece. The officers surrounding him all smiled awkwardly because they knew the camera was grinding away.

"Viva Obregón!" the crowd yelled.

"Long live the Army of the Northwest!"

Carranza, beard flowing majestically, sat outdoors in front of his shuttered house in Monclava, solemnly signing a proclamation—left-handed, from our point of view.

"Long live the First Chief!"

Some boos became mixed in with the cheers. Pancho Villa galloped into view, the all-conquering centaur, grinning and urging his superb black stallion. The audience roared and stamped their feet, so that the theater shook.

"Long live the Northern Division!"

"Viva Pancho Villa!"

We saw a bit of the last battle for Torreón, but on the screen it looked oddly tame . . . a few puffs of smoke from the cannon behind some cactus; a few officers staring straight at the camera, waving gleefully; then long panoramas of the white desert with horsemen straggling through the dust. A scene of some wounded and exhausted men lying against an adobe wall brought a common sigh, like a breath of

/ 211

wind, from the audience. There were no *vivas.* Too many friends had died in too many battles.

After that the movie concentrated on Venustiano Carranza. It showed him riding into Nogales on a white horse. Then he rode into Chihuahua on a black horse. It showed him under a mesquite tree, supposedly signing the Plan of Guadalupe, then at six different desks signing six different proclamations. He visited hospitals and schools. He patted little children on the head and talked to bewildered Indian women who surely wouldn't have understood a word he was saying. It went on for twenty minutes and through a change of reels. "Let's go," Candelario muttered, digging his elbow in my ribs. The audience began to stamp their feet again, then hiss.

"Enough! No more Don Venus!"

"Viva Francisco Villa!"

The booing rose to an uproar as yet another picture of the First Chief filled the screen, prancing into Mexico City on a horse that had been decorated with plumes like a circus animal. He waved in triumph to the wretched crowds. Candelario kept muttering, but that was mild compared to what happened on the other side of the screen. I never found out who, but some outraged officer in the front part of the theater—clearly not a Carranzista—yanked out his pistol. He fired two shots.

I don't know what part of the First Chief's image they hit, but the bullets ripped through the screen, flew about six inches above my head and slammed into the back wall of the stage, knocking off plaster.

"Jesus Christ . . ." I didn't need an invitation; I fogged out of that chair like a turpentined cat. Crawling along the wooden boards, followed closely by an outraged Candelario supporting a stumbling Julio, as if we were in battle and pinned down by a well-fortified enemy, we reached the stage door.

Once we were safe in the street I took a deep gulp of the cool night air. It tasted sweet. It always did when you knew you were lucky to be alive.

"That was some brilliant idea," Julio gasped, when he had his breath back.

Candelario turned on me, shaking a fist. "Do you realize," he yelled, "that if Carranza had entered Mexico City on foot, we would be dead?"

"But if he'd entered Mexico City on foot," I said, trying to calm them down, "he wouldn't have been Carranza."

Comical? A farce? Yes, but so was the whole convention. From the time that it had been announced in July it took six weeks to get it going, and then it lasted well into November of 1914. Zapata and Carranza never showed up, although they each sent plenty of delegates to shout and glare at each other. Zapata never gave a reason for his absence, and Carranza offered such a bagful of reasons that you never knew what he really meant. He sent a stream of formal messages to Aguascalientes, one of which began: "If Pancho Villa could write, or if he could read what others write . . ." He publicly referred to Villa as a dedicated enemy of the Catholic Church, the murderer of William Benton, and a brigand who had tried to overthrow the apostle Madero by force of arms. Villa writhed but held his tongue. I think he truly hoped for peace.

Throughout the first month the delegates struggled to find a solution to the conflict. Green eyes glittering with catlike patience, Obregón played the role of peacemaker. Testing the waters, the convention adopted a halfhearted resolution proposing to remove Carranza, Villa and Zapata from their posts before they appointed an interim President of Mexico. Marching before the delegates, hair washed and mustache curried, Villa proclaimed, "You are going to hear sincere words spoken from the heart of an uneducated man. Francisco Villa will not be an embarrassment to those of good conscience. He seeks nothing for himself! I want the destiny of my country to be bright. *I will go!* Let history say who are Mexico's true sons."

Tiny Obregón, all smiles, reached up and hugged him. He must have thought that if everyone left, he would be president.

Now, in the political arena it became a matter of "After you, señor." Zapata, filing his spurs down in his mountain stronghold of Cuernavaca, never bothered to reply. Carranza continued to run the government from his hotel in the capital as if nothing had happened. He wanted the Northern Division to disband before he took the train to Veracruz.

"If I leave that scheming sonofabitch behind me in Mexico," Villa muttered, "he'll find some excuse to change his mind." So Villa went before the convention with a more forceful solution. Tears streaming from bloodshot eyes, he proposed that he and Don Venus face a firing squad together, thus effectively ending their dispute, at least in this world.

Predictably enough, Carranza announced that he would decline the honor. The idea was a sham, he said, and masked Pancho Villa's true desire to rule Mexico. The next day the convention met and elected an interim President of Mexico—a bullnecked lawyer named Eulalio Gutiérrez who had been a dynamiter of trains for Obregón up in Sonora and finally occupied some government post under Carranza, although it was well known that the First Chief disliked his plodding sincerity. Few had met the man, and therefore few had developed a reason to dislike him. That was his great advantage, which obviously couldn't last for very long. Sure enough, Carranza refused to recognize Gutiérrez as the legitimate President of Mexico. "I will continue," Don Venus proclaimed, "to fight the enemies of Mexico."

Like boys at a Sunday sandlot baseball game, it was time to choose up sides. Our generals met early one November afternoon in Villa's hotel room. The air was hazed with smoke and thick with the smell of horses and old sweat. Everyone wore medals distributed by the convention, except Felipe Angeles, who came dressed in a brown sweater with leather elbow patches and his black riding boots. Angeles, the most sophisticated among us, reflected not the enthusiasm of the revolution but its impotence. He assumed a forbidding air at the meeting and even spoke sharply to Villa.

"Why do you think no agreement has been reached here, Pancho? Have you wondered? I've come to a simple conclusion. Everyone in Aguascalientes struggles now for the fruits of victory. Each man aligns himself in a way most advantageous to his personal interests. Idealism is dead."

"Not with us," Villa said.

"So what do we do?" Urbina demanded. "Sit back and let these pantywaists parcel out everything we've fought for? Or do we fight them so that we can keep it?"

"Fight who?" Angeles asked. "Where's the enemy? There's no battlefield, no dictator. Huerta and Orozco are gone. Carranza has no army. What has Obregón done to us that we should fight him for?"

"Not to us," Villa growled. "To the people. What he did in Mexico City is unforgivable."

"Obregón wants to be President of Mexico," I said. "Why not let him, chief? You always say you don't want the job. What Obregón did in the capital may have been bad, but he's still a revolutionist. He hasn't taken sides since the convention started. If he forms a government with you behind him, President Wilson will recognize it the next day. You can have anything you want. You would stand at his right arm as a conscience, a protector of the people."

"I've said a dozen times," Villa replied, "that a military man shouldn't be president."

Angeles smiled thinly. "But it's well known that Obregón's only a chickpea farmer turned general."

Rodolfo Fierro was there but he said nothing. Urbina thumped the table so hard that the ashtrays spilled. "If it comes to a fight with Obregón," he yelled, "we'll beat the shit out of him!"

"Zapata controls the south," Villa said thoughtfully. "I control the north. If Obregón's fool enough to ally himself with Carranza, whatever army they've got is wedged between us. Felipe, you're the strategist—work out a plan to deal with it. If this fucking convention can't make peace, I'll meet with Zapata and we'll do it ourselves."

Peace? He didn't mean peace. He meant war. Angeles looked at him bleakly. Our meeting came to an end, and so did the glorious Revolutionary Convention of 1914. General Murguía, who had defended Torreón against us, went over to Carranza with an entire Federal division that had been hiding out near Puebla. He hated Villa for defeating him; any enemy of Villa's was automatically his friend. Then three of our own generals defected, with their brigades, in return for God knows what promises from Carranza. That blow penetrated even deeper when one of them trumpeted to the American reporters the true story of the Benton murder and his part in falsifying the execution orders. Carranza's staff packed up the treasury's printing presses, carting them off in the direction of Veracruz. Enraged by the theft, President Gutiérrez conferred with Pancho Villa and appointed him Chief General of the Army of the Convention. We found out later that he bore a grudge against Obregón, who had once told him, "If you were as skillful a lawyer as you are a dynamiter of trains, all your clients must be serving life sentences."

Obregón made his final decision, I suspect, in favor of what he considered the lesser of two evils. He had all the captured German equipment that had landed last May on *Ypiranga*—enough barbed wire, rifles and bullets to equip an army of fifty thousand men. Abandoning Mexico City, he issued a manifesto calling for all of Mexico's good sons to rise up with him and Carranza against that monster of treason and crime, Pancho Villa.

"Our native land implores us to resist evil!" Obregón cried. "To struggle until we conquer, or convert Mexico into a vast cemetery . . ."

Villa read these words with flinty eyes, and then, to those of us present, he said, "We'll go south. The time has come to meet Emiliano Zapata."

That afternoon I went alone to see Villa. I had promised Hannah and myself that I would leave when the revolution had triumphed, when we took Mexico City. The triumph seemed a hollow one, but now at last we were about to enter the capital. The end had come, and it was time to go. I wondered why I felt so dejected . . . empty of desire.

I held firm and told Villa my resolve. His yellow eyes glittered. "I want your blessing," I said. "Before I go."

I hadn't known I was going to say that. I hadn't realized how important it was for me.

"Why are you doing this?" he asked sharply. "Do you think your luck's run out? Do you think you'll have your balls shot off on some battlefield?"

"That's always possible," I said. "But that's not my reason. Hannah's waiting for me in El Paso. I'm going to marry her. You always knew that. You always said it would happen."

He looked at me oddly for a moment, as if he didn't quite believe me. But then his eyes softened.

"Good, Tomás. I'm happy for you. Of course, you have my blessing. I owe you that and more. But I'll miss you. . . ." A bleak and puzzled look suddenly crossed his face. I realized then that nothing had worked out the way he had planned, either. He had thought that once he had whipped Orozco and sent Huerta fleeing, the revolution would be won. He had planned it perfectly, and he had succeeded. But something had gone awry. The rules of the game had been changed. Perhaps he was frightened . . . I saw something in his eyes that could have been fear, as if his imagination had faltered and events had raced beyond his control. I was moved by his sadness. I loved him as a man, and I wanted to see him prevail.

"You were right," he murmured, breaking into my thoughts. "You argued that we should join forces with Obregón, let him be president. If not, we'd have to fight against him. And it's so." He looked at me shrewdly. "But it still makes no sense to you."

"You could have made a deal with him, that's all I meant. It would have saved a lot of lives and grief."

"A deal? I'll tell you what kind of deal it would have been. He would be president, and I would be marked for a bullet. No, everything's clear now. I have to smash him, have him shot by a firing squad. Carranza, too. And then I've got to find a man to rule this miserable country. It won't be me—I'm a soldier, not a governor. But somewhere in Mexico there must be a man like the little Señor Madero, and I'll find him. Then I won't make the mistake I did before. I'll guard his back."

His words gave me heart. He was a man who needed clear objectives, and now once again he seemed to have them. I wished I could be there to see how it turned out. Life with Villa certainly was never dull.

"Is Zapata the man?" I asked.

"No," he said thoughtfully, "I don't think so. Zapata is like me. Born to fight, not rule." He gave me a tired smile. "Do what you must, Tomás. I told you, you have my blessing."

I made another decision then. I may simply again have smelled my destiny.

"I tell you what, chief. Let me come with you to Mexico City. I've never been there. They say it's a great city. I want to meet Zapata. I've met everyone else who seems to matter, and I'm curious. After that, I'll go."

 " 'Tis time to fear when tyrants seem to kiss."

On a fine December day, full of birdsong, Candelario and Julio and I strolled down the tree-lined Avenida Juárez in Mexico City, sightseeing. A squad of brown-skinned Zapatista soldiers in floppy white cotton trousers followed us at a distance, gazing up in awe at the tall buildings

216 /

with their barred French windows. We had just reached the stone plaza in front of the National Palace when a clanging of bells reached our ears. A brilliant red fire engine turned the corner, tires screeching on the slickly paved street. Firemen hung from both sides, wearing scarlet uniforms and peaked caps.

The Zapatistas behind us ducked for cover among the linden trees, raised their rifles to the hip and fired. One of the firemen bounced on the pavement, then began to crawl toward the shelter of a doorway.

Candelario ran to help him. Julio and I flung ourselves toward the little men crouched behind the trees, our pistols drawn.

"Don't shoot him! For Christ's sake, stop!"

The Zapatistas looked up slowly, their soft eyes bright with alarm. "But my colonel—those are Federals—"

"No, no," Julio panted. "Firemen. They have red uniforms too. They put out fires. With water—see the hoses? Go help the man you've shot . . . get him a doctor."

When they were gone, we looked at each other. These were Villa's potential allies. "No wonder they never left Morelos," Julio said. "They're not soldiers. They're backward children."

Following Obregón's flight to the east, the Zapatistas had come up from the south to occupy the capital. The citizens expected the occupation to be far worse than the systematic rape perpetrated that summer by the Obregonistas, for the mountain men of Morelos had been depicted as bloodthirsty savages who skinned fair-haired people alive and ate iguanas for breakfast. But they arrived without bugles or drums and filed silently down the boulevards, never firing their guns in the air as the more exuberant warriors of the north were prone to do. They entered the glittering establishment of Sanborn's on the Paseo de la Reforma, called the capped-and-gowned waitresses "Esteemed lady," asked to be shown the proper way of holding the cutlery and then paid their bills with silver coins. Around their necks they wore silver crosses and jade amulets against the evil eye. They were polite to the more rowdy soldiers of the Northern Division and in exchange for a few extra cartridges would offer them bags of marijuana. The Zapatistas smoked it day and night, which may have accounted for their simplicity.

Following the shooting of the fireman—a fine example of Zapatista judgment—I saw a sight early one morning that typified Zapatista justice. In the gray dawn light, propped against the Monument to Motherhood off Avenida Insurgentes, waiting for the garbage cart to come and haul them away, lay three blood-soaked bodies in big braided sombreros and the floppy white cotton clothing of Morelos. Centavo coins had been placed on the eyelids of the three corpses, and to avoid any mistaken speculation as to who was responsible, a hand-lettered cardboard sign was pinned to each Zapatista's hat, signed by a Zapatista colonel.

The first sign said: "This man was shot because he was a traitor."

The second said: "This man was shot for stealing."

The third said: "This man was shot by mistake."

Emiliano Zapata set up his headquarters in a modest hotel on the outskirts of the city. He told all journalists in the briefest possible words that he supported President Gutiérrez, hoped that land would be given to the people, and looked forward to meeting the great revolutionist of the north, Pancho Villa.

But the next day, as we approached the city, Zapata scurried back to the mountains of Cuernavaca like a frightened hare. The meeting didn't take place until a week later.

During that week I played the role of tourist, and Pancho Villa that of unrequited lover. His second day in the city, at a bullfight, he was introduced to a twenty-year-old girl named Conchita del Hierro, a sloe-eyed orphan whose parents had died of typhus during the summer occupation of Obregón. Now penniless, she worked as a receptionist in the Hotel Palacio, and she was under the guardianship of her aunt, an imperious woman named Isabel del Hierro. The girl was rather beautiful, I thought, and more refined than Villa's usual choice of wife, although she had the powerful breasts and tawny features that he always admired. I was at the bullfight too, sitting between Villa and Conchita's Aunt Isabel, and after the introduction, before the toreros appeared to circle the ring, the lady leaned toward me and stage-whispered in my ear, "What a marvelous man your general is! One hears so many tales of him, one hardly knows what to believe. But he is so masterful! So simple, yet so obviously complex. What a pity," she sighed.

"What is a pity, señora?" I asked.

"That he's married."

"Why is that a pity?"

"Because, Major, I have made a study of the stars. General Villa is a Gemini, is he not? My niece Conchita is a Sagittarius. We think we control our own fate, but we are often in the hands of superior forces. Conchita and your general were destined to fall in love and marry."

She must have known something. For three days Pancho Villa squired Conchita del Hierro about Mexico City, to parties and dances and little lunches in bowered hotel gardens. He even went riding with her through Chapultepec Park in the early morning to pick flowers, as if he were a botanist. I watched lazily from a distance, wondering if wedding bells would soon be ringing after a priest had faced the wrong end of a pistol. On the fourth day I dropped by Villa's house, a spendid three-story colonial mansion on Calle Liverpool that had been owned formerly by a Huertista banker, to find out when our meeting with Zapata would take place. The chief welcomed me eagerly, then fell into a leather chair like a bull cleanly killed. His eyes were bloodshot, and his cheeks, usually so ruddy, were pale.

"Tomás, I'm glad you haven't gone yet. I must talk to someone. I have a terrible problem."

"What's Carranza done now?"

"Piss on Carranza—I can deal with that."

The story then poured out like a waterfall. As he talked he kept lighting cigarettes, stubbing them out half-smoked on the arms of chairs and tabletops, so that by the time he had finished the floor was littered with butts and ashes and the carpet had been scorched in three or four places. He never noticed.

He was in love with Conchita del Hierro, and as far as he could tell, she returned his affections. He spent about five minutes describing to me how beautiful he found her, how intelligent, how sympathetic and sensitive. He had never met a girl like her. He was ready to die for her bones, as the Mexicans say. She was only twenty, but she had the wisdom of Cleopatra and Sheba combined, the courage of Joan of Arc, the queenly bearing of Victoria. Naturally he had asked her to marry him. The result was not what he expected.

"She told me I was married already, and so the answer was no. I explained that Luz was like a sister to me, and the others—" He dismissed that gang with an upward movement of his hand. "But still she said no, and when I persisted, she began to leak tears. Tomás, I can't stand it when women cry. Luz did a lot of that in the beginning, but not anymore. She's learned. But when Conchita cried, my heart nearly broke in half. Naturally, I changed the subject. She could ask me to get down on all fours and moo like a cow, and I would do it."

The next day, he continued, Aunt Isabel paid him a visit, and they lunched in the garden of the Hotel Palacio. Villa had bought a new dark green tweed suit and a polka-dotted bow tie, and he wore the shiny boots that gave him corns. With a man in love, I realized, anything is possible. Señora del Hierro arrived in a magnificent white lace dress that revealed as much as possible of her white bosom, probably intended to remind Villa that under Conchita's blouse there dwelled the same splendors. Birds chirped in the patchy sunlight of the little garden, which they had quite to themselves, Villa having ordered it closed to everyone else. The señora began the conversation over her sherry by relating to him the troubles of the del Hierro family, who had owned silver mines near Zacatecas. They had never mistreated the mine workers, she stressed, and therefore weren't as rich as some of the other owners, but their historical kindliness was of no avail when the revolution began.

"So I gathered she needed money," Villa said to me, "and I immediately wrote out a draft for five thousand pesos. But there was more. She thanked me, and then she explained that Conchita was religious and would be glad to give herself to me in marriage . . . if I would divorce my other wives. The stars had foretold our union, she said! Can you imagine? Conchita was destined to marry a great man astride a prancing black horse. I told her it sounded like she would become the next Señora Carranza, but the old bitch didn't even smile."

"Will you do it?" I asked.

"Marry her, yes! Divorce the others, no! Tomás, I'm their light-house and their shepherd. Can a lighthouse darken its beam? Can a shepherd turn his back and leave his flock bleating in misery—dis-honored? It would be unthinkable. And yet I love this girl—I *must* have her."

He waited for me to comment, but I wasn't particularly moved. I sat on an antique wooden footstool, restlessly scuffing my boots at a pile of ashes he had dropped on the carpet. It struck me that he had more important things to worry about, but I knew the power of love and how it twisted the imagination.

"Can't you have an affair with her," I suggested, "and let things take their natural course?"

"She's willing," he said darkly, "and she's already given me a little taste of her honey. I suppose she thinks she can trap me that way. She's getting advice from the aunt, I'm sure. But what hold can a man have on a woman if she's not his wife? She can leave him anytime she pleases. Look at that Indian one you had, that Rosa. She left you, didn't she? Could *you* stop her?"

"It wasn't quite the same," I said unhappily.

He ignored that. "Tomás, I offered Conchita my love and my name. Don't you think that's honorable? But she still won't marry me! I thought of going to a *curandera.*"

"For a potion?"

"They say it can work. Some men carry a dead hummingbird in their pocket, or put the leg of a beetle in the girl's glass of soda pop. You can also use powder made of crushed bones from a human skull, but too much of it makes her crazy. I've seen a *curandera* in Durango treat a bad dose of clap by rubbing the pecker with a live black chicken. The chicken became crippled. The pecker stood up and was fine. What should I do?"

He was quite serious, as I found out later, but clearly pessimistic. Besides, unlike most men, he wasn't bent on seduction without mar-riage. Beyond stating the obvious, I couldn't help him.

"Have an affair, chief. You'll get tired of her, just as you do in your marriages. Then you'll pay her off, just as you do with your wives. It all comes to the same thing in the end. Meanwhile," I said, "pay more attention to the war, or the revolution, or whatever you call it these days."

That wasn't what he wanted to hear, and he realized he wasn't going to get any more solace from me if he kept up his laments.

"It helped me to talk to you, Tomás," he said, a bit coldly, "even if we didn't find an answer. Now, what can I do for you? Why did you come by?"

"I'm ready to head for Texas. I wanted to know when we're going to meet Zapata."

"Tomorrow," he said. "It's been arranged—at Xochimilco. Be ready to leave at dawn."

The village of Xochimilco was a Zapatista stronghold near the floating flower gardens south of Mexico City. We rode on horseback, with a cloudless sky and the sun like a ripe tomato rising above the snowy peak of Popocatépetl. Trotting through cobbled streets that smelled of sizzling corn oil, Villa tilted his hat back and closed his eyes. Despite his troubles with Conchita del Hierro, his mouth drooped in a lazy smile; through the figurehead of Gutiérrez, he ruled Mexico. That wasn't what he wanted—he had always said so—but it didn't seem to displease him.

On the edge of Xochimilco we were met by Professor Otilio Montaño, the burly schoolteacher who had translated all of Zapata's thoughts into the Plan of Ayala. It was the best revolutionist document I had ever read, because it was the shortest. While the horses drank from goatskin buckets of water brought by Indian women, children ran out with wreaths of poppies and roses that they dumped in our path. The sun shone brightly on a breathlessly hot morning; the scent of the flowers was overpowering. Villa began to sneeze.

"My hay fever is coming back." He turned to me, groaning quietly. "I'll be dead by the time we get there."

The village band of Xochimilco, a few trumpets, a tuba and a bass drum, played "Las Mañanitas," and then the legendary leader from Morelos appeared, sauntering down the dusty main street with his retinue as we dismounted in front of the schoolhouse. I had seen pictures of Zapata, a former melon grower and army sergeant, but I still wasn't prepared for the man in the flesh.

Pancho Villa had come dressed in the clothes he had worn in the northern campaigns—his tan sweater with its frayed elbows, baggy khaki pants and riding boots, and the cool pith helmet that was now stained much the same color as his shirt. The rest of us, except for Rodolfo Fierro, wore our Texas scout hats and cartridge belts. Zapata looked as if the finest tailors in Mexico City had prepared him for the occasion and sewn his clothes around his body. His black *charro* pants were so tight that his private parts bulged like an apple with a thick stem, and the seams glittered in the sunlight with oversized silver buttons. He wore a brilliant lavender shirt, a blue neckerchief and a short black silk jacket from whose pockets protruded two scarlet handkerchiefs. He was a short man, and his pointed Spanish boots sported four-inch-high heels. The gold-braided twenty-gallon sombrero made it dangerous to come within two feet of him without risking that the brim might cut your throat. His mustache extended beyond his cheeks; his dark eyes were large, liquid and mysterious. Candelario whispered to me, "He looks like the leader of a mariachi band."

/ 221

But Villa, eyes leaking tears from the bouquets of flowers the children had pressed into his arms, ducked under the sombrero and gave Zapata the promised *embrazo*.

"Señor General, today I realize my dream. I meet the chief of the great revolution of the south."

In a languid voice, Zapata replied, "And I meet with honor the chief of the Northern Division."

Arm in arm they strolled into the schoolhouse where a large wooden table, scratched with the initials of children and lovers, had been placed in the center of a small classroom whose flaking walls were yellowed with age. Termites worked busily in the wooden beams overhead, so that peppery brown dust dropped steadily on our papers. Zapata had with him his brother Eufemio, Otilio Montaño, three generals and a journalist named Paulino Martinez. We all sat down, while the band gathered in the corridor and began to play. The big bass drum boomed in my ears, and it was hard to hear what the two chiefs were saying.

"... a beautiful sombrero, Señor Zapata. It must keep you very cool in the hot weather."

"Very cool."

"I used to wear a sombrero, but in battle . . . hard to see the enemy if . . . what? A present from my wife in Chihuahua. Teddy Roosevelt . . . at San Juan."

Candelario whispered again in my ear, "Don't you want to go to a cantina with me and get drunk?"

I shook my head. I had waited too long for this. Shy as a girl and boy introduced by their families for the purpose of marriage, the two great revolutionists continued their historic discussion. Finally the talk edged round to the subject of Carranza, and it was as if the boy and girl had discovered they both loved cherries and hated prunes. Each in turn damned the former First Chief, men who slept in soft beds, drank chocolate instead of black coffee and were oblivious to the suffering of the people.

"No man can be a true revolutionist, General Zapata, if he hasn't slept under a mesquite tree on a cold winter night."

"That's true, General Villa. The people still don't believe it when you say to them, 'This land is yours.' We must teach them."

"In the next life, Señor Zapata, I'll be a farmer myself. I believe there is going to be another life . . . but if there's not, I have forty thousand Mausers, seventy-six cannon and sixteen million cartridges for this one. And thirty thousand men who know how to use them."

"You are a fighter, Señor Villa. There's no doubt of it."

"What else can a man do?"

"You don't want to rule Mexico, Pancho?"

"No more than you, Emiliano."

That point was settled. The fencing was over. The band struck up with "Adelita" for the second time. Zapata, in his soft voice, murmured something that I didn't hear.

"Well, is there a more private place?" Villa asked eagerly.

We withdrew to a little classroom on the second floor, leaving most of the retinue behind. Zapata and Villa mounted the wooden steps first, boots thumping, arms linked together, still murmuring in each other's ears. None of us could hear. Angeles, Urbina, Fierro and I were behind them, followed by three Zapatista generals who looked very much like their chief except that their sombreros were smaller. We all sat down in the classroom.

". . . good," Zapata was saying. "After we've stood Obregón against a wall, we'll pick the man together."

Immediately we realized that something had been settled on the staircase amid those unheard whispers and soft squeezes of arms. Between the first and second floor the two generals had agreed to join forces in war against Carranza and Obregón. This was a decision that would affect millions of lives, cause thousands of deaths, but it had been accomplished swiftly, simply and privately. Urbina, when he realized what had happened, grinned widely, showing broken teeth. Angeles looked startled. He had been ordered to work out a strategy; but then he had not been consulted.

"For the moment we'll let Gutiérrez stay on as president," Villa said. "When we've defeated our enemies, we'll have an election. One man, one vote. Any woman who can sign her name will have the vote too. In that, we'll even be ahead of the gringos."

Zapata shrugged. He waved his hand languidly, an instant convert to suffrage. Now the talk became more practical, as the two men bent their heads together behind children's desks and swiftly planned the military campaign. They did it alone, as they seemed intent on doing everything alone.

The strategy was simple. Villa would strike to the north, against González and Obregón. Zapata would march east and capture Puebla, then descend the eastern Sierra Madres to tropical Veracruz on the Gulf of Mexico, destroying whatever army Carranza might have mustered. "Find Don Venus," Villa said, "and stand him against a wall." He would need cannon, Zapata declared. Villa nodded emphatically. Felipe Angeles cleared his throat to voice his opinion, but the chief silenced him by raising his palm. Clearly Villa felt that this was a time for only the heads of armies to speak.

"There is another matter to discuss," Zapata murmured. He explained that during the convention a onetime colonel of his had defected to the side of Obregón and was now in Mexico City, appointed by Gutiérrez to some official position. He asked Villa to find the man and deliver him to Cuernavaca to be shot.

"With pleasure, *compañero.*" Villa turned to Fierro, who sat, as always, attentive and silent, yet somehow managed with his calm gaze to project an air of indisputable menace. "Make a note of that, Rodolfo," he said, and Fierro nodded. Then, as if he were taking orders for delivery of inanimate machinery, Villa addressed Zapata again. "Is there anyone else?"

"Yes," Zapata said. "I have a list."

"Good. So do I."

The man who headed Villa's list was Paulino Martinez, the editor of the newspaper in Cuernavaca, who had published articles several years ago damning President Madero as a weakling and charlatan. That had been Zapata's expressed opinion too, but it seemed that insults which would be forgiven on the part of the great general of Morelos, our new ally, were enough to condemn his lackeys to execution. At that moment Martinez sat downstairs in the schoolhouse, joking with Candelario.

Zapata was affable about it. "You can have Martinez. I don't want you to think I'm a difficult man to deal with." This time Zapata turned to Fierro, whose reputation was known and whose role in the proceedings was clear, and said, "Do you know the man, Colonel Fierro?"

"No, Señor General, I've not had that pleasure."

"I'll introduce you later," Zapata said.

"That's very kind of you," Fierro replied.

They understood each other perfectly, and I had the feeling that they would make a fine pair. Even Villa frowned slightly, but said nothing.

Matters of war and vengeance being settled, we all clumped downstairs to a restaurant where the town authorities had prepared a little banquet of hot chile, roast kid, pulque and beer. Halfway through the meal Villa made a little speech that began, "You are going to hear sincere words spoken from the heart of an uneducated man. . . ."

And then Paulino Martinez, a florid, slant-eyed man—with no way of knowing that his general had just traded away his life—rose to heap praise on the occasion. "This date," he intoned, "should be engraved with diamonds in our history. It is the dawn of our salvation because two pure men, men without duplicity, men born of the people, know their griefs and fight for their well-being."

Villa smiled crookedly, and I lost most of my appetite and couldn't finish my kid and beer. I remembered Hipólito, back in the stockyards of Torreón, saying that the revolution was turning to shit. I had hoped he was wrong; but so had Paulino Martinez.

After the meal Zapata called for a bottle of Hennessy cognac. He poured two tumblers and set one in front of Pancho Villa, who frowned.

"*Compañero,* you know that I don't drink."

"You must," Zapata said softly. "To seal our friendship."

Villa hesitated, then tilted his head and drained the glass dry with one swallow. Fresh tears burst from his already red eyes. "Get me some water, for God's sake. . . ."

Such was the historic meeting of the men whom the people called the Centaur of the North and the Attila of the South. They agreed to meet in a few days in Mexico City at the National Palace, and in the middle of the afternoon we called for our horses and left for the capital.

We rode in silence for a while, each with his own thoughts. The mountains and plain were covered with a golden light haze that turned first smoky blue, then dull violet. Finally, as it chilled, the peaks stood out sharp against a slate sky, and the land seemed a soft velvet brown. There was a last dying flash of green color. On the outskirts of the city we dismounted to piss. Villa slouched over to where Angeles, Urbina and I stood together. Our breath blew puffs of vapor into the cold evening air. Villa stuck out his jaw toward Angeles.

"Well, Felipe? You wanted to speak in Xochimilco and I stopped you. What was it?"

"I don't think you want to hear it."

Even in the gloom, Villa's eyes glittered. "Speak your mind."

"Very well." Angeles straightened his shoulders under his thin sweater. "I don't like the man we met today. He reminded me of the young French officers I knew in Saumur, the ones who wanted to fight duels instead of battles. And he insulted you by forcing you to drink. But I now speak only as a military man, and as someone whose opinions in these matters I hope you respect."

"Felipe, get on with it." Villa shuffled his feet. "I'm freezing my ass off."

Angeles got on with it. He felt it was a serious strategic mistake to have given Zapata the task of taking Puebla. Venustiano Carranza was a relentless politician. Obregón was not a bad general. Given time, they would organize their forces, make promises they couldn't keep and rally the dissident generals throughout the country. "Throw the Northern Division against Carranza at once," Angeles counseled. "And stop only after we've defeated him and pushed his General Murguía into the Gulf."

"Zapata will do that. He said so."

"Pancho, I've studied his campaigns. I've spoken at length to his officers, and now I've met the man himself. There's no doubt he's a patriot, a good revolutionist. He's a brilliant guerrilla fighter. He attacks with surprise, he harasses his enemy from all sides, he withdraws cleverly. But does that make him the general of an army that can cross half of Mexico? Has he ever commanded a complicated battle such as Torreón? He captures villages and garrisons! He's never even left the south!" Angeles shook his head. "You've seen his soldiers, for God's sake! They're halfwitted peasants! Whenever they stop to rest, they blot out what few brains they have with marijuana. Once they leave Morelos and find themselves in flatlands and tropics, without their women and their safe hideaways . . . will they stay to fight? If they suffer a bad reverse, will they regroup? I don't think so, Pancho."

For a while Villa seemed to consider this seriously. But then he said, "Zapata asked to go to Veracruz. I've promised him half my artillery. If I go back on my word, how can I convince him that we're partners in war?"

"You shouldn't be partners," Angeles said flatly. "That was your mistake. You should be in command."

"I am," Villa said, annoyed.

"That wasn't obvious. If so, why is he going after Carranza while we're chasing after isolated brigades in the north? Carranza's no general, but he has plenty of men, and Murguía to command them. González and Obregón are like hats hanging on a rack. The rack is Carranza, and the best use of our forces is not to pick off the hats one by one, but to topple the rack. Then all the hats will fall."

Villa frowned. "If Zapata can't give Carranza a bath in the Gulf, we'll come down and do it for him. What do you think, Tomás?"

He had turned to Tomás Urbina, not me. Urbina tugged at his drooping mustache. As the last scarlet band of sunset vanished in the gloom, I couldn't see his eyes. If I had, perhaps I would have understood.

"Let's go to Chihuahua and fight González," he said. "We're always lucky there."

"I'll think more about it, Felipe," Pancho Villa promised, but it was clear to all of us that he wasn't about to change his mind. We mounted our shivering horses and trotted off in the bright starlight toward Mexico City. Tomorrow, I thought, I'll say my good-byes. Then I'd head for Texas. Whatever Villa did from now on, I would have to read about in the newspapers.

Conchita del Hierro and her aunt occupied the top floor of Villa's house on Calle Liverpool. The second floor, in a picturesque state of disarray, was Villa's, and the ground floor was given over to the conducting of government business. I had been quartered with Candelario and Julio in a heated apartment not far away. I strolled over to Calle Liverpool through the gas-lit streets, and Villa took me upstairs to his second-floor office, so strewn with documents and petitions that I wondered how he managed to live in such chaos. When I commented on it, he said, "I know where everything is. However, it's true that if I were to die or lose my memory, the Gutiérrez government would collaspe within hours." Dropping into a leather chair, he hunched forward to clasp his hands. The light of a single lamp cast harsh shadows on his face, making him look older, a man weighed down by the need for decision.

"Tomás, I know you're going. I have one more thing to ask of you . . . one final favor. It won't take you very long, and if there was anyone else I could trust as I trust you, I would. But . . . you'll see . . . only you can . . ."

He broke off, and I waited, trying to appear patient. But he seemed nervous. He got up and began to prowl the room, rumpling his already unkempt hair. Lines of worry slashed from the tip of his runny nose to the fleshy lips.

I was already uneasy about the whole meeting. God knows what Hannah was thinking, knowing that I had promised to return when Mexico City fell. Why, I wondered now, had I delayed even this much? Would she tolerate it? Women were supposed to sit and wait, but for how long?

There were three things, Villa said. I was going to El Paso anyway.

"When you get there, go see Luz. I'll give you a letter stating that you speak on my authority. She likes you—she'd probably throw anyone else out on his ear." Then he flushed a dusky red. "I want a divorce, so that I can marry Conchita. Ask Luz, and find out her terms." He thrust his jaw forward, clamping his teeth so that his cheekbones jutted through the puffy flesh, as if he understood his cowardice and needed to show the face of a resolute man.

"Do you want a drink, Tomás? I should have asked you before. That banker left me a bar that you wouldn't find in the best hotel in the city."

"No, thanks. What else?"

"Will you do this for me with Luz, as a favor?"

"What are the other two things?" I asked.

"One of them," he said, "is a delicate matter. You'll have to come back into Mexico, but not too far. Do you know the town of Parral?"

"West of Chihuahua City, in the mountains."

On a certain day, he explained, in about two weeks, the German military attaché to Washington, who also dealt with Mexican affairs for his government, would show up in Parral. His name was Franz von Papen. He had asked for a meeting with Villa, or with someone who had Villa's full confidence.

"It won't take you long," Villa said. "You can meet Candelario in Chihuahua City and ride over there and talk to the man. Then write out a report and give it to Candelario to bring back to me. Then you can go up to Texas again to your Jewish sweetheart."

"But what's it all about, chief?" I asked, puzzled.

"I can't tell you everything because I don't know it myself. This Von Papen got word to me through a third party. All I know is that he has a proposal to make to us on behalf of his government. It may be something so bold, so much to the benefit of the revolution and the people, that it makes my head spin. I swear you to secrecy on this, of course."

"But the Germans aren't your friends," I reminded him. "They supplied Huerta."

"Because he was in power. Now I am. Don't ask me any more questions. It will all become clear. I'd see this fellow myself, but there are too many eyes watching, and it's the most confidential sort of business. He'll be expecting you in Parral at a place called Hacienda de Los Flores." He glanced at a crumpled piece of notepaper. "It's on Calle Chorro, in the home of some old German woman called Elisa Griensen." He leaned forward, his eyes glowing in the lamplight like gems. "That's it. Will you do it?"

I looked at him for a long moment. "What if I say no?"

"That's your right. You'll still have my blessing. If you have a son, I'll be its godfather. It will lack for nothing. If you name it after me, that would please me even more."

If I did what he asked, I realized, I would be in El Paso at least a week before it was time to leave on the diplomatic errand. Hannah would know I was back for good—we could even set a date for the wedding. There was no fighting now in the north, so there was no danger of an ironic and untimely end. A meeting, no more. Nothing very complicated or risky. Still, I held back. . . .

"You said three things. That's only two."

"The other one is nothing." But he blushed again. "When you meet Candelario, check on the gold in the laundry room of the Fermont." We were to take one sack, he explained, wrap it securely so that it didn't jingle, put it in a locked trunk and carry it to Parral. Candelario would then bring it to him in Mexico City when he delivered my report of the meeting with the German. That was an innocent enough task, and I understood well enough that the money was for Conchita and her aunt. I had thought it was the revolution's treasury, but if he had given part of it to Candelario and me, I suppose he had the right to dip into it himself when the need arose. His generosity, so long ago in Chihuahua City, now began to take on a new and more subtle meaning.

One final favor, he had said, when I first arrived. It didn't seem much to ask.

"All right, chief. I'll do it."

He sighed with obvious relief. "I'm grateful, Tomás. I don't know who else I could have sent."

Then something occurred to me. I would still be Villa's man when I reached Parral, but I was a gringo. This German military attaché, Franz von Papen, would certainly see that. Even if I carried the right papers, wouldn't he suspect they were stolen, and that I was a spy?

Villa placed both his hands on my shoulders. I felt their weight and their power. The Griensen woman, he had been told, was a middle-aged spinster who had lived in Mexico for many years. She would be there to interpret for us, so I could speak Spanish all the time. There were many Mexicans with foreign names.

"Yes, the name can be explained, but—"

"Tomás, have you looked in the mirror lately? You look like a Mexican. You usually think and act like a Mexican. A very smart Mexican might realize after a while that you were a gringo, but a visiting German would have to be gifted with the sight of a witch to tell the difference. Believe me, there's nothing to worry about."

Had I changed so much? I may not have been the callow youth who had jutted out his jaw to seem more of a man—but if not, what was I? While I pondered that, he went on to explain that he would have letters ready for me by noon the next day and a special travel document with his seal and signature. "In the name of Colonel Tomás Mix. I can't have a lowly major dealing in my name with foreign governments. Now you can retire in real style. When you're in El Paso, buy yourself a decent uniform. Get rid of those moth-eaten pants. You look disgraceful, worse than when I first met you. You're not a broken-down cowboy anymore, and you never will be again." He ground another cigarette into the carpet. "Are you sure you won't have a drink?"

I asked him for a double whiskey. *Colonel Thomas H. Mix, Retired.* I wasn't yet twenty-four years old.

Around midnight Pancho Villa and I embraced for what I thought would be the last time, and we said goodbye. I weaved my way back through the dark streets, half-drunk and chortling to myself. A free man . . . almost.

20

"Know of your youth,
examine well your blood."

Swinging down off the train at the Juárez railroad station, saddlebags slung over my shoulder, I scanned the crowd of unfamiliar faces. I felt a tap on my elbow. A voice said severely, "Colonel Mix?" and I turned to face Hipólito, who embraced me like a brother. After three days on the train my hide had soaked up enough dust and coal smoke to make me considerably whiffy on the lee side, but he didn't care. It was December of 1914, more than a year since we had taken the city by riding the rails backwards, and Hipólito looked even fatter, dressed in the expensive glad rags of a successful businessman: a smartly pressed new gray herringbone worsted, a matching vest, maroon string tie, white shirt with starched collar and gold cuff links in the shape of a pair of dice, and pointed black shoes.

"*Pendejo!* How are you?"

"Pretty good," I said, "all things considering. And you?"

"Judge for yourself. How do I look?"

"Like you're on the way to a whorehouse."

"Now that you've brought up the subject, how are the ladies? And Candelario?"

"The ladies are fat and sassy. Candelario's so worn out you could stuff him into a drainpipe."

Hipólito had a car waiting, a black Cadillac roadster with a chauffeur also dressed in black. On the way to his house he told me that he and Mabel Silva were married now. I congratulated him, and then he explained that the chief had just telegraphed with fresh instructions that I buy some sort of uniform for myself, befitting a colonel.

"You have an appointment tomorrow at my tailor on Mesa Street. He's a Jew, from somewhere in Poland, and as you can see by looking at me, a genius. Which reminds me . . ." His smile dimmed, then faded. "I have bad news. Felix Sommerfeld is dying. Cancer of the lungs, although no one dares to say it in so many words. But it's not good. It's very bad."

That was a shock. Hannah may have written, but the mails were something less than dependable.

"It happens to all of us, Tomás. But his ugly daughter, who thinks my brother is a beast, is in excellent health. She's panting for you like a bitch in springtime. I stopped by to tell them you were coming, although I didn't say exactly when."

"That's good." I was thinking about the letter in my pocket and Luz Corral; I wanted to get that over and done with. I hadn't seen Hannah in eight months—another day wouldn't make any difference. Not exactly a lovesick knight panting for his beloved princess . . . and I wondered why. The Cadillac bumped across the International Bridge. I told Hipólito I had quit, and he pounded my back.

"You did right, Tomás. The revolution doesn't need you anymore."

Did it ever? Or was it I who had needed the revolution? I had little time to think about it; he had my old room ready for me at his house on Montana Street, and that night I regaled him with tales of the campaigns, described the meeting with Zapata, and then after the third bottle of burgundy I rolled off to bed and slept like a cowhand just come off a cattle drive.

In the morning we went to his tailor next door to the Texas Grand Theater. I was fitted for a lightweight tan uniform such as the officers at Fort Bliss might wear, tucked in at the waist, with gold eagles on the epaulets. It seemed a bit of foolish frippery to me, in view of my retirement, but I had learned from Candelario never to look a gift horse in the mouth; and in any case I would need it for the meeting with Captain von Papen.

That afternoon I walked up North Oregon Street to the house that Villa had rented for Luz Corral. A five-passenger Hudson stood in the driveway, and there was a porter watering the lawn. I wore my faded Levi's tucked into my boots and a jacket that smelled of not just the train but the trails of Chihuahua and the dung-filled streets of Xochimilco.

Luz Corral remembered me, greeted me kindly and took me into her kitchen, where she fussed over me and fed me apricot pie and fresh milk as if I were a schoolboy. She was simply dressed in a yellow cotton frock with woolen stockings and brown shoes. Her gray eyes brimmed with curiosity.

"And how is my Teo?"

About then I realized the enormity of the task that Pancho Villa had given me, and there was nothing I wanted to do more than offer my apologies, thank her for the pie and sneak out of that kitchen like a thief. It was no man's job but his, and no one else should have come. On the other hand, I hadn't complained when he asked me. Not being in the habit of seeing things too clearly when they first showed themselves, I had just dumbly nodded, and now it was too late to back out.

I told Luz Corral that her husband was very well indeed, comfortable in his house on Calle Liverpool, up to his ears in the affairs of government and the successful conclusion of the revolution.

"Is he eating well? Is he getting enough sleep? Does he wear his hat against the sun?"

She treated him like a schoolboy too. I assured her that he was in good health, wouldn't part with his pith helmet even for one of Zapata's sombreros, and then dug in my back pocket and produced the letter that he had asked me to give her. She broke the seal and read it.

"He says you have an important message for me."

"Doesn't he say what it's about?"

"He says that I'll want to discuss it with you, and that I'm to trust you completely and give you my answer in detail. He says he's spoken to you from his heart with the sincere words of an uneducated man. I wonder why he always thinks that the words of an uneducated man are sincere." The corner of her mouth tilted in a whimsical smile.

"Please go ahead, Colonel. Tell me what it is."

"I wish you'd call me Tomás."

"Very well . . . Tomás. What does Francisco want? Is it a divorce?"

I started to stutter and wave my hands, and I knocked over my glass of milk quite by accident.

"I thought so. Here, don't do that. Let me get a dishcloth and mop it up. Don't use your sleeve, for heaven's sake! I'll pour another glass for you. Be calm, Tomás. It's not the end of the world."

"Thank you, señora."

"We've been married five years, and this will be the third time he's asked me. The first time was only six months after our wedding day . . . he met this *soldadera,* the one they called Adelita, and he thought he was in love. Well, he may have been—I can never tell. But she wouldn't marry him, and that nearly drove him crazy. Then she gave him a terrible disease, which Francisco cured with a black chicken. That calmed his passion, naturally. He changes his mind from one moment to the next, as you know . . . although usually for good reason." Luz Corral's eyes sparkled at the memory, and she spoke idly in a soft, clear voice, as though she were telling tales she had read in a book.

"After that," she said, while I sat at the kitchen table with my eyes round as marbles, "he met a young woman named Pilar Escalona. She was from Chihuahua City, where Francisco worked for a while as a butcher. As a reward for his services in 1911, Señor Madero had given him the concession of all the bulls killed in the ring, and he sold the meat. It isn't really fair of me to call him a butcher, and he turns absolutely pop-eyed when I use that word. Don't ever mention it to him, Tomás. He'll get angry and know that it comes from me."

"I won't, señora. I hate to make him angry."

"Anyway, he met Pilar Escalona while she was studying to be a bullfighter. She was a very tall, very pretty Indian girl. She turned Francisco's head so that he couldn't see straight. He married her, of course, and when I found out there was an awful scene. He said, 'If you're going to be unpleasant about it, let's get a divorce,' and so I yelled at him like a woman who sells garlic in the market. I had the child then, you see. I left with her for Texas, to let Francisco get it out of his system and because I was ashamed of my behavior. Then Orozco got after him and put him in prison, and he escaped here to El Paso, as you know."

She startled me then by bursting out with a peal of raucous laughter. "Pilar Escalona followed him. When she got to the border and told the gringo Immigration people that she was the wife of Francisco Villa and had come to join her husband, they said: 'But, señora . . . his wife is already here in Texas!' 'Well,' she screamed, 'I'm his wife too!' But they explained that in the United States a man couldn't have more than one wife. And they wouldn't let her into the country as Señora Villa, only as Señorita Escalona. When I heard about that, I demanded a paper saying that no matter how many times he managed to get married in Mexico by putting a pistol to a priest's head, I was his only legal wife. And I got it. So you see, Tomás, I'm used to this sort of thing. Who is she this time?"

I took a deep breath and told Luz Corral what I knew about Conchita del Hierro, although it wasn't much.

"Poor Teo," she murmured. "He must be very unhappy that the girl won't marry him."

"He's miserable."

"But why is she making such a fuss? Doesn't she realize that if he marries her, he'll leave her? He always does, you know. . . . Once he gets what he wants, he loses interest."

"That's what I told him too."

"He's had a hard life—much more so than people realize. He ran away when he was fourteen to drive a freight wagon in Chihuahua, and when they caught him they whipped him and put him in jail. Then, of course, he killed the man who raped his sister and became a bandit. He learned to see a cave behind a bush where other men saw nothing, and if he stole a cow and roasted it, he had to dig a hole to bury the carcass. He had a lonely life. Whenever he acts foolishly now, I try to remember all that. You mustn't condemn him too quickly for his actions, Tomás."

I sat silently for a while, wiping the milk from my mustache with a white cloth napkin.

"What am I to tell him, señora? He's asked me to find out your terms for the divorce. Forgive me—I wouldn't offend you for the world—but I've got to send him an answer."

"I won't divorce him," she said. "Do you think that if I did, and he married this Conchita, she would let him marry other women as I do?"

"I wouldn't bet on it."

"I love him too much to let him make a fool of himself. Tomás, I think you're intelligent and have a warm heart. So you'll understand."

"You're a remarkable woman, señora. You accept things as they are. Not many people can do that."

"My husband's road is a long one. He grows weary and stops to pray in many churches, but he worships in only one cathedral. I could never rob him of that true faith."

I digested this morsel and found it satisfying. I stood up. "I'll give him your message."

"Tell him we miss him, and we'll come whenever he calls."

She asked me if I wanted more milk and pie, but I explained that I was going from her house to see my family and Mama would be hurt if I didn't eat until I let out two notches in my belt.

"You're a good man, Tomás," she said gravely. "But you look unhappy. Don't get killed."

I remembered the Indian women wailing that to their sons as they marched off with us in the desert of Chihuahua, when we first crossed the Rio Bravo two years ago. Why did I look unhappy?

"The revolution's almost over, señora. I'm just doing a few favors for your husband, but I've quit."

"I knew you were clever," Luz said, kissing me.

Things happened quickly then. The next morning, keeping one eye skinned for that fellow who had tried to shoot me nearly a year ago, I picked up my new uniform. Then I went to see Sam Ravel in his office, to find out more about Felix before I showed up on his doorstep. Some strands of gray had begun to show in Sam's black hair.

"You look splendid, Tom. Better steer clear of Bliss, though. If General Pershing sees those eagles he'll figure that within a year he'll be saluting *you.*"

/ 233

"I've already quit, Sam. I'm just putting in a bit of overtime."

"Smart man," he said, and I was glad everyone thought so. "How soon will it be over?"

"Most people guess by the spring. But most people are usually wrong."

"Yes, I've noticed that too." He gave me a wintry smile. "But now that Gutiérrez is gone—"

"Gutiérrez? Gone where?"

As he spoke in his easy drawl I found it difficult to believe that so much had happened in just a few days. But volcanos don't erupt gradually; they do it with a suddenness that sends everyone running for their lives.

Sam told me that Villa, true to his word, had signed the order for the execution of Paulino Martinez, the journalist. Fierro had carried it out with the aid of a firing squad. President Gutiérrez became enraged at that and other political executions, and also at what everyone but he had seemed to understand from the beginning—that Pancho Villa was running the government from Calle Liverpool. In the middle of the night, driving a *campesino's* wagon and carrying thirteen million pesos stolen from the national treasury, Gutiérrez made his escape. When he reached his home in San Luis Potosí he declared that he was now loyal to Obregón.

"And where the hell is Obregón?"

"He turned up somewhere near Puebla, with a big army. To stop Zapata."

I remembered Felipe Angeles' worries, but I said nothing to Ravel. He seemed to think the situation was under control. Pershing had already called Villa "the man of the hour," and Ravel offered his opinion that if the chief could strike quickly and avoid killing any more Englishmen, Mr. Wilson would be more than glad to accept him as President of Mexico. Wilson's concentration was elsewhere, on the war in Europe and the growing peril of German submarines.

"Now tell me about Felix," I said.

"They just brought him home from the hospital."

"I'm on my way to see him."

"How about you and Hannah?"

"We're getting married," I said, "and I'm going to take over the business. You and I will be partners, Sam."

That pleased him, and he solemnly shook my hand.

Mrs. Sommerfeld opened the door for me and almost started to cry. Hannah was out riding, she explained. "Would you like to say hello to Felix? He heard you were coming. He's asked for you, Tom."

I had never been upstairs in this house; the davenport was more my territory. It was cool and pleasant up there, richly furnished. A lot of good it would do Felix. He was dying, and you could see it. He didn't look like a frog anymore, except for his greenish pallor. He was so thin he could have taken a bath in a shotgun barrel. He wore a little black skullcap on his head, and there was a Hebrew prayer book on the bedside table next to a syringe and some bottles of pills. The room smelled of decay and laudanum. His watery blue eyes fixed weakly on me as I forked a chair beside his bed.

"Well, Tom . . . can't give you a birthday party this year."

"You'll be around awhile, Felix. You're a tough bird."

"Smoked myself to death," he whispered. "Told Sarah to send the funeral bill to the Murad Company." A little smile wrinkled the transparent mask of his skull. "How are you, Tom? You staying?"

"Yes," I said. "You're stuck with me now."

"When's the wedding?"

"Soon, I hope. If she'll still have me."

"She will." He coughed harshly out of his rotten lungs, closed his eyes for a moment, then opened them and rattled a sigh. "I remember in Columbus how I laughed at you. Wet behind the ears . . . full of piss and vinegar. I liked you a lot." He began to cough again. "You changed, but it was good to see."

"You should rest, Felix."

He beckoned with his fingers, and I saw that under his pajama sleeves hardly any flesh remained on the arm. His body was so bony it hardly made the counterpane rise. I leaned closer and sniffed the sour odor of laudanum on his breath.

"I had a son once. Before Hannah. Died young, in the cradle. Wish he'd lived . . . wish he could have known you."

My eyes were blurred now. I had always liked Felix. He had always been straight with me. Treated me, I realized, like the son he had lost and never seen grow to manhood. That's what he was trying to say to me.

"I'll rest now, Tom. Take care of yourself, and Hannah." I clasped the bones of his cold, skeletal hand and then left the room. Alone with my thoughts and a cup of coffee that Mrs. Sommerfeld gave me, I sat in the parlor awhile and then walked out on the veranda to wait for Hannah. A fresh breeze stirred the linden trees on the street, and the foliage cast fat dark gray shadows on the pavement. I had never seen a man I cared for turning into a rotted bag of skin. War was awful, no doubt of it, but there was something to say for the way it put a period to your troubles.

Hannah came back in about an hour, wearing jodhpur boots, derby and tucked twill riding jacket. Her cheeks were flushed from the desert air. I was in deep shadow, and she didn't see me until she mounted the steps of the veranda and shook her hair loose from under the hat. It was an unguarded moment . . . her cupid's-bow lips were parted, her blue eyes a little lonely. When I cleared my throat she clapped a hand to her mouth, as if she had seen a ghost. But then she rushed softly across the creaking floor, into the shadows and into my arms. The smell of horse and woman flooded my nostrils, and she started to cry.

"Oh, Tom . . . thank God . . ."

Later that day we walked through the hot streets of El Paso to San Jacinto Park and sat on an iron bench there, eating vanilla ice cream cones we bought from a vendor. Birds warbled in the chestnut trees, and the shade covered us like a cool umbrella. Hannah had become quieter and certainly looked thinner than when I had last seen her. Chin down, she studied her hands, then fixed me with a mournful look.

"It was such a long time, Tom."

"For me too."

"You left in April. You said it would be all over by summer, and then we'd be married. Now it's nearly Christmas. . . ."

"I know, Hannah. I'm sorry." The words lacked proper weight. I wasn't sorry at all. For her, yes, but not for what I had done. That had only been what I wanted to do. I felt a great listlessness and ennui, as if I were somewhere else, outside my skin, and the man here on the park bench wasn't real, was a sham.

"You're always sorry," she said, with bite. "You'll be sorry when you look at me one day and there's an old maid staring you in the face. Sometimes I think you're more engaged to Pancho Villa than you are to me. What do you think I do when you're not here? I wait. I sew. I do the crossword puzzles. I practically *live* at horse shows. I'm *bored*, Tom! Tell me—are we getting married while Daddy's still alive?"

I took her hand, but she was still angry and she shook it loose. The ice cream broke from the cone and fell into her lap. She uttered a little screech and jumped to her feet, so that the milky vanilla rolled down the length of her dress, then plopped on her suede shoes.

"Just look!"

I yanked out a bandanna, which awakened memories, and tried to wipe it off her shoe. But she pulled away, sitting down swiftly. She let the ice cream stay where it was, evidence of her misery. Then I smiled.

"We'll get married whenever you like, dear. Next week, next month. I love you, Hannah. I'm not engaged to Pancho Villa anymore. I quit the revolution." I didn't bother to tell her that I had to go to Chihuahua City and Parral on those last two errands—it would have spoiled the moment.

All the flash left her eyes; they glistened with tears. Her voice grew soft.

"Oh, Tom . . . you've made me happy."

So it was settled. A winter wedding, she said, right after the first of the year. Quiet, with just a few friends and the family. I kept nodding in agreement. I found a clean part of the bandanna—most of it was wet with vanilla ice cream—and dabbed at her stained cheeks. I remembered the tears sliding down Rosa's cheek that last night in Zacatecas. I hadn't been able to wipe those tears away, so this was a form of penance.

"I'll go tell my folks," I said, as I gently kissed her cheek. "That will make it official."

Mama and my sister embraced me. Papa pumped my hand, but then he frowned. I asked him what was the matter.

"I keep thinking that those people killed Christ."

"That was a long time ago. And it's just a rumor."

"People still believe."

"Hannah had nothing to do with it, Papa."

Hipólito cleared the debris from his parlor and gave a small engagement party for us on New Year's Eve, as we all considered it unseemly to hold it in the Sommerfeld house with Felix dying one floor above the festivities. With my back pay I bought a little diamond ring at a Juárez jeweler who owed some favors to the revolution, slipping it on Hannah's finger just before Mabel Silva announced that the buffet was ready. So many tongues wagged at me, and I had to shake so many hands of people I didn't know, that I was busier than a one-armed man saddling a green bronc.

Hannah clung to my arm, a single orchid pinned to the breast of her red silk dress, her hair falling in chestnut ringlets to bare shoulders. She was a virgin, even after the one night in Hipólito's back bedroom. I understood the sacrifice she had been willing to make that April night. She was a hot-blooded girl with some lively desires, but in those days, all things considered, she had gone awfully far with no guarantees.

I loved her for it. In fact, I was going to marry her for it.

The next morning Hipólito shook me awake. He clamped a mug of black coffee in my hand and waited patiently until I had survived the first two swallows, which nearly boiled my gullet but served to shake my brains back into working order. Then he told me the news that had come in on the wire to our commander in Juárez, who had sent a white-faced captain straight across the river at dawn.

Four of our brigades had been stationed in Guadalajara, the second largest city in Mexico, when a Carranzista general named Treviño suddenly appeared with five thousand men and a regiment of artillery armed with new German cannon. The battle had lasted only three days, but when it was over, half the Northern Division was in flight. They had retreated in an easterly direction to the town of Irapuato, where Villa heard the report and then ordered the commanders shot.

"Our men had no will to fight," Hipólito explained gravely. "They were confused. No one knew where Pancho was. Their artillery had been shipped to the south, to Zapata. Treviño came on them without warning. He went through the brigades like butter. He hanged all the prisoners."

"Jesus. What's happening in the south?"

"Obregón took Puebla back from the Zapatistas."

He told me that last bit of news almost as if it were an afterthought. Of what importance was a southern city like Puebla compared to a defeat that had befallen the great Northern Division? With Villa occupied in the north, Carranza had seized the opportunity to make new promises, and in Mexico, even more than most places, the last promise shouted loud enough was the one to echo in a man's ears. Carranza signed a pact for government aid to the newly organized national trade union, which promptly supplied four brigades of worker-soldiers. When Obregón attacked Puebla, the white-shirted Zapatistas occupying the city realized they would have to hold their ground or die. The Belgian cannon were too complicated for them to use. When the guns began to jam, they abandoned them. Like ghosts, they melted away into the surrounding mountain fastness. Through the forests and over back trails, they drifted back toward the safety of their *patria chica* in Morelos.

So Villa and the bulk of the Northern Division were surrounded by three powerful Carranzista armies—Treviño to the west, González to the north, Obregón to the south. I groaned.

"Felipe was right—your brother's a damned fool. And where was Zapata? At his tailor's? How could he let them give up so easily?"

"He was in Mexico City when they heard the news of Puebla. His garrison panicked. They say he went back with them to Morelos."

"What do you mean, 'they say'? Has Zapata quit? Is it true or not?"

Hipólito smiled. "You know better than to ask such a question, Tomás. The answer is always: 'Who knows?' "

I knew what he meant. You had to be there to find out. I swung out of bed, reached for my boots and uniform, then hesitated. "Has anything happened in Chihuahua?"

"Urbina is there. The north will always be ours."

"If we can stop Obregón."

"We?"

I wonder now if I had been waiting for such news all along. It chilled me, but it also stirred something in me. My resolve and my loyalty had only been asleep. Why hadn't I seen it? I had fought with Villa all throughout the good times, the times when we won the battles and took the cities, and now that things had suddenly turned sour I had absented myself. Villa's plan—the man himself—was stumbling, failing. I had forgiven him everything up until then, but I hadn't forgiven him his inability to make the most of victory. *"Once he gets what he wants,"* Luz had said, *"he loses interest."* No, not interest, but clarity of vision. That's when I had shied away, sunk in the trough of my despair over Rosa and my cynicism over the antics at Aguascalientes. I had quit too soon, when he still needed me. I had once believed in his revolution—not a whim, but a belief that had been built over years, despite mistakes. And even— yes—despite villainy. I still believed, and I had to go back. Would Hannah understand? Beyond the certainty of desire, did *I* understand? If I didn't go back I would be guilty of a second cowardice, a turning away. Once was enough for a lifetime.

"What time does the train leave for Chihuahua City?"

"Nine o'clock, Tomás, as always. Which is to say, anytime after nine o'clock."

I had to move swiftly or not at all, I knew that. I had barely enough time for Hipólito to drive me to the Sommerfelds. He waited in the car while a maid roused Hannah from bed. She met me halfway up the staircase. The white silk handkerchief round her head slipped a bit, and I saw that her hair was wrapped tightly in iron curlers. Then her sleepy blue eyes widened as they focused on my rifle and saddlebags at the foot of the stairs.

"Oh, no, Tom. *Why?*"

"Because I've got to do it. Got to do it now. I'll be back."

"No!"

I told her what had happened in the south. She stared at me, uncomprehending.

"I have to finish what I started. All my life I was a quitter. I can't do that anymore."

"You're quitting *me,*" she cried. "You promised! I'll be humiliated, I'll look like a fool! We told everyone we were getting married next month! You *can't* go."

"Hannah," I said, seizing her hands. "Try to see me as a whole man, not just the man you love. I want to be a whole man. If I don't go, I won't be."

"I don't care about that!"

"But I do," I said, a little coolly.

"And don't you care about *me?*"

"You know I do that too."

"No! I don't know anything anymore! All I know is that you're leaving! And you swore you'd stay!" Her eyes glittered with something like desperation. "Last April, Tom, you got me into your bed. And all those times here in the house . . . Doesn't that mean anything to you? I gave you everything I had . . . you don't even care . . ."

"That's not true, Hannah. I didn't seduce you. I hope you don't hold that against me. And I didn't even—I mean, you're still—"

"No," she cried, "I'm not! That's not so! It *did* happen!"

Did she really think that? The mind plays tricks; I know that now. Perhaps she had convinced herself. Perhaps, I realized, she had only done it in the first place to clamp me in a tighter grip.

She looked at me more calmly, although her eyes were still hot with resolve.

"If you go now," she said, "I won't wait for you. It will be over, Tom."

"Oh, Hannah," I groaned. "You don't mean that."

"I do! I'll consider myself free. And you'll be free too. You can stay in Mexico! You can *live* in miserable Mexico! Why don't you do that?" she said cuttingly. "Find some Mexican girl who'll wait for you while you chase around the country with Pancho Villa. That's what you need, Tom. You don't need me. I wonder—did you ever?"

A massive burden suddenly lifted from me. I felt as if I were gazing at a stranger. A beautiful and once beloved girl, but still a stranger. It was as if she receded from me in space—still visible but far away . . . fading. In her place, close to me—*she* had brought forth the image, for I would have struggled against it—I saw a browner face, dark eyes, a sweep of sable hair.

To Tomochic . . . If you want it, you will have to come for it. You know where it is buried. . . .

Something became clear to me in that moment, an understanding I could only deny at extreme peril. Hannah had been the dream of my youth ever since I could remember. I had conjured her into form even before I met her in the lobby of the Commercial Hotel. She was something I had read about by a campfire, and I always saw her that way, despite our episodes on the davenport—a poetic image of idyllic love. But if I wanted to live with her for the rest of my life, why had I always left her? The rest of anyone's life, I realized, begins *now.* And now, once again, I was leaving. I had sustained my image of her because I had never been willing to test the dream against wakefulness. Rosa and I had been together for two long years, through separations and battles and all the bizarre events of the revolution. That was real, that was good. When she left me in Zacatecas, I had been lessened as a man. What might have come of us, what could *ever* come of us, I didn't know. We were strangers, creatures of the planet who had met by accident and cleaved by need. So were any man and woman. And in the harsh light of day, even more, so were Hannah and I.

Rosa was no princess in a tower, but she had worked herself into the fabric of my life and I couldn't push her out . . . and didn't want to. That was my fate, at least for now, and it was time I stopped ducking it.

But I was still in the grip of some chivalric notion. I said, "Hannah,

I have to go or I'll miss my train. You're upset. I don't think you mean what you're saying."

"I do, Tom. Of course I'm upset. God! I'm *more* than upset! But I meant every word."

I gave her another chance.

"I'll be back when it's over, Hannah. Let's not decide anything until then."

"You've decided already, Tom. You're going!"

"I have to run. Goodbye, Hannah. I'll write."

"Don't bother!" she shrieked after me as I backed down the steps, then turned and ran out the door into the sunlight.

The motor of Hipólito's Cadillac was idling. As he stepped on the gas pedal he turned to me. "Tomás, your face is bright red. Are you feeling all right?"

"Awful," I said. We raced toward the International Bridge. He drove recklessly, leaning on the horn, ignoring pedestrians and traffic alike. "No, wait—not awful. Wonderful, Hipólito. And awful too. Awful *and* wonderful."

I was part of the revolution again. I wasn't going to live happily ever after and bounce babies on my knee and have Luz Corral and Sam Ravel tell me how clever I was, but it didn't matter. I was going to do what I had to do. As for Rosa, I was clear in my mind about that too. I knew where to find her, and I would go.

At ten minutes after nine, just as the train for Chihuahua City gave its final high-pitched whistle, Hipólito shoved me aboard. The train wheezed out of the Juárez station, and in a few minutes we were out in the desert, picking up speed. I loved it: the rippling heat, the brown horizon, the stainless blue sky. This was where I belonged . . . for now.

The railway car rattled and banged, and the broken seat dug into my thighs. As soon as I had my wits back I dug into my saddlebags to haul out my pistol and cartridge belts. I broke open the rifle and slipped a box into the chamber. In revolutionary Mexico, you never knew.

21

"Take all the swift advantage of the hours."

Candelario waited for me in Chihuahua City at the Hotel Fermont. He wore a sheepskin coat and dusty trail clothes, and he was polite enough not to comment on the starched newness of my uniform. He had received Hipólito's wire only ten minutes ago. He explained that the military situation was changing by the hour, and the roads were not quite as safe as they had been a week or two ago.

/ 241

"Don't worry," I said. "After Parral I'll still keep you company. I won't let any harm come to you."

"Well, now I can sleep nights. But you were quitting. That's what the chief told me."

"I changed my mind."

He sighed. "And I thought you had more brains than the rest of us. What made you change your mind?"

"I would have missed you, you hairy ape."

"You're not well, Tomás."

"I'm very well. I'm better than I've been in a long time. Listen, do you know what I've got to do in Parral?"

He scratched his beard. "I know we've got to get a sack of gold here, that's all. As for Parral, I'd just as soon you didn't tell me, unless you need my help. The more I hear about the chief's doings these days, the more confused I get."

"Where is he right now?"

"In Zacatecas, getting the Division organized. Or Irapuato. It's hard to keep track of him. He's changed, Tomás."

"How?"

"Well, he's worried. He never used to worry before."

The gold was still in the laundry room of the hotel, exactly as we had left it. The gold never changed. It gleamed dully and mysteriously in the soft light of the basement. There was something almost frivolous about the task, considering the gold's destination and the news from southern battlefields, but at least it wasn't taking us out of our way. The chink and jingle as we hauled a sack from one corner reminded me of the day and night that Candelario and I had spent counting it, and the two other sacks buried behind the corral of Rosa's house up in To-mochic. From the glint in Candelario's one good eye I could tell he was thinking the same thing.

"You'll have your restaurant soon, *compadre.*"

"That's pleasant to believe, Tomás."

He had already bought a black trunk with a great brass lock, and we loaded the sack of gold Spanish pesetas into it and stuffed the edges with sheets and dirty towels so that there would be no telltale rattling. Candelario ground out the cigarette with the worn-down heel of his boot.

"Urbina's giving us horses and an escort to Parral. Let's be careful when we meet him."

The main boulevard, lit by flickering torches, was filled with whores and drunken soldiers. You knew who was in command here. Urbina, with a week-old growth of beard, met us at Doña Luisa's Station Hotel, where he had arranged for us to stay the night. The lobby was empty and forlorn. Occasionally from the darkness there came the sound of a random gunshot or the snatch of a ballad sung off-key. One of Urbina's great Spanish swords clanked at his side in a silver scabbard, and he wore three bandoliers stuffed full of brass cartridges, so that when he walked he wobbled from side to side with the weight he carried. He was drunk, of course, and his small eyes rolled back and forth in their sockets, like black marbles.

"What the hell's going on?" he demanded. "I'm sitting here in this miserable town with three thousand men and no ammunition. I've got dynamite, but you can't shoot dynamite from rifles." Pulling his huge pistol from its holster, he spun the chambers. "Can you stuff a stick of dynamite up here? I'll tell you, without mentioning any names, I'd like to stuff this pistol up someone's ass. Where is Pancho Villa? Someone told me Irapuato. Someone else told me Guadalajara. Who should I believe? These days, everyone lies. I heard that we were supposed to go north to Sonora and take Agua Prieta. How can I move three thousand men in any direction without ammunition? I've got the rifles, but no bullets. I've got the trains, but no coal. Son of a whore, this is crazy weather! It's too cold, and my rheumatism is killing me. The horses are hungry, and I can tell you, I'm fed up. What have you got in that trunk?" He grinned devilishly. "If it's good whiskey from Texas, you'd better open it up. I'm the new collector of taxes in Chihuahua. I haven't got anything else to do, so I've decided to get rich. You think that's a bad idea? If you do, tell me. I haven't got a better one, but I'm a reasonable man. I'll listen to anyone's opinion."

"There's no whiskey in the trunk," Candelario said calmly. "Just dirty laundry."

Urbina spat in the general direction of a spittoon and missed. "Look at that fancy trunk! Are your clothes stitched with gold thread?" At the mention of the word, a crafty look spread over his features, which were those of a black-snouted fox. "You visited the Hotel Fermont, didn't you?"

Candelario yawned. "Let's get to the cantina and have a drink."

Urbina said thickly, "It's my duty to inspect everything that passes through Chihuahua. Open the trunk. If it's laundry, I'll get you a woman to wash it. Do you want a woman, by the way? This city's lousy with them. I found a pretty one the other night, coming back from the river. A young hellion, not very willing, but they're often the best kind. Tits like melons. Look! She gave me this!" He pointed proudly to a scabbing welt on his cheek. Then he turned on me. "Who has the key to the trunk? You or this other peasant?"

"I have the key," I said. "But the dirty laundry belongs to the chief. He wouldn't want me to open it."

Thumping a fist against his thigh, Urbina exploded into harsh laughter. "Now I know you're lying! The only dirty laundry that Pancho Villa has got is right next to his skin. I'm the commanding general in the state of Chihuahua, so don't make me shoot you for disobeying an order. Open that fucking trunk."

"I can't do that, General Urbina."

"You can't?" He flashed a smile that showed his decayed teeth. "Or you won't?"

I said quietly, "With respect, the chief doesn't want the trunk opened until we reach Mexico City."

Urbina sniffed, then snarled like an animal. I could swear he smelled the gold.

"Fuck your respect. You sound like Fierro." He turned to Candelario. "*Compañero,* if I shoot this gringo ass-kisser, will it upset you?"

"It will upset him a lot more," Candelario said.

"Then you have no objection?"

Swaying slightly, Urbina once again pulled his pistol from his holster and once again spun the chamber. The brass cartridges gleamed. I don't know if blood can actually run cold, but that's the way it felt; an iciness that spread from the heart into the limbs. The great temptation was to reach for my own pistol, but it would have been too late.

Candelario spoke thoughtfully. "If I were you, my general, I wouldn't do it."

Urbina spun around. "Do you think I fear Pancho Villa? There's no man on earth I fear," he cried, slurring his words. "I love him like a brother, but the word *fear* isn't in my vocabulary. Now tell me the truth, you bastard! What's in the trunk?"

Candelario shrugged and said, "Gold."

"By God, I knew it!" Urbina's eyes blazed in triumph. "Why didn't you say so in the first place? Candelario, what an intelligent man you are! And honest! I like that! Oh, yes, I like it a lot! Now I don't have to shoot him, you see? *Válgame Dios!* Gold! From the Banco Minero, right? Let's have a look!"

The big pistol swung away from where it had pointed at my belly. Leveling it at the brass padlock, he pulled the trigger. The shot boomed in the hotel lobby, echoing down the corridor, and the padlock splintered apart. Drunk or sober, Urbina could shoot straight. I took a half-step forward—but Candelario's hand lightly touched my arm, holding me back not so much by force as by suggestion. Urbina holstered his pistol. With a grunt of pain from his rheumatism, he bent to the trunk, the bones of his bad knees creaking in protest. He wrenched the shattered padlock loose from the hasp, thrusting open the top of the trunk with such violence that he nearly unhinged it.

"Christ! It *is* laundry!" He began tossing out the towels. "Shit! But now . . . wait. There's more. . . ." His fingers gripped the side of the sack, and he squeezed. He felt the hard edges of the peseta coins and heard the heavy chink as they slid one against another. He turned to us, on his knees now, and his eyes burned with a bright fever. Reverently he whispered, "You know, I almost thought you were joking. But it's true! It's the gold from the Banco Minero. I've caught you red-handed. What bad people you are. A pair of fucking thieves to boot! How much have you got?"

"Count it," said Candelario. "But take off your hat first. Show some respect for gold."

Dutifully Urbina swept the sombrero from his head and thrust his hands into the sack. He started spilling out the coins. *"Cómo están bonita!"* he murmured. "How beautiful they are!"

Candelario's pistol appeared in his hand, then spun. Barrel extended—the way any Brazos cowhand would do it, so that he wouldn't relinquish the grip of the handle and the possibility that he might have to squeeze the trigger to finish off the ruckus he was about to start—he laid the notched sight across the top of Urbina's skull where the bushy hair was thinnest. Candelario was tough enough to hunt bears with a switch, and when he buffaloed Urbina the general squawked once in distress, then fell headfirst into the trunk across the gold, limbs twitching, out cold.

"Were you worried, Tomás?" Candelario asked, smiling.

"You certainly took your time."

"It was either that or shoot him. This is the most stupid sonofabitch I've ever known. But we'd be even more stupid if we stayed around and waited for him to wake up. Don't you agree that it would be wise to leave town?"

I took my first easy breath since we had walked into the Station Hotel. "What about the escort of soldiers?"

"We don't need them. I know the way to Parral. Doña Luisa!"

An old crone with stringy white hair and steel spectacles appeared in the doorway from the hotel kitchen. The smell of garlic and sizzling corn oil followed her.

"The illustrious Señor General Urbina has regrettably passed out," Candelario explained. "Do you have a bed for him?"

"Aieee! The poor one!"

"As you can see, he fell into our trunk. If you'll be kind enough to show us an empty room, we'll carry him there."

Doña Luisa led the way; Candelario, having had second thoughts, told me to stay with the trunk of laundry and get it securely closed once again. He thrust his powerful arms under Urbina's and dragged him, sword clanking against the furniture, through the lobby and down the hallway to an empty room. He was back in a few minutes, sweat dripping from his forehead. I had found some rope and tied up the trunk.

"Come on, Tomás. She's blind as a bat, but I think she smelled the blood on his hair. Even a blind Mexican knows the smell of blood. When that drunk wakes up, I want to be far away."

With the trunk and the letters of safe-conduct that Pancho Villa had given me, we hustled round to the military stables. From the stable sergeant we commandeered the six healthiest-looking horses and a pack mule. While I saddled them, Candelario ran out to buy a bottle of mezcal and some tamales wrapped in cornhusks. We strapped the trunk to the mule and moved slowly out of town, through the darkness, toward the pass of San Martín. This was the road Rosa had taken, a year ago, to bury our gold in Tomochic.

A sky full of icy stars glittered down on us, and a freezing wind whipped out of the sierra. I remembered the year we had spent in the desert of Chihuahua, trying to warm our bones by a hundred campfires. The underfed horses blew steam, nickering in protest as the grade began to rise, and I kicked the belly of the old roan I was riding to show him who was boss. The skinny pack mule trudged in front of us, surefooted but slow. Once through the pass, we would have to turn south and descend into the desert if Parral were our destination. When we reached the turnoff I slowed the roan and laid a hand on the horn of Candelario's saddle.

"Let's go to Tomochic first," I said.

In the gloom of night I couldn't see Candelario's eyes. "Is there time?" he asked, and his voice was a shade hoarser.

"If we don't stay long."

"How long can it take to dig up two sacks of gold?"

"That's not it. The gold will just get us killed. You said so yourself. We still have no place to hide it that's any better than the corral."

"Then why—?"

"I'm going to get Rosa."

He sighed. He must have instantly understood the doggedness of my purpose, and sensed that it was unalterable, for after a second sigh and some muttering in the murky dark, he kicked his horse forward, toward the west. The mule had stopped. I laid a bullwhip on its back, and we moved deeper into the silent, night-mantled mountains of the Tarahumara sierra.

The drab walls of the village cut the fringe of the horizon. Between rocks pitted with huge eroded cracks, with a stream trickling below, a narrow ledge along the incline served as a mountain trail that led down from the high sierra to Tomochic. I knew what I would do, I knew what I wanted. Whatever she said, whoever she was with, I would beg her to come back to me.

Dogs showed their teeth in welcome. The village, a lusterless collection of huts, seemed somewhat cheered by the radiance of the rising sun, but at best it was a somber place in a dreary little valley. The revolution hadn't penetrated to these mountain pueblos, except as sons and fathers might have gone off to fight and not returned. We were a martial pair, but our weapons were sheathed and I tried to nod in a friendly manner. The girls we passed looked dumpy and dull of eye, bowed at the shoulder from grinding corn and washing clothes. The walnut-brown Tarahumara women, wrinkled as burnt boots, wore tattered rebozos; the old men, frayed white cotton shirts that flapped in the breeze. With worried eyes, they watched us ride by. Tomochic was another of those places that had been only a name to me. Was this where I had banished her? Rosa had been born here, lived here, but she might as well have come from the far side of the moon. I understood now what it had meant for her to live in the Hotel Fermont and then in our hideaway up on La Sierpe.

She had described the location of her mother's house, and it was no trouble to find it—a hut much like the others, that couldn't have contained more than a single room and a chimney. In that room a man and woman would live, make love, birth their children, grow older and die; and the children would follow suit. A pair of thin mustangs stood in the corral behind the hut, pawing the turf nervously. They smelled a gringo. When I dismounted a Tarahumara woman came to the rude, wooden-slatted door. I saw Rosa's face in hers. She was a woman only in her thirties, but already the dugs of her once robust breasts hung low and her hands were gnarled like those of a crone. Her rump and thighs were thick, her brown neck corded, her face puffy. She may have been handsome once. She may have been as pretty as Rosa.

I tried to glance over her shoulder into the shadows of the hut, but I saw nothing.

"Señora . . ."

I introduced myself, and then, not knowing what else to say, I blurted, "Where is Rosa?"

Her eyes betrayed no recognition of who I might be, and her voice showed no emotion. She spoke Spanish with difficulty. Rosa was not there, she said.

"When will she be back, señora?"

"She is gone."

"But where?"

"Quién sabe?"

Gone? I didn't want to believe it. Not after I had come this far, with such longing and resolve. "But when? How long ago? Where did she go? To Chihuahua City, or just to some village? Please, señora . . . I'm her friend. Tell me all you know."

The woman shrugged her shoulders. A while ago, she said. She had come. After a while, she had gone. She had gone once before, for a long time, and come back only once, with a mule. A strange girl, Señor Colonel. She comes and goes. She is hardly of the village. It is not easy to say what she will do, or if she will ever be back.

I wanted to rage at her easy acceptance of what to me was near-tragedy . . . but what good would it do? She wasn't responsible. She knew nothing more than what she had told me. Rosa had come. Rosa had gone.

"Señora, please answer. Did she go alone?"

"Always alone, Señor Colonel."

/ 247

"Where should I try to find her?"

She shrugged. She tried to smile, perhaps to comfort me, and I saw decayed brown teeth.

I walked back to where Candelario waited by the horses, and for a moment I laid my cheek on the hard flank of the roan, needing to feel some heartbeat of life. When I looked up, Candelario was studying me intently.

"She's gone?"

"Yes."

"To where?"

"Her mother doesn't know."

"Alone?"

"I asked. Yes, alone."

Candelario coughed uncomfortably. "And did she take the gold with her?"

"I didn't ask." I swung into the saddle. "The gold is hers—she can do what she pleases with it. I don't care if she took it or not."

"Half of it is mine," Candelario reminded me. "*I* care. I told you, Tomás—"

"Damn it," I said, my voice rising, "what the hell do you want to do? Dig in the fucking corral, with the whole village watching? If it's not there, there's nothing you can do except cry. If it is, you're stuck with it. You can't leave it—you can't take it with you. So let it be. Hope that it's there," I said cruelly. "Maybe that will get you safely through the rest of the revolution."

He looked at me angrily. He hadn't deserved that outburst, but I didn't care. I jammed a knee into my beast's flank and turned him, snatched the bullwhip and flicked it over the mule's laid-back ears. I had left Hannah. Now I had lost Rosa. I wanted to get to Parral, do what had to be done and then go fight. The horse and mule surged ahead, back toward the sierra, struck by brilliant yellow bursts of the morning sun, with Candelario following in silence.

Parral, in the cup of the valley southwest through the mountains, formed itself vaguely out of a cottony dawn mist. Not far from here, Pancho Villa had been born. We were cold and hungry. I stopped a ragged peasant who was leading a mesquite-laden burro into the town and asked him how to get to the Hacienda de Los Flores on Calle Chorro, which is where Villa had told me the old German woman lived and where I would find Franz von Papen. Doffing his sombrero, the *campesino* scratched the lice in his gray hair. He offered his deepest apologies: he had been born near Parral and lived there for forty years, but it had never been necessary to learn the names of the streets. Who would bother? If we could perhaps trouble ourselves by describing the persons we sought and give their occupation, he would be honored to offer his services in guiding us there. A foreign woman named Griensen, I told him. What she did for a living, I couldn't say.

"Una gringa? Alta? Una güera, con ojos verdes? Con muchos caballos buenos?"

All foreigners, unless they were heathen Chinese, were considered by the *campesinos* to be gringos, and I had no idea whether the old woman was tall or fair-complexioned with green eyes, or had many good horses; but I said yes, that was the one, figuring that even if it wasn't she could still direct us to the right place. The man led us out a cobbled side street. Just as the sun appeared weakly over the mountains and the valley was flooded with pink light, we reached the flat, rose-colored façade of a house with a huge carved wooden door and a copper cowbell hanging from a length of rope. Like the faces of Mexicans themselves, the front of a Mexican house told you little about what lay behind the blank walls. Candelario gave our guide a few centavos; he saluted us and went on his way.

I yanked on the cowbell, and it pealed richly in the thin morning air. In a few minutes a wooden slat opened and the dark brown, hooded-eyed face of an Indian porter peered out at us.

"Is this the house of the Señora Griensen?"

*"Cómo no?—*why not? At your orders, señores."

"Colonels Mix and Cervantes would like to speak with the señora."

"Cómo no? When will they arrive?"

I realized then that the last thing in the world we resembled were staff colonels in the Army of the Convention. Riding those bucket-headed nags four days from Chihuahua and Tomochic, wearing our black serapes and dusty trail rags, we could have been a pair of wandering pulque sellers or soldiers from any one of the dozen armies that ranged over Mexico. Candelario, who was in a fractious mood anyway, did the sensible thing. Slipping his rifle from its scabbard, he pointed it through the slot at the porter's suspicious face.

"Open the door, you fool, or I'll blow your nose out of both your ears."

"Cómo no?" the man said, and did as instructed.

We walked our sore-footed horses through the tall portal into the courtyard, the pack mule following. As soon as we were inside I realized why the place had been named Hacienda de Los Flores. Flower gardens meandered in all directions, with neat beds of white roses, orange dahlias, geraniums of all shades, spiderlilies and blood trumpets, and those blue morning glories that the Mexicans call "Mantle of the Virgin." Purple bougainvillea climbed all over the stately house with its grilled windows and rough stone walls, and there were red coral trees and towering royal poinciana with orange butterflylike blossoms. The grass was as green as a carpet of emeralds, sparkling with early dew.

/ 249

Macaws and lovebirds sang in cages. I had never seen anything so lush, or smelled anything so fragrant, not even in Mexico City.

A woman appeared in the doorway under a trellis covered with grapevines, carrying a Mauser rifle at her hip, with a slim brown youth of about eighteen at her side. From the wood-seller's description she had to be Elisa Griensen, except that she didn't fit Villa's description—she wasn't old at all. Candelario's weary horse switched its tail and chose that moment to dump a load from its rear end onto one of the dahlia beds. The woman didn't smile.

She was tall—as tall, I guessed, as I was—probably in her mid-thirties, with fair but suntanned skin, high cheekbones, a handsome curved nose, very yellow hair and narrowed green eyes that raked us up and down as though we had just stumbled out of a Juárez cantina. She wore a white Indian blouse with embroidered flowers, a long brown leather riding skirt, trail boots and a flat black Spanish riding hat. Hostile as she looked, she was still a splendid sight for any traveler.

"What do you want?" she said crisply, holding that Mauser steady on my belly button. Lately, people were doing that far too much for my liking.

"With apologies, señora . . . is it possible that you're Elisa Griensen?"

"I am."

I adjusted my thoughts. What difference did it make if she were young rather than old? "Colonel Tomás Mix," I said, "at your orders. And this is Colonel Cervantes. General Villa asked us to call on you. I'm sure you know why."

She still failed to greet us with any warmth, and I realized she probably thought we had come across the real colonels in the sierra and murdered them for whatever few pesos they carried.

"Do you have any papers of identification?" Her voice was husky, flavored with a German accent.

"In my saddlebags. With your permission?" Reaching into my neatly folded uniform, I extracted Villa's letter. Elisa Griensen read it, looked us over again with that keen eye and kept frowning. Her eyes flicked to the uniform that now lay on the grass next to the pile of dung.

"Is that yours?"

"Yes, señora. The uniform, not the other."

That brought a flicker of a smile to her face, but the rifle didn't come down. "Put it on," she ordered. "Let's see if it fits."

I slipped obediently out of the saddle, picked up the wrinkled jacket with the gold eagles and then the striped pants, but then I hesitated.

"Where would you like me to change, señora?"

"Right here, where I can keep an eye on you. Don't worry. I've seen a man in his underwear before."

I didn't doubt it for a moment. Candelario chuckled insolently behind me as I struggled out of my serape, then stripped off my cartridge belts, dirty brown shirt and Levi's. When I sat down on the grass to work my feet out of my boots, I was embarrassed to see my big toe sticking out of one smelly sock. I stood up in my tattered vest and droopy gray underpants, teeth beginning to chatter in the morning cold, then quickly slipped into the pants and buttoned the jacket of the uniform. It occurred to me that the chief had been blessed with some shrewd foresight, and I was grateful to the little Polish tailor for making such a perfect fit, including that neat pocket on the left side that kept my privates snugly in place.

"My, don't you look splendid."

Elisa Griensen smiled, showing a set of white teeth. She lowered the rifle. "My apologies, Colonel. You looked a little young, that's all. The uniform seems to fit you, so you must be the man we're expecting."

"And *my* apologies, señora." I gallantly waved a hand at the dahlia bed, where the horseshit steamed gently in the cold air.

"It will make the flowers grow more quickly." Her bell-like laugh chimed in our ears. "You all look as if you could use a bath, and then some breakfast . . . or the other way round, if you're starving." She wrinkled her sharp nose. "No, have the bath first, if you don't mind. You smell like the hind end of a mule. Then we can eat and talk. I have a friend coming who wants to meet you. He's late too, so it worked out fine."

She ordered the young man to lead the horses to the stables. He was the son of the porter at the gate, Patricio, who hefted the trunk on his back and showed us to our quarters. He was all smiles now that Candelario hadn't shot him.

We were given two fine rooms at the rear of the house, with big beds and warm, handwoven Oaxacan counterpanes. There was a thick gray carpet in our room, with geometrical designs that I had seen once in a photography book about Mexican temples, flowered chintz curtains, and bunches of dahlias and red zinnias in Chinese vases. We had a bathroom too, and when a maid turned the big bronze tap in the shape of a horse's head, hot water gushed out. Using a jug of kerosene, Patricio swiftly kindled a fire in the grate of the bedroom fireplace, then heaped on some mesquite logs. When he and the maid had gone, Candelario turned to me, his one good eye gleaming. On the way down from Tomochic we had barely spoken, but now something had happened to take his mind off his sack of gold.

"You like this, Tomás?"

"It's better than Doña Luisa's Station Hotel."

"Don't rush with our business, whatever it is. Let's stay a few days. The mountain air agrees with me."

"How do you know she's not married?"

"So much the better. The best soup is cooked in a used pot. If her husband were here, it was he who would have come to the door." He crouched by the crackling fire, rubbing his hands together.

/ 251

I laughed. "What makes you think she fancies you?"

"Experience, Tomás. On the gate of every woman's vulva, God has written the list of all those who may enter. And sometimes, through a magic I don't pretend to understand, this list reflects itself in the eyes. In the garden, when you were busy dressing yourself in your beautiful uniform, I looked into her eyes and she into mine. I saw the shadow of my name."

"All right, but only if there's time. The man I have to see has messages for the chief."

"Make sure you understand the message perfectly," Candelario said, crouched by the fire. "Life is short, as I've told you before, and it's a sin to miss the small pleasures that offer themselves on the path toward the grave. A man rarely regrets what he's done, but what he *could* have done, and didn't!—this is what torments him when his hair is white and his pecker rises only at dawn when he has to piss." He spoke calmly, rubbing his hands near the flames to get them warm. "I'm older than you. Not smarter, of course, and perhaps not wiser. But I've faced death. When I was shot at Juárez, I felt a cold wind blow through my heart, which almost stopped beating. One never forgets that wind. So . . . talk slowly. For the sweetness of life and because I, your friend who saved your life in Chihuahua, and whom your foolishness may have cheated of his fortune, ask it of you. Did you notice the maid, by the way? Her name is Francisca. She is very pretty. She looked at you with great appreciation."

I nudged him away with one boot and bent to warm my own hands.

"Take your bath, you fool. You have the mind of a goat, and she told you what you smell like. I'm sorry about the gold, although I'll bet you fifty pesos it's still behind the corral. And I'm also sorry," I said gruffly, "that I yelled at you. I was upset. I'm still upset, but I'll get over it. One thing more." I raised a warning finger. "This woman is German, and so is the other man I've yet to see. They don't know I'm a gringo, and the chief doesn't want them to know. This man may be a friend of the revolution . . . and right now, I suspect, we need every friend we can get. He may be able to help the chief beat Carranza. So watch your tongue."

"I'll keep your secret, Tomás. It's a bargain." He grinned slyly, triumphantly. "What a pleasant stay we'll have here!"

**"I will find you twenty lascivious turtles
ere one chaste man."**

Breakfast in the big sunstruck kitchen was flapjacks smothered in wild dandelion honey, rashers of sweet smoked bacon and a platterful of scrambled eggs so laced with chile they brought tears even to Candelario's glass eye. Freshly shaved and shampooed. Candelario in his best rumpled khaki jacket and I in my uniform, we felt more like Villa's colonels and less like foul-smelling fugitives from Urbina. Elisa Griensen didn't do the cooking, but she told us that she had taught the art to Francisca, and we heaped compliments on our hostess while the pretty Indian girl heaped the flapjacks and bacon on our plates.

I learned that Franz von Papen had been delayed but was due in a day or so—fortunate, given our own late appearance. Candelario stroked his curly black beard; it was so clean it squeaked. "How shall we pass the time until he arrives, señora?" he asked. "Can you suggest something? What is there to do in Parral?"

"There's an old church nearby in Atotonilco. Otherwise," Elisa Griensen said, "not much. I can take you out riding, but I don't expect this desert is any different from the desert you've been through."

"It would still be my pleasure to accompany you," said Candelario, in his smoothest manner. "I love old churches, and the desert even more."

"You'll come too, Colonel Mix?" she asked.

"Tomás was brought up in the city of Juárez," Candelario explained. "As a child he was thrown badly from a horse. Poor fellow, the memory lingers. He can't stand the beasts except when it's necessary to get from one place to another and there's no railroad. He won't want to come."

That didn't sit too well with me, for I liked to think I could give Candelario a mustang and outride him bareback on a burro, but I held my peace.

"A pity," Señora Griensen said. "Oh, there's a *charreada* tomorrow at the bullring. Perhaps that would amuse you?"

A *charreada* was roughly the Mexican equivalent of a rodeo. "With pleasure," Candelario crooned.

The Griensen woman fixed me with her curiously light, penetrating green eyes. "It's strange, Colonel Mix, that you should fight for Pancho Villa and yet you don't like to ride."

"I'm his confidential aide, señora."

"And you don't bear a Spanish surname."

"My grandparents came here from Ireland many years ago. Unlike General Obregón, they didn't bother to change their name."

"I like the Irish," she said softly. "A manly race, I've always thought. What a pity you don't ride."

After breakfast Candelario strapped on his spurs and stuffed his rifle into its scabbard. Elisa Griensen changed from her embroidered blouse to a blue denim shirt, and they cantered out into the desert on two fine pintos that Patricio brought from the stables.

Having nothing much else to do, I wandered through the sunny flower gardens, bending now and then to inhale the powerful perfume of roses and tiger lilies, and then asked Patricio if he would show me the horses. He led me down a gravel path to where they munched from feedbags in their stalls. These were the best stables I had seen since Texas—each horse had plenty of room, hay and fresh grass. They were freshly shod too, their coats shone and not not one of them looked as if he had been sick this winter. Besides the two pintos she had a Morgan stallion, an Appaloosa, two young bay mares and one colt, and a big-chested gray quarter horse with chunky hindquarters and fine, sinewy legs, the kind that never go lame.

From there I meandered through the house, which proved to be as splendid as the woman who lived in it. The sitting room had Chinameca and Otomi pottery, a couple of bearskin rugs and a mahogany piano, and the wide pine boards of the floor were covered by at least a dozen fine Indian rugs. I asked Francisca for a cup of coffee and took it with me to the library. Books in German, Spanish, English and even French lined every wall from floor to ceiling. Francisca kindled a fire, and I settled into a red-leather easy chair. I needed the chance to do some more brooding about Rosa. It made no sense to have come back to Mexico, a free man, bent on begging her forgiveness, and then find that she was gone. Having seen Tomochic, I understood now why it had been impossible for her to stay. I looked into the leaping flames for a clue. There was none.

But I would find her. I didn't know how, but if I had to hire a hundred men and scour a hundred cities, I would do it.

Books are a balm to most miseries—you can almost always find some poor soul who's got more woes than your own. I read a favorite chapter from *Gulliver's Travels,* leafed through Shakespeare in German and then started a novel by a fellow named Sterne, which kept me chuckling although I couldn't make hide or hair out of the story, except that the hero actually described his own birth. After an hour's reading I grew sleepy and left a bookmark in my place. I wondered why an educated and handsome woman like Elisa Griensen had carved out this little oasis for herself in the wilds of northern Mexico.

They came back in the late afternoon while I was taking a siesta, and we didn't meet again until suppertime. Candelario, although he had missed a night's sleep, looked doggedly determined to pursue his quarry but couldn't help yawning from time to time, especially after we had downed a bottle of German white wine and stuffed ourselves with Francisca's jugged hare. Elisa Griensen had changed into a black silk blouse and her shining bundle of yellow hair was piled neatly on top of her head. By candlelight her cheekbones glowed with a coppery flush, and her eyes sparkled with the pleasure that a handsome woman usually feels in the company of two attentive men. I knew how Candelario felt about blondes, and this one was as natural as a sunset. If he worked himself between her sheets, I thought, I'd have a devil of a time getting him to heft that trunk of gold with me to Mexico City or Irapuato, or wherever Villa was by then.

Mostly to keep the conversation away from my Irish ancestors, I asked Señora Griensen the question that had sprung to my mind in the library. What was she doing here in Parral?

It turned out that she had been born in a town called Nuremberg in a part of Germany called Bavaria, where the men wore leather shorts and didn't do much except farm and hunt and go to cantinas and stamp their feet while they drank beer. She came to Mexico when she was eighteen to visit an uncle who was ranching in Chihuahua, fell in love with the country and then with a young Mexican cattle baron named Zambrano. They had one child together, a girl, who was in school now in Berlin. Zambrano died of a ruptured appendix ten years after they were married, and she inherited the hacienda in Parral as well as some few thousand acres of good grazing land to the north.

"I wasn't meant to live alone," she said simply, "so I married again . . . a bit too quickly, perhaps. He was a lawyer, a great believer in Francisco Madero. In 1911 he was shot by a firing squad at the orders of General Huerta. I haven't married since. I think twice is enough, don't you? In any case, I have my daughter, who comes to visit me every summer, and I have the ranch and my horses. A pity you don't like them," she said again to me, wrinkling her nose a trifle. "You certainly smell of them."

"I visited the stable," I confessed, but I was annoyed. The Griensen woman smiled at me.

"Did you see Willie? That's the Appaloosa. Isn't he a beauty? He's my favorite. So silly, and gentle as a lamb. Rather like you. I named him after the Kaiser, but you mustn't tell that to Captain von Papen when he gets here."

I ignored her barb. "I liked the Morgan. And that gray quarter horse is a fine animal."

From the other side of the candlelit white tablecloth that stretched across the oak dining room table, Candelario yawned. Taking it as a signal to make myself scarce, I excused myself on the pretext that I was still bone-weary from crossing the sierra. I was glad to get out of there anyway; Elisa Griensen had a way of getting under my skin.

I read *Tristram Shandy* in bed for an hour or so until the heavy wooden door opened to admit Candelario. He took off his clothes without a word and then, wearing his long johns, slipped into his bed. I looked at him.

"Tenochtitlán," he grumbled, "wasn't built in a day."

"Didn't you tell her your name was on the list written by God on her vulva?"

"Shut up and go to sleep, Tomás."

The next day was one of those warm, crisp, blue winter days—no trace of cloud and the air rich in your lungs—that makes you fall in love with the desert if you don't know what it can do to you when it turns mean. The sky burned so brightly that my eyes ached to look at it. Just before lunch Elisa Griensen announced again that she was going to the *charreada,* and she invited us once again to keep her company. Candelario had already accepted; and then, so did I. I decided to have some fun . . . and a little innocent revenge for the way she had been digging at me.

A Mexican *charreada* is like an old-time American rodeo in some ways, and in a few other ways it isn't. Rodeos started when cowhands on roundups got to arguing as to who was the fanciest rider and the fastest roper, or who could ride that slant-eyed mustang that had already broken the trail boss's leg. I had roamed for two years with Colonel Miller's Wild West Show from Oklahoma City as far west as Tucson. Once you learn to rope a calf or ride a fishtailing bronc, it's not something you forget. But in Mexico a *charreada* was a kind of free-for-all rassling show, with a lot of yelling and betting and even more tilting of the pulque jug. They had the usual saddle-bronc and bareback riding, roping and bulldogging, but there were no judges and fewer rules.

I spent most of the morning behind the stables with a pigging string and a thirty-foot coil of rope I borrowed from Patricio. It was a good maguey rope made from the fiber of the century plant—extra hard, held a wide loop and could be thrown fast. After an hour I had that loop dropping round the fence post every time. Of course, a fence post wasn't a bawling, ridge-running calf.

Elisa Griensen came out and watched for a while. "You're good at that," she said. "What are you practicing for?"

I gave her a lazy smile. "Well, señora, I figured if you'd be kind enough to lend me that gray quarter horse of yours, I might try a little roping out at the *charreada.* "

Tilting back her flat-brimmed Spanish hat, she looked down her nose at me as though my head came to a point. But then a playful little smile curled up from her wide mouth.

"That's serious business, Colonel. You could get hurt . . . very easily."

"I'll be careful. I sure like that horse."

"But aren't you frightened?"

"Well, that's been on my mind. I've got to get over that. I'm tired of General Villa making fun of me because I'm scared of horses. I should have got right back on when I was a kid and that stallion throwed me. Now's my chance, you see, and I don't want to miss it."

She kept trying to talk me out of it, but the more she argued the more I turned stubborn. Finally, with a merry laugh and tossing her blond hair, she agreed.

After lunch I saddled the quarter horse, whose name was Maximilian, tightened the cinches and then loosened them a notch to give his back some air. He felt fine between my legs; he was frisky but he responded to every touch, and by the time we reached the bullring I had the idea we were friends. The stands were already packed, for even in the midst of the revolution Mexicans didn't give up their favorite sports. Elisa Griensen went off for a minute to talk to some people, and when Candelario swung down off the back of the pinto he was riding, I heard a familiar jingle in his pocket. I leaned down.

"Hang on, amigo . . . is that what I think it is?"

"You're going to win, aren't you, Tomás? I thought I might make a little bet. For the two of us."

"Candelario, I could just as soon make a jackass of myself. I'm a little out of practice."

"It's only a few pesos. The chief will never miss it. And if he does, we can replace it from our own gold in Tomochic, which you're sure is still there."

"Who will you bet with?"

"I'll find someone. Any man from Parral will bet against a panty-waist from Juárez."

Patricio stayed with the horses while we paid our fifty-centavo admission, squeezed into some seats next to a gang of half-drunk soldiers from one of our brigades, and then Candelario and I went round behind the barrier to the chutes. It took only a few minutes to find the man in charge, and when I told him I wanted to enter the calf roping, he agreed right away. I asked him if there was a fee, and he looked at me in a puzzled way and said, "No, señor, of course not. For what should you pay?" I should have known right then what I was in for, but as usual I ignored the danger signs.

A band started blaring spirited music, and then the bareback-bronc riding got under way. The horses were all flat-eared mustangs brought straight out of the Sierra Madres to town, and there wasn't a single *charro* who could stay on any of them for the full ten seconds. The crowd cheered mightily as one fellow after another dropped onto the spine of his critter and then soared up to see what the moon was made of. Most of the bets, I guess, were a matter of which of the riders could crawl out of harm's way behind the barrier faster than the last man. Everyone was having a fine time. Mexicans always do when they have a grip on a pulque jug and can smell horseflesh and there's a hope of blood.

When the saddle-bronc riding started they announced that roping would be next. I worked my way through the noisy crowd back to the chutes, to draw my calf. But there wasn't any draw. There weren't any calves.

Three other fellows had entered the event, all local boys from Parral. They had already made their choice of what they cared to rope, and they weren't calves or trough-fed dogies. They were full-grown steers—

/ 257

Chihuahua longhorns. Now I understood what Elisa Griensen had meant when she said I could get hurt very easily. I never had developed any motherly love for bovines, but these were the worst. They could run like a deer, fight like a cougar, dodge a rope like a jackrabbit and scheme like a Piute sneaking up on an Apache camp. They were long and lean, lithe as snakes, mean to the bone, half-wild and half-savage, and they had a third half that was pure crazy.

The one that had been left for me was a mottled brown beast as ugly as a tar bucket, showing a spread of dirty horn that I calculated to be nearly five feet in length, roughly the shape of a double-bladed Turk-ish sword. After roping them, they had to be tied down, too. I decided this was no sport for Mrs. Mix's wandering and not very clever son, and I'd gracefully withdraw. But then I remembered that Candelario proba-bly had a bet down by now. It was a matter of honor. I had to try.

While Patricio checked the bit and cinches on the quarter horse, I watched my competitors do their stuff. The first man rode down on the careering longhorn in no time at all but looped his rope a shade too high and caught a handful of air as the steer switched those big horns down in the turf. The *charro* tried again with his second rope, got one horn clamped down almost to the rosebud and vaulted from the back of his pony. The steer whirled that young fellow round in a circle and set upon him. The crowd jumped to its feet, screaming. Before half a dozen men had sprinted from behind a barrier to drag the rider away, the horn had raked him from knee to ankle and cut a furrow right through his leather chaps, spiking the tendon. Blood soaked the sand. That foolish man would limp for the rest of his life.

"Don't worry," I said to Maximilian. "I'll worry for both of us."

The next man took too slow a dally and the horse let the steer drag it halfway across the arena before the rider tumbled off. The fellow after that managed to make a nice hooleyann toss and actually rassle the beast to the ground—and then the pigging string slipped from his teeth and got swallowed up in boil of dust, so he let go. The crowd gave a halfhearted cheer. They must have felt cheated. No one had been killed or gored for at least ten minutes.

It was my turn then. I got my knees locked down tight and tied the rope snug on the horn. I knew I wouldn't have much time, and I'd need a wide loop.

"You ready, Maximilian?"

Maximilian snorted that he was ready. It gave me faith that he listened to me so carefully. I hoped he was as good a horse as I thought. Wiping the sweat from my eyes, I bit hard into the pigging string.

The mean brown longhorn shot out of the box. I kicked with my spurs and was out there on the sand faster than a rummy reaches for a bottle, whooping and bearing down on that mean critter, and taking one twirl with the rope to throw something halfway between a washerwoman loop and a hooleyann, because those horns were awfully wide and I wasn't trying for a common head ketch like the other riders.

The steer turned nicely toward me; he had to, because I'd cornered him. I turned Maximilian until we were neck and neck galloping round the ring, with him pinned between us and the barrier. If he veered now, I would regret it. I heard the crowd roar, and I smelled that longhorn's musky rotten breath when he whipped his ugly head round to see who was dogging him—we were that close. I threw the rope over his right shoulder, giving it a little twist so that it landed just a shade to the right of his forefeet. I don't think I've ever seen a finer loop settle better on a pair of churning legs—one of them, anyway—and it snugged perfectly back against the rosebud. I yanked back on the bit, reined to the left and braced myself against the coming calamity. Maximilian planted his thin legs, took the strain with me and didn't budge more than a foot when the steer bellowed, twisted, reversed himself in midair—then hit the ground like a boulder dropped off a mountain.

The air whooshed out of him like a busted balloon. I vaulted off, grunted from the shock and ran down the rope while Maximilian kept the slack out of it and dragged that big hunk of foundering beef right in my direction . . . that quarter horse was something else. Keeping clear of those gigantic horns, I dived at the belly of the steer in not quite the most graceful move you'd expect to see in a real rodeo with just a four-hundred-pound calf at the end of the rope—Ty Cobb sliding headfirst into second base is about the best way to describe it—and whipped the pigging string round his flailing hoofs in a three-legged cross-tie before that ton of bawling wilderness knew what had happened to him.

The crowd let out a yell that could have been heard in Chihuahua City. That kind of dirty roping and mean cowbusting was something they didn't often see in Mexico. I hadn't done it too often up in the Brazos, either, because if you made a one-legged ketch on a steer you were apt to break its shoulder. But it was the only way I was going to survive those horns, and it had worked. I jumped up from the dust, back on Maximilian, and let out a war whoop. I was champ of Parral. And for a whole morning I hadn't thought of Rosa. . . .

By the time I had the gray cooled down and handed him back to Patricio, and worked my way back through the hot sun to where Candelario and Elisa Griensen were sitting on the shady side of the arena, I guess about two hundred people had thumped me on the back and yelled at me, *"Mucho! Mucho!"*—which was the biggest compliment they could pay a roper, or even a torero. There were no rules, and I had done the job. I was grinning like a jackass.

Candelario gave me a bone-cracking hug. Elisa Griensen looked at me in a way that was both disturbed and disturbing.

"You lied to me," she said quietly.

"Only a little, señora—" Coated with dust and sweat, I was still puffing from the ride. "I was scared to death, that's God's truth. And I never said I couldn't handle a rope. Anyway, that Maximilian is an animal a baby could rope with. I've got my courage back, señora." Turning to Candelario, whose smile was so wide his teeth almost bit the wax out of his hairy ears, I asked, "Did you get our bet down?"

"A hundred pesos in gold, amigo. You see my great faith?"

"Yes, but I don't see the money. Who took the bet?"

He blushed. "No one had that kind of money to bet. Gold is very valuable. But the Señora Griensen didn't share my faith, so she made the understandable mistake of betting against you."

"Oh . . ." I frowned, then turned to her. This wouldn't do—it was confession time. "Señora, I'm sorry. I didn't know that. You're right, I lied. It wasn't fair. I don't think it would be right to take your money."

"I didn't bet money," Elisa Griensen rasped, angling a hard look at me with those eyes that were the color of winter grass. "I bet the damned horse."

"Which damned horse? You don't mean Maximilian?"

"Unfortunately, I do."

I stared at her, then drew a deep breath and let it out. "Señora Griensen, I can't take him."

"Yes, you can," she said evenly, and now there was a warmer glint softening that jade hardness. "A bet is a bet. I've lost some and won some, and I never welsh. No one's ever ridden that quarter horse the way you did, and perhaps no one ever will. You may have tricked me, but that's my fault. He's yours, Colonel. Just treat him well. Tonight we'll celebrate."

Clearly she meant it, and I made a decision too. I turned to Candelario.

"The chief once said you can't divide a woman in half—we won't go into the reasons for that. The same thing's true of a horse. I rode him and risked my neck. He's mine. I'll pay you a hundred pesos in gold for your half."

"In gold!" Candelario bared his teeth and whistled through them. "I know which gold. *Madre de Dios! Qué cojones!*"

"Is it a deal?"

"Yes," he grumbled, "it's a deal."

So I owned a quarter horse. I would pay for that later in a way I couldn't foresee—and not in gold.

When Elisa Griensen made up her mind to something, I discovered, trying to stop her was as risky as braiding a mule's tail. With the excuse that Captain von Papen might show up that evening, she broke out the French champagne. I had bathed in water as hot as I could stand it to keep some of the day's soreness from working too deep into my bones, splashed on some cologne I'd found in the bathroom, and over the bubbly stuff we got right down to a first-name basis. I was still feeling a little guilty over the trick we had pulled, although it had really been Candelario's idea so that he could get close to her calico, and I had just gone along with it for the fun . . . but she wouldn't hear any more apologies.

She raised her glass of champagne in a toast to me. "When you called that stallion a Morgan, I should have known. I wasn't born yesterday. You ride like a devil. You haven't always been a *charro*, have you?"

"No," I confessed, "I was a baby once."

Francisca brought another bottle of champagne. Soon the corks were popping like gunshots on a border raid. That tornado juice crept up on you with soft feet and I knew my tongue was getting thicker and my head full of feathers, but I kept up the pace, glass for glass. I told a few tales about riding with Pancho Villa, and when I was in the mood I guess I could color up a story redder than a Navajo blanket. Elisa was a good listener too, and had the knack of making a man think he was a descendant of Homer rather than a pie-eyed windbelly. Around midnight Candelario just let his ears hang down; after cheering me to victory in the day's festivities, he didn't have enough vocal power left to bend a smoke ring.

Then Elisa coughed once, looked Candelario square in his good eye and called the turn.

"You must be tired. Don't let me keep you up."

He muttered something meant to be cordial, made a bow of sorts and obediently vanished.

In the candlelight Elisa's eyes looked like leaves of a tree freshly washed by summer rain. She took me by the hand and said softly, "Come, Tomás."

In the first place, I was drunk. My head felt light and my tongue heavy. In the second place . . . how could I say no? And why? I had done her a wrong, cheating her out of that quarter horse, and in turn she had fed me a dinner fit for a lord and popped the cork off her best champagne. And, whether I liked it now or not, I was free. Hannah was off my conscience, and Rosa may have been lost to me forever.

And in the third place, or fourth, drunk or not, I knew I wanted her. With those green eyes and wide shoulders, her shapely small breasts pressing against the white Indian blouse, she was a beautiful and bedazzling woman. I had watched her breasts for the last two days, bobbing freely under her shirt as she rode or walked, and I could swear I smelled their perfume. She moved like a proud queen, tall and sure, and that was the way she led me upstairs, as if I were about to be crowned at her side.

Her bedroom was a big airy room with graceful antique mahogany furniture that looked more French than Mexican, an oversized four-poster matrimonial bed with carved columns, and lacy white curtains stirring in a breeze that blew through the balcony windows. Candles burned in black iron holders on the bedside tables. When we got inside she locked the door, kissed me so that my head felt even giddier and then peeled off her clothes. She tossed them carelessly on a chair. When I did the same, she hauled me through the curtains into the four-poster. The puffed pillows and even the pale blue sheets smelled of fresh flowers. Her body was long, narrow-hipped and tanned, neatly made and strong, and her breasts were all I had imagined—small and soft, with big nipples that seemed to fill my mouth. Her unpinned hair spread out on the pillow like a shower of fine gold thread.

It was a merry frolic by candlelight. Elisa Griensen had an appetite that would have shamed a cowhand after a trail drive through a blizzard, except it wasn't cornbread and clabber cheese she hungered for. She was all woman, that German lady, and not afraid to show it. I wondered how long she had been without a man. She was too much of a prize, I reckoned, to stay lonely for very long, but that night she gave me the impression that she was starved. We wandered deep, unbosoming our little fears and our great pleasures in the candlelight. At the end, with a lightning cry that came first, galloping hard in our embrace, she flooded the room with song. It became a duet.

We fell asleep in each other's arms. The next thing I knew she was whispering gently in my ear to get up. It was dawn . . . it would be better if our overdue visitor didn't find me in her bed.

I staggered downstairs in the first gray light, listening to a wind moan from the desert, feeling like the frazzled end of a misspent life and wondering how Candelario would take it when he realized I had bedded the lady of his choice—the sort of thing that Mexicans don't take too sportingly, as I had found out in Ascensión a long time ago. I didn't think he'd go so far as swearing a vow to kill me, but after what had happened in Tomochic I'd hate to have made yet another dent in our friendship.

Our bedroom door was bolted from the inside. I gave a few light taps, then a good thump with the toe of my boot. There was some muttering. Finally, naked as a gigantic brown worm, Candelario opened the door a crack.

"Ah, it's you . . . be quiet, if you can."

I nudged into the room. From under the counterpane of his bed I saw the black hair and dusky peaceful face of Francisca, sound asleep. I smiled, rolled into bed, turned out the candle power in my brain and passed out.

23   "Wisely, and slow."

I had a dream that I heard bedsprings creak, and then the sun poured in through the flowered chintz curtains, too brightly for me to ignore it. When I opened my eyes a slit, Francisca was gone and Candelario was already pulling on his boots. I decided to try out my tongue and see if it still flapped.

"How do you feel?"

"I will never drink again," he said solemnly.

"But you had a good time?"

"It was diverting. I knew already, when she served us breakfast and brushed against my sleeve, that it would happen. On the vulva of every woman—"

"You told me that before. You're still plastered. So you were on Francisca's list?"

"My name was written in large letters."

"Listen, my friend"—my voice came out as a croak—"I have a confession to make—"

"Confess nothing. I know all. I was mistaken when I first looked into Elisa's eyes. Sometimes that happens. It may have been that the sun was blinding me, or that my good eye was turned the wrong way and I misread the name. Did she entertain you in the proper spirit, Tomás?"

"She was *mucho*," I said gravely.

"So I suspected. The man who picks the bad bull often has the luck to draw the best mount." He sighed, then grinned evilly. "Are you still in such a hurry to leave Parral?"

I put my jaw in a sling and didn't answer. I had to chew all this a bit finer before I could swallow it, and my head ached too much to make a decent job of it. How complicated my life had suddenly become! I had walked out on Hannah, which had freed me but still pained me. I had gone to find Rosa in Tomochic, my heart at the high tide of love, missing her, wanting and needing her, spinning a web of plans . . . a web that had been swept into the dust. But I had sworn to find her, no matter how long it took. And here I was, not four days after being practically a married man, first to one woman, then to another, fluffing Elisa Griensen's fur and loving every minute of it. No, I wasn't in a hurry to leave Parral. The song of that German lady's roused and cheerful passion, the friendly ways she had known to give pleasure as well as take it freely— the taste of all that was as sweet in my mouth as the champagne was sour in my belly. I was the least likely candidate I knew for the role of Don Juan, but it looked to me as if that was the man whose gluttonous shade I had become, and the Hamlet in me was long dead, buried somewhere between Mexico City and the Rio Bravo.

All brushed and curried, blond hair massed on her head like a Sunday School teacher, Elisa was waiting for us at the breakfast table, and there was a man sitting with her, drinking coffee heavily laced with milk, his pinky extended slightly into the air. He was about forty, with a long nose and mellow brown eyes, a bristling military mustache and eyebrows so bushy they looked like part of a Halloween costume that had been glued to his forehead. Dressed in a beautifully cut gray tweed suit, he made me feel like a shabby hobo from the wrong side of the railroad tracks. I hadn't bothered to put on my uniform and was still wearing my steer-roping clothes.

"Colonel Mix, Colonel Cervantes . . ." Elisa said. "Permit me to introduce Captain von Papen."

The captain shot instantly to his feet, clicking his heels like the crack of a rifle. He saluted. It took me a moment to realize that I was the focus of his attention, since I couldn't remember the last time anyone in the Mexican army had saluted me, and I always regarded my rank as a private joke between me and Pancho Villa and my friends. To a German officer, however, it was the real thing.

I returned the salute and in his guttural schoolbook Spanish he said, "I am honored to meet you, Colonel. With your permission, may I sit?"

"Certainly. Just make yourself right at home."

"May I finish my coffee, sir?"

"You sure can. I need to eat and recuperate before we talk. Mind if we join you?"

"I would be honored, Colonel."

Then he rattled off a few sharp words in German to Elisa Griensen, and she turned to Francisca, who was blushing at the stove, and in a few minutes we hunkered down to the serious matter of flapjacks and bacon and a pot of hot black coffee. The Kaiser's business with Pancho Villa would just have to wait until I'd got rid of my hangover.

After lunch, Von Papen and I settled ourselves in the library over a brandy, with Elisa there to interpret when the going got tough. Candelario had vanished . . . I could guess to where. Von Papen asked if I spoke any English, and I said, "A little," so he told me he would speak that language, and if I missed anything he was sure Frau Griensen would help out. That suited me, since I realized it would give me two chances to chew my cud before I spat it back in Spanish. His English was flawless, and he spoke it like a London lord, which was natural because he had learned it there. Of course, if he didn't want me to understand he had only to drop into German. The only words I knew in that language I had learned in bed last night, and they wouldn't fit into this conversation any more than a whore into a white wedding dress.

The captain and I had already chewed the fat about lesser matters, and I knew now that he had gone to cavalry school in Hanover and been an officer in the Westphalian Fifth Uhlan Regiment, and then a permanent member of Kaiser Wilhelm's General Staff for nearly two years. Washington was his base now, but he had been an observer for his government when the Americans had dropped anchor and shot up Veracruz. He had toured the port facilities there, inspected all the gunboats and cruisers, and been given a young American captain as his personal guide, a fellow named Douglas MacArthur.

"He was remarkably kind. It's extraordinary how open the Americans are about their situation. One suspects them of being Machiavellian, but in fact, upon reflection, one realizes that the armor of naïveté may be as potent a weapon as the poison of deceit. Eh what?"

The captain was as full of verbal lather as a soap peddler, and I had to be careful that I just didn't keep nodding dreamily and let on that I understood his drift. He took out a miniature gold comb on the end of a gold watch chain and began to run it through his mustache. When he finished his grooming he fished out a monocle. It hung from a black velvet string, and he screwed it deliberately into his right eye so that one bushy eyebrow arched halfway up his forehead, peering at me like an owl from a cottonwood tree. I had never seen that except in the movies. I was impressed.

"Perhaps," he said gently, "you would be kind enough now to tell -me what you already know of my proposal to General Villa. It will save us a great deal of time."

"I've got plenty of time," I told him, which might not have been the case if good fortune hadn't fallen on my plate last night. "So why don't you start from the beginning?"

He went into his prattle, which was like rain falling on a tin roof. The Germans, he explained, were going to win the war in Europe. "Destiny, dear fellow, demands it." The Kaiser's dignified cousin, King George Five of England, knew nothing about modern warfare, and the French were a nation of decadent drunks. The attitude of the Kaiser was that the European war was really no business of the United States, whose great enemy was in truth her current ally, Japan.

"In fact," Von Papen informed me, "we know that it is the plan of the Imperial Japanese government to invade the United States by way of Mexico, once an accord has been reached with the ruling powers of your country, whoever they may prove to be." He went on to explain that the Japanese monkey men cared nothing whatever for the sufferings of the Mexican people. *"Die gelbe Gefahr,* the Kaiser has called them—the yellow peril. Beware of them, Colonel. Don't listen to their silken overtures. Indeed, if any foreign power comes to you in your hour of need, it should be we Germans, who have always venerated the culture of a proud people cheated by history."

He paused to let that sink in, and then he edged a little closer to the point. He said, "Colonel, have you by chance ever looked at a map of Mexico in the year 1844?"

I admitted I hadn't, not lately.

"The borders of your country, sir, extended as far north as the American states of Kansas and Colorado. They included all of Utah, California, Arizona, New Mexico and, of course, Texas. Imagine! All this the Americans took from you, first with the Texas Annexation and then in the Mexican Cession of 1848, which snatched away what I can only term as the paradise of California. Even today, as you must know, the ubiquitous Mr. Hearst owns half of the state of Chihuahua. American Smelting and Refining, Standard Oil . . . these are all-too-familiar names in Mexico. The mind boggles, dear fellow! How can you possibly think of these people as your friends?"

I realized now that I was talking to a very persuasive man, and I was glad it was me listening to his spiel and not Pancho Villa. His lingo was so polished you could skate on it, and if I were truly a Mexican colonel and hadn't been born in Pennsylvania and bred in Texas, I might well have been ready to place my hand on his bible and get his religion.

"What it comes down to, Colonel, is that Mexico must make a choice. One hopes, an intelligent one."

He then let slip the notion that other elements in Germany, with whom he had no sympathy, were hoping to finance Victoriano Huerta's return from Spain for the purpose of a coup against the feuding revolutionists. "The deeper purpose of this," he said, fiddling with his monocle, which had slipped a trifle, "would be to divert Mr. Wilson's attention from the European war and force yet another intervention in Mexico. From our point of view, needless to say, that would not be unwelcome."

That puzzled me, and I thought it was time to speak up, with the hope of getting him to tell me what in hell he was driving at.

"With due respect, Captain . . . I don't see how that works. Wilson doesn't like Huerta, but if the old drunk came back it would never make him intervene. That Veracruz thing didn't work out too well for the United States."

"That may be. One hopes so. I don't like Huerta, either." Von Papen sipped his brandy. "In any event—and more importantly—I believe in your revolution, and so do the people in Germany who really count. I believe that Francisco Villa is the revolution's ultimate leader. What if the revolutionary forces could stabilize themselves under such a man? What if they could declare solidarity with Germany? That would simplify matters, eh?"

For who? This fellow could probably talk a pump into believing it was a windmill.

"Captain, I still don't see it. Why should that help Germany? The

Americans might get damned annoyed, but if it was no more than a declaration of solidarity, Wilson would just send a few more divisions to Texas and tell his factories to churn out more rifles. He sure wouldn't declare war."

Sipping his brandy, Von Papen pretended to think that over. Then he said, "You may be right. But there is one thing Villa could do to provoke it."

"And what's that?"

"Declare war on the United States. *Make* war . . . with German arms and German money."

I took a shaky breath. "But, Captain, if we did that—it would light such a fire under Wilson's ass that he'd go to war with you as well!"

"Ah, but not in Europe!"

Suddenly I saw his point. His point, our army.

"Come on, Captain," I said, smirking. "Why should Villa do such a thing? What is poor Mexico to gain by making war on the United States other than more bloodshed . . . more suffering? There's everything to lose. But what's to gain?"

"I should think," he replied calmly, "that in the hour of victory the main thing she would lose would be the adjective you applied to her. She would be proud Mexico, not poor Mexico. With Germany's help she would take her rightful place among the world's great powers."

"Those are pretty words. I'm not sure Pancho Villa would be impressed by them."

"I've never met the man. What would impress him?"

The whole idea had begun to horrify me, but I was too curious to hold back.

"A specific promise. Not for himself. For Mexico."

"How about Texas?" Von Papen said, without even pausing to think. "Arizona. California. Her lost territories." He smiled, as I gasped.

I had to call time out then. This had gone far beyond my anticipation and to the limits of my imagination. I hadn't known what to expect, but it surely wasn't a proposition that the Northern Division join up with the Krauts, then invade Texas and get it plus California as a prize!

Already I imagined General Pershing peering through his binoculars at our whooping, charging brigade, muttering to his aide, "That crazy fellow on the chestnut looks familiar to me. See if our snipers can pick him off. . . ."

I strolled alone through the orchard to mull things over. Then we met for tea and biscuits, and after that we wandered off to the library. I settled back into the soft red-leather easy chair and put my feet up on an ottoman.

I got the jump on him this time before he could begin to lather up.

"Captain, I think I understand the situation now . . . what you'd like General Villa to do. I know the army of Mexico, especially the Northern Division. I've fought for it for two years, and I didn't get to be a colonel at my age because I parted my hair in the right place. Our soldiers are as brave as the next man, when they're fighting for land and liberty. *Their* land . . . *their* liberty. But they're not much interested, the way you Germans are, in fighting to take over some other fellow's backyard. It's my opinion that they wouldn't get ten miles inside of Texas before they'd have more troubles out of Black Jack Pershing's army than Job had boils. And when Scott wheeled out the light artillery, they'd just turn around and hightail it for home. Now, that's no way to win a war."

Elisa translated my Spanish into a flowing German, while Von Papen started currying his mustache again.

"Colonel Mix," he said, when he finished spiffing up, "ten miles inside the border would be more than enough. A single mile would do. We wouldn't expect you to fight a major campaign. We would merely expect you to strike and then regroup to a more secure position." Thinking I was Mexican, he of course avoided the word *retreat*. "Such an act of incursion would be sufficient to bring the American army after you, and then you need but wait for the inevitable."

"What might *that* be?" I asked, more and more amazed.

"Our intervention on your behalf, followed by American surrender to German military power. Our submarines can blockade their eastern coast. Our troop transports can reach it. Once we have brought England and France to their knees, our full might will be thrown against the United States. It will be a matter of weeks before there is a negotiated peace. Mr. Wilson has no stomach for a serious war. And you will recover all that you lost in 1848."

Time, I thought, to nail this down. "Would you put that in writing?"

"At the proper time," he said cordially.

I nodded and asked where he, as a cavalry officer who knew the Texas border, thought the Mexican army could strike most effectively for the common cause. He smiled beautifully then. As far as he was concerned, I was netted and ready to be fileted.

"General Villa would surely know that better than I," he said, with a nice deference.

"He's always open to advice. You say you've never met him?"

"I've not yet had that honor."

"Oh, he's the most reasonable man you're ever likely to come across. Always eager to listen, always ready to take help from the right people. And speaking of help, what exactly are you prepared to offer?"

"Give us a list of your needs."

"No, Captain," I said firmly. "Give us a list of what you can supply. And when. And by what method of transportation."

"But surely, Colonel, you can't expect such a commitment at this stage."

"It's not what I expect. It's what General Villa will require. If I come back empty-handed, he might get to thinking he's buying a pig in a poke and that all we did up here in Parral was punish the air. And that might not suit him."

He thought that over for a while, then chattered something in German to Elisa, who nodded. He turned back to me.

"Are you in a great hurry, Colonel? Can you give me a week? Perhaps even ten days? I would like to send some cables, and they must be coded, and the response is not always as swift in your country as one might wish."

It was my turn to look at Elisa, and I broke into rapid Spanish that I knew he wouldn't follow. "Frau Griensen," I said, "can you stand my smelly hide around here for another week? Or would you rather we skipped to a hotel in town?"

"There's no hotel here where you'd be comfortable, my colonel, and I like your smelly hide." And then, just as Von Papen swung his monocle back to look for my reaction, she winked.

I cleared my throat dramatically. "It seems to be in the interest of my country and my general to stay. What about you, Captain?"

"With your kind permission, Colonel, I will return to Juárez. Our communications facilities are better there."

"You've got my permission. I don't know what we'll do here, but it's been a long and fatiguing war. Colonel Cervantes says the mountain air suits him. We'll wait here for you."

"Soldiers deserve a rest and rarely get one," Captain von Papen replied sympathetically. He stood up, stiff as a steel bar, cracking his heels together again. He saluted me.

Right after tea, with his Mexican escorts roweling their horses and firing their rifles gleefully into the air, Von Papen set out for Chihuahua City to catch the northbound train. As soon as he was out of sight, vanished into a fog of alkali dust, Elisa took my arm. She walked with me into the shade of her bountiful garden and threw a crafty smile at me.

"What a good actor you are, Thomas," she murmured. "You may have missed your true profession. I almost applauded."

She had spoken to me in English.

"What are you talking about, Elisa?" I answered gruffly in Spanish. "I don't understand."

"Did you enjoy *Tristram Shandy?*" She paused. "I've been following the progress of your bookmark. Oh, don't look so worried and conscience-stricken. I know you're not a spy sent by General Pershing. If Villa gave you his trust, that's good enough for me."

I kept frowning, while she kept smiling. Eventually her smile conquered, as smiles do. And this smile was on the face of a beautiful woman.

"Did you tell Von Papen?"

Elisa laughed, and squeezed my arm. "He wouldn't have understood. These military people are so damned stuffy. I'm German, but I've lived here most of my life. One's sympathies change. Whatever I did was in order to help my country, and my country is Mexico. It just struck me that Mexico might be helped more if this meeting took place than if Captain von Papen bolted because he wouldn't believe Villa would send a gringo." She smiled at me. "Now, I myself think the gringo was an inspired choice. And how would the gringo feel about a siesta?"

That week, one of the more memorable ones of my life, passed quickly—too quickly. Candelario was content. He had his Francisca, who stroked his beard lovingly and rubbed axle grease on his back when he got drunk and took a nasty fall from the pinto, and eventually moved in with him after asking permission of her mistress. And I had Elisa.

This was new to me, and wondrous—a powerful word but an accurate one. I had never known a full-grown independent woman before, someone at the zenith of her beauty and power. She played no games with me . . . at least none that I didn't enjoy.

"I want you to know who I am, Tom, so that you won't make any serious mistakes or have too many illusions. I'm thirty-seven years old, and I've had a bellyful of the world. I haven't seen and done everything, and I hope I never do—but what's happened to me has been enough to make me glad I lived. I value my independence above everything. I won't let any man, or anything, take it from me. I mean," she said, shrugging, smiling softly, "I'll put up a hell of a fight." She lay back on the sofa, smoking a cigarette. I watched the blue smoke swirl in front of the crackling fire.

"My first marriage," Elisa went on, "to Zambrano, wasn't a very good one. He was *muy mucho, muy Mexicano.* You know what I mean. I didn't cope too well. I could now, but not then. My only excuse is that I was young. He went haring off after the ladies, and I got back at him by having affairs with men. With a woman too, but only once. She was a girl from Berlin, my cousin, who came to visit. I'd always adored her, a schoolgirl crush, and it came to fruition. It ended, she went back, but I've never regretted it—I did it with a whole heart. And I see you're shocked."

I wasn't. I don't think anything she had done could shock me, because she wasn't the least bit ashamed and she made it sound natural. It was just something beyond my comprehension, and I said so. She smiled.

When Zambrano's appendix burst, as she had already told us, she married again and lost her second husband to one of Huerta's firing squads. "That hurt," she said succinctly. "He was a good man—much

270 /

older than I and far wiser. And then I went through what the English call 'a bad patch.' I didn't want anything to do with men, but they came round, as they always do to a woman on her own. Bringing me God's gift in a pair of tight trousers." She laughed merrily. "I turned them all away. I'd learned a long time ago that promiscuity wasn't the answer—not for me. I needed someone, and I was willing to be chosen, but I wanted the right to choose too. There's more than one revolution, you see. So I had to do a bit of kicking and scratching, which isn't my style. I think I achieved a reputation in Parral as a tough *hombre*. The buck nun of Los Flores." She chuckled again. "And I loved it as much as I hated it. What I hated was the loneliness, although I've discovered that human beings are constructed in such a way that they'll get used to anything, no matter how *in*human. Like war," she said carelessly. "But never mind that. Getting back to me, what I grew to love was my bloody independence. And *that's* a trap too. Believe me! The ego soars! You grow a little arm-weary patting yourself on the back. It's so damned silly . . . and so damned necessary. It's the key to your life, but it's a bore to make it a *way* of life. But I did. And still do. Can't help it. I warn you."

She fell silent awhile, but I knew she wasn't waiting for me to speak. She was mulling something over in her mind. I liked to watch that process of thought: I liked the changing shadows in her green eyes and the tightening of little muscles around her lips.

Then she said quickly, "I want you to know something else. No illusions, no serious mistakes—isn't that what I said? But still." Again she hesitated before she spoke. "That time, when I wore the nun's habit—I'm not speaking of the dead past. It's lasted right up to now . . . that is, until the night after the *charreada*. You're the first, Tom, in two years. Long years, I might add. Good years, but not the easiest ones."

I believed her instantly. She flattered me, but it wasn't her intent. She wanted me to understand her and to be a shade more careful than I might have been otherwise. She was as vulnerable as I.

"But why *me*, Elisa?"

"Because you didn't take me for granted," she said. "Not before bed, not during, not after. You have some style, Tom, not just with Chihuahua longhorns and German staff captains. I like almost everything about you . . . so far," she said, warier now, pulling back, but with a little smile.

"You don't know me yet," I answered.

"I have a good sense of smell. Age and experience, my sweet, have to provide some benefits."

No one had ever called me "my sweet" before Elisa, and nothing can move a man to lay out the raw truths of his life more than a woman who beats him to the punch. She hadn't been shy; neither was I. I told her my story, what little there was. I didn't leave out my courtship of Hannah or my living with Rosa and my visit to Tomochic. I didn't leave out the corral in Torreón. I must have spoken for hours—not at one time, but over the course of our days and nights and even in the pearl light of dawn after we had wakened and made love. Elisa always listened. She was a woman of substance, and I knew she could help me.

"Oh, Tom!" she burst out. "These past years, you've *lived*. You're learning! What good does it do to keep on torturing yourself? It's not what you do that counts, it's how you do it. With what spirit! Don't you think, sometimes, that this life is a kind of game? Unlike any other, I mean, with rules that you have to make up for yourself. You play to win, but you sure as hell better enjoy playing or it makes no sense."

I reflected on that for a while. We were sitting in the library, with snifters of brandy. A good hickory fire blazed in the grate, fragrant and warm.

"I suppose you're like me," she said. "You were brought up to be good, and truthful, and faithful. Isn't that so? But to what? To other people's idea of goodness, and truth, and fidelity, and heaven knows what else." She tossed some stray yellow hairs from her forehead and spoke soothingly. "In the end, Tom, I think there's only one judge of your life on this earth. That's the man standing in your boots. He stands alone, and he's usually damned lonely. No one else can see his vision. No one else has the right. Certainly not the knowledge."

"I suppose if you put it that way," I said, "no one can judge Rodolfo Fierro. But I don't care. I judge him. He's a murderer. And I don't think those men in the corral at Torreón thought much of the game *they* had to play." I sighed; I never seemed to stray far from that memory. "And what about the *campesinos,* the ones who live in places like La Perla? You can't tell a starving man that life is a game. You can't tell a mother of fifteen Indian kids that it's a game and she's a fool if she doesn't enjoy it. I mean, you can—but if there's a rock handy, you'd better duck."

"I don't mean that, Tom."

"I see. You mean for people like you and me."

"For anyone who can crawl out of the rut they were born into. Damn it, it's not easy! But some people do it. They don't spend their lives acting out a morality that they don't believe in. They don't inherit—they create! And you know I don't mean they have the right to be cruel, or to cheat for the sake of gain. Unless," she said, grinning, "it's for a good quarter horse. . . ."

"But why not?" I said, trying to follow her thinking. "If I believe in that, if those are my rules, if that pleases me, why in hell shouldn't I?"

"But you *don't* believe in it."

"No," I sighed, "I don't. Except for a quarter horse."

"And you surely have the right to take pleasure when it's offered to you with no strings attached. And give it in kind. I do what I please, Tom. I take the consequences, and I can live with that. If I make a mistake, no one pays but me."

"But what do I do now, Elisa? With you, I mean. Can't you see? I'm falling in love with you."

It was a simple confession of simple fact, and she took it that way, without comment or fluttering of eyelashes. I suppose she had known without my having to say it.

"Stay here with me," she said, "until Captain von Papen gets back from Juárez. And then do what pleases you, whatever it may be. Just make sure it's because you truly want to, and not because you feel obliged. Don't do anything for that reason."

"I feel obliged to Pancho Villa," I said, changing the focus. "Does that make it wrong to keep on fighting for him?"

"You believe in his revolution, don't you? Doesn't it make you feel you can look yourself in the eye without flinching?"

"You put it well."

"If your obligations are the same as your desires, you're a lucky man. You can be whole."

I tried to see how that applied to my being torn between Hannah and Rosa in the past, and now so suddenly involved with her, but I got all muddled up. I told her so.

"Ah, you're young," she said gently. "But that's no crime. It's something we all have to pass through, like Tristram Shandy kicking from the womb. Don't think about it too much. The answers will come to you when you're not thinking. Trust them when they come. Meanwhile, finish your wine. Come to bed."

Elisa Griensen wanted to sing again. I would oblige, and I had the desire to match the obligation. So I felt whole. Not terribly enlightened, but certainly lucky. The pleasure was unsullied by guilt or longings in any other direction. I tried not to think about Rosa. She was there, somewhere in Mexico and somewhere in the core of my mind and heart, but she wasn't here. And I was. Elisa was a calm island bounded by warm waters in the midst of a turbulent sea. The revolution didn't touch me during that week. I had a taste of what peace might be like, and it suited me as much as the other. So I was torn that way too but didn't know it.

We would talk out by the stables, working on the horses, or riding through the desert, and then sometimes in the bedroom before we lit the candles on the bedside tables and crawled under the perfumed sheets to romp in the shadows. Elisa was a full-grown woman in ways I realized I wasn't yet a man, and the twelve years she had on me made a difference as wide as the Rio Bravo. But we met in the middle of the river and swam with the current. She was just steadier, more sure of herself, and content to let things happen without yanking too hard on the rudder. Many an hour we spent in the library, I deep in *Tristram Shandy* or dipping into some other book she thought I might like, and she sipping her brandy. Sometimes she read aloud to me, a long passage of a poem that she liked, and one evening, her cool cheek pressed against mine, we read that scene from *Romeo and Juliet* where they wind up killing themselves from the pain of lost love. There were tears glistening in Elisa's green eyes when we had finished. She was a fine woman, hard on the outside and hard in the core, but with plenty of softness in between.

The next morning we were riding Maximilian and the Appaloosa in the hot haze of the desert, and we reined up in the shade of some cottonwood trees to let the horses cool down.

"Elisa, I've been thinking. You know me now. Am I the right sort of man to ever get married?"

"I may know you, but I can't answer that for you."

"I don't think I really know anymore what the word *love* means," I said. The confession cost me something. "A man says he loves fried chicken, or his folks, or his offspring—and that's clear enough. Simple desire. Not so simple habit. But loving a woman is something different. It's a kind of crazy feeling . . . it hardly ever makes you feel peaceful, or easy inside your own skin."

"Is that what you want from love? To feel peaceful and easy?"

"I sure don't want to feel *un*easy."

"Do you think real love has to make you feel a little crazy?"

Laughing, I said, "It tends to, doesn't it?"

"No law says so."

"If you were younger, Elisa—" I stopped there, wishing I could bite back the words. She looked quickly away for a moment at the rippling horizon and the blast furnace of the sky, and I couldn't see her face. But when she swung it back to me, she was at ease again.

"If horses had wings," she said lightly, "we'd fly to the moon. If I were younger, Tom, I'd still be married. And even if that weren't so, I'd be a different person. You might not feel the same way about me. We all change. Sometimes things happen, and the happening makes the moment right. So don't fret about if and maybe. Think about what you've got, what you're doing, and hang on to it or do it with a whole heart . . . or move along. Life is short," she said, echoing Candelario, only with a touch of bitterness in her voice I had never heard before. "Too short to play the fool. Too short to . . ." She clamped her mouth shut a moment. "Well, just too short. You'll find out. Look!" She pointed over my shoulder.

A horseman came bobbing out of the heat haze, black against the white glare of the desert, sun flashing off his spurs. It was Candelario on the Morgan, coming up at a brisk canter. I let go the stock of my rifle.

Captain von Papen was back, he said, and waiting for us at the hacienda.

Our talk took longer than it should have because, as usual, Von Papen sowed a big crop of words before he got round to what I was waiting for: the list of supplies that the German government was willing to provide Pancho Villa. He had it typed in Spanish on some plain white paper, folded into a plain white envelope, and it was unsigned, but as soon as I read it I knew it would serve the purpose. The list included everything from new 7.62-mm Mauser rifles and gas-boosted light machine guns to 88-mm field artillery and Mercedes-Benz trucks—in enough quantities to equip an army of fifty thousand men. I had only one idea in my head: that there might be a way to get the arms without invading Texas.

"I'll give this to him, Captain. How should General Villa contact you when he's made up his mind?"

"I'll find him," Von Papen said.

He didn't waste any time after that but took his leave as soon as he had clicked his heels and exchanged salutes with me, and then he fogged out of there in another dust cloud toward Chihuahua City. I doubted I would ever see him again—but I was wrong.

It was my turn then to leave. I could have stayed on at the Hacienda de Los Flores for another week, or even longer, and been more content than a bee in a clover patch, but I knew that Pancho Villa would be somewhere around Irapuato fretting for the news, as well as the gold for Conchita. Still, I told Candelario we wouldn't pull stakes until dawn.

So I had one more night to curl up against Elisa and drink her honey. I woke in the first fuzzy gray streak of day feeling worn out as a fresh-branded calf. Elisa was already in the kitchen frying a skilletful of eggs and brewing a pot of black coffee. Long goodbyes, I realized, wouldn't be her style.

Candelario and I had decided to skip Chihuahua City and a run-in with Urbina, who might still be nursing the lump on his skull and a feeling for us that wasn't exactly motherly love, and head southeast for Torreón where we could pick up the southbound train. The revolution and human nature being what they were, Maximilian was too fine a horse to leave behind in some Torreón livery stable, so I told Elisa we would ride the nags we had come on. They had been well grazed and had put on some weight in the ten days we had been lazying around. I asked her to keep Maximilian for me until I came back. A little smile crinkled her tanned cheeks so that her dimples flashed.

"You think you'll come back, Tom?"

I looked up from the kitchen floor where I was packing my bag. "I'll come back. I wouldn't leave a fine horse like that and just forget about it. I'll be back . . . if I'm still welcome."

"You'll be welcome," she said huskily, then turned away toward the stove.

It was a frosty morning and the horses still had humps in their backs, so after we ate we saddled them and let them soak for a spell to forget their friskiness. Even when I forked my saddle, that roan I'd picked up in Chihuahua had to iron out a few kinks and show me he wasn't keen to leave a comfortable barn. I knew how he felt. We wheeled to and fro in the dust outside the stables until the animals settled down. Our trunk of gold was strapped to the pack mule. A cold wind blew off the sierra, and I bundled up in my serape. Patricio opened the gate.

I had told Elisa I would be back. The meaning of that hadn't escaped me, even though the resolution and the strength of the desire had surprised me. I hadn't lied to her. I would do it . . . somehow. I wanted that badly. I loved her. I had only told it to her once, that day in the library, and she had never responded in kind—but that didn't matter.

Francisca, shivering, waved to Candelario from the kitchen door. Elisa wore the same outfit as the morning when we first arrived, with a blue rebozo thrown over her wide shoulders to keep off the chill.

"Go well, my sweet." She looked up at me as the horse pawed the turf.

"I won't forget you, Elisa."

"I hope not."

"And I'll be back."

"You told me that already. Don't promise anything, Tom. I don't want promises."

There was no more to say that wouldn't be a lie. I didn't know what the future would hold. We were going to fight a battle somewhere, and that always meant there might not be a future. But for the first time in my life I felt fully purged and at ease inside my skin. That was Elisa's gift. I wondered if I had given her anything of equal value.

If I were alive, I would come back. I knew it. I tried to tell her that with my eyes. Not a promise. A declaration of need. Maybe love, in the end, was no more than that. No more, but no less. She smiled fondly up at me. We kicked the horses out of the gate and trotted toward the unfriendly desert stretching south of Parral.

 "I see you stand like greyhounds in the slips."

from THE SCHOOLTEACHER'S JOURNAL

Fort Bliss
March 18, 1915

To continue my chronicle of events:

. . . Obregón's third occupation of Mexico City, following his defeat of Zapata at Puebla, was perhaps his most memorable. Swiftly he wreaked his vengeance on the merchants who had refused to pay the twenty million pesos he had demanded on his last visit. Men disappeared in the middle of the night or were snatched openly from their offices, never to return. All schools were closed, all public transportation halted. The Catholic Church then began to reap the fruits of one hundred years of loyalty to the wielders of power. Obregón's soldiers sacked the churches, riding their horses up the aisles and smashing statues of the saints with the flats of their swords. Drunken soldiers wandered down the street, heads bizarrely thrust through religious paintings, or draped heavy gold crucifixes round the necks of the dead rats that piled up in the garbage heaps on the Reforma. More than two hundred priests were thrown into prison and held at ransom.

Everything of value in the city was shipped by mule and train to Veracruz, which Carranza had just declared to be the new capital of Mexico for the simple reason that he was there. No food was allowed into Mexico City, not even the shipments sent by the American Red Cross. All was given to Obregón's Constitutionalist Army, camped to the north by the great pyramids of Teotihuacán with trainloads of rifles, artillery and barbed wire—all that had come off *Ypiranga*. In order to eat, the poor had but one choice: join the army. In the space of ten days, Obregón received twenty thousand voluntary enlistments. Those men and their families were then fed.

As soon as Obregón had the men he needed to go with his arms, he headed north to do battle with Pancho Villa.

March 30, 1915

. . . The latest report is that Francisco Villa has joined his army at the railroad junction of Irapuato. Obregón is now in Celaya, only thirty miles to the east of them.

The two principal armies of Mexico thus face each other across a barren flat plain in the area called the Bajio. If there is to be a battle that will decide the future of Mexico, it must be now. Whatever the result, the Bajio will never be barren again. It will be watered with blood, and the decaying flesh of men will make the land bloom as never before.

25   "And lay the summer's dust with showers of blood."

The flat plain rippled in the heat, making me dizzy. Three months had passed since I had left Elisa Griensen in Parral. Now, through the blaze of an April morning we were advancing toward the city of Celaya, to do battle with the army of Obregón. I tried not to think of Elisa because I had learned that if you wanted something too fiercely and too steadfastly, you almost never got it.

I had almost completely stopped thinking of Rosa, and perhaps that was the reason why, sooner than I dreamed, I was able to find her. Or, more accurately, the reason she was able to find me. The battle may have been the test, the trial.

A few strawberry fields had been trampled into rags by the artillery caissons, and just ahead of us some freshly planted wheat was about to receive the same bruising. Wagonloads of shells rattled forward, the drivers shrieking, while sweating soldiers wheeled their horses to lay quirts across the backs of stumbling mules. A chorus of bugles shrilled, telling me to do God only knew what. I was mounted on a young and skittish bay. Julio cantered up to me, his face a narrow mask of dust. His eyes raked me up and down, resting briefly on my two cartridge belts and then more intently on my saddlebags.

"Are there any more bullets in there, Tomás?"

"Just what you see." I tapped my pistol. "This is loaded, but . . ."

He understood I had no spare shells for it. "Son of a whore," he growled. "The cannon better shoot straight today."

"Pray," I said. I had faith in the cannon and our gunners, but not in the shells they were going to fire. Most of our supply of Belgian-made shells had been exhausted in the second battle of Guadalajara, which our western brigades had again lost to Treviño, and the artillery now depended on shells manufactured in a little factory Villa had built in Torreón. Last week in the few skirmishes near Celaya, most of our shells had flown wide, or long, or short—you had no way of knowing in advance—and two of them had jammed the guns and rendered them useless. But the worst blow of all was that Felipe Angeles wasn't there to nurse them back to life.

Returning from Parral, I had found Pancho Villa in Torreón, at the Hotel Salvador, anxiously awaiting the completion of the factory that would make his cannon shells. The chief gave me a potent welcoming *embrazo,* vigorous enough for me to feel the muscles beneath his fat. But he didn't seem terribly surprised when I told him I'd come back to stay.

"War gets in a man's blood, Tomás. He hates it when he's surrounded by death and suffering, and a little interlude of quiet is certainly desirable . . . but nothing matches war. It corrupts your senses, and there's nothing you can do about it. You would have found that out eventually—you would have thought back on this time as the best years of your life. I confess, I'm only truly happy when I'm fighting or getting ready to fight. My only hope is to wear myself out. To grow old. Or to be killed . . ." He sighed. "I knew that in Mexico City. That's why I behaved so foolishly about Conchita. Love may be the only substitute for war. They're disgustingly similar."

"And where *is* Conchita?" I asked. I hadn't seen evidence of her in the suite.

"Gone." He waved a hand in a mock gesture of goodbye. "I grew weary of her tears, and all that piety. You were right, Tomás. It wouldn't have lasted, even if I had married her. I don't need a woman now. I'm going to fight Obregón."

My mouth must have gaped open in astonishment, because he blushed. I hunted for words. "In that case you're lucky that Luz said no to me! To *you,* I mean. No divorce."

"Yes, it was lucky," he admitted. "But I suspected that's what she'd say. Under the circumstances I had to try, didn't I? Was she angry?"

"Not really. She treats you like a backward child."

"Don't be impertinent, Tomás."

"I didn't mean to be. I'm just stating a fact. As you said, she's a remarkable woman."

He took the chest of gold from us without comment; he hardly seemed to remember what it had been for. When Candelario and I told how I had nearly lost my life and how we had dispatched Urbina in order to rescue it, he only shrugged.

"You did the right thing. That's Urbina's fate. He can no more stop being a bandit than a loser can walk out of a poker game."

He was more interested in my report on the talks with Franz von Papen, and he read the German's list carefully. But then he stuffed it into his pocket with a batch of telegrams. "You were clever, Tomás. I'll have to think more about this. This German is certainly imaginative, but I don't dislike the gringos enough to make war on them. And paper is cheap. Promises cost even less."

In that he echoed Elisa, and I knew what he meant. But I was relieved that for the time being we weren't going to invade Texas.

After that I moved into the Hotel Salvador and marched off with Villa every morning to the telegraph office at the railroad station, from where he conducted his preparations for the campaign against Carranza. A storm had been blowing up ever since Felipe had counseled against trusting Zapata's army in the southern campaign, and in Torreón, beginning in February, the weather grew dark indeed. Felipe didn't rub it in, but he looked so generally mournful and disgusted that you knew exactly how he felt. Lounging in a wooden swivel chair as reports clicked in on the telegraph key from all over the country, he said with great conviction: "Don't be distracted, Pancho. You've committed yourself to gaining full control of the north. That may have been foolish when we were able to strike at Carranza, but it's done. Keep to the plan."

"Obregón grows stronger every day," Villa said. He prowled back and forth on the concrete floor of the office, chewing cigarettes more than smoking them. His shoulders were hunched, his teeth bared. "The sonofabitch has thirty thousand men. If I let him alone for another month, he'll finish training his workers and have forty thousand."

Angeles argued patiently that the shortage of ammunition made it foolhardy to attack. In Celaya, Obregón was closer to his supply base in Veracruz, and Villa was farther from his own in Juárez. "Make him come to you. Draw him far away from where he's comfortable. Harass him en route. Order Zapata to attack his rear and push him northward."

"*Order* Zapata?" Villa howled. "That fucking Indian, with his tight pants and ridiculous hat? He's worse than useless!" Villa had finally admitted it. He rolled back and forth across the little room, boots stirring up dust. "I've got to attack!"

But all the reports, Angeles argued, indicated that Celaya was fortified and entrenched, that Obregón was well dug in and that his army had just received a fresh shipment of a hundred machine guns. Unlike Torreón, the open plain before Celaya was crisscrossed with irrigation ditches for cover.

"If the attack fails—"

"You talk too much of failure," Villa said angrily. "Isn't it true that Obregón will never fight unless he's entrenched and fortified? That's his style . . . cowardly as it may be. And it's mine to attack." His chest swelled; his eyes glared redly. "I'm a man who came into this world to attack. And if I'm defeated by attacking today, I'll win by attacking tomorrow."

Felipe wasn't impressed. "You risk the entire Division."

"And whose is it to risk? Do you think I sit on a hilltop," Villa said cruelly, "with some cannon that can't shoot straight? The Dorados will lead the attack on Celaya, and I'll lead the Dorados. In a week's time the church bells in Celaya will ring to celebrate our victory. If not, I'll be dead. Then the Division is yours. You can do as you please with it. That's what you've always wanted, isn't it?"

Insulted, but keeping his temper in check, Angeles swung his boots off the desk and stalked out, leaving Villa to chew his cud alone.

That afternoon outside Torreón, while Angeles was testing a batch of the new homemade shells in his cannon, one of them exploded. Bitter smoke swirled round. Angeles' horse bawled in terror, hurling himself backward so that Felipe couldn't get clear of the stirrups. The horse fell heavily. When the men pulled Felipe free, his face was gray as ash. He had lost enough skin to make a saddle cover, and his leg was broken in two places.

When Villa heard about the accident, his eyes bulged. Sweat burst from his forehead in greasy drops.

"He did it on purpose—damn his soul! To spite me! To keep me from attacking Celaya!"

I flared at him. "You just heard that his leg is broken. The bone is sticking right through the skin."

"Oh, my God." Villa mopped his brow with a bandanna. "Poor Felipe . . . let's go see him."

When we got to Felipe's bedside, Villa went down on his knees, clutching one of his prized bags of peanut brittle and offering it as though it were the relic of a saint. Humbly he asked Angeles to forgive him for the nasty things he had said at the railroad station. Angeles, in great pain, handsomely replied that he couldn't remember a word.

The chief issued a stern order to the surgeons. "Take care of this man as if he were me. Do you hear?" He looked as though he wanted to leap onto the bed and give the stricken general a hug, but we could see that at the slightest touch Felipe's face turned even whiter. So instead, Villa kissed him fervently on both gaunt cheeks.

"The battle of Celaya will be dedicated to you, my friend. It will be the decisive battle you always preach. And I'll have crutches made for you from the bones of Alvaro Obregón."

Our line facing Celaya spread across the plain of the Bajio for four miles, a mass of men and horses with an occasional drooping Mexican flag, the infantry in the center and the cavalry holding the flanks. I remember that date well—April 6, 1915. Not a blade of grass stirred, and the sun beat down with a terrible fury. This was the brutally hot time of the year on the central plateau. The horses were listless, the men on edge. The women were in Irapuato, thirty miles away; this time they would not be allowed near the battlefield. It had been a long time since I had been in battle; not since Zacatecas. But I felt no fear. I never had, at least not since Fierro had ordered Juan Dozal to shoot me if I failed to load his pistols.

Then the vanguard of Obregón's cavalry came into view through the haze. A tin bugle brayed. Julio shouted, "Come on, boys! Plenty of the bastards for all of us!"

I pulled my hat to a fighting angle and drove that bay pounding across the plain, firing my rifle at the blurred shapes in front of us. A golden cloud of dust soared skyward. Bullets flew around my head, but it wasn't those bullets I worried about: it was the one that couldn't find a way around me.

Obregón's cavalry broke at the first charge. Blood boiling, yelling like Comanches, we rode over their fallen men and ground them into the earth like lumps of dung. Men in battle are no longer sane: what seems proper at another time has no purchase when the bullets fly.

"Look at the bastards run! Don't let them get away!"

The cavalry rolled forward through the smoke, rifles yapping, the earth seeming to tremble under the drumbeat of hoofs. We must have crossed five miles of crushed wheat and barren plain. The horses were staggering, wild-eyed from the bite of gunsmoke. Obregón sent out column after column—each time we charged at a gallop—each time they broke before our assault. A mule-drawn wagon rumbled through the dust to where Candelario had halted our advance. With Rodolfo Fierro shouting orders, four grinning men leaped down, spilling cartridges from wooden boxes. We crowded round, stuffing our saddlebags. The men from the wagon rolled out two barrels of water and split the staves with an axe. Men drank greedily, and it felt as if fresh blood flowed through my body.

Thin smoke floated through the breathless air of five o'clock—the worst hour of the day.

Candelario shouted an order to mount. The plain squirmed with men and horses as the Dorados again climbed into their saddles, clicked cartridges into the chambers of rifles, sheathed sabers, soothed their horses. Pancho Villa came riding up at a trot, face hideously stained with dust and sweat. Like a general in a painting, sword in hand, he broke forward to the head of the troop. The Dorados thundered after him.

A hot gust of wind struck me in the face as we spurred up the first ridge . . . and then the world seemed to burst apart.

My horse was hit, sliding down to his knees in a puddle of his own blood and squirting piss. Vaulting clear, I smacked into the dirt behind him. The air swarmed with bullets, and there was a steady rattling sound as of sewing machines run amok. Beyond the ridge lay an irrigation ditch. That was where they were, bedded down neatly in the trench, the slim black barrels of the machine guns nesting among piles of sandbags. The plain in front of the ditch was covered with rolls of coiled barbed wire that ran in either direction for a mile. This was how they were fighting in Europe. I had seen pictures in the newspapers. So had Obregón.

To have had my horse shot from under me was a blessing I only understood a minute later. The rest of the Dorados hit the barbed wire at a gallop, horses bawling with terror as the barbs ripped into their guts. Men were falling from saddles like wormy apples in a high wind. The machine guns chattered angrily, and I felt the bay's dead body quiver at the impact of fresh bullets. I hunched down, hardly daring to peer up for fear that my head would be torn from my neck. A man crawled by me, arm shredded from elbow to wrist, eyes glassy with pain. Another man stood up, shook his fist furiously, then toppled like an axed tree.

I heard Pancho Villa's shout from afar. "Come on, boys! Form up! For the love of God, keep going or they'll kill us all. . . ."

I threw myself over the blood-soaked flank of my horse and fired into the smoke. Villa's voice, raging and swearing, rang out above the gunfire. A troop of Dorados burst through the haze to fling themselves at the barbed wire. Quick as hell would scorch a feather, the saddles began to empty. The machine guns stabbed from side to side. Like steel rain, the bullets cut through the troop. I could see a few horsemen stagger to the edge of the trench. Then Obregón's troops rose up to greet them with bayonets. Tumbling men were blown down by rifle fire at less than ten yards. Dying horses pawed the dust. Great tears rolled from stricken eyes down long brown faces, gasping the last terrible breaths of life. I fell prone in the dirt, reloaded and began to fire. The barrel of my rifle rested on an outflung forearm, burning a purple welt that the dead man would never feel.

"*Go back!*" a voice cried. And then another nearby moaned in fury, "My nose! Where's my nose? *Oh, Maria! . . .* the bastards shot off my nose!"

I became aware that fewer men were in front of me. More shambled back. One fell nearby, his back torn open by bullets. In a minute or two the flies had settled on his tongue. I fired steadily at whatever showed itself beyond the barbed wire. I would have stayed there, on that shredded patch of earth, until one of the little puffs that sent the dust flying finally reached me to put an end to my madness. But a horse's hoofs drummed close by, and I looked up to see the hot eyes of a man staring down. His face was blackened by powder. He still clutched his sword, the blade red with blood from tip to guard. It was Pancho Villa. He had been to the trench and back, and he was unharmed.

"Tomás! Jesus Christ! *Here . . .*"

A powerful arm gripped me by the shoulder, hauled me up behind his saddle. I clutched at his chest, felt the pounding of his heart. The horse lurched toward the rear. Crying like an angry child, I leveled my rifle behind me and fired one last shot into the dust.

They shelled us until it grew dark. Our own cannon boomed in reply, but the spotters reported that our fire was falling short of the city and the enemy guns.

"Not the guns!" Villa screamed at the man who had brought the report. "Not the city! *Destroy the barbed wire!* Oh, Felipe," he groaned. "Why aren't you here?"

The sky became blue velvet, the sun a brilliant, obscene orange. The wounded straggled by, bound in bloody rags, dragging their rifles. Some tried to grin and make jokes; some hummed love songs. A few wandered aimlessly and had to be set back on the path. The sun sagged, grew fat and red, then vanished gloriously. The day snuffed out like a match, leaving only gray wisps of smoke. From a little ridge behind an alamo tree I could see the flare of the enemy guns, like dancing cigarette tips. Dim forms loomed in the shadows, whispering.

"It was hard . . . a death trap! I'm not ashamed to tell you I threw away my rifle. But now I regret it, because tomorrow . . ."

Men sucked water from their canteens and built little corncob fires, crouching round them on their haunches. I stumbled past and a soldier hailed me. "Hey, *compañero!* Are you hungry? Have some tacos. They're cold, but it's better than eating smoke, eh?"

The men bivouacked round the fire gave me a part of their food. The tortillas were like cardboard. I ate them quickly and muttered my thanks. In battle and after, men take strength and find courage from the presence of others. I began wandering.

"Have you seen Colonel Cervantes? . . . Do you know Julio Cárdenas? I'm looking for them. . . ."

I found Candelario in the shelter of an alamo tree, rubbing axle grease on the gashed flanks of his horse. His uniform was mottled with dried brown blood, but his luck had held.

"I'm glad to see you, Tomás. It was better in Parral, wasn't it?"

He told me that Julio had been wounded in the leg, but not badly. He had been sent back to the hospital train in Irapuato. I limped off a few steps and curled in a lump by a fire where a few men were softly singing. I fell instantly asleep and dreamed of Elisa Griensen.

I woke only when the sun popped brightly over the plain leading to Celaya. Men lit little fires, putting up coffee. Others tossed under their serapes, muttering in protest. A sweating officer galloped among them.

"Get up, boys! Sons of whores! Come on, my little ones! Come on, my lambs. . . ."

The troop began sifting toward the horses. A few Indian women slid out of the brush with black water jars on their heads. Their aprons were full of fresh tortillas. Candelario silently offered me a tin mug of hot coffee. I said hoarsely, "What's happening? What are we going to do?"

He looked at me with mild astonishment. "We're going to attack. What else?"

I limped round the plain until I found a trooper standing by a remuda of cut-up horses with tick-infested bellies. The man's head was swathed in bloody bandages that were black with flies. He had an idiotic look on his face.

"*Compañero,* whose horses are these?"

He looked at me blankly, and I had to repeat the question. "Ah," he answered, "they are the horses of men who didn't come back. Very fine horses, señor—the horses of the Dorados. I would give you one, but they are being saved for officers." His voice grew martial. "Don't try to take one from me. I would have to shoot you." He had no gun.

"I'm a colonel. I'll take that black."

"My colonel . . ." the man sobbed. "My head hurts. I don't think I can fight anymore."

"You don't have to fight. Go back to Irapuato. But first, give me that black horse. . . ."

The man began to sob as I took the reins of the black and led him away. A sword had been looped with a piece of red velvet across the saddle horn. Gouts of dry blood hung from the horse's nostrils; with my bandanna and a bit of water from my canteen, I wiped them away. A wagon jolted back through the wheat field for a fresh load of wounded, and I directed them toward the man who clutched the reins of the remuda.

Pancho Villa appeared on a gray stallion, weaving a path through the campfires. "The infantry can't advance," he told me quietly when he had dismounted. "I can't send men out to be killed before they can fire a shot. Tell the officers that the cavalry is to carry them—one man behind each rider. We'll take them as far as the barbed wire. Then they'll dismount and get through it. The cavalry will follow. Tell them Celaya will fall today." He shook his fist at the sky. "Tell them Francisco Villa swears it! If not on the first assault, then the second. But it will fall!"

Villa mounted and spurred away. The ground boiled with a scramble of men and horses. Mules were lashed insanely as they tugged at lumbering caissons. The gunners tore away the canvas. Officers ran to and fro, yelling for shells, checking fuses. Villa came pounding back, eyes streaming tears from the smoke.

"*Closer!* Not here, for Christ's sake! Get down on the plain! . . . Follow me!" He slammed spurs into his horse, while the soldiers once more hitched the guns to the reeling mules.

The sky had become a faultless blue vault. Birds sang sweetly in the bushes. Our cannon began to pound at the trenches. At nine o'clock the cavalry surged forward, each rider bearing an infantryman who carried sticks of dynamite. The plain was covered with bodies already starting to swell and bubble. The man mounted behind me spotted a black earthenware jug under a maguey plant. He begged me to turn my horse a few steps to pick it up. Candelario rode only a few yards to my right, with another soldier in the saddle behind him. We moved toward the earthenware jug at the same time, and then Candelario pulled out his pistol and fired, shattering the jug into a dozen pieces. It had been full of milk, which the yellow earth soaked up instantly.

"Poisoned!" Candelario yelled. "They've left them all over the plain for us. Arsenic!"

Rifle fire rattled—a bugle blared. Brutal and blinding, the sun beat down. The infantry rushed forward, swallowed by the smoke, appeared again as dim shapes, then vanished behind gentle curves of land. Cannon whomped gutturally, and we heard once more the tapping of machine guns, like a flock of angry woodpeckers in a forest of oaks. The wounded stumbled back, and when they were past us Candelario gave the order to charge. A throng of men plunged forward, spurs ringing, flags flying in the breeze. Bending low, pistol in one hand, saber and reins in the other, I put steel into the black's side. The horse trumpeted with fear, but I had him in a gait he couldn't break, knees pinned so hard into his heaving flanks that I could feel the knock of his heart against my thigh. And we broke suddenly through the acrid smoke that hid the trenches.

Our cannon had blasted the rolls of barbed wire into a crazy tangle, but the shell craters had made it easier for the infantry to crawl forward, toss their bombs, then dart forward again to the next crater. Bleeding from the wire, they vaulted over the lip of the first trench to fall upon the defenders. I couldn't stop my horse in time. He tried to clear the trench in one leap, but his forelegs struck the far dirt wall, and amid the roar of guns I heard the bones snap. He bawled with the pain. I was pitched clear.

The heat of the guns and the stench of scorched flesh had turned the trench into a cauldron. I jumped to my feet and thrust the point of my sword into an Obregonista soldier who was trying to crawl from under an overturned machine gun. These were the bastards who had been killing us, who had left arsenic for us to drink. . . . I spitted him through the neck, and blood spurted as from a broken pipe. Pulling the sword free, I slashed with the wet blade at another man who was firing his pistol toward the barbed wire.

Candelario, from on high, standing in his stirrups, screamed at me. I turned, and a gun exploded in my face. My hat whipped off my head . . . an enemy officer towered over me, face striped with blood, the steel of his bayonet flashing. My pistol clicked empty. I had no room to swing my sword. I jumped aside; the bayonet slid by my neck, so close that the coldness of its steel burned like a hot iron. Butting and flailing, shouting curses, I clutched at the man's legs and twisted him to the earth.

"No!" I shrieked. "Goddam you—no!"

"Tomás! Out of the way!"

As I reeled backward, Candelario leaned down from his horse and swung his saber. It broke through flesh and gristle, nearly severing the man's head from his body. Blood gushed over my boots like a spilled bucket of red paint. I staggered to my feet.

Suddenly, unexpectedly, the afternoon was silent. The firing had stopped. A few dazed men crawled through the dust, whimpering softly.

We had won the trench. . . .

I stumbled out of it and found my horse. Both his legs were broken, but he was still alive. I shot him through the head. A riderless chestnut, with a white flame between his ears, nosed the earth a few yards away where some broken shoots of greenery had been blown by the breeze. The reins trailed on the ground. Snorting, the horse raised its head, gazing at me with half-dead eyes. But he would do. I settled into the hot leather of the saddle that had been exposed to the sun and looked down to see bodies, heads flung back, limbs spread like scarecrows.

And then Candelario's weary call reached us. "To Celaya, boys! Let's go! *To Celaya . . .*"

A daredevil squad of Dorados reached the city plaza. One of our men climbed to the belfry of the cathedral and rang the bells, just as

Pancho Villa had promised Felipe Angeles. Then the man was killed by machine-gun fire.

The main body of cavalry was still working its way across the plain when the irrigation ditches began to fill with water. The water trickled at first, then began to flow, and finally slashed in a torrent of loose brown mud that leaped across the fields. Horses slipped, bucked in fear and fell. No one seemed to understand what was happening. The advance halted. Mired in the mud, the brigades came under fresh artillery fire. Our own troop, far in advance, found itself cut off. From behind the railroad station, about a mile away, galloped a fresh battalion of Obregón's cavalry, cunningly concealed there as a reserve. They struck when we were exhausted. Half our men were dead.

Candelario and I galloped through the smoke to find Pancho Villa. "Chief, we can't hold!" Candelario cried. "There's no support from the right. Our battalion to the left is retreating. Let's not die defending a lousy ditch! Let's attack the bastards!"

A shell exploded fifty yards in front of us. "Order your men back," Villa said grimly. "This isn't a defeat. I can stand a defeat, but not a slaughter."

Our main force, bogged down in the ditches and bracketed by the enemy guns, was being blown to shreds. The rest of us wheeled our horses, scooped up what infantrymen we could and picked our way back among the dead, across the battlefield and waist-deep in water through the trenches where we had fought with fire and sword . . . fought for nothing. Despite the thump of cannon and the whistle of bullets, I sagged in the saddle. My eyes closed before I could will otherwise. I might have fallen asleep if the soldier riding behind me, whose name I never bothered to ask, hadn't talked at me, again and again, in a high brittle voice that had a touch of madness.

"Keep going, my colonel! Don't fall off! You heard what the chief said. A defeat is nothing! We'll fight again tomorrow. Don't fall off, my colonel. We'll win! You'll see! Tomorrow, we'll win. . . . Tomorrow. . . ."

A week later we attacked Celaya again and got whipped worse than the first time. Green flies clustered on our wounded, and rats gorged themselves on the corpses. Between battles Candelario and I picked lice off each other that were nearly as big as grains of rice. The Northern Division, exhausted, stumbled north toward the city of León.

Felipe Angeles, on crutches, begged Villa not to attack again. "Go further north, my general. Make Obregón follow you to the border. Stretch him out . . . then we'll have him where we want him."

But Villa wanted revenge and badly needed a victory. He executed a fine maneuver by night, cutting the railway line and surrounding Obregón's army, which had occupied León. There, in heat that rarely dipped below a hundred degrees, we fought for forty days. Obregón's right arm was shattered by one of our shells. The pain was so great, we heard, that he tried to kill himself, but his pistol was empty. His luck held. He had the arm amputated and pickled in a jar of alcohol. In each of those battles he defended himself the same way, with barbed wire and mounted reserves that pounded down on us after we had struggled for half a day to take a line of trenches. In each of the battles Villa attacked as before, always muttering that "the known road is the good road." By the time we limped northward from León we had more than ten thousand casualties. Obregón ordered all the Villista prisoners shoved into corrals, where they were machine-gunned to death. Unlike Fierro, he had no need to prove his marksmanship.

We kept moving north. In June we fought at Aguascalientes in another awful battle and lost. We lost Zacatecas in July and retreated north toward Torreón.

In the battle for León I was knocked unconscious by an exploding shell. I was put on the floor of a hospital train filled with dying men and taken to the military hospital in Torreón, the same hospital that had housed Miguel Bosques and the doomed prisoners. I stayed there more than a month. Two ribs were broken and my shoulder dislocated. I mended slowly. After a time the body rebels against punishment. If it heals too quickly, it knows it will only be hurt once again.

Candelario visited me in the hospital before he left for Chihuahua City, where Villa had ordered him to check on our gold. He told me that Yvette and Marie-Thérèse had packed up and headed back to Columbus. He looked bewildered. *"Válgame Dios!* I'll never understand women!"

"There was never any future in it, amigo."

"I loved them both. It's not over, Tomás. As soon as we start winning again, I'll go get them. The whole world loves a winner."

Felipe Angeles hobbled in to visit me too, bringing a bottle of port, some cold cuts and glacé fruit. I didn't know such things could be found in wartime Mexico, but Angeles had sources that were denied to the rest of us. He wore a gray broad-brimmed hat and a shirt of olive-drab wool; in Felipe's dress as well as his manner there was always that autumnal quality. In a few days, he told me, when the doctor removed the cast from his leg, he was going to Washington, D.C., as the chief's emissary.

"What for?" I asked.

"To influence people." His American friends, he said, believed that the United States government hadn't given up hope of finding an alternative to Carranza as the next President of Mexico. William Jennings Bryan, the former Secretary of State, had remarked that despite his losses on the battlefields, "Villa was perhaps the safest man to tie to."

"What does Bryan know," I asked, "that we don't know?"

Angeles smiled. "He's a teetotaler, Tomás. So is the chief. Draw your own conclusions."

"My conclusion is that men seem to take more care in picking their enemies than they do their friends."

"How would you like to come with me?" Angeles asked. "If I requested you, I'm sure it could be arranged."

"You don't need an interpreter," I said. "You speak better English than I do."

"But I don't think as a gringo. Sometimes I fear that I don't even think as a Mexican. You would be useful, Tomás. And good company."

I was flattered. But I remembered my one diplomatic mission, the meeting in Parral with Franz von Papen. "It's not for me," I said, keeping to the track of my destiny. "I don't really know what good I'm doing here, but. . . ." I shrugged.

Angeles nodded, his spirit submerged in a gentle melancholy. "You're probably right," he said. "Stay here with the chief. He needs his friends."

He left then, and I never saw him again.

A few days later, when the remnants of the Division began trickling into Torreón, the doctors realized that the hospital beds would be needed for new wounded. Because I was a staff officer I was consulted, not ordered.

"Well, all right. If it's necessary, of course I'll go."

"In a day or two, my colonel," the doctor said. "There's no rush yet. I just wanted you to be prepared."

I wasn't afraid. I was just glad to sleep twelve hours a night and have my food brought to a bedside table. I wondered about Parral, if I would ever see it or Elisa again. The ward was cool. Outside, the July sun beat down. I passed the time by writing slowly in my journal. I wished I had brought *Tristram Shandy* with me. I still had Shakespeare, warped and taped, the spine reglued, but his darker sentiments were all that got through to me now. I needed comfort, not unsparing wisdom.

The next morning, when I woke in the early light, I felt a presence near my bed. The warm sun streamed through the dusty cracked glass of a window. Something soft in the air—a musky scent. A presence. Still half asleep, I was about to murmur Elisa's name. But luckily I turned and opened my eyes.

"*Rosa . . . ?*"

"Yes, Tomás."

"Am I awake?"

"Yes, Tomás. I hope so."

She hadn't changed much except that she looked thinner. Her dark eyes had the same glow, her long black hair the same luster. Absurdly, considering my state of shock, I realized that in less than a month she would be seventeen. That and other inconsequential thoughts invaded my mind and turned it to mush. Where had she come from? How had she found me? She wore a plain gray dress—her best, for it had no patches—a red scarf knotted loosely round her throat and plain leather sandals. Oh God, I was gladdened, and I was dumbfounded.

"Rosa, I can't believe it!" I clasped her hands. "Are you all right?"

"Very well. Are you badly hurt, Tomás?"

"I shouldn't even be here. They want me to get out. Where did you come from?"

"Zacatecas. And then by train to Torreón. I arrived last night."

Nearly a year had passed since she mounted the mare and rode off from me on the hill of La Sierpe. I had gone to find her and failed. Had she come for me, or had she another purpose? Was she en route to somewhere else?

"I knew you had been to Tomochic," she said.

"Rosa, I don't understand. . . ."

I still could barely believe it. She was like a mirage, a will-o'-the-wisp delusion. But I listened to her murmuring voice, a real voice, as she told the tale of her wanderings.

News came late to the remote sierra hamlets such as Tomochic. In the winter, after the melodrama of the Revolutionary Convention at Aguascalientes, she had remembered my final words. "*. . . when there's peace, I'll go back to marry Hannah.*" The convention had collapsed in ruins. There was no peace. She needed to cling to hope, to believe the letter more than the spirit of my words. She knew I might have gone to Texas, but then again—

"*Si Diós quiere,* God willing, you might have stayed. There was no way to know." She sighed.

"I regretted leaving you in Zacatecas, Tomás. That was foolish. I should have tried to convince you to stay with me, but I felt too much pain. And I was too proud to beg, which was wrong. 'Perhaps,' I told myself later, 'if I had stayed until he was ready to go, he might have changed his mind. He might have been unable to leave me if I had thrown myself at his feet and torn my hair and threatened to kill myself, as any sensible Mexican woman would do.' " She laughed softly. "It was very hard for me in Tomochic, Tomás, thinking such thoughts. My mother thought I was crazy, or sick with a strange disease that I had brought back from the war. She treated me like an idiot. I saw no one. For many months I did nothing. I spoke to myself at night, alone in the corral. I thought that perhaps one night you would come for your gold. I didn't want to miss that chance to see you. I did have a kind of disease, you see. And then, when I got a bit better, when I thought finally to search for you, I heard that Francisco Villa was in Mexico City. It was far to travel, and I was frightened. I had lost much confidence. But I was unhappy in Tomochic, and Chihuahua City was close. So I went there in the new year."

In January? I had been there too, to get the gold and meet Candelario. She was close to me, and I hadn't known it but had gone instead to Tomochic.

If the Northern Division went anywhere, she thought, they would go to Chihuahua City. And she would be waiting for me. For the first time, telling this to me, she allowed herself a small smile. I think, like me, she didn't quite believe she had finally found me.

In Chihuahua City she found work, washing laundry for the occupying brigade. She waited, but no one came. Not Pancho Villa, not me. One evening at dusk, returning from the stream where she washed the soldiers' clothes to the hovel that she shared with two families, she was stopped in the street by two drunken officers.

"They were Urbina's officers," she said. "He held the city then. It was dark and I couldn't see their faces, but I could smell the pulque on their breath. I ran away, through the streets, when I understood what they wanted, but I tripped and they pulled me into a doorway of a hut that had been shelled. I fought, Tomás. I struggled as best I could. I ripped one of them in the face with my nails, so that blood flowed as when pigs are killed. I pray he carries the scar forever. But there were two of them, and they were too strong for me. In the doorway of the hut, they raped me."

Pain struck my chest as if screws had been turned, and I groaned. *In January!* Urbina's officers, she thought. But I knew better. *I found a pretty one the other night, coming back from the river. . . . Look, she gave me this. . . .*

I didn't tell her. Rosa raised her eyes and looked at me calmly.

"I felt nothing, Tomás. It was awful, but I felt no shame. It was very dark, and I closed my eyes so that I couldn't see them and would never remember their faces. In the war, I knew, such things happened. Still, I realized I could no longer stay there or it would happen again, and the next time, I knew, no matter what the risk, I would not permit it. I would fight until I was dead. So, when I felt better, I went back to Tomochic. Then I found out you had come looking for me. *Mi capitán!* I wept and beat my breast that I had ever been fool enough to leave . . . but still my heart soared. Now there was hope. And I set out again to find you."

By then she knew there had been fighting in the south and it had gone badly for Villa. On a moonless night she dug up the trunk of gold buried behind the corral. From one of the sacks she took a handful of coins and tied them in a pouch that she put under her head scarf. All the rest she replaced, then smoothed the dirt over with a shovel.

"It was your gold, Tomás, not mine, and I had vowed to the Virgin that I would never touch it. But I needed it for the trains, and food. I decided that you would forgive me, and I would have to take my chances before God. Some risks are necessary."

She reached Irapuato and learned how the Division had twice assaulted Celaya and twice been repulsed. By the time she reached León that battle was over too. The army of Obregón blocked her path. She had to be careful, for not only Urbina's soldiers would offer an animal welcome to a pretty Indian girl on her own. Always a train journey behind the battles, she made her way north, to Aguascalientes and then Zacatecas, from pueblo to pueblo, stopping any stray wounded Villistas she could find and telling them that she sought her husband—a major, a gringo. Did they know him? Was he alive?

"It might be yes, señora . . . and then again . . ."

"I feared you were dead, Tomás. I feared that even more than I had feared that you had gone to Texas and married. I had to know." She raised her head, brushing away the gossamer film of tears. "And then I came here to Torreón. They told me the Division still held the city, but I didn't truly believe it until I arrived. I found Julio at the Hotel Salvador, as before. He told me you were alive and in the hospital. That, indeed, you had gone back to Texas many months ago, and then returned. That you had not married. I wept . . . this time for joy. And here I am. As you see me."

I remembered that she had spoken those same words to me by the lake in Ascensión after she had told the tale of her young husband's death. I clasped her hands. "No, Rosa, I didn't marry her. I came close, but your shadow stood between us."

"And have you found another woman?" she asked quietly.

"No," I said, smiling. I would learn from Elisa and make my own rules.

"Then will you have me as your woman, as before?"

"I came to Tomochic to ask you that, Rosa. You know I will."

"The thing that happened to me in Chihuahua City—"

"You didn't have to tell me that," I said. "But you did. What happened doesn't matter. We never have to talk about it. I love you."

"It was worth everything to find you, *mi capitán.*"

She pressed her head down on my chest, and I felt the flow of tears as I had felt them on the banks of the Nazas River when she cried for another lost love. I never wanted her to cry again. I wanted to hold her, and comfort her, and keep her safe from all the evil in the world.

"I think I have forgotten to speak English," she whispered, after a while. "Although sometimes, when your presence was strong, I spoke aloud to you in your language and made up your answers. But it was not easy. You said funny things. I would like to learn again. Can you tell me how you say *te quiero?*"

"I love you." I had never taught her that. There had been no need until now.

The doctor wrapped my ribs with fresh bandages, and I left with Rosa for the Hotel Salvador, where a room was waiting.

* * *

With my back pay I bought her a new dress and deerskin riding boots for her seventeenth birthday. Nothing had changed between us except that we were closer than ever before. And now, instead of Hannah hanging at the far side of my fantasies, there was the beckoning vision of Elisa Griensen. . . . In the dark of my mind I couldn't lie. Elisa didn't simply vanish because Rosa returned. It wasn't frivolous. Greedy, perhaps. But far from being punished, I was rewarded . . . or so it seemed, for a time.

26

**"What! wouldst thou have
a serpent sting thee twice?"**

Pancho Villa greeted me in his suite at the Hotel Salvador. Surprisingly, he didn't look too bad. He had lost weight fighting in the heat of the Bajio, and his waist was almost trim. The sagging jowls had firmed. He paced the carpet of his suite in the Hotel Salvador like a man with a purpose.

"Tomás, I knew you had been wounded at León, but I didn't know how badly. I thought you might have died. I'm glad that's not the case."

"So am I, chief. What are we going to do now?"

"I'm going to keep fighting these bastards. Did you ever doubt that? Did I ever lack a plan? I've learned a trick or two from that one-armed chickpea farmer. The next time I fight him it's going to be in a place of *my* choosing. If it's a city, I'll starve him out. If it's out in the open, so much the better. I can use barbed wire too."

His words cheered me, for I had been wondering ever since Celaya if he could adapt to the change in battle tactics. Obregón was fighting a modern war, learning from the Germans what worked and didn't work in the mud of France. We were still shouting, *"Adelante!"* and charging across open plains. I realized how much faith I'd had in the chief. He had forged a strategy and followed it nearly to the end. He had said to Angeles that he was a man who came into this world to attack, and if he was defeated by attacking today, he would win by attacking tomorrow. His own bullish bravery had defeated him; his rawness of vision had shattered his morale. His imagination had faltered. "If they hadn't brought a curve ball into this league," he seemed to be saying, doggedly and before every losing battle, "I'd still be hitting home runs."

After every defeat I had thought, These are things armies have to go through. It's a test, and we'll weather it. The tide turns, then turns again. Obregón is ruthless and scheming, Carranza is just another Porfirio Díaz. We'll win the next time, because we're on the right side—or else there's no justice. But why should there be? When I was a boy I had believed that life was fair. If you brushed your teeth, told the truth and worked hard, you would be rewarded. You might even be happy. I knew better now—except for my life with Rosa. There I had no complaints, no doubts, no forebodings. We had spent three days together in the hotel room and on the boulevards of the city, and all was well again between us. She was no mirage, no will-o'-the-wisp. She was flesh and blood, and mine. It seemed miraculous. I told her everything that had happened to me in Aguascalientes, Mexico City, El Paso and Parral, and then on the battlefields of the Bajío . . . except for my interlude with Elisa Griensen.

"What will your chief do now?" Rosa asked. "Can he still win?"

"Mexico's a big country," I said. "There are plenty of men to fight for him. And he always comes up with a plan."

So his words that August morning of 1915 in the Hotel Salvador gave me fresh heart. We had only to maintain our strongholds and flanks in the north—Chihuahua City, Juárez, Monterrey and Nuevo Laredo—and dig in here in Torreón. If we could rest, he said, shore up our defenses, patch up our brigades, if we could defend Torreón successfully against Obregón's assault, that would turn the tide. A single victory . . . that would do it.

"But first," Villa said to me, "I have one thing to do. It's on my mind, and I'm losing sleep over it. Have you heard about Urbina? And the gold?"

"I've heard plenty about Urbina," I said bitterly.

"I sent him a wire," the chief raged. "I ordered him to reinforce us at León! That bastard—he never showed up! He went down to Jiménez with his brigade, to levy taxes and find new women, but he ran into one of Carranza's pantywaist generals named Treviño. He challenged Treviño to fight him alone, *mano á mano,* but Treviño told him to kiss his ass. Urbina was drunk, I have no doubt. When the shells started falling around his head, he retreated back to Chihuahua City."

Villa had begun to smoke. Again he chewed the cigarettes one after another, more than smoking them, spitting out pieces of paper and tobacco.

"And then, when the sonofabitch got to Chihuahua City, he dynamited the laundry-room door in the Fermont! He took the gold from the Banco Minero—the revolution's treasury! Now, when we need it the most, to buy new guns! He went off in a cloud of pulque to Durango. He has a hacienda there called Las Nieves, where his mother lives. The one he always tries to shoot."

Rodolfo Fierro appeared, tall and composed, smooth-skinned and handsome, silver spurs jingling, in brown leather hip-high boots and full bandoliers over a wrinkled gray jacket. He had fought at Celaya and then at León, where they said he had been as brave as the chief, leading a charge that had almost broken the defense on the thirty-fifth day of the fighting. I hadn't seen him since then, and I hadn't missed him. But I no longer feared him; he had received an order in Juárez that he could never disobey. He nodded coolly to me.

"We're going after Urbina," Villa announced. His round head bobbed up and down on his thick shoulders, and his eyes narrowed. "To Las Nieves. Tomás, how is your shoulder?"

"Mending, chief."

"I want you with me. You can tell what's there and what's missing."

"How do you know he took the gold with him to Durango?"

Villa laughed harshly. "He hasn't the brains to think of leaving it somewhere else. And he'll want to count it each morning and every night. It's unlikely he spent it—he makes his own aguardiente at Las Nieves. Tomorrow at dawn we'll go." He turned to Fierro; it seemed they had already discussed this. "Rodolfo, take a company of two hundred good men. Urbina may not receive us so graciously."

I thought the chief had better things to do, but I didn't say no; I had my own scores to settle. And so, in the midst of the war, with men deserting every day, with the Division in blood-soaked disarray and Obregón less than a hundred miles to the south, we set out the next morning across the Sierra Madres into the state of Durango. Such was the power of gold and vengeance.

August was the worst month of the rainy season, and the rain poured down throughout most of the journey, turning the mountain trails to mud. All of us were soaked, and the bandages round my ribs became so cold that when we halted for supper I had to peel them off and throw them away. A thick morning fog blocked our vision the next day; during the afternoon the sun was only a white blur behind the haze. We arrived the second night and camped a few miles from Las Nieves.

Fierro and Julio rode ahead to scout the hacienda. An hour later they came back to report that lights burned in the main house, and guitar music could be heard. All the horses were in the stables.

"He's having a little fiesta with his officers," Villa said. "They're drunk, but they'll fight well when they're drunk. We'll wait until dawn. By then they'll be asleep."

Las Nieves was more than a hacienda: it was a pueblo, and Urbina owned it. His house was huge, aswarm with pigs, chickens, tame deer and children. The only store in the pueblo was at the hacienda, and the *campesinos* had to buy their corn and cigarettes from Urbina or his administrators. He owned them, body and soul, and his mother kept the books. He was a hell of a revolutionist, I thought, and wondered what was passing through Pancho Villa's mind. He was godfather to several of Urbina's sons by various mothers, and between battles he had visited here for baptisms. They had been bandits together—had slept in caves, fled from the *rurales*. They had been like brothers.

Fierro must have been thinking the same thing. Wrapped in his damp serape, he approached Villa by the campfire. In its flickering light his smooth face was the color of blood.

"Pancho, I don't want to make any mistakes. In the morning, what is it that you want done?"

Villa flicked his hand impatiently. "He's a traitor. For all I know, he may be planning to go over to Carranza. There's only one punishment for traitors."

"I understand," Fierro said.

Before dawn, in the milky fog, we drifted down the slope toward the hacienda. The horses' hoofs made hardly a sound on the wet earth. The great main house of Las Nieves covered the top of a mesa, the bare mountains behind it wreathed in drifting vapor. No lights showed now. A single farmer passed by on a burro, but when he saw us he made the sign of the cross and quickly reversed direction. As soon as some light filtered between the peaks across the yellow plain, Villa locked his feet into the stirrups.

"Let's do this," he muttered.

We trotted across an open dirt square past a pigpen. A tomblike silence came from the house, and then Villa raised his pistol and fired a single shot into the cold air. It boomed like a cannon, and almost immediately there was an answering barrage of rifle fire from all sides. The men yipped wildly, swooping down on the hacienda.

A half-dozen men lay around in the huge main room, slumped in heavy upholstered chairs and with their heads on the table. A few squawking chickens fluttered out of our way. Empty bottles lay on the concrete floor; the fire in a tiny grate had gone out. Waking slowly, the men raised their gray faces to see our guns. The chill of death hung in the room, but their drunken sleep had saved their lives.

From the rear of the house came the loud sound of shots. Leaving a handful of men to guard the prisoners, we surged down a dank hallway toward the bedrooms. We heard cursing . . . more gunfire . . . the crash of breaking glass. An angry young man, with a gray-haired woman cowering behind him, loomed in a doorway. He carried a leveled rifle, and I shot him where he stood. The woman fell back and began to crawl under a rumpled bed.

"That's Urbina's mother," Villa said, taking time out to instruct me in the midst of the fight. "She fucks the soldiers when her son sleeps. In case no one told you, that's why he always wants to shoot her."

Urbina, wearing his long johns, had been sprawled asleep in a bedroom with one of his mistresses. When he snatched a pistol from under his pillow, Julio shot him once in the shoulder. Then Urbina recognized him and cried out, "For Christ's sake! Julio, are you crazy? It's me!" He threw the pistol away and charged into the hallway, bushy hair all in a tangle, clutching his bloody shoulder. The sight of the man chilled my heart. When he saw Pancho Villa his little eyes sparkled, and he flung out his arms.

"Pancho! Thank God you're here! I was almost killed! This must be my lucky day. . . ."

I was flabbergasted, for Villa returned the embrace. When the two men parted, the seeping blood covered Villa's shoulder as well.

"*Compadre,*" he said thickly, "you're hurt. Is it bad?"

"I'm not dead, so it can't be that bad." Urbina clenched his teeth and put a hand to his breast, under the wound. "But the bullet's still in there." His eyes swiveled to lock on my face. "You!" he cried. "You gringo bastard! I've a score to settle with you—" He shook the fist of his good arm at me. "You and that one-eyed ape disobeyed my orders! You put a knot on my head that a rat couldn't run around. You hurt me! I was unconscious for two days! And you ran off without knowing whether I was dead or alive! Did you think I was going to steal your damned trunk? I told you, I was collecting taxes to buy ammunition and coal. We could have bargained a little, couldn't we? But you're a gringo, you don't understand how we do things. . . . You hurt me," he snarled.

"I should have killed you," I said. For a moment Urbina looked startled, and so did Villa. I still had told him nothing of what happened in Chihuahua City with Rosa.

"Let's go into the kitchen," Villa muttered. "We'll see what we can do for your shoulder."

On our way a woman ran out of a room and fell to her knees, flinging her arms about the chief's legs. "Señor General! I've just given birth to a baby boy. Not three days ago! Will you baptize him? I'm going to call him Francisco, after you."

"I'm not a priest, señora."

"But you are General Villa! You can do anything! God smiles on you!"

"Later, yes," Villa grumbled, "if you insist."

In the kitchen he shooed everyone out except Fierro and me. There were still hot coals in one of the charcoal pits of the range. He put a kettle of water on the fire to boil and then ripped off Urbina's shirt to inspect the wound. Straddling a chair, Urbina bit his lip with the pain.

"It's bad," Villa said. "It looks like it hit the bone. I don't think I can get the bullet out. Is there a doctor nearby?"

"About twenty miles . . ."

"Let's clean it up first. You know, I came here to shoot you."

"Because of that damned gold?" Urbina chuckled hoarsely. "I'm keeping it safe for you, Pancho. That fucking Treviño had five thousand men and three dozen cannon not thirty miles from Chihuahua City! He would have dynamited that door faster than I did. And then, think—it would have been lost forever!"

/ 297

"You ran away," Villa said grimly. "Treviño saw only your ass."

"Ran away?" Urbina thumped his other fist on the kitchen table. "I don't know the meaning of the word! My men were being slaughtered! I had to regroup."

"Here?"

"I had to think what to do next."

A bitter smile curved from Villa's lips. "You don't have to think, *compadre*. You have only to follow my orders. And why didn't you reinforce me at León when I sent for you?"

"I never got the wire."

"How do you know I wired?"

"Pancho, my shoulder's killing me. For Christ's sake, don't ask so many difficult questions. It makes my head ache." He glared at me again. "That's your fault, you gringo dog. I have headaches now, to go with my rheumatism."

Villa finally asked him, almost as an afterthought, where he had hidden the gold.

"In the stables. I have three good men guarding it."

"You *had* three good men. Tomás, go see if it's all there."

Urbina growled again. "Don't trust him, Pancho."

I didn't reply but went outside into the foggy morning, where a chill wind blew off the sierra. In the stables a few of our men were playing poker with a dog-eared pack of cards. The smell of leather, grease and sweat hit my nostrils. Ignacio, whom I remembered from the battle of Torreón, sprawled on a heap of hay, drinking from a bottle of aguardiente. I ordered him and the others to stand guard outside.

The gold was there, buried deep in the hay, in the same flour sacks Fierro had requisitioned outside the Banco Minero. There were three sacks missing; it could have been worse. Ignacio poked his nose in.

"My colonel, the men are having an argument, and they ask you to settle it."

"If I can."

"I say your country is at war with England and Germany, over in Europe. The others say it's not so."

"The others are right."

"You're not at war?"

"I'm at war, but America's not. Not yet."

"Then how do the gringo soldiers pass the time?"

"Practicing. Ignacio, don't let your men get drunk."

When I got back to the kitchen I found Fierro sitting on a stool, cleaning his fingernails with the point of a butcher knife. He looked vexed and out of humor. The kettle had boiled and Villa had cleaned Urbina's wound, but he had not been able to extract the bullet. The edges of the hole were a raw pink—at least it hadn't been one of the soft-nosed lead bullets. He and Urbina were seated at the oak table, reminiscing about the days when they had been bandits here in Durango. "Luis Campos . . . ," Villa was saying. "I remember him well. We were on the run from the *rurales,* and we stayed at his house. But they were after him too, and when they came to get him we had to shoot our way out. So he's dead. . . ."

"Hanged by Murguía," Urbina said mournfully. "Do you remember after that, when we worked in the Del Verde mine? We slept in those filthy limestone holes. You had gangrene in your foot—I had to sell my saddle to pay for the doctor."

"But I kept working. I needed the lousy peso a day." Villa had seen me enter, and now he turned to me. "Tomás, was it there?"

"All but three sacks, chief."

"How much did you steal for yourself?" Urbina asked me, his lip curling. I didn't answer, just glared coldly, and Villa ignored him too. He gave a windy sigh, then turned back to Urbina.

"*Compadre,* we'll have to take you to the doctor. After that we'll decide what to do."

"After that," Urbina said, "let's go after Obregón. I want to fight again."

"You won't run away?"

"Why would I do a thing like that?"

"You did it once, didn't you? We'll have to make sure." Villa chuckled malevolently. "Rodolfo, tie a noose around his neck before he gets on his horse. You hold the other end. I want him to have a taste of what might have happened."

He looked disgruntled for a moment, but it was clear that for old times' sake he had granted the pardon. Urbina grinned. My hand tightened on the butt of my pistol, then relaxed. I had thought of killing him. But then I would have to tell them why, and betray Rosa's secret. I knew I had no right.

Villa found a spring wagon behind the stables and loaded it with the gold. He disappeared for a few minutes to baptize the child, having discovered that the woman was one of Urbina's daughters. Just as the sun broke through the haze to warm our bones, we forked our horses and the troop set out on the trail. Then Villa had one last thought for Urbina. "I want you to be comfortable, my friend. You can ride in the wagon with the gold . . . the gold you so kindly kept safe for me."

Urbina, amid various grunts and complaints, waddled to the wagon and settled himself on top of one of the sacks, a hangman's noose looped snugly, but not too tightly, around his neck. Fierro had fashioned it himself, and the other end was tied to the horn of his saddle. He and Villa and I rode behind the wagon, with the troop of men out in front. The men were muttering among themselves. Before Urbina snugged himself down he pointed to the rope and called out jovially, "Don't forget about me. Don't wander off the trail, Rodolfo. . . ."

/ 299

Rodolfo Fierro didn't bother answering, and he never smiled. He finally gave voice to what was on his mind.

"My general, with respect—this is wrong. The man is a traitor."

Villa's face darkened. That reminder wasn't what he wanted to hear. But there was no way he could escape Rodolfo's calm words.

"And the punishment for treason has always been death. There can be no other."

A sullen look, boyish in its petulance, crossed the chief's face. "What proof do I have," he growled, "that he meant to keep the gold?"

"You said in Chihuahua, in the Banco Minero—in front of us all, as I recall—that any man who breathed a word about the gold would be shot. Now half the Division knows he stole it. And then there's the matter of what he did at Jiménez. He ran away from Treviño. And he failed to come to León when you sent for him. He got your wires."

The lines of anxiety deepened on Villa's swarthy face. He had handled Urbina poorly, and he knew it. When a general loses one battle after another, he's not at his best in other matters.

"And there's this," Fierro said. "If you let him live, what will our men think?"

"That he tricked me," Villa muttered. He realized now why they had been grumbling among themselves; they were more than puzzled that we had come all this way to shoot Urbina and now were bringing him to a doctor to save his life. But the worst thing about this business, for me, wasn't the gold; it was that Urbina had failed to show up at León. He had been too busy hunting for stray women and collecting the last taxes in Chihuahua City.

Fierro hammered away. "Four men were killed defending the gold for him. And yet Urbina lives."

"If he doesn't fight for us," Villa muttered, changing course as he felt the weight of Fierro's argument, "he'll wind up fighting for Carranza, like the others. I can smell it."

Urbina heard none of this. He sprawled on the sacks of gold, one arm clasping his wounded shoulder. He looked as if he were falling asleep, despite the jolting of the wagon on the trail. The sun had vanished and the sky was soggy with impending rain.

A little desperate, Villa turned in his saddle toward me. "What do you think, Tomás?"

He knew that if any man would counsel mercy, it should be me. But he was wrong. And yet something stopped me from pronouncing the sentence. If I were to do that for a false reason, it would be a trickery I couldn't live with. If Urbina were to die, it had to be for treason.

"Don't make me condemn him to death," I said. "That's your job."

Villa nodded glumly. "All right. He's a traitor. Traitors die." He drew his pistol.

He raised it in the direction of Urbina, who had begun to snore in the wagon. The middle finger curled reluctantly around the trigger. He was going to shoot him in his sleep; he didn't want to see his eyes. But after a moment, his finger quivered . . . then slowly uncurled, like a worm from a hook. He let the pistol drop, shoving it back into his holster.

"I can't do it," he murmured. "I must have a sentimental streak somewhere. Rodolfo . . . use the rope."

The rope stretched slack about fifteen feet from the horn of his saddle to Urbina's neck in the spring wagon. Fierro checked his stirrups, patted his sorrel's neck, then dug his right knee hard into the flank. The sorrel wheeled, almost knocking me askew in the saddle, and then Fierro spurred him round the other side of the wagon. It was cleverly done . . . he must already have been thinking about it before he received the order. If he had just galloped back along the trail he would have dragged Urbina after him, tearing him to pieces on the stones. But Fierro had his code. Despite what he had done to Benton, he believed in a quick death.

As I stared, Urbina's body flung itself across the sacks of gold, slamming hard into the planks of the rattling wagon. His hands flew to his neck to get rid of the rope, and he snatched the hangman's knot just as it began to bury itself deeper in his throat. The team of horses pulling the wagon trotted gently along, the driver half asleep on the box. Fierro spurred as far as he could until the rope was taut and Urbina, eyes popping, was wedged in a ball against the wooden slats. Then he slowed the sorrel and hung there, trotting in pace with the team.

Dancing a strangulation jig, Urbina kicked his legs fiercely, fighting for life. The wound in his shoulder flowed red with fresh blood. His tongue bulged. He wasn't able to speak, to remind Villa how they had fled from the *rurales* or worked together in the Del Verde mine. But his grip on the knot was too powerful; he was refusing to die. The sorrel strained against the rope, mud spurting up from his hoofs. Urbina kicked and jumped, and his pop eyes glared with fury.

"Stop!" Villa cried to Rodolfo. "You've bungled it, you fool!"

The rope began to relax. I kicked my horse and bolted forward, drawing my pistol. The purple tongue had already begun to edge back between the slitted lips; the limbs gave a last kick of relief, and Urbina's onyx eyes blazed in demonic triumph. He thought now he would live.

"No, you bastard," I whispered, and thrust the barrel of the pistol between his eyes. I pulled the trigger—the pistol roared, smoke curling. Urbina slumped suddenly, tiredly, with what seemed a third black eye above his nose and his bloody brains spewing out against the boards of the wagon.

Warm sweat rolled down my face. I turned to Pancho Villa. A vein in the center of his forehead stood out like a piece of thick blue twine.

"It's done," I said.

/ 301

With one sleeve he wiped his eyes, then shoved his horse forward to the main body of men. Fierro trotted back to the wagon. He untied his rope from Urbina's mangled neck and dumped the body in the road for the buzzards.

Rosa was avenged. But when we reached Torreón in the fog the next morning, I forgot about that. While we were gone, hunting gold and Urbina, Monterrey and Nuevo Laredo had fallen to the Carranzistas under González. Our new commander in Chihuahua City, Calixto Contreras, sent word that Treviño had begun to bombard him; he doubted that his single brigade could hold out. Five hundred more of our soldiers had deserted from Torreón. Our scouts reported that Obregón was pushing north with thirty thousand men and was only fifty miles away. Villa sank down on the pink silk cushions of the settee in the Hotel Salvador, head in his hands. God no longer smiled on him.

"Everything's falling apart, Tomás. Since that damned convention, nothing's gone right for us. I'm starting to think that Obregón may be smarter than I am. . . ."

I knew how it pained him to say that, but now I believed it too. I felt a sense of waste more powerful than any I had ever known. The banners of the revolution were in rags. We had less than seven thousand men left. Torreón was our stronghold, but with Obregón fast approaching, it wouldn't be for long.

"If I defend the city and we lose it," Villa said, "that will be the end of the Division. The end of hope for the people. Obregón will turn this country into a charnelhouse."

For three days he brooded alone, seeing no hope. I wondered if he would give up. This was a test of his resources and the scope of his mind. Finally he called me and Candelario and three of his generals to his room. When we entered, I saw the change. He hadn't bathed and during those three days he must have sweated constantly in the summer heat, because he stank. But his eyes gleamed with a resolve that I hadn't seen since we had been in Ascensión and he planned the campaign to take Chihuahua.

"We'll stay here a little longer," Villa told us, "because I don't like to move an army in the rains. And perhaps Contreras can hold out in Chihuahua City, which may change things. But if not—listen! Here's what we're going to do."

Obregón, he explained, had always considered the northwestern state of Sonora as his fiefdom, but now Obregón was far afield. Sonora was almost unguarded. The main Carranzista garrison there was in the desert town of Agua Prieta, across the border from Arizona, and it was commanded by General Chao, the man with the ivory-handled pistol, as well as a certain Colonel Calles.

"So we'll go to Sonora," Villa announced, grinning. "On the way we'll raise the Yaqui nation. They hate Carranza. First we'll cross the high sierras . . . then all we have to do is lick that bucktoothed geography teacher at Agua Prieta. That won't be hard—for a change we won't be outnumbered. With the American border at our backs, Obregón will have to come at us head-on, if he dares. He can't surround us, as he could do here, and we can fight forever. We'll destroy him! I'm going to fight a diplomatic war too—any day now, Felipe Angeles arrives in Washington. I've written to General Scott at the War Department, asking him to arrange for Felipe to see President Wilson. The gringos will help us, I feel it in my bones. As soon as we have enough men and arms, we'll strike east into Chihuahua. We know how to fight there, and we still hold Juárez. It will be hard to do it all over again, but we can. And what *can* be done, *will* be done! That I swear to you. The people of the north will support us—we won't count anymore on this idiot Zapata. This will be a new beginning of the struggle. The real revolution will triumph."

His energy swept us all before him, and late into the night we planned the campaign and the equipment we would need. Villa looked as if he hadn't slept, but he was tireless and thorough. I was elated. God had to smile on such a man.

He waited as long as possible, hoping that Contreras could hold out against Treviño. But Chihuahua City fell. Then in September we heard Obregón's cannon. On the floor of his suite, Villa spread out the tattered maps with their faint smell of mildew. "Here," he said, eagerly scratching a broken fingernail in the upper left-hand corner, not far from Texas, on that dotted line separating the states of Chihuahua and Sonora. "We'll cross the sierra here, from Casas Grandes, into Sonora. The pass is called the Cañon del Púlpito. It's twelve thousand feet high, and no army is supposed to be able to get through it. So it will be unguarded. If we time it right, the rains will be over and the bad cold weather won't have begun. God willing, we'll get through. That's the first step to victory."

I looked over his shoulder at the maps. As his fingers traced our path northwest from Torréon through the desert, and then across the forbidding mountains to Sonora, my heart beat more quickly in my breast. Our route would pass through Parral.

27   **"So shines a good deed
in a naughty world."**

October rain beat on the tiled roof, and a chill north wind rattled the windowpanes. Lying in the big four-poster bed with Elisa Griensen curled in my arms, I had no thought of wind or weather.

The seven-thousand-man army had been camped outside of Parral for the past two days, resting and provisioning itself for the crossing of the high western sierra. Rosa was in the camp. She had traveled at my side for nearly two weeks over mountain trails that we had taken to avoid any Carranzista garrisons. Parral was still in our hands, and the remnants of Contreras' brigade had joined us there. But we couldn't stay long if we wanted to outrace the winter weather. Shamelessly I left Rosa in the camp, telling her I had to do business in town for the chief and I would come back just before we marched north. On the long trek from Torreón I had convinced myself that I needed Maximilian . . . a good horse might get me safely through the Cañon del Púlpito. By the time we reached Parral I knew there was a deeper, simpler reason. I wanted to see Elisa. I wasn't proud of myself. I was the same faithless man I had always been, but I had to do it. Life was short.

I tugged at the cowbell in front of the Hacienda de Los Flores at dawn, just as I had done seven months ago with Candelario. Once again Patricio opened the wooden slat and peered out with his hooded Yaqui eyes. Two minutes later, in the library, Elisa was in my arms, and we were kissing and murmuring each other's names as if they were the most precious words in the world. She unpinned her yellow hair, letting it tumble below her shoulders. It was longer than I remembered it. She knew how I loved the way she did that—that wanton shower, as if all barriers tumbled at the same time.

"So you came back for your horse," she murmured.

"Yes. For Maximilian. I told you he was too good a horse not to ride again."

"Oh, Tom. You're bad. Do you know that?"

"Why? I'm doing what pleases me."

"You learn too quickly. That frightens me. Do you want to go upstairs?"

"To ride my horse?" I said wickedly.

"Yes . . . bad." Her green eyes sparkled, the little crow's-feet around them crinkling into a fan. "But I love you for it."

For two days and two nights I buried myself in the magic of her body and heard her song. But she was wrong; I didn't learn quickly, I only acted impetuously. And there was no consistency to my deceit. I told her about Rosa's return to Torreón and that we were together again. Before, with Hannah playing the role in my life that Rosa now occupied, I had been honest with Rosa. Now that I had committed myself to Rosa in almost the same way I had once done to Hannah, I chose to lay my soul bare to Elisa. It eased my conscience considerably that I could admit the truth to one of the two women in my life. Perhaps that's why, through the centuries, mistresses had been held in such high esteem.

"Will Rosa go with you to Sonora?" Elisa asked.

That had been troubling me ever since we left Torreón. There would be some women on the trek, but crossing the sierra was perilous. And on the other side, in Sonora, the land was so barren that Villa already worried about feeding his army.

"I know the Púlpito," Elisa said. "I rode up there years ago with Zambrano. The crossing is awful, and if it snows you won't get through."

"But it's only October."

"Last year, in November, a party of Mormons was trapped. They froze to death."

"I should send her back to Tomochic," I said, sighing. "She won't like it. Neither will I."

Elisa leaned back in bed, propped up on the scented pillows. Her belly was flat and brown—she liked to tan herself on the balcony in the late afternoon and sometimes take her siesta in the sun. She said she woke up feeling drunk, as if the gods had violated her while she slept. I watched the muscles of her breasts stretch, the nipples going a little flatter. We had made love already, and now we were both ready to sleep. The Division was leaving next evening at sundown. She ran a finger lightly across my lips. But I could see she was thinking of something else, and I raised my eyebrows.

"Rosa could stay here, you know," Elisa said.

"In Parral?"

"At Los Flores."

"With *you?*" I laughed nervously. "Elisa, I couldn't do that."

"Why not?"

"Because . . . first of all, I'd be using you . . ."

But that wasn't the reason for my reluctance. The real reason was a gut fear at the thought of the two women in my life coming together, meeting, living under the same roof. And yet when I thought of sending Rosa to Tomochic, I knew that would be cruel. At Los Flores she would be both comfortable and safe. For Rosa's sake I wanted it, but still I hesitated.

"I wouldn't have offered," Elisa said, "if I didn't mean it. It's a big house. There's plenty of work to do."

"I know it will be good for her," I explained. "For you, I don't know. But it will surely complicate *my* life."

"It needn't. And don't worry about me—I could use some company. It's for you, my sweet. I'm taking the risk. So should you."

Then it was hard to refuse. I was at the point of asking her, if Rosa stayed, whether she would be willing to pick up where I had left off and help with her reading and writing. But she was already offering a favor beyond value, and I couldn't in conscience ask for more.

"I don't want her to die in Sonora," I said, thinking aloud.

"Then bring her here tomorrow."

Later I had second thoughts and a gallery of fears. I would miss Rosa; the separation had no time limit. I would have to talk her into it. I remembered her crossing the mountains to Tomochic with our gold—she had no sense of personal danger. But she would probably be frightened of Elisa—that elegance, a strange house, a woman strong enough to live on her own in Mexico with no man in sight. And then . . . what if she discovered the truth? Elisa would never tell her, but women had a sense of smell that went beyond male understanding. The only man I knew who had it was Pancho Villa. If she found out why Elisa was keeping her, she might pack her saddlebags and head into Sonora on her own. Remembering what had happened the last time she had gone hunting for me, I didn't want her to do that.

I rode back to camp early the next morning. Our men were sprawled the length of a fertile valley in a place called Cuevecillas de Abajo, surrounded by low mountains filled with caves. The rains had turned everything green, and the remuda grazed well. By our campfire Julio sat cross-legged in front of his silver saddle, plaiting a horsehair rope. Candelario was still at the hacienda with Francisca. A sour down-turn of the lips made Julio's face look more than ever like a pitted tomahawk.

"What's happened?" I asked. "It can't be good."

"The chief got a message. Our garrison in Juárez went over to Carranza."

"Damn!" That was our only port of entry to the United States—it had been vital to keep it. "Are we still going to Sonora?"

"*Hombre,* there's more reason than ever. Agua Prieta's just over the border from Arizona. We've got to buy bullets and shells."

"How is the chief taking it?"

"Not well, Tomás. Keep clear of him today."

I found Rosa by a little stream that ran past a yellow cornfield, beating on our laundry with a mesquite branch. Her back was bent like a thousand Indian women I had seen from Ascensión to Xochimilco. A few more years of that and she would never be able to straighten it. If I had any doubts, that sight erased them. A thin sun forced itself through the haze. She looked up at me, sweat beading her lip, smiling from her clear brown eyes.

She listened carefully while I explained what I had in mind, and she said what I thought she would say.

"I am not afraid of the pass, *mi capitán.*"

"Rosa, do it for my sake. I'm worried."

"You have a feeling?"

"A feeling? You mean a premonition?"

"Yes."

I nodded. It wasn't really true, but it would do as a reason.

"I believe in those," she said.

"Then stay. This woman is a good woman. She's an old friend of mine."

"You're sure it's not something else, Tomás?"

"Like what?" I asked, guardedly.

"Do you want me to go back to Tomochic?"

I laughed. "No. I want you to stay here and wait for me. After we've taken Agua Prieta, if I'm still alive, I'll come back for you."

Swiftly she made the sign against the evil eye, but then she nodded.

That afternoon I took her to the Hacienda de Los Flores. She mounted a cinnamon-colored bay that we had picked up in Torreón, and when we had ridden through the gate Elisa was there to greet us, standing by some azalea bushes that were inflamed a shocking red-pink by the hazed sun. She wore her leather Spanish riding clothes, and I saw her eyes rake Rosa up and down, taking in all that lushness and youth. Rosa dismounted gracefully. She had grown a couple of inches since I'd known her—she was seventeen now—and her body had become more slender and womanly, her face more serene. The image I carried of her mother intruded for a moment, then mercifully vanished. Rosa couldn't properly be called beautiful, but she carried herself as if she were. Life was never easy, but she valued it.

Elisa gave her a good greeting. It had occurred to me that she might treat Rosa like a servant and be aloof from her. But I needn't have worried.

"Señora, I'm grateful to you. I won't be any trouble."

"You'll be just fine, Rosa," she said calmly. "We'll be friends."

They made a fine pair, the regal blond woman and the black-haired Tarahumara girl. It made Elisa look older and Rosa younger, but not in a bad way. Something stirred in me, but I couldn't quite understand it, or perhaps didn't want to. Not then.

"I'd better head back."

I realized that I had outfoxed myself as far as any final farewell to Elisa was concerned, and I surely wasn't going to snatch Rosa's arm and march her off to a siesta in Elisa's house. The three of us, with Patricio, went around to the stables, where I saddled Maximilian. He was always glad to see me, and his eyes rolled in his head as if he thought we were going off to rope another longhorn in a *charreada*. But this time we were going to fight in Sonora. It wasn't right to expose a fine horse like that to shellfire and barbed wire, but I had been riding an easily spooked young piebald, and I wanted to have brave flesh under my legs for what was going to happen. Elisa had understood; she had insisted that I take him.

"Try to bring him back, Tom. He's yours . . . but I wouldn't mind seeing him again."

With those words she was telling me something else. Leather creaked as I bent down from the saddle and kissed her on the cheek, inhaling her perfume. Then I bent in the other direction to Rosa. The sun sloped toward the western mountains, fringed by swollen gray clouds. The birds warbled in their cages. The women walked with me to the gate.

Patricio opened it for me. I trotted off toward the camp, looking back once over my shoulder to see Rosa and Elisa standing close together, waving, struck by an odd brown light that made them look as if they were in a photograph—a picture to be engraved in my memory perhaps forever. Motionless, wrapped in dark shawls, hands frozen in the air, smiles fading, faces a trifle blurred in the gathering dusk . . . and dear beyond belief.

Amid a wild blaring of bugles and the steady martial thump of a single drum, the column left Casas Grandes. We headed westward in a cold thin rain toward the Cañon del Púlpito.

We had moved north much too slowly, picking up more men, until in Casas Grandes we had nearly nine thousand. But only two thousand, with Villa in the lead, trotted toward the sierra. We had to secure the pass before the main body could follow. The Dorados had been organized again under Candelario, whom Villa had promoted to general. We had commandeered wagons and pack mules and carried two batteries of field artillery and thirty machine guns, as well as the wagon full of gold.

The land sloped steadily upward. An icy rain beat fiercely down—a gully washer, a stump mover, a real frog strangler. Soggy clouds humped overhead and rolled menacingly across the plain. I hunched in the saddle, feeling the drops trickle through every chink in my armor and fight their wet way into every pore, murmuring all the while to poor Maximilian that it would end . . . it would end soon. Just before darkness came down on us like a thrown blanket, we made camp at a place called Ojitos.

Stiff and cold, we woke to a gray morning. We could see the forbidding peaks of the sierra and feel their raw wind. Nothing grew there, and the cold numbed. Sometimes in the high sierra, as Elisa had said, winter came early. Men lashed the shivering mules. The wagons creaked and we started forward again.

A few wretched peasants lived in the foothills. That night, before attempting the climb, we camped in a desolate valley under a moonless sky. The stars glittered frostily overhead. We built a fire to warm our bones, and then Candelario said, "Look!" He pointed into the blackness, and I heard the flapping of wings, a thousand of them. Then came a distant mournful cry.

"What are they?"

"Cranes, Tomás. Flying south."

I could see them now, gray shapes flowing like silk across the firmament. "They're beautiful," I murmured.

"It means bad weather," Candelario explained.

"Maybe snow," said Julio, who always thought the worst and was usually right.

In the morning the sky looked like a blanket of lead. We climbed all day through the passes that led to the Púlpito, over bare rock under that gray heaven. It was high enough to make noses bleed. The wind struck our faces and we had to bend almost double, serapes clutched tight, or it knifed between the eyes and made the head ache. Rattling wagons bounced from boulder to boulder, horses whinnying in protest. Men had to tighten cinches, use both quirts and spurs. Dreaming of lost meadows in Parral, Maximilian tried to raise his long gray head to look at me for help, but the wind beat cruelly on him and he ducked down again with a melancholy snort. Ahead of me, borne back by the blast, came the voice of a man who bravely tried to sing.

> Si Adelita me fuera por otro,
> La seguiría por tierra y por mar . . .

In the afternoon it began to snow. Fat flakes drifted across the trail, and soon all view of the mountains was cut off. The chill penetrated more deeply. The rocks ahead grew whiter, although the horses' hoofs trampled slush and mud. Each new peak showed through the gloom like a ghost shrouded in a white sheet. It was beautiful . . . but there was no more singing.

We had to make camp that night in the snow. The men were so hungry that Villa ordered spare horses slaughtered for food. The next morning the mules were shoved into their traces and we moved into the pass.

The Cañon del Púlpito took its name from a giant needlelike rock that soared at the beginning of the pass in the shape of a church pulpit. The trail itself had been carved from rock by the Yaquis a thousand years ago. It wasn't the only way to cross from Chihuahua to Sonora, but the Carranzistas would never dream that an army could pass through the Púlpito. The canyon was only five miles long, but it was also, in places, only fifteen or twenty feet wide, with sheer drops on one side and vertical stone cliffs on the other. I wondered myself if it were possible. The trail twisted right and left, up and down, like a snake with a broken back. The horses' hoofs struck sparks off the rock and rang through the defiles, echoing and re-echoing, so that I wanted to clamp my ears shut but didn't dare let go of the reins.

Draped in fog, the needle of rock towered over us like the fist of a demon from hell. A cry was raised, muted by the snow but echoing back and forth between the walls of the canyon. *"To Sonora! . . ."*

How many such cries? How many cities? Once it had been *"To Torreón!"* In Mexico there was always someplace to go, somewhere else to fight.

An artillery piece tipped over first. The caisson skidded on one of the hairpin turns, then slid toward the edge as the mules brayed in terror. Finally teetering, then toppling, it bounced down with a series of awful ear-shattering crashes into the rocky bottom of the cut. One of the teamsters leaped to safety. One held the reins until the last minute, struggling valiantly and uselessly . . . and then went down with the caisson, screaming his rage. In Mexico there were always plenty of men left to die.

It was cold up there . . . too cold. I was glad I had left Rosa behind; more than ever now, I knew it had been the right thing to do. My fingertips under my sheepskin gloves were starting to freeze, and as the snow struck Maximilian and nestled in his mane, it turned to ice. He whinnied pitifully. For a while I kept as close to the cliff face as I could, afraid to look down into the canyon, but then the snow began to loosen the overhanging rocks. One of them, the size of a fist, tumbled down to bounce off the scabbard of my rifle. Maximilian shied—his hind hoofs slipped. By the time he regained his balance we were in the middle of the trail. Julio had been forced to spur ahead to avoid collision, and my heart pounded in fear like a jackhammer. More rocks flew down, then ricocheted off into the defile, booming. "Single file, Tomás," Julio called nervously. . . .

We spread out down the center of the serpentine path. From ahead I heard another fearful crash, then more screams. A munitions wagon had tumbled, carrying both mules and driver into the abyss. I had once hated the desert. Now I would give anything to be back in it.

Long before darkness, Pancho Villa called a halt. We would have to camp in the middle of the Púlpito. Just after sunset, which we couldn't see but knew had happened because the grayness had turned inky black, Villa and Rodolfo Fierro came walking back along the rocky inner wall of the trail, inspecting the damage. The night was dark enough to keep the bats in their caves, but Fierro carried a lantern. In the wavering yellow light I could see icicles forming on Villa's mustache. He took me to one side, crouching with me by the fire we had built under an overhang against the cliff. The wind blew, and threads of snow whipped at our eyes.

He yelled into my ear, "Tomás, we've lost three cannon . . . and a wagonload of bullets! How do you like our Sonora winter?"

I had to shout too. "In Texas, chief, we call it hog-killing weather! A blue norther! Comes down from the North Pole with nothing to stop it except a barbed-wire fence!"

He hissed even closer in my ear, but not quite so loud. "Some of the horses won't last the night. The teamsters' hands are already frostbitten. The Yaquis say the last half of the pass is the worst part—narrower, with sharper turns. I want you to go back."

I wondered if the cold had affected my ears. They felt like glass—I didn't dare touch them.

"The gold!" he shouted. "*The gold.* I can afford to lose a few more cannon. But not the gold."

The sacks were too heavy to carry in the saddle or be grasped in a man's arms. Horse or man might stumble.

"Back to where, chief?"

He thrust his frozen hands so close to the sputtering twig fire that I thought he would scorch them. I bent to hear him.

"If you get back through the pass, the only safe direction is north. The first pueblo is Ascensión. You remember it, don't you?"

"I remember. We were there a hundred years ago."

"I was thinking of the lake. Gold is indestructible, I'm told—but I've been lied to so often I don't know what to believe. Is it true?" he shouted.

I stamped my feet to keep them from getting numb. "Yes, chief," I yelled. "It never rots! It will outlive us all!"

"Wrap the sacks tightly with wire and rope, then dump them in the lake. Not too deep, not too shallow. We don't want anyone else to stumble on them, but we want to be able to haul them up when the time comes."

He would keep two sacks, which he might need in Sonora, and take his chances that they got through. The rest would stay in the wagon. At dawn Rodolfo Fierro and a squad of men would go back with me through the eastern end of the pass.

I felt an old touch of unease. Fierro and I had never had our reckoning, and after Villa's orders in Juárez I had felt safe. But he wasn't the man I wanted for company on any long journey. "Let me take Candelario and Julio too."

"I need them to fight at Agua Prieta."

"You have nine thousand men to fight. You need men you can trust to bury the gold."

In the swirling snow he looked at me steadily for another minute . . . then nodded his head in agreement. "Make sure you know exactly where you sink it. Pick out markers on separate banks. I've seen surveyors do that."

A fresh blast of wind ripped up out of the canyon. The snow had almost stopped falling, but now I felt something harder and more biting begin to flail my cheeks. The snow was turning to sleet. Villa bent to light a cigarette from the fire, which looked as if it might expire at any moment.

"Luckily"—he had to shriek now against the wind—"the wagon is near the rear of the column! You can start at first light!"

"And where will we meet, chief?"

"In Agua Prieta, if all goes well. If not, then on some cloud. I'll be . . ." The rest of his words were lost in the wind.

"What?"

"I said, I'll be the fellow with the four wives and the harp!"

My voice was about to give out too. I roared back at him, in the freezing wind and sleet of that hellish place, "Do you really think, after all you've done, you'll still get to heaven?"

With a chuckle, he answered me, not very loudly this time, but still

I heard him. "Yes, why not? I'm not a bad man. And I've done my best."

His cigarette went out. And then, with a hiss, so did the fire.

Going back through the Púlpito, the horses were half frozen. Their legs and hocks were sore, and they left a trail of blood from walking in crusted snow. The sleet turned to icy rain. But we plodded on through the dark day, the wagon of gold sliding in the mud, sometimes wandering almost to the edge of the precipice before the driver could shriek at the mules and haul them back in time. Toward evening, as we moved lower into the eastern passes of the sierra, the wind eased and the rain became a misty drizzle. That night, near Ojitos, we slept like the corpses of drowned men.

In the morning patches of blue sky peered from among the clouds. The crags of the sierra blazed white in the sun. I smelled dust, and the breeze made it feel like spring. We slit the throat of one of the spare horses and grilled steaks for breakfast. Julio ate his horsemeat raw, blood dripping from his lips, patting his lean belly in satisfaction. He felt brave again. From the rest of the meat we made jerky. Fierro kept apart, and no one minded—Julio and Candelario had as little use for him as I. Less, as I soon found out.

That night we reached Ascensión, camping by the lake very near to where I had first found Rosa. The town itself was almost deserted; the revolution had sucked it dry and then abandoned it. I spent an hour by the campfire, rubbing the stiffness from Maximilian's muscles, and then let him out to graze with the other horses. He looked thin, but he had survived. The same, I suppose, could be said for the rest of us, except that I had lost my voice shouting at Villa.

At dawn I surveyed the lake. It looked lower than I remembered, but memories can deceive. Although it was a cool day the sun was shining, and the surface was a bright blue-green with pools of a more sandy color. Those would be the shallows, to be avoided. Wind kicked up a few whitecaps. I stepped over to the driver of the wagon and told him we were going to dump the sacks in the lake.

He looked surprised. "But they contain flour, my colonel."

Of course, I realized, Villa hadn't told them. "The flour is poisoned," I croaked. "We have to make sure no one eats it."

"Why not leave it for the Carranzistas?"

"They may fight that way," I said, remembering the arsenic at Celaya, "but the chief still wants to get to heaven."

He shrugged contemptuously. As far as he was concerned, killing the enemy in any way possible would lead straight to the pearly gates.

"We'll dump them far out," I explained, "so we can't use the wagon. You and your men can go into town and see what's there."

"But there's nothing, my colonel."

"Look hard. There may be some pulque, or a woman."

The soldiers went off on their horses, whooping and hollering, toward Ascensión. Candelario, Julio and Fierro began unloading the sacks of gold from the wagon, paying scant attention to me as I stood on the shore, looking for landmarks. In my mind I drew a line from the dead jacaranda tree, where Rosa had first gone down on her knees to me, to a thick clump of barrel cactus on the far shore. Off to the right, about a mile away, I spotted a gutted mud hut and a stand of maguey. The maguey would be there long after the hut was gone. A channel of frothy green water snaked out between the sandy patches, almost as far as the middle of the lake.

"Let's ride through that. If each of us carries a sack, it will make six trips. I'll tell you when to let go."

Julio blushed. "Not too deep, Tomás. I can't swim."

"Ride close to me. Candelario?"

"In my past life I was a dolphin."

"Rodolfo?"

"It's of no consequence." He meant that unlike the others, there was no possibility of his falling off his horse.

Julio and I trotted out first, our stirrup irons nearly touching, an unwieldy flour sack full of gold clutched in our arms behind the saddle horns. The bubbly green water was more shallow than I had realized, and the horses were no deeper than their hocks and knees. I wanted them at least belly-deep before we dumped the load. I veered off toward one of the sand-colored patches to try my luck, and Maximilian nickered with fright. I had to put steel into him, and even then he snorted and tried to buck. The gold swayed, almost fell.

Julio called sharply. "Tomás, it's quicksand!"

Maximilian had smelled it. There was a sucking sound—thick, juicy and evil. One hoof and fetlock of his foreleg came up brown, caked with the treacherous gumbo. I wheeled him quickly and kicked my way out of there, trying to soothe him. Up on the Brazos I had seen a remuda of horses and a herd of twenty cattle go down in quicksand in the space of five minutes. We had saved some, but the rest died pitifully. I yelled hoarsely to warn Candelario and Fierro who were behind us—they might have seen but not understood. Candelario waved, then spoke some words to Fierro.

Maximilian plunged deeper, up to his ribs in the foul-smelling green water. Jerking my head to the right, I sighted the maguey in a reasonably parallel line to the far shore of the lake. "Here!" I shouted. I heaved my sack of gold off to the right. It struck the surface with a splash that soaked my Levi's—then sank swiftly, the ripples spreading. I heard another splash to my left as Julio let go. A cloud of mud rose from the bottom, and the sack was nowhere to be seen.

One by one we carried the sacks to the middle of the lake, then dumped them. Maximilian's hoofs threw up a fountain of water that made a rainbow against the rising sun. Each trip took more than ten minutes—five out, five back. My mind wandered, and I began to daydream of Elisa. In the rainbow of water I saw her neat breasts, her lemon-colored hair, her sandy bush and red lips dripping honey. The musky salt smell of the lake bottom was like the smell that came from between her thighs. Then I conjured up Rosa—brown flesh covered with a sparkle of sweat, the candle glow making a patch of light on her brown forehead, a curve of hip. . . . and I saw the photograph again: the two silhouettes frozen at the gate in parting. My pecker stiffened in my pants. I neared the shore and shook my head like a dog, disgusted with myself.

Julio, at my side, turned and gazed back at the lake. He had left his hat on the shore, so that he shaded his eyes against the sun with one hand. When he hissed my name I twisted in the saddle.

White cat's-paws rippled the water. Candelario was coming toward us, saddle empty of the last sack, head thrown back, a black and bulky shape against the glare. Farther out, chest-deep in the lake, legs out of sight but thrashing and churning up mud, Fierro's sorrel neighed terribly. Rodolfo clutched the sack of gold with one arm. His quirt was in the other hand, and he was whipping the horse's belly. I couldn't see his face.

"That's green water . . ."

"With quicksand under it," Julio said.

Rodolfo had drifted to the left to find a fresh place where he could dump the last sack. The channel veered there, narrowed, then must have deepened, and the mud stirred by the horse's hoofs had hidden the telltale patch of brown. I spurred toward him, with Julio following.

"Rodolfo!" I yelled. *"Drop the gold!"*

He couldn't hear me, or he was too absorbed in whipping his horse. He was locked into his stirrups and wouldn't let go. Now I realized he couldn't swim. His back was toward us, his broad shoulders hunched over the withers. The horse was squirting piss. Stifle and tail vanished from sight, and he sank even lower.

We reached Candelario, who sat unmoving. I had lived in a bog camp with cattle—I knew what to do. Taking Maximilian out there would be murder, for he could sink into the goo as easily as the sorrel. Fierro was about thirty feet away from us. I kicked my feet loose from the stirrups, bent to wrench one boot loose—then pushed it at Julio.

"What are you doing, Tomás?"

"They'll fill with sand!" I worked the other boot loose. "Take it, goddammit!"

"I can't hear you," Julio said.

I yelled at Candelario, "Sling a rope around me!"

Fierro thrashed in the water, hip-deep, and the sorrel screamed with mounting terror. Candelario leaned close to lay a hand on my arm. "Tomás," he said calmly, "this is no loss. The man is still your enemy, no matter what. Leave him be. No one but us will know."

They had always despised Fierro, and to them that must have been reason enough to let him die. In the corral at Torreón, Fierro had called death a reasonable answer to a generally unsatisfactory life. And yet, as the lake closed round him, he struggled to preserve it.

I dropped the boots and vaulted from the saddle into the cold water. Wriggling out of my Levi's, I snatched the rope off the horn. The sorrel was braying like a burro, head pointed toward the sun at an impossible angle. Only his loins and croup showed above the bubbling brown surface. Fierro whipped him about the ears with the quirt. He still forked the saddle, and the water had reached his crotch.

I shook out the rope to build a loop, then doubled it, keeping the noose open. I couldn't save the horse with a head ketch, even though I knew Fierro would hang in the saddle until hell froze over. The only way to haul a horse out of bog was by the tail, which was strong enough to take the strain. But the tail was long gone under water. A head ketch would likely break his neck. I had to go for Fierro himself.

His back was turned. I whirled the rope by the honda over my left shoulder, then to the right and up over my head and tossed out a hooleyann with a corkscrew roll. It whirred through the bright air and dropped neatly over Fierro's shoulders, pinning his arms. I planted my stockinged feet into the cold gumbo, took a fast dally around my thigh and yanked as hard as I could. Fierro flew backwards out of the saddle. I hadn't meant to do any damage, but I was in a hurry and it happened that way. I felt him stick for a moment in the stirrups—then he shot free.

The sack of gold thumped off, kicking up a fountain of spray. At the same time I heard a whirring over my own head, and a wide loop settled around me and snugged tight against my ribs. The knot bit hard into the soaking wet shirt. Glancing back, I met Julio's grin; he took a dally with the other end around the horn. Candelario was twirling a second rope in case Julio had missed.

The rest was easy: they hauled on me, and I hauled on Rodolfo. He came bouncing backwards through the water like a hooked whale, swallowing a few pints of muck and brine on the way. When his head popped up above the surface, although he was nearly out cold, I could hear him sputtering and gasping, but then he went back under the next second. It might have been funny if that poor sorrel hadn't gone under at the same time. Some obscene gaseous bubbles floated on top of the murky cloud where his head had been, and then they subsided. He was in his grave. Rodolfo had been luckier.

I beached him at last, near the jacaranda tree. After I caught my breath I knelt astride his back and began to pound the water out of his lungs. The others crowded round, interested now. My mending ribs ached again from Julio's rope, and the turn I had taken around my naked thigh had skinned off enough white hide for a lady's purse. Water dribbled from Rodolfo's slack mouth. Candelario vanished from my sight for a few minutes. When he came back he had my boots and trousers, slimy with mud.

Rodolfo vomited green water into the dust. His eyes rolled in his head. His face looked like the peaks of the Púlpito after it had snowed, with a touch of blue twilight color. He worked himself up on one elbow, trying to reach down toward his boots. But he fell back, turning even paler. His voice was barely a whisper.

"My leg . . ."

He wore riding boots that reached almost to his crotch. When Candelario started to tug the left one off, Rodolfo let out a howl, then bit his lip until he drew blood. Julio pulled out a hunting knife and slit the leather down to the shin. He worked the boot off more gently than I thought he would, while Rodolfo's shoulders jerked from the pain. The foot hung at a crazy angle. "The ankle is broken," Julio muttered.

Coming out of the stirrup it had jammed, then snapped—the kind of fall that every cowhand feared. Rodolfo rested for a while, getting his breath back, staring at his ruined ankle. Then his tawny eyes fixed on mine. "It was your rope. . . ."

I didn't want that man owing me a damned thing. "I didn't save your life," I reminded him. "I just postponed your death."

Later that morning we held a little council of war. Our soldiers had come back from Ascensión, unable to find either pulque or a woman, and they sat around by the wagon, smoking cornstalk cigarettes and waiting for us to give some orders. Rodolfo was flat on his back under the jacaranda tree, beyond earshot, grunting every now and then like a hog. We had no painkillers, and none of us knew how to set an ankle bone. If we didn't get him quickly to a doctor, he would wind up a cripple. "We can't leave him," I said, and the others gloomily nodded.

Candelario wanted to head south to Casas Grandes, leave him there with a doctor, then ride for the Púlpito and try to catch up with the Division. That idea chilled me even before I felt the wind. Julio thought we could make our way westward across the desert, evading the Carranzista patrols, to join up with the chief outside Agua Prieta. "I'm a general," Candelario shouted. "I'll decide!" Finally I butted in.

"Hang on a minute there. Damn it, Candelario!—I mean, General Cervantes—can't you just shut up for a second?"

Crossing the desert toward Agua Prieta, I said, meant we would be hemmed in between two armies who would shoot at anything that moved. Going back to Casas Grandes involved a gamble that we would find a doctor.

"We'd have no problem," Candelario grumbled, "if you hadn't

been stupid enough to throw your rope. Not south, you say. Not west. Should we grow wings?"

"Let's ride north!"

"Tomás, you swallowed too much of the lake. North leads to Juárez. The garrison surrendered. Treviño will honor our arrival with a firing squad."

"But we'll cross the border, General. Into the United States!" Scratching a map in the dirt, I began plowing up furrows with one grubby finger. "A few miles east of Columbus, I figure. Then we haul Rodolfo to a doctor in El Paso. After that we take the train to Arizona, and when Agua Prieta falls . . . why, we just walk across the border and meet the chief!"

Candelario clamped both my shoulders, and his good eye sparkled. "My brilliant friend! If I insulted you, forgive me. I like it—I like it a lot! I can stop off in Columbus to find Yvette and Marie-Thérèse!"

Julio objected; he pointed out that the border was guarded by Pershing's cavalry. They were supposedly friendly to us, but they wouldn't be pleased to see twenty-odd armed Villistas whooping across with a wounded man in a wagon.

"We'll send the soldiers back through the Púlpito," Candelario said excitedly. "The three of us are enough to get Rodolfo to Texas. Tomás is right—he needs a decent doctor."

There was no argument, no more talk of Fierro as a burden. When Candelario's cock twitched, the whole man followed.

28

"The path is smooth
that leadeth on to danger."

I never counted the miles I journeyed back and forth in Mexico during the years I was a revolutionist with Pancho Villa, but if I had been selling patent medicine on the way I might have made a fortune. And if I had a dollar for every time someone fired a shot in my direction, I could have retired on the interest.

Rodolfo traveled in the spring wagon with Julio driving, and by nightfall we neared the border. All that jolting across the desert didn't help Rodolfo's ankle, which had swelled up and had the appearance of a colorful sunset, but to give him credit he never said a word, just smoked all my supply of tobacco and sometimes bit hard on a piece of boot leather. He had fever. Candelario wanted us to camp near Columbus so he could go north on the Deming road and find his lost whores, but when he felt Rodolfo's head he realized there was no time now for partying or pleading.

A rusting barbed-wire fence marked the border. At dawn we cut a hole through it and then about a mile later turned eastward on a trail marked with stones. This was home—the United States—not that it looked any different from Chihuahua. We didn't see a human face, just a few ganted steers wandering across the railroad track when we passed into Dona Ana County. To the north, the peak of Mount Riley appeared out of the morning heat haze, suspended in a golden mist. Then the land became greener, and there were rolling hills. We must have been ten miles from El Paso in the late afternoon when the mules laid back their ears and the horses snorted uneasily. A moment later we heard three single snaps of a rifle coming from the hills ahead of us. Julio had been sleeping on the seat of the wagon, the reins looped about his wrist. He woke up quickly, grabbing for his rifle. Candelario already had yanked his own Mauser out of the scabbard and was working the bolt.

"Take it easy!" I yelped. "This is the United States! Those might be cowboys or soldiers."

"Then who are they shooting at?" Candelario rapped back.

"We'll find out soon enough. They're right up there in our way."

He didn't put down his rifle. Knowing the value that Mexicans put on a life, and their tendency to shoot first and figure out later who it was they had hit and whether or not it had been a mistake, I decided to ride ahead and see what was happening. I wanted to get to El Paso, but I didn't want to kill any American citizens in order to do it. Under my sombrero and Mexican colonel's eagles, no matter who I rode with, lived a Texan.

I nudged Maximilian over the first rise, just as two more shots snapped crisply and echoed through the hills. Ahead, in the cut, the Rio Grande twisted in a northwesterly direction, sparkling in the sun, no more than thirty yards wide with heavy bushes on both banks. I knew the place now. There was a little settlement farther on called Hot Wells, and a big cattle ranch lay to the north. I didn't like exposing myself this way, but I wasn't carrying my rifle and I hoped that whoever was doing the shooting, if they had spotted me, could see that my intentions were peaceable. My uniform was stuffed into my saddlebags, and except for my Levi's I wore the dusty clothes of a Mexican vaquero. I could see a few adobe huts baking in the heat on the far side of the river, where the railroad tracks of the El Paso & Southwestern turned southward in a glittering curve. An eagle coasted against the high arc of sky. He let out a thin scream.

A bullet whistled by, zinged off a stone, and a moment later I heard the crack of a Springfield—it made a more high-pitched sound than a Mauser, a Remington or a Mannlicher. I tumbled out of the saddle, whacked Maximilian on the rump and ate some gritty dust. Three more shots echoed among the hills. I didn't see what they hit, but my ears told me they were aimed in my general direction.

Candelario and Julio came sliding up on their bellies, taking cover behind some rocks.

"Who are they?" Candelario hissed.

"I can't see yet," I said. "I think they're on the near bank of the river. In the bushes."

"Soldiers or cowboys?" he asked, chuckling.

"Don't shoot, General. They may be making a mistake."

Hombre, a worse mistake would be to let them kill us."

Another volley cut loose, this time six or seven rifles. The puffs of smoke drifted up from the bushes below us about two hundred yards away. The bullets whined over our heads like a swarm of bees.

"They might be Mexicans," said Julio, commenting on the accuracy of the gunfire. I poked my head up. Down on the far bank of the river I saw some pale brown shapes lying near the bushes—they looked like dead quail.

"They're hunters. I'm going to show myself." I dropped my rifle and scrambled to my feet, waving my arms over my head and jumping from side to side on the balls of my feet in case the men in the bushes decided to keep shooting. I must have looked like a nervous clown. A moment later there was movement behind the bushes. Then four or five men showed themselves, crouching down on one knee with their rifles leveled. They wore flat-brimmed scout hats, khaki breeches and tight leggings: the uniform of the United States Cavalry.

"Hey, down there!" I yelled in English. "Don't shoot! I'm an American!"

The soldiers began jawing to each other, until finally one of them cupped his hands to shout back. "Who are you?"

"We're coming down," I called, then turned to Julio. "Get the horses and the wagon. Candelario, let's go down and powwow."

"I don't like it, Tomás."

"I speak their language, don't I? And you're a goddam general in the Northern Division. Lower your rifle. I'll take care of everything."

He sighed, meaning that he would put his fate in my hands with a bare minimum of faith, and we trudged down the hillside through the brush. The soldiers waited for us on the riverbank. Their scout hats were lowered against the sun, and a few still bent to one knee with their rifles covering us. As we got closer, more showed themselves; they were at least twenty, and I saw their horses tethered downriver in the shade of some mesquite. They raised a red and white swallowtail pennant with two stars and a number eight, which I guessed meant the Eighth Cavalry. One of them, wearing whipcord breeches and high leather boots, lowered his dust goggles. I groaned, grasping Candelario's arm.

"What's the matter, Tomás?"

"I know the officer."

"But that's good!"

"No, it's not."

It was that damned Lieutenant Patton, the man who had restrained Miguel Bosques from shooting me on Stanton Street a year and a half ago. He stood apart from the others, tall and slim, legs planted wide on the earth, hand resting on the butt of his holstered pistol. His face was as tanned as a butternut. He was a fine-looking soldier; he just wasn't one I wanted to meet. There must have been half a dozen lieutenants out patrolling this part of the border between El Paso and Columbus . . . why did I have the luck to run into *him?* I had to do this the hard way, so I strode right up to him.

"Hello, Lieutenant. Real nice to see you again."

He squinted at me with the puzzled air of a man who knows a face but can't yet place it. Then he said, "Ahhh! . . ." and he nodded, sticking out his jaw. "Mix, isn't it? You're Captain Mix."

"Colonel Mix now, Lieutenant. And this is General Cervantes of the Mexican Army of the Convention. Also, commander of Francisco Villa's Dorados."

Everyone knew of the Dorados. Patton was a soldier, bred to discipline, and he couldn't help himself: he threw his right hand up in a brief, snappy salute. Candelario knew enough to return it, in a sloppy fashion, and I did the same. Patton dropped his hand and then raked us up and down with a critical glance. Candelario—one-eyed, black-bearded, scruffy as a ragpicker—clearly wasn't his idea of a general. And I knew what he thought of me.

"What's all this about, General?" he said in that high-pitched voice I remembered well.

"The general doesn't speak English." I stuck out my own jaw and planted my hands on my hips. "Let's back up. Godammit, I want to know why your men were shooting at us! You could have killed me!"

He looked at me in the same scornful manner I remembered from El Paso. "If we had wanted to kill you, Mix, we would have done it. My men fired warning shots. There are bandits on the border around here. We couldn't know that you were Villista officers."

He would have died before he called me "sir," or even "colonel," and what he really wanted to say was that as far as he was concerned the only good Mexican was a dead one; but he assumed from the angle of my jaw and the hoarseness of my voice that I was fighting mad . . . and he didn't yet know how many men we might have on the other side of the hill. Still, he wasn't taking any guff. That wasn't Patton's style.

"You're in United States territory, and I want to know what the hell for." He jerked a thumb over his shoulder, toward the border. "Your war's down there."

"Lieutenant," I said, "we have a wounded officer in our wagon. He has a broken ankle, and fever. We were north of Ascensión when it happened. The nearest surgeon's in El Paso."

Julio had appeared over the crest of the hill with the wagon and our horses.

"Why didn't you take him to Juárez?" Patton asked.

"The Carranzistas hold it. If we went to Juárez, our officer would lose more than his leg. And he'd have company."

"How large a force are you?"

I waved in Julio's direction. "What you see."

"Let's have a look at this man," Patton said, when the wagon jolted closer. He treated me as if he were the colonel and I were the lieutenant. He strode over, shot a quick look at Julio and then peered in at Fierro, who was awake, propped up on one elbow and glaring at the soldiers. Fierro kept one hand under his serape, and I knew the finger would be wrapped around the trigger of his pistol. But he kept his mouth shut. His face was white except for a high flush on the cheekbones. His forehead glistened with sweat. The ankle was dark purple and swollen to the size of the calf.

Patton's eyes locked with his. Then he turned to me. "What are the names of these two men?"

"Colonel Cárdenas and . . . the wounded man is Captain García."

He nodded. "The man's obviously a soldier, and he'll lose his leg if you don't get him to a doctor. I'll send a detail downriver with you to El Paso. If you try any monkey business, they'll be under orders to shoot."

I couldn't figure him out. He was doing the right thing in the wrong spirit. "Take it easy," I said. "You're not at war with us. The last time I met Black Jack Pershing he took me and Pancho Villa to a baseball game, and then we had pineapple upside-down cake at General Scott's."

He stared at me for a while, then smiled as if something had only just come clear to him. "When did you last see a newspaper, Mix?"

"Is there news?" I asked uneasily.

"Sober up and listen." His smile faded. "Mr. Wilson finally made up his mind. Four days ago, the United States recognized the Carranza government—which means that for Mr. Wilson, and for General Pershing, and for me, Venustiano Carranza is the legitimate President of Mexico. Which also means that Pancho Villa is now nothing but a goddam outlaw. He's had his last shipment of rifles and his last pineapple upside-down cake at General Scott's. As for the rest of you people, you're all officers in an illegal revolutionary army. That army is the enemy of a duly constituted government recognized by the United States. You hang around in this country after you've delivered your man to the doctor in El Paso, and we'll hand you over to the Carranzista authorities in Juárez. In your particular case," he said, "it will be a special pleasure. Your purpose is humane or I'd do it right now. I'll give you and your gang of pirates forty-eight hours. Then get your ass across the border. And don't come back."

We reached El Paso at dusk, the soldiers trotting along behind us under the command of a tight-lipped Apache scout named Sergeant

Chicken. After I told Julio and Candelario what Patton had told me, there was no more to say. Carranza, in the eyes of the United States, was President of Mexico. We were outlaws. No news could have depressed me more, other than the death of the chief. I wondered if he knew. Even if he licked the Carranzista force at Agua Prieta, he couldn't use Douglas as a port of entry. The Americans would supply Obregón, and we would be back where we were two and a half years ago in the desert of Chihuahua, having to steal every bullet and tortilla. It just didn't seem possible . . . but I knew Patton wasn't lying.

Sergeant Chicken's orders were to let us go when we reached the city limits. We crossed into Texas over the Borderland Bridge, and the Apache scout watched us disappear down North Mesa Street. There were a few El Pasoans sauntering along the sidewalks in the cool evening air, but when we came clopping into view they ducked into the nearest doorway or behind parked cars. I couldn't blame them—we were a ragged, barbarous trio, and Rodolfo's face, peering up over the sideboard of the wagon, looked like the joker's in a pack of cards.

We brought him straight to Hipólito's house, and I pounded on the door. Hipólito came out, jowly and red-eyed, wearing an undershirt, his paunch hanging over baggy duck trousers. He didn't look like the man I had known.

"Tomás! But this is good! And these other two! *Madre de Diós!* It must be Christmas! What do you bring me, a wagonload of pulque?"

"A wagonload of Rodolfo Fierro."

An hour later Fierro was in a dimly lit little hospital on Third Street in Little Chihuahua. The doctor said he could save the leg; gangrene hadn't yet appeared. There was nothing we could do after that except go back to Montana Street, where Mabel Silva brewed coffee and fried some chickens, and Hipólito told us all he knew.

A conference on the so-called "Mexican problem" had been held in Washington, attended by the foreign ministers of all interested parties. Carranza's envoys hadn't been invited, but they came anyway and hung around to assure the delegates that Don Venus would guarantee the property rights of foreigners under his new regime. It sounded like Porfirio Díaz all over again. The only one who raised any fuss was General Hugh Scott, but no one listened. Felipe Angeles had never managed an interview with President Wilson. The American people were fed up with the Mexican rumbling and more interested in who was slaughtering whom in Europe.

On October 19 Wilson recognized Carranza as the de facto leader of his country. Patton was right. With the stroke of a pen, we had all been made outlaws.

"It's what Wilson always wanted to do," Hipólito said, "ever since my brother murdered that Englishman. But naturally, being a politician, he couldn't do it as long as Pancho looked to be the next president. After our garrison surrendered in Juárez, he could see that the tide had turned for good . . . at least, that's what he thinks. Don Venus is back in the capital. Obregón controls the rest of the country. What's left to us? A few pueblos, just like the old days." He hawked, spat neatly into a brass cuspidor, then turned to Candelario. "What are our chances in Sonora? Don't lie to me . . . not too much, anyway. I need some good news."

"We hold the Púlpito," Candelario declared. "We've got nearly nine thousand men. If we win at Agua Prieta, we'll take all of Sonora. You know your brother—he'll never give up. He always has a plan." Candelario's tone turned a little cruel. "What are you worried about? You're not going to fight . . . you haven't fought in a year. You've lost your casinos, but you must be a rich man by now. Enjoy your good life here in Texas."

Hipólito's face darkened at the insult. But then a sheepish smile spread over his pudgy features.

"If that were true," he said, "we'd be drinking champagne instead of tequila. I made a lot of money but I gambled too often at Touché's."

"I thought the wheel was rigged," Candelario said, perplexed. "Couldn't you read the marks on your own cards?"

"Pancho said the purpose of the revolution was to correct such abuses." Hipólito laughed. "I did, and the house percentage killed me. I'll go to Sonora with you and fight."

Candelario embraced him. All was forgiven, and all was well again.

"The problem is supplies," Hipólito said gloomily. "No more bullets. No coal."

I thought fleetingly of Franz von Papen, wondering if Villa was doing the same. Then I said, "We'll have to see Sam Ravel and Felix, if he's still in business. They'll figure a way to get things across the border. They always did."

Hipólito looked even gloomier. "Tomás, I thought you knew. Felix died last April. And Ravel switched sides. He's supplying Obregón."

We were all depressed, but that night on the porch of Hipólito's house, after we let the air out of a second tequila bottle, Candelario announced that he was leaving for Columbus early the next morning. "I'm going to find Marie-Thérèse and marry her," he said drunkenly. "Yvette, too, if she's willing."

"You're married already," I reminded him.

"If the chief can have three wives, why can't I? There must be some privileges that go with being a general."

I pointed out that the girls would probably never leave the United States for Mexico.

"Then I'll stay here," Candelario decided. "This crazy lieutenant won't find us. I'll shave off my beard. I speak a few words of English, and I can learn the rest—I'm just as smart as Rosa. I like the United States. I like the movies. I'll get a job on a ranch. Or I'll open a restaurant. I have some money put away somewhere," he said, leering.

"I'll be your partner," Julio said glumly, snatching the bottle. "Hipólito, stay with us. You're too fat to fight. You'll just get killed in Sonora."

Hipólito rubbed his belly. "I could lose weight."

"You'll lose plenty," said Candelario, "when you're lying dead in a well. You can be a waiter in my restaurant."

"Mabel doesn't want me to fight, either."

"So that settles it." Candelario uncorked yet another bottle, took a swig and passed it to Julio. "We're retired. We'll all get fat and rich. If you're not rich, Tomás, if you can't get a job as an actor, you can always get a free meal at my restaurant. This is a wonderful idea. Why didn't we think of it before?"

"Because you were never so drunk before," I said.

"Are you serious? I've been drunk for a year, at least between battles. What else is there to do in life except fight and fuck and drink?" He peered at me carefully, as if he saw me through a haze—which was probable. "What are you trying to say, Tomás?"

"That I'm going to Sonora."

"To fight?"

"Well, not to fuck and drink."

"You believe this lieutenant will really come after you if you stay here?"

"That's not it. I haven't given up. Neither has the chief. So what if Carranza's president? Huerta was president before him, and we licked Huerta. The revolution's not dead . . . it can't die as long as Pancho Villa lives."

"Jesus," Candelario muttered to the others. "He's become more Mexican than the rest of us."

"No," I said, "I just remember why I joined up with you idiots in the first place. Anyway, the second place. And that hasn't changed."

But the next morning before the rest of us were awake, Candelario left on the train for Columbus. After we had thrown buckets of water over our heads to cure the worst part of our hangovers, Julio, Hipólito and I went to the hospital on Third Street to see how Fierro was doing. The doctor told us he had saved the leg, and he thought the bone would heal well enough so that Rodolfo could walk and ride without any trouble. Then I went to Sam Ravel's office in the Toltec Building. I had to try and talk him out of switching sides.

I had a garden of reasons, and I plucked them out one by one, weeds and all, and slung them across his desk. But Sam just tapped his fingers impatiently.

"Things change, Tom. That's something you've got to realize . . . for your own sake."

"Why? What do you want me to do?"

"Villa hasn't won a battle since before the convention. He's finished. Can't you see it?"

"Not if he can get arms. The people will always be with him. And he's the only one who really gives a damn about the people."

"That's how Hannah used to talk when she was a kid. Tom, wake up! The people backed Villa when they thought he was a hero, when they believed he could win something for them. Now they see he has feet of clay. He's lost! Not even the *campesinos* will support him after this. I'm not supplying Obregón because I think he's any better than Villa . . . I'm doing it because he and Carranza are the only ones left who can lead Mexico out of its bloodbath. You're an intelligent man, and you've got a future. Don't turn your back on it. I need you in Columbus, and that offer I made to you still goes, no matter what happened between you and Hannah. You should take it."

I felt no small irritation at his quick change of sides—even if he had what he considered a decent reason—and even more at the fact that he thought I would go along with him.

"You want me to work for you against Villa? No, Sam . . . if that's waking up, I'll stay asleep."

"But you were going to quit last December! You were going to marry Hannah after the new year! What the hell ever happened to make you stay down there?"

"I got more involved," I said, keeping it simple.

"And you don't even ask about Hannah."

I couldn't explain all that to him. Besides, I had already heard from Hipólito that she was well and thriving, and that my fleeing to Mexico hadn't ruined her life or driven her to a convent. I may not have loved Hannah anymore, but I respected her ability to survive and track down whatever it was she wanted in life.

"Will you see her?" Sam asked.

"I don't want to play games," I said. "It's over between us."

"She talks about you an awful lot. If you wanted . . ."

"I don't want."

We shook hands, even though he was going to supply bullets to men who would try to kill me with them. I suppose he didn't think of it that way, if at all.

"If you change your mind, Tom, let me know."

"I won't. Take care now."

"I'm sorry about all this."

"Well, business is business, as they say."

His handsome smile faded a bit at that. I regretted the remark right away—we had been through a lot together, horse-trading and jawing over bottles of brandy and cigars. I had always respected the man, and he had helped to save my life by the Stanton Street Bridge. But I didn't apologize. There are some things you can't do and still lock eyes each morning with that fellow in the shaving mirror. I had started to get a glimmer that when things busted apart at the seams, what kept you whole inside your own skin was a blind—some would say senseless—loyalty to the people who counted on it. There certainly wasn't much else that lasted.

When I woke early the next morning, I heard Candelario's raucous voice. I pulled on my boots and stomped into the front room. He was drinking coffee with Julio, and their blanket rolls, saddlebags and rifles were piled by the door. Julio was stuffing cartridge boxes among the socks and shirts in his war bag. Mabel Silva was in the kitchen. I smelled eggs frying in butter.

"What's going on?"

"Ah, Tomás!" Candelario sighed. "When did the course of true love ever run smooth? I found them at Doña Margarita's whorehouse. They say business has picked up—the cavalry has been reinforced at Camp Furlong. Yvette looks well, although Marie Thérèse has grown a little too thin. We spent a pleasant night. I fucked them both, vigorously. But they both declined the pleasure of marrying me, and they won't come to Sonora. They seem to have lost faith in the chief's future. They send their love and many kisses. Do you want them from me, or do you take my word for it?" He grinned, showing his broken teeth.

I pointed to the blanket rolls. "What are you doing now?"

"The train for Arizona leaves in an hour. Hipólito's gone to the bank to get the rest of his money."

"I thought you were all staying in Texas."

"Amigo, we were drunk—didn't you know that? It sounded like a good idea at the time. And how could we let you go alone? Besides, none of us are good for anything but fighting."

"You drink pretty well too," I said.

"I fuck even better. Not that it does me much good."

"You had me scared the other night," I admitted.

"You? Scared? That's hard to believe, my friend. Doubting, yes. Scared, never. I know you too well."

We stabled the horses, piled into Hipólito's Cadillac and bumped across town in the sunshine to the railroad station. When we got near it, turning into Dallas Street, we heard the rumble of horses' hoofs on pavement and the dragging of boots. Hipólito hit the brakes.

"What's *that?*" Candelario muttered.

The cross street was blocked by policemen and wooden barricades. Beyond them a mass of Mexican soldiers marched in ragged formation toward the station; they wore sombreros and cartridge belts and carried the usual varied assortment of rifles, and they were singing "La Cucaracha." A crowd had gathered. The clop of hoofs grew louder, and when we looked beyond the soldiers we saw hundreds of horses and mules being herded down Wyoming Avenue toward the staging yards. Vaqueros were cracking bullwhips; horseshit steamed on glistening tar. I couldn't count the men, but within our view there must have been at least a battalion.

"Who are they?" Julio murmured.

"How should I know?" Candelario scratched his beard so vigorously I thought he had discovered a nest of fleas. "Let's ask. Tomás, you go. Speak English. Be clever."

Quickly I jumped out of the car and trotted up to the nearest barricade. A red-faced copper in a blue uniform stood there, waving his billy at the crowd to keep them in check.

"Are we being invaded?" I asked. "Which one is Pancho Villa? How come the army's letting these chiles march through town?"

"Uncle Sam's orders, lad. A free ride for them on the El Paso & Southwestern."

"But who are they?"

The Mexicans, he explained, were part of a brigade under the command of a General Manzo, who fought for Carranza. I must have looked horrified. "It's all right," he said. "Carranza is President of Mexico." The soldiers were headed for Arizona, where they would cross the border to reinforce the town of Agua Prieta. "Pancho Villa's going to attack it, see? They're running an excursion train to Douglas this afternoon so the folks can watch. Got any plans? You should go. It'll be a hell of a fight! You'll never see anything like it again."

Maybe not. But I understood now. Obregón had been unable to send men westward on the Mexican side of the border—Villa had succeeded in blocking the passes. So Carranza had prevailed on Wilson to use a simpler route: through the United States on the El Paso & Southwestern. Villa, unless he knew, was riding into a trap.

I went back to the car and told the others. Candelario shouted, "This Wilson goes too far!"

"We can't get on that train," Julio groaned. "Someone will recognize us."

In a vision, the idea came to me, the idea that would sink me and seal my fate. I blurted to Hipólito, "Can you get hold of any dynamite?"

"Probably. What are you thinking?"

"We can dynamite the tracks between here and Douglas."

"Tomás! That's brilliant!" Candelario whacked me on the shoulder. "But why the tracks? Let's blow up the train!"

"You clown, there are Americans on board. We'll just do the tracks."

"Do you know anything about dynamite, Tomás?"

"What is there to know? You light a match to the fuse."

/ 327

"Jesus," Candelario said, "who's the clown now? Dynamite is complicated stuff. We don't want to blow ourselves up. We want this to *work.*"

"We'll buy it at Heid Brothers," Hipólito suggested. "They'll tell us how to use it."

"Yes," I said, "explain to them that we want to blow up the El Paso & Southwestern."

We all looked at each other, nonplused.

"You three go to Heid Brothers," I decided. "Buy some wire and fuses. Plenty of dynamite too. Put it in the wagon, then get the horses and meet me back at Montana Street."

"Where are you going?" they asked.

"To see Rodolfo. I have an idea."

I took a taxicab to Third Street and found Rodolfo sitting on the edge of his bed in the hospital ward, fully dressed except for his boots, his ankle in a cast, and looking grim.

"What's the matter?" I asked.

"I don't like it here," he said. "I'm bored."

"Well, I've got a problem. This might perk you up." I had remembered that he was an expert with explosives—he had blown up the tracks at Tierra Blanca to keep the Federals from getting too close to Juárez. I told him quickly what we planned to do. He listened carefully, eyes averted, while he stroked his black mustache.

"It can be done," he said, when I had finished. "It's very simple, if you know how."

"Then tell me."

"What kind of dynamite did you tell Hipólito to buy? White powder? Frozen? Nobel's or Pyrolith?"

"What?"

"Tomás, they're all different. Different density, different blasting caps. Dynamite contains nitroglycerin. Out in the desert, where it's hot, it can explode before you're ready to have it explode. Did you tell Hipólito to buy slow or fast match fuse?"

I shook my head slowly.

Rodolfo sighed and said, "Hand me one of my boots. Let me lean on you."

"What are you doing?"

"Coming with you."

"You can't ride, Rodolfo."

"Why not? It may be uncomfortable, but I can do it. It's better than sitting around here all day. I can be back by nightfall if we don't go too far."

"What will the doctor say?"

"Fuck the doctor."

He had grit, no doubt of that. He leaned heavily on me, one arm thrown over my shoulder, and we got outside to the street where I had kept the taxicab waiting. He clamped his teeth shut and held tight.

An hour later, with a wagonload of dynamite, we all trotted out of town. Rodolfo's foot in its plaster cast dangled awkwardly out of the stirrup. He never complained. I despised the man, but still I had to admire him. We kept an eye out for Lieutenant Patton and any other cavalry that might be patrolling the border, but no one crossed our path. The empty desert stretched along the railroad line south of the river, the long yellow ridges wavering in the heat. The sun burned fiercely down. This was part of me: the naked desert, the drumming of hoofs, light flashing off lifted rifles, even the tightness in my chest. The crisp air filled my lungs, and if we hadn't cautioned ourselves to silence I would have let out a war whoop.

We picked a desolate spot west of Hot Wells, and Rodolfo showed us how to plant the dynamite at intervals on a hundred-yard stretch of roadbed. We set the caps, connected a length of fast fuse and payed it out fifty yards to a spot behind a little hillock of chaparral. After we had tethered the horses to some mesquites, Julio lit a cigarette and touched it to the fuse. It sizzled, then caught and set off, writhing like a snake, in the direction of the tracks. We all hunkered down and stuffed our thumbs in our ears.

There was a marvelous loud bang—then, in rapid succession, three more. Dust and chips of steel flew over our heads. We ran back, shouting with glee. There was certainly no more need to keep quiet.

The railbed looked as if it had been shelled by artillery, and the rails themselves were torn apart like twisted paper clips. Smoke drifted southward on the afternoon breeze. Candelario was jumping up and down with pleasure and clapping Julio on the back.

"Let's stay," he said, when he calmed down. "I want to see the faces of those Carranzista bastards when they get off the train."

"What if they see *our* faces?" I asked.

"We'll be behind the hill. And they'll think whoever did it was long gone."

They were as excited as children at the prospect of fireworks on the Fourth of July. The best I could do was talk them into rolling some dead trees out on the tracks and piling them about fifty yards ahead of the wreckage, so that the engineer could slow down in time and not get himself killed.

The train came clacking along at about two o'clock in the hot afternoon—a long train, maybe seventy or eighty cars, most of them open and filled with men and horses and cannon.

"Watch!" cried Candelario. "Just watch!"

The engineer spotted the trees and ripped track in plenty of time.

The wheels screeched and threw off red sparks; the whistle screamed and blew puffs of white smoke into the blue sky. It was very colorful, very beautiful. The train stopped, and the engineer and brakeman hopped out of the cab with two Mexican officers. They all bent to the tracks, shaking their heads and tugging at their mustaches.

"One of those has got to be a general," Candelario whispered passionately. "We could pick them off before they knew what hit them."

I clamped a hand on the barrel of his rifle and glared at him.

"All right, Tomás. All right . . ."

The engineers and Mexican officers were soon joined by a handful of American officers in khaki and whipcord, all of whom studied the damage and jabbered back and forth for a good ten minutes. They didn't have a repair crew aboard. Jesse James was long dead; no one blew up railroad tracks anymore in the United States. They stared around into the desert, but our cover was good and the horses were even farther out of sight. One of the Americans walked back to the first open railroad car. I saw then what I had missed before—the gondola was filled with horses and men of the U. S. Cavalry from Fort Bliss. The gate fell down with a thin bang, and the cavalry came tumbling out—about forty of them, mounted and armed, wheeling in the sand. I recognized Lieutenant Patton on a brown roan.

"I think we'd better get out of here," Candelario said.

Crouched low, we scurried back to the horses, boots kicking up little puffs of dust, spurs jingling in the silent afternoon. We were still out of sight, but we wouldn't be for long.

"Leave the wagon!" I shouted. We helped Rodolfo to mount. The five of us settled into the saddles and galloped away into the desert. It didn't take a genius to figure out there was only one safe direction: northwest. The train lay southeast of us. Beyond that was El Paso. I looked back over my shoulder. The cavalry had spotted us—a soldier was waving and yelling, although I couldn't hear his voice. I heard the bugle, though, braying a clear, sweet call, not the kind I was used to hearing down in Torréon and Celaya. This fellow had had some music lessons.

The desert of Dona Ana County lay ahead of us for twenty miles. Beyond it we could see Mount Riley and the blue haze of the Potrillo Mountains. Our horses were still fresh and the cavalry would never catch us . . . if we kept going in that direction. Maximilian thundered over a burning river of sand. Once we were safe in the Potrillos, I realized, we could bend around to the southwest into Luna County, turn south of Florida Peak and point ourselves toward the Arizona border.

What we couldn't do was head back east toward Texas . . . not if we didn't want to fight a losing battle against Patton and the Eighth Cavalry. And if Patton had seen me, I could *never* go back. I had committed a crime on U. S. soil against U. S. property. I was a fugitive now from my own country.

Part Three

The Yanks are coming,
The Yanks are coming,
The drums rum-tumming everywhere . . .

—"Over There"

29

**"His bruisèd helmet
and his bended sword."**

I never claimed to be a historian of the Mexican Revolution. Men and
events passed before my eyes. What other things happened, or were
supposed to have happened (according to the history books and newspaper accounts I've read), were things I only heard about, then and
later.

But I was there. I saw; I listened. If anyone can tell me otherwise,
let him speak. Let him say, "No, señor, you were deaf and blind. It
couldn't be as you say. It was *this* way." But I can only tell what I know,
from the time I volunteered as a revolutionist to the time—three years
later, to the day—that I switched sides and joined the United States
Cavalry to hunt down Pancho Villa.

After we dynamited the railroad tracks to delay Manzo's brigade,
we outdistanced the cavalry with ease. For a few days, fearing that they
would have patrols farther south to seal off the border, we camped by a
little stream in the foothills of Mount Riley. Fierro rested his ankle.
Julio shot a deer and we skinned it, ate venison steaks and cured the rest
in the sun. We rode back one evening toward the southeast and saw the
red glow of soldiers' campfires down by the river.

Candelario coughed politely. "It's my fault, Tomás. If I hadn't
wanted to see them get off the train, this wouldn't have happened. I
didn't think."

"You're not the only one." The price for blowing up the railroad, I
reckoned, would be ten years in Yuma Prison.

"Well, it's pleasant in the mountains. The air is good for the lungs. I
wish we had some women with us . . . but life is rarely perfect."

"Really? I'll try to remember that."

A week later we skirted Big Hatchet Peak and crossed the Pyramid
Range. We reached Douglas, on the border between Arizona and
Sonora, on November 5, 1915, two days after the battle of Agua Prieta.
Out in the desert, Indian women were still stripping the dead. I took off

my sombrero and cartridge belts and rode into town to find out what had happened. Everyone in Douglas seemed to know a few details and was happy to tell the tale, and the rest we learned later.

The day after we blew up the tracks a repair gang had swarmed out from El Paso, so that within seventy-two hours the trainload of Carranzistas reached Douglas and the brigade was able to cross the border to Agua Prieta. But our effort was wasted—down in Sonora the main body of the Northern Division became trapped in the Púlpito. The gorges split open in flood, carrying men and horses to an icy death. Frostbite crippled thousands. It took Villa nearly a month to put things right. Then, having lost all element of surprise, he still attacked Agua Prieta. He could approach it only from the south over a flat plain, densely barricaded with barbed wire twenty feet thick, and then a stretch of desert that was sown with land mines—a nasty welcome. The Division left three hundred men and their horses on the wire, and those who got through had their legs blown off and whimpered for mercy. That night, determined to attack—for he had been born to do it, as he had told Felipe Angeles—Villa cleverly sent burros and mules ahead of his sappers to detonate the mines. The brigades advanced cautiously behind them and got through. But at one o'clock in the morning, as the men surged forward through the craters among the afternoon's dead, the plain was flooded with yellow light. Three giant searchlights on the parapets of the town blazed across the battlefield, sweeping in enormous arcs. Bullets and cannon shells followed their beams. The blinded Villistas shook their fists helplessly and died. From the rooftops of Douglas the trainloads of sightseers, shivering in the night air, raised a cheer . . . then they emptied their flasks of whiskey.

That was the last attack. Villa's lips foamed with curses at the gringos. By then he knew about the brigade that had crossed U. S. territory. And where had the searchlights come from, if not Douglas?

A week after Agua Prieta, like a bull bleeding from the lance of the picador, he threw the remainder of his crippled force against the Carranzista garrison at Hermosillo, the capital of Sonora. The Division was nearly wiped out. After the battle, two thousand men deserted. No one knew how many men Villa had left. No one even knew if he were alive.

We picked a lonely stretch of desert west of Douglas and jumped across into Mexico. For more than a month we wandered around under a blazing sun like four lost members of the Israelite tribe in Sinai, asking any lone *campesino* we met if he had seen anything of Pancho Villa. The pueblos were empty—ovens cold, water tanks dry. We heard rumors of a battalion camped somewhere in the desert but found nothing but bodies ravished by buzzards and skulls turning white in the desert sun. It was one of the awful times of my life. The days ran on endlessly. There seemed no purpose to them other than hunting for a moribund army, whose remains—or graves—we were almost afraid to find.

Come Christmas (according to the days I had scratched off on a page of my notebook), we camped on the banks of the San Pedro River, a trickle running north toward the Arizona border. Candelario wakened me at first light with a present of two hardboiled eggs. In return I gave him my last box of safety matches.

"No, Tomás, I can't take it. Half will do."

"Leave me one. I've only got tobacco for one more cigarette."

Why go on? I thought again of Rosa waiting for me. And Elisa.

"This makes no sense," I told the others. "We'll never find the chief. And even if we do—what then? The war is lost."

"My brother will have a plan," said Hipólito. "He always does."

"Tomás is right," said Julio. "It makes no sense." He turned to me. "What should we do?"

"Go home."

"Yes, we can do that. But what about you? You can't go to Texas now."

"I'm going to Parral," I said.

"I can't go home, either," said Candelario. "And not you, Julio. Not any of you." He spoke quietly to the others. "If the war is lost, if Obregón and Carranza have won, the first place they'll look for us will be at our homes. They'll come to find all the officers who fought for Pancho Villa, the ones who might lead the next revolution. I'm a general now. You three are colonels. For Christ's sake, Hipólito, you're Pancho's brother."

Julio scratched his dusty head. Hipólito and Fierro said nothing.

"You have the only chance, Tomás," Candelario said. "No one knows you in Parral except the Griensen woman. Maybe we should all go there."

"Let's keep looking for Pancho," Hipólito begged. "One more week, until the new year."

The others agreed, and so did I.

Later that morning, east of the river, we saw a layer of dust on the horizon. Soon the sun glinted off bayonets and bridles. A score of men rode toward us, wearing khaki rags and faded scout hats. Half-empty cartridge belts were strapped across their bony chests.

"Who are you?" one of them called.

"Don't answer," Candelario cautioned. He called back, "Who are *you?*"

"The Northern Division," the man yelled, seeing that they outnumbered us. "We fight for Pancho Villa!"

"So did we," muttered Candelario, under his breath, "when we were younger." We put our knees into our horses' flanks and galloped into the camp.

There were five hundred gaunt and silent men there. The chief gave a faint murmur of joy. "I thought you were all dead. . . ."

/ 335

Candelario grinned through a mask of dust. "They can't kill a one-eyed man. And Tomás is so clever—even the bullets salute him before they fly the other way."

The chief wiped his eyes with one sleeve while we told him where we had been and all that we had done. An hour later Franz von Papen rode into the camp from the direction of Nogales. The patrol that had found us had been looking for him. He and Villa had made a Christmas appointment in the desert of Sonora.

A daytime moon curved low in the sky. A thrush sang in an ash tree. Ragged men with bronzed faces and ivory teeth walked slowly to and fro, leading their horses to the river. Pancho Villa sat cross-legged, an old Marlin rifle in his lap, listening to Franz von Papen's insistent voice. The chief was gravely occupied in killing the fleas in his shirt. The ash trees, with their dark green crests, kept the desert sun from beating us into the earth.

Villa pinched the last flea between thumbnail and finger. Von Papen pulled his tortoiseshell comb from the pocket of his herringbone jacket and began to curry his mustache . . . again.

"General Villa, I don't know what more to say to you. You have nothing, and I offer you everything. But mostly, I offer you irrefutable logic. We Germans are your friends. The Americans have proved that they are your enemies."

I translated, as I had been doing all day.

"Captain," Villa said, sighing, "there's just one thing I don't understand. Well, no, there are many . . . but this one comes most readily to my mind. If you Germans are our friends, then why did your Colonel Kloss teach Obregón to flood the trenches at Celaya? Why does Obregón use German cannon? And why did your Major von Hesse advise the Carranzistas to plant a minefield in front of Agua Prieta, which killed so many of my men?"

"Who told you this, sir?"

"General Scott. Last week in Nogales."

"And you believe him?"

"Scott has never lied to me."

"There's a first time for everything, General Villa. And even if it's true, you must realize that there are good Germans and bad Germans. There are factions in our country, just as there are in yours."

"I'm hungry," Villa said. "Let's eat dinner. Would you like some tacos?"

"With pleasure. But without chile, please."

"Without chile? Señor, in Mexico you might as well ask for a desert without rocks, a summer without rain . . . and a general without fleas."

After lunch and a short siesta, the discussion resumed in the shade of the ash trees. Hens cackled in the huts, and a few soldiers, taking advantage of the same shade, snored like trombones. Von Papen repeated all his arguments, even to the point of a discourse about the monkey men of Japan who were slavering at the mouth when they thought of invading the United States from Mexico.

"Well, I don't like them, either," Villa said. "I can't tell them apart from Chinamen, for whom I have no use at all. In fact, when I think of it, I don't like any foreigners who come so far to stir up trouble. Mexico is a pot with too many spoons."

I translated this faithfully, and Von Papen frowned. "General Villa, an attack on Columbus would cost you little. It could win you everything. And you need to win *something*, I think. May I ask how many men you now have under your command?"

"I have five hundred loyal soldiers in this camp," the chief replied. "Throughout Mexico, a hundred thousand. They only wait to hear my bugle, and then they will rise."

"But you have no arms. No money."

"I have gold."

"Your men wear rags."

"That doesn't stop them from shooting straight."

"Then shoot, señor. Shoot your enemies."

"I've half a mind to shoot *you*," Villa said, "and send your head to Colonel Kloss as a Christmas present."

Von Papen's gentle smile seemed to ascribe the threat to a quaint Mexican sense of humor. I was more pleased than disturbed—it meant the chief was feeling more like his old self. Just then he sprang from his crouch and tossed away his cigarette. "Captain," he said, "I'm going to confer for a few minutes with your old friend, Colonel Mix. Then I'll give you my decision."

Von Papen saluted. Villa and I withdrew to the shade of another tree. A mangy dog was sleeping there, but a hard nudge from Villa's boot sent it slinking away.

"Tomás, what do you think?"

"Chief, I'm a gringo. The last thing I want is for you to go pumping bullets into Columbus. Aside from my personal feelings, Pershing would come after your scalp and hang it from the flagpole at Fort Bliss."

Villa chuckled. "He'd try, although he'd never catch me. Do you think I'd shoot Americans? I'd rob them, yes. I've already sent the Lopez brothers into Chihuahua to stop a mining train that's coming south from El Paso. But attack them? Why? Wilson, yes. I'd gladly hang him side by side with Carranza. No, I'm talking about this pantywaist German. Should I shoot him or not?"

"You were serious?"

"Didn't you hear him insult me? He said my men wore rags. He meant me too."

"But it's true. Look at us."

"Truth isn't at issue. It was an insult."

"If you shoot him, it will give the Germans an excuse to invade Mexico, or they'll get Wilson to do it for them."

"All right. I'll just kick his ass back to Nogales. Or I would, if my corns didn't hurt."

We walked leisurely back to where Von Papen waited in the shade of the ash tree, standing in the formal at-ease position, but the forward hunch of his shoulders betrayed his eagerness.

"Captain, I've made up my mind," Villa said. "I'm not going to shoot you—a decision I may regret, but I'll stick to it. For that you can thank Colonel Mix, as others have had reason to do in the past . . . or as they would have had reason," he sighed, "if I'd listened to him. As far as this other business goes, you're right. Except for Scott, the Americans are no longer my friends. But the devil you know is better than the devil you don't know, and I'll be damned if I'll let even one more ass-kissing, heel-clicking German into my Mexico."

Greatly relieved, I translated into English, although I left out the last part.

Von Papen frowned. "This decision is final, Colonel Mix?"

"Nothing in life is final, Captain, except the end of it. But if I were you, I wouldn't debate it anymore now. General Villa's corns are bothering him."

Von Papen saluted, clicked his heels and strode off through the dust to his waiting escort, a trio of Germans in civilian clothes and a pair of Yaqui guides. They mounted their horses and rode off at a trot toward the border.

A few days after my arrival a roaming company of our men under Ignacio García charged across the line at Nogales, shouted insults at the gringo troops, then let off a few exuberant shots well wide of the mark. Taking aim, the cavalry's sharpshooters dropped three men from their horses at five hundred yards. Ignacio, with awe in his voice, reported to the chief, "Señor, their bullets had eyes. . . ."

Then on January 19, in Chihuahua, the Lopez brothers fell upon a train full of gringo engineers heading south to one of the American-owned mines that Obregón had allowed to reopen. The Villistas barricaded the track at a place called Santa Ysabel. Seventy men swooped through the coaches, grabbing not only the $25,000 payroll but all the baggage and even the passengers' lunches. When the mining engineers protested, Pablo Lopez became angry and herded them outside. "Let's have some sport," he said to his men. "Let's kill gringos."

The eighteen engineers were lined up at ten paces. One of them, a man named Holmes, made a break for it. As bullets whistled round his head, he fell into the bushes near a dried-up riverbed, where he feigned death. Pablo gave a mercy shot in the head to the seventeen men lying by the tracks, and Holmes made his way back to El Paso and told the grisly tale. Villa protested his innocence.

"It's a tragedy," he said, in a message to Scott in Nogales. "Lopez and his brother exceeded their orders. If I find them, I'll shoot them."

But in El Paso a mob heading for Little Chihuahua had to be turned back by Pershing's troops, and martial law was declared along the border. By then we had moved across the Sonora desert to the pueblo of San Rafael, not far from a pass that led through the low sierra into Chihuahua. We were a hunted band of outlaws, a meandering heap of broad sombreros, dirty khaki, faded blankets and underfed horses. We certainly weren't an army that was going to retake Mexico, and I saw no sign yet of those hundred thousand men who were going to rise at the blast of a bugle. We had more desertions every day, and the chief finally told his officers they were free to leave if they wished. He announced that he would give Carranza six months to make good on his promises to the people. I wondered what that meant. Had he given up? Was it an admission that Obregón had licked him for good? He didn't say. As for me, I kept thinking of Rosa waiting for me in Parral at the Hacienda de Los Flores. Why was I wandering here when I should be headed there? I had been granted freedom of choice as well as the next man.

I bearded Villa one afternoon in a little adobe hut on the outskirts of San Rafael, which he had decided to call Divisional Headquarters. He was scribbling letters to the American generals on the border, still pleading his innocence and vowing death to the Lopez brothers. Outside the hut two Yaqui women were shelling corn, and some dark clouds had massed on the horizon.

"Chief," I said, "I think you should give up. Get some guarantees from Obregón and quit fighting. Hell, we're not even fighting. We're just hanging around."

A white flash of lightning ripped across the sky, and the roosters stopped crowing. Villa glowered. "I've given Carranza six months to get something done. When that time is up, if he's succeeded, we can think about guarantees."

"He's started land reform."

"A start is not a finish."

"The Chinese say that a journey of a thousand miles begins with a single step."

"Since when do you quote to me from Chinamen? I don't like the way you talk, Tomás. Every day you sound more like a gringo."

He wasn't friendly. He had been cankered and irascible ever since we had found him in the desert. It suited him even less than me to hang around doing nothing. It sapped the will and made a man feel useless.

He was used to power, and he had none; he got that power from attacking his enemies and building schools, and now all he did was issue denials. He folded his arms across his cartridge belts, and his yellow eyes, even in the shadows, glittered waspishly. More lightning crackled toward the horizon. The green lances of young corn rustled in the wind, fighting for life, and a dove wept far away in the dry riverbed.

"You're bored, Tomás. That's what's unsettled your mind. It's the same with me. Do you want to fight? Is that it?"

"I want to make a decent peace and get on with my life. So should you."

He ignored that. "We have only five hundred men, but we had less when we took Casas Grandes. We've got to make a start. Felipe's still in Washington. Once we fish our gold out of that lake and get it to him, he'll buy bullets and arms. What is it that Chinaman said? 'A journey of a thousand miles begins with a single step.' That's not bad, for a Chinaman."

"Our men are half-starved. And even if we had the bullets, who is there around here that we could fight?"

Villa took the cigarette I had built for him and slid it between his lips, then lit it from mine and puffed thoughtfully. "We'll find someone," he said.

30 "Be bloody, bold, and resolute."

from THE SCHOOLTEACHER'S JOURNAL

Culberson's Ranch, New Mexico
March 15, 1916

Early one morning I was having coffee with Lieutenant Patton in his office, prior to his drilling the troops and my going to work in the stables, where I help groom and feed the new Arabians that have come down from Oklahoma. The lieutenant was in one of his talkative moods, busily telling me how his father, after graduating military school in Virginia, almost joined Hicks Pasha's expedition to Egypt in 1877.

"Which was a damn good thing," he said. "I mean that he *didn't* do it. Because the expedition was wiped out. To the last man, Miguel! If he'd gone, hell, I wouldn't be alive today . . . sitting on my fat ass in this desert, hunting quail."

He went on then with his usual complaints about Mr. Wilson, and then to the subject of the weather, which grows hotter every day—and then his hay fever, which knows no season—and finally, for about the third time, the incident that happened last week with one of the men from the machine-gun platoon he had helped to train. I listened patiently, although now I knew most of the story by heart.

The lieutenant had been walking back from the polo field when he found a loose horse wandering across the parade ground, where a Curtiss Jenny was soon due to land, there being no other field. He marched down to the stables and discovered the name of the man responsible. After he found the culprit asleep on his bunk, he dressed him down in front of the men and told him to run down to the stable, tie the horse and then run back.

"Well, either he didn't understand or else he was just dead beat, and he started to walk. I got mad, and I yelled, 'Run, you lazy bastard! Goddam you, run!' Which he did, bet your boots. But then later in the day I got to thinking that it was an insult I'd put on him—everyone listening and all that—so I called him up before the other men who'd heard me swear, and I apologized. The thing is, I know now *why* I blew up at him that way." He slammed his riding crop into his palm. "Because I'm stagnating here! *Stagnating!*" His voice rose in its almost feminine squeal. "Down here on the border, godammit, you *drift*. And if a man like me starts to drift, he busies himself with all kinds of chickenshit details which may seem of moment, but they're not. And he's lost. . . ."

In such a mood, which is common with him, he veers back and forth between soliloquies about both present and past. He began castigating Mr. Wilson again—a man, he claims, who represents an ideal rather than a personality—and he compared the President to his grandfather. "He was a brigadier general. He commanded the advance guard in Earlie's raid on Washington, D.C., and his command was the only Southern force which ever camped within the city limits. He was killed at the battle of Opequon in 1864, but before that he could have taken Washington with just the Twenty-second Virginia Infantry . . . but he hesitated. Worried too much. Didn't do it. And he could have!"

The lieutenant's conclusion was that his grandfather didn't have the military mind in its highest form of development, because he was swayed by ideas of right or wrong rather than those of necessary strategic policy. A revealing statement, which he seemed about to amplify . . . when a bugle sounded. Not a clear call, but a strident, thrilling blast, as if the bugler didn't know what to blow but knew that some noise was necessary. An alarm, perhaps.

Lieutenant Patton dropped his pipe and snatched his gun belt, buckling it round his waist as he ran out the door. I peered after him into the hot sunlight, but the lieutenant was already out of sight, headed no doubt in the direction of the bugler. A motor ambulance stood by the post gate, its engine idling. A few mule-drawn escort wagons were pulled up behind it, and with them a troop of sweaty horses just back from branding at the remount depot. Officers and men were shouting and kicking up dust.

I waited nearly an hour for the lieutenant to return. When he did, his face was flushed a deep salmon-pink. His eyes were shining. He rubbed his hands together gleefully, like a man about to carve an exceptionally fine roast.

/ 341

"He did it, Miguel! That damned fool *did* it! Attacked Columbus last night! Killed five soldiers and a dozen civilians!"

"Who attacked Columbus?"

"Pancho Villa! Slocum beat him off at first light! Thirteenth Cav's going after him! *Ya—hoo!*"

It hardly seemed joyous news that nearly a score of people had been shot dead, but of course I understand Lieutenant Patton's jubilation. It heralded combat, and that was his dream. Pipe in hand, pacing the office, he told me what he knew. At four o'clock in the morning, after knifing the sentries on the border, Villa had struck at Columbus. The cavalry's rifles were under lock and key, the officer with the key nowhere to be found, so the men had to smash open the weapons locker with axes. One soldier in the stables killed a raider with a baseball bat, and the kitchen cooks defended themselves with pots of boiling water and cleavers. A dozen Mexicans were burned alive when the Commercial Hotel caught fire. The telephone operator in the Hoover Hotel, although her baby was clasped to her breast and she was struck in the face by flying glass, got through to Deming and summoned aid. The cavalry rallied and struck back. At dawn the Villistas fled, leaving a gutted town. Why had they done it? On Villa's part it seemed madness. Pablo Lopez and his brother, who had massacred the train at Santa Ysabel, had been recognized. Major Tompkins, with a troop of horses, set out in pursuit and penetrated fifteen miles into Mexico before he ran out of bullets.

"Tompkins claimed they killed a hundred of them! Do you realize—this is war! The big question is, will the Eighth Cav go?" Patton grew a shade paler. "If I don't go, I'll . . . why, I'll just die."

The rumor is that the army will send a force consisting of nine cavalry regiments, infantry, trucks, one regiment of mounted artillery and a troop of Apache scouts, and the First Aero Squadron. But some units will have to stay behind to guard the border. If that is the fate of his own Eighth Cavalry, Lieutenant Patton says he will resign his commission and raise polo ponies in Pasadena.

Luckily, the following day, he was Officer of the Day. He was smoking his pipe on the porch of the headquarters building after lunch when he learned that the Eighth Cavalry would definitely *not* go to Mexico. Despite the midday heat he rushed immediately to the regimental adjutant and asked to be recommended to General Pershing as an aide. Then, in a sweat, he flew across the compound to the major who has been appointed adjutant general of the expedition and repeated his request. Finally he buttonholed Lieutenant Shallenberger, his friend and one of Pershing's two regular aides-de-camp, begging him to put in a good word.

In the late afternoon, while he sat around sneezing and biting his nails, he was summoned to the general's office. Pershing was busy dealing with logistics and newspaper releases. He had no time for pleasantries.

"What's all this about, Lieutenant? I'm being hit from all sides about you."

"I want to go to Mexico, sir."

"So does every officer worth his salt." Pershing's bony face revealed no sympathy. He was a Missourian, and you had to show him. He was one of three officers in the history of the U. S. Army who had been promoted directly from captain to brigadier general—in his case by President Roosevelt. It wasn't favoritism; it was merit. "What exactly is so special about you," he asked Patton, "that you should receive consideration?"

"What's special," Patton blurted, "is that I want to go more than anyone else! Beyond that, sir, I'm a Distinguished Marksman, Master of the Sword in the whole army, and I know more about cavalry tactics than . . . well, I know a lot. I've learned some Spanish too—I mean more than just *buenas días*. And . . . and . . ." Here Patton saw that the general was unmoved by his plea, and was about to dismiss him and return to his paperwork and the ringing telephones; and here, in a fit of desperation, Patton's fateful idea came to him.

"There's something else, sir. Something special. I won't bore you now with the details, but I happen to be personally acquainted with a colonel on Villa's staff. He's an American, a renegade. Soldier-of-fortune type. A cold-blooded killer to boot. He was one of the Villistas who blew up the railroad last October. If I can make contact with this man—and I've got an idea how to do that—he could be of extraordinary use to us. He has no more morals than a rat, but I might be able to persuade him not to fight against his own kind."

Pershing grunted, shuffled the papers on his desk to one side and tented his thin, liver-spotted hands. "What's the man's name?"

"Mix. Colonel Mix. He's much too young to be colonel. He probably curried favor."

"Suffering catfish," Pershing said. "I know this fellow."

"You do?" Patton's mouth hung open.

"I met him here at the post, at General Scott's house. Villa was there too. Just after they took Juárez in 1913."

Patton remembered then that Mix had told him he had once had tea with the general. But he had not believed him.

"I see . . . Well . . . how do you judge the man, sir?"

"Young. Probably more competent than most. Idealistic. A bit simple-minded. Very close to Villa. Why do you say he's a cold-blooded killer?"

Patton quickly related the story of the massacre in the stockyards of Torreón.

"Good God . . ." Pershing shook his head sadly. The subject of wanton death was more than distasteful to him. Six months ago his wife and three daughters had been burned to death when their home in San Francisco caught fire. Only his small son survived. It had made the general melancholy and turned his already gray hair a yellowish white, but it was not a subject he would discuss.

"Do we want such a man working for us?" he asked Patton.

"Sir, it's war. We're going to be in a hostile country. No roads, poor maps,

/ 343

hardly any water for the first hundred miles. We'll lick them, but we've got to have good Intelligence. Well, you know that—you campaigned down there against Geronimo. I've studied that very carefully. I've also heard a tale that the Germans may be backing Villa, that they may have helped him organize this raid—start a diversionary second front that will keep us out of France. Now, I think—"

"That will do, Patton. I'll let you know."

The lieutenant hurried back to the stables and brought me with him to his office. He began to sneeze ferociously. Whenever he was nervous, not only did his voice rise but his hay fever attacked him. While he brewed tea he told me the story of his proposition to Pershing.

"What do you think, Miguel? Will you help me?"

"How can I do that?"

"If—lousy, rotten *if!*—if Pershing takes me along—and by God, he's got to!—I'll have to make good on this thing about Mix. The idea just came to me, bango, like that, but it's a first-rate one. Don't you understand? Even though the man's a swine, there's got to be a spark of patriotism in him. And if there's not, I'll pay him—out of my own money. What the hell else is it good for? That should do the trick, and he can give us the sort of information that might be worth millions. The problem is . . . I've got to reach him."

The lieutenant looked at me eagerly with his watery blue eyes. After another sneezing fit, he poured the tea into two white mugs and handed one to me.

"Here. It's Darjeeling. The best."

I stared at him. "You know that this man killed my brother. And two hundred other innocent men."

"Yes, I know that. War is hell, Sherman said. And it makes strange bedfellows."

I took a shaky breath. "If I ever found him, Lieutenant, I would kill him."

Patton disregarded me. "If Pershing makes me his aide," he said, "I'll need a striker. To take care of my horses, uniforms, brew tea, keep the tent neat. So you'd be part of the expedition. I can't reach Mix, but you can. And then you can bring him to me."

"Lieutenant . . . I can't."

"Look here, Miguel. I've got to say something straight—man to man. You owe me quite a lot, and you owe even more to the U. S. Army. We pulled you out of the desert, gave you a decent life, fixed up your arm. That was from the goodness of our hearts, because that's the American way, and you don't owe a goddam nickel to me or the army. But if you have a chance to pay that debt with service . . . well, you should damn well make an effort."

Face flushed, he waited for my answer. There was certainly reason in what he said, but he asked too much. For two years I had nurtured the thought of revenge in a way that the lieutenant, brought up to be a soldier and a good American, could but poorly understand.

"I'm grateful to you," I said. "And to the army. I might have the best of intentions, but if I came face to face with Major Mix, or the other one, Colonel Fierro, I don't think I could act reasonably."

"You're a grown man, Miguel!"

"I've made a vow to God, on the sacred memory of my brothers. I can't break it. If you feel I'm ungrateful and you dismiss me from my position, I'll understand. But I couldn't do what you ask."

Lieutenant Patton clenched his fists, not in anger but in frustration. He turned his back, paced the length of the office, glanced up at his medals and diplomas, then swung back to me.

"Would money change your mind?"

"I didn't hear you say that."

His cheeks flushed even more, and he came up to where I sat on the other side of his desk, my tea growing cold in the mug. He tried to lower his voice so that it didn't squeal as much as it had been doing.

"I have only one more way to ask you. That's to beg. And I'm doing it. My career's at stake. More than my career—my whole life. This is my last chance in the army."

I knew how hard it was for him to say that, and I was moved.

"Let me think about it, Lieutenant. You don't have to beg."

He threw the dice once more. This time he rolled a high number.

"When it's over—I mean if we get through to the man and he does what I ask him to do—you can do as you please. I won't interfere again, as I did on Stanton Street. You have my word as an officer."

At five o'clock the next morning the telephone rang in Lieutenant Patton's house up on Military Heights. General Pershing came directly on the line.

"Patton, how long will it take you to get ready?"

"Five minutes, sir. I packed last night."

"I'll tell you a brief tale," Pershing drawled. "In ninety-eight I was an instructor at the Point—a lieutenant. Policy had it that no instructors were to go to war. I applied through channels for an exception and was turned down flat. So I went AWOL to Washington, knocked on the door of the Secretary of War, who was a friend of my father-in-law, and got myself sent to Cuba. If you repeat that, I'll call you a liar. You'll be my aide-de-camp with Shallenberger. Be down here by seven o'clock."

That morning, Punitive Expedition Headquarters issued Special Orders Number Two, relieving Lieutenant Patton from duty with the Eighth Cavalry. Once again he rushed to the stables to find me.

"Will you come? I've got authority for a striker and two extra horses."

"If you put it that way, yes. You know I want to go."

"Then it's settled. That's dandy! That's really fine!"

He said nothing more about his plan to find Pancho Villa through Mix, and neither did I. Perhaps, I thought, he had given up the idea. It was certainly farfetched, and the more I considered it the more I realized that if ever I tried to ferret out the man in the wilds of Chihuahua, my own life would be at forfeit. Mix understood my intentions—if he were given the opportunity, why should he hesitate to still them forever? I would accompany the expedition because I wanted to be with the lieutenant. I felt linked to him now in a way that was difficult to fathom. It was almost as if we shared a destiny, and I didn't want to be left behind while he sought it. He was a man of great talent and enormous ambition. I confess, for all his singlemindedness, he fascinated me. He may have been a Johnny-One-Note, but so was I.

That morning he met with the general's other aides to divide their tasks. He loaded all the staff horses on the train that would take them to Columbus, and in the afternoon he coded telegrams with a major from the Intelligence unit. At dusk we all piled into several staff cars and drove to the railroad station. I had never been that close to General Pershing before. He paid no attention to me. I was the lowest of the low, an officer's servant.

By then we knew a great deal more about the raid on unsuspecting Columbus. Although he had denied it, it was assumed that Villa was wreaking vengeance on the United States for having recognized the Carranza government and helping to defeat him at Agua Prieta; and he had probably hoped to steal rifles and ammunition at Camp Furlong. Colonel Slocum now claimed that Villa had led the raid himself; the bandit general's burly form was easily recognizable. The rumors of German involvement continued; the names of a Colonel Kloss and a Captain von Papen were most often mentioned, but there was no hard evidence. In the fighting one hundred sixty-seven of Villa's soldiers were killed by the Americans' accurate fire. Most of the bodies were soaked in gasoline outside the town, then burned to char. Colonel Slocum was in some disfavor because he had disregarded a warning from some Mexican vaqueros that Villistas were camped only a few miles from the border. Major Tompkins, on the other hand, had already been recommended for the Medal of Honor for pursuing Villa into Chihuahua and receiving, in his words, "a slight wound in the knee, and a bullet through the rim of my hat." He described the accuracy of the Mexican gunfire as "remarkably atrocious."

The American people cried out for vengeance. The State Department, on orders from President Wilson, authorized the expedition immediately—"with the sole object of capturing Villa and preventing further raids by his band, and with scrupulous regard to the sovereignty of Mexico." Carranza telegraphed to Washington that he was in complete accord "if the raid effected at Columbus should unfortunately be repeated." In the heat of preparation, no one paid much attention to that careful wording. We were going to fight! Nothing else mattered.

Our train reached Columbus late at night. The town still smoldered, and the stench of burned flesh struck my nostrils. I had no desire to see the piles of dead; in Torreón I had seen enough for a lifetime. Lieutenant Patton, however, made an inspection by lamplight before he unloaded the general's baggage from the train. He then had to wait until five o'clock in the morning to get the horses off—Caterpillar tractors were being unloaded first, for grading the dirt roads of

Chihuahua. Then he collapsed for an hour in the barracks, where I had slept fitfully among a gaggle of snorers. I was not the only civilian. The army was so short of transport that it had advertised all over Texas and New Mexico for trucks, and in most cases hired their drivers and mechanics with them.

"It's a fourth-class army," Patton said to me bitterly, when he woke and leaped into his baggy khakis. "But this war will turn it into a first-class one. What a chance for the cavalry!" At that thought he brightened and rushed out shivering toward the mess hall for a cup of coffee and some toast. The night had been so cold that the water in our canteens had frozen.

The day grew warm and chaotic. Army units piled in from all directions— the Seventh Cavalry from Alamo Hueco and its machine-gun troop from Douglas; the Sixth Field Artillery from Fort Huachaca; a dozen others. Columbus was the main staging area, and from here the expedition would split into two forces. The Eastern Column of four thousand men, wagons and trucks, led by Colonel Dodd of the Second Cavalry, would strike south through the town of Ascensión to Casas Grandes. The Western Column under Pershing, with Patton accompanying him—nothing but cavalry and field artillery—would cross the border fifty miles westward at a place called Culberson's Ranch. Lacking the cumbersome wagons, we were expected to travel swiftly through the desert and hit Casas Grandes from the west. The idea was to catch Pancho Villa's army between the two forces.

At noon Lieutenant Patton received orders from Pershing to take two Fords and seven Signal Corps men and drive to a place called Los Cienagos, to pick up a Telefunken radio set which he was to deliver to Culberson's Ranch.

"Come along, Miguel!" he yelled, sweeping a bedroll under his arm.

The cars bounced over dry tracks through the desert, passing some motor ambulances and trucks en route, the Stars and Stripes flapping on every one of them. I wondered about Patton's words earlier that day, that it was a fourth-class army. Word had already reached us that Carranza was enraged at the nature of the expedition; we had been forbidden the use of all Mexican railroads. Villa was rumored to have less than a thousand men, and by the time our reserve reached us in Casas Grandes we would have more than ten thousand, plus cars, trucks, artillery, even airplanes. But the deserts and mountains of Chihuahua were Pancho Villa's home. He knew every adobe hut and stand of cactus, every cave and dry riverbed. Almost all of our soldiers, including Patton, had never seen combat . . . never seen the desert of Chihuahua. We picked up the radio and reached Culberson's Ranch shortly after eight o'clock. The Seventh Cavalry were already bivouacked in their pup tents; the Tenth were pounding tent pegs. It was very neat and orderly. I smelled the odor of five thousand horses picketed in long lines, feeding from bags of oats, snorting and stamping their feet in a darkness lit by hundreds of yellow lanterns. My fears were calmed. These were Americans—disciplined and organized, with almost unlimited resources. The men had proved at Columbus that they didn't panic under fire, and their own marksmanship was something that Villa could only barely comprehend. He would surely be punished for his madness.

We ate beans and hardtack in the Tenth Cavalry mess hall. Just as we finished, Lieutenant Shallenberger trotted in. He had arrived from Columbus with Pershing and the last of the Eleventh Cavalry.

"George . . . Black Jack wants to see you. On the double, at the ranch house. He says to bring your striker."

As we drove along the bumpy track through the camp in the darkness, I quietly asked the lieutenant why he thought the general wanted me along.

"Probably wants to talk about that idea I gave him." Patton touched a finger to his lips, meaning not to discuss the matter of Colonel Mix in front of Shallenberger.

The ranch house was the center of considerable activity: by the steady light of Coleman lamps, mules were being hitched in their traces to wagons which would follow the column, and a line of Quad trucks was being loaded with sacks of oats and hay for the horses. Inside the house oil lamps and candles cast harsh shadows. Shallenberger led us across the wooden porch and into the main room, decorated with the heads of buffalo, bear and elk. A blaze crackled in the huge fireplace.

General Pershing, flanked by two staff officers, sat at a desk, leaning forward in earnest conversation with a man seated opposite him. For a moment I didn't recognize him. He wore the dusty faded clothes of an American cowboy, he had dark unruly hair and the back of his neck was tanned like a walnut. After we entered, he turned. His face moved from shadow into light. His eyes flooded with worry and flicked back and forth between me and Lieutenant Patton.

It was Colonel Mix, whom I had last seen on Stanton Street as a major. My fingertips tingled, and I felt a chill run from the back of my neck down my spine.

Pershing returned Patton's salute. "Here's your man," he said, smiling frostily. "Showed up in Columbus just before we left. How about it, George? Do we shoot him or enlist him?"

Mix looked more than worried when he heard that. And Patton, for once, had no reply.

31 "And one man in his time plays many parts."

In March, Villa decided to go fishing for gold in Lake Ascensión. With it, Felipe Angeles could buy arms, and we could recruit a thousand more men and attack one of the border towns—not head-on, as he had done at Agua Prieta, and not with an army, but from the flanks, at night, unannounced.

"Juárez," he said thoughtfully. "I'm always lucky at Juárez. . . ."

We were trotting in a dusty column toward Ascensión, when a band of men under Ignacio García galloped out of the desert. They had been sent in an easterly direction as an advance patrol. At first, when he heard Ignacio's report of the raid on Columbus, Villa just threw back his head and guffawed.

"I don't believe it. Lopez probably got drunk and wandered across the border to shoot a cow. The gringos are very touchy these days, since those engineers were butchered."

"No, my general." Ignacio calmed his horse, still lathered with sweat. "It was a real battle. They say forty or fifty of their soldiers were killed. They say we lost two hundred men."

"We're here, aren't we? Do you see two hundred men missing?"

Ignacio looked around at the column straggling through the alkali haze. His lips began to move, as he began counting. Villa became impatient.

"Stop that, you fool. Tell me what you know and who told it to you."

Ignacio related what he had heard from two separate groups of Yaquis: that the raid on Columbus had taken place before dawn, that Villa had led it himself and that a regiment of U. S. Cavalry was riding into Chihuahua to bring him back, dead or alive.

"And how long ago did I do this thing?" Villa asked, astonished.

Ignacio counted on his fingers with the same maddening seriousness. "Two nights ago, señor. Maybe three."

Villa gazed northward at the heat rippling the horizon. "We'd better find out more about this," he said gravely.

He ordered Julio to take five men, ride hard for Casas Grandes and see what they could learn there. We slowed our pace and moved cautiously toward Ascensión, reaching it only at dark. We camped by the lake. The night had a foul smell, as if the waters of the lake had been poisoned. Around midnight, as Villa was pacing the turf by a little fire, Julio and his men galloped out of the darkness. One of the horses crumpled to his knees, black blood oozing from the nostrils. Like hen hawks on a setting quail, we swooped down on Julio.

He squatted on his haunches, took a deep breath and said, "It's true, chief. Almost everything that Ignacio heard, except that everyone tells a different story about how many were killed. Columbus was burned to the ground, that's certainly a fact. Worse . . . Pershing is really coming after us. But not with a regiment of cavalry. With twelve thousand men! Cavalry, trucks—even airplanes! Can you imagine? I've never seen one."

Villa's face in the firelight looked blood-red. "Who told you this?"

"Some Mormons were there. They just got back from El Paso. One of them had a brother in Columbus."

"Why do they think we were the ones who did it?"

"Pablo Lopez was recognized. Martín too. And the colonel of the garrison swears you led the raid. He recognized you. It was supposed to be for revenge, and to steal rifles."

From our cut-off and lonely part of the world it seemed a ridiculous story, but we understood the implications. The gold would have to wait. We rode south through a cloudy night to Casas Grandes, and at dawn we finally found the telegraph operator. Villa composed a denial to Pershing at Fort Bliss, and then a second message addressed to President Wilson himself.

"How will the wires get through?" I said. "They have to be routed by way of Juárez."

"I didn't think of that. But we'll send them anyway. This is a crazy business. What do you think really happened?"

"Well, *someone* attacked Columbus. Maybe it was really the Lopez brothers. You said you'd shoot them for what they did at Santa Ysabel. Maybe they went over to Carranza."

"Carranza . . ."

"It was dark. Anyone can yell *'Viva Villa!'* Anyone can ride a black horse and put a pillow under his shirt to look like you."

He shot me a look of reproof. "I've lost weight, Tomás."

"Colonel Slocum doesn't know that."

"I still don't understand it. Why would Carranza bother to do such a thing to me? I have only four hundred men."

"But a hundred thousand will rise at the bugle call. That's what you said to Von Papen. If Carranza believes it too, this is a fine way of getting rid of you. The U. S. Cavalry will do the job for him."

He laughed. "Even twelve thousand men can't find four hundred, not if the four hundred know where to hide. And not if they're led by me." He sank down on his heels in the dust. "I don't believe Carranza is behind this. He'd piss blood at the thought of gringos invading Mexico, even if their aim is to catch me. You remember how he yelled when they landed at Veracruz?"

That made sense. "Then who did it, chief? If it wasn't us, and if it wasn't Carranza . . . then who?"

Pulling at his mustache, Villa squinted into the glare outside the telegraph office. I could see that all his senses were alive. He had been beaten on half a dozen battlefields by Obregón, humiliated and reduced to a poor wandering bandit; but now he was challenged by something larger than the problem of where to water the horses or how to find enough stray chickens and tortillas to feed four hundred tapeworms— and it suited him. It made the blood move in his veins. It was as if he had been waiting for the worst to happen, and this was it; and now he could be himself again, because the worst was over.

For a moment he shut his eyes. I knew what he was doing. He wasn't thinking. He was letting the breeze talk to him, letting it tell him how to hit the empty cartridge in the wall, and in which column the gold was hidden. I waited a reasonable length of time . . . perhaps two minutes.

"What do you smell, chief?"

"The German. The one you stopped me from shooting in Sonora. Do you think Lopez did this on his own? Why? He has no reason. To solve a crime, you have first to see who it benefits. The German is the answer. This is what he hoped for."

It was farfetched, but so was everything to do with Von Papen and his idea that Mexico recover her lost territories. He wouldn't even have to promise that to Lopez. Von Papen was a man who kept his branding iron smooth. He would only have to pay enough cash and make some sort of oily-tongued guarantee that Lopez would be sheltered from Villa's wrath.

"We'll never know," I said.

He brooded for a while, kicking his feet in the dust, picking at the raw skin of his thumbs. "All right," he decided, "let the gringos come. Their soldiers will die in Chihuahua. They shoot well, but not if they don't have targets. We'll do what Zapata does—hit them from all sides, then withdraw. They'll have to build a cemetery in Mexico as large as Fort Bliss."

A feeling of alarm spread through my chest, almost as if I had swallowed a hot pepper. I knew that Villa meant what he said. He had nothing against the United States or the American army—it was only the government in Washington that he hated now—but if he was attacked he would fight back like a hound dog against a grizzly, slashing until he dropped. And I realized that if he did that, I couldn't fight with him anymore. I couldn't put a bullet in the stomach of an American soldier who was only doing his job for fifteen dollars a month. These weren't Redflaggers who skinned Yaqui feet, or Obregonistas who shot children in Mexico City over a sip of water. These were my own kind. They said in the old days in Texas: "Another man's life don't make a soft pillow at night." I had known that at Hot Wells, after we blew up the railroad and I wouldn't fire at Patton. I had known it even before that, after Torreón. I would have to quit Pancho Villa and the revolution, and I didn't want to do that yet.

These last months, watching Carranza make a mess of things in Mexico City, hearing *campesinos*' tales of Obregón's further cruelty, I had come to the belief that Villa had made one other mistake that none of us had understood. Despite his denials, he was the right man to rule Mexico. No one else had the simplicity of motive, the backing of the people, the ruthlessness to deal with the politicians who wanted to hack and carve up the country just as Díaz and Huerta had done before them. He had to have his chance, and I had to convince him to seize it. It might take a lifetime; but a lifetime in Mexico was short, and I had no better way to spend it. Neither did he. It wasn't a reckless spirit that moved me—it was stubbornness and knowing where I belonged on this earth, at least for now. The thought startled me, as true thoughts always did.

But before any of that happened, there were a few minor obstacles in the way. One of them seemed to be the United States Army.

"That wire will never get through," I said, "but you've got to get word to Pershing that you didn't raid Columbus. I met him at Scott's house, and I don't believe he's the kind of man who forgets people. I'll go up to Columbus. I'll find out what really happened there. I'll tell him you didn't do it."

"He won't believe you," Villa said glumly.

"Then we're no worse off than now. Give me a letter with your seal. At least you'll be on record."

Villa frowned. "You blew up their railroad outside of El Paso. You told me about this damned lieutenant who recognized you. If you go up there, they'll arrest you."

"I can sneak across the border east of Columbus. How can they prove I planted the dynamite?"

"No, Tomás. It's too risky."

"Chief, it's a slim chance, but it's just about the only one we've got. I don't want Pershing to hang you. And I don't want you lining up your sights on his belly button. If you do that, your revolution's finished. So let me try."

A cold wind blew at my tail, and I bellied through the brush, crawled through a ditch and found the barbed wire. The night was dark with just a sliver of moon. I snipped the strands and peeled them back so they wouldn't score Maximilian's flanks, then went back and fetched him, and we padded softly into New Mexico.

Around midmorning I reached Columbus. Everything we had heard was true. The U. S. Army was on the move, stirring up more dust around the town than Noah's flood could have settled. Horses, wagons and trucks were everywhere; officers were shouting orders; and a few thousand khaki-uniformed soldiers were either bivouacked by their pup tents or massing into different formations. The town itself looked like the plagues of Egypt had visited it, and I smelled smoke and scorched flesh. The Commercial Hotel was gone. Peache's, where I had lunched with Sam Ravel and Felix Sommerfeld, was nothing but some charred timber and a black hole in the ground. I could see why Mr. Wilson was upset.

I kept an eye skinned for Patton. I still hadn't made up my mind how I was going to go about this when a hard-looking officer of about forty-five, with a thin gray mustache, detached himself from a troop of cavalry and strode over to me. I must have looked like some lost buckaroo from a cattle camp just suffered a die-up in the herd. He smiled up at me in the saddle and said, "What's your problem, cowboy? You here to join up? Are you a scout?"

"I'm looking for General Pershing," I explained.

"Are you now? Well! Black Jack's just a mite too busy to accept your enlistment personally, but he'll be flattered you asked for him. I'm Major Tompkins, Thirteenth Cavalry. Cowboy, if you'll just head over toward those Quads—that's a truck, see, with wheels and an engine?—someone will take care of you."

"Is there a Lieutenant Patton anywhere around here?"

"He's left for Culberson's Ranch. You want to see him?"

"No, sir, I want to see General Pershing. I have a message for him from Pancho Villa."

Tompkins shook his head sadly. He had no time to waste with chuckleheaded cowboys like me, and he just jerked a thumb in the direction of a big tent where a great many people seemed to be hurrying in and out. I strode over there, and a young officer, Lieutenant Shallenberger, took my message and my name, gave me a funny look and said he would see what he could do. I recognized him right away—he was the lieutenant who had been on the porch with Hannah that long-ago day I'd come courting. But he didn't know me at all. I guess I had changed.

I waited for the better part of the day, except for a time when I wandered over to a loose feed bag and snagged it for Maximilian, and then helped myself to a plate of scrambled eggs that the cooks in the mess tent were handing out. I still kept an eye out for Patton, but my luck held and he didn't show up. About five o'clock, sitting cross-legged in the dirt, I heard a familiar granite voice. I looked around and spotted the man striding out of the tent. They called him Black Jack because he had once commanded the all-Negro Tenth Cavalry, and he was supposed to be so tough he had three rows of jaw teeth and holes punched for more. I'd heard a story that when he was a boy in Missouri his mother had walked out in the yard where he was roasting corn and said, "Watch out there, Johnny! You're standing on a hot coal!"—and he had looked up, without moving, and drawled, "Which foot, Mama?"

But he was the man I had come to see. His shoulders were squared; he wore summer khakis, hat and leggings; and he chewed on a cigar. I yelled his name.

Pershing skidded to a quick halt, and his head snapped round. You didn't yell at a brigadier general that way—not unless you were a major general.

"Sir, excuse me. I'm Tom Mix. We met a while back in General Scott's house at the fort. Do you remember me?"

Pershing's angry gray eyes grew a lot more interested than I thought they'd be. "Indeed I do," he rasped. "Well, I'll be damned! What's your rank now? Do I have to salute you?"

"Not yet," I said, "I'm just a colonel. I've come here from Ascensión. I've got a message from Pancho Villa."

"Hold on a minute, Dodd." He turned briefly to the colonel at his side, who was staring at me as if I were a cracked egg. "Come inside, Mix. I'm willing to hear this."

I followed him into the tent and took the offered camp chair. While he paced up and down and worked the cigar back and forth between his teeth, I told him my story—that Villa had been nowhere near Columbus when it was raided and that I had a letter from him swearing to it. Pershing read it and listened carefully to what I said. Every now and then he blinked, but he never asked a question. I had the uneasy feeling he was just waiting politely for me to finish, and then he was going to put his boot heel between the cheeks of my butt and kick me all the way to Mexico. But instead, when I was done, he stood up, laid his palms flat on the rickety table between us and fixed his eyes on me with an intensity that might have withered a cactus or melted a bar of iron.

"I don't believe a word of it, Mix. But it was a good try. No, don't argue. You're wasting your breath." He leaned even closer, and I smelled the dead cigar. "Now look here . . . I don't know what you really want, and I don't know anymore who you really are. Or for that matter, *what* you are. But I'm leaving in about five minutes for Culberson's Ranch. I've got an officer there who wants to make a proposition to you—one that I'd personally, for your sake, and professionally, for mine, like to see you accept. I've got room for you in my staff car. Will you come?"

That floored me, but my mama hadn't raised a total nincompoop.

"Who is the officer, sir?"

"Lieutenant George Patton. You've met him."

I started hunting for reasons to make myself scarce. But then I decided this was the wrong man to play games with.

"Sir, Lieutenant Patton and I are not on friendly terms. Indeed, we've met, but it was never a pleasure for either of us. The reasons don't bear discussing, although the original sin—if I can put it that way—was mine." I cleared my throat. "Sir, I'd rather not hear his proposition, if you don't mind."

Pershing's eyes grew even more piercing, and I felt lower than a snake in a hole under a rock.

"I know about the prisoners at Torreón," he said. "And I know you blew up the El Paso & Southwestern. You're in a hell of a lot of trouble with quite a few people, Mix, but I give you my word that if you ride with me to Culberson's Ranch, no harm will come to you. You might even end these hostilities before they rightly begin, which would suit me just fine. I may be a general, but I don't like to see blood, be it Yankee or Mexican, spilled for no damned good reason. And you'll have the chance to make up for what you've done. Now, will you come?"

A faint heart never filled a flush, and I said I'd go.

Miguel Bosques stared at me like a moonstruck Piute who had seen an ancestral ghost. I knew him, of course. You don't forget the face of a man who has pleaded with you for his life and later pointed a gun at you. Patton, standing next to him in puttees and riding boots, had a whole battalion of expressions fighting a pitched battle on his face; and then he began to sneeze, one blast after another, so that he had to pull out a khaki handkerchief and bend almost double, pressing it to his nose. I kept my eyes on Miguel Bosques. He wasn't armed, but that was the way he had started out on Stanton Street too. He wasn't as wild-eyed as that time, but the way he pressed his lips together made me think he was suffering from toothache.

I didn't much enjoy Pershing's remark to Patton about whether he wanted to shoot me or enlist me, but he had promised me I wouldn't wind up feeding the grubworms, so I just smiled feeblemindedly treating it as a rich joke. Let him think I was missing a few buttons between the ears. Under the circumstances, considering the risk I took, that wasn't far off the mark. But I had decided that no matter what those risks, they were worth it if I stood any chance at all of keeping the cavalry out of Mexico.

When Patton had finished sneezing, Pershing said: "Lieutenant, your man Mix has been very obliging. He came here voluntarily, and I've granted him immunity for whatever he's done . . . while he's with us. Bear that in mind. Now, take him with you. Talk to him. Tell him what you told me. Then report back here."

"Yes, sir," Patton said, saluting. He gave me a light shove. I stumbled out the door, with him and Bosques close behind.

Two minutes later we were hunkered down in the dirt near a big truck that some troopers were loading with coils of telephone wire. Patton had placed a hissing Coleman lantern between us, so that the light turned his flushed face a shadowless yellow color, like buttermilk. It was chilly out there, and the sky swarmed with stars. Patton had taken Bosques aside for a few seconds and murmured something to him; after that, Bosques only spoke when he was spoken to. He looked plumper and softer than when I had last seen him, and I guess he had taken kindly to American grub and a feather pillow. I pretty much understood now what had happened to him after he had escaped Torreón.

Patton wanted first to know what the general had told me.

"He said you had a proposition for me. I came here to tell him that Pancho Villa didn't raid Columbus. We were over in Sonora when it happened. Villa thinks the Germans paid the Lopez brothers to do it." I told him that we had met up previously with Captain von Papen in the desert and he had put the same proposition to us, but Villa had turned it down cold.

Patton smiled. "And did General Pershing believe you?"

"No, but that don't make it a lie."

He fiddled in the dust with his fingers, as if he wanted to smooth it out to draw a map. But he didn't; he was just nervous.

"Look here," he said. "Villa and Columbus are one issue, and you're another. You heard the general . . . for the time being, you're off the sharp end of the hook. But I want to ask you something before we get down to business. After you blew up the El Paso & Southwestern, we chased you into the Potrillos." Patton had filled a pipe from a leather pouch, and when he got a fire going he tipped his blue eyes up over the bowl and looked at me keenly. "We shot to kill. You didn't return the fire. How come?"

"I fought for Villa against Orozco and Huerta," I said. "And then against Obregón and Carranza. I'm a revolutionist, but I'm an American too. Pennsylvania-born, Texas-bred. I pledged allegiance to the flag every day in El Paso High. There's no way I could ever shoot an American soldier."

Patton wagged his head up and down. He had the air of a circling buzzard who had spotted a crippled calf. I built a cigarette and waited. He puffed on his pipe, sending up clouds of nut-flavored smoke.

"Mix, you're a smart fellow," he said, after a while. "You're not blind. We're going after Villa, and nothing's going to stop us. Maybe he didn't raid Columbus personally, but he's responsible." He waved a hand around him at the line of trucks whose engines sputtered in the darkness. "We've got ten thousand men, here and in Columbus, ready to move."

"Lieutenant, Villa's innocent, and you're making a terrible mistake. But if you don't believe me, all I intend to do is ride back down there and tell that to him. And then I'm going to retire from the field, so to speak . . . if Villa and the U. S. Army have no objections."

"We just might let you do that," he said. "If you cooperate."

I bit shallow on that. Pershing had given me immunity, but it wasn't an open ticket to paradise. I still couldn't go back to Texas unless I wanted to break rocks for ten long years in Yuma. But I didn't see exactly what kind of cooperation Patton had in mind. He surely didn't need one more rifle added to those ten thousand, and even if he did I was less disposed to fire on Candelario and Julio than on the Thirteenth Cavalry. I got to wondering if he was going to ask me to scout for them, but I had already spotted a dozen Apaches in the camp as well as a couple of Mormons who had lived in Mexico most of their lives and knew northern Chihuahua even better than I did. So that wouldn't make much sense. I was about to blurt out my feelings on the matter when a little voice tickled the vacant space between my ears and told me to shut up . . . let him ride the point on this sally. I was pretty pleased with myself. It wasn't often that I had that kind of sense.

He got tired of waiting for me to say something. Squatting around that Coleman lamp, the game had become interesting.

"Mix," he squeaked, "let me tell you the deal I've got in mind. A damned good deal, especially for you. You interested?"

"Depends," I said.

"I wouldn't ask you to fire at the men you rode with. I'm a soldier. I respect your feelings on that score. Am I right?"

I hesitated and then gave a light shrug, as if the matter was of no great importance. He brightened up even more.

"Like you said, you don't want to see Americans get killed. Whatever you've done, you love your country. Isn't that so?"

"I'm an American, if that's what you mean."

"You hear a marching band play 'The Star-Spangled Banner,' it thrills you, right? You salute. Or put your hat over your heart?"

"Every time."

"Well, look here. Villa was finished even before this happened, but now ten thousand of the finest soldiers in the world are riding into Chihuahua to get him, and believe it . . . they will succeed. My point is this: sooner is a damn sight better than later. The quicker it's over, the less blood will be spilled. Once we get to him and take him to trial . . . why, that's the end of it! All we want is him and a few others. We have no reason or authority to fight his men after that, and the expedition will be over. You say Villa is innocent, that he didn't attack Columbus or authorize the raid. All right, fine. If he didn't do it, that will come out in court. It will be an American court, and you know he'll be innocent until proved guilty. That's the American way. If he's guilty, he'll pay the penalty under law." Patton wiped his brow with a khaki handkerchief. "But if he doesn't surrender, there'll be a hell of a war. If we have a hard time finding him, a lot of Mexicans will die. Men you know well. And a lot of Americans too—men you don't know. But if you did, and if you knew their mothers and wives and sweethearts, you wouldn't want to be responsible for their deaths."

He waited, and I couldn't help but nod. I'd had a hand in too many deaths already. But I had begun to sense his drift.

"You can prevent all that, Mix. You can save a thousand lives on both sides, keep hundreds of good men from being blinded and crippled and having their gonads shot off. You see where I'm heading?"

"Not exactly, Lieutenant. Spell it out for me."

"I want you to help us find and capture Pancho Villa."

My mouth hung open a moment. "That's *all?*"

Patton banged on. "You can lead us to him. If you do, you'll have the satisfaction of saving all those lives on both sides. Besides that, we'll grant you a full pardon. Blowing up the railroad will never have happened. And you'll go down in the annals of your country, not as a traitor, which is what you deserve up to this point . . . but as a goddam fucking four-star American hero! How about that?" He smiled benignly, showing all his heroic teeth. "Now, think about it, Mix. Cogitate. Don't answer too quickly."

I didn't intend to. All that flapdoodle and flagwaving had set my teeth on edge. Find and capture Villa! If I helped him do that, there would be more than one four-star hero in the future annals of the American military. They would make him a general, or at least a captain, for suckering some dumb cowboy into leading the cavalry to Pancho Villa.

But chinked among those high-pitched patriotic phrases, there had been a certain amount of good horse sense. And he had planted an interesting idea in my head.

"Lieutenant, let me take a walk. This is a big decision to make. You're right, I need to think. I want to see if my horse is okay too."

"What's he need? Feed?"

"No, but he might be spooked by now, smelling all those dark-complexioned fellas. The white ones too, come to think of it."

He was eager to please. The three of us piled into a Ford, with Bosques in back, and bounced down to the big tent where I had tethered Maximilian.

"That's a fine quarter horse," Patton said. "I noticed him at Hot Wells. Arizona-bred?"

"Chihuahua. Gift from a German lady in Parral. Now I'm going off to cogitate, like you said. Give me time. This ain't easy for me."

Alone, I led Maximilian into the cactus, where he could sniff the desert and feel more at home. He wasn't spooked, he was too smart for that. I was the one now who shied at shadows. I was still remembering things that Villa had said to me . . . that the cavalry shot well, but not if they didn't have targets. *"We'll hit them from all sides, and they'll have to build a cemetery in Mexico as large as Fort Bliss."*

I patted Maximilian, looked up at the stars and murmured to him in Spanish, "What do you think, old fella? Want to be a horse spy?" He snorted comfortably, and the cold night wind blew.

"I'm in trouble," I confessed, "but I can get out of it. That suits me, because I wasn't cut out to be a fugitive, and one day I want to go back to Texas. But that's not all. This gringo lieutenant's given me an idea. He wants me to lead him to the chief. Now, you know I wouldn't do a thing like that . . . I'd sooner die. But *he* doesn't know that, and I'm not going to tell him. Now, listen hard, Maximilian. Suppose I said yes to him? Told him I didn't know exactly where Villa was right now . . . but I could ride back down and find out. And suppose that wherever I told him and the U. S. Army to ride, with all their trucks and cannons, there was . . . *nothing!* Nobody! Pershing would never find the chief, and Pancho wouldn't have any decent reason to go after old Black Jack and try to skin his hide. None of those wives and mothers in Texas and Oklahoma would have to see their men come back on a stretcher with their gonads shot off. That crazy Candelario wouldn't get his other eye plunked out by a Colt machine gun. A lousy war, but no killing! Sure as hell less than if I said no and quit the revolution. Suppose I did that, Maximilian? I'd still be a kind of hero, wouldn't I? Nobody would know it—but does that matter? What do you think? Have I lost all my buttons?"

He snorted again. He loved me to talk to him. But I didn't quite understand his answer.

"Maximilian, I see I'll have to be a bit more specific. First of all, am I loco?"

He snorted and waved his big gray head from side to side in the negative, eyeing me from those tear-shaped brown orbs. His forelock fluttered a little in the wind. I had a hand on his chew muscle. I hoped I wasn't guiding him too much.

"Good. Now here's the second question. The first answer was real satisfactory. Listen hard, and think before you nod yes. Should I lead General Pershing and the U. S. Cavalry on a wild-goose chase through Chihuahua? If they find out, I'm a dead colonel. If I've got nine lives, I may have used up eight of them already in this damned revolution. Is it worth the risk?"

He rolled his eyes, sniffing the cold air. The smell of bacon and dung floated out from the camp.

"Come on, Maximilian. I haven't got all night. Loosen up, amigo. Tell me."

I gave just the gentlest tug to his hackamore. He dipped his head and whinnied.

"Good boy. That's what I figured you'd say."

I led him back to where Patton waited with Bosques, leaning against the chassis of the Ford. I thought at first I would bargain with him and debate the ethics of it before I gave in—that was what any good writer would make the actor do—but when I saw how eagerly he greeted my return from the darkness I realized I could spare the theatrics and get right to the point.

"Lieutenant, I'll do it."

I thought he might jump up into the air and click his heels. He had spirit. I liked him a lot more than I did that German captain. He stuck out his hand and pumped mine in a firm grip.

"You won't regret this," he said.

"Let's hope not," I replied. "If Villa finds out, he'll hang me so high I could look down on the moon."

"Now you can tell me. Where *is* Villa?"

"Well, he *was* in Casas Grandes . . . which doesn't mean he's still there. I'll have to go a ways before I find him, and I can't take a regiment of troopers along with me."

"Where do you think he'll go?"

"Anywhere in Chihuahua. Maybe even Sonora. He never tells anyone what he's got in mind. You have to be there to know. He might split up his men."

"How large is his force?"

"Maybe four hundred."

"Shithouse mouse! They told us more than a thousand!"

"Well, whoever they is, they told you wrong."

"Four hundred will be a hell of a lot harder to find than a thousand. . . ."

"If they split up, it'll be even harder. It'll take a little time."

"We want only Villa. And five others."

"Which ones?" I asked.

"The Lopez brothers. They were with him at Columbus. Those two who were with you at Hot Wells—General Cervantes and Colonel Cárdenas. We believe they were at Columbus too. They'll all get a fair trial. And that other one, if he's alive—Colonel Fierro. A story's got round that he was drowned in quicksand in some northern lake."

"He's alive," I said.

Bosques' face hardly changed expression, but I heard him draw a quick breath. "Is *he* going with you?" I asked Patton.

"He's under my orders."

I turned to him. "Bosques, there's something you need to know and I need to tell. That time in Torreón, at the stockyards—if I had refused to load his pistols, Rodolfo Fierro swore he would kill me. I was a week-old captain, and he gave me an order. I tried to get out of it. I just didn't try hard enough. I'm ashamed of what I did, which isn't going to make up for your brother getting killed, and all those other poor souls . . . but that's the story. Short. Not so sweet."

"You heard him, Miguel," said Patton.

"I've made a promise," Bosques said, nodding at the lieutenant. "I will keep it."

"Good enough for me." I turned back to Patton. "Where is your army headed?"

"That's no secret. Casas Grandes, by way of Ascensión."

"I'll meet you there as soon as I know where Villa's hiding out."

"And if we move on?"

"Ten thousand gringos can't hide in Chihuahua, Lieutenant. There won't be an Indian between here and the Yucatán who won't know exactly where you are."

Patton saluted me and said, "Good luck, Colonel," which pleased me no end.

I rode through the night to Casas Grandes.

Julio brought me out to a canyon in the mountains west of the town, where a pleasant little waterfall coursed down into a hot bubbling pool that smelled of sulphur. The chief was bathing there and he was glad to see me; after all, we had both worried that I might be stood up against a wall in Columbus and shot. Some doves cooed in the crannies of rocks, and I stripped down and dove into the pool with him, relishing the chance to wash the dust off my hide. His brown flesh glistened in the sunlight, and he was flapping his arms, making noises like a walrus.

"I saw Pershing," I said. "He didn't believe me."

He seemed to accept the news. If anything, his calmness worried me—it might mean that he was looking forward to scrapping with the cavalry. So I described the camp at Columbus. I didn't want him to think that the American army was coming with just a regiment of green horse soldiers and some broken-down Dodge trucks.

"Ten thousand men . . . ?" He whistled between his teeth. "To find just *one?* They must be crazy."

"Well, they have a tendency to overdo things. Bigger and better, that's the American motto. But they're coming. That's a fact."

"I won't fight them if I don't have to," he said. "We'll let the desert and the mountains do the job. But if they *do* find us, and they attack . . ."

"Listen, chief, I'm glad you feel that way. I know you don't want to kill gringos just for the hell of it. So here's what I did."

As we were drying our bodies on some rocks in the sun, I told him about Patton's proposition. His eyes grew large.

"And you agreed?"

"Why not? If you go south, I'll lead them east. If you ride east, I'll make sure they'll hunt in the south for you."

He gave me a stinging wet slap on the shoulder.

"Clever, Tomás! I like it! Tell me more!"

I explained about Pershing's plan to send the two columns south from Columbus and Culberson's Ranch, squeezing our forces between them.

Villa chuckled. "That's a good plan! It would have been a good battle too. But a bloody one. We'll just have to disappoint them. We'll ride south."

That afternoon, back in Casas Grandes, our whole band of four hundred men trotted off toward the sierra in the direction of Bachinava. I figured the cavalry would have left New Mexico by then. I thought of them wending their way through the desert, stringing telephone lines behind them all the way, and wondered how they would like those Chihuahua buzzards sitting on the wires, staring down with bold, hungry eyes. With his supply lines stretched thin as a rubberband and no Villistas in sight, Pershing might just give up and go home. When I was an old man I could rock in my chair and tell my grandchildren: "I once stopped a war. Had a little help from some lieutenant, but it was me that did it, kids."

Whose grandchildren? Rosa's and mine, I figured. That's what I had in mind now when this was all over, if I could rid myself of the vision of Elisa Griensen. It kept recurring in all my fantasies, usually at the edge of things, but sometimes at the center. And sometimes I saw both her and Rosa as I had left them at the gate, waving their farewell in the brown light of dusk. For two years I had struggled, sometimes without even knowing it, between a dream of Hannah and the reality of Rosa. Now that struggle seemed to be beginning all over again, but with new combatants. No . . . I amended that. No one was in battle except me, and I had no antagonist other than my nature. I knew that even then, at the age of twenty-four.

Villa broke into my thoughts with some of his own. We were in the mountains, on the way to Bachinava. Riding south suited him perfectly, he told me, because he had received word from a Yaqui deserter that a small Carranzista garrison had occupied the town of Guerrero, about seventy miles west of Chihuahua City. They were supposed to be guarding a stock of new Mauser rifles and bullets. We needed arms, so we would attack them. And then he had just heard a report that Carranza, in Mexico City, was hopping up and down like a scalded dog, furious at Mr. Wilson. "Maybe the gringos will decide they're fighting the wrong man," Villa said, with a new gleam of hope in his eye. "Especially when they realize I don't intend to fight back. Maybe we can make war together on Carranza. I would enjoy that. I'll let Pershing keep command. I'll just advise him and eat his peanut brittle."

He kept on dreaming. He was always in a good mood before a scrap.

The next night we fell like wolves upon the sleeping garrison at Guerrero. The fight was brisk and mercifully short. We captured the rifles, three machine guns, a storehouse of ammunition and a dozen cases of tequila. We had a gang of young Yaqui recruits with us, and that wet stuff drew them like flies to sugar.

Just as the sun was about cordwood high, one of our scouts reined up outside the village and yelled to Villa, who was standing near a little graveyard admiring the stones. A force of a hundred Carranzistas cavalry, he said, was riding like hell down a trail from the direction of Anáhuac. Villa turned idly to Julio. "Do you have any men who are still sober?"

They organized about forty of the Dorados and rode off in a swirl of dust to stop the Carranzistas. After fifteen minutes we heard some distant rifle shots. Half an hour later Villa and a dozen men came cantering back, grinning through their sweat. Candelario, Hipólito and I were sharing a bottle of tequila in the cemetery, our backs propped against the gravestones.

The chief dismounted, wiping his forehead with a bandanna. "We picked them off from the top of a little hill. They must have thought we had a thousand men. They turned tail and ran like jackrabbits. Julio and the others are chasing them."

Bullets whined off the gravestones, biting out hunks of mica and splintering the wooden crosses. The eye of a horse standing off to my left blew apart, spurting blood. I flopped down on my belly behind a stone, wishing it were a bigger one. Villa looked more annoyed than worried. He knew, from a hundred battles, that nothing could hurt him. He didn't bother to duck for cover.

"Some of them got away into the hills when we chased them," he explained. "They must have circled round the town—"

He stood a moment in the blaze of the sun, squinting up at the forest. Then, barrel-chested, pigeon-toed, rolling from side to side, he moved toward his horse. The horse was tethered to an orange tree that grew from the cobbles in front of the storehouse. Villa was trotting toward it when he was hit. He gave a weak cry, then sprawled forward on his face in the dirt between two wooden crosses. His pith helmet flew off his head to clatter across the cobbles.

Hipólito and I reached him first. We dragged him quickly across the street to the safety of the storehouse. Candelario yelled at the men inside. "You drunken bastards, go out there and shoot those people! But be careful. . . ."

The wound was in the leg, a bad one. The chief had been running, and the bullet must have struck him as the leg was raised. It had torn the flesh behind the knee, exiting lower down where it smashed the shinbone. The exit hole was as large as a plum tomato, oozing blood and chips of white bone. Villa, lying on his belly on the floor, slipped a bandanna between his teeth and bit down hard.

"Go outside, Tomás," Candelario said. "See what's happening."

I edged out the door and found that our men had taken cover and were firing haphazardly into the hills, but now there was no return fire. By the time I returned, Villa had decided that he would leave in a wagon with Hipólito and Fierro and head south toward the mountain village of Pahuirachic, hoping to find some kind of doctor on the way. Candelario would assume command of our forces, waiting for Julio and the missing Dorados to return. "You'll find me," Villa gasped, his face gone chalky from the pain.

But before we could move or do anything, another Yaqui scout came belting into town, crying out that yet another column of hostile soldiers was riding down a different trail toward Guerrero.

"Now who the hell are *they?*" Candelario said, annoyed at the interruption. "Tomás, let's mount up and put a stop to this. We can't let them attack us until the chief is out of here. Hipólito, don't move him until we get back."

Some of our boys were hauled from the different huts where they had been drinking tequila, and soon we had about a hundred mounted men milling about the square. Candelario spurred up to me and told me to ride ahead with the Yaqui scout and pick a spot for an ambush.

We galloped down an arroyo and then up a steep hogback on the west side of town. There were bluffs that extended back to the range of sunstruck mountains, and the little valley beyond was cut by more arroyos, filled with pine and juniper trees, hard to traverse. The Yaqui explained that the trail ran along the edge of the next bluff. I told him to hold Maximilian, and I crawled through the pines and then scrambled up to the bluff. I heard distant hoofbeats. Half a mile, I judged. I flopped down with my rifle cradled in my arms and peered down the narrow trail, flanked with cedars.

I saw dust rising . . . then khaki uniforms and flat-brimmed hats came into view. The lovely red, white and blue of the American flag flew in the forefront of the column. A pole next to it carried the blue swallowtail guidon of the Seventh Cavalry.

"Son of a whore," I said aloud and then scrambled back as fast as I could. I hopped into the saddle, gave Maximilian a serious jab and we went haring back, swooping down the hogback into the juniper arroyo where our men were advancing at a trot.

I reined up to yell at Candelario. "It's the United States Cavalry! Let's get the hell out of here!"

His good eye widened. "Impossible! How many, Tomás?"

"A regiment!"

"They're supposed to be at Casas Grandes. How did they get down here so fast?"

"Should I go ask them?"

We galloped back to the town and found Hipólito carefully loading his injured brother into a wagon with one of the captured machine guns. "It's the gringos," Candelario explained. "A full regiment!"

Villa's eyes fixed directly on me. "How is that possible?" he gasped. "Why are they this far south?"

"I don't know," I said, feeling miserable.

Candelario wheeled his horse, then laid a quirt across the mules. The wagon jolted off, and Villa fell back on his blankets, groaning. Six men rode with him as escort. Hurriedly, for the cavalry would be on us any minute, Candelario divided the rest of our force into three groups. His would ride east, another group would climb westward into the sierra, a third toward the southwest. There was no way to get word to Julio, who was still pursuing the Carranzistas. I realized that Candelario had sent no one in the direction Pancho Villa had taken toward the little village of Pahuirachic. The slow-moving wagon would travel unmolested.

"Ride with me, Tomás!" Candelario bent low over the withers. The Seventh Cavalry sighted our dust, put spurs into their horses and swooped down the trail after us, pennants flying.

I learned later that the Seventh was under the command of Colonel Dodd, who was sixty-three years old and due to retire in a year. Pershing had got word of us from some Carranzista informers, and Dodd's men of the Seventh had covered fifty-five mountainous miles in eighteen of the last twenty-four hours. They would have found us even sooner if they hadn't become lost on the trails south of Bachinava, where they had been hit by a gale and then had to hack their way through a snow slide. The troopers had been living on frijoles and parched corn for two days, and their whiskers had grown icicles. But they were the Seventh Cavalry—they kept coming.

It became a running battle, and there was no way Candelario's men weren't going to shoot back. Hoofs rang and drummed on the turf. I lay flat on Maximilian's withers and never looked behind me. The cavalry killed and wounded twenty men before the big Oklahoma horses gave out, and those of us who were left plunged into a ravine and quirted our way up a slope that led to a pine forest. We trotted another two miles before we decided we were safe. Then we reined up in the shadows to take a breath and count the missing.

Dodd, I found out later, hadn't lost a single trooper. Only five of his men had been wounded, none of them seriously. The cavalry later claimed they had killed more than fifty Villistas and wounded twice that many.

I began to wonder why Pershing needed a spy when he had in me, instead, a dumb cowboy who would tell Pancho Villa not to worry.

32 "An you lie, sirrah, we'll have you whipped."

Dodging the Seventh Cavalry for more than a week, Candelario and I didn't catch up with Pancho Villa until we reached the mountain pueblo of Pahuirachic, a collection of hovels in a valley of hawthorn trees. We were trotting through the forest about a mile west of Pahuirachic when a Yaqui scout popped from behind some dark green firs and hailed us. He brought us to a little cave.

Hipólito, squatting on his haunches outside, told us of their flight from Guerrero.

"The trail was rough," he said, "and there were rock slides. When Pancho woke up in the wagon, I thought he might die. We had to make a litter for him. Four men carried it, and whenever we stopped I lifted him in my arms. Each time I wiped away his tears, the men looked the other way. Then it started to snow. We couldn't go on. *Hombre,* it was cold! We laid Pancho under a black oak tree and gave him all our blankets."

The snow melted. The little band of fugitives pushed slowly across

/ 365

the sierra to Pahuirachic, and Villa himself spotted the cave on a mountainside behind some scrub. None of the others could see it until they were nearly in front of it. The chief's leg may have been a ruin, but his eyes were those of a fox. Once, when the weather cleared, an airplane flew overhead and circled the village. From Hipólito's description, I knew it was one of the Curtiss Jennies of the First Aero Squadron. Hipólito feared that some of the local Tarahumara had been paid by the Americans to spy for them, but there was no way Villa could be moved until he recovered strength and the wound stopped festering. In the village they found some permanganate of potash, and it seemed to help. Villa grew weaker every day, but still he told the men what to do; from all his years as a bandit in the Sierra Madres he knew the tricks of survival. The cave overlooked a little cup of a valley with a good waterhole. Deer and wild fowl came sometimes to drink, and Villa ordered the men to gouge out the eyes of any they caught. Blinded, the animals would stay close by the water. When the men in the cave needed fresh meat, they had only to go back at night and kill it.

Hipólito led us inside to crouch down beside the chief. His baggy pants had been cut nearly to the hip and the wound cleansed with peeled blades of the nopal cactus, then wrapped in cotton bandages. But from knee to ankle the leg had turned black. The cave smelled of coonshit, and Pancho was stretched out on a bed of blankets and pine needles. It reminded me of the first time I had seen him on the cot in the hut outside Juárez, except that then the evidence of his power was simply being held in check, whereas now it had vanished. A brushwood fire crackled to keep out the dampness. He was pale, and he seemed frightened. Still he managed a small smile, which faded as we told him the tale of our flight from the cavalry at Guerrero.

"And Julio?" he said weakly. "Did he get back?"

"We couldn't look for him," Candelario replied. "We were riding to save our ass."

"So we're all scattered. . . ." Villa thought for a while, sweat beading his forehead. "I'm going to stay here. There's no place else to go. If I don't get well, I'll die . . . it's as simple as that. There's no doctor for a hundred miles."

"How about Parral?" I said.

"That's the first place they'll think I've gone. The *curandera* there is known throughout Mexico."

"And Chihuahua City? You need a doctor, not a wich."

He propped himself up on one elbow. "Tomás, even if I could travel that far, and sneak into the city, which is possible, and find a doctor who wouldn't turn me over to Carranza, which is also possible . . . how would I get past the gringo cavalry? Their patrols will be covering all the roads and trails. If they catch me their doctors may cure me, but then I'll hang for something I didn't do."

He lay back, breathing shallowly.

"Listen, chief," I said, "the cavalry still trusts me. It was just bad luck that led them to us at Guerrero. They probably don't even know that you're wounded. I'll go back to them. I'll tell Patton that I know where you are. North, or south or west—anywhere but Chihuahua City. And then you can go there."

"All right, Tomás," he gasped. "Do it. I may not go, but at least they won't come to Pahuirachic. Lead them far from here, so I can get better in peace. Or die in peace."

"You're not ready for harp lessons, chief. In a month or so you'll get your bristles up and go shoot some Carranzistas. You'll feel real perky again."

He gave me a wan smile and squeezed my arm. His revolution was over. He was the great maker of plans, and now he had run out of them. He wouldn't be shooting any Carranzistas or sharing any peanut brittle with General Pershing. He wouldn't build any more schools in Chihuahua. I was sure of all that . . . then. I went outside, clapped Hipólito and Candelario on the shoulder by way of goodbye and hit the north trail.

Bachinava, where I found the cavalry, was jammed with vehicles, horses and men. A line of dusty disabled trucks sat at various angles on the plaza, most with broken springs and flat tires, bent suspensions and cracked oil pans. The desert and the mountain trails of Chihuahua had taken their toll. A dozen hostlers were working nonstop in the morning heat, shoeing horses and inspecting them for shinbone and other ailments. The men were camped in pup tents on the hillsides, and most of them sat around oiling their rifles, putting salve on their sun-blistered faces, jawing, playing cards or eating wolfishly out of their tin mess plates. I saw a few reporters too, listening and busily taking notes. The smell of hot biscuits reached my nose and set my mouth watering.

Some Negro soldiers came back from where I had sent them to find Patton. He wasn't in the camp, they said—he had gone out duck hunting. I wandered around a hillside and down toward the pup tents, when suddenly I whirled at the sound of a voice—a woman's voice—shrilling my name.

Yvette came bounding across some rocks, holding onto her skirts, dyed blond hair flying and a big smile on her painted face. I hadn't seen her since before the battle of León, last April—a year ago. She grabbed my hands and planted a wet red kiss on my mouth.

"Tom! *Chéri!* 'Ow are you? What you do here?"

"I might ask you the same question, Yvette," I said, getting my wits back, "but I guess I'd have to be some kind of bonehead not to know the answer."

"It's *merveilleux* to see you, Tom! My sister, she is here too—but she is busy now."

"I'll bet. Tell me, don't they have regulations against this?"

"Maybe yes, maybe no. *Le plus probable . . . qui sais?* You see how much I learn in Mexico? But a very nice major have arrange it all for us. There are five girls. The men are so bored, Tom! They try to build a baseball field, but there is no flat ground. They have nowhere to spend their money. And if we are not here, they rape the señoritas, which the major says is very bad. Ah, *chéri!* So good to see you! You stay awhile, *en souvenir de bon vieux temps?"*

"Another time. I'm waiting to see someone. Give my love to Marie-Thérèse."

"Je comprends. You are married now?"

"No, that's not it. That didn't work out, Yvette."

"Rosa is with you?"

"In spirit. The flesh is a long way away."

"You see Candelario? He is not dead like the other one?"

"I just left the old randy buck . . . in Parral. Which other one is dead?"

"Your *chef.* The fat one. Pancho Villa."

"Who says?"

"They argue. Some say it. The Indians tell them he is wounded."

That was good to know. I hadn't intended to mention that to Patton, but now I could give him the more gory details, and he might swallow the rest of the story.

"Yvette, I have to go. Good luck to you both."

"Chéri, je t'aime comme toujours. Don't get killed."

War was hard on some, kind to others. Yvette and her sister would never complain. I went back up to the square, and in about an hour Patton showed up and found me sitting outside the mess tent with a plate of jerky and brown biscuits. Miguel Bosques wasn't with him, which didn't exactly bring tears to my eyes.

"Mix, I'd just about given up hope. Thought we'd have to hang you when we found you in Texas." He chuckled. "Come on with me, man—tell me everything."

Walking through town past the mules and supply wagons, I spun the yarn of Villa's being wounded at Guerrero.

"That confirms our reports," Patton said. "Where is he now?"

"In Parral, to see a *curandera.* He split up his force. Cervantes is in a place called La Bufa—way west—with two hundred men. Fierro took the rest east, toward El Sauz."

I had hit on that one because the chief had said Parral would be the logical place for him to go, and it would draw Pershing well south of both Chihuahua City and the cave in Pahuirachic. If I could get them to go west and east as well, they would hunt forever.

"Let's go tell the general," Patton said.

Pershing had established his headquarters in a small hacienda on the edge of town. There was a garden, but it hadn't been watered in months and flower petals lay in rank heaps. When we got there Pershing was sitting in the shade of the patio with his boots up on the edge of a stone fountain that had dead bees floating in its stagnant waters. He was eating an orange and talking to Major Tompkins, the doughty, hard-looking man I had first met when I hit their camp in Columbus—the officer who had led the counterattack right after the raid. Pershing wore a khaki blouse open at the throat and a thin brown sweater with frayed elbows. Patton told him I had brought definite information that Pancho Villa was wounded and hiding out in Parral.

"Parral!" Major Tompkins slammed a fist into his palm. He turned to his general. "I told you he'd head there! When he was a bandit, he always holed up in Parral. Now we've got him!"

Pershing shifted his frosty gray eyes in my direction and let them rest on my face for almost a minute. If he can read my mind, I thought, I'll face a firing squad.

"How do you know this, Mix?"

"I just left him a few days ago."

"How many days ago?"

"Two. No—wait. Make it three."

"Where did you see him?"

"In the mountains near Guerrero."

"Which village?"

"No village, General. Somewhere in the mountains."

"How many men did he have with him?"

"Maybe thirty."

"Who were the officers?"

"General Cervantes was there, but he left for La Bufa. So was Villa's brother, and Rodolfo Fierro."

"What about Colonel Cárdenas?"

"Broke away from us at Guerrero. Took off after some Carranzista general."

With a grunt, Black Jack pulled a military map from his battered pigskin briefcase. He punched his finger into the brown area northwest of Parral.

"You see this range? We've had reports that Villa's there, hiding in a cave or some peasant's hut. Somewhere around Pahuirachic or San Nicolás. They say he can't move. How does he intend to get to Parral?"

Unable to restrain himself, Tompkins broke in. "General, excuse me. Those goddam reliable reports aren't worth a fart in a windstorm! So far they've told us that Villa is everywhere and nowhere. Here's a man who's seen him and knows he's heading for Parral!—and that's what I've said all along he'd do! Now if I go down there with two troops of the Thirteenth and a dozen pack mules—a flying column—I can get to Parral around the same time he does. The farther south we go, the more trouble we have. Bad supplies, tough trails, higher mountains. And a more hostile people. A larger command couldn't conceal itself. A flying column can punch through."

The general didn't reply, but turned again to me. "Where in Parral will he stay?"

"I don't know that yet. But if I get there ahead of Major Tompkins, I can find out. Although in my opinion, sir, you should send a larger force."

"Oh?" Pershing showed his teeth in a thin smile. "And what's the basis for your opinion . . . Colonel Mix?"

The basis was that I wanted to steer the expedition away from Pahuirachic. But I had to think of something else that was likely.

"Parral's held by a Carranzista garrison, but there are fifteen thousand civilians in the city. They think of Villa as one of their own. What's two cavalry troops in your army? A hundred men, maybe a bit more. They might surprise Villa, but they might get cut up awfully bad if they don't. Once you're in Parral, it's hard to get out. It's in a valley. There are only three trails that lead in or out."

"And why do the people in Parral think so much of Pancho Villa?"

"He was born nearby, and he built a school there four years ago. They never had one before that."

"A school?" That tickled Pershing's fancy. "What is he, a general or a construction worker?"

"He's a revolutionist. That's the kind of thing he does."

He chuckled and said, "I suppose nobody's all bad." Then he turned to Major Tompkins.

"Frank, take four troops, not two. I'll send units from the Tenth and Eleventh to cover your rear. The Seventh can head over to La Bufa. The Fifth will look around El Sauz. Now that we know where Villa's going, the main force will sit right here."

That suited me perfectly.

All the while Lieutenant Patton had been sweating in the sun, hands clasped behind his back. Now he piped up. "Sir, with your permission, can I accompany Major Tompkins' flying column?"

"Why, George?"

Patton's voice rose nearly an octave. "I want to see some action, sir."

"Permission denied. I want you to take a troop and ride east toward Rubio. Sergeant Chicken and the other Apaches say there are Villistas somewhere in the desert, foraging and recruiting and raising hell. He thinks it may be Julián Cárdenas. Could you recognize him if you saw him?"

"He was driving the wagon I intercepted at Hot Wells. Thin man, about thirty. Black eyes, drooping mustache. Looked mean and surly."

"Find him for me." That made me uneasy, but I didn't have time to dwell on it because Pershing turned to me and said, "Mix, you'll go with Major Tompkins."

"Me?"

"You know the trails. You say you know the town. Guide him there. Discover where Villa's hiding. Do your job."

"What if any of Villa's men see me riding with your cavalry? My life won't be worth a dish of beans."

"We'll give you a uniform. No one will recognize you." That was settled, and he turned once again to Major Tompkins.

"Frank . . . find Pancho Villa. Wounded, alive or dead. But find Villa and bring him back."

I was glad to be rid of Patton, although Major Frank Tompkins was no easy substitute; it was like swapping a wolf cub for its mama. But he warmed up to me on the way south when we started talking about horses. He was riding a beautiful little black called Kingfisher, a young Arab stallion whom I had admired for his springy step and alert head. Tompkins was a Minnesotan who had joined the cavalry straight out of military school and then served in Arizona and the Philippines—one of those old-line officers who had graduated the hard school of the frontier where a soldier was taught to consider his horse first and himself last, and where once on the trail he would stick to it until the quarry was run to earth or he was out of bullets. He was a demanding officer, but he treated his men like human beings. They had smuggled along a few bottles of tequila provided by the Chinese peddlers in Bachinava. One of his platoon leaders, Sergeant Richley, reported this fact to Tompkins, and the first time we bivouacked the major made a little speech.

"Now look here, boys—I know all about the tequila. I'm not an unreasonable man, and I know you might need a little drink at reveille to clear your throats . . . and maybe another at morning mess to wash down the beans . . . and of course after cleaning up his horses a man has to wipe the stink from his lungs. A sociable drink at supper is okay, and one or two along the march for stamina . . . and maybe a couple more to help you get a decent night's sleep. But none of this constant nip, nip, nip, and sip, sip, sip! There's a limit."

The trail I picked led south through the sierra, a steady uphill climb through a barbarous land. We had started in the afternoon, and it grew quickly cold with a wind whipping and whistling between the peaks, so that the men unrolled their blankets and threw them over their shoulders like Yaquis. Above nine thousand feet it began to snow, and horses' hoofs slipped on round stones that they couldn't see. The beasts panted and blew clouds of thin vapor. The troopers had already suffered thirst and sunburn in the desert. Now their lips cracked from the cold, their noses bled from the altitude, their heads ached from the wind.

We quickly picked up the tracks of about twenty ponies, and Sergeant Chicken, the Apache scout who had herded us from Hot Wells to El Paso last October, said they were Villistas. A short, sinewy man of

/ 371

about fifty, he was the oldest of all the scouts, who sported names like Hell Yet-Suey, Skitty Joe Pitt, B-25 and Loco Jim. Chicken had long greasy black hair, a nut-brown face and bloodshot eyes, and he wore a red silk neckerchief with a silver concho slide. He sang to himself all the time, his neck veins bulging, wailing words that none of us understood. Years ago he had fought with the Chiracahua against Pershing, and when he said, "Villistas," Tompkins believed him. So we pressed on into the darkness, and the wind became a gale. Snow flailed our faces and turned my forehead icy. When the trail grew rockier and more narrow, we had to dismount and lead the horses. We had been in columns of squads, but now we pushed along in single file, trying to keep in touch with the horse in front, stumbling on the hidden stones like blind men. The trail wound through a rocky chasm, turned about in the opposite direction, then corkscrewed up the steep slope of the mountain.

Tompkins was right behind me, leading his stallion. "Jesus Christ," he said, "this is worse than a Montana winter. And in the daytime it's worse than an Arizona summer! What kind of a country is this?"

"One you shouldn't travel in at night," I told him, shouting to make sure he heard me above the wind.

"Villa does it," he yelled back. "What Villa does, the cavalry can do!"

"Major, he's in a hurry. We're not. Let's stop this foolishness."

Luckily the snow had eased by then. The clouds parted to reveal a moon and we came to a flat place with a grove of oaks. Tompkins grumpily called a halt—he knew it was getting too hard for the horses. The men bivouacked, building little fires in the grove. The horses were fed their grain and picketed to graze. The wind howled with greater violence than before. It knocked over the tin cups, filling the meat cans with sand and gravel; it blew the kindling right out of the fires. We chewed a meager meal of hard bread and jerky, and Major Tompkins gave me some of his *pinole,* parched corn ground to powder and mixed with water, which he said tasted like a combination of birdseed and chickenshit but was plenty nourishing. He also showed me a trick I had never seen. He dug a shallow trench the width of his body, built a tiny fire in it that was useless to cook on, but when the earth was warm enough to suit him he raked the coals away and crawled in with his saddle and Kingfisher's bridle. He pulled his blanket over both lips of the trench. He had learned that in Montana, he told me, in the winter of eighty-nine. I tried it and started to sweat. It was too damned hot in there.

When the wind died down for a while, Tompkins poked his head out and asked me if I would care for a belt of tequila as a nightcap.

"Major, I wouldn't mind a little ice-cold lemonade if you've got it. I'm roasting in this hole. In Chihuahua this is the way they cook sheep."

He chuckled, and I heard the bottle gurgle a couple of times.

"How long you been in Mexico, Mix?"

"Three years to the day that Columbus got raided."

"You ever make any sense out of their politics?"

"They're all thieves, except Villa."

"That's just what General Scott says. He likes the man. I can't figure that out."

I thought I had better amend my statement somewhat; I didn't want to sound too enthusiastic for the quarry we were supposed to be hunting.

"If you don't like what Villa stands for, Major, he's a thief too. But Mexico's a funny country. They're so poor down here they make the Apache look like bankers. I've heard it said that 'to steal is to live, and not to steal is to fall into the pit the devil dug for cowards and honest men.' I guess you could say the politicians are less cowardly than most."

Tompkins chuckled and took another swig. "You a Republican, Mix?"

"Hell, no. I'm a Texan."

"If that means you voted for Mr. Wilson and the Democrats, you made a big mistake. I talked to some of these Mexicans up in Casas Grandes, and they hate our guts. They look on us as invaders. We're here to rid them of a bandit, and all we've accomplished so far is to make the people think of him as a hero. I've heard some of them—Carranzista officers, by God!—say they'd consider it a national disgrace if we capture him. And I lay that situation right at Mr. Wilson's doorstep. If we had Taft in the White House there wouldn't have been a Columbus raid. Then there wouldn't have been a need to freeze our asses off in these mountains, because the Mexicans would have held the U. S. of A. in respect instead of contempt."

"I don't know too much about that, Major. The truth is, I was too young to vote. Sleep well, sir."

I curled in my trench, which had cooled down a bit and was nicely comfortable. Soon I would be in Parral. I didn't much relish showing up with troops of the U. S. Cavalry, but once I had dispatched them to some more southerly point I could get about the other pressing business of my life. Now that I was on my way, I knew even less than before what I would do. I missed Rosa. She was the best thing that had ever happened to me, and I couldn't imagine anything better. But I missed Elisa too. I listened to the night wind blow—it bore no messages—and worried myself to sleep.

Come morning the sky was frosty blue and the wind only ghosted through the canyon. The soldiers cooked bacon and hardtack in their mess kits and then fed and shod their horses. There were no more oats so the horses had to eat corn, which they hated. The Chihuahua corn had little pebbles in it, and each man carefully spread the feed on his blanket and picked them out before putting it in the nosebag. Once a horse bit a pebble he would snort in disgust and stop eating, no matter how hungry he was. Tompkins told me that on the march south to Bachinava the difference in temperature—sometimes seventy degrees from day to night—had killed more than fifty of the brutes. Even the ones that were left had thinned down so that their ribs and withers stuck through their skins. The mountain trails wore out their shoes, and if they stubbed their toes on the rocks they would often cast the iron free.

The third day out the troopers became grumpy. We were still in high country with gray clouds that floated past our faces and sometimes swallowed men whole. We had no coffee or sugar, only hardtack, potatoes and cowboy dough—flour, water and a pinch of salt fried in bacon grease. It was good grub for a hungry man, but all I craved were some tacos and guacamole laced with chile. I guess my stomach knew even better than I did which side I was really rooting for.

On the fourth morning we were somewhere near Pahuirachic, and I was beginning to feel jittery. I hoped we wouldn't run into any more tracks or some hungry Indian who thought he could pick up a good meal by telling that Villa was nearby in his cave. A gale blinded us with dust. As we passed out of a gorge onto a sheet of volcanic rock that rose toward a pine forest, we heard the sound of a sputtering engine. Every man in the column looked up. A minute later an airplane, a Martin Model S, appeared over the mountains from the south, buffeted up and down by the whirlwind. It couldn't have been more than three hundred feet above our heads, and I ducked mine down and got ready to hit the dirt. Just as it flew over us, bucking and jumping like a beefsteaked mustang, it shot upwards, did a somersault, then plunged toward the forest of pines. In a few seconds it vanished from our sight.

"Come on!" Tompkins yelled to his advance guard.

We had taken a good bearing, but as we spurred up the rocksheet we expected any second to hear a fearful crash and then find a mangled aviator.

What we found was the ship rightside up, uninjured, sitting prettily on a brown meadow strewn with rocks. The propeller turned over a few more times as we dashed up, then shuddered to a stop. The pilot, whose name turned out to be Lieutenant Christie, climbed out on the wing and jumped to the ground. When he took off his goggles we saw he had the face of a cherub—bright blue eyes, ruddy lips, and he'd never had to pay hard cash for a razor strop.

Tompkins reached him first and slid off Kingfisher. "Good Lord, boy! I thought it was taps for you! How did you get out of it?"

"God had me by the hand," Christie said.

"He sure tossed you up and down before He let go. Are you okay?"

"Got anything to eat?" Christie asked.

While we fed him he told us he had just spotted a force of about thirty armed Mexicans moving between Pahuirachic and San Nicolás on a mountain trail. That was the main function of the Aero Squadron in this campaign; to deliver messages and scout for enemy troop concentrations.

"Villistas?"

"Beats me, sir." Christie explained he had been unable to follow them because of the downdrafts and the whirlwind.

Tompkins wasted no time. "Lieutenant, we're going after them. Can you fly out of here, or do you want to join us?"

"I can't leave my ship, Major. When the wind dies down, I'll take off for Bachinava."

"Good luck, then!" Tompkins jumped up on Kingfisher, and off he went, across the meadow and through the forest, with me thundering after.

I was more than disturbed; I was demoralized. I didn't know what I was going to do. I *knew* who it was, and if the Thirteenth Cavalry fell upon the chief while he was moving camp, he wouldn't stand a chance. He would be outnumbered and probably being carried in the litter, which meant he couldn't even try to escape. And I would be riding with the men who would capture or kill him. That thought made me want to howl, and it gave wings to my imagination. We had to slow down between the pine trees, and I kicked Maximilian up to Major Tompkins.

"Sir, let me go ahead! There may be a good way to bushwhack them. If we come on them like a thundering herd, they'll head in ten different directions into the brush."

"What brush?" Tompkins pointed at the rocky mountain slopes.

"For Villa there's always brush."

Tompkins cocked an eye at me. We pounded onto the rock face. "Take Sergeant Chicken with you," he yelled. "Don't fire your rifle! Just locate them and report back! We'll follow!"

"Yes, sir!"

I hoped to avoid Chicken, but Tompkins was already waving to him. The Apache jumped smoothly onto his mare and trotted over from the troop waiting on the trail. The bugler was already sounding "Boots and Saddles." Tompkins repeated the orders, and Chicken and I galloped off together toward Pahuirachic.

There wasn't much to know about Apaches—they didn't let you know much—but if you were brought up on the border you understood two things about them. They hated Mexicans; and as scouts they could track a bee in a blizzard or follow a wood tick on solid rock in the dark of the moon. They could tell by twigs and bent grass just how long ago an animal had passed by, and if it were a man they could tell you the color of his hair. There was no way I was going to fool this dark old fellow galloping along at my side. We shot through the huts of Pahuirachic, scattering chickens and pigs, and then Sergeant Chicken took the lead on his mare and veered off the trail into a stand of juniper. He raised one hand. We stopped in the shadows to dismount.

The warm air was silky and still, and some drowsy shafts of sunlight floated through the trees. Chicken murmured to me so softly that I could hardly hear him, "Maybe fifteen, twenty men . . . They ride at a slow trot. Maybe two, three hundred yards ahead."

I craned my neck around the trunk of a juniper, listening to the rustle of the leaves and peering through the green shadows. There was nothing. "You see them?" I asked.

"Saw the tracks," he said.

I had been looking so hard for tracks I had nearly scraped my nose on the rocks. I heard a fluttering sound and snapped my head up to see some blue quail dotting the sky between the trees. When I looked down again, Chicken was ten yards away. I had never heard him move. His mare was as silent as he was—an Apache horse. I trotted up to him with Maximilian, breaking a few branches underfoot on the way, so that he turned with an annoyed look.

"Where we going, Sergeant?"

"Closer. Take a look. Then go back. For Christ's sake, cowboy— clam up."

If God had held Lieutenant Christie's hand, He still had a spare hand to guide this sinner through the forest. We crept between the trees about fifty yards over a cushion of moss until we reached the edge of a glade and some bare rocks. Not twenty feet away, a rattlesnake coiled in a crevice, sunning itself. Its head swiveled noiselessly round, the green eyes glittering, I slid my pistol from its holster. Sergeant Chicken saw what I was about and grabbed my arm, showing filed teeth that rightly belonged to a shark.

"Don't kill that there snake, son. Let it live. It might bite a Mexican someday."

He was grinning in his predatory way and thought that was the end of it, but he didn't fathom the depth of my intentions.

"I can't *stand* them varmints!" I cried. "Oh, little Jesus! Look, he's ready to strike!" I yanked my arm loose from his sinewy grasp, raised my pistol, didn't aim, fired . . . and missed that rattler's head by a good two feet. He whipped himself back into the crevice. The sound of the shot shattered the tranquil air of the forest, and the bullet whined off the rocks. Then the snake slithered out again and headed toward us.

"Fucking half-wit!" Chicken hissed.

He leaped back and ran for his horse, ground-tied to a fallen juniper branch. I yelled, "I'll go this way!" I clutched Maximilian's reins and jumped down on the rocks, then headed at a run toward the trail. That rattler would need wings to catch me. And I had warned Pancho Villa.

Bullets sang above my head, and one zinged off the gray boulder where I ducked for shelter. I reached up to whack Maximilian on the rump, and he bolted across the trail into the junipers. Something tugged at my hat—it sailed off my head, cartwheeling through the dust. My scalp burned where I had been creased. Now look here, I thought—this is ridiculous. Villa and Candelario and the rest of them hadn't recognized me: they had heard the shot, caught a glimpse of my khaki uniform and figured they were being attacked by the cavalry. It would have been an ironic conclusion to my revolution if I had led Tompkins to Villa's hiding place in the sierra, but it occurred to me that it would be even more personally disappointing if by trying to warn them I wound up looking like a chunk of Swiss cheese doused in ketchup. Raising my hand over the boulder, I wigwagged my pistol.

"Chief! It's me! Tomás! Don't shoot!"

Two more bullets chipped sparks off the stone. Then I heard the nasty rattling of a machine gun and saw little explosions of dust advancing down the coulee off to the right of the boulder, marching right past me in an orderly but blood-chilling progression. I was used to this, but that didn't mean I liked it. Warm blood already tickled my ear. I kept the cheeks of my tail pressed tightly together to avoid my body getting more alarmed than my brain wanted it to be. And any minute, with all this hullabaloo, Tompkins and the cavalry would come barging up the trail and fall on Villa, with me squeezed in the middle.

I looked off to the right again, to see how the machine gun might be traversing, and spotted the rattler sliding down the rock face in the sunlight, wriggling purposefully to where I hunched behind the boulder. From under cold green eyes his forked tongue darted out of a satanic mouth. I fired at him and missed. He slithered forward, and that did it for me. I shoved off hard to the left, bent low and soared down the cliff onto the trail. tumbling in the dirt like a rodeo clown. The breath flew out of me . . . pain ripped through my arm.

"Damned fools!" I yelled. "Cut it out! *It's me!*"

Just before I reached the shelter of the junipers, staggering along on all fours, bullets worrying the air all around my head, I shot a glance down the trail in a last hope that they'd recognize their lost gringo *compadre* and come loping up to give me a hug and a decent apology. I saw them clear enough. . . .

But it wasn't Villa and Candelario. A dozen Carranzista soldiers blocked the trail some fifty yards away, with an officer on a black horse waving a quirt and yelling at the machine gunners to kick the barrel over in my direction. I felt like God, having finally seen what was lying there in His hand, had opened His fingers and shaken it loose like some kind of bug.

I dove into the forest. Maximilian saved my bug's life. He nosed toward me through the trees, nickering with pleasure. I jumped up and pulled a dirty trick. I had seen Geronimo do it back in Oklahoma in Mr. Miller's rodeo when he went after the buffalo. I grabbed the horn of the saddle with one hand and the stirrup iron with the other, stretching myself flat along Maximilian's flank so that he was between me and the Carranzistas, who were firing wildly into the forest. With one spur I kicked his rump . . . off we went at a trot between the junipers. It was an uphill slope and I couldn't see a thing, just smelled sweat and horseflesh. The low juniper branches slashed my shirt straight down the back and took half my hide with it.

He was a smart horse, and a lucky one—or else the Carranzistas couldn't see his smoky shape in the hiding shadows of the forest. We reached the head of the slope and broke into a little sunlit glade. It was quiet there. I could only hear Maximilian's snuffling and my harsh breath, and feel his heart, big as a coconut, beating fast beneath the hard gray hide. I worked my way up into the saddle and jammed my feet into the stirrups. Gulping warm air, I leaned down, kissed him between the ears and thanked him.

"I'd do the same for you, amigo, if I could."

We got out of the glade quickly, and I chose a gentle descent through some hawthorns, then came out of the forest onto a burro path. It looked to me like it wound around the mountain back in the direction of Pahuirachic. Shooting began, back where I had come from, and I guessed that Sergeant Chicken had led the cavalry back to the Carranzistas and they hadn't yet realized they were fighting on the same side, or were spoiling for a scrap and didn't give a damn. Not my fault. I used my sleeve to wipe the blood off my ear and cheek, and eased Maximilian into a slow trot south toward Pahuirachic. These mountains looked more familiar to me. Villa was nearby—I decided I would drop in on him and tell him what all the shooting had been about.

It took me nearly three hours to find the cave. You couldn't see it from a distance, not unless you had Pancho Villa's eyes, but I remembered some stands of dead maguey in the ravine below it, and the water hole, and eventually I found them. By now my back smarted and stung from where the branches had scored it, and I thought I might have busted my shoulder when I jumped from the rattler's path onto the trail. I sipped warm water from my canteen, changed out of my cavalry uniform, stuffed it into the saddlebags and began to climb the slope. It was awfully quiet . . . no sound but crickets in the brush and a breeze feathering through the ravine. A few buzzards coasted far up above the crest of the hot blue sky. When I reached the cave I was out of breath.

The cave was empty. For a minute I thought it might be the wrong cave. Then I caught the faint smell of disinfectant and coonshit that still lingered in the dampness, and when I poked around in the dirt I found bits of eggshell and charcoal from an old fire. It was the right cave. I figured they had been gone for about a day or two.

Hunkering down at the entrance, I gazed round at the stony brown mountains struck by the afternoon sun. The silence was sweet and soothing, soft as a snowfall. It was pleasant there, and surely peaceful. A man could do much worse. Down below, beyond those distant peaks, crazy men wanted nothing but to kill each other. They froze at night, their tongues hung out by day. Up here, none of that made sense. If I stayed, I could live on the mountain, trap quail and deer, never have a care or enemy in the world, and no one would shoot at me. A hermit's life might be the best that this earth could offer, and I even had William Shakespeare in my saddlebags for company. By the time I worked my way through to *The Tempest* and *Henry VIII,* I would have forgotten all the good parts of *Richard III* and *The Merchant of Venice* and could start all over again.

It tempted me for about five minutes, and then I understood that I was a creature of the flesh, and there were too many people back in that lunatic world whom I wanted to hug and smile at, and I came to terms with something in my nature and said aloud at the sky, "I'll take the bad with the good . . . hell, that's all there is."

Getting shot at all the time is no tonic, but afterwards it does tend to make you think straight about why you're pleased not to be dead. I slid down the rocky slope between the cactus plants. The skin of my back had been peeled away in the forest, my head was bloody and I thought my shoulder might be broken or out of joint. I hoisted myself into the saddle. I knew where I wanted to go, what tempted me more than the mountain. The women I loved were in Parral. The cavalry was headed there too. I was glad to be rid of them for a while, but it might be an intelligent idea—if I wanted to keep on Patton's good side, and if ever I wanted to live in Texas—to be there when Tompkins arrived, so I could shore up my credibility by spinning some yarn about first the rattlesnake and then the Carranzistas chasing me. Hell, wasn't it partly true?

Partly true, in a world full of loonies and hunters and liars, like myself, seemed like gold.

33   " 'Tis true:
there's magic in the web of it."

Patricio let me in at the gate of Los Flores and walked a weary Maximilian around to the stables. The lovebirds and the macaw screeched in their cages. Elisa, in demin and boots just as I had imagined her, slid out the door and spotted me standing there in her garden.

"Tom! Oh, Tom . . ."

I must have looked like a motherless calf that had bawled its way through a barbed-wire fence and then had a losing argument with a bobcat. She moved to embrace me, then held back. I looked over her shoulder toward the pink stone of the hacienda, hot in the morning sun, and didn't see Rosa. But she couldn't be far, and I thought I heard footsteps moving quickly on gravel.

"It's all right, Elisa. We're old friends. You can kiss me."

She looked fine—lean, suntanned, hair yellow as fresh butter. She came into my arms and hugged me tightly, so that I felt the heat of her breasts beneath the denim. I smelled faded perfume behind her ears. I thought, this is what it's like to come home. The vanilla orchid vines had their flowering now, in May, and the blossoms of the African tulip flowed nearby to the ground. I often wonder, at this distance of years and space, if it would have changed things had Rosa been the one to come to the door. Because, already, my heart was being rent and tugged.

"You look like hell, Tom. Are you all right?"

"Sleep and a hot bath are what I need. Where's Rosa?"

She came round the corner of the house in the shade of the poinciana trees, then stepped off the gravel path into a flood of sunlight. Barefoot, she wore a white cotton dress and some silver Indian bracelets I had never seen before. It had only been three months, but it was a different Rosa. Her black hair was swept up in a thick bun atop her head, and her coffee-colored skin shone as if she had freshly scrubbed. She carried a notebook and pencil. She looked thinner, but what had changed most wasn't something you could point a finger at and say, "That's new. That's different." She was a young woman now, not a girl. I cut loose from Elisa and held out my arms. Dark eyes shining, she flew across the grass.

"Tomás . . ."

She smelled of Elisa's perfume, and the musk of her black hair was even more familiar to me than those other canary-colored strands. This was home too. I had carried all that in my mind, never forgotten the sepia photograph of the two women by the gate, hands frozen in good-bye. I looked over her shoulder and saw Elisa's eyes still smiling, a kernel of sadness in the sea-green depths. Rosa drew back.

"Are you hurt, Tomás?"

"Hell no. I'm wild and woolly and full of fleas. Got moss on my teeth, and I hugged a grizzly bear so hard he begged for mercy. I've been eating eggs out of an eagle's nest, and the eagle's so scared she hides. I rode a panther bareback. Rattlesnakes have bit me and crawled right off and died. I just took in too much territory, that's all."

They both brought me to the house, where I worked off my sweaty boots, slapped the dust from the seat of my pants and stretched out on one of the leather chairs in the big cool room, full of fragrant white roses and lilacs in Chinese vases. This would be any man's idea of heaven, once we got the sleeping arrangements sorted out. If I had my way, I realized, I'd never leave.

Elisa parked me in the room where Candelario and I had slept when we had come over the mountains from Chihuahua City with the sack of gold. She and Rosa fussed over me in a way that made me purr. I must have stunk like a whorehouse in a heat wave, but after a hot bath I was fresh as a powdered babe. They fed me veal in lemon sauce and fresh buttered spinach and black bread, and I drank half a bottle of cold white wine that made me dizzy. My shoulder wasn't busted, but it was bruised to the bone and I was practically a one-armed man. Rosa put a paste of mustard and wild herbs on me; that took the sting away. Elisa cleaned the scalp wound and wrapped my head in a white bandage. I looked like that fellow in the Revolutionary War—the American one—beating his drum on the way to Bunker Hill, or wherever he was going.

I was glad to be alone that night. I was worn out and wouldn't have made good horizontal company . . . and besides, that was a situation I hadn't yet figured out how to handle. Rosa was my woman, but she had made no move to claim me. More to the point, I hadn't claimed *her*. Now that I was here, a sense of well-being had descended upon me. A hasty move, I realized, could put an end to that. I wasn't pawing around for turmoil anymore, but if Rosa had worked herself into the fabric of my life, as I had decided a long time ago, Elisa was woven in that fabric now too. I didn't want to start unraveling until I was dead certain what was right for each of them and for me.

I slept ten solid hours and woke to the sun, feeling stiff but perky. Over a breakfast of flapjacks and coffee I told them all about my adventures and how Major Tompkins and the flying column of the Thirteenth Cavalry were due to descend on Parral looking for a man who wasn't there. Rosa, wearing a blue cotton dress and a silver comb in her hair, just sat quietly smiling at me. Military moves were beyond her concern.

But Elisa understood more and didn't like it. She leaned back to tap her riding crop on the table. She told me then that Carranza had issued an order to his garrisons to keep the Americans out of the cities—by force if necessary.

"The people here hate Don Venus. They love Francisco Villa. If they think the cavalry's hunting for him and about to find him, they'll resist."

"The cavalry can hunt all they like. He's not here."

"Tom, how will the people in Parral know that?"

"I'll find Tompkins and head him off. Tell him Villa's scooted."

"He may not believe you. And there may not be time. They may just attack."

"Attack? No chance. That's not the American way, Elisa," I said, quoting Patton and feeling proud.

/ 381

After breakfast we went to the library, where I could stretch out more comfortably on a leather chair and ottoman, and when Rosa left for a while to look after one of the pintos who had a case of distemper, I asked Elisa how things had gone between them. I had noticed that note-book and pencil in Rosa's hand when we first met in the garden.

"It was the way I thought it would be, Tom. We're friends. You didn't tell me you'd started to teach her to read and write. That was good of you. When I found out, I took up where you left off."

So what I had wanted had come about without my asking. If only all things in life were so ordained! Elisa, straddling a hardback chair, wore her tight blue denim shirt with nothing on beneath it, whipcord breeches and carved riding boots. It was the kind of working outfit that wasn't meant to tempt a man, but it had the opposite effect on me. Every time she shifted in the chair I saw those lithe muscles press against the cloth.

"Can I ask you something?" she said.

"That's not like you, Elisa. When were you ever shy?"

"All right. I'm not. You're back, although no one knows for how long. What do you want here?"

I knew exactly what she meant, and I didn't want to fudge. But I didn't know the answer. I had come back to discover it.

"One thing's sure," I said. "I want a little harmony in my life. And I don't want to hurt anyone. Not Rosa, not you. Does she know about us?"

"I suspect she guesses. But I never told her."

"If she guesses, or knows . . . is she jealous?"

"Tom, a woman isn't a female man. Rosa doesn't think that she owns your body."

"And the rest of me? My feelings? They're not constant, either. They never were. I love Rosa, and what I feel for you—if it's not love, Elisa, then I don't know what to call it." I made an important confession then, and a discovery. "I used to think I wasn't greedy," I said, "but now I know that's not so. I don't know how to deal with that. I came back to find out. You and Rosa each give me something, and whatever it is, I need it. Until I sort myself out, I can't give equal value."

"Did you stop loving Rosa," asked Elisa, "when you were here with me?"

"No, I didn't. Isn't that the problem?"

"But you're a warm-blooded man, Tom! You don't love wisely, but you love well. With a whole heart! You may not see that, but I do. So does Rosa."

I became distracted for a moment when the morning wind blew the curtains apart so that the sun burst into the room and turned her hair into fluttering gold. She had moved to share the ottoman with my feet, legs tucked beneath her black riding boots, one hand resting on the Indian carpet. I fished in my pocket for the makings of a cigarette.

"Well, Tom. There you are," she murmured at me. "Divided, although that needn't be."

"Can I sew myself together, like a torn shirt?"

"You can try."

"And what do I do while I'm here? Would you keep me on if I had Rosa in my bed?"

"I don't own you, either."

"My mama brought me up to have better manners, Elisa. I'm your guest."

"And my house is yours. I knew you'd come back, and I knew that Rosa would be here for you." She beckoned to my hand, and I gave her a puff of my cigarette.

"You're aces on kings, Elisa. So tell me this. How would Rosa feel if I went off to your four-poster? Assuming, which I don't, that I was invited."

"Ask her," she said, a merry light flickering in her green eyes.

"I couldn't."

"Tom, you're a clever man. You may try to play the happy-go-lucky cowboy, but it doesn't wash. You know how to get what you want."

"Do I? No. Things just happen to me, and it seems I usually don't have much choice."

"Nonsense," Elisa laughed. "You always choose. I don't know anyone, and never did, who *makes* things happen the way you do. That's why I know you'll be all right whatever you turn to—in this house, or anywhere." She rose gracefully and began to pin her hair. "I've got to go. The mare's in foal. She needs Aunt Elisa."

She left me there with something to think about. I strolled through the orchard and listened to the wind blow across the desert. But thinking was one thing . . . coming to conclusions was another.

After supper the three of us dropped comfortably into the leather chairs in front of the fireplace, sipping coffee and brandy. After a while we heard a tinkling of the gatebell . . . then, a minute or so later, a squeal from Francisca. I hoisted myself out of my chair and took my holstered pistol down from the peg by the mantelpiece. A man was chuckling softly in the garden. Francisca was giggling.

I stepped outside into the cool air, and in the twilight I saw a broad shape I would have known anywhere. Setting Francisca aside, he thumped up to me.

"Tomás!"

"Candelario! What in hell are you doing here?"

"Visiting the pleasant places of my youth. What else?" He gave me a hairy embrace, and I inhaled a week's sweat. "And you, Tomás? The same, I presume?"

"I went back to Pahuirachic, to the cave, but you were all gone. Some damned Carranzistas skinned my hide a few times with a machine gun, and I needed a hot bath. This was the nearest tub."

"And the water here is just the right temperature. You devil!"

"Come inside, *coño*. Get warm. Say hello to the ladies."

"Tomás! Not a devil. *The* devil."

By then he was inside the front door. In the lamplight I saw how weary and thin he looked, black beard bushier than before and filled with gray dust. He took off his hat, smiling craftily at Elisa and then Rosa. *"Buenas nochas, señora y señorita.* My warmest compliments. I have a great favor to ask of you . . . in a moment." He turned back to me. "The chief is worse, Tomás. That's why I came."

"Didn't he go to Chihuahua City? I thought—"

"We would never have made it to Chihuahua City. There were gringo soldiers around San Nicolás. We brought him here. He's waiting outside the town." While I gawked, he bowed again to Elisa. "Señora, I have a message from General Villa. He humbly requests the hospitality of your house and an introduction to the *curandera* at Atotonilco. If not, he will die or lose his leg. I beg you, for old times' sake—if you've forgiven me for helping to cheat you out of your quarter horse—or just from the goodness of your heart, which I know to be beautiful, sweet and kind, to let him stay."

"Of course," Elisa said, and glanced meaningfully at me. My mouth still gaped open. Then it began to function.

"Candelario," I blabbered, "I told Patton—I told the cavalry—that the chief was coming here! To Parral! I didn't know . . ."

"And so he has," Candelario said gloomily, after he had digested it, "which makes you a prophet. But now he'll have to stay. Another night on the road, or in a cave, will kill him. Let me get Hipólito, and then we'll all put our heads together and decide what to do about this. You know my opinion of you, Tomás. You're a genius. You always think of something."

Pancho Villa didn't arrive until midnight, when the city of Parral was asleep. Hipólito and three soldiers silently brought him in through the gate on his litter; he was exhausted, and they took him straight to bed. Candelario moved his gear in with me, and Elisa put up a cot for Hipólito in a spare room behind the stables. The rest of the escort, with Rodolfo Fierro in command, rode stealthily out of town for the little caves at Cuevecillas de Abajo, where we had camped last October before setting out for the Púlpito. At two o'clock in the morning I met with Elisa in the library.

"Have you got an idea, Tom?"

"Not a one. But it'll come to me."

"You'll let me know?"

"Oh, you bet. First tell me about this *curandera* in Atotonilco."

"Her name is Doña Maria. She's more of a *bruja,* a witch, than a *curandera*. She's very old, very difficult. I don't think she'll come here, even if it's General Villa. We may have to take him there. Atotonilco's a strange place—there's an old church built on the ruins of a Toltec healing ground, with stone heads of the Toltec gods. People come from hundreds of miles and wear crowns of thorns. They whip themselves. Some come all the way on their knees."

"Do you believe in all this stuff, Elisa?"

"What works, works. It will help a lot if Villa believes."

"Oh, he does." I remembered the tale of the black chicken and the clap.

"I'm very tired. Goodnight, my sweet."

I kissed her in a brotherly fashion and went off to my room. Among all the comings and goings, Rosa had slid off to bed too. She slept upstairs, in the same part of the house as Elisa. I collapsed into the cold sheets, while Candelario snored, and lay there in the dark trying to think of a plan. Sleep came first; inspiration was shy.

At dawn I woke in a sweat, saddled Maximilian and rode northward out of town in the cool gray morning. I guessed that the flying column of the Thirteenth would arrive tomorrow at the latest, although Pershing had given orders not to hurry, and I knew now that Tompkins would happily stop en route to clean up any pockets of Villistas he heard were roaming the mountains. I didn't see anyone except some half-naked Yaquis straggling along the trail and a toothless old *campesino* on a gray-bearded burro. I asked them all if they had heard of any cavalry coming this way, but they all shrugged.

When I got back to Los Flores, Candelario and Hipólito had already ridden off to make the arrangements with Doña Maria. Rosa met me in the garden and told me she had brought breakfast to Pancho Villa in his bed.

"How is he?"

"Bad, Tomás. He didn't even try to pinch me."

"And how are you, *cariña?*"

Rosa hesitated a minute. "Tomás, there is something you must know. Try not to be angry. . . ." She lowered her eyes. "In Torreón, the last time, after I found you, I wanted to have a child by you. And I tried." Then she looked up, boldly yet sadly. "I never protected myself. But I know now what I thought might be true when I was with my husband. I am barren. I wanted to tell you this before . . . before you decided anything."

As always, the way she spoke, the things she said, touched me to the core.

"How can you be sure, Rosa?"

"We did it so many times." She chuckled. "I can be sure."

"Maybe it's me."

Her eyes widened. "Impossible. You are too *macho.*"

"But you're too *hembra.*" It meant female, as *macho* meant male.

With her fingertips she touched my cheek. It was warmer than a kiss. Then she smiled, and I saw something of the old naughty sparkle in her eyes.

"I know about you and my friend, Tomás."

"What friend?"

"Señora Griensen. Our friend. Elisa."

"Oh? What do you know? And *how* do you know?"

"She didn't tell me. She would never do that. I have a good nose, like your chief. I know that when you were here you slept with her."

"Oh. You do, eh? Well, look, Rosa—"

"I don't mind. She owed nothing to me. She is a beautiful woman. If she were ugly or had a mean tongue, I would mind. You chose well. So did she. How could a man resist? Or, for that matter," she laughed, "how could she?"

I cleared my throat uncomfortably, although I was grateful beyond measure. "I didn't sleep with her last night, Rosa, or the night before. Maybe you thought I did, because I didn't come to you. What I mean is . . ." My voice trailed off.

"You can," she said. "She loves you, Tomás. And she wants you."

"Well . . . Jesus!" I snorted like a horse, waving my hands awkwardly in the air. "How about that? Thanks! Don't you want me too?"

"Of course."

"Then—"

I couldn't finish. These women were unmanning me with their kindness. What lay behind it? Something, I was sure, that I didn't understand. But Elisa had said that a woman wasn't a female man. And even if a man had made such an offer, I wouldn't have been all that sure. Then I remembered something Elisa had told me long ago, when we first met, about her cousin who had once visited her from Germany.

"Rosa, did anything happen between you and Elisa?"

"Happen? I don't understand, Tomás."

I stammered, searched and finally found the words to ask.

Rosa smiled. "No, *mi capitán.* That never happened, although it could have. But she loves me. And I may love her. I don't really know. And it may be," she said enigmatically, "that it doesn't really matter."

I had carried the conversation to the limit of my understanding—then. I couldn't ask any more questions, and I didn't want to offer any more answers. "Rosa," I said, "I have to go see the chief."

I tapped softly on his door. After looking at his leg, which was a mess—the skin blackened and the wound suppurating—I told him how I had so cleverly misled the cavalry in the direction of Parral. He was too sick to really understand.

"These things happen," he said weakly, "although you don't seem to be as lucky as before. But neither am I. We'll worry about it when they get here. I had to leave the cave . . . I knew it even before the Carranzistas showed up. Too much cave air thins the blood and gives you gout. There was a rain dwarf in there too. He was trying to kidnap my spirit. Remind me to tell that to Doña Maria. When is she coming?"

"Later, chief." I wondered if his mind was going too.

When Candelario and Hipólito returned they brought bad news. Doña Maria wouldn't come. If the chief wanted to see her, he would have to journey to Atotonilco. They had arranged the visit for this evening.

Villa sighed. "I have no choice. If I refuse now, she'll put a hex on me."

All day we waited. I steered clear of Rosa and rode out again in the late afternoon on the trail to Pahuirachic. The Carranzista soldiers patrolled the hills, so I had to leave my rifle and cartridge belts behind; I put on a ragged shirt and baggy pants borrowed from Patricio. But there was no sign of Tompkins or his scouts.

When it grew dark Candelario and I lifted Villa onto his horse. Elisa came too, but Rosa stayed behind at Los Flores. We couldn't carry the chief on the litter for five miles, and when we rode into the desert he began to cry again from the pain.

The sun had set and the desert horizon was a dark rich blue, then a layer of soft rose shading to a band of cream. The Toltec heads of Atotonilco stared at us in the light of a full moon. Pilgrims camped outside the church on the stone terraces. In the ivory light I could see the crowns of thorns they had wound about their heads, the rope whips dangling from their belts, the bloody knees. There were hundreds of them and they made no sound, just watched us pass by. These were people whom the revolution barely touched; they believed in something else, not of this world.

Elisa led us around the side of the church to an adobe hut. A young girl came out, carrying a candle. This was Doña Maria's granddaughter, and she beckoned us inside. Candelario lifted Villa off the horse and carried him again like a child, half-unconscious. Hipólito stood guard outside with the little girl, and the rest of us entered.

The hut was only two rooms—the main one, and an alcove with an unmade bed—and as full of cigarette smoke and the pungent smell of marijuana as a Juárez cantina. There was hardly room to move around, and you had to stoop to avoid knocking into strings of garlic and other paraphernalia that hung from the wooden beams. I nearly banged my nose against a dried hummingbird before I settled next to Elisa on a wooden box. Bones hung on strings, scraps of meat rested in little bird-cages. Shelves were crammed with dead toads, herbs in shoeboxes, snakeskins, hunks of hair, paper cutouts of angels and devils, buzzard feathers, dolls stuck with pins, bowls of withered flowers, playing cards and amulets against the evil eye. The room was lit by two flickering candles. A white, three-legged mongrel dog with no tail lay on the dirt floor, gnawing a huge bone that looked as if it came from the leg of an ox—or a man.

Doña Maria sat spread-legged on a rumpled bed in one corner, her back propped against pillows, smoking a cigarette. She looked about seventy-five, with sweaty gray hair drawn into a pigtail, a beaked nose, dark eyes set in a bony Indian face. She wore copper earrings and a copper bracelet around one thin wrist. A wrinkled dress flowed down to her ankles over a swollen belly. She stroked an orange cat and fed it bits of meat. Another cat crouched on a shelf over her head, between a photograph of Francisco Madero and a wooden statue of Jesus Christ, staring down at us with mad eyes.

A pudgy, greasy-looking man in the clothes of a *campesino* sat on the edge of the bed with an old violin balanced on his lap. Elisa whispered to me that this was Doña Maria's son. He stood up slowly as Candelario helped Villa across the dirt to the bed, and with a gasp of pain the chief sat down and faced the witch.

"Doña Maria . . . do you know who I am?"

"Francisco Villa."

"Can you help me?"

In a cracked voice she said, "If you want to be helped, anything's possible. Why are you so afraid?"

"I'm not afraid of you, señora," Villa whispered sadly. "But I'm afraid I'm going to die."

"Then you will. I can't help you if you're afraid. Have you seen a snake, a mad dog, a charging bull or any other terrifying sight lately?"

"No, señora, I haven't."

"Have you stumbled and struck a rock that you might have offended?"

"That's possible."

Candelario crouched next to me now. "Tomás," he whispered in my ear, "this woman knows everything. I'm sure the chief has offended a rock."

"In that case," I whispered back, "I'm a dead man. I've bounced off a dozen of them lately. And I've seen a snake too."

Maybe that would account for all the troubles that were yet to befall me. In the light of what Doña Maria did that night, I've always wondered.

"There's more," Villa said to her unhappily. "I've been living in a cave. And a rain dwarf shared it with me. He may have attacked me in my sleep."

She shook her head. "I don't think I can help you. Not if you're afraid."

"Please try, señora. I'll give you anything you ask."

Doña Maria gathered her skirts and got to her feet—the cat jumped off her lap and ran to a dark corner. Standing, she was tinier than I had realized. She began muttering to herself in a language I didn't know. I looked quickly at Elisa, who murmured through clenched teeth: "Tzotzil. She's a Tzotzil Indian. From the south."

Turning to Villa, the old woman spoke again in Spanish.

"Do you know how I became a *curandera?*" Of course, she would never identify herself as a *bruja,* a witch. "When I was seventeen I became ill. A mad dog crossed my path, and I couldn't get well. My bones ached until I thought the dwarfs were sucking the marrow. I didn't want to eat. One midnight I woke and found a bowl of dead flowers at the foot of my bed. Then a cock began to sing, and an old man covered with running sores came into the house. The dwarfs told me to lick him from head to toe. I did this disgusting thing, and in the morning I got out of my bed feeling hungry. After that, I got well. I soon started curing others. Do you believe that story?"

Villa nodded vigorously.

"Good. First I'll try to end your fright. Then I'll pull the cave air out of your body. If that works, curing your leg will be easy."

She waddled into the center of the room, so that I had to draw back my knees and lean against the damp wall. When she came close to me I smelled rotten eggs. The dog was in her way—she kicked it smartly in the side, and it slunk out of the hut. Her son handed her a knotted mesquite stick, and Doña Maria began to beat the ground, raising up dust. Then she turned to each corner of the hut, and called out: "Come! Come to your house! Don't be lazy! Don't be frightened! Come directly to your house!"

Candelario whispered, "She's calling for the chief's soul. His fear has driven it away."

When she was satisfied that her message had been heard, Doña Maria picked up a bowl of water and dumped some dead flowers in it. She handed it to Pancho Villa.

"Now shut your eyes, señor. You're a general, aren't you?"

Villa, with his eyes closed, nodded.

"You command many men?"

"Not so many now, señora. But in times past, thirty thousand."

"Then you know how to command. Don't speak . . . but command your soul to return. Command it to kick the fright out of your blood, as I kicked the dog out of the room."

I could see Villa's eyelids tighten, and the muscles of his back grew tense. He was silently commanding. A strange energy seemed to flow from him.

"Open your eyes." She peered closely into them, and then she smiled, showing brown teeth. "You see? You're not frightened anymore.

Your soul is back in place. That was easier than I thought it would be. You have much faith."

Villa wagged his head brightly. But I didn't see how that festering leg was going to respond to a shout or a command.

"Now," said Doña Maria, quite pleased with herself, "we'll see if you've really been invaded by cave air."

She ordered Villa to take off his shirt, then snatched an egg from a shelf and rubbed it all over his back. When she was done she broke the egg and poured it into a glass of water. The white of the egg rose immediately, whirling about. Little bubbles formed on the surface. Doña Maria grunted; he was obviously shot through with cave air. From another shelf she took a doughnut-shaped gray stone, placed it against Villa's chest, then bent and began to suck through the stone. After a minute, she straightened up and spat on the floor.

She continued for nearly half an hour, sucking at his chest and stomach, then his back, spitting out the cave air each time. I grew sleepy. I looked at Elisa, but her eyes were on Doña Maria. They never wavered. Candelario hardly breathed. When she was finished sucking, the *curandera* brushed Villa's chest with a handful of geraniums and pepper-tree twigs. She straightened up, her old bones creaking.

"There! How do you feel?"

"Stronger," Villa said. "The cave air seems gone."

"Seems gone? Or *is* gone?"

"It's gone," he said forcefully.

"And you're no longer frightened that you'll die?"

"I will live, señora, and get well."

"Now I understand why you're a great general. And now," she announced, "we can cure your leg."

She instructed Villa to lie down on her bed, on his back, and then nodded to her son, who tucked the violin under his greasy chin and began to play. His bow squeaked across the strings with one jarring note after another—a strange song, if a song at all, that made the hairs on my neck stand on end. It was like no music I had ever heard, and I wouldn't care to hear it again. He fiddled all the while that the witch performed the operation.

First she called in the granddaughter, whispering in her ear. The girl went out and returned with a squirming sack, which Doña Maria placed at the foot of the bed. She turned to Candelario, Elisa and me.

"What you will see is sacred. If you tell anyone, your blood will turn to bile. You'll have headaches that will make you wish you were dead. No *curandera* will be able to help you. Swear."

I swore, and so did Candelario and Elisa. And I've never told a soul, not until now, when it no longer matters.

After that she began to chant again in Tzotzil, and while she chanted she unwrapped the bandages from Villa's leg. The girl took them, yellow with pus, dark with dried blood, and threw them out the window. Villa arched his back at the pain. The cat on the shelf stared down at him, switching its tail.

The leg was still black, and the wounds on both sides, where the bullet had struck and exited, had turned an angry red. Doña Maria bent the leg slightly so that she could see better. Villa groaned.

"Your fear is gone," she murmured. "Remember, your soul is back in place." She beckoned to the girl, pointing to a crumpled pack of cigarettes on the table. The girl put one in her mouth and lit it from the candle flame, then handed it to Doña Maria, who bent over the bed. She inhaled and began to blow gray smoke into the wound. I glanced at Candelario.

He leaned across to whisper, "So that when the sickness escapes, it won't infect us."

The rest went quickly, and in the candlelight it was hard to see exactly how it was accomplished. From a pile of parrot feathers Doña Maria drew out another cigarette, hand-rolled in brown paper, which she gave Villa to smoke. She told him to inhale deeply and take in as much air as smoke. Villa puffed hard, and I could smell the marijuana. Doña Maria unknotted the sack the girl had brought in and took out a young chicken, its legs tied with string. She muttered the whole time. Her son fiddled. The girl handed her a pair of rusty scissors. Holding the squawking chicken by the throat, she rubbed it over Villa's wound on both sides of the leg. He smoked and never said a word. Then she stabbed the chicken in the neck with the scissors. The bird shrieked . . . blood dripped on the wound. Villa's eyes rose dreamily to gaze at the beams on the ceiling. The girl darted into the alcove and came back with a kettle of hot water and some clean rags. Doña Maria spread more chicken blood from the wounded knee down to the ankle.

"The devil must be fed," she hissed to Villa.

More Tzotzil gibberish followed. The fiddler's fingers began to pluck at the strings of the violin. Chanting, the witch tossed the bleeding chicken in the dirt and laid her gnarled hands on the open wound, one in back of the knee, one on the shinbone. The girl blew out one of the candles, and foul black smoke plumed in the air. The room grew darker, and the girl crept closer to the foot of the bed where the chief lay. I really only noticed her then for the first time. She had wild black eyes and a harelip. She couldn't have been more than thirteen, and she never spoke.

Then Doña Maria shrieked, *"The devil will come out!"*

While I strained to see, the girl bent swiftly in the shadows. From the sack she plucked a second chicken, and with a rapid slash of a knife she cut it deeply from gizzard to pope's nose. The bird's guts and hot blood exploded outward, drenching Villa's leg. Doña Maria shrieked again . . . she fell forward, grabbing at bits of meat and clots of blood, scooping them up as if they were pouring from the leg and not from the chicken. The girl had already thrust the writhing carcass back into the sack.

"Here is the devil! Look, señor! *Look now at your devil!*"

Gasping, Villa tried to sit up. Pinned as he was by the witch, the best he could do was arch his neck forward and stare in wonder. She held up a morsel of the bloody guts.

"A bad devil, señor! The worst I've seen . . . *but it's out!*"

Swiftly she began to wipe away the mess with a rag, throwing the pieces of guts into the bowl of dead flowers that had cured the chief's fright. The girl kept pouring hot water over the rags, and the witch kept wiping at the wounds. I had almost heaved my own guts, but now I edged off the wooden box and moved slowly across the room in a crouch, toward the bed. Candelario and Elisa were right at my side.

The leg was still stained with blood, but it was no longer black. The coloring had faded to a reddish-gray. The angry holes were pink now, and the pulpy flesh inside was white with only a few specks of chicken blood. When Doña Maria wiped the flecks away, the wound showed itself clean.

In the chief's pale face, his eyes gleamed—the pupils dilated and very black. He looked at us eagerly. "It's cured," Candelario whispered.

Villa thumped back on the pillow.

"The bones will knit well," Doña Maria said. "Tomorrow he will walk. In a week he will ride as before. He will not limp. He won't conquer his enemies, but they will never conquer him. He will die from many bullets, with his hands on something large and round. He will be happy when he dies, and it will be quick. I don't know when it will happen . . . but not soon." Her eyes were glazed.

When she came out of her trance she and the girl finished cleaning up, bandaged the wound, and Villa walked outside, supported by me and Candelario. He mounted his horse in the cold night air. He never groaned once.

She charged ten pesos, plus three for the fiddler, which Hipólito paid in silver. I doubt if it covered much more than the cost of the two dead chickens. But Elisa told me they would make soup for a week.

The next morning Villa woke early, hobbled out into the garden and then to the stables, where I was saddling Maximilian and Elisa was tending to her mare. I was wearing a straw sombrero and the baggy white clothes of a *campesino,* for I meant to ride out and look for the cavalry.

"Why are you dressed like that, Tomás? Are you about to do honest work and plow some fields?"

I stared at him with astonishment. The color had returned to his face and he was using a borrowed hickory cane, but it was obvious that he felt hardly any pain. Doña Maria had turned me into a believer, no matter what hocus-pocus she conjured up to do it. In my time I had used a bit of hocus-pocus myself.

Villa limped over to Elisa. "Señora Griensen, I haven't had a chance to truly thank you. Excuse my bad manners. You are a saint."

"In the next life," she said, smiling. "In this one, unfortunately, too many pleasures are denied to saints."

Villa looked at us both, then winked. "I know what you mean, señora."

"General Villa, my house is yours. And if I were you, I'd use it. Stay indoors until dark. Tomás may bring us some unfriendly visitors." Her gaze shifted to me. "Or have you thought of something to keep them away?"

"Not yet," I said grumpily.

I rode out on the trail once more, thinking again about Doña Maria and realizing that there were more than a few things on this earth that fell beyond my understanding, when suddenly, between Parral and a little pueblo called Santa Cruz, over a distant hill I spotted a plume of dust fouling the chaste May sky. The plume became a pillar, and under it, into my view, came the flying column of the Thirteenth Cavalry—a sweaty group of khaki-clad, unshaven men and steaming horses, led by Major Tompkins, Sergeant Chicken and a Carranzista officer.

Tompkins raised his hand and the column halted. I cantered up to him. To my surprise he was smiling. He thrust out his hand and gave me a hearty shake.

"Well done! You're alive and kicking! I'm glad to see you, son! Are you all right?"

I had almost forgotten about the bandage wrapped around my head under the sombrero.

"I had a little scrap up at Pahuirachic with those Carranzista troops. They cut me off from the column. I got knocked out, and when I came to . . . you were gone."

"Chicken told me you got spooked by a rattlesnake. Just as well you took a shot at it—otherwise we would have met them head-on, gotten all cut up by that machine gun. Damned fools! They still think we're an enemy . . . except for this man. This is Captain Mesa from the garrison at Parral. He claims Villa can't possibly be there. General Lozano's got the town sewed up tighter than a button on Lieutenant Patton's britches. No one can get in or out, and no one has, least of all Pancho Villa."

Mexican junior officers have a natural tendency to tell you what you'd like to hear. But I nodded smartly.

"He's right, Major. Villa's scooted. Headed for Durango, I heard. If you hurry, you can get onto his trail. Chicken's sure to pick it up."

"Son, I'm not in that much of a hurry. The men need rest and the horses need forage. Captain Mesa says both are available in Parral. Plus a warm welcome, and a cold whiskey and soda, and a hot bath—all of which would be mighty refreshing."

This would never do. I cleared my throat. "Major, it's likely to be the other way round. The bath will be cold, the whiskey and soda warm, and the welcome might be hotter than you'd appreciate. The people of Parral are just about ready to revolt against this General Lozano. And they don't like us, either."

I had taken the chance that Mesa didn't speak English, and by the blank look on his face I saw that I was right. But Tompkins shook his head. He was coated with dust and he hadn't shaved. "The captain's also promised to give us a sack of real coffee from his stores. That's an offer I can't resist. I'd give my Christian soul for a cup of hot coffee. And while we're there, we might as well search the town for Villa." He raised his hand. "Col-ummm . . . ho . . . oh!"

The cavalry surged forward. I had to spin Maximilian around to avoid getting knocked down by Sergeant Chicken, who had been giving me black and crabby looks from his bloodshot eyes ever since I'd appeared. And so we headed toward Parral, where, as I saw it, Major Tompkins' lust for a hot cup of coffee was about to bring him Pancho Villa's head on the saucer.

34 "Knock there, and ask your heart what it doth know."

The Thirteenth Cavalry's arrival in Parral was an occasion, and no secret, and by the time we had clattered and clopped through the town, leaving piles of dung steaming on every street, it seemed that half the population was gathered under the trees, in the dappled sunlight of the main plaza, to gawk at us. Tompkins left two troops on the trail, Troop M by the railroad station, and he rode in with Troop K. General Lozano's headquarters was under some stone arches next to the bank, and a gang of his soldiers had cleared away the taco sellers and taken their places on the cobblestones, rifles at the ready. The plaza had a raised park with wooden benches shaded by leafy eucalyptus trees, and the park was full of Carranzista soldiers too. Across from the bank, on the plaza, stood the little brick public school that Pancho Villa had built for the children of Parral. I had an uneasy feeling.

General Ismael Lozano marched out of his office in full-dress blue uniform complete with red sashes and epaulets. He was a fat pig-eyed fellow with only one arm. Tompkins, who spoke some Spanish, introduced himself.

"And why are you here, Major?"

"At the invitation of your Captain Mesa, señor. And to provision ourselves—for which, naturally, we'll pay you. In Mexican silver."

Lozano shot a dirty look at Mesa and then said: "Accompany me to my office, if you please, Major. This will have to be discussed."

Tompkins tugged me by the arm. "Come along, Mix. If he rattles too fast, I'll need your help."

We climbed some rickety stairs to the general's office, which had big French windows opening onto a balcony overlooking the plaza. No sooner did I poke my head out the window to get a view and a whiff of breeze than a mule hitched to a heavy cart came bolting down the street toward the cavalry—some citizen's form of protest and a way of starting mayhem. A yell rose from the crowd, but a big Yank from Troop K lumbered quickly into the path of the cart, grabbed the mule by the bit and brought it to a halt.

"Whoa there, Carmencita!"

The cavalry, dismounted by now, started to laugh. The crowd looked disappointed, but that simmered them down.

Lozano and Tompkins had seen that too, over my shoulder. The major slipped his holster more forward on his belt.

"This is the problem," the general said. "The people of Parral are unhappy that your soldiers are here in Mexico. For that matter, so am I. Intervention by the armed forces of one state into another is against international law. I must stress this so that you fully comprehend. You are not welcome here."

"Translate that for me, son, while I think of what to say."

I did, and then Tompkins nodded.

"Okay, General. I appreciate your opinion. As soon as my men have provisioned themselves—I have a list right here—we'll be on our merry way. That is, after we take a look around for Pancho Villa. We had a report that he was here a while ago. He may have left some men behind."

Lozano's eyes gleamed with interest. Unlike Mesa, he didn't think that Villa's presence was impossible. He studied Tompkins' list.

"You should not have come here, Major. But I wish to avoid an incident. If you will be good enough to camp outside of the city by the railroad station, the supplies will be delivered to you. And then we shall conduct the search for this bandit together. Under my command, if you please."

My heart sank—I had hoped Lozano was going to insult him and kick us out. Nothing was going right for me today.

"Good enough," Tompkins said. He saluted, and for the first time the fat general smiled.

"Viva Villa! Viva Mexico!"

The shout came from the street through the open French windows—at first one or two voices, then a swelling chorus.

Lozano said, "I suggest we go right now."

"I take your meaning, General."

We thumped down the stairs double-time. As soon as we reached the street I understood what was happening. Troop K, at an order from Sergeant Richley, had mounted their horses; the crowd had bunched up and were shaking their fists. Most of the blue-clad Carranzista soldiers had retreated to the little raised bandstand in the center of the park. But a group of white-shirted citizens had come marching up from a side street, and they were the ones making the trouble. They were led by a tall, green-eyed woman in a black sombrero, denim shirt, black pants and riding boots. She carried a Mauser hip-high. That was the way I had first seen her at the front door of the hacienda, so I knew how the soldiers felt. She didn't give the impression that she was one of the weaker sex fooling around at grown men's games. She urged the townspeople toward the uneasy troopers.

"Are you men or goats? Are you citizens of Parral? Then tell these gringo bastards to go home!"

Tompkins' lingo was good enough to understand most of it. He spoke out of the corner of his mouth to me. "Who's she?"

"A tough lady. German, used to be married to a Villista. I think it's time to leave town."

"Richley! Get those men out!"

Just at that moment Elisa raised her rifle and squeezed off a shot, well above Troop K's heads. I looked hard at the people surging around her, but she had had enough sense not to let Candelario or Hipólito come along. The bullet banged off the copper sign above the bank. Rushing up with a horse, Captain Mesa helped to hoist his general into the saddle.

"I will lead your men to safety," Lozano wheezed to us.

Elisa was still turning the air blue with curses. I hoped Tompkins couldn't understand the shades of meaning, although Lozano certainly did, and for all his pompousness he was even grinning a little. The troopers kept quiet and held their fire; there was no way they would shoot at a wild-eyed beautiful blond woman, even if she was telling them they were sons of whores, goats and one-balled faggots.

The trouble came from the most unexpected quarter: the Carranzista soldiers. Troop K had begun to retreat, with Tompkins, Richley, the pack mules and me bringing up the rear. Captain Mesa and a troop of his blue-uniformed men stayed behind with us. The sun beat down, and the swallows in the plaza chirped like a troop of disturbed monkeys. Lozano was at the head of the column, winding up a steep cobbled street. I lost sight of Elisa. The citizens and the Carranzista soldiers, who had moved out of the park and into the street to control the crowd, jostled and shoved each other. The outnumbered soldiers gave way grudgingly—they were not overly fond of the people of Parral, who had made no secret of their loyalty to Pancho Villa. Machetes flashed, striking sharply against the steel of bayonets. Then Captain Mesa, tired of being pushed around and perhaps beginning to fear for the safety of his soldiers, shouted an order. Carranzista rifles cracked . . . women screamed. I saw a white shirt blossom with blood. Tompkins yelled ahead at his men to hold their fire, to retreat to the railroad station and join Troop M. Lozano, hearing the shots, came galloping back, brandishing his sword. But it had got beyond the control of any one man.

Now a few citizens of the town had pulled pistols and were firing back at the Carranzista soldiers. Bullets whistled in every direction, some of them chipping stone off the walls above our heads. It was hard to tell whether they were aimed at us and who was doing the firing. Tompkins and I reached the crest of the hill, above the railroad embankment. The horses' hoofs rang out on the cobbles. A messenger came galloping up from Lozano.

"Señor Major, the general requests that you withdraw!"

"What the hell does he think we're doing?" Tompkins snapped. "Look here—your soldiers are shooting at *us!*"

When we got down to the embankment we turned, and now the Carranzista troop under Mesa was running down the street toward us, whooping and hollering. They must have decided, in the end, that the real enemy had white faces.

Tompkins, purple in the face rather than white, turned to Sergeant Richley. "Sergeant, give me your rifle . . ." He stood up and yelled at the charging soldiers, "Damn it, you people! Get back!"

The answer was a wild volley of shots that slammed into the embankment . . . all but one bullet, and that one gored Richley in the eye and flowered out the back of his head. He had been lying on his stomach, with only his head exposed to see over the rails. He made no sound; he just slumped over. I didn't think of it then, but he was the first American soldier of the Punitive Expedition to be killed in Mexico. It happened no more than five feet away from me. Tompkins turned to hand him back his rifle, saw the puddle of blood and knew immediately that he was dead.

"Troop M, fire at will! Troop K, withdraw!"

The battle lasted about an hour, while the Yanks steadily withdrew along the trail to Santa Cruz. The troopers had one more man killed and six wounded. About twenty Carranzista soldiers were killed, and later I found out that in the melee on the plaza they had shot four citizens of Parral. With all that smoke and confusion and dust I became separated from Tompkins, and of course I never fired my rifle. Elisa was out of her mind, I decided . . . and for all I knew then, she might have been shot by one of Mesa's men. After we passed the railroad station I veered off behind a water tank and then, when the firing slackened, ducked my head and whipped Maximilian across the tracks and down a smelly back alley that led to Calle Chorro. I wanted no more to do with the cavalry.

I threw the reins to Patricio and ran across the gravel into the house. The coolness was a balm. I heard voices in the library. Elisa sat on an ottoman, the rifle across her lap, her face dappled with sweat. Villa sprawled in a red-leather easy chair, drinking a mug of steaming coffee. Elisa looked up at me quickly.

"It worked, Tom!"

"Worked?"

"The cavalry's gone. They won't come back. Your chief is safe. Isn't that what you wanted?"

Well, I suppose she was right, and she had a right to be proud and think of herself as a hero. Where I had failed, she had succeeded. That may have irked me a trifle, but what dismayed me considerably was the realization that two Yank troopers and some fairly innocent citizens of Parral had been killed in order to achieve our purpose. The soldiers, who had only fired after they had been fired upon, were as undeserving of death as the citizens. Elisa didn't seem to understand that, or didn't seem to care. I was sure it had never occurred to Pancho Villa.

I let Elisa know what was on my mind. She flushed a little, but then she said, "Tom, it had to be. We just couldn't foresee it."

"You thought Tompkins would leave peaceably?"

"He tried, didn't he? How could anyone know the Carranzistas would shoot at the crowd?"

Villa asked, "Where are the gringos now?"

"Heading north," I said. "They've had enough of Parral. They don't want to kill Carranzistas or Mexican citizens, chief. They only want to kill you. They won't be back."

He turned to Elisa, smiling. "You saved my life, señora. If I had medals to give, I'd give you the biggest one, made of pure gold. For the moment you have only my thanks. And my loyalty to the grave."

I grunted and stomped out of the house to the stables, where I smoked a cigarette, cleaned up Maximilian and muttered to myself for the better part of an hour. It wasn't for this that I had left Texas and come back down to Chihuahua, and it certainly wasn't why I had agreed to stay on with Pancho Villa and play at being a spy. Maybe the reason I hadn't wanted to fight at Guerrero had been more than just my worry about Rosa and Elisa. What sense did it make? We'd kill some of them, they'd kill some of us. In between, a few cavalrymen would die too. What had started as a battle for land and liberty had become little more than a bloody game. It could go on forever, and the chief would keep believing that when he blew that one bugle call, a hundred thousand would rise. It wouldn't happen. I wondered if there were that many whole men left in the country to fight.

I was sick of killing, sick of being shot at, sick of running. I had come back from my mountain lair at Pahuirachic to find a different destiny. It was here, I was sure of that. I was tapped out, fed up. A stove-up cowboy—too tired to fight, but not too dumb to quit.

That night I was roaming the garden, still muttering and trying to make peace with myself, when Rosa came out of the house to find me. I hadn't seen Elisa all evening; she had stayed out of my way, and I took my meal in the kitchen alone. I didn't have much appetite, but I managed to guzzle almost a full bottle of wine, and then I had a brandy to wash it down.

Rosa, without a word, pressed her body against mine so that I inhaled the perfume of her hair. Villa was back with Hipólito in his room behind the stables. Candelario would surely sleep with Francisca. I took Rosa with me to my room, bolted the door, and we undressed. I made love to her . . . not with much joy, but it was better than I thought it would be. It was a way to kill the voices in my mind. It had been a long time, but neither of us had forgotten how to please the other.

Afterwards, she sighed. "Don't be sad, Tomás."

"I can't help how I feel."

"In war, men die. It's to be expected."

"Not this time. It didn't have to happen." I stubbed out my cigarette.

"They would have found your chief. That's all Elisa was thinking about. You would have done the same."

I might have . . . that was true. I had gone over this a dozen times already in my head and muttered versions of it to Maximilian. But nothing helped.

"I'm not angry at *her,* damn it. I'm just upset because two Americans died. And didn't have to! They didn't even want to shoot. They held their fire until one of them got killed."

"In battles, *mi capitán,* many have died. My husband. Thousands more."

"I guess I'm just tired of it all, Rosa. I wish to hell I could go home."

"You can."

"No, I can't."

Rosa was silent for a while, stroking my bare back, careful to avoid the strip of peeled hide that had scabbed and begun to heal. When I thought of all the times I had been skinned and shot and nearly blown up—at Torreón, Celaya, León, Pahuirachic—I was lucky to be whole.

Then Rosa spoke, even more gently than before. "There is one thing, Tomás. Elisa doesn't say it, but I do. If you get angry, which I hope you don't, I ask your pardon. If you hadn't come here first, and then if your chief hadn't followed, this would never have happened. If he had not chosen this house—which he did because of you—the señora would not have had to do what she did. The two gringo soldiers would not have died. The fault lies with you and General Villa."

I put a hand to her lips. Of course, she was right: Elisa had just been an instrument of our purpose. She had been brave . . . braver than I would have been. She had faced a troop of the U. S. Cavalry, with no way of knowing that Lozano wouldn't order her shot.

I had to make it up to her, but somehow this didn't seem quite the right way to go about it, with Rosa curled next to me in the darkness.

The next day, at first light, Elisa rode south into Durango with Patricio. A while ago she had made an appointment to buy an Appaloosa stallion, and she didn't return until evening.

In the late morning Villa strolled out to the stables and saddled his albino mare, then rode around the corral for half an hour. His leg hurt, he said, but he could bear it, and riding a horse would help to cure him. Back in his room he unwrapped the bandage and showed me the wound. It was pink around the edges and starting to scab.

"In a week, I'll be able to leave. And do you know what I think?" His topaz eyes gleamed; he had shaved, and his skin looked fresh and healthy. "I think our fortunes have turned. This Pershing coming to Chihuahua was the best thing that could have happened. Who could have foreseen it? The people hate the gringo soldiers, and they love the fact that they can't catch me. Ten thousand against four hundred! . . . It makes the blood sing. They will rally to me even more than before! What I told that German wasn't a lie . . . when I blow the bugle, a hundred thousand will rise. Eventually the gringos will leave. The people will be sick of Carranza and Obregón. The true revolution can begin again! And we'll win."

Oh, no. Enough was enough. He had been licked on half a dozen battlefields from Celaya to Guerrero, by Obregón and Chao and even Colonel Dodd, and he still couldn't admit defeat. Whatever we both had wanted wouldn't happen now—the future was in the hands of other men. If the ideas of the revolution were good, they would survive defeat. They might even survive victory. He had done his best, but he was a loser now.

"The first thing we'll do, Tomás, when I'm well, is get our gold out of Lake Ascensión. Then we can buy rifles and bullets and cannon. We'll attack Juárez. . . ."

I left him there, working out his plans.

When Elisa returned she was busy with the new Appaloosa, gentling him down around the mares. Dinner was as long as a rainy Sunday.

Finally, after a brandy, Rosa and the men went off in different directions. Elisa started to go too, but I caught her arm.

"Will you have one more drink with me?"

We settled down in the library, where we had spent many an evening. I coughed a few times.

"Oh, don't look so sheepish," she said. "I hate that. Spit it out." There was a sharp edge to her tongue, more than just weariness, and she didn't seem as hangdog as yesterday.

"Elisa, I got you into this, and I blamed you when I should have been blaming myself. I just wanted to say I was sorry."

"I accept your apology. I don't feel too well myself about the way it turned out. You can go." She cocked a pale eyebrow at me and drew up a corner of her mouth. "Rosa's probably waiting. Don't keep a woman waiting too long, Tomás."

So she knew about last night. That, I realized now, had been inevitable. She was mistress of the house and could figure out where everybody was and wasn't. But hadn't she given her blessing? I downed the cognac in one swallow. "Elisa, if you're angry, tell me why. You owe that to me."

"Not angry. Disappointed. You didn't go to Rosa last night. You went away from me. I don't like that."

I let out a groan. "Elisa . . ."

"It was childish."

"Maybe so. I was feeling low. Obviously, sooner or later, it had to happen."

"What's done is done." Her green eyes glinted. "But now *I'm* the one who feels low. I'm the one who went out on the street the other day, and innocent people got shot because of it. I've been feeling rotten ever since it happened. And I need a shoulder to cry on too. If need's the key to open that door you've shut ever since you got back, I've got plenty of it."

Ever since I got back? Hadn't she understood my confusion? Words, I realized, were never enough. "Let's go upstairs," I said, bold as a bull firing out of the chute.

"Let's do that."

"Want to finish your drink?"

"I don't need *that.*"

She led me upstairs. The big four-poster gave us plenty of room to stretch and curl and tangle our limbs. She cried a little before we made love, but I think they were tears of gladness as much as sorrow for the hard time she had been through. The tears that came afterwards were from pleasure. Before my brain fogged over I had one long and unbalancing thought.

Last night, Rosa. Tonight, Elisa. No qualms, no bad feeling in the bones. What did that make me? A rake? A great lover? A cocksman like

Candelario? A man who liked coffee *and* tea? Was it need or gluttony? There had to be a reckoning.

The morning after I slept with Elisa, Rosa was in a cheerful mood. She cooked a breakfast of sizzling lean bacon and fried eggs and hummed to herself all the while as Candelario boiled the coffee and I made toast in the charcoal oven. Later, in the library, she read to me in English from a school reader. She kept glancing at me warmly, and there was no sign that she knew what had happened. On balance that suited me, even though I felt a stir of guilt at her innocence—because if I had to dash back and forth calming one of them down each time I wound up in the other's bed, I would be as miserable as a razorback hog stropping himself on a fence post. Not that I meant to continue that dangerous game—Elisa one night, Rosa the next. Oh no! I had reached a decision. The part of me below the waist might be able to handle it for a while, but my nerves would last as long as a keg of cider at a barn raising. In the end I would lose them both, as well as my self-respect. And I didn't care what Elisa believed—there *was* such a thing as right and wrong, at least for me. And there still is, although perhaps my definitions have changed. Started to change even then. *Especially* then.

It was a lazy day. Patricio told us that Major Tompkins and the cavalry had headed straight north, licking their wounds. Elisa and I worked with the horses, introduced the new Appaloosa to the other mare, did some shoeing and plaited some fresh maguey ropes. Villa rode around the corral for another half-hour. Candelario took a siesta with Francisca. I wondered if I should be heading back for Bachinava in order to point Patton and Pershing in some other interesting direction . . . but I was in no hurry. They still had a lot of scouting to do around La Bufa and El Sauz.

In the late afternoon Rosa and I went into the orchard to pick oranges so she could squeeze fresh juice for the chief. She smiled at me sweetly.

"I meant to ask you earlier, Tomás . . . did you have a pleasant night?"

"Did I what?"

"Did you sleep well?"

"Uh . . . on and off. I had funny dreams." I bent to the basket of oranges, but from the corner of my eye I saw her grinning.

When I began to blush furiously, she gave a merry cackle. Then she said calmly. "Last night I had a dream too. Do you want to hear it?"

"I'm not sure I do. Damn it, Rosa, what are you crowing about?"

"In my dream you wandered through the hacienda. You found yourself at the door to Señora Griensen's room. You went right through the door, as if it were made of air, and into her bed. And you told her you were no longer angry at her. It made her very happy."

"Rosa!" I yelled. "Damnation! You had an ear at the keyhole!"

"My room is next door," she said. "The walls are thick, but I am not deaf."

"And you're not angry?"

"Not if it pleased you, Tomás. And not if it pleased the señora."

I took the risk. I couldn't lie now. "Well . . . it did. Yes, it surely did."

"That's what my ears told me."

"And you're not angry? You're *sure?*"

She smiled at my discomfort and laid her fingers on my cheek. "I would be a foolish girl to be angry, if the man I love and my best friend in the world gave each other pleasure. You're not displeased with her anymore, nor she with you. It was not wrong of you, Tomás."

This simplicity made my head ache. I had been brought up to be jealous—not that I'd had much opportunity before I left Texas—and to believe that a woman had equal rights in that department. Mexicans weren't much different, and their women would kill for love. Rosa had to be one in a million. Well, one of two in a million. I couldn't believe my luck, and knew enough not to scratch at it.

But that evening one question remained. Where to go? Everything had been discovered, confessed and apparently forgiven; there could be no more sneaking around in the dark. Freedom is always poorly organized, and I recalled an old maxim that the females of all species are most dangerous when they appear to retreat. And, I thought, when they appear to agree with each other. I might be able to double-talk Urbina and Patton and Major Tompkins, but with these two women I would never get away with it. And didn't want to. That's what I worried about . . . and should have known that the worry would bear no fruit I could eat. The women were in charge here. That was hard to accept at first, but I've learned worse lessons in my life.

Dinner was by candlelight at the big oak table: a raucous and jolly feast. Villa, now that he was mending and making new plans, which he loved almost as much as fighting battles, reminisced about his days as a bandit and told a tale about hiding out with Fierro and Urbina in the ghost town of Las Palomas, near Bachinava—he had been more frightened of the ghosts, he said, than of the *rurales.* Wine gurgled from the bottle. The bones of Francisca's jugged hare were picked clean. Finally Villa yawned. Hipólito's head was already slumping, and Candelario was ready to hunt for his Francisca, who wouldn't be hard to find. We drank a last toast to Julio, wherever he was, and then they all bowlegged off to bed, leaving me at the table to make my way with Rosa and Elisa.

"Well . . ." I cleared my throat a few times. "Fine dinner. Really fine."

Hands behind her head, Elisa leaned back, smiling sociably, showing that long white throat. "You've had enough, Tomás?"

"Stuffed. I truly am."

"A cognac?"

"That might just cut a breathing hole through the meat and potatoes."

In the library she poured three amber tumblers. Rosa, her face already flushed from the wine, waved her hand in protest.

"Not so much, señora. You know what it does to me."

She wore a simple white cotton dress that revealed the strong swell of her bosom. Elisa was in white too—an Indian blouse and flowing skirt, so that the color of her hair by candlelight seemed even more pale and lemony. Neither of them showed any desire to quit the field and make it easy for me. I started to feel uncomfortable. I didn't have it in me to march off with one and leave the other sitting there to twiddle her thumbs. My cowardice in this situation, which I had thought might have gone off to hibernate for a while, woke up with a vengeance and began to yell for elbow room. I excused myself to take a leak, and while I splashed into the bowl I sorted things out as best my fuzzed brain would allow. There was only one thing to do . . . make some excuse and head for a cold bed. I buttoned up and wandered back to the library, starting my speech as soon as I entered the room.

"Well, I'm kind of worn out and—"

But Elisa stood by a bookshelf, alone, smiling at me, hands outstretched. I glanced around the room.

"Rosa felt dizzy and went to bed. Come upstairs, Tom. If you're tired, we can just sleep."

I breathed a private amen. Still, I thought, where can it lead? How could Rosa go on accepting it? How could *I*?

"I'm sorry I didn't get to say goodnight to her. . . ."

Elisa handed me the oil lamp from the table and followed me upstairs—that well-traveled route. In the shadows of her bedroom she unbuttoned my shirt and kissed me on both nipples. They popped right up through the hair, and I tingled from scalp to toes. My pecker didn't remember that I had claimed to be worn out . . . it rose up quick as a poked cat. As usual, there wasn't much connection between my supposedly finer parts and the lower region. Like Candelario, I was cursed by lust. I remembered what Rosa had told me about hearing through the walls and resolved not to make my usual ruckus tonight.

The breeze blew through the balcony curtains, and a nearly full moon stood clear in the velvet sky, casting its light across the four-poster.

"Blow out the candles," Elisa said.

She took off her clothes, and the moonlight bathed her with a porcelain glow. She unpinned her hair—the gesture I loved. The golden storm fell about my shoulders. My pecker quivered against her belly, and she squirmed. When we stretched out on the bed and I began to kiss her breasts, she groaned loudly.

"Elisa . . . shhh . . . ! Don't make a racket."

"What's the matter?"

"Rosa can hear."

"Do you really think so?"

"Yes. I'm sure of it. She told me."

"But the walls are stone. Three feet thick." She reached up behind her over the carved wooden headboard and rapped her knuckles hard against the wall. A hollow thump resulted. Some flakes of white plaster fell off.

"Elisa . . . she'll hear! That's her room!"

My pecker might have dwindled then, except that her other hand had it in a feathery grip, one oiled finger peeling back the foreskin and gently stroking. Before I could say anything more, she pulled me up next to her and drew my lips into the warm cave of her mouth. I loved her mouth: it was wide, and the lips were full, carved, with a hardness to the edges and a softness in the inner pink flesh. Her tongue slid over my gums and then inside my teeth. I just let go, relaxed, let her thrill me. I began to drift into a state that was half agonizing, half utter peace, the state that anesthetized your mind and made you know with total certainty—which could never last—that the mind was the enemy of all true pleasure, and this feeling that ran from earlobes to toes was a poor human's revenge for all the conundrums that God had set before him on the dusty earth. It was a state that didn't last long; it brought you suddenly, man or woman, to a craziness that you would not have thought possible. Here was a magic that even Doña Maria couldn't work.

A distant creaking sound got through to me . . . then the click of a latch. I heard steps on the carpet—bare feet. I wanted to turn, but Elisa's strong hand gripped my neck and slid up to press my mouth harder into hers. Sweat popped from my forehead. Whatever I mumbled was lost between her lips. Then a third hand—gentle and cool—touched my hip, and I believe my hair almost stood on end. I couldn't speak . . . not even if my tongue had been untrapped.

A garment rustled. The breeze of it falling to the carpet raised goose pimples on my arms. A body, cooler than the hand that had announced it, pressed softly against my back. I felt the fullness of Rosa's breasts on my shoulder blades, felt her breath in my ear.

My eyes bored wildly into Elisa's, which were half-closed—but the moonlight didn't allow her to lie and I saw the edges crinkle. Her mouth beneath mine widened in a smile. I worked my lips loose.

"Rosa must be cold," she murmured, before I could speak. "Make room for her, Tom. . . ."

That's how it happened to me in Parral, in the house of flowers. It was my twenty-sixth year. Given a grace that few men merit, I wasn't contrary enough to say no. *"Divided,"* Elisa had said to me, *"although that needn't be . . ."*

I loved them both. They returned that emotion, and they loved each other. How it would work or what would come of it, I didn't know—but there was no more need for an inquisition. The women ruled in this house, and they didn't torture themselves. They weren't female men.

Elisa took a third pillow out of the closet and put it on the bed. For a week the three of us slept together: cool nights, siestas in the warmth of the afternoon when the sweat of our bodies so mingled that you didn't know who was where or who was doing what to the other. For a couple of days Rosa had her curse and retired to sleep in her room. But she wasn't shut out; it was her choice. One night soon after that Elisa had a headache—or said she did—and sent me next door to Rosa's bed. In the morning at the kitchen table, over a pitcher of orange juice and a skilletful of eggs, there were still only smiles and laughter.

Laughter . . . not just then, but at the scene of the crime. The morning after our first night together, at dawn before we made love again, they laughed until I thought they would either weep or wet the bed. At least that's what Elisa claimed would happen if I didn't stop making an ass of myself by asking questions.

"Poor Tomás," Rosa giggled, after she had quieted down a bit. "I worried you might think it was a ghost."

"Ghosts don't smell like that. Ghosts don't have . . . well, they don't do what you did to me. You're wicked and scheming women, both of you. Jezebel and Lady Macbeth. Delilah and Circe."

"No," Elisa said. "It was an inspiration."

"You knocked on the wall, didn't you?"

"Oh, that. Well, by then it was settled. But if we'd asked you in the library, would you have come upstairs with us both?"

"Yes," I said, "I've always wanted this, ever since I left for the Púlpito. I just didn't know it. I wasn't able to think that way. If I had," I confessed, "I probably *would* have said no last night. God! That would have been awful! That would have been a sin!"

I didn't quite understand all that I wanted to say, but I understand now. In my time since then I've known men who wanted such an arrangement in their lives, either because they were divided in their desire—although that was rare—or because their lasciviousness was unchecked and they were driven to crack the bounds of what was permissible and common. Some were hungry to prove their manhood; some were jaded, unable to make love any other way; some were voyeurs. But there was no spontaneity; all of them plotted their moves in advance, some cajoled and even begged, and I knew one man in Beverly Hills who used opium to seduce his wife and her sister. Where was the joy? I never understood. That's not how it was at Los Flores. I planned nothing. I wasn't heroic and purposeful, as Pancho Villa would have been had he wanted such a thing. But I was *ready*. No guilt impeded me, no obsession consumed me. I took what came, took it wholeheartedly, and so did they. We were innocent partners in our desire. We were happy. After a while the gods must have frowned.

To love and be loved by such women, with no green-eyed devil of jealousy sharing the bed, no barbs, no worry that one was being cheated at the expense of the other . . . this was a blessing. If each had not made a separate peace with her own life, it would not have worked. But work it did. And Elisa had said, when we rode to Atotonilco: "What works, works."

I never had to question the direction of either tenderness or lust, because there was enough to go round and in that time I loved Rosa and Elisa equally—not the one less than the other, never the one more. Which isn't to say that they weren't different in their ways and needs, or that I didn't sometimes spend my sweat in an unbalanced way. That was a matter of mood and occasion, even opportunity, and they understood it without my having to make excuses. When my blood was up I could go on for an unconscionably long time, and one night, when I had got at her again, Rosa groaned and said, "I'm worn out, Tomás. You're a bull. This time, if I may, I will watch." She giggled. "I can learn much, *mi capitán.*"

It was true: Elisa had the knowledge of a grown woman, and she didn't mind exhibiting it. Rosa was as quick to learn that as she was to read and write. So she watched, and did something to herself that I wouldn't have thought possible. But why not? She was an innocent. She had never left her own country, but still she was an explorer. Then, the next afternoon, something extraordinary happened.

I took Elisa from behind, while Rosa straddled me to rub her fur against my thigh, hands cupping the weight of her own breasts. Elisa flattened out and rolled over on her back, mouth red from the bite of her own teeth, breath coming quickly. I moved behind Rosa, who lay on her side . . . and then Elisa pressed against her, kissed her and bit one swollen brown nipple. That startled me for a moment . . . what would Rosa do? Before, at other times, one had held the hand of the other, or gently stroked an arm, but this was different. It roused me powerfully and I fired into Rosa like a cannon, while she gasped into Elisa's mouth, threw her buttocks back at me and thrust her hand between Elisa's thighs. The little devil. I no longer saw her as quite so innocent. Bed doesn't do much for man's vision of women's delicacy. But it wasn't wrong—nothing could happen in that bed that was wrong. They loved each other as sisters, as kindred souls, as beautiful women, and now all that could find expression and voice. Elisa cried Rosa's name and mine in a way I knew too well. There was magic in that moment.

/ 407

Gazing down at them, I felt rich. I didn't own their bodies or their minds, but I owned this moment, this sight, for memory and age. One was so fair, the other dark. One was young and the other womanly . . . one rounded, the other slender. The swelling bosom, tipped so sweetly, softened against the small white breasts, the only place but one where the sun never tanned Elisa's skin. The black hair mingled on the pillow with the pale gold. The rising musk of their bodies dizzied me. They kissed each other lightly—now, afterward, there was nothing but friendliness between them. I was apart, a momentary stranger, but it didn't trouble me a hair. I felt as if I had bestowed a blessing in return for what I had received.

In that time—not then, but when I was alone once in the garden—I thought of Hannah and what a fool I had almost been. How close I had come! If I had married her I would never have been content. It wouldn't have been her fault. I would have known that and stayed with her . . . grown a bitter man, dreaming of what might have been. Now I had found something else—a life that would have shocked many, but not those who were living it. It wouldn't be an ambitious or profound life, but it would be mine, not one forced on me by habit or sloth. Not one I could resent. I would work hard—we would breed horses here and live off the land. Already we had begun to make plans. How long could this last? That didn't matter. We would see it through to its natural end. I had given enough of my energy to war.

Life was short . . . that refrain beat in my ears. Dreams blurred, the body withered. We all returned to dust. What was wrong in grasping at pleasure if it caused no pain?

But I wasn't alone in the world, and no one but Elisa and Rosa knew the changes that were taking place inside me. One evening when Villa called me to his room, Candelario and Hipólito were already there. The chief was oiling his pistol, and he looked well rested, with color in his cheeks and a purposeful glitter in his eyes.

"This has been pleasant," he said to me. "The kindness of this woman is beyond value. But in war there's a time to rest and a time to move on. I can ride now, my leg grows stronger every day. I've decided what we'll do."

"And what's that, chief?" I dropped down on the edge of his bed and looked at him worriedly.

He was going to fight again, of course. He would never give up. Our old friend Colonel Medina, who had vanished from sight for a while, had appeared in the town of San Juan Bautista, south of Chihuahua City, with three hundred loyal men. "That's all I need to begin," Villa explained. "But I won't make the same mistakes I've been making. We'll fight in Coahuila, to the east, far from the cavalry. All we need is arms.

Tomás, you'll go north with Candelario and Hipólito. Go first to the gringos and send them west into the sierra. Then get our gold out of Lake Ascensión. I can't fight without arms and equipment . . . saving that gold was the smartest thing I ever did. Hipólito will carry it to Texas and find new Jews. It won't take long, but however long it takes, it will be done." He paused, and I saw the familiar narrowing of his eyes, catlike and perilous. "What's the matter, Tomás?"

"I'm finished with it," I said.

"You don't want to fight?"

"Not anymore. I'm going to stay here."

He digested that, considered awhile and then said quietly, "I understand. I thought that might be the case, and I can't blame you. But why? Have you lost faith in me?"

"No," I said, "but I've got faith in something else, and it's stronger."

Still he frowned. "Tomás, no one knows exactly where the gold is except you. Candelario has an idea, but he's not sure. And no one else can send the cavalry in the wrong direction. They still trust you."

He was right, of course. And it wouldn't take long. After that, I would be free.

"I'll do that much," I said. "Then I'll come back here."

"That's all I ask. You had my blessing a long time ago, in Mexico City. I don't withdraw it, because I see that you don't withdraw your love for me."

"Never, chief. When do you want us to leave?"

"Tomorrow. Pick up Rodolfo and the rest of the men on your way out of Parral. They'll ride to Texas with Hipólito. I want the gold well guarded."

So I said goodbye to him for the second time in my life, although I never believed for a minute that I wouldn't see him again. And I was right.

That night I told Rosa and Elisa I was going in the morning. "A week or two is what I figure. Then we'll go up to Tomochic and get our own gold. I want to start on new stables, a bigger corral. Tell the Indians we want to buy mustangs. Wild ones. I can break them."

They might have talked me out of going, but they didn't try. They believed me when I said it was the last thing I would ever do for Pancho Villa . . . and I was right about that. They couldn't know what evil would befall me.

At dawn Elisa woke me. Rosa was already dressed, pinning up her hair. I left my Shakespeare on the bedside table, not as proof of my intention to return, but as a charm . . . as part of me.

"Don't come out to the gate," I said. I kissed them each quickly, gently, on the lips. "I have a good enough memory already. I'll be back soon."

"Just come back," Elisa said.

We rode out of the gate as the sun rose, and I felt as if I were leaving my home. That's what it had become. And after all these years and all the houses, all the diamond-studded spurs, all the wives and all the goings, I still miss it. I've never had a better one.

35 "Hoist with his own petard."

from THE SCHOOLTEACHER'S JOURNAL

Casas Grandes, Chihuahua
June 14, 1916

The United States Army has been in Chihuahua since March, more than three months. The Punitive Expedition is a failure. Trucks break down constantly on the roads, automobiles boil over in the heat, horses suffer from distemper. Eight planes of the Aero Squadron have crash-landed because of mechanical difficulties. With rare exceptions, we cannot find any Villistas. Last month a thousand men were sent east to El Sauz and west to La Bufa. They heard rumors which seemed to confirm Mix's reports, but they came back empty-handed. "It looks like we've got Pancho Villa surrounded," General Pershing remarked, "on one side."

After the fiasco at Parral and the continuing fruitless search, Pershing decided to move his headquarters north to Casas Grandes, in order to bivouac closer to his supply base. As soon as we reached here we were told by General Treviño, the commander in this area, that if American troops moved in any direction other than north it would be construed by Señor Carranza as an act of war against the Mexican government. So Carranza threatens, Wilson demands and Villa—wherever he is—undoubtedly laughs.

As for our young spy, there are two schools of thought. Tompkins believes he is a fine fellow and admitted privately to several officers that if he had listened to Mix's advice, the unfortunate incident at Parral would never have happened. He points out that Mix was wounded in our service at Pahuirachic, saved our men from a bloody encounter with a hostile Carranzista machine-gun troop and, despite his weakened condition, made great effort to rejoin the flying column outside of Parral and keep it from entering that unfriendly city. Lieutenant Patton, on the other hand, has grown uneasy. He had a talk with Sergeant Chicken, Tompkins' old Apache scout, who told a strange story about Mix and a snake, and a shot which alerted the Carranzistas.

"And how come, if he was so badly wounded," Patton asked me, "he was able to get all the way to Parral? I mean, hell, if he could do that, why didn't he rejoin the column on the way down from Pahuirachic? They wouldn't have been hard to find for a man who claims to know the trails. And if Villa wasn't there, how did Mix *know?* How do you prove a negative? Didn't anybody ask that? Where's the sonofabitch gone to now? Tompkins says he was probably wounded again, but no one saw it happen. Chicken thinks he scooted back into Parral. But why? I've got to talk some more to Frank . . . there are too many things I don't understand. If that goddam cowboy shows up here again, which I doubt, I'll put him on the carpet myself. By Jesus, I will!"

He has also come up with another disquieting thought, based on one of Mix's unguarded remarks and the ongoing rumor that the Germans sponsored the raid on Columbus and may still be active in Chihuahua.

"The woman who shot at the Thirteenth in Parral . . . they say she was German. She raises horses. Didn't Mix tell me he got that quarter horse in Parral, a gift from a lady friend? Wasn't she German? And he admitted he'd met this Captain von Papen. Do you see the connection, Miguel? I know it's far-fetched, but that smart-ass cowboy could be working for the Germans! Godammit, this whole thing was my idea, and if something's rotten in Denmark it'll be *my* ass that Black Jack kicks. Maybe all the way back to Texas," he added gloomily.

But that was in Bachinava. Now we are in Casas Grandes, and we know more. This evening, Lieutenant Patton and I and twenty men of the Thirteenth Cavalry will set out on a mission that may prove more worthwhile than the entire Punitive Expedition. We may, after all, find Pancho Villa.

It started when Patton scored his great coup of the campaign. . . .

One day, about a month ago, while still at Bachinava, a troop of the Eleventh Cavalry rode out to hunt for Colonel Julián Cárdenas, second-in-command of Villa's famed Dorados. Patton was detailed to accompany them because he was the only man among us who had ever seen the Villista colonel's face—an incident that happened outside of El Paso long before we entered Chihuahua. He was certain he could recognize him again, and the troop captain had remarked, within Pershing's hearing, "If they've got a mustache, all greasers look alike to me." Cárdenas had been ranging the countryside, looting ranches, recruiting volunteers for Villa and skirmishing with Carranzista patrols. He was reported to have more than a hundred bandits under his command and was already responsible for the deaths of thirty government soldiers. He was stubborn and resourceful, even though apparently cut off from the main body of Villa's men, which we now believed to be farther south, where Treviño's order forbade us to hunt. But Cárdenas had been on the Columbus raid. Other than Pancho Villa himself, he was one of the four men whom Pershing had been ordered to bring back dead or alive. The latest report, from the Sixteenth Infantry, had placed him near the ranch of San Miguelito, north of the pueblo of Rubio.

When Patton went with our men to San Miguelito, the scouts spotted several armed Mexicans galloping into the hills in a westward direction. The troop chased them without success, then retired to the ranch, where they camped. Patton, ever eager, took a long walk about the corrals and outbuildings to familiarize himself with the topography. He even drew a little map for his own use. The troop rode back to Bachinava.

About ten days later, headquarters staff realized we were running out of corn. Pershing directed the lieutenant to take three Dodge cars, one corporal and six privates of the Sixteenth Infantry, and an interpreter and buy corn from the haciendas lying to the east of Lake Itascate.

"How about it?" Patton said to me as he loaded his Springfield. "You don't *have* to come . . . but you might enjoy a luxury auto ride in the desert. Get some suntan!" He laughed shrilly. "And we can poke around for this fellow Cárdenas. I'd give my eyeteeth to catch him. We need something to cheer up the men and stop this bad press."

The day was terribly hot, the earth gray and bare. Not a cloud in the sky offered the prospect of rain. Our corn buying went poorly. In the pueblo of Rubio, Lieutenant Patton began asking questions as to the whereabouts of Cárdenas. He didn't expect truthful answers; he told me later that he was only trying to interpret the language of evasiveness. Each time he asked if the Villistas had returned to San Miguelito, the *campesinos* lowered their eyes before they said, as expected, "Who knows, señor?"

"Let's go there anyway," Patton said. "I have a hunch. Now listen, boys—" He gathered us around him. "I was at this ranch just a week ago. It's a big place built around a courtyard. There are only two ways to get out. Through the main gate facing east, or from the windows on the western wall. The gate's most probable, if they want to cut and run toward the mountains like they did the last time. We'll drive right up in the three automobiles. We'll stay in them and surround the house."

"Stay in the cars?" said the corporal.

"That's correct. Shoot from them if we have to."

"Sir, we're infantry. We don't shoot from moving cars."

"Then we'll try something new," Patton said. "Call it a motorized action."

"Never been done before," the corporal said fatuously. But Patton calmly issued his orders for the deployment of the vehicles.

Our scout drove the lead Dodge, carrying Patton, three soldiers and myself. As we topped the rise about a quarter mile from the hacienda, Patton ordered the driver to step on the gas. With dust boiling out behind us, we raced across the desert. Three old men and a boy were skinning a cow just inside the front gate. When the boy saw us, he bolted for the house.

A minute later, just as we reached the gate, three armed horsemen dashed out. Patton yelled, "Halt!" He drew his pistol, but the horsemen charged by toward the north face of the hacienda, where they almost collided with the second Dodge full of our soldiers. The horsemen wheeled and began firing at us. One bullet ricocheted off the hood. Patton leveled his pistol and shot three times. He told me later that it was the first human being he had ever shot at.

"Out of the cars!" he shrieked. "We've got 'em!"

I sprinted with him around the house. I had no intention of killing anyone, but I was caught in the surge. Other Mexicans were breaking free now, and our men fired at will, dropping two. Patton shot first at the horses to prevent escape, then coolly took aim at the fallen rider as he scrambled to his feet. All this time, the three old men continued to skin the cow.

One of the riders, a wiry fellow who had lost his sombrero, ran quickly toward the desert. When he was about twenty yards from us, Patton cried out in a quivering voice: "Stop or I'll fire!" The man's stride broke. He wheeled round, trying to raise his rifle. Spread-legged, face mottled with excitement, Patton leveled his pistol and fired twice. The man stumbled forward, then fell to his knees as if he were praying. As we approached him he lifted a hand in apparent token of surrender. The dark eyes in his poxed face looked stunned and confused. He tried to raise his pistol, but before he could fire he pitched forward in the dust.

When the fight was over we had killed three men; perhaps ten others had escaped. Patton showed the bodies of the three dead Mexicans to the old men who had been skinning the cow.

"This one is Julián Cárdenas . . . isn't that so?"

He pointed with the tip of his saber to the body of the pockmarked man he had shot. He had been struck twice in the chest with .45-caliber bullets and was muddied with blood. The men finally nodded.

"By God, I knew it!"

We lashed the three dead men to the hoods of the cars and drove back to camp. In one room of the house Lieutenant Patton had found a silver saddle, which the old men, voluble enough now that they realized they were in no danger, claimed to be the property of Cárdenas. The lieutenant reported the action to General Pershing and asked permission to keep the saddle as a souvenir. Pershing agreed, although his lips curled with distaste when he saw the bodies slung across the hoods of the cars, like bagged deer.

A *New York Times* reporter named Elser interviewed the lieutenant late that afternoon, but it was not until two weeks later that we read the newspapers. Elser called the incident "one of the prettiest fights of the campaign" and labeled the action a new type of combat for the American army. Patton and his men had fought from automobiles, leaping directly from them to open fire. It was ironic, Elser pointed out, that a dedicated cavalryman should be the first to employ a moving motor vehicle in an attack—he may have struck a blow to make the horse obsolete in modern warfare. When he read this, Patton frowned.

"I hate to admit it," he said, "but the man's not entirely wrong. Depends on the terrain. Mobility is everything. I've got a lot of new ideas . . . if only they'd listen to me."

Now he is a hero, and for him at least the campaign has been a success. He was promoted to first lieutenant.

Then came our worst defeat, at Carrizal, when Captain Boyd and the Negro troops of the Tenth Cavalry made a foolhardy attack against four hundred entrenched Carranzista troops armed with machine guns. We suffered twelve dead, including Boyd, and twenty-three men were taken prisoner. I remembered Boyd well—he was the officer who had greeted me when I crossed the border after escaping from Torreón. It was never quite clear why he had attacked the government troops, although there must have been some grave provocation, but the War Department was furious. General Funston, Pershing's superior, accused him of "a terrible blunder." That action effectively ended the campaign. From then on, after being forbidden by Treviño to venture in any direction but north, we sat in Casas Grandes and prayed for rain, and the newspapers began referring to our ten-thousand-man army as "Pershing's Punitive Patrol."

But one hot morning, as Lieutenant Patton was writing a letter to his wife and I was busy hanging his shirts out to dry on a line we had rigged between the tent and a mesquite tree, Tom Mix arrived in the camp at Casas Grandes.

"Good to see you, Mix," the lieutenant said cheerily. "Where have you been? I've got a letter for you."

The letter had arrived some weeks ago in the mailbag from Texas. It was in a feminine handwriting, and while our young spy sat on a cot and read it, I studied him. He had grown older since I first met him in the stockyards of Torreón. That mask of innocence had faded from his windburned face, but his eyes were clear and he seemed more at ease, more sure of himself—more of a man now than a youth. If I had had no reason to hate him, if he had not loaded the pistols that had killed my brother, I might have found him an appealing man. He had a certain wry and pleasing expression; yet underneath it one sensed a lack of frivolity, a tempered metal that no longer bent so easily.

Mix read the letter twice, smiled wistfully, then tucked it in the back pocket of his Levi's.

"Well, Lieutenant . . . thanks. Now, what did you ask me?"

"Where have you been?"

Parral, said Mix, recuperating in the home of a *campesino*. In the retreat he had fallen off his horse, injuring his shoulder again.

"Where's Pancho Villa gone to?"

"West of here, in the high sierra. You can get there through a pass called the Púlpito. He's gone to Sonora to meet General Cervantes."

"How do you know?"

"I bumped into some Villista officers on my way up here. There's one named Colonel Cárdenas—he was up at Hot Wells, driving the wagon. I met up with him in Buenaventura. He's headed west now with a hundred men to join up with Villa."

The lieutenant looked only momentarily startled; then he recovered himself. "You met Julián Cárdenas?"

"That's right."

"How long ago?"

"Maybe four or five days."

"You're sure it was him?"

"I know him well."

For a minute Patton looked away, into the glare of the blue sky, obviously trying to control his emotions. He cracked the knuckles of both hands.

"I see. Look here, Mix, if I can persuade Pershing to send a regiment of cavalry through this pass into Sonora, will you go along with us? We'll need a good scout. And you're the only man who can show us where Villa might be."

"I can join up with you on the other side of the Púlpito. But I can't start out with you. I've got to ride up to Ascensión . . . on something personal."

"Let me talk to General Pershing," the lieutenant said coolly. "Let's see what he thinks. You stick around my tent until I get back. Come along, Bosques. . . ."

Mix agreed to do that, and I strode off with Lieutenant Patton toward the general's headquarters in his big tent on the edge of town. Patton looked grim. I wondered why he hadn't arrested Mix on the spot. He said nothing, and neither did I; the situation was all too clear.

Pershing was with two other officers, but Patton asked to speak to him alone. The general put on his campaign hat to shield his head from the sun, and we stepped outside the tent. Patton began to sneeze, and it was only after a series of hard blasts and half a minute of honking into his handkerchief that he was able to get a grip on himself and speak coherently. His face was flushed, and his voice was as high-pitched as ever I had heard it.

"Sir, that fellow Mix is in the camp. I've just talked to him. He's not a spy for us at all. He's still working for Pancho Villa. I take full responsibility."

Pershing frowned out of his lean face. "What the hell are you telling me, George?"

The lieutenant repeated most of our conversation with Mix, including his claim to have spoken to the dead Julián Cárdenas five days ago. "Bosques heard every word. Mix has been leading us up the garden path. He's a goddam traitor! To his flag and his country! Despicable sonofabitch!" Patton's eyes glittered. "Villa was never in Parral. Or if he was, Mix tried to decoy Major Tompkins out of there. And then he rode back to warn Villa. The whole while our men were hunting at La Bufa and El Sauz, he was laughing at us."

"That's a nice mess," said Pershing. He was angry, but he controlled it well. "Where is this fellow now?"

"Back at my tent."

"You didn't place him under guard?"

"He still thinks we trust him. And I have a plan. I think I can locate Pancho Villa."

"Your plans with this damned cowboy haven't panned out too well so far. How the hell do you propose to find Villa?"

"Mix will lead us to him."

Pershing looked exasperated. "You just said he's still working for the man."

"I don't mean voluntarily. I think they're in touch. Mix said he was headed up to Ascensión, which may be true or false. But if I can follow him, sir, I may get lucky."

/ 415

Pershing considered for a while, then shook his head. "He's bound to spot you. You can't hide a troop of cavalry, much less three automobiles. Go back and arrest him."

Patton straightened his shoulders. "I didn't mean a whole troop of cavalry. Just a few men under my command. Once we know where Villa is, I can send a scout back for the troop. I'll tell Mix that you're going to take a regiment west through this pass into Sonora, and he can meet us later—that was his idea. He'll believe me. Then when he leaves camp, I'll follow him. There's hardly anything at risk." Patton thrust out his jaw. "Sir, I have to do something to make up for my stupidity. Give me that chance."

Pershing said, "I think we should have the man court-martialed."

"If he doesn't lead us to Villa, I'll save you that trouble."

"Stay calm, George. I need to conjure on this. Can you stall him until evening?"

"No problem. Bear in mind, sir, that the press thinks of the expedition as a failure. The Secretary of War's having a bad time of it in Washington. If Mix leads us to Villa, the expedition will be a complete success. All the glory will fall on your head, sir."

"Get out of here, George. There are times I think you're a damned fool. Or else you think I am."

Patton saluted smartly and drew me away through the dust toward camp. He was still red-faced, his eyes were watering, but he punched his fist several times into his palm.

"He'll do it," he muttered. "I know he'll do it. . . ."

I didn't know if he was referring to General Pershing or Tom Mix. When we got back to the tent, Mix was standing by his horse, reading his letter yet again. Patton calmly told him the general needed more time to think about it; he wanted to consult his maps and his scouts.

"Can you come back about seven o'clock? Do you have a watch?"

Mix smiled pleasantly. "I don't need a watch. Never did own one. I'll be here at seven."

He mounted smoothly on his gray and trotted off in the hot morning, past the corrals where the soldiers bivouacked, toward the town. We quickly lost sight of him. "The swine," Patton murmured. "I had all I could do not to slap his face. An American citizen! He makes me want to puke."

The lieutenant waited all day, skipping lunch. He told me he had no appetite. He chewed his fingernails instead, oiled his saber and cleaned his rifle, although both already sparkled. His hay fever attacked him hourly, so viciously that he had to sit down in order to sneeze. Each time he finished he looked red as a lobster. When he wasn't sneezing he smoked his meerschaum pipe.

"If Pershing gives me a green light," he said to me, "I want you to come along. You brought me luck with Cárdenas."

By six o'clock he had practically no nails or tobacco left. Pershing hadn't specified a time, but Lieutenant Patton couldn't bear the waiting any longer. We went round to the big tent, and Lieutenant Shallenberger ushered us in. Pershing sat at his field desk, looking up bleakly as Patton saluted.

"Sir?"

"All right," Pershing said, "you can do it. But I don't want you tear-assing off on your own. You might run into trouble, like Boyd. Take twenty men. Pick 'em yourself. Tell the packmaster to provision them for three days. After three days, no matter what, I want you back."

Patton glowed. "Yes, sir!"

"Remember, you can't go south of here—at least not more than a few miles. If Mix heads that way, call off the pursuit. If you do anything foolish," Pershing said gruffly, "I don't want to know about it. But if you can find Villa . . ."

He didn't have to finish. They exchanged salutes, and we left the tent hurriedly. Patton raced round to where the Thirteenth Cavalry was bivouacked and selected twenty men under a veteran sergeant. He wanted seasoned men with a better than average reason to fight, and they had all been in the retreat at Parral. He had them lead their horses and the pack mules to a corral near the edge of the camp, on the route Mix had taken when he left that morning. Then we went back to the tent to wait. I worked on my journal. Patton paced outside, watching the sun dip toward the horizon. The cloudless sky grew violet, while the sun turned bloody orange and lost its round shape. Patton began to sneeze.

The sun set, gossamer pink streaks firing up from the mountain peaks. It was seven-thirty. The lieutenant listened to the ticking of his watch. He shifted the holster at his hip and continued to pace. At eight-thirty Mix still hadn't showed up.

"Damn that fucking cowboy! He's got no watch!"

"Lieutenant . . . he can tell the time by the sun and the stars. His watch never stops."

"Then why isn't the sonofabitch here?"

"Maybe he changed his mind. Maybe he smelled what you know."

"He couldn't have! How could he?"

"I don't know, Lieutenant."

At nine o'clock Patton made up his mind. We saddled our horses—his a big brown with a broken blaze on his forehead, mine a smaller red roan—and we rode out to the corral where our twenty men stood in the cold air, smoking their cigarettes and wondering what had happened to us.

"We're riding out, Sergeant," Patton said. "Have your corporal bring up the rear with the pack mules. I want as little talking as possible. Saddle up—column of twos. We'll take the west trail toward Ascensión."

36 "They kill us for their sport."

A Dodge drove by, its isinglass curtains buttoned into the tonneau, but I couldn't make out the face of the officer inside. For the third time that morning, as I stood sweating in the sun, waiting for Lieutenant Patton and Miguel Bosques to get back from the general's tent, I read Hannah's letter. It was dated April 5, 1916—more than two months ago.

Dear Tom [she wrote],

You will no doubt be surprised at receiving this epistle from me, especially in view of the fact that you have never bothered to write to me, but I have learned in life that, for the sake of one's conscience, the golden rule is better obeyed than flaunted. I am doing unto you as I would have wished you had done unto me. I am writing to tell you whither my life has chanced to lead.

To still your wonderment, I know of your whereabouts through a letter that Lieutenant Shallenberger, an old beau of mine, wrote to his sister, who is my friend.

I cannot tell you how astonished I was! To think, after those long years when you remained loyal to General Villa—at the expense of your loyalty to yours truly—that now you should fight against him! The delicious irony of it! I remain shocked.

Yet I feel, somehow, it is evidence that you have grown in your estimation of what is right & good for a man to do. Perhaps, in a way, you are atoning for past errors of judgment. Whatever your process of thought, you have my blessing. You fight now for a just cause against a man who has proved himself to be what I oft claimed him to be: a murderer of innocent men, women & children.

Now, here is my news. On Aug. 4 ult. Daddy passed away. He was in great pain at the end, and he asked for you several times. The funeral was attended by hundreds of friends & many who did not even know him but wished to show respect. I miss him terribly.

But even an ill wind blows some fresh breeze. . . .

My mourning o'ershadowed the grief I had felt at your parting that awful day, more than a year ago. (Is it so long? How time becomes meaningless!) Perhaps you were unaware of that grief, but I think now you must face it. I will not burden you, Tom, with a recounting of the nights & days that I wept into my pillow, or beat my breast or tore my hair. I will not tell you how I lost weight, fell ill with the grippe & suffered. You do not want to know these things. They are private to a woman who has been lied to & abandoned.

For I believed, even when you left, Tom, that you might come back. I prayed that you would. You cannot imagine my distress. Young men besieged me & tried to distract me—I had two proposals within one week, and each time broke down in tears. But my prayers were not answered, perhaps not even heard. In time, I ceased. I accepted the reality of our parting.

Tom, I loved you more than I thought a woman could love a man, but you did not truly love me in return. I gave you my all, and you cast it away. That stain will never be erased from my body & soul. You could have come back, but you chose not to. Your love for me was incomplete. More than me, you loved the life you lived, and as long as Pancho Villa existed for you as a heroic figure, you would never give up following him for a decent married life with the woman you claimed to love.

And now to the heart of my message.

I set you free, Tom. I put it down in these indelible words. You are free. I am engaged to a fine and honorable young man from a good family in Houston—let him be nameless, so that you will never be tempted to contact me—and after our marriage am moving to that city to start a new life.

I trust you wish me well. I will keep your engagement ring as a memento of happier times, a memoria in aeterna *rather than* une mémoire de lièvre, *and I will always remember you fondly—especially as I first saw you so long ago in the hotel in Columbus, so young, so handsome, so shy. The hotel, like our love, is now a burned shell.*

I cannot write more or I will begin to cry all over again. Bless you, Tom. I salute you for having broken free—alas! for us, too late!—from that madman & bandit.

Stay well, and don't get killed.

Affectionately,
Hannah

Even on the third reading I felt no shame, and my heart was about as empty of regret as a church is of cowhands. Two proposals in a week wasn't bad at all. It certainly meant she had been out and around last winter and not cooped up all the time with her wet pillow and torn hair. I did wish her well in her marriage and wished I could tell her that too, but that was not to be. Princesses lived in fairy tales. Women lived on the earth.

Patton's reedy voice shook me from my reverie. He stood there in front of his tent with Bosques, explaining that Pershing wanted until evening to make up his mind whether the cavalry would ride to Sonora. He seemed oddly distracted.

"All right, Lieutenant . . . whatever you say." I promised I would be back at seven.

On the way out of camp, heading toward Casas Grandes, I passed the men bivouacked in their pup tents on the edge of the desert. Under that brassy sun they were a forlorn and grumpy-looking lot, but they would cool down in the Cañon del Púlpito. At least none of them would get shot at over there. That thought made me feel as righteous as a preacher. I scanned the tents for some sign of Yvette and Marie-Thérèse; I didn't find them and was about to leave, when I spotted the familiar figure of Sergeant Chicken, wearing his fringed buckskin vest and flat black hat with an eagle feather, ambling along smoking a cigar.

"Say, Chicken . . . how you been? How's life treating you?"

"Pretty good, cowboy. Seen any snakes lately?"

I chuckled, and this time so did he.

"You know those two whores that were down in Bachinava? French girls? They still around?"

"They're here," he said. "Ask too much wampum. Bad medicine, them two."

"You don't need to powwow that Apache pidgin to me, Chicken. I know how smart you are. Where can I find them?"

"Cost you five U. S. bucks, cowboy. No takee pesos. Wham-bam, thank you, ma'am."

"Point the way."

He told me they lived in a little hut behind the encampment, but it was too early in the morning for them to be in business. I went round there anyway, leading Maximilian, and banged on the door. Marie-Thérèse came out after a minute, wearing a raggedy white nightgown, blond hair in a tangle, cursing until she saw that the intruder was me.

"*Chéri!* I miss you the last time! 'Ow wonderful! I wake Yvette."

"Don't mean to disturb you—"

"We are disturb by worse all the time. It's okay. Come in. It's a mess, you don't mind?"

"This is me, Marie-Thérèse. I don't mind."

Yvette crept out of her cot and unknotted the bandanna she wore wrapped around her head to keep out the morning light. She hugged me too.

"Ah, Tom! You look fine. . . ."

"I've been taken good care of, Yvette."

"You are still with Rosa?"

"Sure," I said. "Practically a married man." I didn't tell that I was with Elisa too; they might have been whores, but they could still be shocked. "Candelario's here—not far, anyway. He wanted to come to camp to hunt you down, but I told him he'd get put to bed with a pick and shovel instead of a kiss if they spotted him."

"Ah, yes . . ." Yvette crossed herself. "Like poor Julio."

I sat down slowly on her cot, taking her warm hand in mine.

"What do you mean, Yvette? What do you mean, like poor Julio?"

Marie-Thérèse said to her, *"Le pauvre, il ne savait pas."*

"Speak English," I demanded. "Is Julio dead?"

"Oui, chéri. He is dead."

No, life was never fair. He had ridden off from Guerrero without even a wave of goodbye, and I had never seen him again. And now never would. I sat there in the hut while my eyes fogged and my heart beat in my chest like a tired drum.

"He was killed down south," Yvette said softly. "At a little ranch. It was quick, Tomás. One shot, they say. By that Lieutenant Patton."

I looked up quickly. Even through the misery that poured through me, I felt the stir of alarm. They told me what they had heard of the fight at San Miguelito. For a week it had been the talk of the camp.

"I have to get out of here," I said quietly. "It was good to see you both."

Yvette kissed me on both cheeks. *"Je suis désolée,* Tom." Then Marie-Thérèse kissed me and said she was sorry too. "Give our love to Candelario," they called.

I mounted Maximilian and trotted toward the town. Patton had known. When I spun that yarn that Julio had told me Villa was in Sonora, he had known right away. But he had said nothing. I didn't understand it at first and didn't work too hard at it—my mind kept jumping back to Julio, lying dead in the dust and then lashed to the hood of a car. *Patton.* Damn his soul! Damn him to hell. . . .

Now, after all this time, I remembered the name of the third musketeer. It was Athos, the melancholy one.

Candelario and Hipólito were waiting for me in the hot foothills west of town, hunched in the shade of some manzanita trees. Fierro stood guard, mounted on his buckskin stallion. He walked with a limp now, but he rode his horse with the same straight-shouldered grace. He always wore the same clothes: white Stetson, riding boots up to the thigh, a gray jacket with silver buttons, silver-dollar spurs and criss-crossed cartridge belts.

All the way back I had thought about Julio, my boyhood friend, who had fought at my side in the wrecking yard at Torreón. The revolution had claimed many lives but never one so close. We had been lucky. There was an end to luck. There was an end to everything. Hipólito gripped my arms strongly.

"What is it, Tomás? Say it."

I don't know how long I had been standing there.

"Julio's dead," I said. "Shot near Bachinava, by the gringos."

Death was something we all faced, and no one could shake his fist and swear at God that He had tricked us. Candelario took a little walk into the hills and smoked a cigarette. Hipólito turned his back and fiddled with his saddle, tightening the cinch, then loosening it, then tightening it again. "Shit," he said. Fierro spat into the dust, then looked away at the mountains.

After a while Candelario came back. He had made his peace, but his voice was flat and drained. "The others are waiting for us. Let's go get the damned gold and split up. Come along, Tomás. This is the last thing you have to do for us."

We approached Ascensión from the southwest. With our escort of twenty men we raised a cloud of alkali that could be seen for miles on that empty desert. No breeze blew. It hadn't rained here for nearly a year, and the buzzards strutted, gorging themselves on dead cattle and prairie dogs. In a drought, cows went mad and broke their horns hooking trees and rocks, or went blind. The ground had cracked under the heat so that giant fissures gaped between stands of cactus. The unpitying sun coasted toward the peaks.

The usual old men squatted in the dust, and two Yaqui boys again played leapfrog on the back of a sow. I missed the sight of the old women bearing water jars from the lake. It had been seven months since we dumped the gold in the green channel between the bars of quicksand. We left the men and the wagon on the edge of town and skirted it at a trot, rifles resting across our saddles, scanning the desert in the fading light. But there were no signs of Carranzistas or the cavalry.

We trotted along a burro path past ruined adobe huts. I recognized the house where we had lived before we attacked Torreón. The orange tree that had grown through the roof was lifeless. Far off to the right I saw the derelict hut that marked the line of sight.

"Where's the damned lake?" Candelario muttered. *"Válgame Dios! Son of a whore!"*

There was no lake.

Now I understood what I had seen when we had dumped the gold. But I had only seen it with my eyes and not my brain. The waters had been steadily receding. That was why they had looked so brown, and the smell that had filled my nostrils the night we had camped here in March had been the smell of mud and rotting carcasses. The drought had finished the job. The lake had become a stagnant bog. We could see the bleached skull and ribs of a longhorn, picked clean.

Without a thought to quicksand, we spurred down the bank into the flatland. The setting sun had turned the bog a lovely brownish-pink. The gumbo sucked at Maximilian's pounding hoofs. Carrion crows flitted overhead, cawing insolently. A few pools of brackish water glistened in the unearthly light.

There was no gold, either. We searched what had been the lakebed until dark, when there was nothing more to see. We pounded back and forth on the stinking mud, but our curses could never bring back the waters of Lake Ascensión or the sacks of gold. Finally Candelario came drumming up beside me to clutch at my reins.

"It's no use," he gasped. "But who took it?"

"Someone who's a long way from here."

"Let's ask the old men in the town," he said.

They knew nothing. They shrugged. *"Quién sabe, señor?"*

But the boys leapfrogging over the sow in the cool darkness were eager to talk. They remembered. It had happened about two months ago, when there had still been water in the lake, but it had sunk to a level where the strange humps, like the swollen bellies of dogs long dead, had been noticed by some poor Tarahumara camped on the edge of town. The Tarahumara were too poor to own horses. They had waded out in their bare feet and discovered that the objects weren't dogs at all. The boy who spoke knew what they were.

"They were sacks of corn, señor. Someone had stored them there. It was a very bad place to store corn, but in these times, as you know, people do foolish things. The corn must have been rotten. But these Tarahumara were so poor and so stupid that they didn't care. They carried the corn away, one sack at a time, into the hills. It seemed very precious to them. They never came back."

Hipólito bared his teeth. "We'll go to every village in the sierra. We'll see which ones look prosperous, where they've built new houses. We're bound to find it if we look long enough."

Candelario laughed grimly. "And pigs will fly. Do you know what those Indians will do with our gold?"

"Spend it. What else can they do?"

"They'll do nothing with it," Candelario said. "On what should they spend it? They know it belongs to someone else, and that someone will come here one day—as we've done. If they spend it, people will ask: 'Where did you get it, señor? Who did you kill for it?' The soldiers will come to ask more questions. The Tarahumara have been in the sierra for a thousand years, and they'll be there another thousand years. They'll bury the gold in those mountains. They'll tell their children where it is, and the children will tell their children. A thousand years from now, if there's still an earth and a Mexico, some fools will dig it up. I'd like to be there to see how they fight over it. I know what gold does to your brains."

He was right, and we all knew it. It would have taken us a year to search.

Hipólito, with Fierro, was meant to have loaded the gold in the wagon and taken the escort of our soldiers to Texas. He no longer needed company. "But I still have to go," he said gloomily. "Angeles is waiting for me."

We built a little fire on the edge of town, and by its red glow I told them the tale of how I had tried to trick Patton into riding to Sonora, and how he had discovered my lie.

"You're not as clever as you used to be," Candelario said. "The chief was right. Too much fucking dulls the mind." He gave me a bitter smile. "Will you ride with us to San Juan Bautista?"

"What for? Without the gold, the chief can't buy guns. Without guns . . ." I shrugged. "It's finished, Candelario. Why fool ourselves? It's really finished this time."

Hipólito embraced each of us in turn, and I told him to give my best regards to Mabel Silva and not to make too many babies. "I'll name the first one after Julio," he promised, and then he rode off in his dusty blue suit with the cartridge belts wrapped around his potbelly, looking exactly the same as the first time I had met him outside the hut in Juárez.

An unlikely villain, if ever I knew one. His portly figure grew dim and then vanished. I would never see him again.

We threw sand on our fire and ground out the coals, and then the three of us trotted back to where the men camped on the southern edge of Ascensión. Huddled by their own crackling fire, its sparks arcing into the sky like June bugs, they softly sang a ballad of lost love. I had heard hundreds of them, and they always touched me.

"Let's sleep here," Candelario said wearily. "This has been a bad day. Tomorrow can't possibly be worse."

We helped grind out the soldiers' fire and then bedded down. It was a warm night, and crickets chirped on the desert floor. As the fire died, the darkness became absolute. The stars swarmed overhead, the Milky Way thick as cream. It was a beautiful night, so calm that it seemed impossible to relate to death. And yet death lurked there—I smelled it. The very calmness was frightening. The crickets ceased their chatter. The desert was strangely silent. Fierro had withdrawn as always to a place of his own.

Candelario spoke. "So, Tomás . . . it's really over for you."

There was no barb in his voice. He knew my mind. I think he loved me deeply, as a man loves another man, and I felt the same for him.

"Yes," I said. "It's over."

"We'll miss you."

I didn't want to think too much about that, so I chuckled. "Don't you have the feeling the chief can get along without my advice now? I haven't done too well lately."

"My friend, it was always good to ride with you. When I open my restaurant, wherever I go, you can come and have a fine meal. With wine. Shall I set two places or three?"

"What do you think? You're the one who told me life was short. I believe it now."

"Your luck gets better all the time—but it will never be as good as mine. You've got to lose an eye for that." He chuckled in the darkness, but he had spoken with a certain wistfulness. "How will you live down there, Tomás? What will you do?"

"Horses. That's what I'm good at. We can enlarge the corrals and breed mustangs. We'll sell them over in Chihuahua City. Our gold will come in handy." I sat up and looked at him; I had an idea. "Come with me to Los Flores. We'll go by way of Tomochic. You can shave off your beard—no one will recognize you. Open a restaurant in Parral."

"Do you know," he said, "that under my beard I have a weak chin?"

"That's hard to believe, Candelario."

"But true. I was ugly . . . not that I'm so handsome now. That's why I grew it in the first place."

"Will you come?"

"I have to go to San Juan Bautista and tell the chief what happened. Later, yes . . . I think I'll come." He thought for a while. Quietly he said, "If anything happens to me, unlikely as that may be, give my sack of gold to Francisca. She made me comfortable, and she asked for nothing."

"What about your sons becoming lawyers?"

"Without me around, Tomás, they'll become nothing. They'll spend it on tequila and women. They have my blood."

I wonder if he knew. We both ground out our cigarettes and punched a hollow in the saddlebags to make better pillows for our heads. The horses snorted on the picket line.

The next morning, fortune ceased to smile on her favorite soldier. Before sunrise one of the men shook me awake. "My colonel, there's something blinking in the hills. To the west—there."

Dawn puckered the eastern sky, thin fingers of gold slanting through the mist. Darkness crumbled, the phantom shapes of cactus and stunted trees emerging in pale shadow. But enough yellow light flowed across the desert to show us the small flash at which he pointed. It might have been quartz or a patch of alkali, but then again it might have been a rifle barrel or field glasses. It was far off in the foothills that sloped toward the dun-colored mountains.

"Let's not take any chances," said Candelario. "Let's make ourselves scarce."

We shouted the rest of the men awake; they grumbled when we told them there would be no coffee. Saddling the horses, we swung up on their backs and trotted off toward the south. Our route would bring us closer to the mountains than I liked, but there was no other way. The grazing had been poor, and we needed to move onto higher ground where hummocks of stubby grass chinked between the rocks and where we knew there would be water holes. The glint of light in the foothills had vanished. As the sun crept higher, I began to sweat.

An hour later we wound our way upward along a trail bounded on both sides by rocky escarpments. Here, God knows how many years ago, the earth's crust had heaved and fractured. The brooding, bronze-colored mountains sheered up from slate cliffs . . . primeval, untenanted. The sun raged down on them, flashing off quartz, mica and limestone, then flowed across the tan plain. This was the Chihuahua I knew best, a landscape for which I felt that strange affection that one feels for a place linked with hardship. I listened to the soft footfalls of our horses in the dust. A rock fell somewhere far off, with a faint echo. I felt the flinty taste of fear . . . knew suddenly, certainly, what was about to happen. I put my knee into Maximilian and veered left off the trail, where it widened through a defile toward the desert, yelling for the others to follow. . . .

Rifles cracked from the escarpment. Two horses screamed—two

riders fell. I saw the peaked olive-drab campaign hats peering over the rocks, the hats with their wide brims and chinstraps; the pale faces; the spurt of bright red and curl of smoke from the Springfields. Candelario rode ahead of me, Fierro just behind. The men trailing us wheeled in confusion, trying to control their horses. Another man spilled from the saddle. Candelario tucked his rifle under one arm and pumped bullets toward the rocks, face contorted, beard flowing in the breeze like the mane of a black lion. The horses stumbled up on a rubble of shale, ready to plunge down the slope toward the desert, where we could run clear.

I bent low, the horn of the saddle grinding into my ribs. Candelario's cheek shattered apart in front of me—blood and bone sprayed into the air. He pitched off to one side, boots jerking from the stirrups, body flopping and twisting, the spread fingers of one hand trailing in the dust. His horse began to crumple. With both arms I reached out and gripped him, hauled with all my might to free him from the saddle. I heard his voice, muttering, *"Son of a whore . . ."* Then his hand clutched the thick gray ruff of Maximilian's mane, and I swung him up in front of me like a giant two-hundred-pound rag. A mask of red dirt covered half of his face. I flew over the top of the shale and crashed down the hillside behind Fierro, whose horse's flanks bled from the steady jab of his spurs.

Down we plunged . . . down into the desert, with the echo of rifles cracking off the rocks. The barren peaks were turning gold in the sun. The earth tilted. Hot sand scoured my face. I buried my head in Candelario's body. Under me, Maximilian's stride lengthened to a gallop.

At last I looked back over my shoulder, where a fan of thin dust trails spread over the plain . . . our men, scattering like spokes on a wheel from the hub of rifle fire. I knew it was Patton. I never saw him then, but still I knew.

The desert, flanked by black humps of mountains . . . a land like a great knuckled paw thrust into space. The horses sweated. Gray clouds loafed along the mountaintops. The air grew oppressive, our shadows faded. A flash of lightning licked toward the cloud banks, and thunder rumbled. The first shower of rain cooled the horses, and I raised my face toward the sky. A pair of buzzards flapped to the branch of a mesquite, black wings tucked tightly down, motionless under the flogging rain. I slowed Maximilian and then dismounted, while Fierro waited.

I laid Candelario on the desert floor. Soaking my bandanna with rainwater, I tried to swab away the blood from his face. The blood, mixed with dirt, had grown dark and stiff.

"I can't see," he whispered.

The bullet had struck up through his cheek, destroying his good eye. He was blind, he was dying. He would never grow fat, never own his restaurant, never see his sons become lawyers.

The rain pelted down. "You'll be all right," I said. Oh God! I clenched my fists and took deep shuddering breaths.

I hadn't seen Julio die, and so it was unreal to me. But Candelario made up for that. I didn't care anymore that death came to us all. Those were words. He had been my brother. We had counted gold, been shot at in the Morelos Theater, blown up the railroad, found both our names inscribed in Parral. Images spun through my mind. The trenches of Celaya, where he had saved my life, a lobby in the Station Hotel. I cared that the best were gone, the worst survived.

"*Hombre,*" he whispered. "Go. Leave me in peace."

I thought I would have to shoot him the way I would shoot a crippled horse. But he was considerate, even at the end. A little rattle came from his throat. Through the blood I couldn't see his eyes glaze, but I felt him stiffen, then go slack. I was gripping his shoulders in the rain when he died.

Fierro's calm voice seemed to come from a distance. "They're not far behind," he said. "Leave him now."

The rain eased. Hard gashes of sunlight swooped down to stain the desert, so that the shadows of the horses flowed like a moving stream. Sunset bled over the land, turning the desert crimson. Then the wound closed, and night fell like death.

37   "Still ride in triumph over all mischance."

from THE SCHOOLTEACHER'S JOURNAL

Chihuahua
June 17, 1916

The lieutenant positioned us perfectly and made only one mistake: he let me keep my rifle. It was sheer good luck that the Villistas had ridden into the foothills, but they must have had a destination south of Casas Grandes and this was their only route.

They came in single file, silently, three riders ahead and the rest bunched behind, faces in black shadow under their sombreros. When they were less than a half-mile distant, Patton, squeezed down between two boulders, worked goggles over his nose and reached for his field glasses. The desert light was so strong that the horses seemed to swim legless on a rippling sea of white water.

"I can see Mix," he murmured, "but where's Villa? *Goddam!* The man out in front looks like Cervantes. How are your eyes, Miguel?"

His were watering and red-lidded from losing a night's sleep. I took the glasses from him and adjusted the focus. I watched the dark faces drawing closer, lacking expressions, mouths clamped tight under their mustaches against the dust. He was right: I didn't see Pancho Villa . . . but I knew the man behind Mix. That smooth face and those almond eyes had haunted my dreams.

"Third in the column, Lieutenant, is Colonel Fierro. The one who shot the prisoners in Torreón."

He grunted impatiently. "Yes, but do you see Villa?"

"He's not with them. He would lead."

"Hold your fire," Patton called calmly to his men. "Let them pass. Be silent."

Our horses were tethered behind the cliff. Hardly a breeze blew. The riders were a hundred yards away now. The shuffle of hoofs in the dust reached our ears . . . the creak of saddle leather, the click of iron on loose shale. Somewhere a rock fell, dislodged by a trooper seeking better cover. Mix yelled, then spurred his horse. . . .

Patton would have let them go. He wanted them to lead him to Pancho Villa. But that meant nothing to me. Whatever promises I had made about Mix, I had made none about Rodolfo Fierro. Mix had only been his instrument, I knew that now, but for Fierro I felt an engulfing hatred. To have him in the sights of my rifle and to let him go would have mocked my vows, my brother's memory, the deepest purpose of my life. A red haze rose before me. I pulled the trigger of my rifle.

"Damn you, Bosques!" Patton cried.

Alive, unharmed, Fierro spurred his horse quickly after Mix, over the rocky scarp toward the desert. The troopers took my shot as a signal; they began firing. Cervantes swung his rifle toward us. The rest of the Villistas tried to turn their horses, to bolt back down the trail. A trooper to my left, clutching a bloody chest, dropped his Springfield. . . .

When it was over, Lieutenant Patton climbed to the escarpment, peering through his field glasses.

If you do anything foolish, I don't want to know about it. But if you can find Villa . . .

Perhaps Pershing's words came back to him then. Perhaps he remembered his Confederate grandfather, who had hesitated at the gates of Washington, D.C. *He didn't have the military mind in its highest form of development, because he was swayed by ideas of right and wrong. . . .*

His face warped with anger. He lowered the glasses, clenching his fist so tightly that the knuckles showed white. Then he plunged down the cliff, sliding on shale, shouting orders to his sergeant. He was to lash the three bodies on pack mules and take the prisoners to Casas Grandes.

"Go back to General Pershing," Patton said. "Tell him I may find Villa. Tell him I've taken only my striker."

The lieutenant and I mounted our horses and galloped over the escarpment. With the field glasses we could see faint puffs of dust far to the south on the desert. After a while it began to rain.

38 "But, since I am a dog, beware my fangs."

The second day out from Ascensión, when we mounted into the sierra, I hung over the lip of rock for a long, thoughtful look at the two men who had followed us across the desert. Patton was easy to recognize. After half a minute I knew that the other fellow had to be Miguel Bosques.

The earth was wet from the rains, and we couldn't hide our tracks. That afternoon, north of Bachinava, it rained again—a gully washer with rolling clouds, ropes of white lightning, gusting wind and earsplitting thunderclaps. To add to my troubles, the thunder spooked Maximilian. He shied off the trail and threw a shoe against an outcrop of rock; it was from a hind hoof, and in the high country he couldn't do without it. I had a spare pair, but I didn't carry any anvil and bellows and I had to plate him cold right there on the mountain trail.

I had begun to sort some things out in my mind, and when I stopped work for a minute I turned to Rodolfo, who sat cross-legged in the mud, massaging his bad ankle.

"We'll split up now," I said. "I'm going south. You can pick any direction you like, but you can't go to San Juan Bautista."

He hadn't known my plans . . . he hadn't been at Los Flores. "Where are you going?" he asked, surprised.

"Parral."

"Francisco Villa is at San Juan Bautista."

"I know where he is. And if you go there, you'll lead this damned lieutenant right to him. That's why he's following us."

"I won't lead him anywhere that I don't want to," Fierro said. "Tomorrow, or when it pleases me, I'll kill him."

I should have known. He would pick the time and place, just as he had once said he would do it with me.

"Listen, Rodolfo. Clear the potatoes out of your ears and hear me well. This Lieutenant Patton may want me dead, but I don't mean to return the favor. I want to lose him, not kill him."

That wasn't easy to say, but that was the only way I could live. No more killing, I had decided. Patton had killed Julio and Candelario, two men I loved, but he was a soldier and for him they had been the enemy. I might hate him for it, but I didn't lust for revenge like Bosques. I needed to get off the wheel.

I shoved Maximilian against a boulder and leaned on him hard, so that his weight shifted. Lifting the hind leg, I ran a hand down to the hock, then jammed it between my teeth and hammered the shoe home. Maximilian snorted. The hoof was tender.

Fierro considered for a while. Then he spoke in a maddeningly gentle way. I would rather he had snapped or spat, but then he wouldn't have been Rodolfo Fierro.

"Tomás," he said, "I've known you a long time now. Once I threatened to kill you, and I would have done so if the chief had not stopped me. But you threw your rope to me at Ascensión. The others would have let me die, but not you. I confess that puzzled me for a while. Finally I accepted it and understood. I consider you my friend."

His friend . . . maybe the only one he had, other than Pancho Villa. But he was wrong, terribly wrong. I would rather have been friends with a scorpion.

"No," I said quietly. "I despise you."

"Why?" he asked, genuinely puzzled. "You've killed unarmed men. You're not squeamish anymore. You shot Dozal, then Urbina. And others. You never even knew their names."

With the claw of the hammer I twisted off the point behind the shoe and then hammered the nails into the crease. I lowered Maximilian's leg. Testing the hoof in the mud, he nickered agreeably. There had been no devilment.

"I had reason," I told Fierro. "And I never enjoyed it, like you."

"But it has to be done. These men following us are our enemies— even more so than Urbina. And they want to kill you, as much as Dozal did. I understand your feelings—one of them is a gringo. So I'll do it. I've already chosen the place. It's the same as in Torreón. You don't even have to load my pistols. You have only to not interfere." He clambered awkwardly to his feet and limped toward his horse. "No, whatever you do," he said, over his shoulder, "don't interfere. That would be a mistake."

I went about my business of stowing the rasp and clinching hammer in my saddlebags. I knew how dedicated he was to the short life and the quick death, and he wouldn't change his mind. No more killing, I had said. But I had forgotten about Rodolfo Fierro.

We rode higher into the mountains, making camp at dark. We couldn't build a fire, but the night wasn't cold and I was comfortable under my blanket. Fierro stood guard for a few hours while I slept, and then he woke me. I squatted a few yards away with my back against a juniper tree. When he finally began to snore, I stood and peered down at him. A few raindrops from the leaves fell on my neck. I slid my Colt softly out of its holster.

Candelario and Julio were dead. Why should Fierro live? *The best were gone, the worst survived.*

He was on his back, hands on top of his saddle blanket. I leveled the gun and held it pointed at the middle of his chest. A rising moon offered enough light. His death would have passed from my mind like the shadow of a buzzard flitting across the sand. No one would mourn him. Patton and Bosques would live. I would have paid one debt that I had owed ever since Torreón.

I holstered the pistol and walked among the juniper trees, listening to the soughing of the night wind and the patter of drops. The shapes of Maximilian and the buckskin, side by side, bulked from between the trees. There was no one near.

I hadn't been able to do it in the dark, while he slept. Candelario had been right the first time, in that Juárez cantina. I was a *pendejo*.

I stayed with Fierro. If I had left him alone there would have been nothing to stop him from bushwhacking Patton and Bosques anywhere he chose. Why did I care? I suppose, despite everything that Patton had done, I respected him. He lived and fought like a soldier. I could damn his soul to hell a hundred times, but I could never blame him for lining up the sights of his rifle on the men who had been my best friends. To him they were enemies; he couldn't help that.

As for Bosques, he was a man for whom I felt more than a measure of responsibility. I hadn't been able to save his life at Torreón, and I had come to regret it. Perhaps I could make up for that now.

But even beyond that, I couldn't let go, the way a man who's played in a big poker game until nearly the end can't get up and leave just as the stakes are raised to life and death and the cards come flicking across the table. I couldn't turn my back. I wanted to play the final hand.

They found us north of San Juan Bautista in the ghost town of Las Palomas. In the sunny afternoon as we trotted into that eerie landscape of ruined buildings and abandoned mine shafts, Fierro reined up and swung lightly off his horse.

The region was one of rolling hills with scrub that had started to green in the summer rains. It was one of the few places where the old Spaniards hadn't bled the land dry. Thirty years ago Las Palomas had been a thriving city of twenty thousand souls. The gold and silver mines tapped out first, then the cobalt and zinc. The soil was too dusty to grow anything except dwarf maize, so the people went too. It was as if the bones of a city had been scoured clean by buzzards and coyotes, or been bombarded for a month by a thousand cannon. There were cobbled streets, dusty roads, an abandoned plaza and the walls of fine stone houses, dazzling white in the sun—but no one lived there except the lizards. Windows, like blinded eyes, gaped on all sides of roofless ruins with jagged walls. The walls were held together by creepers that had grown from the dust to support the stones. The mountain wind sighed among piles of rock.

"I know this place," Fierro said. "Pancho and I hid here ten years ago with Urbina. The mine shafts go into the hills . . . not straight down, as you would think, but level. They wind back for a mile. When you turn a corner, it's pitch-dark. Black as you've never known black to be. Come along, Tomás. I'll show you something."

He seemed to have no worry that Patton and Bosques would arrive before he was ready.

"See? It looks like a castle. It belonged to Luis Terrazas."

We were on a dirt road at the outskirts of the town, where the wrecks of houses were larger and more scattered. He was pointing at a brown turret a hundred yards away, with a battlemented walkway. To our right was the great hole of a mine shaft, an oval black patch against an alkaline hill, leading back to an inky darkness.

Fierro dismounted, looping the buckskin's reins around the branch of a mesquite tree in front of the mine shaft. The horses had grazed during the night, in the sierra. I swung off Maximilian and tied him to the other side of the mesquite, unbuckled the cinch, hauled the saddle off his back and laid it on the ground. I didn't believe that we would have to hightail it out of here. We would either go at leisure, or not at all. Following Fierro, I jumped down into the sloping cut shaded by the castle. Across the road stood a single two-story house with four windows on each side. Blue sky shone through every window. A ruined stone staircase led up from the earth, then ended in space—a bizarre comment on human effort. I understood now what Fierro intended to do. The horses, in plain sight, would serve as bait.

I should have killed him the night before. Before he shot the prisoners at Torreón he had calculated the wind, the distance, the angles. He had known from the beginning what he would do with me in Las Palomas. I laid down my rifle to fish some Bull Durham from my pocket, and when I looked up over the makings, his pistol was pointed at my belly. He reached out carefully and grasped the barrel of my rifle, sliding it toward him through the dirt.

"With your left hand, Tomás, take your pistol from the holster. Use one finger. Put the pistol at your feet."

He didn't have to kill me—he had only to disarm me. The blood rushed to my cheeks.

"Rodolfo . . . there are two of them. You can't do this alone."

"Why not? I'm an excellent shot, as you know. Do as I say."

If I tried to yank out the pistol and gun him down like some old-time western shootist, he could kill me. Pancho Villa would never know. I slid the pistol out slowly, as he instructed, and let it drop to the ground.

The corner of his lip curved in a little smile. "Good, Tomás. Now, my friend, go across the road. Get behind the wall of that house. Stay there. It would make me nervous to have you close by, and this time I don't have Dozal to watch you. Who knows? You might interfere with my aim."

Walking through the dust, I felt the sweat spread across the small of my back.

I settled down inside the roofless house. Through the ragged masonry of the window I could see Fierro's face, a dark plane under the shadow of his gray Stetson. He was about twenty yards away. I smoked three cigarettes and cursed steadily while we waited. I didn't want these men to die. In about an hour, Lieutenant Patton and Miguel Bosques came riding out of the foothills to the north.

A mile distant, they were a wisp of dust on the lion-colored plain. A twisting wind had blown up to ransack the prairie, blowing tumbleweed and twigs, whining through the broken stones of the houses. Rain clouds were already lumbering in. The swirl of dust grew larger, and I made out two peaked cavalry hats. They could see our horses tethered to the mesquite. Then they veered off the trail and vanished behind a butte.

Patton was clever; he had proved that already. He would circle and come at us from the other direction, with the ruined houses to shield him. They wouldn't know where we were, but they wouldn't think we were close to the horses. Fierro counted on that. I waited five minutes, and then, as if a tap had been turned, fresh sweat began to pour down my forehead. I was sitting here in a shell of a house, with busted windows on every side, a staircase leading to nowhere . . . everyone's target. I wasn't armed. I had to watch while three lunatics tried to kill each other. The wind kept blowing, the weed kept tumbling. I inched my head up over the rubble of the window.

From off to my left two rifles cracked in the gray air . . . seconds later, cracked again. The shots had been unhurried. Under the mesquite tree up the road, the buckskin fell without sound, shot through the head. Maximilian staggered. With a brief cry he sank to his knees, shook his head . . . then crashed in the dust. Like red wine from a vat, blood pumped from his ripped heart, splashing and then coursing down the incline of the road. Patton had shot the horses to make sure we couldn't ride away.

I screamed, "You bastard!"

In a windy silence, my voice echoed among the ruins. The stone above my head shattered, showering my scalp with bits of plaster and rock, and I heard the hateful snap of a Springfield. Then more shots slammed into the wall. Boots slid over rock. The shout had revealed my hiding place, and of course they thought I was armed. One of them was coming for me, while the other covered him to keep my head down. A short life, and I had finally made some sense of it . . . but I would never see Rosa and Elisa again. I crawled toward the staircase and began to climb. A dozen steps, and there was nowhere to go. I looked once more at the sky, then turned, just as Miguel Bosques crashed through the ragged arch of the door.

He stared up at me. Perhaps he had thought to find Fierro. Much later, I recalled his hesitation on Stanton Street, when he had snatched Patton's pistol. He was a poet and a schoolteacher; he had never been a killer. To survive, yes . . . as I had done. But he saw an unarmed man before him, sitting with stricken eyes the way the men had sat in the corral at Torreón. And so he died, unable to pull the trigger on the man he had sworn to kill.

A rifle barked thinly, the echo fading in the gray air. Sheltered across the road behind the cut, Rodolfo Fierro had a clear view through one of the gaping windows. The schoolteacher clapped his hand at the red rose blooming on his neck. He sprawled forward at my feet and twisted on his back, across the staircase.

Thunder broke above my head. Lightning ripped at the sky. The rain poured down as if God had tipped a giant bucket, washing away the blood pouring from Bosques' body. I pried the army Colt .45 from his outstretched hand and vaulted out of a window into a pile of scrub. Crouching low, I ran through the rain toward the safety of the mine shaft . . . and Patton, nestled behind a pile of rocks, squeezed off a single shot. Something shoved me in the side, hurled me to the soggy earth. I heard the high yap of the Springfield. I kept crawling, my shirt ripped from stones and catclaw, my legs caked with gumbo. I reached the mine shaft. *Gutshot,* I thought. I had seen it happen to other men. It didn't hurt too much, and there wasn't much blood. It was never quick. You had time to think before you died.

So I crawled a few yards into the mine shaft and waited to die. But no images came . . . no visions; my life didn't pass before my eyes. I was tired, and there was an annoying throb deep inside of me. The mine was cool and dry. The shaft was a dead place where no man had been for years. Beyond in the rain and gloom, Patton and Fierro stalked each other. Die, you bastards. Keep me company.

A bit of time passed . . . I don't know how long. I still hadn't decided what to think about. If I thought about the good things, I might be too sorry to go. Then, against the glare of gray light that led to the outside world, I saw a man's dim shape. It was there for only a second . . . then it vanished. The rain tore down, dribbled, then stopped. The sky lightened rapidly. The man at the entrance to the mine grew visible, frozen against the oval of pearly light. He was waiting for his prey. He didn't know I was behind him. My heart beat against the stones . . . I wondered dully which one of them it was.

Then the man moved a step backward, seeking more shelter, and I heard the jingle of silver spurs. I called his name softly.

Whispered from the darkness, it still alarmed him. He spun in a crouch, dislodging stones. He couldn't see me . . . but he knew my voice, knew that he had disarmed me.

"Tomás. . . ? Show yourself."

I raised Bosques' pistol, my middle finger wrapped around the trigger. There was no distance between me and the target. Hand and pistol, target and bullet, desire and obligation—all were one. I squeezed off two shots before the hammer clicked on the first empty chamber. The heavy Colt bucked, and waves of sound boomed wildly off the walls of the cave.

I stood, and moved to the entrance of the mine. I nudged the body with the toe of my boot, but there was no responding groan. His eyes weren't even reproachful. Even in death Fierro was calm. A mist steamed from the road . . . the light was fading. Patton was out there, somewhere. I tossed the pistol out into the mud and cried out weakly that he could come and claim his prize.

He built a fire near the mouth of the shaft, not far from the dead horses. In his saddlebags he carried a U. S. Army first-aid kit with iodine and tincture of opium in tiny bottles. He didn't give me the opium, but he said he would if he had to. He heated water on the fire and then swabbed out the hole in my side, dressed it and bandaged it. I yelled a lot, and he told me to shut up.

"Why should I? Goddammit, it hurts." He expected me to act like a soldier—not a gentleman, but at least an officer. Officers didn't complain when they died.

This crazy lieutenant had mixed himself up in my life to an unconscionable degree. From the time I first bumped into him in El Paso right up to now, he had bothered me, used me and hunted me, killed my friends and then shot Maximilian. Good God, he'd even shot *me*. I had every reason to hate him, but I didn't. I didn't hate anyone now that I was dying. I just hated to go.

He lit his pipe, and by the flare of the match I could see the curiosity in his eyes. He didn't understand any of it. By all rights he should have been dead, pitched into a well. You could never fix odds on such a contest, but I think Fierro would have outlasted him.

"Why did you kill him?" he asked me.

"I'll tell you if you give me the opium."

"Not yet. On the way back."

"Back?"

"To Casas Grandes."

"Why would I go *there?*"

"For court-martial."

"Goddammit," I said, "I should have let the sonofabitch kill you. I

/ 435

thought he was a more worthless sonofabitch than you are, but now I'm starting to think I was wrong. If you don't want me to die, Lieutenant, you better give me that opium. I *hurt.*"

He grumbled but gave in. "Just lick the bottle with the tip of your tongue," he told me.

It was a brownish liquid that smelled salty and sweet at the same time and tasted like crushed almonds. In a few minutes all my pain and most of my troubles vanished, and I felt wonderfully sleepy. I laid my head down on a rock and drifted off to dream about Elisa's four-poster, except that it was out in the middle of the desert under a hot sun, and I was sprawled in it with a cool hand stroking my back. I didn't know whose hand it was, and it didn't matter. A machine gun chattered in the distance, and I said, "Don't pay any attention. That's just Black Jack having target practice." When I shifted my head on the pillow, something hard banged into my teeth. I unglued my eyes and saw the rock under my nose, with a pale sun tipping the peaks east of Las Palomas. I had slept all night. Patton was crouched by the fire stirring a pot, but I didn't smell coffee. He was brewing tea . . . and I knew with certainty that I didn't intend to go back with him to face a court-martial. Some army doctor might save my life, but that life wouldn't be worth living. If I was going to die it would be on my own terms, in the place I cared to lay down my bones.

"I've got to bury Bosques," Patton said.

Until then he hadn't mentioned the dead schoolteacher, but I knew he had been thinking about it, and I could tell from the expression on his face that he was more twisted up about Bosques than he was willing to say. He must have felt in some way responsible. Beyond that—although I didn't know it then—they had been friends. I was sorry too that Bosques had been killed—he could have pulled the trigger on me and didn't—but I imagined that if he and Fierro got to the nether regions at around the same time, which seemed likely, he would get some measure of consolation at seeing the company he kept.

"Never mind burying Rodolfo," I said. "Let the buzzards choke on him."

Patton took all the rifles and pistols and headed over to the ruined house where the schoolteacher's body still lay on the stone staircase. He knew I couldn't run away, and I wasn't armed. Or at least he didn't think so. He wasn't a cowboy, so he didn't know the things that a cowboy could do. All he knew was the pistol and rifle and saber. When he was out of sight I got shakily to my feet and lurched across the dirt to where Maximilian and the buckskin lay under the mesquite tree. Their legs were splayed stiffly in the chill dawn air. I didn't want to look into Maximilian's eyes. No, I wouldn't go back. I hauled my rope off the saddle horn and limped back to my place by the campfire. Coiling the rope out neatly in the dirt, I threw a bloody saddle blanket over it and squatted down. My insides cramped once again with pain, and with shaky hands I poured myself a mug of tea. I could have used another sip of opium, but I would have to wait.

When Patton came back from the burial he looked mournful and grim. He was leading the big black and brown cavalry horses. His rifle was stuffed in the scabbard; he had holstered his pistol and buttoned the flap. He drank his tea and then put out the fire with sand.

"Mix, I'll make things easier for you . . . if you give me your word you won't try to escape."

"You'd trust me?"

"You're an officer."

"It's an officer's duty to try and escape."

"If he's able."

"I still can't give you my word."

He looked me over where I sat on the ground, a bedraggled specimen. His lip curled. "I won't have to tie you," he said. "You won't get far, even if you're idiot enough to try."

He turned his back to tighten the cinch on his horse. I grabbed the rope. The loop was as big as I could make it, and I whirled it out with the same head ketch I had used on Fierro in the quicksand of Lake Ascensión, a wavelike toss traveling long to the honda. He heard it whir above his head and he started to turn, but it was too late. When the rope settled I dug in my heels and yanked with all my strength. The pain almost took me off my feet. He had his pistol half out of the holster; his face was bright pink, his blue eyes snapping. But the noose tightened on his arms, and he came bouncing across the dirt, kicking up dust—then left his feet and landed flat, so that all the air broke from his lungs and the dust kicked up as if a shell had exploded. He flopped around, while I played him on the rope and worked my way round in that direction. Before he could shake loose I had grabbed the business end of that Colt .45 pistol, jammed it into his neck and was yelling at him to get up and back off slow, because I thought I might pass out and I didn't know what foolish thing he might do if he had any fight left in him. He did what I told him. He was out of breath and still couldn't speak, but he loosened the rope from where it bound his chest and let it fall to the ground so he could step out of it. He looked ashamed.

Then, without warning, he broke into shrill peals of laughter. At first I thought I had loosened some of his bolts.

"What the hell's so funny?"

"You are," he said, when he had quieted down. "I'm your prisoner . . . but what are you going to do with me?"

I hadn't thought of that, and when he realized it he began to laugh again.

"Patton," I said, after a while, "I'm a desperate man. So stop cackling like a goddam jackass. Just shut up and listen to me."

/ 437

I cocked the hammer of the Colt and leveled it at his chest. He stood in front of me now, hands on the hips of his ripped puttees, legs spread wide in the dust, blue eyes studying me with great concentration. I had settled down with my back against the mesquite tree next to the bodies of the horses. I had the bottle of opium at my side, and I yearned for it the way a rummy yearns for one more shot of red-eye. But I knew what that medicine did to a man's brains.

"I'll listen," he said, "if you'll put that pistol down. I know goddam well you're not going to use it."

I stuck out my jaw. "How come you're so sure?"

"You shot Fierro, didn't you? If you meant to kill me, you would have done it five minutes ago. Now put it down and speak your piece."

He had me there, but for all I knew he might have been as full of tricks as I was.

"All right," I grumbled. "If you give me your word as an officer that you won't grab it. And you won't try and knock me out or anything like that. A truce."

"Yes, yes," he said impatiently. "Get on with it, man, before you drop dead."

I laid the pistol on the ground, but I still didn't pick up the opium bottle. I had a lot of talking to do, and I wanted a clear head. We made a comical pair. I had always admired him as a soldier, and then, for a moment, despite everything he had done, I almost liked him as a man. So I told him everything: why I had agreed to be a spy for him, why I had led the cavalry astray. I must have sounded like a whore bucking for sainthood, but I didn't care.

"And you never worked for the Germans?"

"Go fuck yourself, Patton."

"What about that German woman in Parral, the one who shot at Tompkins' men—"

"Not *at* Tompkins' men. Over their heads."

I told him that Villa had been there all along in Los Flores, hiding out while his leg mended. A witch cured him, I said. That part didn't exactly shore up my credibility, but at least he never called me a liar. And I told him about my talk with Von Papen, and then the second meeting in the desert of Sonora when Villa had sent him packing.

"He didn't raid Columbus. I swear that to you."

He smirked, but I think he believed me about Elisa and why I had misled the cavalry all over Chihuahua. "It worked, didn't it? Tell me that it worked."

But he shut up. He would never give me that satisfaction.

"And now let's make a deal," I said. "Because if we don't, we'll sit here until I die . . . which I don't intend to do, not just yet. I'll take your spare horse and ride to Parral. You can go back. Tell them you shot Fierro and I got away. And then leave me in peace."

We were a fine pair of poker players . . . neither of us with any cards in his hand. What choices did we have? The pistol lay on the ground between us. He couldn't pick it up because he had given his word. I could pick it up, but I couldn't use it.

He saddled Miguel Bosques' horse for me, and he did something then that altered not so much my life but my view of it. It wasn't deliberate, I'm sure of that; his mind just wasn't focusing, and so he didn't think to hunt for my saddle but instead used the one that had been given to Bosques—and his saddlebags as well. I was hurting too much to notice, and if I had I still might not have cared.

Before I climbed up I wet my pinky with opium and licked it lightly. I shoved the bottle into my hip pocket. I felt better right away—drowsy, but able to ride.

"Anyway," Patton grumbled, "you'll probably die before you get there."

"Goddammit, is that all you can say?"

I think he misunderstood me. I was complaining about his lack of imagination, but he must have thought I meant that something more was required for the occasion. Maybe it was. And to give him credit, he supplied it. He reached out, shook my hand and said, "I hope I'm wrong. Good luck to you, Mix."

"Same to you, Lieutenant. Don't get killed."

He was added to the list of people I would never see again, but in this case it was without regret. I trotted off, moaning like a banshee.

I rode all day, half asleep, and bedded down somewhere in the high sierra after I had licked the top of the opium bottle again. I had a bit more for breakfast too.

It was one of those cool and luminous Mexican mornings—blue sky, golden sun—when the world seems reborn. The forest sparkled with light. Green leaves rustled, and the air was a tonic. Fiddling around in Miguel Bosques' saddlebags, I came across his journal.

39

**"Hark! the land bids me
tread no more upon 't."**

I don't remember how I got to Parral. The opium turned my head to mush and I rode in a sweet daze, dreaming of mustachioed devils, yellow-haired angels, the pounding hoofs of creatures that were part man, part horse—and yet a mellowness made it more than bearable. Leaning against a tree to piss, I was able to press my fingers through the bark into the core, feel the living sap at the heart. A heavenly choir, shimmering swaying ladies in long skirts, sang to me from a blue sky; I saw them. They were *real*. I remember some Tarahumara who fed me maize and pulque up in the sierra, and some buzzards that sat on a telegraph wire and flapped round my head with staring red eyes until I clipped one's wing with a shot from my rifle . . . and I remember an owl who hooted all one night and then fluttered out of the forest to ride on the horn of my saddle. Maybe he didn't, but I thought he did.

I reached Los Flores early one evening and tumbled off my horse into a bed of zinnias. From that point on, for a while, I don't remember a thing except the voice of Doña Maria. Elisa told me later that she'd had to get down on her knees to beg the *curandera* to come to the house, and it was only when Doña Maria realized that Elisa wouldn't leave Atotonilco without her that she finally agreed to come. She cast a spell on me, and then a one-eyed *comadrona,* a midwife, dug the bullet out of my innards. Luckily it had passed all the way through and nearly come out the other side. Doña Maria said that apart from everything else, I had *ojo*—evil-eye sickness. Some bad person had given it to me. I thought of Fierro, lying in the mud and staring up at me with his calm, dead gaze. He seemed the most likely candidate.

Before Doña Maria could cure the fever and take the infection away from my guts she had to rub a hen's egg over my eyes, break it into a saucer and pierce it with seven sharp thorns, which blinded the one who had inflicted the *ojo*. Then she chanted, *"Isa ya! Isa ya! Ri ega! Bi esha! Xiyilqua!"*—and after massaging the lower part of my body with an infusion made from the leaves of the rue and pepper tree, she spat a mouthful of aguardiente into my side and sucked it from the wound until the fever broke and the peritonitis went away. I had no fear, she told Elisa, and my soul was still in its correct place, which made things much easier for her.

It took me two months to recover, and Rosa tended me most of the time, changing my dressing and reading to me slowly from *Treasure Island* and some Kipling novels, or sometimes, after the rains, just sitting with me in the shade of the garden with a cool hand laid on my forehead. I asked her to try to read Bosques' journal aloud to me, and she did, haltingly, but when she got to the part where the men were being killed in the stockyards, I told her not to go on. Elisa came by a few times a day and brought me my meals, the kind of gruel a baby eats. I lost a lot of weight and got thin and knotty, like a birch covered with barbed wire. I slept alone.

I kept asking for news of Pancho Villa, but there wasn't any. He seemed to have vanished. Hipólito would be in touch with him, of course, and would have told him the tale of the lost gold. He would know about Julio and Candelario from the American newspapers, which played up every victory of the cavalry, no matter how obscure, as if it were the battle of Manila Bay. Poor Pershing was still sitting up there in Casas Grandes, sending out patrols and following up rumors, and no doubt starting to wonder if he was doomed to live out his command in the wasteland of northern Mexico.

And then one fine morning I woke and asked Elisa to cook me some ham and eggs and let me try a mug of Rosa's coffee. Youth can suffer worse wounds than age . . . I know that all too well now.

After that I got well quickly and fleshed out, and in a couple of weeks I moved upstairs with them. They treated me tenderly and gently for as long as it was necessary. One day I said, "Let *me* do it. I'm feeling a lot better, Elisa."

"That's obvious." She fell back on the bed, exhausted.

After that they only treated me tenderly.

"Men are merriest," Shakespeare wrote, "when they are far from home." But merriment as a steady diet can't compare to tranquillity salted with passion. The rains kept falling, and the desert had its short, splendid season of flowering. Poppies and blue barrel cactus bloomed everywhere; dwarf marigold sprouted where you thought only rocks could grow. The raw land of Chihuahua held me in thrall. Rosa, Elisa and I rode out in the early mornings, and then in the evening we would sit in the library and make our plans. Once we agreed we were going to breed horses, I hired two workmen and set about enlarging the corrals and stables. Rosa grew sleek and put on some weight. A few new tiny lines spread out from the corners of Elisa's eyes.

I didn't want anything to change in our lives, but that was a forlorn hope. In fact, they had begun to change already, although the shift was subtle and never signaled by any dramatic outbursts.

Women are nesting creatures, and I suppose each one needs to believe that she's queen of the nest. Rosa was young and full of a vigorous energy that didn't come quite as easily to Elisa. She knew very well that it was Elisa's nest—we were there at Los Flores only because of Elisa's generosity. Rosa treated Elisa with a certain deference, but I think at heart she believed that I belonged to *her* and that what took place among the three of us was in the nature of a gift . . . *her* gift, to me. Elisa began to sense it. As for me, I had been with Rosa a long time, and I began to realize that my love for her was deeper than what I felt for Elisa. I loved them both, yes—but differently. Elisa sensed that too.

And so even before the next events that befell us, our life upstairs began to take on a different character. There were fewer playful romps in the four-poster than before. Elisa would say she was tired, or headachy, and I would spent those nights in Rosa's room. One day I found that my clothes and books and papers had been moved in there. I never

/ 441

had to ask why or who. Rosa shrugged. She knew too. I think the women may have discussed it between themselves, but I wasn't included. They were making their peace with reality. They weren't female men.

Elisa and I bought another roan stallion from a ranch near Parral, and one hot August day we rode over to Camargo and dickered for a couple of days for six fine brood mares and two wild Durango mustangs. Just before we left, my workmen told me that they had heard news of a battle taking place near San Andrés, to the north, between Pancho Villa and General Treviño. Villa had been licked again, they said.

But in Camargo we heard more. It was Treviño who had been licked, and Villa had driven a whole division south in disorder.

Land and liberty! *Viva el revolución!*

"He must have a new plan," I said to Elisa.

Then two weeks later, we heard, with only a thousand men he attacked Treviño again in Chihuahua City. He freed all the prisoners locked up in the penitentiary, secured sixteen truckloads of small arms and ammunition, and left the city with fifteen hundred more men than when he had entered. A month later he struck audaciously in the same spot, and this time after three days of confused fighting, Treviño fled. The chief moved briefly into his old house, with Luz Corral. Pershing sat up in Casas Grandes and fumed . . . Carranza still wouldn't let him move south. The cavalry had now been in Chihuahua more than half a year.

One blue October day in that fateful year of 1916, Rosa and I rode up to Tomochic with a pack mule and dug the gold out from behind the corral. We had agreed to put her half of it into the horse business and give the rest to Francisca, as Candelario had wished—or else ask Francisca if she wanted a share in the business. We gave a small bag of gold to Rosa's mother as a gift. That was my idea, I'm pleased to say, and that worn-out Indian lady wept and called Rosa *"mi tesora"*—my treasure. Indeed she was . . . and mine too. I loved her with all my heart. But when we got back I thought she looked awfully tired and wan, and I asked if she was feeling sick.

"No, Tomás . . . not really." She smiled at me with large eyes. "I am with child. Did you think I was just getting fat like an old Mexican woman?"

It didn't seem possible. She had always claimed she was barren. But the evidence was there and wouldn't go away. She said it had happened in June, just before I left for the north, after we had begun our romp in the four-poster. More than one barrier had fallen then.

"And does Elisa know?"

"Where men are blind, women have eyes."

"Rosa, that's wonderful!" A father! Since coming to Mexico I had become a revolutionist, a libertine, a colonel, an assassin, a spy, even an orgiast—but never a father. I was thrilled. "Will you marry me now?" I asked.

"It's not necessary, Tomás. It's not a disgrace in Mexico to have a baby and not be married."

"I'm sure it isn't," I said, thinking of the dozen or more children that Villa was supposed to have fathered throughout the land—"but that's not the point. Are you worried about what it will do to Elisa?"

Rosa nodded. I knew it was that.

"Don't," I said. "She may be hurt, but that's something that has to come. She knows I already think of you as my wife. I love you, Rosa. Won't you marry me?"

"Yes, Tomás," she breathed, resting her head on my shoulder so that I might not see the tears in her eyes.

That night I talked to Elisa alone in the library. She was amused at the fact that I had been ignorant for so long, but her laugh sounded just a fraction strained.

"And what are you going to do about it?" she asked.

"We'll get married. I asked her, and she said yes. But now I have to ask you something. Will you want us to leave?"

"Oh, Tom!" She hooted with laughter. "*I* never wanted to marry you! I'm close to forty—I have a grown daughter in Berlin, almost as old as Rosa. No, of course I don't want you to leave. We're in business together, aren't we? And we care for each other. Let Rosa have the babies. Let Rosa be your wife. I'll be old Aunt Elisa."

"I wish you wouldn't call yourself that."

"I won't, *cariño*. Not out loud." She kissed me softly on the lips. "Will you come to bed? I invite you both, for auld lang syne. Now that such momentous decisions have been made, it calls for a celebration."

Rosa wasn't big enough yet to be awkward, and we jumped around like three bear cubs holding a rassling match. Elisa clutched Rosa's hand and sang her lovely song . . . and I thought, it will be all right.

In November Mr. Wilson was elected President again, although Teddy Roosevelt yelled that he was responsible for the Columbus raid and had let the U. S. Army be humiliated in Chihuahua by "a mere handful of bandits." But Wilson promised he would keep us out of the war in Europe, and so the people voted for him. On Christmas Eve Pancho Villa attacked Torreón—again—and took it. That brought back memories. I wondered if the Otomis watched the battle from the same place outside the city. I wondered too if Villa knew where I was, and I thought of going to find him, just to say hello and how-are-you, but it would have been even more dangerous than sentimental, so I stayed put. Villa raised a forced loan from the banks and made a speech saying that if Pershing would come south he'd kick his ass out of Mexico once and for all, and then with the other boot do the same to Don Venus, who was sitting in Mexico City putting all his proclamations together in the form of a Constitution. I read that document in a local newspaper, and it wasn't bad at all. It gave the land back to the people and established the right to strike. Whether those promises would be translated into reality was another story, of course.

In January of 1917 the ten thousand troops of the Punitive Expedition began to withdraw toward the border. They had never found Pancho Villa, although twice, in Guerrero and then in Pahuirachic, they had come awfully close. I guess their Intelligence let them down on that score, and whenever I thought about that I was proud of what I had done. The chief would never have let them take him alive, and a lot of good men would have died trying. Maybe even a certain lieutenant.

Rosa and I got married a month before that, in December, in a little church in Parral. I was a couple of months shy of my twenty-sixth birthday; Rosa had just turned eighteen, so she was officially a woman. Elisa bought her a white lace wedding dress that would have fit the fat lady at the circus, but Francisca, who had decided to go into business with us but still insisted on being a maid, took it in below the bosom, and Rosa looked lovely. After the ceremony we went back to the Hacienda de Los Flores and drank bottles of bubbling French champagne, which made everyone giggle. Elisa grabbed my hand and pulled me into the kitchen.

"Tom, I'm happy for you," she whispered, laughing and leaking tears at the same time. "I want you to know that. I love you both, as much as I've ever loved anyone in this world. And maybe more."

"I adore you too, Elisa. And so does Rosa. You know that."

"Am I still aces on kings?"

"A straight flush. You're the finest woman I've ever known. You've made all this possible. And you made me grow up."

"You can both stay forever," she said. "Just be kind to old Aunt Elisa. . . ."

I hugged her, and then she cried as if her heart was breaking. But through it all, somehow, she kept giggling. From the corner of an eye I saw Rosa step through the kitchen door. She came up to us, and Elisa laid her head against Rosa, as Rosa had so often done against me. The wayward yellow hair tumbled down on Rosa's bare shoulder.

"It's the champagne," Elisa sniffed, between sobs and snorts of laughter. "The champagne always does it to me. And because I'm so happy for you . . ."

In February Rosa's time came. She was so big that when we walked through the garden and let the lovebirds out of their cage, they could sit on her belly. She was a strong, healthy girl. No one seemed worried. The one-eyed midwife arrived at Los Flores around four o'clock in the afternoon, an hour or so after Rosa's labor pains began. All the women gathered upstairs and kicked me out.

Down in the library I poured myself a full snifter of brandy and read straight through *The First Part of King Henry IV* and then *Othello*. It took my mind off the yells I heard.

Toward late evening Elisa appeared at the door, looking pale and as worn out as if she were the one giving birth.

"There's a problem, Tom . . ."

The midwife had poked around and decided that the baby was lying feet down, which was the wrong direction.

"Can't it come out that way?"

"Not easily. We may need your help."

The idea made me jittery, but of course I nodded. I had seen plenty of blood and more than enough anguish, but I didn't want to see Rosa's.

"You can pull," Elisa said, clenching her fists.

"If there's a choice—if it's a question of Rosa or the baby—"

"We know that." Elisa seemed impatient with me. But I knew that wasn't at the root of it; she was just feeling unhappy.

Labor went on for a few more hours . . . Rosa's screams increased in volume. Mexican women weren't taught to be decorous in childbirth. I probably would have flitted into the orchard so that I didn't have to listen, but Elisa had said they might need me. I stayed in the library, trying to read *King Lear*. Sometimes I became caught up in it, but most of the time I had an ear cocked for the next shriek. This was all wrong. Why should she suffer that much? Let me take the pain . . . and God, I prayed, let her be all right. I was no true believer, but like most men, in moments of helplessness I didn't know who else to turn to.

At midnight Francisca descended swiftly in bare feet and told me the señora wished me to come upstairs. I took the stairs two at a time and then slowed down to ease gently through the door into the bedroom. Oil lamps and sputtering candles cast a light in which the shadows overlapped and seemed confused. What I saw was awful. Rosa, on the bed, looked ashen. She was covered with clammy sweat. She was biting on a towel, but still her groans were load. Elisa gripped her bare shoulders. Her thighs were spread obscenely wide, and the baby's legs dangled free up to the knees. The legs were chubby and purple, scarcely human. The midwife tugged at them. The sweat poured down her brown face so that in the lamplight she glistened as though she were standing in the rain. Words choked from my lips and made no sense.

"Pull," Elisa cried.

The legs in my hands were soft boneless pieces of meat. The midwife told me to pull harder.

"But—"

"Harder, señor! Don't be afraid!"

I was ruining my child's body. How could I know that it didn't matter, that he was already dead? As soon as Rosa had forced the body free he began to breathe, but the head was deep inside where there was no air. He quickly suffocated. I thought only of Rosa.

Later Elisa told me that Rosa's pelvis was small. It had no relation to the fact that she was a wide-hipped young woman. It was something you couldn't tell until it was too late. The baby's head was jammed up behind the pelvic bone; it couldn't get through. The labor was over. Her body wouldn't work anymore. No amount of tugging would do it. Rosa was worn out, but she kept screaming.

Finally the midwife shoved me aside and with a high-pitched cry of terror reached in with one bloody hand to crush the baby's head and drag it through. I turned my head away . . . I couldn't bear to see this. Rosa gave a great groan of relief and threw her head back on the pillow, soaked with her sweat. Then I was able to look. Her hand reached up to clutch at Elisa's, and she even smiled.

The midwife didn't smile. She stared down, waiting. She must have known what would happen and dreaded it. She had thrust the dead baby to one side, not even bothering to cut the long, fat white cord. She didn't care about the baby any longer.

The blood gushed out between Rosa's legs—bright red, as if pumped by a vengeful devil. The midwife snatched a handful of white cotton cloths and tried to force them in, to stem the surge. She was bloody up to the elbows. The baby's head had ripped Rosa on both sides. Rosa never knew it—all she knew was that the pain had ended. She didn't feel her life pouring out of her. But I felt and saw it. I understood. So did Elisa. She held Rosa's hand while her face turned the color of paper. Then Rosa grew pale too, but still smiled with relief, even as she closed her eyes slowly . . . even as she died.

I never truly understood it, no matter how many times it was explained to me about the small pelvic cavity and the way she felt no pain at the end. She was only eighteen. She was a big, strong, healthy girl. Her hair lay on the pillow in a wet black tangle, and her lips were slightly parted in that terrible smile of relief. I bent to kiss her, and the tears that fell from my eyes were warmer than her lips.

Elisa rushed from the room and locked herself in the library. I heard the door slam and echo. Francisca, on her knees, began to tear her hair. The midwife crossed herself, marking her breast with Rosa's blood, and said hoarsely, "God must have had a reason."

But what could it have been?

That night in the garden I stretched out on the unyielding ground and wept until no more tears would come. I chewed mouthfuls of earth and spat them out. I stayed there until dawn. Later in the morning, it being a hot country, we buried Rosa and the baby in one grave that Patricio dug behind the corrals. There was no ceremony of any kind. The sun shone from a cloudless blue sky, mocking everything. You couldn't have asked for more glorious weather. Patricio knocked together the coffin, and Elisa took care of putting the bodies in it. I didn't help. I wasn't able to do anything except sit around and stare up at the sky and listen to the birds trilling cheerfully in the garden. I hated being alive.

When it came time for the coffin to be lowered into the hole, my hands trembled. Not that it was heavy . . . it wasn't heavy at all. In death, Rosa seemed to weigh almost nothing. Elisa laid flowers on the pine planks. I placed some small stones there. My throat was twisted into a knot that nearly strangled me, and my eyes blurred again with tears. This was a death I would never accept.

Rosa, how good you were! I remember you by the lake, when you were a child, on your knees in the dust. I watched you grow to be a woman . . . and I've known no finer sight. I remember it all . . .

I remember too much!

And you never displeased me.

After that, for a while, I passed through the turning wheel of time in a kind of narcosis. I would wake up in the morning and whisper Rosa's name, thinking that she was alive but had gone away for a while, and if I invoked her name often enough she would hear and return. My spirit was frozen in a twilight. Elisa's grief was even more mute. There was no decent way to put things into words. We became strangers living in the same house and even, sometimes, the same bed. We couldn't talk about Rosa. It was as if we didn't dare admit she was dead. I wonder if we both didn't feel, somehow, that she had been better than we were, and the fact of her going lessened us because it made no sense that we were alive and she wasn't. To make love seemed wrong. It was a kind of betrayal. It hadn't been like that before, when she was alive, but that was how it seemed now.

But we did it sometimes to try and cheat our loneliness. It wasn't very inspiring. Day by day, night by night, we drifted apart, and neither of us could stop it or talk about it. The shadow of Rosa lay between us like a canyon. For some stubborn reason Elisa wouldn't get rid of the third pillow, and whenever I realized it was there I got gooseflesh and turned my head away. Elisa's song was muted and sometimes, I thought, false. I worked around the corrals. I broke the mustangs from Camargo. Life went on. We had to pretend it was important to eat and sleep and work.

Meanwhile, in that other world of people and events, Mr. Wilson got hold of a secret telegram from Berlin to the German ambassador in Washington, suggesting that Carranza be encouraged to go to war against the United States, in return for which Mexico would be given her lost territories. After some sinkings of American ships by German U-boats in the Atlantic, we declared war. Elisa bought a radio, and every evening she sat by the fire drinking brandy and listening to the news, and after a while I went off to the library and drifted off into a stupor with a bottle of wine. Pershing was going to lead an American Expeditionary Force to France—they were all agreed that he was the best choice because of his experience fighting in Mexico. No one thought the Punitive Expedition was a failure now. They saw it, with hindsight, as preparation for the war in Europe.

One evening Elisa asked me if I would go too.

"I've been thinking about it," I confessed. "I don't believe I will."

"But you're an American."

"I know that, Elisa. And you're a German. Would you fight if you were a man?"

"I'm not a man. I can't think that way."

"I've had enough of fighting. I've been shot at enough for one lifetime. And I don't want to kill anyone—not ever again."

"What will you do then, Tom? I don't think you want to stay here."

It was out in the open then, and I nodded. Too many good things had happened between us for me to lie.

"I'll just go back to Texas and be a cowhand. I can always change my name. They don't draft cowhands. They're too ornery. They can't take orders, and they never learn to shoot straight."

A couple of days later I strewed a few flowers on the grave of Rosa and the baby. Yes, I thought, she never displeased me. And she ruined me for everyone else . . . even Elisa.

I saddled my horse by the gate. Elisa had wanted to give me what was left of the gold, but I refused.

"I'd just spend it on whiskey and wild women. You keep my share. Times might be hard after the war. I came here with nothing. I don't want to leave with anything. That would be wrong."

"You mustn't blame yourself. What happened wasn't your fault."

That was the only time she ever referred to Rosa's death. I just nodded. Maybe it was so. I would never know. I only knew how godawful I felt about it, how hollowed out and barren. I remembered what Bosques had written: that death was Mexico's greatest crop. Villa was still fighting, I knew, somewhere in northern Chihuahua. How many had been killed in all these years? How many were yet to die? I had grieved for Julio and Candelario. I didn't want to count, didn't want to know. Only one death mattered now. I saw every flower and bush that way, as a branch of someone who slept beneath the dust. That was one of the reasons I had to go.

"You'll always be welcome here," she said. "You know that."

"I do know it. Take care, Elisa. I never stopped loving you. I just stopped loving life. One day I'll start again . . . but not soon enough for you."

"Go well, my sweet."

She kissed me on both cheeks. She looked old and tired. I didn't thank her as I had done the first time I left the hacienda. She knew my gratitude, and I think she knew my heart was broken into pieces too small to be of much use to anyone who needed a whole heart. I hadn't lied to her.

She turned on her boot heel and strode back into the house, head high, shoulders square. She was never any good at goodbyes. She closed the door. In all my life since then—and I've done a lot—I never met another woman so proud.

On the way north, on a sunny March day of 1917, somewhere above Bachinava and below Casas Grandes, in that part of Chihuahua I knew so well, a band of horsemen appeared out of the desert. They cut a wraithlike trail of dust along the horizon line; then the trail narrowed and thickened, and they came riding straight for me. I made sure that my pistol was loose in the holster and checked that I hadn't forgotten to put a fresh clip in the Mauser. If this was trouble I wanted to be ready.

The riders, about six or seven of them, wore big sombreros and carried full cartridge belts. The barrels of their uplifted rifles glittered like jewels in the sun. They rode straight up to me and wheeled their horses, tugging at the ring bit as hard as they could. That hadn't changed. And their leader didn't waste any words.

"Who are you, señor? Where do you come from? Where are you going?"

I remembered Candelario's way. "Not so fast, friend. First, who are *you?*"

The man who had addressed me couldn't have been more than twenty-one, with a mahogany-brown face, eyes to match and a flowing black mustache. In my time I had seen a thousand like him. He showed his fine white teeth.

"Captain Luis Zuñiga, of the Army of the Revolutionary Convention. At your orders, señor . . . perhaps. Now, who are you?"

I had been away awhile, I realized. "Captain Zuñiga, help me out. Who runs the Army of the Convention these days?"

"General Francisco Villa, señor. Do you come to join us, to fight for land and liberty?" He had his rifle pointed right at my chest.

"I've done that already," I said, "but I do want to see your chief. We're old friends. My name is Colonel Tomás Mix."

Showing a wonderful sense of trust, he thrust his rifle back into the scabbard, bared his teeth again and threw his hand up to his sombrero in a salute. I gave it back to him.

"And where might General Villa be these days?"

"South of Casas Grandes, my colonel. We ride there. We would be honored if you would join us."

"A pleasure, Captain."

We rode off across the dusty plain. I had never meant to leave Mexico without saying goodbye to the man for whose sake I had first come. I had known he was somewhere around here, and I had been keeping an eye skinned. Casas Grandes suited me just fine.

The new army was camped in the foothills of the mountains ten miles south of the city, which was held by the Carranzistas—about fifteen hundred men, I judged, with the usual women and kids and assorted animals. We reached there well after dark, and Zuñiga went round the campfires to make some inquiries. After fifteen minutes he came back to tell me that General Villa wasn't in the camp. He had gone off to sleep. No one knew where.

"In which direction did he go, Captain?"

He asked the last man he had spoken to, and the man pointed to the east. I knew Villa's habits and didn't think they had changed. I thanked Zuñiga and then spurred my horse off in the other direction, westward.

It led me into some gently sloping hills dotted with saguaro cactus and maguey. A half-moon lit the way, casting ivory shadows on the desert. I didn't try to be quiet but thrashed my horse back and forth on the rocks and kept muttering to myself like an old man with many woes. I didn't want to come on anyone by surprise. After an hour of this foolishness I had almost given up, but then at my back, in the black shadow of a hill, I heard the scrape of boot on rock. At first, when I turned in the saddle, I thought I had been mistaken and the green eyes that gleamed at me were those of an animal—a coyote, maybe an owl.

But then the animal, a two-legged one, gave a guttural chuckle and stepped out of the hiding shadow, pistol held loosely in his hand. It was Pancho Villa.

"I thought it might be you, Tomás. Anything's possible in this life, I told myself. But I couldn't be sure. You have a good nose to find me."

"But yours is better, chief. I'm glad you didn't think it was Carranza."

"Carranza . . ." He spat into the darkness. "Get down off your horse, Tomás. Let me make sure you're not a ghost."

I swung out of the saddle, and he stepped forward to embrace me. He smelled of meat and wood smoke. I think he may have meant what he'd said about making sure I was real; he hugged my ribs hard until I thought they would crack, and then he squeezed my shoulders. He was his paunchy old self, and there was a lot more soft flesh on his arms than I remembered. He must have had a good supply of peanut brittle.

"You're thinner," he said. "I can't see your face so I don't know if you look older. But it's logical that you would. How long has it been now?"

"Ten months, chief. In Parral."

"Come around the hill with me. I have a little fire there. I put it out when I heard you, but the coals are under the sand and we'll get it going again. Then I can see your face and learn more."

I walked my horse around the slope with him, and he got the fire going again, blowing on the coals and adding some cornhusks. The little blaze leapt up. His own horse was hidden nearby in the hills. He wanted nothing to give away his presence, and he had his own nose for sniffing. Squatting on our heels in the flicker of the fire, we studied each other. I was right: he was fatter and his jowls looked flabby. But the yellow light in his eyes was the same—shrewd, restless, the fanaticism always tempered by that childlike gleam of hope.

"You do look older," he murmured. "More than I would have thought. What's happened to you? I know about Julio, and then I heard about the gringos bushwhacking the rest of you. They were very proud of killing Candelario and Rodolfo, but they said nothing about you. I should have known that no one could catch you if you were on a horse. Is there more?"

I decided it would make life simpler if I let him keep believing that the cavalry was responsible for Rofolfo's death. I said that I had been wounded in the chase and had to recuperate a long while, and then I told him about Rosa. He didn't speak for a while. There was nothing that would comfort me, and he was wise enough to know it.

"But you married her first."

"Yes, chief."

"That was good of you. That makes women happy. Perhaps you remembered I'd always told that to you. If so, I'm pleased. If not, it was still the right thing to do. And the other one, the beautiful señora?"

"She's still in Parral. It was over, chief. And I had to go."

"She was *mucho.*"

"Yes. That's what she was."

"And your wound healed well?"

"Doña Maria cured me. And took away the *ojo.*"

"*Válgame Dios!* In that, too, we're brothers. . . ."

I took note that I had graduated from bastard son to brother . . . which meant that somehow, at least in his view, I had grown up. That's why I had come to Mexico in the first place. Well, I did feel old—and worthy of promotion. In my time, for him and for the revolution, I had done my best. That was a knowledge no one could ever take away from me.

"You did well," he said, for he still had the ability to read a man's thoughts. "There was never anyone I trusted more than you. Do you remember when we crossed the Rio Bravo? I thought you wouldn't last more than a month. How long has it been? I can't seem to remember. . . ."

"Four years."

"Is that possible?"

"Yes, it's so. Time runs even while men sleep."

He heaped more cornstalks on the fire and looked at me closely in the rising blaze. "And now? Have you come back to fight for me again? From the sadness in your eyes, it doesn't seem that way . . . but I could still use you. I'm working on a good plan. Angeles is coming back soon. Among the three of us—"

"It wouldn't be any good, chief. I've lost my taste for it."

"I can understand that. A lot has happened. Elsewhere, too. Did you know Obregón quit? Carranza made him Secretary of War. Each day he had to approve a special allowance of five thousand pesos for Pablo González, that lousy general who couldn't cut the railroad line at Torreón. It was for expenses. What a pack of thieves! Obregón always wrote alongside the papers, 'By special order of Don Venus.' So Carranza wasn't sorry to see him go."

"Have you read the new Constitution?" I asked.

"I've had it read to me. The big words give me eyestrain. It's pretty good. Unfortunately, a Constitution is no better than the men who enforce it. And they're a pack of politicians and dogs. I don't even know why I make the distinction."

"And what will you do now?"

He laughed. "You always ask that, as if there's a choice. There never was, you know."

"You'll keep fighting."

"I drove the gringos out, didn't I?"

I think he believed it. . . .

"Of course I'll keep fighting," he said, after a moment of relishing his triumph. "Zapata will too, in Morelos. He's not so bad as long as you don't rely on him—there are many men like that. I'm going to take Ojinaga, so that we can have a port of entry for supplies. And then Juárez. Within six months I'll have ten thousand men. I had to give up Chihuahua City, but I'll take it again, and Torreón too. I'll take all the cities on the railroad. I'll take them and lose them a dozen times if I have to. The defeats are also battles, as I've told you, but from now on there will be more victories than defeats. You'll see. Help me up," he said quietly. "I need to stretch my legs."

I did as he asked, and he arched his body and twisted his arms to articulate the bones in his back. I heard a series of tiny cracklings. He sighed at this evidence of age. "And what about you?" he asked, when he was done. "Candelario once told me that in your misspent youth you thought of becoming an actor on the stage in New York. It's a foolish profession, in my opinion, but still you might do well at it, and they say there's money to be made. Perhaps you could be in the movies. I love William S. Hart, but he's getting old. You could do as well as he did. You can certainly ride a horse better."

So once again he touched and changed my life. He never lacked that power.

"I might try that, Pancho. I don't know. I haven't thought much about it lately."

I had never called him Pancho before, but it came naturally now, and he didn't seem to notice. That may have been deceptive. He noticed everything, I remembered.

"Whatever you do," he said thickly, "you'll always have my blessing. You're a man who will never be at rest, Tomás. You're like me—you need a challenge. Now go. I have to sleep. Tomorrow we're going to attack Casas Grandes . . . again."

I left him there by his little brushwood fire and rode off into the familiar darkness of the desert night. This was the only parting that hadn't truly saddened me. He was doing just what suited him, which was more than I could say for myself. I didn't really want to be a cowhand again; for me that was like cutting along the dotted line. I had come to Chihuahua a youth and stayed to become a man . . . found all I had yearned for, and then lost it. Not many, at the age of twenty-six, could say that. And not many would wish to. They looked forward, not back. That was my problem, and it still is.

A little north of Casas Grandes I let the roan out to graze, then bedded down, hands tucked under my head, gazing up at the cold stars that glittered above Chihuahua. The stunning silence of the night surrounded me—vast, impersonal, wondrous and fine. I seemed to feel myself perched on the earth's crust, and the earth was turning in the black void.

I turned with it—I was its slave—I had no choice. I whispered, "Goodnight, Rosa. Sleep well, my love," and closed my eyes.

The sun woke me, and after I had boiled some coffee and swallowed a few hardboiled eggs, I felt a bit better. A distant patter reached my ears, like the sound of fingernails tapping impatiently on wood. Gunfire. The battle for Casas Grandes must have started. . . .

I rode all day over a rocky alkali flat, dodging sword plants and chaparral, keeping the roan at a lazy walk, trying to figure things out. Pancho Villa's words kept nibbling at the edge of my mind. *You're like me—you need a challenge.* I supposed I was free to take it, if that's what I really wanted. Black Jack Pershing and George Patton were over in the mud of France, and now that we had the Huns to hate, who would care about settling old scores with out-of-work renegade Mexican colonels?

An actor. I had always wanted that since the curtain came down in high school. I wasn't Hamlet caliber, but I had been a pretty effective

/ 453

Fortinbras in my time, cleaning away the debris. I still had Shakespeare in my saddlebags—old faithful companion, he had outlasted everybody. In El Paso I could jump a Southern Railway red-ball freight and be in New York in four days' time. But it was barely March . . . it would be cold up there. They'd have a good laugh when I hauled out my serape to keep warm. And I would have a lot to learn before I could tread the boards of the Shubert with any confidence and some style.

On the other hand, they made movies in California—a sunnier land, I'd heard—and it occurred to me that if I got any work out there I wouldn't even have to speak. I could start out as one of those mangy fellows leaning against the bar in a saloon, or one of the mustachioed outlaws who tumbles out of a window above the livery stable when the handsome sheriff starts fanning the hammer of his six-gun. William S. Hart himself didn't do much more than ride and rope and kiss wasp-waisted women . . . and I'd had some practice in those arts. All I would need was a set of civilized harness. Western heroes didn't wear sombreros and Levi's.

A bloody ball of sun dipped toward the mountains that tumbled about on the horizon in the direction of Sonora. *To Sonora . . .*

To Celaya . . .

To Torreón, again . . .

To Hollywood . . .

The desert lay drowned in rich, soft mist. Somewhere, a coyote howled. The dead slept in the slowly cooling earth of Mexico. Goodbye, my love . . .

What the hell, I thought. The defeats are also battles. Goodbye, my youth—and goodbye, Chihuahua. I flicked a rein. The horse turned west. I rode off into the sunset, singing a mournful tune, and became a movie cowboy.

epilogue

"I have some rights
of memory in this kingdom."

A good twenty years, and then some, have passed. A lot has happened to me since, but I won't go into that. I intended to write about the part of my life when I was a revolutionist with Pancho Villa, and I've done it.

I lost touch with the people I met during that unruly time, but I know what's happened to all of them. . . .

Zapata kept on fighting Carranza, who was now president, although there was no vote. Anytime he captured a Federal army officer, Emiliano crucified him on a telegraph pole or smeared him with honey and staked him over an ants' nest—or, in the rainy season, over a maguey plant, whose thorns would grow a foot or more during the night and drive inch by inch through the man's body. In April of 1919 he was betrayed by some turncoat colonel and lured into an ambush at a place called Chinemeca. He was shot to death in a patio by more than two hundred men.

In May of 1920, scenting a wholesale military rebellion against the corruption of his presidency, Carranza absconded for Veracruz with the national treasury and the dies of the government mint, even the light fixtures from the National Palace. He got as far as the pueblo of Tlaxcalatango, where he went to sleep in a little hut with only a saddle blanket for cover. During the night he was shot to death by a dozen men.

Obregón, who had come out of retirement and declared himself an enemy of Carranza, eventually became President of Mexico. He pursued his policy of trying to offend everybody as little as possible, except for the Church. In July of 1928, sitting in a café just outside Mexico City, he was shot to death by a religious fanatic.

So much for those bastards.

Felipe Angeles returned from Washington to fight for Pancho Villa, but in 1919 he was captured by General Treviño and shot to death by a firing squad. They say he refused to wear a blindfold, and he gave the signal for his own execution.

General Black Jack Pershing, as everyone knows, commanded our A.E.F. during the Great War and covered himself with glory. Major Frank Tompkins, who led the Thirteenth Cavalry into Parral, received the Distinguished Service Cross for his part in that campaign, became a colonel and fought in France, where he was badly wounded. In 1934 he wrote a book called *Chasing Villa*. I read it with considerable interest, but he never mentioned me once.

George S. Patton, Jr. went to France as a captain and got himself into the Tank Service, won the Distinguished Service Cross and when I last heard of him was a colonel at Fort Riley, Kansas. We're never met since Las Palomas, but I knew he would do well.

Franz von Papen got kicked out of the United States in 1916 for being a spy. He returned to Germany as a hero, where he rose to become Chancellor. But under that madman Hitler, the best job he could get was Ambassador to Austria.

One day some years ago, when we were on a publicity tour that stopped in New Orleans, a well-dressed, middle-aged woman rushed up to me in the Vieux Carré. It was Yvette. She told me that she and Marie-Thérèse owned a genteel little establishment on Bourbon Street that catered to the carriage trade, and they were doing just fine. Unfortunately I was in a hurry to get to a radio station, and we didn't have much time to reminisce. I never saw her again.

Hannah Sommerfeld married a Houston oilman and is very active there in charity and cultural affairs, and something called the B'nai B'rith. We're not in touch.

Elisa Griensen had to leave Mexico after the war and go back to Germany to care for her daughter, who had lost a leg in a car accident. So it probably never would have worked out between us. I heard that bit of news from Hipólito, in the only letter I ever got from him. He told me that Mabel Silva had divorced him, and he was living alone in Chihuahua City, running a little poker parlor. His letter embarrassed me; he asked for my autograph.

He also told me that Luz Corral was back in her house, Quinta Luz. She had turned part of it into a little museum, and Hipólito said that for five pesos you could see Pancho's saddle and a good collection of grenades and rifles and photographs. . . .

And that famous bullet-riddled Dodge.

He kept on fighting, of course. He took Casas Grandes and Ojinaga, just as he promised, but then he got licked at Juárez. His new army never got to be more than two thousand men, so he couldn't take another crack at Torreón, which was always his favorite city to attack. He attacked Parral instead, hanging a few Carranzista officials in the little square where Elisa had fired above the heads of the cavalry. But after that he fought only a few skirmishes and guerrilla raids, and in 1920 he finally made peace with the new president, Adolfo de la Huerta—a man he seemed to respect and no relation to Victoriano Huerta, the man we had fought against. Villa sent him a letter which began, "You are about to hear sincere words from the heart of an uneducated man. . . ." and which ended, "Let us begin to discuss the well-being of the republic." The old warrior, in his twilight, must have been tired. The government was generous, even forgiving—they'd had enough of him as an enemy. All of the Villista troops were offered a year's pay or invited to join the new Federal army and keep their rank. Villa could maintain a personal escort of fifty men, and he was given half a million pesos and a hacienda at Canutillo in the state of Durango, not far from Parral. In return he promised never again to take up arms against the legitimate government. It was all in writing, with the usual seals and his fancy signature at the bottom.

In Canutillo he married again—this time with Luz Corral's dressmaker, a pretty girl named Austraberta Rentería. (I think he'd always had an eye on her.) Luz refused to share the house with them. Pancho went into farming, raising blooded stock and a cote of white doves. He grew fat, and his fifty men rode tractors instead of horses. He had a secretary named Trillo, and in Trillo's office, decorated with an oil portrait of Francisco Madero and a bronze bust of Felipe Angeles, they studied economics together and read *Don Quixote*. He kept his word, never again taking up arms or dabbling in politics.

In July of 1923, with Trillo and some others, Pancho drove into Parral for a cockfight and a christening. On the way out of town at the wheel of his Dodge, as he slowed at an intersection to wave to a pumpkin-seed seller who had shouted, *"Viva Villa!"* he and his men were shot to death by a barrage of automatic gunfire that came from a doorway. Pancho was hit by seven bullets . . . killed instantly.

All of Doña Maria's predictions had come true. He had died of many bullets, and the large, round thing in his hands had been a steering wheel. It had been quick. And his enemies had never really conquered him. He was only forty-three years old.

Hipólito arrived in Parral the next day and buried his brother there. It was rumored that the man behind the assassination was Colonel Calles, who had helped defeat Villa at Agua Prieta. He didn't think Villa had ever forgiven him, and he was running for president then. A dead enemy is the best kind.

In 1926 some vandals broke into the grave and stole Pancho's head. I hope it gave them *ojo*.

A while ago the publicity people out in Hollywood prepared a short biography of my life, written in the first person, and I signed my name to it. But I left out the four years I had been Mexico and told them I was still on the rodeo circuit then. No one checked. I figured I didn't need any more trouble from the U. S. Army or the government, which was already bothering me about some unpaid taxes.

When the chief was killed I was in the midst of making a film for Fox called *The Lone Star Ranger*. I read about it in the papers during a coffee break. I had never forgotten him, and I hoped he hadn't forgotten me, even though I had finally quit his revolution in its dying stage. I could almost hear him mutter, as he tugged at his curly mustache and showed a glint of red teeth, *"I'm a man who came into this world to attack.... My only hope is to wear myself out. To grow old. Or to be killed ..."* Silently, I saluted him. Then I went back to work. Work is the best anodyne.

Since then, in Mexico, they've turned him into a forgotten man. I'm sure that the *campesinos* and the old Villistas toast his memory, but the government seems to be ashamed that he ever existed. Every city and pueblo boasts a big avenue, even a school, named after Venustiano Carranza, but not one in honor of Pancho Villa. From my point of view the revolution—and all true hope for the Mexican people to rise from their gloomy poverty—died with him at Parral. Or perhaps even before that, in Aguascalientes, when he didn't see that he was the right man to become president, and when I failed to tell him.

In this country, if you ask anyone about Pancho Villa, they usually say: "A bandit, right? And didn't he once raid Columbus, in New Mexico, and kill a lot of Americans?" I never contradict that. It hardly seems worth the trouble to explain how I know it isn't so, and it certainly wasn't my purpose when I sat down to write this tale of my lost years.

Did I have a purpose beyond a middle-aged man's self-gratification, and the purging of past sins? Probably, but it doesn't matter. The means become the end, don't they? I simply wanted to remember, because there's not much time left, and it's colored gray. And that time was the best time—a fever of the mind, a perpetual intoxication of the blood that you can't find in any bottle. I've looked, and I know.

I was loved then, and I was in love. Not just with Rosa, then Elisa Griensen—but with my very existence on the hot planet. I was young.... doesn't that say it all? Our youth is so brimful with choices, and rarely do we make the intelligent ones that serve us best. How painful it seems, that journey through its startling landscape. But how precious the pain becomes, when it's gone.

And yet I have my memories. When I meet a particularly attractive woman at a party in Beverly Hills or London, I can't help but peer into her eyes to see if my name is reflected there from the list that Candelario swore was written lower down. "Life is short," he said. I can still hear his voice . . . and the others. They speak to me at night, when I'm alone. They call me *"Tomás . . ." or "my colonel . . ."* and even *"pendejo."* Or, in a huskier tone, touched by desert sunlight, one says, *"Go well, my sweet. . . ."*

I've tried, Elisa. I've gone far, and sometimes well . . . although not always.

Another, as if reaching out from deep sleep to make sure I'm still there, whispers in the calm, silent darkness, *"Mi capitán . . . ?"* I see her even calmer face—bright, loyal, and full of grace.

Rosa! I haven't stopped loving you. In your short life you brought me more joy than any other, then or since. I miss you still!

T. M.
Florence, Arizona
October 7, 1940

Tom Mix was driving from Tucson to Phoenix on the afternoon of October 12, 1940. Alone in the car, he swerved to avoid a crew of highway workers. He crashed and was killed instantly.

author's note

This is a historical fantasy, although I prefer the word *romance,* which my dictionary defines as "a novel or other prose narrative typically characterized by heroic deeds, pageantry, romantic exploits, etc., usually in a historical or imaginary setting."

For the most part I have tried to be faithful to the facts of the Mexican Revolution and Pancho Villa's life. The battles, the political conflicts, the characters of such men as Carranza, Obregón and Zapata, are all accurately described. Patton and Pershing were in Chihuahua in 1916 (and the young lieutenant killed Julio Cárdenas in the manner chronicled); so were Franz von Papen, Rodolfo Fierro, Hipólito Villa and Candelario Cervantes, who was shot by the Seventh Cavalry. Elisa Griensen is a historical personage who did indeed lead the citizens of Parral against Major Tompkins' squadron. Felix Sommerfeld and Sam Ravel were two of Villa's purchasing agents in Texas. Luz Corral vda. de Villa, at this writing, is alive and well in Chihuahua City, in the same house I described. Rosa, Hannah, and Miguel Bosques are fictional characters. The stories of the massacre in the stockyards and the gold taken from the column of the Banco Minero, among many others related, are true.

I have changed Tom Mix's age somewhat to suit my purpose as a novelist. But the young actor's role as a volunteer for Pancho Villa is mentioned briefly in several books. They include Ronald Atkin's *Revolution! Mexico 1910–1920* (John Day, New York, 1970); Haldeen Braddy's *Cock of the Walk: The Legend of Pancho Villa* (University of New Mexico Press, Albuquerque, 1955); Ernest Otto Schuster's *Pancho Villa's Shadow* (Exposition Press, New York, 1947); and *Twenty Episodes in the Life of Pancho Villa* (The Encino Press, Austin, 1973), by Elías L. Torres, the man who arranged Villa's retirement for Adolfo de la Huerta. Torres' memoir, based on his conversations with Villa, was first published in 1931.

Almost all historians have assumed—I suppose for the sake of simplicity—that Villa either led or authorized the March 9, 1916, raid on Columbus, New Mexico. But there never has been any proof for that assumption other than that some of the raiders cried, *"Viva Villa!"* Until his death in 1923, well beyond a time of jeopardy, Villa continued to deny it. General Hugh Scott's papers in the National Archives *(Mexican*

Claims Case Files and General Claims Arbitration) reveal a letter dated March 11, 1916, in which he expresses his doubt that Villa was either present or responsible. Dr. R. H. Ellis, one of President Wilson's personal observers on the border, claimed that on the day of the raid Villa was near Sabinas, Coahuila, more than three hundred miles away. "I was with him," Ellis later wrote. In *Pancho Villa: Intimate Recollections by People Who Knew Him* (Hastings House, New York, 1977), Ellis also says: "After the Columbus raid, Carranza soldiers were captured in uniform at Columbus by National Guards. Placed in Federal detention they made statements in writing pleading guilty, and admitting that they were Carranzistas under the direction of Obregón and the German agent, Luther Wertz [who worked for Von Papen] . . . Wertz was finally apprehended in Nogales, Arizona, and taken in custody to Ft. Sam Houston, Texas, January 31, 1918. Under death sentence Wertz exonerated Villa of all blame for the Santa Ysabel massacre and the Columbus raid. This was a written, recorded statement and is in the files at Washington, D.C. Wertz was hanged."

I have been unable to find any such statement. But I can't find any, either, that proves Villa *was* there. Today, at the site of old Camp Furlong outside Columbus, one finds—incredibly—Pancho Villa State Park (with camping facilities). We are either a forgiving people, or else someone in the government knew that justice had not been done.

Was the chief responsible for the raid? Did Tom Mix rise to the rank of a Villista colonel before he became a Hollywood movie star?

It might be yes, it might be no. But most probably . . . who knows?

C. I.
The Springs
January 14, 1982.

The quotes beginning each chapter are from the following Shakespearean plays:

1	"I prithee. pretty youth . . ."	*As You Like It*
2	"The eagle suffers . . ."	*Titus Andronicus*
3	"He may at pleasure . . ."	*Antony and Cleopatra*
4	"Assume a virtue . . ."	*Hamlet*
5	"It is the purpose . . ."	*Troilus and Cressida*
6	"If to do . . ."	*Merchant of Venice*
7	"The web of our life . . ."	*All's Well That Ends Well*
8	"Courage mounteth . . ."	*King John*
9	"The gates of mercy . . ."	*Henry V*
10	"And if words will not . . ."	*2 Henry VI*
11	"And if I have a conscience . . ."	*Henry VIII*
12	"Shall I be frighted . . ."	*Julius Caesar*
13	"Fortune brings in . . ."	*Cymbeline*
14	"And every tale . . ."	*Richard III*
15	"Whose church-like humors . . ."	*2 Henry VI*
16	"Do you not know . . ."	*As You Like It*
17	"The cankers of . . ."	*1 Henry IV*
18	"The bow is bent . . ."	*King Lear*
19	"'Tis time to fear . . ."	*Pericles*
20	"Know of your youth . . ."	*Midsummer Night's Dream*
21	"Take all the swift . . ."	*Richard III*
22	"I will find twenty turtles . . ."	*Merry Wives of Windsor*
23	"Wisely, and slow."	*Romeo and Juliet*
24	"I see you stand . . ."	*Henry V*
25	"And lay the summer's . . ."	*Richard II*
26	"What! wouldst thou . . ."	*Merchant of Venice*
27	"So shines a good deed . . ."	*Merchant of Venice*
28	"The path is smooth . . ."	*Venus and Adonis*
29	"His bruiséd helmet . . ."	*Henry V*